THE HARLEQUIN CREW SERIES

THE HARLEQUIN CREW SERIES

GALLOWS BRIDGE

CAROLINE PECKHAM
&
SUSANNE VALENTI

This book is dedicated to everyone out there who has ever felt like they don't belong.

We hope you've been swept up in this journey and have discovered a piece of home among our Harlequin crew in the dark and twisted town of Sunset Cove.

It's time to read the final pages of their story…

Gallows Bridge

TRAVIS

CHAPTER ONE

Shawn crowed like a rooster, tipping his head back and laughing loudly as Luther Harlequin roared his grief to the hateful sky and lunged forward to try and get to his son. Dead Dogs surged around him, fighting to restrain him while he fought like a feral dog who had been cornered in the street, teeth bared, fists swinging and a savage, reckless pain to his actions that made it more than clear he would die here and now if that was what it took to get to his boy.

Memories stirred in my gut as I thought of my own father for a moment, the question which always hung over me tracing through my mind. What would he think if he saw what I had become in the wake of his death?

My gaze swept beyond the drop at the side of the bridge as Fox jerked and kicked at the end of the rope which was slowly choking the life out of him. My fist tightened at my side, jaw ticking, emotions locked down.

I didn't so much as flinch at the sound of Luther's grief and desperation carving the air in two. I didn't have enough humanity left in me for that anymore. I'd let all of it go a long time ago and was better off for it. It made watching this kind of thing simpler, if not easier. My eyes saw while my soul looked away.

Sometimes I wondered what kind of man I was. In moments like this when my own instincts and inclinations were shut down so hard that I could barely feel them anymore. I'd spent so many years pretending to be this creature of Shawn Mackenzie's that it was hard to grasp the person I truly was without the fake persona shrouding me.

If you embody a hellion for long enough, then perhaps you truly become one.

The wind blew across us, carrying the scent of the sea on it as Luther Harlequin was thrown to the ground, kicked and beaten by ten of Shawn's men as he fought back with a raw and brutal savagery which stirred something in me. Some memory of a family I once would have given my life for just the way he was begging to save his son. It twisted the knife which had long since been lodged inside my gut, that almost feeling of being a part of something more. Family. Love. I remembered it all with a detachment that would have been alarming if I could care about it enough to lament its loss. As it was, I only watched as Luther's blood was spilled onto the cold stone of the bridge while his son kicked and thrashed his final few minutes of his life away, just out of reach.

Yet still I waited. Unmoving. More machine than man as I held myself in check, considering what action I might take next. Wondering what I might do if the choice was my own. But it had been years since I'd been anything like my own man. My sorry ass had been bought and paid for once upon a time, the cost of my life the submission of my own free will. It had been the only offer on the table, and it had seemed preferable to death back then. Now, I just wondered whether I'd been right about that or not.

I glanced at my forearm, my deep brown skin marred by the symbol of this gang I paid lip service to. The false life of the man I pretended to be thrived while the one I truly was rotted away.

I didn't even dream of the day I would be free of this task anymore. I didn't dream at all. Such luxuries had been stripped from me as I waited to find out who I was upon the orders of the person who got to decide such things. I was a lost soul languishing on the whims of those so much more powerful than me, and no doubt one day I'd find myself bleeding out for their cause one way or another, my life worth no more than a pawn on a chessboard, sacrificed for a game I had never had any choice in playing.

Shawn laughed loudly while his men kicked and beat his enemy, his eyes alight with a blazing kind of victory as he took the revenge he had been working towards for so long, enjoying every torturous second of this. If his brother had been a man worth avenging, I may have even been able to understand this need in him to seek out retribution, but he'd been nothing more than an animal who took pleasure in inflicting all the worst forms of pain on those weaker than him. The world was better off without him, and I knew even Shawn understood that. The reality was, Luther had done him a favour when he'd killed Nolan Mackenzie. Shawn's brother was a burden on him, holding him back and bringing far too much attention with the brutal games he liked to play. If Luther hadn't ended him, Shawn would have done it eventually. He'd have had to unless he wanted Nolan to drag us all down with him.

I cut my gaze away from the man screaming for his son's life and took in the still jerking form of Fox Harlequin as he swung from the end of the rope which was secured beside me, blood staining his clothes from the stab wound to his side and his life now measured in moments that were rushing away all too quickly.

The drop beneath him was a long one with a rock-filled river waiting to welcome him into its icy embrace once he stopped twitching and Shawn cast his body away. The sound of rushing water reached me over the bellowed agony of Luther Harlequin as he continued to fight back, even as he was beaten bloody between the group of merciless Dead Dogs.

I flexed my fingers. Aching to do…something, but the person I was and the one I pretended to be had yet to decide upon what that was. Time was running short though. Each second like the toll of death striking as the gates of hell swung open, ready to admit a sin-filled soul or two.

Six years was a long time to spend wearing a face that wasn't yours. Especially when I hadn't even finished growing into a man when I was forced to start wearing it. I didn't know who I was now. So I focused on the one thing I did know; who I belonged to.

My phone buzzed in my pocket and I tugged it out, looking down at the single command in the message I'd just been sent.

Black Sheep:

We stand with the Harlequins.

I dropped the phone back into my pocket, snatched the pistol from my belt and grinned as I was finally cut free of my own noose.

This was the day I left The Dead Dogs behind me. This was the day I found out who I really was. And fuck me, it had been a long time coming.

Shawn's gaze met mine as I jerked the pistol up, his pupils widening as he took in the reality that had just come for him, the laugh dying on his smug lips as he saw the truth of me at long last and discovered the viper he'd invited into his home.

My twisted smile was all the warning he got, the weight of the weapon in my hand a welcome relief and the taste of freedom on the air calling me home. I only had to figure out where that home might be and I'd be safe and dry, brought in from the cold at last.

I fired off three bullets in quick succession, one into the chest of the man closest to me, one at the rope which was hanging Fox Harlequin and one straight at fucking Shawn's black fucking heart.

Shawn jerked aside as I fired, trying to avoid what was inevitable for him now, but a bellow of pain escaped him as the bullet found its home in his flesh. He roared in shock and pain, stumbling back a few steps before his knees

10

hit the edge of the low wall that lined the side of the bridge. He cried out in horror, his arms pinwheeling as he crashed back over the wall, his legs flipping up over his head and he fell from the bridge with a scream of fright.

The men attacking Luther Harlequin whirled to face me just as a pair of distant splashes sounded Shawn and Fox hitting the river. The smile on my face widened as I drew in a breath of fresh air and welcomed whatever this new reality held for me. I wasn't a Dead Dog anymore. I was finally free of that leash.

A beat of silence sounded loudly as the men I'd spent years living and working amongst stared at me in shock, confusion, horror and alarm, finally seeing me for exactly what I was. A snake in their long grass, just waiting for this moment to strike, venom dripping from my fangs and a hunger in my belly that had been building for years.

The first of them recovered from the shock of what I'd done, lunging at me, swinging a fucking hatchet at my head as I ducked aside and shot him in the face with my final bullet.

Blood splattered my cheeks as I lurched forward, ripping the hatchet from his dead grip before he'd even hit the ground, swinging it at the next man to come for me with a bellow of rage.

I was a beast with its tether cut and a creature seeking nothing but bloody, endless vengeance for the things I'd been forced to bear witness to in all the time I'd been caught in the company of these men. I wasn't afraid of bloodshed and gore. But I did take exception to the way they ran their gang and the fallout they left in their wake, so I was happy to finally show them what I'd really been thinking this whole time. The burden placed upon me was finally lifted, and vengeance for all I'd seen them do was coming on swift and violent wings.

Gunshots were fired my way, but I moved fast, ducking and shifting between them, using them as shields and fighting my way towards Luther while swinging my hatchet with reckless abandon at anyone who was stupid enough to get close to me.

Blood spilled, men screamed, and pain lanced along my arm as a bullet found its home in me, but I fought on, all sense of self-preservation gone as I shed the shackles of the false life I'd been living for too long and made it to the man who was now firmly my priority.

Luther Harlequin was fighting for his life, and I saw the shift in the tide within him while he swung his fists with blows that broke bones and shattered jaws, this new reality dawning for him too. He'd thought he was watching his son die, had been willing to follow him into death too, yet now the will of God had changed and everything was possible again. My god just lived a little closer to home than the one he might have been thanking.

I reached him in what could have been a matter of minutes or seconds, all sense of time lost to the heat of the fight, the feeling of blood on my skin and the pain of my injuries. Cuts and bruises had joined with the gunshot wound I'd taken, but I had no time to waste inspecting any of them.

I grasped his tattooed arm and heaved him towards the edge of the bridge, swinging my hatchet to carve us a path through the weight of bodies pressing in on us. I kept my head low as more shots were fired, the confusion and surprise wearing off as both their leader and his second in command failed to give them any orders. But they were soon catching up to the reality of what I had just done, of who had turned on them and what was happening, and we needed to get the fuck out of here before we were overwhelmed and gunned down.

Luther ran with me, though his eyes were full of mistrust. All I could do was smile darkly as I relished this sense of freedom as we made it to the low wall that sat between us and the only hope we had of escape.

"Carmen Ortega sends her regards," I growled, tugging him with me as I leapt up onto the wall and dove straight off the other side of it with a whoop of exhilaration.

Luther swore as he jumped too, the air whipping past us as the river rushed up to greet us, and all we could do was pray there wouldn't be any rocks waiting below.

I hit the surface hard, sinking beneath the water, the sounds of the gunshots which chased after us blocked out as nothing but the roar of the churning river filled my ears. The water was ice cold and the current so powerful that it threatened to flip me over and take control of my destiny, working to disorient me the moment it held me in its grasp.

My foot hit a rock somewhere towards the bottom of the river just as my descent began to slow and I kicked off of it hard, swimming towards the faint moonlight above me with a fierce determination.

I surfaced again, sucking in a deep breath as the ferocious current took hold of me and whipped me away with it, quickly sweeping me away from the bridge and The Dead Dogs who remained on it, yelling threats and firing shots that had no chance of reaching me now.

I still held the hatchet in my hand as I began to swim along with the current, looking ahead of me at the dark water as I hunted for any sign of the men who had joined me down here. The riverbanks were lined with sharp rocks, and even if I could have gotten close enough without my head being dashed against them, they were far too steep to climb. I placed my faith in the flow of the water and prayed it didn't carry me straight to my death as I continued to swim with it.

My orders had been clear anyway, which meant I needed to get to Fox Harlequin. I might have saved him from the noose, but he didn't stand much chance of survival in the freezing depths of this river with his hands bound as the current swept him away and threw him against the rocks.

"Fox!" Luther roared as he surfaced beside me, blood washing down the left side of his face from a cut to his cheek.

"He fell in ahead of us, we need to swim to catch him," I barked, earning myself a string of curses from the leader of The Harlequin Crew who seemed disinclined to follow my orders no matter if I'd just saved his sorry life or not.

But I had my own agenda so I took off, not paying any attention to whether or not he followed as I set my focus on finding Fox Harlequin in the murky depths before he could drown on me. I wouldn't start this free life as a failure. If I wanted any hope of it becoming more than it had been while I languished beneath Shawn's control, then I needed to prove myself with this first task. I needed to show them that the years I had spent in The Dead Dogs hadn't been wasted. I was worth more than another false life at the mercy of some new mad man. I was worth noticing.

I swam harder, using the force of the current to propel me forward as I squinted through the dim moonlight, fighting against the water which continually swelled around me and splashed my face violently, making it nearly impossible to see anything up ahead.

He had to be alive. I refused any other fate for him now. My life was tied with his and my future began now. If he was dead then he had better be prepared for me to come rip him back out of hell, because I was done being nothing and no one. I was ready for something more.

I gritted my teeth in determination, swimming harder, faster, ignoring the bite of the cold water and focusing only on the single goal of retrieving him and proving my worth.

Finally, I spotted him, the sounds of him coughing and choking on the water carrying to me as he fought to try and keep his head above the surface with his hands bound, relief tumbling through my chest as I swam faster towards the sound. The wound on my arm burned from the effort as I forced it to work, disregarding the pain and focusing on my orders.

A shoulder crashed into mine as I swam for my target, and I swung my hatchet around, only pulling myself up short a moment before I could land a killing blow as I found Luther swimming just as furiously at my side, the current forcing us together.

He looked like shit, his face bruised and bleeding from the beating he'd taken, though his green eyes were bright and wild with the truth of his son's survival and the reality of how close they'd both just come to death. There was gratitude in his gaze buried deep beneath a whole heap of mistrust and I just grinned at him, offering no explanation for what I'd done or why I'd done it.

"Keep up, old man," I taunted, swimming on as I kept my gaze fixed on Fox, my target clear and my future riding on it.

"Same to you, little boy," he growled in reply, powering on through the water beside me, keeping pace despite the agony which must have been thrumming through his body.

He reached Fox ahead of me, grabbing him and yanking the noose from around his neck as a choked sob escaped him.

"I've got you, son," Luther growled, a look passing between them that shoved me back into the past and made my heart twist once again, my own father having looked at me like that right before the end. *Fuck.*

"My hands," Fox grunted, coughing again as a wave of water rushed over his face and I made it to them, the three of us knocking into one another as the merciless current swept us on.

"I can handle that," I said, gripping his elbow to hold him still before finding his wrists beneath the water and slicing the rope securing them with my hatchet.

Mistrust flared in the eyes of both father and son, but they didn't have time to question me on my motives as we were tossed into the rapids a moment later.

Water bucked and crashed around us, knocking us apart and sending us rolling through the waves as the river charged towards the sea at a fast and endless pace along the rocky ravine.

I lost sight of everything, my focus solely on my own survival as I fought the current, aiming to keep myself in the middle of the river as it tore through the rocks until I could find a way out of this torrent.

I gasped down air whenever I managed to keep my head above the surface, panic clawing at the edges of my mind as I felt the icy hands of death trying to drag me under, a watery grave awaiting me, beckoning me closer with every passing second.

We were swept further and further down the river, the odd word catching my ear as Luther and Fox called to each other as we went until suddenly my gut plummeted and I was launched over the lip of a waterfall with enough force to make my muscles tighten and a cry of alarm catch in my throat.

I sailed through the air for several breath-taking moments, my heart stalling in my chest as fear of what awaited me at the foot of the falls pressed in on me from all around.

I hit the water hard, sinking beneath it, pummelled by the torrent which cascaded over the waterfall behind me and flipped me over and over, forcing me to lose all idea of which way was up or down, left or right before spitting me out violently and leaving my lungs burning as I swam for the surface again.

I kicked harder as I emerged, taking advantage of the slightly wider pool I found myself in and the reduced speed of the river as I spotted the rocky bank to my left, my hatchet still firmly locked in my grasp.

It would have been easier to swim on without the thing, but I'd grown attached to it. It was one of the first choices I'd made to claim this weapon as a free man, and I found I didn't want to relinquish that taste of freedom just yet.

I hit the rocks at the water's edge with a flare of pain tearing along my side.

With a determined roar, I swung my hatchet at them and lodged it in a crevice as the water tried to drag me away.

My muscles bunched and burned with the effort of holding myself there, the weight of my saturated clothes working to pull me under, but I clung to that fucking hatchet with all I had and began to haul myself out of the freezing embrace of the water.

I heaved myself up and out of the hungry river, the sharp rocks cutting into my skin while I panted with exertion, letting myself laugh as I finally made my way back onto dry land.

I rolled onto my back, water pooling around me from my clothes as I looked up at the stars between a network of tree limbs and gave myself a single moment to relish what I had just done and the beauty of having no idea of what would come next for me now.

I rolled to my knees before getting to my feet and gazed back at the river, spotting Fox and Luther as they swam towards me, the two of them looking more than a little worse for wear, but beautifully alive. I'd done it. The first task I'd been given to prove my worth and I had fucking done it.

I dropped my hatchet, moving to grab a long branch from the ground behind me. I jogged back to the water's edge and lowered it into the flow of the river to help haul them out.

They both caught hold of it and I grunted, planting my boots more firmly as I worked against the pull of the river to hold their weight in place and wait for them to climb out.

Luther shoved his son ahead of him and Fox took my hand, his eyes full of suspicion as he let me drag him up onto the bank before turning to help me heave Luther out too. The gunshot wound on my arm protested at every flex of my muscles, but I knew how to disengage my mind from such things when necessary.

I tossed the branch aside, looking back up towards the waterfall and releasing a breath of laughter as I realised how far down river we must have come. It had to be over a mile from here to Gallows Bridge, and with no roads running this close to its banks, I was confident that The Dead Dogs were long behind us now.

I couldn't help but laugh harder as I looked between the two Harlequins who appeared more like drowned rats than kings right now, dropping back onto my ass and picking up my hatchet as they remained standing over me, all scowls and curiosity.

Luther cut a look to his son, and I waved a hand in encouragement, letting them have a moment for the emotional shit before they had to deal with me. He looked at Fox like the man had come back from the dead – which, in all fairness, he sort of had, and a choked noise caught in his throat as he threw his arms around his boy, embracing him fiercely and murmuring his relief against his flesh as they clung to one another.

Fox sagged in his father's arms, gripping him tightly and returning his sentiments of relief at their survival, their love for each other clear and stinging the old wounds of my past.

When they finally broke up the reunion, they looked to me in suspicion and Fox Harlequin got a dangerous look about him that told me exactly why he deserved his title as the Harlequin Prince. The asshole had just been swinging from his neck, eye to eye with the grim reaper himself, and it didn't even look like he was remotely shaken by his dance with the afterlife, though that bruise around his throat looked all kinds of fucked up and the stab wound to his side was bleeding through his saturated shirt.

"Who the fuck are you?" Fox demanded gruffly though I got the feeling he recognised me just fine and was after my real identity. His voice was hoarse from the rope which had been knotted around his neck, his dark green eyes blazing with all the life he'd nearly been robbed of.

"Hard to say these days," I admitted, pushing one hand through my short dreadlocks and shoving them back out of my eyes while keeping a firm grip on my hatchet with the other. "But I'm guessing the real question you're asking me is, who do I work for?"

"Don't get smart with us, kid," Luther warned, seeming to think I would feel threatened by his macho bullshit.

I'd long since lost the ability to feel fear so I only smirked at him, waving my hatchet to remind him I was the only armed man here. And I might have been younger than them, but I would take a weapon over experience any day. Besides, I'd lived the kind of life you couldn't really measure in years, the things I'd survived, witnessed and endured didn't require decades, but they stacked up all the same.

"Keep your hair on before it starts falling out," I suggested. "Besides, I'm guessing you made a deal to get my help anyway, so I have to assume you already know the answer to your question."

"Carmen?" he asked, a mixture of hope and trepidation on his face, and Fox raised a brow at me as he massaged his throat where the bruising from the rope burns on his flesh already flared angrily.

"Yeah. The two of you officially owe her your lives. Let's hope you're good for the price." I grinned at them as they exchanged a concerned glance, but my attention was snatched by movement on the far riverbank, and I shoved myself to my feet as I spotted fucking Shawn clawing his way up out of the water.

"You've got to be kidding me," I growled. "I shot that motherfucker in the chest. He should be at the bottom of this damn river by now."

Shawn's laughter called to us as he looked right back, clinging on to a tree and using it to support his weight as he pointed across the raging water at us. There was blood soaking through his shirt as he clutched the place I'd shot him, though it looked too far to the right to have done the job I'd wanted to do.

"You Harlequins are like a nest of fucking cockroaches!" he called. "You just won't die easy, will ya?"

"We could say the same about you." Luther took a step towards the water's edge like he fully intended to dive back into that raging hell pit and swim over there to throttle the bastard, but Fox caught his arm to stop him, his other hand pressing to his side where the stab wound Shawn had given him was still bleeding freely. It was hard to tell how bad the wound was, but I couldn't say I'd want to do a whole hell of a lot with a gut wound like that even if it wasn't going to be instantly fatal.

"I need to get back to the cliffs to that blowhole," Fox said fearfully, cutting a look at me like he wasn't sure where I stood now and didn't have the time to waste figuring it out either. "Rick, Rogue and the others need us."

I arched a brow, wondering what he was referring to and whether he seriously thought this favour I'd just done the two of them came for free. A debt was owed now. One that would have to be paid.

Luther cursed and turned his back on Shawn as the two of them rushed off into the trees, leaving me and Shawn to face each other across the river. The Harlequin men either believed we were done now or that I would simply allow them to do whatever the fuck they wanted from this point on. Neither was the truth.

"I see you now, boy," Shawn cooed, raising two fingers to point them at me like a pistol before firing a fake shot, staggering a little and proving that gunshot wound was giving him trouble. Maybe he'd die of it yet.

"I see you too," I called back. "Been looking for a hell of a long time."

"You gonna tell me who owns ya?" he asked but I only smiled.

He'd figure it out soon enough anyway. I doubted there was a single one of his men left alive at this point. The bridge had likely been swarmed not long after we vacated it, or if not, I knew Carmen would be cleaning house soon. She'd played her hand, cut ties with The Dead Dogs, and she didn't leave men breathing when they had grudges who might come bite her in the ass at some later date.

"Well, it ain't you," I pointed out, though that was clear enough for all to see now.

"You're gonna regret crossing me, boy," he sang, looking so fucking smug it made my blood heat and an undeniable need for violence rise within me.

I wrenched my arm back in a sudden movement and hurled the hatchet with all of my strength, aiming for his fucking head as every torturous moment I'd endured in his company whilst watching him for the Castillo Cartel played over on repeat in my skull.

Years of my life stolen by this waste of fucking oxygen. Countless orders followed and bullshit ignored. But I was finally done with him and despite his show of bravado, I could see how deep my betrayal had cut him, and it felt damn good to pull the wool from his eyes at last.

Shawn jerked aside a moment before the hatchet could kill him, the blade lodging in the tree he was using to hold himself up on as a whoop of exhilaration escaped him.

"Yeah. You see me now," I called, ignoring him as he started boasting about being unkillable. I didn't need to stand around and listen to his fucking voice anymore, so I turned away to follow the Harlequins into the trees.

I broke into a run, following the path they'd taken through the woodland, spying footprints and broken branches easily in the silver moonlight. I'd catch up to them quickly enough and I'd be reminding them that we were nowhere near done yet. They had a date with the Black Sheep and she wasn't a woman to be kept waiting.

A lightness filled my chest as I ran, and I couldn't help but smile to myself despite my failed attempts to take Shawn's life. His day would come, and in the meantime, I was going to be reclaiming myself at last.

I was a dog finally free from my chains, and I was ready to return to my true master.

CHAPTER TWO

My scream was torn from my lips in a torrent of bubbles which spun towards the surface of the salty water. I was tossed beneath the merciless waves in the blowhole and thrown against the rocks once more, my shoulder exploding with pain at the sharp slice of them against my skin.

My heart thrashed in panic as I scrambled to figure out which way was up, my body desperate for oxygen and the fear of drowning in this fucking pit of hell eating into me with every passing moment.

The water swelled again, sucking me down and letting me know where the surface was as I began to kick with as much strength as I could in the opposite direction to where it was trying to drag me, moving as fast as my frozen limbs could muster.

A hand gripped mine as I made it to the surface and I sucked in a savage breath lined with icy droplets of salty water that made my throat and lungs burn, blinking up at Chase as he clung to the rocks and heaved me closer with a determined snarl.

"JJ!" I screamed as I managed to take hold of the rocks and haul myself up onto them in the dark, twisting my head to look back down into the pool of black water beneath us. There was no sign of him, and fear welled within me as I looked for my boy, desperation crushing the air from my lungs.

The foam of the waves made it impossible to see anything within the dark depths of the hole which was fast turning into a death trap, and panic clawed at my insides as a sob lodged in my throat and I screamed for the man I loved again.

"He's gone, little one," Chase choked out, those words so filled with pain that they cut me even deeper than the truth in them.

I shook my head in fierce denial, though I knew he was right. He hadn't resurfaced and it had been too long now, far too long.

"He must have been tugged out through whatever tunnel lets the water in," Rick called from the other side of the chasm, drawing my attention to him where he clung to the rocks too, Mutt tucked under his arm and trembling in fear, his wet fur plastered to his body.

"We can't leave him," I begged, shaking my head as the sharp rocks cut into my fingers and the water roared beneath us in anticipation of another swell.

"He wouldn't want you to die for him down here," Chase said fiercely, his grip on my arm tightening painfully as tears spilled down my cheeks and I just kept shaking my head in dumb refusal.

I knew they were right; I knew it and yet I also knew that climbing meant we were giving up. The moment I began to ascend these rocks, I would be leaving Johnny James behind and the mere thought of that was enough to make me feel like I'd be leaving my own soul down here with him.

I can't.

I won't.

My heart was ripping down the centre, and I couldn't find a way to breathe. I'd thought there'd been no force in this world powerful enough to take one of my boys from me, but I'd been wrong. So fucking wrong, and now I was helpless against the wrath of the sea, two of the pieces of my soul stolen away, and I didn't know what to do.

"This is gonna be a bad one!" Rick yelled as the roar of the wave filled the blowhole once more and a scream escaped me.

I gripped the rocks with all I had, terror puncturing my grief as I cowered against them and the surge slammed into us again, working hard to tear us from our perches.

Chase's hold on me turned to iron as we were driven against the rocks, my cheek scraping across them as the ocean took more of my blood in offering and my grief tore through my chest like the claws of a demon trying to prise my soul from my flesh.

Impossibly, we all managed to hold on, the water rushing back down and leaving us dripping where we still clung to the rock wall.

"Climb!" Rick bellowed, and with my heart fracturing and grief destroying me, I did as he commanded, reaching up and grasping the next handhold as I pulled myself higher, tipping my head back to look up at the taunting stars hanging in the sky far above.

Chase stayed right beside me, his arm brushing mine as we climbed up and up, the crash of the water swelling below us making each second seem to drag like an eternity and rush past impossibly fast at once.

I was crying, sobs tearing from me and tears streaming down my cheek. The pain I felt consumed me and left me with nothing but the single task of climbing ever higher and trying to escape this hell.

Rick yelled out for us to hold on once more and I shrank against the rock wall as Chase shifted closer to me, his arm encircling my back as he took hold of the rocks on my other side and tried to shield me with his body.

I looked over my shoulder and locked eyes with Maverick whose jaw was gritted with determination as he crushed Mutt between the rocks and his chest, bracing for the impact of the waves as my little dog whimpered fearfully and huddled against him.

"It's okay, it'll be okay," I called out, not even certain who I was trying to reassure, but Mutt's wild eyes softened a fraction as if he understood me.

The sight of them was stolen from me as the bellow of the surging water deafened us and the wave rushed up and over our heads, spraying out of the hole above us while all we could do was cling on for dear life and hope the water didn't tear us back down with it when it left again.

I was flattened against the rocks once more, my bare toes burning with the pain of the sharp stones cutting into them as I held my breath and trembled in Chase's hold.

The water rushed back again even more forcefully than it had crashed over us, and I screamed in alarm as Chase was wrenched backwards, his arm dropping from around me as he cried out and began to fall.

I snatched his hand into my grip as he tipped backwards, the rocks cutting into the fingers of my right hand as his weight threatened to rip me free of the rocks too.

My muscles burned and my blood spilled, but a defiant roar broke from my lips as my fingernails bit into his skin and he scrambled to regain his hold, heaving himself back against the rocks and swearing while I panted at the exertion of keeping hold of him.

We didn't waste time with words, climbing again, the sharp rocks cutting my fingers and toes with every movement as I wrenched myself up and up.

A sob of relief escaped me as my hand finally grasped the lip of the hole above my head.

I pulled myself upwards and Chase smacked a hand against my ass before pushing me up even faster as the water howled beneath us once more, the rush of it racing closer with every passing moment.

I fell onto my chest as I made it onto the wet rocks at the top of the cliff, another sob choking me as I heaved my legs up behind me and rolled, scrambling back towards the edge to help the others.

A flash of white drew my attention as Rick tossed Mutt up and out of the hole just before the water blasted from it once more, the spray drenching me as I screamed in fear for my boys who were still grasping the rocks within it.

Mutt raced away from the wave with a yelp of fright, and I shielded my face as I was drenched by the blast of water, my shattered heart racing like a bolting stallion as I waited for it to drop away again.

Before the wave had even fully subsided, a hand reached over the edge and I cried out in relief as I lurched forward to help pull Chase to safety, my head lifting to search for Maverick and another cry escaping me as I found him climbing out of the blowhole too.

I leapt to my feet, throwing my weight back and pulling Chase so hard that we fell in a heap as he emerged, his body crushing me down onto the ground with a heavy thump.

I wrapped my arms around him, and he buried his face against my neck, the relief of what we'd just survived tangling with the fear and grief we felt for the two missing members of our family.

"Get up," Rick commanded, taking hold of Chase and yanking him to his feet before grabbing my hand and pulling me up too.

He kissed me hard and fast, his lips crushing mine against my teeth and almost drawing blood with the ferocity of his relief before he was gone again, his hand remaining around mine as he dragged me away from the blowhole.

"JJ!" Chase bellowed, cupping his hands around his mouth and for a brief, soul destroying moment we all paused as if we really thought we might get an answer.

The silence was only broken by another wave crashing up and out of the blowhole, and I flinched at the force of it as we were sprayed with salt water again.

"Our stuff is all gone," Rick cursed, the set of his jaw and the lifeless look in his eyes making it clear that he was shutting down, blocking out his emotions and working on the problems at hand while ignoring all else.

"What should we do?" I breathed, staring at the water spraying from the blowhole and trying to figure out where the hell it came from. "Do you think maybe JJ got washed out or-"

"We need to get to the car and go after Fox. We can call the coastguard to hunt for Johnny James," Rick said decisively. "We just need a phone."

Chase's jaw ticked but he nodded, taking hold of my hand and squeezing it tightly for a moment before we all broke into a run, none of us speaking again because there weren't words for the shit that was happening right now. This was so far beyond anything any of us wanted to believe in. I could tell we were all going to let ourselves fall into the trap of denial until there was no choice left but to face the truth.

Mutt barked as he ran ahead of us, shaking out his fur as he went, throwing looks back to me which were filled with relief at our survival. I just focused on our destination and what we needed to do as I ran faster, ignoring the bite of the stones that littered the path beneath my bare feet, cutting into my skin and trying to slow me down.

Water dripped from our saturated clothes as we sprinted on, and my rainbow-coloured hair clung to my cheeks as my breaths puffed sharply in and out.

The descent down the cliff to where we'd parked close to Paradise Lagoon seemed to equally take an eternity while somehow passing me by in a blur.

Finally, I spotted Fox's truck through the darkness, a strangled cry of relief escaping me briefly before I took in the damage to it. My heart twisted sharply as we made it to the vehicle, the three of us falling still as we found the windows shattered and tyres slashed, the pungent scent of gasoline hanging in the air from the puddle that pooled below the truck where an iron bar had been driven right into the tank.

"Fuck!" Rick bellowed, his rage sending a sharp jolt to my heart as it burst from him.

"What now?" I gasped in horror, fear for Fox and JJ crippling me as the utter helplessness of our situation drove down on me like an endless, unbearable weight destined to crush me.

We were nothing in that moment. Not gangsters or players on a board so much bigger than us, not strong or powerful or unstoppable. Just three bruised and battered beings drenched and bleeding, unable to do a single thing of use while reality closed in around us. The four horsemen had come seeking the end of days, and we'd been foolish enough to think we could refuse them.

"We keep running," Rick growled, barely sparing the truck another glance as he dismissed it. "Until we find someone with a fucking phone or a car that we can steal. We don't stop."

I nodded mutely as his hand latched around mine again and Chase tightened his grip on my left, binding us together in what little way we could manage.

We took off into the night, running barefoot, bloody and dripping wet down the stony path which seemed to stretch away from us into eternity across the cliffside. Every moment that passed us rang like a death toll in my head, and the worst thing of all was that there was nothing I could do to stop it.

CHAPTER THREE

I'd been in a washing machine inside a tumble dryer inside a tornado. My head had impacted with so many rocks, it was a miracle my safety helmet was still strapped in place under my chin. It took me a long time to realise I wasn't spinning anymore, and the heartless sea had finally relinquished me from its grasp. I'd faced its wrath and survived, and I had to thank it for its mercy.

Soft sand cushioned my aching body, endless tiny cuts stinging from the briny water which was drying against my flesh. My breaths were shallow and heavy, but the longer I lay there in an exhausted state, the more even they became.

I could feel a tugging inside my chest that had nothing to do with the assault of the ocean, but I couldn't quite hold onto what it meant. I was dancing on the line of consciousness, and there were only hazy, twisted memories living within me.

I heard a girl crying my name into the dark and the roar of a hungry beast before I was stolen away from her. I felt fingers slipping through mine and the callous laugh of a man I knew I hated through to my core. But the claws in my brain wouldn't release me, keeping me trapped in purgatory, knowing something terrible was happening, yet unable to stop it.

The sea was purring now, lapping at my feet, drawing in and out as deeply as my breaths, as if the monster it had been had shifted into a gentle creature instead. This was the sea I knew and loved, the one I'd played in as a kid with the only people in this world who knew the roots of me. It was coaxing me back to life, guiding me towards them and suddenly my world tipped, and my eyes flew open.

It all spilled in at once.

Rogue.

My boys.

The blowhole.

"I'm coming, hold on," I growled, my voice raw from the salt water I'd swallowed, but my promise still carried a solid weight of truth in it.

I was on a small slip of sand between sharp rocks that jutted up around me, meeting with the cliff at my back and rising towards the blackest night sky I'd ever seen. This was far from The Mile or anywhere that I could expect to find help, and my heart lurched with panic as I tried to get my bearings and figure out how far I'd been taken by the ocean.

I released a raking cough, vaguely recalling doing just that the moment the sea had spat me out, water pouring from my lungs onto the sand. The briny water had left a dry burn in my chest, but it was nothing compared to the flash fire that consumed my heart at the thought of the people I loved stuck in that blowhole. And Fox…

I scrambled to my feet, peeling off the tattered remains of my ripped shirt and binding it around the deepest cut on my arm that must have been slashed open by a sharp rock. I couldn't feel it, only certain I had to stop the bleeding so I could keep moving, return to my family and rescue them. I ran up the beach, making my way to a narrow animal trail that led away from the sand.

Adrenaline and panic fuelled every movement of my muscles. I knew if I stopped moving, I'd collapse and struggle to get up again. So I kept going, forcing myself up the steep bank, my stinging palms grasping at the long grass any time I slipped, dragging myself along and refusing to slow. This was so much bigger than me. So much more than the limitations of my body or the pain in my flesh.

My muscles were burning by the time I finally crested the hill and I spotted the narrow cliff road rising ahead of me. I charged towards it, stumbling over rocks and sand before I hit the tarmac and turned my gaze up to the immense cliff to my right where I knew the blowhole was located. Running all the way up there could take me an hour. I needed a car. I needed to get there as fast as fucking possible. But turning away from them felt like the most painful thing I'd ever done as I made the decision, and I prayed with all my soul it would be the right one.

I ran at full pace along the road, my boots hitting the ground, spitting water from the toes as I went.

The moon lit the way forward, the landscape before me seeming so empty, so fucking quiet that it seemed like I was the only person in the damn world. And that was terrifying because if there was one thing I'd never been, it was alone. I always had one of my friends at my side, and the thought of losing them all in one night was close to suffocating me.

I wouldn't survive that. I couldn't. If they were truly gone then I would soon follow, but until I was certain, I refused to give up on hope.

I rounded a sharp bend in the road and spotted a couple of teenagers making out in a shitty old Cadillac, and I didn't hesitate for a single heartbeat.

I charged up to them, wrenching the driver's door open and bellowing at them like a mad man.

"Get the fuck out!" I ripped the girl out of the guy's lap, shoving her onto the road behind me as she screamed in alarm.

The guy raised his hands as fright made his eyes nearly pop out of his

33

head. I grabbed his shirt in my fists, wheeling him out of the car where he stumbled away from me alongside his girl. I dropped straight into the car in his place, and I was already driving off down the road before I got the door shut, leaving them staring after me in shock.

I sped up the winding cliff road as fast as I fucking could, my knuckles turning white on the steering wheel as I tried not to picture what might await me in that blowhole when I got there.

The bodies of my family, floating there like ragdolls in the water, bashed and bruised, too late for me to save them.

"No," I snarled through my teeth, refusing that fate as I drove into the night, the headlights piercing the dark like the eyes of a demon.

I yanked the wheel hard as I reached the road leading back towards the cliffs and up to the blowhole, the back end swinging out on the dirt road and the wheels spinning violently as I flattened my foot to the floor. Stones and dust were blasted up behind me by the rear wheels, and I shot away again with the old car whining in protest at the violent treatment.

I raced up the dirt road at speed, nothing existing beyond what was illuminated by my headlights, the beams piercing through the bleakness of the night like two blazing rays of hope.

I coughed hard, my lungs on fire and my chest constricting as I did so, but I ignored the pain in my body because it was nothing compared to the agony my heart was in, fear for the people I loved most in this world consuming me.

I wouldn't give up on them. I couldn't. If I had to climb back down into that blowhole myself and heave them out one by one, then so help me I'd do it. Though as I thought of the violent sea that had ripped me out of that hell, my terror over the fate of my family only grew.

I sped around another corner, the hill sharpening at last, my destination seeming less distant.

And suddenly there they were, Rogue with her colourful hair plastered to her cheeks, Maverick beside her with Mutt racing ahead of them and Chase on her other side. They were battered and bruised, but fuck, they were alive.

I slammed on the brakes with relief crashing through every fibre of my being, throwing the door open and the moment their eyes met mine, I felt our connection bursting through the air like a firework.

"Johnny James!" Rogue screamed, disbelief and hope tangling in her ocean blue eyes as she ran at me.

We collided with one another, our mouths meeting like they'd always been destined to be together, and I clutched her against me with all the power left in my body, the two of us trembling at the impossibility of this moment.

Maverick and Chase slammed into the embrace, and I rested my forehead to each of theirs as Mutt yapped and licked my ankles frantically.

"JJ," Chase gasped, his lips grazing against my neck. "We thought… fuck."

"Don't ever do that again," Rick snarled, a thump hitting my back as he tried to express what he felt, but I didn't need the words. I could feel it for myself.

"Fox," I rasped as panic found me once more, all of us breaking apart as we shared a look of terror. There was a gaping hole in our group, and this brief moment of relief died a quick death with the reality of where our brother was and what might be happening to him now.

"We have to find him. We need weapons," Rogue said fiercely.

"Harlequin House," Chase said, his upper lip peeling back in a snarl.

"Fucking Shawn is going to die tonight," Maverick growled, and we nodded our agreement.

We were feral dogs of war with a member of our pack stolen away from us, and Shawn Mackenzie was finally going to discover what happened to those who dared to rile us.

CHAPTER FOUR

I rode beside Luther in the car he'd jacked while Travis sat quietly in the back, lingering with us like a reaper waiting to collect a soul. But I guessed he was the opposite of that, because he'd saved both of ours tonight. Though I still couldn't say I trusted him beyond this moment, because he was under orders. The man was clearly bought and paid for by the cartel, an attack dog lying in wait who had turned on the men he'd been planted amongst for fuck knew how long for no other reason than a simple command from his master. That was what made the damn cartel so terrifying – anyone and everyone had the potential to be owned by them, and their loyalty was something steeped in fear and respect so thick that there was no penetrating it. Who knew what life Travis had lived before the Castillos had taken ownership of him, but it was clear he was a cartel weapon now.

Pain speared through my side from the stab wound fucking Shawn had gifted me, and blood was soaking through Dad's shirt which was still cinched tight around my waist. It was only my most painful wound by a little though, because my neck felt like it had come damn close to snapping when I'd fallen from that bridge, and I gritted my teeth against the ache needling into my flesh as I focused on my family.

Adrenaline must have gotten me this far without collapsing, but I was reaching my limits, the moment of stillness in the car bringing the reality of my injuries crashing down on me all too clearly now. My hands were shaking a little, either from the shock, blood loss or just with the need to act, but I refused to give the demands of my body any attention whatsoever until I had my family wrapped tight in my arms again. No other fate was acceptable.

I'd wanted to head straight to the blowhole, but Dad had talked sense into me, because there was no point going up there to help if we didn't have anything to rescue them with. But with every second that scraped by as we headed towards Harlequin House to get supplies, I knew that could be the moment Rogue slipped from the rocks, the moment Chase lost his grip on her, the moment Rick dived after her and split his head open on a rock and JJ followed him into the dark.

I winced, scrunching a hand up against my eyes as I desperately tried not to imagine any of those things, but they were burrowing so deeply into my skull it was as if they'd already happened.

"Dad," I said roughly, my throat ripped raw by the hanging Shawn had given me, leaving my voice raspy and full of gravel. "Hurry," I begged, though he was already driving three times the speed limit and wasn't taking any prisoners.

Luther's hand dropped onto my knee and squeezed, an echo of familiarity passing between us from when I'd been a kid, a time when I'd loved and needed him. I realised I needed him again now. More than anything. He'd followed me over that bridge and known he could have been chasing my tail into death, but he hadn't hesitated.

He was a good fucking father and I finally let myself forgive him for all the bad shit he'd done, because I was done holding onto grudges and regrets. Life was still buzzing through my veins and that was more than I could have hoped for when my legs had been kicking above that ravine. I'd said my goodbyes, I'd tried to let go of it all, knowing my sacrifice would have bought the people I loved a little longer in this world, a chance to survive if nothing else.

I'd never truly let go though, because I wanted to live. I wanted to make amends and fix all the bad shit I'd spent too long breaking in the name of my stupid fucking need to control everything around me. But what if I'd lost the chance to atone now? If this world no longer held any of the souls within it that I was intrinsically bound to, if death had stolen them from me, it would tear a fissure into me that would never heal. There was no life for me without them. No anything.

Dad looked to my wounds like he was going to make some remark, but he held his tongue, only placing his hand back on the wheel as he drove us to Harlequin House as fast as he humanly could. He slipped back into Harlequin King mode just as he'd taught me to do, to separate my emotions from my actions whenever I could. But the fact that he'd come to the bridge tonight proved to me he could still make choices based on love alone, and those were the only kinds of choices I wanted to make now when it came to Rogue and the others. I'd been cold and callous for too long, treating them all like they were mine to command. But no more. If they still lived, I'd do better. I'd *be* better.

The moment we sped through the open gates, I noticed the beat-up Cadillac in the drive and the lights brightening the windows. Someone was here. Some of my family, or all of them? Maybe one of them had made it out, made it back here to get help. Or maybe it was just a couple of Harlequins who'd had to make a break from somewhere. I didn't know, but hope tore through me all the same.

I didn't hesitate to overanalyse it, spilling out of the car and running for the front door as I gritted my teeth through the pain blazing through every inch of my body.

"Fox!" Dad hollered after me as I threw the front door open, and blood dripped between my fingers as I clasped the stab wound on my side.

Darkness curtained my vision, but I fought it every step down that hallway, my shoulder ramming into the wall as I stumbled. Rogue's name spilled from my lips in desperation, but my voice wouldn't raise enough to carry, and my throat burned from the effort, the bruises forming around it aching from my insistence to try.

Be here. Please be here.

My strength failed me, and I hit the floorboards on my knees, one hand still clutching my side while I braced myself against the wall with the other, leaving a bloody handprint smeared down the white surface as unconsciousness tried to steal me away. But I wouldn't go quietly. I had to save the girl I loved, the boys who were brothers to me in every way that mattered.

A shadow rushed toward me, and she came into focus so beautifully that I swear I was dead already as I stared up at this otherworldly creature who owned me. Her blazing blue eyes were wide as they locked with mine, and my heart thundered its way through the centre of my chest as she fell to her knees and screamed something I couldn't hear.

The darkness was stealing her away from me, or perhaps it was the other way around because I was falling again, tumbling from that bridge into oblivion. It hit me in a moment of terror that maybe I was still there, hanging by Shawn's rope, and this was life's final gift to me. A vision so sweet it simply couldn't be true.

Soft fingers brushed the hair away from my forehead then pushed deeper into the roots, the feeling familiar and long-lost to me. My senses were slow to awaken, and I felt the press of drugs in my system, something to steal away the pain I'd been drowning in before.

A roughened hand squeezed my arm and I tried to swallow the rawness of my throat, but it remained there regardless of my efforts.

"He's waking up," a male voice said, and I tried to lean toward it, recognising JJ and my heart lifted with relief at knowing he was alright.

"Maybe I should get the doctor to give him another dose. He should rest through the night," Dad said in concern, but I groaned in protest to that. I wanted to be awake, to see them all, count the faces in the room and make sure everyone was here.

"I think that was a no," Rogue said, so close that I was certain it was her fingers which were pushing into my hair.

I forced my eyes open as I sought her out, my heart beating furiously as I found her staring down at me, her body curled against mine. She was wearing one of my t-shirts, her hair damp from a recent shower, but the rainbow colours in it shimmered where it was starting to dry. I was in my room, on my bed, and I guessed the Harlequin doctor had tended to me because I was shirtless, my middle wrapped in a bandage which covered the stab wound on my side.

"You're okay?" I asked, but my voice was a scratchy, dry whisper.

"I'm okay," she confirmed, her eyes full of tears. "Are you?"

I hunted for my other brothers in the room, needing to know they were safe too and as my gaze found Rick and Chase, their own expressions filled with relief, I finally relaxed.

"Yeah, hummingbird," I said, lifting a hand to feel her cheek in my palm and my heart rate began to thump more evenly, knowing she was here, that she was alright.

Dad leaned closer on my other side, his hand releasing my arm. "The doctor said you shouldn't speak too much while your throat is healing, kid."

I nodded stiffly, looking to him and a tattooed hand landed on his shoulder, drawing him back a little and letting me see Maverick beyond him. His jaw was ticking as Luther shifted aside to let him get closer and suddenly, he lunged at me, wrapping his arms around my shoulders. I clutched him back as he crushed the air from my lungs, soaking in the strength of my brother's embrace and the love I felt for him rising in my chest to meet his love for me.

Rogue dove into the fray and Chase and JJ followed, squashing me to the bed and only half trying to keep their bodies from pressing down on my wounds as I drew them closer.

"Be careful, for fuck's sake," Dad said, but there was amusement in it and Rick caught his arm next, dragging him down into the dog pile. A yip caught my ear before a little ball of fuzzy savagery leapt onto the bed and started biting my arm. When he'd had enough of that, he scrambled his way between us until he was licking my face and I couldn't get my hands close enough to stop him.

"Hey Mutt," I said, relieved he was alright, but less excited to see him as his tongue sought out my damn mouth.

Somehow, miraculously they were here, every last one of them, and my worst fears that had seemed too impossible to refute hadn't come to pass at all.

I couldn't see and I could hardly breathe either as they held onto me like they'd never thought they'd see me again, and the feeling was fucking mutual.

Rogue managed to wriggle closest to me, her mouth falling against the corner of mine, and I turned my head, consequences be fucking damned as our lips met.

I kissed her hard and she started crying, falling apart as she met my kiss with equal fervour, and I tasted her tears between us. I apologised with that kiss and let all of my love for her spill out, every moment of raging fury we'd shared, every barrier we'd built between each other, every missed opportunity and misunderstanding, it all just melted away in the face of *us*. None of it mattered, it was all petty and foolish, and I'd wasted too much fucking time on all of it, when I should have simply been ready to adore her in any way she wished to be adored.

"Fucking hell," Dad cursed, and Rick boomed a laugh while the weight of the others drew back.

Her soft hands moved over my skin in a caress that seemed to be checking that I was still here with her, solid and real.

Rogue was half on top of me and I wrapped my arm tight around her waist while my other hand cupped the back of her head, refusing to let her go as our kiss turned to something more carnal, more urgent.

"Er- Rogue?" Chase tried, but the curse he let out next told me someone had punched him.

I half laughed, turning my head to look at them while Rogue moved her mouth to my neck, a murmured sigh escaping her as she gently kissed the bruised skin there.

"Let's leave 'em to talk," JJ insisted, dragging Chase out the door as my head fell back against the pillow, and my own personal angel continued to inspect my wounds like they pained her more than me.

Luther shoved Rick ahead of him and my brother's laughter carried off into the corridor while Mutt leapt from the bed and followed them, yapping like he was laughing too. Then the door snapped shut and I knew I had her alone.

Moving made the pain come back, but I did it anyway, rearing up off the pillows and tugging her firmly over my lap to close all distance between us as I took her mouth with mine once more.

Our lips remained locked and she moaned against my tongue, the taste of blood suddenly running between us and I pulled back, realising my lower lip had split open again where Shawn had cut it.

Rogue stared down at me, her mouth wet with my blood and tears drying against her cheeks. She looked furious, like a harbinger of death ready to stalk the earth and unleash the wrath housed within her over me.

"I'll destroy him," she vowed with so much ferocity I felt it down to my bones as she took a wad of cotton wool from the nightstand and gently dabbed it to my lip until the blood stopped running. "I'll make him pay for every mark on you, for all he's done to every one of us."

I noticed her left hand was bound with gauze and her right was badly cut up in places, my fingers travelling to all the exposed flesh of her legs where knicks and bruises marred my little hummingbird. The need for vengeance bathed between us and I could feel it gilding us in an unbreakable strength.

Fucking Shawn had done a damn good job of trying to break us tonight, but here we were, somehow more unshakeable than ever, and as I stared into the eyes of the girl who I had loved for my entire life, I finally found my place in the world. I had always been her warrior, pledging myself to protect her in any way I saw fit, but it had never been my choice to make. It was meant to be hers; I'd just been too fucking dumb to see it. Now that I did, it felt like all the pieces of a shattered puzzle sliding into place in my mind.

How had I not seen it before?

Because I was a stubborn, strong-willed asshole, that was why. But not anymore. At least not in any way that would hurt her again.

I cupped her cheek in my hand as I took in the exhaustion in her eyes and the soul-bursting relief in her expression over all of us surviving this night. There were no words for how I felt, and I didn't think I could have voiced them even if I'd known how to describe it.

"Let me see," I demanded, my hands skimming higher up her thighs, chasing the bruises.

Her throat bobbed before she nodded, lifting my shirt over her head and tossing it away, revealing that she was entirely naked beneath. She inhaled deeply as I traced my hands up her sides, caressing every bruise and mark I found as my cock swelled between her thighs and my breaths came heavier. I was caught between a raging, murderous fury over these marks and an equally maddening desire for her that had my blood heating to a volcanic temperature.

I leaned in to press my mouth to a bruise along her collarbone, her back arching and her head dropping back as a moan left her that sounded more like I'd driven myself right inside her than simply touched my lips to her skin. But I felt it too, the way our flesh sparked with energy, the lightest touch like dynamite exploding between us.

It was chaotic and healing and spoke of everything I should have been for her. But this energy was a potent thing that drove us together to clash time and again too. It could be a blessing when we harnessed it right though, if we wielded it like a gift instead of a weapon.

I followed the line of her collarbone up to her throat, my fingers carving a path up her spine in a slow ascent, feeling each tiny flinch that told me I'd found another bruise.

Death would be the answer to this. I had already promised it upon Shawn, but now I was vowing it upon every one of his men too for standing around that blowhole and leaving her there. This girl's pain was worth a thousand bloody deaths, and I'd deliver all of it in payment for tarnishing her flesh.

I could feel the wound on my side beginning to flare with pain and I released a breath against her skin as I tried to fight it back, refusing to let anything stand between us now.

"Fox," she said gently, pushing me back and I let her hands guide me down beneath her once more, expecting her to reach for the shirt she'd been wearing and withdraw from me.

She'd told me she loved me, and I knew it was true, but that didn't mean things had changed between us. She still believed I was unable to give her what she needed, and maybe that was true, but I was at least willing to try now.

"Rogue," I started, my throat barely releasing the word, and she pressed a finger to my mouth to quiet me.

"You want me, don't you?" she asked, a flicker of doubt in her gaze for a second.

I nodded, capturing her hand and pressing my lips to the gauze covering her palm before kissing every one of her cut and torn fingertips.

More than anything, baby.

She was making it impossible for me not to give away exactly what her body was doing to me, and my eyes raked over her tight nipples and the way her breaths were coming raggedly, seeing the reaction she had for me too.

I wanted to be more for her than I could be in this moment with these wounds rendering me weak, and she seemed to see that in my eyes as she ran her palm down my chest to rest over my heart. She gasped as she found the burn where Shawn had stubbed his cigarette out in the centre of the Ferris wheel tattoo. Her lips peeled back in a snarl, and she dropped over me, kissing the mark again and again until it only burned because of her. Then she ran her mouth down my body, kissing everywhere while carefully avoiding the stab wound on my side before she traced her tongue along the seam of my sweatpants.

I groaned, my hands fisting in the sheets as she drove me to insanity, my injuries keeping me still beneath her and she gave me one sultry look before freeing my throbbing cock and sucking the tip into her mouth.

"Fuck," I gritted out as she ran her tongue around the head of my dick while she started to pump the base of it in her fist.

I watched her in disbelief as one of my fantasies of her was fulfilled right before my eyes, and I wondered if I was just in a drug coma, dreaming this up. It had to be real though, because nothing in a dream could feel this good, and I suddenly had to focus really damn hard as her mouth worked over my shaft, my balls starting to tighten already.

I held her hair out of the way, winding it around my fist as she took me to the back of her throat and a growl left me that was all animal. Her eyes flicked up to meet mine and she slowly drew her lips all the way up to the tip in a move that was nothing short of mind blowing.

Just as I thought I was going to explode from the feeling of her sweet torture, she released me from her mouth and moved further up my body, straddling me with a look of sheer need in her eyes. I wanted to be more for her in this moment, capable of claiming her the way she deserved to be claimed, but as I opened my mouth to try and tell her that, she lowered down until my cock pressed against the slickness of her pussy, and I forgot how to speak entirely.

My hands went to her hips and neither of us blinked as she rested her palms on my shoulders, both of us finally giving in to this after so agonisingly long. I had to have her now, even if I was half the man I usually was, laid weak on this bed. But I could see that didn't matter to her, and it suddenly didn't matter to me either. We just had to join together, there was no force in the world that could stop it.

Our breaths tangled between us, a decision made in our eyes before she pressed her hips down and my cock slid inside her, making both of us curse at the feeling we'd both been aching for from each other for so incredibly long.

Our mouths came together and I drove my hips up, moving deeper, filling her entirely and making her cry out against my lips as I continued to work every inch of myself inside her.

We were damaged and hurt and in no state to be attempting this, but it wasn't some simple desire. It was need. Pure, honest-to-God need that demanded we finally cross this line and become what we had always been destined to be.

We started moving as one, our bodies falling into sync immediately like we were fucking made for each other as we found this deep, heady rhythm that promised me all kinds of oblivion at her mercy.

I tasted her on my tongue and couldn't get enough of how perfect she felt around me, my hands moving to grasp her ass and squeezing that perfect flesh as she rode me. It was achingly slow, the two of us kissing and moaning and pulling each other closer as we got used to this feeling of claiming one another in this wholly unreal way. She rolled her hips in perfect movements which had me hitting that sweet spot inside her, making her moan and stare down at me in a haze of pleasure.

I drew her body flush to mine and she ground her clit against my pubic bone while I applied pressure to her back, keeping her there and driving her towards her climax, her pussy squeezing my cock and begging me to come for her. But I wouldn't finish until she did. I wanted to feel her fall apart for me, to shatter just for me. Only fucking me.

I winced as she laid her weight on my stab wound, but as she tried to pull back, I only held her tighter, refusing to let my injury fuck this up and she gave into my wants, her mouth meeting mine again as she moaned in pleasure.

She started to tremble and I slowed my pace even more, edging her and keeping her orgasm at bay while her hips quickened to try and steal it from me.

"Fox," she begged, and the sound of my name leaving her mouth was so fucking perfect, I had to give in to it.

I raised my hips a little more and drove into her deeply, grinding against her g-spot and making her fist the pillows by my head. Her pussy started to pulse around my cock as she gave in to me with a sultry moan which was by far the sexiest sound I'd ever heard in my entire life.

A smile spilled across my face as she came, moaning and writhing, my name falling from her tongue time and again while I fucked her all the way through it, so close to finishing myself, but not letting a moment of my concentration waiver as I kept her climax going for as long as possible.

She melted against me when it was over and I gripped her hips, only needing two more pumps to finish me and crying out in a noise which was mostly stolen by the rawness of my throat, the intensity of it making my head spin.

Pleasure ran along the length of my cock as I exploded inside her, stilling deep within her as I rode out the last of this life-altering high. It felt like our damn souls were colliding and tangling into something made of the universe itself.

Her forehead fell to mine and I wanted to say so many goddamn things, but instead we just remained like that, staring into each other's eyes and holding one another close.

"Never leave me again, Fox Harlequin," she demanded after we finally caught our breath.

"Never," I swore it, and peace filled her gaze, like she'd been waiting to hear that for a long, long time.

She slid off of me, hooking one leg over my hips while I held her close, and she rested her ear over my heart. It must have been telling her all my secrets, but I didn't care, because I'd never tried to hide the fact that I loved her, I just hoped she realised that I planned on doing so in a less toxic way than I had in the past. And when my voice was back, I would be telling her straight what she meant to me on every single day I was gifted with her.

Life had offered me another chance, and I wasn't going to fuck this one up. No. Starting tomorrow, I was going to begin mending the past and carving out the best future I could offer Rogue and my boys. It was time to live again, time to reclaim our town and make the kids we'd once been proud of the adults we'd become at last.

I woke early, hearing a door shut somewhere in the house and for a second, I was disorientated, reaching for the gun I usually stashed under my pillow, but it wasn't there.

Instead, my hand met another and it all came rushing back to me as I cracked my eyes open and found her there, sleeping on her front, one arm around me while her head lay on the pillow we were sharing, her other arm firmly under it.

Her rainbow hair had dried in soft waves, tumbling all around her on the pillow, and a little frown creased her forehead like it often did when she slept. I'd know that after the number of times I'd snuck into her room to watch her at night since she'd come back to us, and I still couldn't find it in me to feel bad about it. Since she'd returned, my obsession with her had deepened, my constant fear that she would slip away from me sharpening. But with her here now, I suddenly didn't feel afraid of that anymore.

She had chosen me. Not in a sense that didn't include the others, but in a way that somehow didn't feel like I'd expected it to before last night. I'd thought I'd feel her missing the others, I thought I'd only experience a piece of her if I were to have her too, but it hadn't felt like that at all.

I rolled slightly towards her and pain engulfed me like a fireball, the realisation that the painkillers had worn off hitting me hard. My flinch didn't even make her stir, though I knew this girl slept like the dead, so I couldn't say I was surprised.

I brushed my fingers along her shoulder, my jaw tightening at the bruise I traced before I leaned down to kiss her awake. She didn't stir though, and a smirk quirked up my lips as I did it again. And again.

Giving up on that, I slid out of bed, gritting my teeth through the pain as I moved across the room into the ensuite. I managed a rough shower, keeping my bandages dry and just using the shower head to get myself clean before returning to my room to dress. Rogue was still asleep, looking seriously tempting curled up on top of my sheets, the curve of her bare ass begging for my touch. But I left her there, pulling on some sweatpants and stepping out of the room.

The sound of the coffee machine carried from the kitchen downstairs, but I didn't head that way, moving to the office instead and slipping inside. I had something I needed to do, thoughts burning in my mind which were begging to get out, and while my voice was failing me, I'd have to do it another way.

I shut the door and moved to sit at the desk, swearing as the wound on my side seared. I took a piece of paper and a pen, writing down my thoughts, spilling it all out, trying to say everything I would never have gotten a chance to say if I hadn't made it down from that bridge.

It was ironic really, because it had taken me swinging from a fucking rope by my neck to get to this point, and it really shouldn't have. I'd been too pig-headed for too long, turning a blind eye to the needs of my family, and bulldozing them with my needs instead. Sure, I'd protected them in ways, it hadn't all been bad, but I'd become too controlling, I'd stopped separating my boys from the crew and acted like I was their king, not their brother. It was time to start being the right kind of friend at last. And that could only begin once I'd bared my heart to Rogue.

When I was done, I folded the piece of paper into my pocket and stood up, jolting at the sight of Maverick in the doorway, his arm rested against it and a look of bemused intrigue in his eyes. He was shirtless, his endless display of tattoos on show, and the board shorts he wore hanging low on his hips. He had gauze taped over his right bicep where Shawn's bullet had grazed him, but apart from a few cuts and bruises, he didn't look too worse for wear.

"What are you up to, Foxy boy?" he asked as I walked towards him, trying to fight the look of an injured pup off my face as I met him man to man.

"You'll find out soon enough," I rasped, resting a hand to his shoulder and he looked down at where it sat before looking back up at me.

"Fucking hell, we're gonna hug, aren't we?" he asked, like he was disgusted by the thought, but he was the one who drew me into his arms, and I clapped him on the back with a light laugh, though it came out as throaty and choked.

"We'd better not let Luther see us doing this," he teased, just as my eyes fell on that very man as he came up the stairs.

"Too late," Luther announced, smiling widely at us for a second, but as Maverick released me, my stab wound flared with pain and his smile fell as he saw me wince. "Downstairs. I've got your meds ready and a coffee waiting. The doctor will come and see you again if you need-"

"I don't need to see him again, I'm fine," I insisted in a whisper which hurt like a motherfucker.

"Stop talking," Luther demanded, and I huffed out a breath, but I knew he had a point. I didn't want to fuck up my vocal cords for good. "At least you're looking well rested."

"Yeah, Rogue tells really good bedtime stories, doesn't she brother?" Maverick taunted and I narrowed my eyes at him, wondering if he'd already guessed what had happened between us or if he was just being his usual, dickish self.

"Did I hear the word coffee?" JJ asked through a yawn as he stepped out of his bedroom and I noticed Chase following him, the two of them apparently having slept in together.

I wondered if Maverick had joined them too. I guessed we'd all needed someone last night after everything. And as Mutt came trotting out of the room next, I assumed that extended to him as well.

"I made a pot," Luther confirmed. "I thought that cartel fella might fuck off once I gave him a cup, but he's still laying outside on a sun lounger like he lives here now." Luther scored a hand over his face. "He isn't going to leave until I go with him to see Carmen, but that can wait a little longer. Come on, get the wildcat up and I'll cook us some breakfast. You all look ravenous."

"She won't wake up," I breathed.

"I'll get her up," Maverick said confidently, striding down the hall and I lunged after him, not wanting the evidence of what we'd done shown to him before she decided it herself.

The movement was too much for me though and I doubled in on myself as I stretched my wound, and Chase steadied me while I tried to get past him. He was limping again, and I guessed the strain of what he'd been through in the blowhole had flared up his old wounds.

"*Wait*," I hissed, but Maverick was already throwing the door open and running into the room like he was about to dive bomb her.

"Oh holy fuck," Maverick boomed then he laughed so loud that it made the roof rattle.

"What?" JJ jogged after him, and I staggered after them as Chase kept a hand on my shoulder.

"JJ," I tried as he made it into the doorway and Chase and I stepped up behind them, all of us looking in at the sleeping form of Rogue on the bed, perfectly naked, and seriously fucking incriminating.

Rick stood beside the bed, looking to me with an arched eyebrow and a smug as pie look on his face that was all taunt. I glanced down at Mutt as he squeezed past our legs, took one look at Rogue then glared straight back at me accusingly like he knew the truth.

"Well look what we have here," Maverick said. "What the fuck happened to her clothes, Foxy boy? Damn mystery, that is."

"Fuck off, Rick," I ground out, my hand going to my throat and drawing Chase's gaze.

"Did you two…" Chase started, looking weirdly hopeful.

"Of course they did," JJ said, rounding on me with a wide smile. "I don't even need to call on my sexth sense for this one, the truth is everywhere."

Maverick tossed a blanket over Rogue then threw himself on top of her like the blanket had made it more acceptable to do so.

She cried out with a yelp, and he rubbed her face into the pillow with an obnoxious laugh. "Morning, dirty girl."

"Jesus, Rick." JJ ran forward and wrestled him off of her, offering a few playful punches as she rolled over and threw plenty of her own, though hers were more savage considering she'd just been woken up and that was never something Rogue let go lightly.

She wrapped the blanket around herself as she wriggled her way out from between them, leaving JJ and Rick shoving each other on the bed. I thought about pointing out that that was where Rogue and I had fucked, but then again, they were assholes and didn't seem to give a damn anyway, so I stayed silent.

Rogue took one sleepy-eyed look at me, blushed then ran away into the en-suite and slammed the door.

"Oh my God," Chase laughed, nudging me with his elbow. "You've made her go all girly."

53

I shrugged him off, turning to head downstairs, but my three brothers chased after me, not letting this go.

"Did you find clarity between our girl's thighs, brother?" Rick asked while I ground my jaw and ignored him. "Did her pussy talk some sense into your cock?"

"Maverick," Luther snapped as we entered the kitchen and my brother boomed a laugh, but thankfully didn't say any more on the subject.

We all sat around the kitchen island and my dad handed us coffee, clapping Rick around the ear as he placed one down for him. Though Maverick just smiled like he didn't even mind it.

"So you're…with Rogue?" Dad asked me hopefully and my lips tightened as every nosy fucker in this house looked to me.

"Not the time, Dad," I muttered, sipping my coffee, though he seemed to take that as a yes, grinning widely as he moved to fill Mutt's bowl with treats. The little dog came scampering up to him, eating all of them despite the fact he always rejected those treats when I gave them to him.

I stole a glance out at Travis who was lounging in the sun with his shirt off, looking like he might just be asleep, though the tightness of his grip on the gun in his hand told me otherwise.

"What's his deal?" I asked Dad and Luther frowned.

"He wants me to go with him to see Carmen. I demanded a moment with you all this morning, but I'll have to leave soon," Dad said.

Rogue appeared in a baggy blue beach dress, moving to sit between Chase and JJ while her eyes kept meeting mine and little smiles passed between us as Rick fetched her coffee. Yeah, I was feeling like a smug asshole right about now, the memories of last night all too fresh in my mind. I didn't even give a damn that Chase and JJ kept smirking at us like idiots.

Luther took Mutt out to the beach, but I suspected he was going to smoke as he took a lighter with him when he went, and everyone else's eyes fell to me.

"Luther told us what happened last night," JJ said darkly, his gaze falling

54

to the bruises around my throat.

"You're the fucking Terminator, you know that?" Chase said with a smile which didn't quite touch his eyes.

I released a breath of amusement as I swallowed a mouthful of coffee, noticing Rick looking at me with his brows pulled together and a dark intensity about him.

"I wanna start making a list of everything we owe Shawn death for, then tick 'em off one by one when we deliver them back to him," Maverick said in a deadly voice which promised retribution for my injuries. It was hard to believe he'd finally returned to me, the boy who'd go to hell and back for me as I would for him. We were brothers through and through, and it felt like our bond was somehow even stronger than it had been all those years ago when we were kids.

"We'll do it together," Rogue added, and we all nodded our agreement, a deal struck and forged in iron here and now. We were going to bring fucking Shawn to his glorious end, no matter what it took.

"Oh, good gracious," Miss Mabel crowed as she entered the kitchen in her nightgown. "I must have slept fourteen hours! What on earth happened last night? Did you find my diamonds?" She looked between us, seeming to notice the wounds we were sporting, and the blood drained from her face.

As Rogue explained, guilt stirred in me in at how we'd failed her. Mabel had entrusted the secret location of her diamonds to us, and we'd fucked up royally.

"I'm sorry, Miss Mabel," Rogue said sadly. "Shawn took the diamonds."

Mabel gasped, holding a hand to her chest like she'd been stabbed there. "That dirty rotten blaggard. How dare that filthy little shit take them!"

She looked a little faint, steadying herself on JJ's shoulders and I got up to cook some breakfast for her before she passed out.

"Are you all okay?" Mabel asked, looking over our injuries as tears welled in her eyes. "I feel terrible. I should never have sent you there."

"We're fine, Mabel," Rogue promised, guiding her to a chair where the old girl let out a little hiccup of sadness.

"Sometimes I think those diamonds are cursed," she croaked.

"It's Shawn who's the curse," Rick growled, and Mabel nodded, sniffing as she drew her shoulders back.

"Well, we must make a plan." She slapped her hand down on the kitchen island. "We must hunt him down, take our diamonds back and offer him a merciless death."

"Hell yes, Miss Mabel." JJ grinned.

When I had her breakfast ready, she bustled back to her bedroom, demanding Chase carry it for her on a tray and he pouted as he did as she commanded.

Luther came back inside with Mutt in his arms and the little dog scrambled his way free, leaping at me, licking my leg before savaging it in a friendly fuck you.

"Alright, old man, I'm gonna need to take you to Carmen now to pay your debt," Travis's voice carried from the doorway, and I looked over at him, his gaze pinned on Luther. "She's likely growing impatient at this point."

"Well, she can hang on a little longer," Luther growled, but I met his gaze with a shake of my head, knowing the last thing we needed was to upset the damn cartel.

"Go," I insisted, and he frowned, but the idea of his refusal bringing the cartel to our door was not one I wanted to indulge in. I knew Carmen wouldn't hurt him, and whatever she wanted from him was undoubtedly well within Dad's skill set.

"So, you're Carmen's man?" Rogue asked and Travis nodded, a slight smile shifting his lips.

"Through and through," he said.

"Well, I guess I owe you a thanks," she said, and a little surprise crossed his features before he shrugged.

"I work under orders. If you want to thank someone, you'd better speak to Carmen Ortega," he said.

"I will," she said, and Travis's brows lifted a little at the conviction in her voice. "Me and her have a connection."

"You might be in Carmen's favour right now, but don't go thinking she keeps friends. She operates from the top, alone. She doesn't keep anyone in her life who isn't useful to her, so be sure to remain useful," Travis warned before turning to Luther. "Come on, old man. Do you need your walker to make it to the door?"

"Fuck off," Luther gritted out before giving our group a last look over before pausing on Rogue. "You look after them, wildcat."

"Sure thing, big man," she said and they exchanged a warm smile before he turned to leave with Travis.

"Come back here when you're done," Rick commanded him, and Luther's lips hooked up at the corner as he glanced back over his shoulder.

"Careful, son, that almost sounds like you care about me." He walked out the door after Travis, and Rick shook his head, though he didn't contradict him.

The front door snapped shut as they left, and Rogue wound her hand around mine. Chase returned to the kitchen, leaving Miss Mabel in her room with the TV blasting old re-runs of Dawson's Creek. The old girl had a bit of an obsession with the show.

"So, are we all fucking Rogue now, or what?" Maverick asked bluntly and Rogue punched him in the arm.

"Not now," she insisted. "I don't want to talk about it now. Let's just... snuggle."

"Snuggle?" JJ's eyebrows raised in amusement as she trailed away into the lounge.

"Whatever you want, little one," Chase said and the rest of us nodded in unison.

"Anything," I rasped, and she looked back at us in surprise as we moved to follow, seeing us for what we were. Her soldiers to command, her men in arms. We were bound by her, willing to fight and die for her. She need only give the word. And it looked like she finally knew it.

Rogue, Rick, Chase and JJ sat around me on the couch, all of us cuddling up under one blanket even though it wasn't really big enough.

And for the first time in so long, it was finally us again. The real us. The five kids who loved each other more than any normal people loved one another, who couldn't sleep easily without one another close. My brain couldn't function enough to figure out the more complicated relationship shit right now, and I didn't care to. All I wanted was the closeness of my family and the knowledge that their hearts were all still beating powerfully in their chests.

"Are we safe now?" Rogue asked, her hand finding mine beneath the blanket and her fingers threading between mine. She looked from me to the others like she couldn't believe we were all here, alive. I was having a hard damn time believing it myself.

"We're safe, pretty girl," JJ promised.

All the things that needed to be done could wait until tomorrow. Luther would have locked down this house with every Harlequin he could muster, and no doubt a whole host of them were out hunting for Shawn too.

"Shawn's probably gone to ground already," Chase said, his upper lip curling. "Fucking cockroach that he is."

"Fucking cock, more like," Rick growled.

I slid my hand into my pocket, taking out the letter I'd written earlier and handing it to Chase, knowing he had entrusted his letter to me once, so I was happy to do the same.

"Will you read that out?" I asked hoarsely and he frowned as he took it, unfolding the page.

"What is it?" Rogue asked, stroking Mutt's head as he started to fall asleep.

"My truth," I said, looking her in the eye and squeezing her hand.

"Hummingbird, I love you," Chase read. "You already know this, you've known it your whole life, and I could spend days excusing myself of my misgivings because of love. But I would be wrong to do that. So fucking wrong. It's taken death to realise that we're just a flash of light in the face of eternal oblivion, and whatever my purpose is here on this floating rock that's hurtling through eternal space, I know it has everything to do with you." Chase paused but I didn't take my eyes off of Rogue as she gazed at me, her eyes gleaming. "So long as I'm here experiencing this existence with you at my side, I know those huge, impossible questions don't matter anymore. I know that what we had as kids is worth fighting for, and I can promise I will try with everything I have to fit into this new version of us. Because the thing is, all that matters is that we're here somehow, existing together in this tiny fraction of a moment which is nothing among the vastness of everything. But it's all we have, and I'm done wasting our seconds, letting them slip away and vanish before my eyes. From this moment forward until my very last in this world, so long as we're here, wanting each other, I am yours. Because maybe there is no divine creature out there who made us, maybe all of this is just maddening disorder that will never make any sense. But you, Rogue, you make sense to me. In fact, you're the only thing that has ever made sense to me. The one thing I have never had to question or doubt. I may not exist for any particular purpose in this world, but I am choosing you as my purpose. I will make your happiness my meaning on this earth. I promise I will enrage you sometimes, and you will enrage me, and there will be days when we're at each other's throats like hungry wolves. But I don't want it any other way, because it's our truth, our raw love and hate for each other coming together as one. Maybe we're the chaos of the universe given flesh. But isn't there something fucking perfect in that? And in true Fox Harlequin fashion, I have to make a demand of you. Tell me you'll have me, hummingbird, because I'm yours, every wretched piece of me."

Rogue gazed at me while quiet hummed through the room and I didn't even feel embarrassed that all of them had heard that, it was the way it should be, all of us sharing in each other's truth. No more deception or things left unsaid.

"You already know the answer," she said croakily, leaning forward to kiss me but I captured her chin, holding her lips a hair's breadth from mine.

"Say it anyway," I growled.

"I'm yours, you're mine. All of us belong to each other," she glanced to the others, and I stole the kiss, guiding her attention back to me, embracing each and every one of those words.

Soon, last night would be the past, just painful memories that we'd recover from. But I was okay with that, because our future shone like a ray of sunshine ahead of us, and starting today I would shape myself into the man I'd once planned to be. I'd keep my promise to Chase and hold our family together no matter what. I would work to fully mend the rift between my adopted brother and I, and I'd forgive JJ for the lies he'd weaved in this house.

But most of all, I would offer Rogue whatever she wanted from me. I would be her protector, her friend, and love her in any way she wanted to be loved by me. My heart was in her hands now, and that was where it belonged.

The Oasis Clubhouse

LUTHER

CHAPTER FIVE

I got into my black Dodge Challenger, the sports car I loved but hardly ever got to drive, waiting as Travis strode around to the other side and climbed into the passenger seat.

I hit the button for the A/C, not wanting the windows open for this conversation as I started the engine and waited for the electric garage doors to roll open.

"Is Carmen still at the mansion along the coast?" I asked, breaking the silence and he nodded.

"I doubt she's too happy you've kept her waiting," he added, looking down at his phone while shooting off a text which I had to assume was either to her or one of her men, letting them know we were on our way.

"Rogue mentioned you've been in The Dead Dogs for a good few years," I said, looking him over as I waited to pull out of the drive, wondering what he'd done to earn himself that kind of position of trust at such a young age.

Travis shrugged, leaning back in his seat and spreading his legs wide as he made himself comfortable. "Shawn was never going to trust anyone easily.

They needed someone young enough for him to know I wasn't a cop, and someone motivated enough to stay loyal to them no matter what."

"Oh yeah? What kind of motivation do you have?"

The silence stretched as I started us down the road and I thought he wasn't even going to answer, but then he simply shrugged.

"I was of the belief that I would rather remain alive than be butchered by the Castillo Cartel. And I had something of a point to prove too."

I grunted, acknowledging that made sense even if it was fucked up. But that was the world we lived in, and if he was under threat from the cartel then he had likely done something to get himself in that position. It was dog eat dog out here, he'd simply chosen a pack to hunt with.

"And they just had you keeping an eye on Shawn? Do they do that with all the gangs they have dealings with?" I asked, unable to help scouring mentally through the ranks of my men, suspicion clouding my thoughts as I considered each of them.

"And the ones they aren't working with too," Travis said, smirking at me.

"I don't suppose you want to tell me who in my house is spying on me then?" I grumbled and he laughed.

"Even if I knew, I wouldn't. I told you, I'm Castillo Cartel through and through, cut me and I'd bleed their name all over the floor of this nice car. I'm their property, there's no way out for me now even if I wanted it."

"But you don't?" I questioned. It seemed like he'd been given little choice but to join up to this life at a young age, so I would have expected daydreams about another life from him. It was something I dealt with within my own crew after all. Blood in, blood out. Though that didn't automatically mean death was the only exit. On occasion, I let men buy their way free of the life at the cost of killing someone I needed gone, the evidence of their crimes recorded just in case they ever tried to turn on me after the fact. But there was no point in holding on to dead weight, and a man who dreamed of freedom that was denied him was never going to be loyal in the way I required, so it made sense to deal with that issue the way I did.

Travis breathed a laugh, shaking his head. "No point in questioning options that aren't there. I'm just glad to be done with fucking Shawn."

He didn't offer me anything further on what he expected to be doing from here on out, but I wasn't surprised. Why would he? He probably had no idea himself anyway, and I could tell he was mostly glad to be free of Shawn's command.

"How about you, old man?" Travis asked, his head tipping as he looked at me. "You ever thought about giving it all up? Retiring somewhere sunny… well, I guess you have sunny covered here, but maybe just somewhere with less people looking to kill you all the damn time?"

The corner of my lips hooked up, my shoulder lifting as I kept my eyes on the road.

"I doubt I'd be well suited to retirement." I had considered change though, not that he needed to hear about that, but I'd spent thirty odd years ruling over these streets, running the crew and being the boss. It was a long time to stay in one place, and occasionally I considered branching out – not so much leaving the crew, more finding new ventures to involve them in. But it was hard to give much thought to changing a strategy that worked so well. Maybe once Fox and Maverick finally got their shit together properly, I'd hand the reins over to them and try something different. That had always been the plan after all, to leave them with my empire when I died, so it wasn't unthinkable to imagine I could do so sooner. I guess I'd never really expected to live into my forties, let alone much beyond them, so it hadn't seemed like something I should concern myself with.

"I dunno, I can picture it now, you with your pipe and slippers, reading the newspaper while looking out over the balcony from the room in your retirement home. You must be starting to feel the aches and pains in your joints at night already, won't be long before you'll be using a cane."

"Yeah? Well, I could use it to beat your ass whenever you came by to visit, so I guess it would come in handy," I shot back, only making him smile wider.

"At least you're admitting you'd need the advantage of a weapon to take me on," he said, seeming endlessly amused by the turn of this conversation and I sighed.

We passed beyond the edge of the town limits, leaving Sunset Cove behind, and making some small talk to fill the air, but Travis was young, cocky, arrogant and I was far too used to commanding respect from assholes like him to be tolerant of too much of his shit.

Travis had absolutely no boundaries, casually rummaging through the glovebox and door pockets until he found himself a stick of gum, then he had the cheek to offer me some of it after the fact.

I sighed, swiping a hand down my face, and focusing on the road ahead. It had been a long damn night and I was dead tired. I could have done without this conversation with Carmen, but of course I had no choice in it. When Carmen Ortega called, all men stood to attention. Unless they wanted to risk her wrath anyway, and I might have been a lot of things, but I wasn't fool enough to cross her.

We finally turned off the main road, following a private drive past several guards who eyed us suspiciously but let us pass, the greenery closing in around us the further we went until we eventually spotted the huge, white mansion standing up on the cliff ahead.

I pulled up before a set of tall, wrought iron gates, looking straight into the security camera perched there as I got out of the car to wait in the heat of the sun for one of her minions to let us in.

Four armed men stepped out from a guards' booth set to the left of the drive, barking instructions at us in Spanish before stepping through the gates and coming to pat me down.

I bit my tongue as I waited for them to finish checking me over, noticing the way they eyed Travis as if he were a stranger to them too, though they didn't search him the way they did me. I had to assume he hadn't exactly been present in their organisation while planted with Shawn, but he didn't seem the least bit concerned about their mistrust or uncertainty. In fact, he took his time observing the mansion at their backs as if they meant little to him at all.

"This way," a man bit out, jerking his chin in a command for us to follow and we fell into step behind him, walking beneath the shade of a row of palms which lined the path up to the front door.

Exhaustion pressed heavily on me as I walked and I gritted my teeth against it, knowing I needed to be on top of my game here. I rolled my shoulders back as I fought to keep my instincts sharp and my focus clear.

We were led up onto a wide porch and the man opened the door there, taking us past another set of guards before leading us to a huge, imposing white staircase which spiralled up to the floor above. The entire place was decorated to perfection, money practically dripping from the ceiling. The fine art that was either hung on the walls, or standing on individual pedestals each called to me on some soul deep level. I couldn't say I'd ever had much interest or appreciation in such things before, but it was impossible to deny the effect some of them had, or the way they demanded attention as we passed them.

At the top of the stairs, the guard led us to the left down a long hallway with arching doors leading off of it, the white wooden floorboards thumping beneath our feet and announcing our arrival. The place seemed more like a luxury hotel than a home, but that didn't really surprise me; Carmen was a woman who demanded the best of everything.

Pepito stood outside one of the doors ahead of us, his back ramrod straight and gaze fixed on the wall across from him. The man was like a wall of solid muscle without a single thought in his head to accompany his bulk beyond his devotion to the woman who I had to assume was beyond that door.

He eyed us intently as we arrived before him, his cold gaze raking over me then Travis, any thoughts he may have had about the two of us remaining locked up tight inside his mind as he didn't show so much as a flicker of reaction to our presence.

"She's ready for us?" asked the guard who had led us here and Pepito nodded, stepping aside to allow us access to the white door at his back.

The guard opened the door, bright sunlight filling the huge suite beyond as it streamed in through a tall window and an open door which led out onto the balcony.

We followed him into the room and my spine stiffened at the scent of sex tainted by the sweetness of Carmen's perfume, and I stumbled as I caught sight of the man lying in the huge four poster bed to our right.

My lips parted as I took in his muscular body, the sheets barely covering his cock where he lay tangled in them, sleeping like the dead, not seeming to have any idea that he had company. There were scratches on his chest and arms, the marks of fingernails gouged there in passion, and I noted a bruise around his throat too.

The bed was in complete disarray, white sheets tangled and torn like a pack of animals had been let loose on them, and yet I could tell that whatever had been done in that space had been only of the most amorous designs.

My chest tightened at the sight of him, something utterly predatory coming to life within me and making my jaw tick with rage. The desire to rip him from the bed hit me as I was struck with anger that wouldn't let go of me, burrowing deep and reminding me of the way I felt right after a kill when blood still stained my skin and I was nothing but the worst of me.

"Levántate, Paulo," barked the guard who had led us here, clapping his hands aggressively and jerking the man in the bed awake. "No seas tonto y márchate cuando ella acabe contigo."

The naked man shifted upright, blinking around in confusion before glancing at the gun sitting on the nightstand like he planned on grabbing it, but he didn't, swiping a hand down his face instead as he took in his surroundings.

Travis snorted in amusement, and I shot him a dark look.

"Lo siento, señor," Paulo muttered. "Debo haberme quedado dormido."

"I don't care what excuses you claim, get your shit and go sleep it off somewhere else. I expect you back at the gates by noon," the guard hissed, and my jaw tightened further as I realised the naked motherfucker was another guard, someone she saw regularly and not just a meaningless conquest she'd brought back here for a night between her thighs.

The man in the bed shoved out of it, his muscles flexing as he snatched his scattered clothes from the floor, yanking his pants up to cover his irritatingly large cock before fisting his shirt, boots and gun and striding for the door at a quick pace.

I turned my head as I watched him go, pushing my tongue into my cheek as I took in the scratches that marked his back too, my mind unable to help but wonder if he'd been able to make her moan for him. I doubted many men would be up to the task of satisfying a woman like her. Not that I'd ever given it much thought.

"Miss Ortega will speak with you on the balcony," the guard announced, heading across the suite and forcing us to follow.

We stepped through the long, billowing curtains that lined the sliding door which opened onto the balcony, and I squinted against the brightness of the sun after being inside.

The guard declared our presence then turned to leave without another word, leaving us to look at Carmen where she was sitting at a metal table that had been laid out with breakfast. Pastries, toast, fruit, a jug of freshly pressed orange juice and a pot of coffee all prepared like some kind of offering for a queen while she just sat there with her toes balanced on the metal railing that lined the balcony, her eyes on the view of the sea below.

She was wearing a pale golden nightdress, the silk material barely skimming the tops of her brown thighs and clinging to the fullness of her breasts with a line of lace trimming the edges of it. Her dark hair was down, though it still appeared perfectly styled, hanging around her shoulders and making her appear a little more human than usual.

"Do you plan on leaving us standing here all day?" I asked when she didn't so much as glance our way, and I noticed her fingers were trailing back and forth over a scar marking the side of her neck.

She blinked at my words, releasing a heavy breath and turning sultry eyes on me like I was testing her patience.

"What's the matter, Luther?" she purred, her voice rich with her Mexican accent. "Don't you enjoy being made to wait?"

I cleared my throat, understanding the jab without needing the elbow I got in the ribs from Travis to remind me of it.

"Fox was injured," I explained, my words clipped and anger still needling at me. I knew I should have been watching my words with her, thanking her on my knees for what she'd done, but I couldn't help the irritation I felt at being brought to her like this, with some man she'd fucked asleep in the other room and her not even offering me the respect of looking me in the eye as she spoke to me.

"But not dead," she pointed out, reaching for a glass of orange juice and lifting it to her lips as a gust of warm air swept around us, whispering promises of the scorching day to come.

"No," I agree, nodding my head. "And I understand I have you to thank for that."

"And yet you aren't thanking me," she said, the warning in her tone clear.

"Thank you," I said earnestly, the emotion in my tone evident and she finally turned her head to meet my gaze. "Truly. I can't ever repay you for what you did, but if there is anything at all-"

"You know nothing in this world comes for free just as surely as you know that I don't offer out favours from the goodness of my own heart." A breath of laughter escaped her at the mere thought of that.

Her eyes shifted away from me to Travis who had taken it upon himself to lean on the balcony railing while we spoke, acting as though he was right at home here in the nest of a viper with the scent of sex on the air and the threat of death staying close to us.

"Travis?" she questioned, taking him in. "I hadn't realised you were quite so…" she trailed off, though the look she gave him wasn't difficult to assess, her eyes running down his frame in a way that set my jaw grinding once more and a growl rolled up the back of my throat that I was unable to fully contain.

"Do you fuck all the men who work for you?" I snapped, unable to help myself for some insane reason, and her attention shifted back to me as a laugh tumbled from her lips.

"Only the ones who seem capable of keeping up," she retorted, not in the least bit rattled by my accusation, her sexuality a powerful tool just like always.

"Is that a challenge?" Travis asked her flirtatiously, and the desire to punch him had my hand curling into a fist at my side.

"Always," she replied. "And not one that many can rise to."

"How about the Casanova we just chased out of here with our arrival?" I asked, uncertain why I was pursuing this line of conversation when I knew there were far more important things we needed to get to.

"Raul?" she asked casually, her eyes flicking towards the bedroom briefly before moving back to us.

"Pretty sure his name was Paulo," Travis said, his grin widening as he watched her, and her lips twitched with amusement while I felt inclined to kill something again.

"Mmm," she agreed, though it didn't seem like she knew either way. "I suppose he was adequate."

"You seem like a woman who deserves more than adequate," Travis purred, giving her a look which seemed all too much like an offer to me.

"Is there a point to this line of conversation?" I ground out before she

71

could reply, and I ended up hurling Travis over the fucking balcony.

"I believe you were the one who took an interest in it in the first place," Carmen said.

"I was merely pointing out that bringing us to your bedroom where a man you just fucked is still sleeping seems like an odd way to conduct business," I bit out. "I assume you summoned me here for a reason beyond trying to get a rise out of me with this bullshit."

"Is that what I was doing?" Carmen asked, her amusement clear, though her voice seemed laced with threat all at once. "Because from where I'm sitting, it seems like I was left waiting for you for hours after I so graciously came to your rescue when you begged me for my help. I killed an entire gang for you, Luther. My men eradicated every last Dead Dog on that bridge after you took yourself for a swim. I saved your son from certain death, not to mention the fact that I saved you too. So excuse me for finding a way to pass the time while I waited for you to come and offer me your gratitude. I didn't realise that you expected me to be waiting here for you in a veil, guarding my precious virginity like my cunt is the holy grail and any man to drive their cock into it would be granted eternal life."

My attention was drawn to the small knife she now somehow held in her hand, the sharp point twisting back and forth around her fingers as she toyed with it, the threat there clear. I had pushed her to the limit of what she would tolerate from me and if I didn't repair this situation, then it would end with that blade lodged somewhere irreparable.

I blew out a breath and forced the tension to fall from my shoulders, holding my hands out in surrender.

"I meant no disrespect," I said, the truth of my words piercing through them. "And you have to know how grateful I am to you for Fox. I'm here to pay whatever price you require of me for that kindness."

Silence stretched as she assessed me, her dark eyes seeming to drink me in, chew me up and spit me right back out again in the time it took for her to decide upon what to do with me.

"Sit," she sighed, waving a hand at the two chairs opposite her and setting the knife down beside the fruit bowl like she hadn't once intended to have threatened me with it. "You're giving me a neck ache."

Travis strode straight forward, pulling a chair out for himself and dropping into it before making quick work of pouring three cups of coffee for all of us.

I was slower to follow suit, knowing I was treading a fine line here and battling to get control of myself. It had been a long twenty-four hours.

"Here, old man, drink a cup of this and get your head on straight before I have to watch the lady gut you," Travis said, placing a cup down before the empty chair which Carmen had indicated for me and I dropped into it in silence, fighting the urge to reply to him while I kept my eyes on her.

Carmen accepted the cup of coffee he held out for her, their fingers brushing as she took it from him, and I forced myself to drink my entire cup without saying a single word. It wasn't like I gave a shit who she fucked anyway. And if her choices were fuckboys like Travis, then I wasn't surprised she found herself unimpressed by them when it came down to it. A woman like her needed a real man to teach her body what it needed, but that really wasn't my problem.

"You didn't kill all of The Dead Dogs," I pointed out as I placed my cup back down on the table. "Shawn is still out there."

"Fucking Shawn," Carmen huffed, her eyes moving to the sea once more. "He is harder to kill than a cockroach it seems. Even so, that hardly negates your debt to me, and I trust that your sons can handle a single man without further input from me?"

"My sons?" I questioned, wondering why she didn't expect me to handle him myself, and the smile she gave me said I'd just hit the nail on the head.

"We have payment to discuss, Luther," she said sweetly. "A life for a life. And even at that I am being generous because I really gave you far more than just your son back, didn't I?"

I nodded, knowing this had been coming and prepared to pay whatever I had to for her help. I hadn't called on her lightly, but she had been my only chance of saving him at the time.

"What do you want from me?" I asked while Travis took a slice of apple from the bowl on the table, popping it into his mouth and crunching loudly without once asking permission to take the food, though strangely, Carmen didn't seem to mind.

"I don't want anything from you, Luther," she said, those sinful lips curling as the wind picked up a lock of her hair and tossed it across her face.

The urge to lean forward and shift it aside gripped me like some form of insanity, but I managed to hold myself still and let her brush it away herself.

"I don't understand," I admitted, though the low chuckle coming from Travis said that he did.

"A debt like yours is steep indeed, Luther," Carmen said simply. "And like I already said, I require a life for a life."

"You want me to kill someone for you?" I asked, relief tumbling through me at the simplicity of that request. Killing I could do. I could make it as bloody as she wanted too, though I was surprised that she only desired something so easy from me, making me wonder if the target was important - law enforcement or a judge perhaps?

"There is a man I wish to kill," she agreed just as Travis leaned across the table and held a slice of apple up to her lips.

She eyed him for a moment, his over confidence clearly surprising her, but the hesitation was brief, and she shifted forward, taking the apple into her mouth before sinking her teeth into his thumb too.

"Fuck." Travis yanked his hand back with a curse, but the look he was giving her said he hadn't been the least bit put off by the strike of pain, and that only pissed me off more.

"Who is he?" I asked, wanting this interaction over and relishing the opportunity to kill someone, because I sure as hell felt the need for bloodshed rising in me with every moment I lingered in their company.

Carmen's eyes shifted between me and Travis, her voice lowering as she leaned closer to us across the table, and I found myself unable to look anywhere but into the depths of those soulless eyes.

"I have such big plans for us," she breathed conspiratorially. "Plans that have been in motion for a long, long time."

Something about the darkness in her tone as she said that reminded me of the story she'd told me about La Princesa all those years ago, and what her father's men had done to her. How she'd risen from beneath his thumb and had killed everyone on that boat before tricking the rest of the cartel into believing she'd been nothing but a frightened child who had miraculously escaped the carnage.

It struck me then who else she might want to take her revenge upon. The man who cast fear into the hearts of everyone on this side of the border and the other. The man everyone claimed was a true demon given flesh to house his rotten soul. The one who pulled her strings and made her dance for him.

"You want to kill the leader of the Castillo Cartel?" I breathed, the words barely leaving my mouth in fear of someone overhearing them, the reality of what she was dragging me into weighing me down like a lead weight crushing my chest. No one went up against him and survived. No one.

Carmen smiled at me again, leaning back into her seat and raising her cup of coffee to her lips.

"Bravo, Luther," she purred. "I think I am going to quite enjoy owning you."

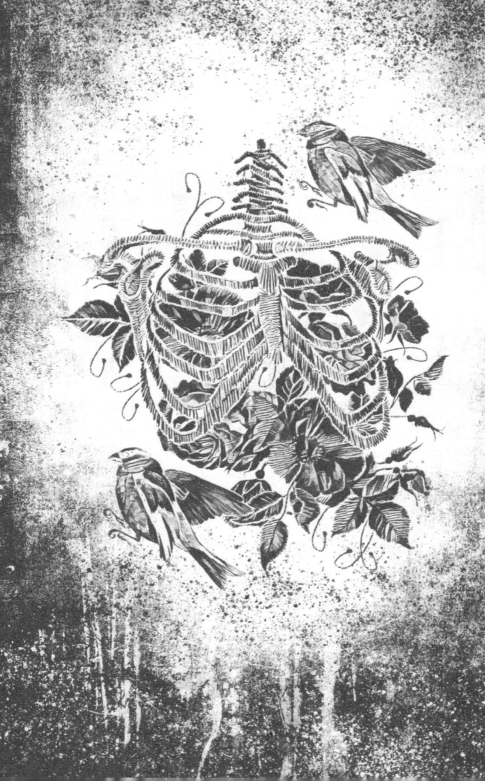

CHAPTER SIX

I'd never considered myself a bisexual kind of man. But when Luther Harlequin had been in a world of turmoil on his knees before me over the hanging of his boy, I had to admit I'd had a stirring or two towards him.

There was no greater feeling in this world than breaking people who proclaimed to be unbreakable, and he had been one of my crowning jewels there for a moment.

But then I'd gone and been betrayed by that piece of shit Trav, and here we were. In the wake of it all, I suppose you could say I was incensed about it all. I'd had the Harlequin Prince swinging from my own rope, and the fallen king before me, shattering to pieces oh so beautifully.

But my victory wasn't to be, no, it was snatched away from me by fucking Travis, a man I'd trusted down to my roots. Well alright, there weren't any men in this world I'd declare to trust, but Trav had been a good boy, he'd been in The Dead Dogs for years, dutifully serving me and reaping the rewards of that servitude. Turned out, he'd been planted there by the Castillo Cartel themselves all along, deceiving me like a rat among mice. Couldn't say I wasn't a little flattered by Carmen Ortega's attention though; she clearly saw me as a worthy adversary, a man worth keeping an eye on.

I suppose it wasn't surprising really, she was only a woman after all, and she kept her position secure in the cartel by surrounding herself with a host of violent men ready to die at her feet if she commanded it. That was the power of the pussy right there. A danger all men should heed. It was what made me invincible, because it was far too many a man's weakness, whereas I was free of that burden, never letting myself get too attached to one pussy in particular.

I looked over at my momma at the far end of the trailer, the scent of stew cooking in the small kitchen as she hummed softly, trying not to disturb me. But I'd been severely disturbed indeed since I'd dragged myself out of that raging river after I'd been shot in the chest by traitorous Trav, though thankfully it had hit my right side and I'd somehow managed to avoid rupturing anything fatal. Lucky, that was me.

Despite my injury, I'd gotten myself to the road somehow, stolen myself a car and gotten far away from the gunfight, picking up my momma on the way and leaving Sunset Cove behind. The Dead Dogs were gone, destroyed, fucking eradicated by that cartel bitch.

Now, I was stuck in a trailer with nothing but Momma and my pretty, pretty diamonds for company.

This wasn't the end of my story though. I'd get back on my feet soon and regroup, but there was one thing I was certain of, I was done with Sunset Cove. With the cartel clearly aligning itself with the Harlequins, my plans of total domination in that town were done.

I huffed in frustration over that, defeat not sitting too well with me. But I'd forge this loss into a victory given time, I just had to come up with a new strategy.

There was a knife sticking out of the wall beside me and endless holes all around it that I'd put there whenever I thought on my failure, whenever I got too fucking furious about it and needed an outlet. But I wasn't an emotional kind of man, I wasn't gonna weep over my loss, I'd accept it like the admirable fella I was, and think on how I'd secure my wins in the future.

It was obvious really. Rogue Easton was the beating heart of those boys, the thing that would break them in one fell swoop. I was a damn fool for not leaving town with her the moment she stepped through my door at Rosewood Manor. But I'd had a taste of power for a moment there, I had seen the possibility of seizing control in that town, and I'd always been an ambitious man, so I could hardly be blamed for shooting my shot.

Things were different now, so I had to adapt my plans to the current situation, and there was really only one thing to do. I'd take their girl from them, run far, far away where they could never find me and spend a long, sweet time breaking her. And maybe when I was done having my fun with her and she was back to sucking my cock daily like a good girl, repenting for all her sins, then I'd carve her up real nice and send her home to her boys in pieces. Yeah, that seemed like one helluva consolation prize, and I wasn't afraid of starting anew. I'd find a town somewhere steeped in crime and sin, then I'd learn who ran it and plant myself in their nest like a pretty little cuckoo egg, just waiting for my moment to hatch.

Though as I thought on that plan, it didn't seem quite fitting. It didn't have quite enough flare, not enough pizazz. No…there had to be something better. Something more catastrophically torturous that I could land in the lap of those Harlequin boys once Rogue was in my grasp. I didn't have the patience to wait years to deliver my punishment, no, I needed retribution for the mockery they'd made of me. I needed them to know who held the might of the world in his grip. And that was me. Always me.

Momma eventually brought over a bowl of stew and laid it down on my nightstand with a hunk of bread. She sat on the edge of my bed, brushing a few locks of hair away from my face and looking at me like I was still her sweet angel boy. Poor, foolish woman.

"How are you feeling, bubba?" she asked, handing me some painkillers

79

along with a glass of water.

"Not so good, Momma." I swallowed the pills down and she placed the glass on the nightstand as she gave me a sympathetic look.

"My poor darling," she sighed, tucking a lock of red hair behind her ear. "Momma will get you fixed up in no time, don't you worry about that." She squeezed my hand then got up and started tidying around the place like the good woman she was.

It wasn't the first time she'd picked a bullet outa me and it likely wouldn't be the last. She knew how to mend me right, but I was growing impatient already as I stewed here on my thoughts.

I slid my hand into my pillow, taking out the pouch of my diamonds and pouring them into my palm. They were fat and beautiful, five little beauties twinkling in my hand. This was an empire in the making right here. A fresh start. But it was no good to me without my sugarpie back under my control, ready to die for me so sweetly so I could claim a final, irrefutable victory over the Harlequins. I was becoming somewhat obsessed with the idea, and I was damn vengeful now too. So what was my triumph over them worth?

I pushed the diamonds back into the pouch, all barring one that I rolled between my finger and thumb before making a call on the burner phone Momma had gotten me.

I knew a lot of bad people, and they knew a lot of bad people too. All I had to do was put out word of this shiny little bounty on Rogue Easton's head, and I'd have someone dragging her to my door bound, gagged and all mine by the end of the week.

A diamond for the girl who could ruin the Harlequins? Seemed like a more than fair exchange. So I was going to let the monsters loose and let them do my dirty work for me.

Let the hunt begin.

CHAPTER SEVEN

My dreams were violent, throwing me here and there like I was caught up in a stormy sea until suddenly it spat me out and I woke with a jolt, a hot sweat rushing over me as I realised I was gonna hurl.

I lurched out of the tangle of limbs I was locked within on the couch, racing for the nearest bathroom down the hall. I shoved the door open, crashing to my knees and retching over the toilet as I spilled a tide of seawater and half digested food into the bowl.

My head spun and my throat burned as I heaved time and again, everything coming up until there was nothing left. A hand pressed to my shoulder, and I groaned as I realised I had a witness to this shit show, burying my face against my arm where it rested on the toilet seat.

"You good, man?" Chase asked and I relaxed a little, thankful it was him.

Chase wouldn't mock me tirelessly for this shit like Maverick might, and I didn't want Rogue to see me weak. Fox? Well he'd start fussing, fetching me water and playing daddy. Chase would sit it out with me until I told him what I needed. That was the way of him. He understood that the company of one of our crew was all we ever needed, no matter what pain we were facing. It was how he'd survived his dad's wrath, seeking us out and bathing in our company, forgetting the darkness that awaited him at home.

"Yeah," I said at last, lifting my head and spitting into the toilet bowl as acid coated my tongue. "Better now."

I got up and he stepped back in the small room to give me space, resting his shoulder against the door while I rinsed my mouth out in the sink. He didn't even react to the scent of vomit in the air as he moved to flush the toilet, and that was that.

He jerked his chin in an offering to follow him and I did, letting him lead the way out into the hall and down to the back door which let out onto the porch. Outside, the air was thick with heat, the afternoon sun baking the world dry and setting the waves sparkling.

Chase dropped down to sit on the porch steps and I sat beside him as he took out a pack of smokes and propped a cigarette between his lips. He tugged a lighter out of his pocket which had a skeleton riding a motorcycle on it, but it slipped from his fingers, bouncing down the steps and hitting the sand at the bottom.

I moved to get it, before he could, shifting onto the step beneath him, before turning back and igniting the flame, holding it out to the end of his smoke. He leaned into it, inhaling deep until the cherry glowed and I watched him suck all those toxins down into his lungs with a frown lining my brow.

"You ever think about quitting?" I asked, moving to sit beside him once more, spinning the lighter between my fingers.

"Yeah, I've thought about it," he said as he took the cigarette between two fingers and exhaled a line of smoke.

"And?" I pushed as he toked on it again.

"And then I stopped thinking about it." He snorted a laugh at his little joke, and I knocked my shoulder against his.

"You'd quit if Rogue asked you to."

"Yeah, probably," he agreed. "But she won't. She gets it."

"Gets what?"

He played with the cigarette in his hand, his brows low as he decided on his next words.

"Look." He shifted so he could get the pack out of his pocket, handing it over to me. "What do you see?"

"A squashed cigarette packet?" I said dryly and he scoffed.

"Marlboros," he corrected. "My sweet ol' Daddy's favourite smokes. The kind I used to steal from him even though I knew I'd get a punch in the face for it, or a strike of his belt. But I still did it. Still risked it, even though Fox and Maverick got cigarettes easy enough, hell, even you could pickpocket them off your momma's clients whenever you fancied. I stole them though, because it was the only thing that I could do against him. My defiance. It's addictive that. The reminder of how I kept defying him, how I shared these very cigarettes with my best friends, and this taste-" He inhaled deeply on his cigarette before letting the smoke out as a smile twisted up his lips "-it brings me right back there again, JJ. It's my happy place, all wrapped up in a cancerous little stick which will likely be the death of me one day if I don't catch a bullet in my head before then, or end up back in a goddamn blowhole being dashed to pieces on the rocks. But if I give these up, I'll be giving him up. That kid with his defiance and his perfect little life with his friends. It feels like now more than ever, I'm becoming him again, so I'm holding on real tight to it. And that includes these." He took the packet back from me, tucking them firmly into his pocket while I thought on that.

"I think you should stop," I said at last, and he glanced at me with his features skewing.

"I think you missed the point of my story."

"I cried a river over your story, Ace." I smirked. "But I still think you should stop. Because yeah, those smokes remind you of the good old days, but they keep you trapped in memories of your asshole of a daddy too. Why are you punishing yourself?"

A tight V formed between his eyes, and he looked away from me like I'd landed a little too close to the truth. He said nothing, but I sensed what he was thinking anyway, and I wasn't gonna let him hide away from me.

I caught his chin, yanking him back around to look at me and his throat bobbed with emotion.

"J," he begged, but I wasn't letting go of this.

"He's still in your head," I growled, tapping his temple. "You think I don't see it?" I ran my thumb around the curve of his unseeing eye, finding it absolutely goddamn beautiful to look at. It was an ocean of pale blue, and the scar cut through his eyebrow and cheek in an X just gave him a look of pure grit that was badass. "You think I can't tell his voice is in your ear every day, telling you you're nothing. And I know Shawn played on that, Ace. I know he got deep in your head too, but I'm not gonna let him keep you in this bullshit cycle of negativity in your mind. You are one of the best people I know. Fuck your mistakes, we've all made them. I love every piece of you, and so does Rogue, so does Rick, and Fox. So stop listening to the villains in your head and start listening to the people out here who matter." I leaned in and kissed him on the forehead, my fingers scrunching tight in his dark curls as he leaned into my touch.

He yanked me against him, resting his chin on my shoulder and crushing me in a fierce embrace that made it hard to breathe.

"JJ, you have no fucking idea how scared I was when you disappeared in that blowhole. I thought you were gone. I thought I'd never see you again and I can't tell you how damn terrifying that was. Thank God for your stupid fucking safety helmet."

"Hey, don't throw shade on the helmet," I joked, but my voice cracked with emotion as I clung onto him.

A creak on the wooden boards behind us made me lift my head and I found Maverick moving to join us, his shirt off and his feet bare. He didn't smirk or laugh at finding us holding each other, he dropped down on my other side and wrapped his arms around us too.

"You and your fucking safety gear," he muttered as the two of them crushed me between them.

"You always were Captain Adventure, even when we got way too old for going off hunting the cove for buried treasure," Maverick taunted. "I've never been so grateful that you're such a fucking nerd."

"Fuck off," I laughed, and Chase chuckled too as we broke apart.

Maverick leaned across me, swiping the cigarettes from Chase's pocket, just like old times, memories tossing us back to that youth we were all so desperate to reclaim.

I figured screw it and stole one too, pushing it between my lips, and the three of us sat side by side as we watched the waves draw in. It was so beautiful here; golden sand rolling down to meet the caress of stunning blue waves, all bathed in endless sunshine and hiding so much of the dark truth that lurked in every shadow. Home. The only one I'd ever want.

"How do you reckon Fox is gonna cope with all this? Do you really think he's all in now?" Chase asked after a while.

"I'm sure gonna have fun finding out," Maverick muttered, and I elbowed him.

"Give him a break, the dude almost died for us," I said, my heart squeezing at what Fox had nearly sacrificed. The idea of losing him was unbearable, unthinkable.

"Key word: almost. And so long as my brother is still breathing in this world, I have the eternal right to keep terrorising him." Rick grinned, but as I looked to him, I saw the creases around his eyes and the tension in his posture. His smile fell away as he smoked and the weight of all we'd almost lost last night fell over us.

"His letter was killer," I commented, and Chase nodded his agreement.

"I could write a better one," Maverick said.

"Go on then," I dared.

"Maybe I will," he said with a shrug.

"You couldn't top Fox's," Chase said, catching my eye as we played one of our favourite old games. Pitting Fox and Maverick against one another was too damn easy. We'd gotten them to do all kinds of shit in the name of their rivalry when we were kids simply by stating that the other one could easily outdo them.

"I fucking could," Maverick insisted. "I bet I could make Rogue all weepy over me, and she'd be so in love with me that she'd take me away somewhere for a full weekend just so she could show me how wet my letter made her again and again."

"You're full of shit, Rick," Chase goaded, and Maverick nearly snapped his cigarette in half as he shot a glare at Chase.

"Oh yeah? I'll fucking prove it," he said, and I shrugged dismissively.

"I'll believe it when I see it," I said.

"You will see it, and you'll eat it too when she cries on me," Maverick said cockily, offering me his hand and I shook it easily.

"Deal," I agreed, cracking a laugh that Chase echoed.

I yawned as tiredness fell in on me again and I stretched out my aching limbs, examining my bruises. The cut on my leg was bandaged up good now, but the painkillers were wearing off and I planned on drugging myself up then napping again before dinner. Chase had only taken his when Rogue had slipped them between his lips and poured water in his mouth, caressing his cheek while she did so.

Maybe I should have faked a little more resistance to them if that was the kind of treatment it would earn me. Though if my pretty girl was gonna pour a drink between my lips, I could think of something with much more alcohol in it that I'd prefer, and if I was asking for things then I'd love to get her to dance for me while she did it. Yeah, that seemed like a sweet new goal to adopt, and with life offering us another chance to make shit right, I could see things actually swinging that way soon.

"So is this it? We're good? We're safe? We're...happy?" I asked in surprise, realising we were finally all together in this house, every one of us on board with this crazy ass new relationship forming between us too.

"Shit," Chase breathed in disbelief.

"Fuck my life, did we all just become besties again?" Rick said dryly, though a smile played around the corner of his lips.

"BFFs forever," I taunted.

Chase sighed, letting smoke coil up from his lips towards the sky. "Well thank fuck for that."

CHAPTER EIGHT

The sound of low voices reached me in sleep, and I groaned groggily, rolling on the couch, my cheek pressing to the bare chest of one of my boys, his arm winding around me lovingly.

"I'm just trying to understand the boundaries here," Rick's voice came from across the room. The warm breeze floating over me made me think he'd opened the sliding doors and was out by the pool.

"I don't know what you want from me," Fox muttered. "I've said I'm in. I understand that she needs all of you too, that we all need each other, so why are you pushing at me?"

"Because I don't wanna go stepping over some invisible line you've drawn in the sand by accident and end up making you cry or some shit," Rick replied.

"Fuck off," Fox muttered in that half-exasperated tone which was so familiar from our childhood. He and Rick used to butt heads all the time and this had been a common outcome; Rick pushing too far and Fox cursing him out as he walked away from the fight. Unless of course he didn't walk away and the two of them started brawling, but I was guessing that in Fox's currently healing state it wouldn't come to that.

"I'm serious. Can I kiss her with you in the room or will you end up getting all weird over it? And this isn't me asking for permission, I'm just wondering what you're going to do when it happens."

"I'm not going to stop you from kissing her," Fox replied irritably, though raising his voice only made it come out hoarser.

"No, I know you're not. I'm bigger than you so I'd just kick your ass if you tried, I'm just wondering if you're going to try."

"I said no already, and I'm bigger than *you*, so check your fucking facts."

Rick scoffed and JJ breathed a laugh into my hair, pressing a kiss to my forehead while I snuggled closer.

"Okay, so I can kiss her. What about getting her on her knees to suck my dick? Will that make you all stabby, or are you on board with that?"

"Maverick," Fox warned, but of course Rick didn't stop.

"If we're all in a room together and she starts riding your cock, is it or is it not acceptable for me to take her ass at the same time?"

A loud smack sounded followed by Rick cursing loudly and barking a laugh.

"See, we're finding your limits. I need to know these things, because me, Chase and JJ are all about sharing her. I like them watching me fuck her, I like watching them fuck her, I like taking turns and I really like it when she takes all three of us at-"

"For fuck's sake, Rick, will you just stop with that shit?" Fox snapped and I opened my eyes, making a move to get up but JJ tightened his grip on me, the mischievous look in his eyes as they met with mine saying he wanted to keep me for a bit longer.

"I should go out there," I said in a low voice.

"Nah, pretty girl, let them fight it out like we always used to," he murmured in reply.

"I remember when they used to get into it, you, me and Chase would usually just leave them to it and go get ourselves into trouble," I replied with a smile. "But this is about me, so-"

"Did you call, little one?" Chase asked, sitting himself up on JJ's other side, his hand brushing over the nasty looking graze on JJ's ribs briefly as he frowned at it, and I was reminded forcefully of the fact I'd nearly lost him too.

"Shit, J," I breathed, leaning in and brushing my lips over the deep bruises that were blossoming beyond the graze. "You must have been terrified when that wave ripped you out of there."

I kissed the bruise again and he released a sigh, the sound of Fox and Rick's continued bickering over how many dicks Fox could handle watching me with fading away as JJ's fingers pushed into my hair.

"I was more terrified of the thought of never seeing any of you again," he said, the slight tremor to his voice showing the truth of that statement.

"We would have been lost without you," Chase said.

"That's because we're a package deal," I replied. "It's all or nothing. Always has been."

JJ nodded, his fingers sliding through my hair again as he cupped my chin and made me look at him. "Being here is like a dream," he admitted, his eyes sliding to Chase. "Even if some of it hurts like a bitch." He nodded to the ragged skin and deep bruises on his side, and I dropped my mouth to kiss the edge of them once more.

"Does this help?" I teased, feeling his muscles flex beneath the pressure of my lips.

"Yeah," he sighed, pure contentment in his tone.

My heart leapt as I felt the roughness of stubble against my cheek and I turned my head, finding Chase leaning over JJ too, his mouth brushing against the edges of his bruises as well.

JJ groaned softly, his other hand pushing into Chase's dark curls, and I bit my lip as I looked into his eyes, wondering where this new tension between

93

the two of them might end up leading.

Chase cocked a smile at me like he could read my mind, his gaze remaining locked with mine as he pressed a kiss to JJ's chest again, his mouth a little lower this time.

JJ released a shuddering breath and as I ran my hand down his chest, I found his cock rigid beneath his shorts, the groan he released as I gripped it letting me know how much he craved a release.

I began to kiss my way lower while I heard Rick assuring Fox that he would send him plenty of sex tapes of me with him and the others to help him desensitise himself like he'd been doing with the last one he sent.

Fox spluttered something incoherent, and their argument moved away from us as Chase followed my mouth down JJ's abdomen, his kisses mimicking mine all the way.

I peeled JJ's shorts back, fisting his cock with a hungry moan as I took in the perfect length of him, gliding my hand up and down the smooth skin while I watched Chase paint more kisses down his abs.

JJ watched the two of us with a raw, heated expression that made wetness gather between my thighs and I bit my lip as I slid from the couch to kneel before him.

I pushed JJ's thighs apart as Chase dropped down beside me, licking my lips as I salivated over the idea of tasting him.

Chase brushed my hair back over my shoulder, his eyes locking with mine as I lowered my head, a deep growl rolling up his throat as he watched me slide my mouth around JJ's cock.

"Fucking hell," Chase breathed, his hand moving to his own dick as he rearranged it, his eyes on my movements, the desire in him palpable.

Chase closed in on me, his mouth dropping to my neck as he began to suck and kiss at the tender skin there, his hand shifting around the curve of my ass until he was skirting it over my rear, passing it by to find the wetness of my pussy.

I moaned around JJ's cock and Johnny James bucked his hips, making me take him right to the back of my throat.

"How wet is she, Ace?" he panted, his hands still fisting in both of our hair, his grip tightening on Chase's curls as he made him tip his head back so he could answer the question.

"She's so wet I bet that both of us could fit inside her pretty pussy at once," Chase growled and the thought of that made everything inside me clench just as he drove two fingers into that very wetness.

I tipped forward, balancing myself on the couch with one hand as I arched my spine to give him more access, raising my ass and moaning around JJ's shaft.

Chase shifted closer to me, kissing my neck again as he continued to play with me, his thumb stroking over my ass as he pumped his other fingers inside me.

I released my hold on JJ's dick, taking my hand from the base of his shaft where I'd been stroking it in time with the motion of my mouth as I reached for Chase too, pushing my hand into his sweatpants and seeking out his hard length.

Chase bit down on my neck as I rolled my thumb through the moisture on his tip, his other hand moving to brush against my cheek before taking over for me with JJ.

Johnny James cursed as Chase slowly began to move his hand in time with my mouth, the two of us working together to get him off while still using our hands on each other too.

It took me a few moments to find a rhythm between the bobbing of my head in JJ's lap and the thrusts of my hips back onto Chase's hand while I jerked him off too, but before long we all just came to it together.

JJ growled my name as I sucked on him, Chase's name a breath that followed it, making my pussy squeeze at how hot that sounded, the feeling of Chase helping me destroy him making me so wet that I couldn't help but whimper again.

"You like that, little one?" Chase teased, nipping my ear before shifting his hand down to caress JJ's balls, making him groan even louder. "You like us doing this together?"

I nodded, moaning my agreement as I took JJ to the back of my throat again, my lips brushing Chase's knuckles and making him curse as he watched me.

Chase skimmed his thumb over my ass again and I moaned, pressing back into him in encouragement until he sank it into me, his hand taking ownership of that too as he began to pump me harder.

"Touch your clit for us, pretty girl, I can help hold you up," JJ growled, his hand fisting in my hair to support me so I could take my free hand from the edge of the couch.

I met his honey brown eyes as I did what he wanted, moaning loudly around his shaft, and pumping Chase more firmly in my hand.

We were all closing in on our undoing, the three of us working on each other in perfect synchronisation as JJ began to lift his hips into my movements, pushing the back of my head down and forcing me to take him deeper.

I moaned even louder as Chase drove his fingers into me harder too, and I sucked on the tip of JJ's cock, flicking my tongue to force an orgasm from him just as mine exploded through my flesh.

The salty taste of his seed washed over my tongue and I swallowed it down greedily, letting him tug me off of him by my hair and looking at Chase just as he leaned in to kiss me deeply, his fingers sliding from my body while I trembled in the wake of my climax.

My tongue danced over his and he growled at the taste of Johnny James on my lips before I broke the kiss and dropped to take his cock into my mouth too.

JJ took hold of my hair again, forcing my head down onto Chase while he gripped JJ's shoulder in return and before long, he was coming as well, tipping his head back with a low groan that made everything inside me tighten in the most delicious way.

My body hummed with satisfaction, some of the aches from my cuts and bruises seeming to fade while pleasure rode through my flesh. Chase groaned his approval, his fingers caressing my cheek before he drew himself out from between my lips and tugged up his shorts.

"You think they're done arguing yet?" he asked as he got to his feet with a cocky grin on his mouth, tugging me upright with him.

"Are they ever truly done?" I replied, the words like an echo from our past when this situation had once been so familiar to us – though the games JJ, Chase and I had played to entertain ourselves while Fox and Rick hashed it out had never been quite like that before.

The sound of Maverick laughing loudly from the kitchen made me look around and I was fairly certain that it was of the taunting, asshole variety.

"Come on," I said, keeping hold of Chase's hand and reaching for JJ's too, tugging him up to stand with us as he rearranged his shorts. "There's something I need to do."

They didn't question me as I led the way out through the closest patio doors and into the sunlight, a deep inhale filling my lungs as I focused on the feeling of the sun kissing every piece of my skin.

I didn't stop until we made it to the edge of the pool, my toes curling over the lip of it and my gaze falling on the deep, blue water before I exhaled again.

"You want to go for a swim, little one?" Chase questioned.

"I think that all of us have good reason to fear the water after what we survived in that blowhole," I said slowly, my eyes moving over the still surface as I let myself remember the punishing force of those waves as they slammed into me repeatedly, trying to tear me from the rocks and hurl me into oblivion. "But I also know that I love the water. I love the sea and swimming, the surf, the waves, all of it. Shawn has taken far too much from me already, and I don't plan on letting him have this."

JJ shifted his weight beside me, and I knew this had to be the hardest for him. He'd been torn out through those rocks, held at the mercy of the water and ripped away from the people he loved by it. Memories of that had to be scratching at the inside of his skull, threatening him with that fear all over again. But I refused to let Shawn have this.

I let go of their hands, pulling the shirt I was wearing over my head so I stood there fully naked, a dare in my eyes that forced both of them to drop their shorts too before I took their hands again.

"On three?" I asked, looking to Chase for a moment before fixing my eyes on JJ whose jaw had locked, his grip on my hand tightening.

"One," Chase said firmly, his thumb rolling over my knuckles.

"Two," I added in the next breath, my muscles tensing in anticipation of the jump.

A long pause hung between that number and the next, JJ's throat bobbing uncertainly before he squeezed my hand, a steely reserve hardening in his honey brown eyes.

"Three," he breathed and just like that, butt naked and free of the shackles that fear had tried to bind us with, we jumped.

The warm water enveloped us as we sank beneath the surface and I kept my eyes wide, a swathe of rainbow hair sweeping all around me as I looked between both of my boys with a big grin on my face, relief tumbling through me as I found them smiling right back. The water skimmed over my naked flesh, feeling so damn good, and as natural as breathing.

I released my hold on their hands, kicking off the blue tiles lining the bottom of the pool before swimming towards the far end of it beneath the surface, the thrill and freedom I always felt in the water surrounding me like an old friend, promising not to let me go.

I came up for air just as a hand locked around my ankle, a wild scream escaping me as I was tugged beneath the surface once more and I kicked out at

Chase, forcing him to release me.

When I came up again, JJ instantly dunked me under, the three of us fast falling into a splash fight as we yelled and laughed.

It quickly became clear that this game had now evolved as they both took the opportunity to pinch my nipples and bite at my neck between tossing me across the pool and shoving me beneath the surface. My laughter pitched to outrage as they began to gang up on me.

I turned and started swimming for them, spotting the hose that was curled by the backdoor, the idea of shooting them with the icy cold spray all kinds of appealing.

But as I made it to the edge of the water and started hauling myself up, Chase appeared, slapping my ass as I almost made it out, the wet smack making a half scream, half moan escape me as I arched my spine, my ass pointing up at the blue sky.

JJ grabbed my hips as I tried to climb out, his teeth sinking into my other ass cheek just as I spotted a pair of black sneakers stopping right in front of my nose and we all fell entirely still.

"Jesus," Luther's low growl made me tilt my head back to look up at him through the wet strands of my brightly coloured hair, my nudity suddenly seeming a lot less liberating as I wondered just how bright that handprint on my ass was, because he was definitely getting a clear look at every round inch of it. Oh, and then there were the teeth marks… "Is there a good reason why the three of you are butt naked in my pool, screaming and hollering like a pack of dogs when there's work to do?"

"Would it make it better if I was wearing a hat?" JJ asked, his hands still gripping my hips, the position we were in making colour rise to my cheeks like I was a naughty kid who had just been caught by her dad.

"No, Johnny James, it would not," Luther rumbled just as Rick and Fox stepped out onto the patio.

"Hey," Maverick barked, pointing at the three of us while striding closer.

"What have I told you fuckers about starting any orgies without me?"

"For the love of God." Luther swiped a tattooed hand down his face as he turned away from us and I quickly wriggled away from JJ, kicking him when he refused to let go and climbing out of the pool.

Rick hauled me up, grabbing a handful of my ass and pressing his tongue between my lips as he dragged my soaking body against him, not seeming to care one bit that the water was saturating his clothes, or that his dad was standing right there.

"Here," Fox said, nudging me with a towel and I pushed Rick's chest to force him back, breathing a laugh as he cursed me before finally relenting and letting me go.

Fox stepped in to take his place, wrapping the enormous towel around me so I was covered from neck to ankle, all tied up like a burrito.

Luther still had his back to us, and he headed for the metal table closer to the house, dropping into a seat. He didn't look our way while muttering something about getting his pool cleaned.

"Are you gonna tell us what the cartel wanted from you, old man?" Maverick called after him, but Luther waved him off.

"It's complicated. I'll get into it when I've eaten something."

Rick rolled his eyes and I snorted at the way he and Luther had so easily fallen back into their old father/son relationship despite everything that had passed between them. It was super cute, even if I didn't dare voice that opinion out loud.

"How are you feeling?" I asked Fox as he tucked a strand of my wet hair behind my ear and a smile lifted the corner of his lips.

"Better," he lied. Or maybe he was just talking about the way he felt about us because there was a warmth burning through me when I was this close to him now that I'd been aching for for a long damn time, and the relief I felt at finally claiming it was palpable. "Go get dressed. Lunch is on its way out and we have things to discuss."

I nodded, hesitating a moment before leaning in and pressing my lips to his. Fox smiled against my mouth, his lips moving over mine like we had all the time in the world and a knot in my chest unfurled as I realised I'd been expecting him to be angry after seeing Maverick kiss me too. It seemed like he really was all in with this now though.

I lifted a hand to brush my fingers over the bruise darkening his neck in a circle, a murderous energy rising in me over what Shawn had done to him.

"The great Fox Harlequin," I whispered, running my hand down to the bandages covering his side, barely grazing over it in case I hurt him. "Still standing even when he's seen the other side of death."

"There was nothing waiting for me in hell, baby," he murmured, the roughness of his voice making my heart pinch at the pain he must have been in. "When the Devil calls my name again, it'll be listed right after yours."

"I'm going to hell, am I?" I smirked and he slid his hands down my back, squeezing my ass with a look that was all filth.

"I think the angels might let you through the pearly gates, hummingbird, but the four of us are damned," he said darkly, sending a shiver fluttering up and down my spine. "I guess we'll be taking you with us, or breaking down those gates to come hunting for your soul."

"Might as well pick hell, beautiful. There ain't no orgies in heaven," Maverick said, apparently listening in on our conversation as he stepped closer and Fox's lips tightened as I laughed.

I broke away from Fox, leaving him to cuss Rick out as I hurried into the house, scampering up the stairs and finding Mutt upside down and fast asleep in the centre of my bed, his tongue lolling to one side of his little doggy mouth.

I jumped into the shower to rinse the chlorine from my skin then quickly tied my hair into a messy knot, pulled on a pair of booty shorts and threw one of Rick's tanks on over the top of it. The grey material was soft and smelled like him with an image of a shark riding a wave emblazoned across the front of it, the huge arm holes showing off a pretty impressive amount of side boob.

But I was all for tempting my men closer to me, so I saw no issue with that.

I headed back downstairs, wincing a little at the tenderness of my bruises as I made my way out onto the patio once more, finding the table now full of food and my boys and Luther sitting around it, though JJ was notably missing.

"What's on this lettuce? Hot sauce?" Miss Mabel cried from somewhere inside the house.

"It's just a Caesar dressing I think," JJ replied from the same direction.

"Well, it tastes like the wrong side of a sailor's ass. I'll stick to enjoying my food without it, thank you very much."

"Are you sure you don't want to come and sit out with us?" JJ asked her.

"And shrivel up in the sun even more than I have already? No thank you."

"Okay. Well, just call if you need anything."

"I am aware of the way to play this needy old lady game, don't you worry," she assured him, and I laughed as I reached the table where the others were all filling plates of food I had to assume Fox had prepared, even though he should have been resting.

"There's a seat right here for you, beautiful," Rick purred, catching me by my waistband and yanking me down into his lap before dropping his mouth to my neck and biting down hard enough to make me gasp.

"Do you think we could eat without the sideshow?" Luther asked dryly as he glanced our way, and I batted Rick off as I dropped into my own chair between him and Fox.

Chase gave me a roguish smile as he handed over a plate filled with all the best things, and I fell on my meal like a ravenous beast without waiting for anyone else to start.

JJ strode back out onto the patio, his fingers trailing over my back as he circled the table, the touch somehow intimate despite its brevity, and I threw him a smile around a mouthful of my salad. He dropped into a seat on Rick's other side, biting down on his bottom lip in that utterly filthy way only Johnny

James could ever pull off. I found myself blushing like a freaking virgin despite knowing full well all the sinful things I'd already done and would do again with him.

Fox dropped his arm around my shoulders, drawing my eyes to him and I frowned as I took in the paleness of his face even though he grinned like he wasn't suffering from blood loss and wasn't in all kinds of pain from his wounds.

"You should be resting," I pointed out, though the idea of the great Fox Harlequin taking a sick day did seem more than a little unlikely.

"My ass is in a chair isn't it, hummingbird?" he questioned reasonably, and I huffed out a breath before spearing a heap of food onto my fork and lifting it to his lips.

"At least let me look after you," I demanded, taking in the amusement in his green eyes as he parted his lips obligingly and let me feed him.

"Holy shit, beautiful, did you just offer out food from your own plate?" Rick mocked from my other side while JJ hushed him dramatically.

"Shh, don't spook her. This is like watching one of those wildlife shows where a lion starts looking after a baby deer instead of just eating it. I need to see if she flips over to the attack or not," he said, and I shot him a glare.

"I'm not a baby deer," Fox muttered, but I shoved another forkful between his lips that silenced him again. He was supposed to be resting his vocal cords after all.

"You'd better mind out, JJ," I warned him. "Or I might just take your plate to make up for what I'm offering out from mine."

The others laughed at me even though I was being deadly serious, and I reached over to grab a handful of French fries from the basket in the middle of the table, stuffing them into my mouth and chewing obnoxiously before tossing a few extras to Mutt.

"You do know that isn't really good food for dogs, don't you?" Fox asked and I whipped around to scowl at him next.

"Err, Mutt isn't just some dog," I snipped. "He is a street urchin just like me. He eats what he can, when he can, and he needs to taste a French fry from time to time to help him stay connected with his roots."

"The food I buy him costs more than the food I buy myself," Fox grumbled. "It's organic and high in omegas and-"

"And no one wants to eat caviar all day even if it's the cure to premature aging and sagging fanny flaps," I interrupted. "Because stinky fish eggs are still stinky fish eggs at the end of the day, and they are never going to be deep fried, overly processed potatoes."

"I chipped those potatoes myself," Fox pointed out. "So they're not overly processed."

"Hmm. I thought they tasted a bit weird," I agreed, making his expression darken while Maverick barked a laugh, dropping an inked hand onto my thigh and squeezing roughly, drawing my eyes to him.

Luther cleared his throat before we could take our argument any further, and we all looked to him as his eyes strayed from Fox's arm that was still draped around me to Rick's hand on my thigh before skipping between Chase and JJ too.

"On second thoughts, I don't want to know," he muttered, shaking his head and concentrating on his food once more, causing a breath of laughter to fall from my lips.

"It's simple really," JJ said anyway, his heated eyes on me, drawing me into his gaze and taking me hostage. "We're in love with her. All four of us."

"Always have been," Chase added, drawing my focus to him and I smiled as I looked at him sitting upright in his chair, not an eyepatch in sight, his scars fully on display and that old confidence he'd always exuded returned. I knew as soon as we were out of this house, that confidence would wane again though, and I wished I could restore it to him fully.

"And she's in love with us, aren't you, beautiful?" Rick added, squeezing my thigh again, the tightness of his grip awakening all kinds of fantasies that I fought to keep firmly inside my head and away from my expression.

"Yes," I agreed simply, and Luther looked up at me, his eyes searching before he finally nodded, accepting that as the truth.

"Well," he began slowly. "I don't really want to know how you figure out the mechanics of all that, but if it's what was needed to reunite my family then I can't say I have any objections to it."

Rick grinned in that asshole way of his. "We mostly all just go at it like-"

I punched him in the gut hard enough to wind him and Chase laughed loudly at his expense while Luther swiped a hand down his face, shaking his head.

"All I care about is seeing you smile like this again," he said firmly, making sure that Maverick didn't feel the need to go on with that explanation while his focus fixed on Fox who really was smiling like the boy I'd once known better than my own soul. "And if I haven't apologised enough for my part in what tore you all apart in the first place then I'll do so again. I might seem like an old man to you assholes, but I was a dad younger than you are now. I had a gang to run and danger knocking on my door every other day. I wanted a good life for my boys, and I wanted to protect you from the world too. I saw this bond in all of you, and I never could have predicted it could resolve itself this way. I saw only heartache awaiting you in a future where the four of you hungered for the same woman, and I'll admit that my own experiences with my brother tainted my take on it. I fucked up. I ain't perfect. But if last night taught me anything then it's that I gotta hold on tight to what counts because it can be gone in a damn blink."

We all said nothing as we openly stared at him, the words he was speaking both too late and yet somehow seeming like an offering. Like a possible future where we all truly moved on from what had happened ten years ago, and everything in between and just looked to the here and now. I wanted Fox and Maverick to have their dad back in their lives the way he had once been. He loved them even if he hadn't always shown it in the best of ways, and it was clear that he was hurting for his actions now. I just wanted all of us to stop suffering for the past. It was time to let it go.

"Stop trying to distract us with this soppy shit, old man," Rick said suddenly, and I laid my hand over his where he still gripped my thigh, feeling the tension in his body as he warred with the idea of forgiveness, while the scars of what he'd endured in prison refused to let him claim it. "Tell us what the cartel want in payment for their help."

Luther's expression flickered at the change in topic and he leaned back in his chair heavily, a breath expelling from his lungs.

"You don't wanna know," he said, and I could tell he wasn't just saying that to bullshit us or fob us off. Whatever price Carmen Ortega had requested for the help she'd given us was clearly a steep one. It was also clear that he had agreed to it, though I guessed it wasn't like he'd have had much choice in that.

"I do," Fox demanded, and I could tell he was feeling the sting of his father's silence on the subject.

"You can trust us," I swore.

"It's not about trust," Luther said firmly. "What she wants me to help her do…" He shook his head, his eyes lifting to the blue sky above us and the look on his face letting me know just how dangerous it was. Luther Harlequin was a damn force of nature, unmovable and impenetrable, yet I could see the concern he had over this task painted into his features like drops of water spilled on sand.

"I'm keeping you out of it," he said fiercely as he looked back to us. "All of you. Not because I don't trust you, but because I want to protect you. I can't have you near this, and if you value your bond and what you've just reclaimed with one another then you won't try to pry into it. I want to keep you as far from this fucking production as possible until it's done. And even then, I'll likely keep my silence on it. Do you understand?"

"No," Fox said predictably, the crack in his voice making Luther wince, his eyes dipping to the bruises ringing his son's neck.

"You know this ain't up for negotiation, kid," he said. "Besides, you said you're out of the crew, and this is crew business."

"How convenient, seeing as you ignored my resignation up until now," Fox rasped.

"Yeah, well that's life, ain't it? You wanna join the crew again?" Luther asked with a hint of hope in his tone like he'd just figured out how to snare Fox back into his position.

I glanced at Fox as his jaw ticked, the stubbornness in him clearly urging him to agree, but then his eyes trailed over my boys before landing on me and he shook his head.

"No, I'm out. Keep your secrets," Fox said, though there was a note of concern to his tone. "You wouldn't tell me anyway."

"True," Luther said, a lilt of amusement in his voice. "I'll get you back in somehow though, kid. You're the best leader this town has ever seen."

"Bullshit," Maverick hissed.

"By all means prove you're a better one, Rick," Luther offered, opening his arms. "You want back in the Harlequins?"

"Fuck no," Maverick growled. "Are you sure you know what you're doing, old man? Keeping secrets is just the kind of shit that got us into the mess we made for ourselves years ago."

"It's not your burden to bear. This won't touch your heads, I swear it. And it ain't gonna fuck up anything in this family, I promise you that. I'll pay my dues to Carmen then we'll put all this shit behind us. So you all just go on with your happily-ever-orgy or whatever the fuck this is." He gestured to us with a fatherly smile that said he was delighted by it, and as weird as that was, I kinda liked having his approval.

Rick muttered his agreement, clearly not wanting to get any deeper into shit than what we were already dealing with, and after a few poignant seconds, Fox nodded too.

"Alright. I trust you," Fox said. "But if there comes a point when you need my help-"

"I know," Luther agreed, but something told me he wouldn't be asking Fox for anything when it came to whatever Carmen wanted, no matter how desperate he was. This had been the price of his son's life and he was more than willing to pay it, whatever it took.

"Alright then, so we just have Shawn left to deal with," Chase said, his jaw grinding, letting me know that Shawn's ongoing survival was pissing him off just as much as it was me.

"He's in the wind now," JJ said mysteriously. "Healing up and hiding out. Most of his men are dead and the cartel have a price on his head. Any sane man would cut and run."

"Do you think he would run, hummingbird?" Fox asked me and I shook my head.

"No way. Shawn doesn't lose. Even now, with everything he'd hoped to claim here in tatters, he won't admit defeat. He'll be coming for us harder than ever. He knows he's failed in his plans to take this place from us, so he'll be going for the jugular now."

"Which means he'll be after you," Chase pointed out, his gaze fixed on me as protectiveness washed through his expression.

"Yes," I agreed, even though I knew it would only make the men sitting at this table more overbearing than ever. I swallowed down the fear that was threatening to clog my throat, facing this head on and drawing strength from the power of the men who surrounded me. "And he probably won't want to waste any time with me like he did the last time if he does manage to get to me."

"We need to draw him out," Rick growled.

"We should play him at his own games." Chase nodded. "But it would help if we knew where to start looking for him."

"Mia might have an idea," I said, my mind going to the girl who was currently recuperating from her time with Shawn in my trailer. "She was with him for a while and the way he was abusing her...I think he got off on having her close, at his mercy and jumping to fulfil his whims whenever he wanted. Maybe she heard something that might give us a clue as to where he would go, or who he would seek out in this situation."

"Seems like a long shot," Rick said dismissively.

"She's been asking to speak to you," I said, pinning Rick in my gaze while unspoken hurt and jealousy passed between us for a moment and he frowned, leaning in to cup my cheek in his large, inked hand.

"She was a means to an end, beautiful. You know that, right? Me and her weren't ever anything real. And she was using me just like I was using her. I wanted to get close to her stepdaddy and she wanted an escape from her privileged, boring life. She mighta convinced herself that there was more to it than that, but it was shallow, empty. We never spoke about anything that counted and she never saw me beyond what she was pretending I could be."

I nodded, my gut twisting with sympathy for the girl who had gotten muddled up in our world as I wondered if she wished she'd never tried to seek out the thrill of the dark in the first place.

"You still owe her a conversation," I pushed, and he sighed, nodding.

"I guess I can manage that," he agreed. "Though I doubt she knows shit about Shawn."

"It's worth a try," I replied because we had nothing else to go on, so I was willing to at least ask the question.

"Okay," he agreed, and we went back to consuming our meals, that decision made even though there were a hundred left looming over us.

There was only one thing that really counted now. We needed to find Shawn and end this for good. Because there was a future awaiting me here that shone so brightly I could hardly believe it was really mine for the taking. All four of my boys had finally accepted what my heart had known since we were just kids kicking the sand together, chasing endless waves towards a bright blue sky.

We were meant to be together. And I was gunning for my happily ever after.

109

CHAPTER NINE

After another night of the Harlequin doctor prodding and poking at us, tending to everyone's injuries, we'd all crashed out in Rogue's bed and I'd woken not five minutes ago with JJ's leg hitched over my waist and Chase's forehead against mine.

It had taken me a good few seconds of sleepiness to realise neither of them were Rogue, my hands roaming until I'd met a little too much muscle and far too much cock for my liking.

Rogue had instead been nestled against Fox's chest on the far side of the bed, and once I'd untangled myself from the bro hug I'd been wedged in, I'd planned to steal her from my brother's arms and disappear into one of the other bedrooms with her.

But then my gaze had fallen on Fox's throat, that bruise turning a vicious kind of purple and blue which made me feel acutely violent towards fucking Shawn, and all kinds of uncomfortable about stealing our girl away from my brother's arms when he looked so damn peaceful with her curled up with him.

So, instead I'd come downstairs, made myself a cup of coffee and now

I was sitting out on the patio by the pool, the sky still speckled with stars, but the tint of light to it telling me dawn was close.

I had a notepad and a pen before me on the table and a sour expression on my face. What the fuck was I even doing right now? I didn't write bullshit mushy love letters like Fox and Chase did. But goddammit, now I'd been challenged to, I had to write the best one that had ever been presented to Rogue Easton, and I wasn't gonna back down on it.

Currently, the words 'you look like the moon' sat on the page, and the longer I stared at them, the more insulting they seemed. *You look like a big white circle in the sky, yeah real fucking romantic, douchebag.*

I tore out the page, screwing it up in my hand, not even wanting to look at those bullshit words. Nah, this wasn't me. I'd told her my truth and it wasn't some pretty poem designed to make her heart flutter or some shit. It was raw, full of pain and the twisted reality of our pasts, tangled into one perfect thing that made up *us*. The others may have had a way with words, telling her how she compared to a summer's day or some bullshit, but Rogue wasn't just summer and light and all things good. She was dark too, all carved up inside and full of anguish.

It was the want in her eyes that I found most intoxicating. This need for something real, thrilling and cataclysmic all at once. It was a wildness to her that could have roused the titans from their slumber with a desire to claim it from her. She held such fucking magic about her, and it had drawn me to her the first moment we met, inciting a need in me to seize it too. The only way to feel like that was with her. I'd experienced every thrill in this world, come damn close to death a thousand times, and nothing made my heart beat with passion and fury like she did.

It was her gift, and something about her being in the company of all of us made that gift stronger every day, made it flourish within her until she damn well shone. And I planned to keep her shining until there were no more todays or tomorrows left.

Damn, that was good. What was it again? I tried to grasp the words I'd been thinking, wanting to lay them on the page for her, but they slipped away like sand through my fingers.

Fuck it, it was probably just some bullshit anyway.

I lifted my revolver from the table where I'd left it, flipping open the cylinder and pouring the bullets out into my hand. I slid one back in out of habit, my fingers moving in the familiar pattern they had taken countless times as my mind drifted elsewhere.

I spun the cylinder without looking where the bullet was placed, slotting it back into the gun with a click that reminded me of all the times I'd pulled the trigger on myself and never been offered death.

"Rick?" Rogue's urgent voice snapped me out of my thoughts, and I jolted in surprise as she collided with me, wrestling the gun out of my grip with frantic breaths falling from her lips.

I let her take it, gazing up at her in surprise as she backed away from me, her eyes blazing with unshed tears as she held the gun behind her back. My heart was wrung out in my chest as I realised what she thought and I shook my head, rising to my feet and reaching for her, but she stumbled back like she assumed I was coming for the gun.

"I was just messing around, beautiful. I'm not playing roulette," I promised, and it was the truth through and through.

Her throat bobbed as the backs of her heels reached the edge of the pool. She was only wearing my grey tank, the hem of it falling down to her thighs and tickling the tattoo of a skull there that was housed within a triangle.

"Come on, baby girl," I said gently, letting my arms fall to my sides. "Do you really think I'd leave you now?"

"I don't know," she admitted in a terrified whisper. "Sometimes I dream that you're all gone, that I'll wake in cold sheets and realise I never found you again."

"Come here," I growled, but she shook her head, shuffling even further back so she was right on her toes at the edge of the pool.

"Knowing you held this gun to your head over and over again, and each one of those times could have meant you leaving this world, makes me fucking sick, Maverick," she snapped, fire igniting in her gaze as that wildness in her came out, and I bathed in the glow of it.

"I'm here now. I didn't leave. Death didn't want me." I smirked, but she bared her teeth at me, not liking the joke.

"How can I know you won't leave me?" she hissed. "That you won't just pick up this gun and check out one day?"

"I told you, I'm yours. I'm here. I'm not going anywhere," I swore, but she shook her head again like she simply couldn't accept that.

"It doesn't feel real," she admitted, and a fat tear slipped from her eye and fell down her cheek. "None of it does. I'm gonna wake up, Rick, I just know it. Then I'll find myself back with him, with fucking Shawn, and I'll realise that I was never strong enough to escape him."

Rage scraped through my chest at that. "Bullshit," I snarled. "You're stronger than all of us, and you're gonna prove that to him too when he's down in the dirt with your finger pulsing on the trigger of the gun that'll take him outa this world for good. You got that?"

She looked lost, uncertain and I despised that. What had happened in the blowhole had clearly shaken her, the fear of nearly losing us all too much. And hell, I got it. I still didn't think I'd quite processed how close I'd come to saying goodbye to two of my brothers forever, but we were still here and that was what mattered.

"It's not real," she breathed again, and I lunged at her, having no other thought in my head but proving to her that I was as real as the ground beneath her feet.

I slammed into her and she gasped a second before we hit the water, sinking deep into the pool as I locked her against my body and kicked until we reached the tiled base.

I hooked my fingers in a filter on the wall to keep us there and her hair swept out around us in a swirl of rainbow colours, a stream of bubbles pouring from her lips.

Rogue's eyes met mine as she wriggled in my hold, but my arm was latched firmly around her body and I wasn't letting her go.

She'd released the gun, the thing sitting on the base of the pool a few feet away and I had no intention of retrieving it.

I held tight to her as I waited for her to stop fighting, her eyes finding mine. The bubbles slowed as they left her lips, only a few of them drifting free now and slipping away towards the surface.

I could hear my pulse thundering in my ears, and that was the point of this, the two of us so awake, so alive as we played chicken with death, making it impossible to deny the realness of us.

She looped her hands around my neck, her thumb finding my pulse point as I released the last of the breath in my lungs, letting it sail away towards the surface. A stillness fell over our limbs as I held us there, peace finding her expression and soothing the ache in me too over her fears. I would be here, always, there was no better reason to stay in this world than her, she had to know that.

The beating of my heart grew frantic, and she jerked in my arms a little, glancing up towards the surface above, but we were just getting to the best part.

I kept my grip on the filter to hold us down, moving over her so she couldn't float up as I adjusted my grip on her, shifting my hand to grasp the back of her neck and watch the way her eyes sparked with an undying thirst for life.

When my lungs burned and the ache in my body reminded me how deeply fucking alive I was, I let go of the filter and kicked upwards for the surface, Rogue swimming with me as we raced for air, the need to live a potent, perfect thing.

We gasped down lungfuls of oxygen as we breached the surface and

Rogue started laughing, my own laughter answering hers as adrenaline spun a web in my veins. I dragged her close, my mouth coming down on hers between frantic breaths and the warmth of her body pressing to mine.

"Real," I promised her, and I tasted her smile as she slid her tongue between my lips.

I kissed all the lasting worries away from my girl and eventually we swam to the edge of the pool, pulling ourselves out and sitting on its edge with our legs hanging in the water.

"Thank you," she said, taking my hand, lifting it to her mouth and placing a kiss to my inked knuckles that made my chest swell.

"When the sun rises, we'll watch it together," I said, nodding to the sky as the promise of dawn swelled within it.

"Is that an offer?" she asked, biting her lip as mischief danced in her big blue eyes.

I grinned in response to that, shoving to my feet and tugging her up too. "Yeah, it's a fucking promise, beautiful. But we don't have much time." I broke into a run, heading into the house, sopping wet and leaving a trail that would make Foxy boy go into mother hen mode when he woke up, but I didn't give a flying fuck as I dragged Rogue after me down the hall, shoving the door open to the garage and racing down into the dark.

I snatched the keys to my motorcycle and jumped on it while Rogue swung her leg over the back, her thighs clutching mine as she held onto my waist. I took her helmet off the handlebars, passing it back to her and not letting her refuse it as I pushed it onto her head before putting on mine.

Then I started the engine, barefoot and wearing nothing but my shorts, pressing the key fob which opened the garage door, the one I'd swiped off of Foxy's keys so he'd had to go and get himself a new one made.

I drove us out of the garage with a roar of my engine, the seat vibrating beneath us as I headed for the gate and swung a mocking salute to the Harlequins on duty who let us through.

Then we were sailing down the road, riding hard and fast as we raced to meet the dawn.

There was one place I thought of heading to watch it, though I'd have to get a fucking move on if we were gonna make it there in time before the sun peeked over the horizon.

The rush of warm air helped dry us out a little and the scent of the sea called to me in a way that reminded me of home. A home I finally belonged to again, one without hate and bitterness tainting everything about it.

I didn't know when it had happened, maybe at some point down in that blowhole when I'd realised life might not offer me another chance to make things right with Rogue and the boys I'd spent my youth loving like family. And though I couldn't change the bad that had happened, or even forget it, maybe I could let go of it, forgive it, put it to rest at long last.

With my girl's arms around me and memories of being a teenager sweeping through my head, doing just this, and feeling freer than a fucking bird, it became easy releasing it all, making peace with my regrets, my vengeance. Today was the first day of the rest of my life, my new life. And as I made it to the blackened husk of Sinners' Playground and the sun spilled over the horizon beyond the hills to the east to a cheer from Rogue that made me smile like a damn idiot, I knew it was going to be a day of redemption. My fresh start.

After we'd enjoyed the sunrise, we returned to Harlequin House, fetching clothes and food. I stole Rogue away again before the others woke up, knowing what needed to be done as I drove us toward Rejects Park.

Rogue wore a little white playsuit with a pale blue bikini underneath, her hair tied up in a knot on her head and JJ's pink sunglasses on her face. I looked less interesting in a pair of black board shorts and a white t-shirt with a mandala skull on it, but Rogue kept brushing her hands over me like I looked irresistible, and I looped my arm around her waist and tugged her close as we headed into the trailer park. Being able to walk around my old streets without being shot at with the girl of my dreams on my arm was a headfuck, but of the best variety, that was for sure.

I was forced to let go of my girl as she spotted her friends gathered around a firepit which was currently unlit.

I folded my arms as the squeals and hugs commenced, waiting for Rogue to return to me, but instead I found a group of girls running towards me and I was suddenly surrounded.

"Fuck, you look even bigger up close, dude," Di said, looking me up and down.

"He's like a big ol' bear, ain't he?" Rogue smirked, elbowing me.

The blonde one, Lyla, cocked her head, looking a little wary of me as she remained a step behind the first. "You're not here to like, kill someone, are you?" she breathed, looking both frightened and excited by that idea.

"He's on a strict no murdering diet right now. If he can sever three less heads this month he'll get a gold star," Rogue said with a grin and my gaze hooked on her mouth as she wetted her lips.

"Jesus, he looks at you like he's gonna eat you," Di said, and a redheaded girl, Bella, squealed a laugh before draining the last of her bottle of beer. It wasn't even nine am yet.

"I do eat her. Regularly," I said. "Don't I, beautiful? Just this morning I had you for breakfast, spread over my bike while the first rays of dawn warmed my back."

Rogue didn't even blush, raising her chin and moving forward to swat my cheek in a warning. "Are you trying to embarrass me in front of my friends, Rick? Because they've heard every dark and dirty detail about you."

"And the others," Lyla added with a snort.

"What about how Fox Harlequin fucked her just after he was almost

118

hung on Gallows Bridge and had a nice, deep stab wound in his side too?" I offered and they all shared a look of surprise before turning to Rogue with a demand for details in their eyes. I boomed a laugh, tossing my arm over Rogue's shoulders, and speaking directly into her ear. "If you wanna give them a play by play of everything we do to you, I'll have to come up with some very shocking ways for us to fuck you to add a bit of drama."

She looked up at me under her lashes with a challenge in her eyes. "If you think you're up to it."

"You're gonna regret saying that," I murmured through a smile, and excitement built in her gaze that said she hoped I fulfilled that promise.

Rogue made plans to meet her friends after we were done here before leading me away through the trailer park, my mood taking a dive as I considered what I had to face now.

The trailer Rogue had taken ownership of was blue and kinda cute looking in a girly way – though I doubted a place as small as that would have ever been big enough for someone my size to call home.

Rogue moved to knock on the door, and I ran a hand over my short, dark hair as I decided how to handle this. I'd been known a time or two to avoid confronting my demons, but I'd pledged to do just that today, and I wasn't one to back out on a decision once it was made.

Mia opened the door, wearing jeans and a plain white t-shirt, her face bare of make-up. I expected to witness pain in her eyes, the trauma of all she'd been through at Shawn's hands, but instead I found resilience there, and I was glad of that.

Her eyes widened as they fell on Rogue and she rushed down the steps in a blur, dragging her into a hug. "Hi."

"Hey," Rogue said, straightening in surprise before winding her arms around Mia and hugging her back.

Mia's eyes moved to me, and her features pinched a little before she released Rogue and brushed some imaginary dirt off of her jeans. "Um, would you guys come inside? There's stuff I need to say, I guess you do too?"

"Sorry would be a good start," I grunted, rubbing a hand over the back of my neck as Rogue looked to me with a sad sort of smile on her lips. "So... I'm sorry."

Mia nodded, moving back inside and we followed her into the little trailer which was decorated in pastel tones, all of it feminine and pretty and I could see Rogue here, understanding the draw it must have had for her even if I was instantly proved right in my thoughts about my size as I had to duck to get through the door.

The girl I'd used to get closer to Kaiser Rosewood looked at me now with an ache in her gaze that made me feel ten shades of shitty about how little she'd meant to me. I'd thought it had been the same for her, but maybe if I really looked closer at it, I'd have known she was getting attached.

Mia caught my wrist and I turned to her with a frown, her eyes darting to Rogue in a question. "Are you with her?"

"Yes," I said immediately, the truth as plain as day anyway, and I wasn't about to sugar coat this for Mia. She deserved the truth, and that I could give her. "I'm in love with her. Have been since I was somewhere around eleven years old, I'd say. Or at least, that was about the time I understood what kind of love it was I felt for her. The one you get no say in, and you don't want to either. Fate chose her for me, and I lost her for a while, but here she is again, and I won't be letting her go this time."

Rogue was behind me, so I didn't catch her reaction to that, but I watched Mia's face shift from hurt to understanding as she nodded.

"I knew the second I first saw you two together there was something deep between you. But I thought...well, I thought we had something too, you know?"

"Mia," I sighed, leaning back against the wall and trying to find the right words for this. It wasn't me, all this plain talking, owning up and seriousness, but I'd manage it. The girl had been through hell after all. "I was an asshole.

120

Still am actually. It's kind of my thing. Some part of me broke a long time ago, and I took out my anger and hate over that on everything around me. I wasn't capable of loving anything anymore because I lost everything worth loving. Now I have it back." I glanced over my shoulder at Rogue and found her looking at me with her soul bleeding right there for me to see. I reached for her hand, winding my fingers between hers and drawing her closer as I turned back to Mia. "I've left a pretty messy trail of destruction throughout my past, and I'm sorry you got wrapped up in that, you're honestly one of the only people I have an apology for. But there it is. If you'll have it."

Mia's eyes travelled between us and a glimmer of hurt rose in them before it was replaced by a wall of strength. "Yeah, I accept it. I mean, I knew we were done. I guess, I just needed some closure. I suppose I have it now." She looked to Rogue, a grim kind of smile twitching her lips. "Are you okay? Did Shawn hurt you bad?"

"Shawn hurts everyone," Rogue said darkly, and my fingers locked tighter around hers, a burning need for vengeance rising within me. "But I'm good. Are you?"

Mia tucked a short lock of dark hair behind her ear, taking in a shallow breath. "I mean, I'm not great. But I'm doing better. The girls here have been real good to me, but I don't wanna stay in this town any longer, there's too many bad memories here for me now, so I'm leaving to go and live with my cousin in Florida this weekend." She seemed relieved at that and some of the weight seemed to lift from her shoulders as she looked to my girl. "Thank you for letting me stay here. I won't forget what you did for me. If there's anything I can ever do…"

"It's done," Rogue said firmly. "We went through enough shit. Be free, Mia. Go start a new life, forget this one."

"Will you stay here?" she asked.

"Yeah," Rogue said, glancing up at me. "It's my home. I'm gonna cut Shawn right out of it and make him pay for what he did to us."

I really liked hearing her call this town her home again, and I liked that it felt like mine too. At long fucking last. I was back in the place I belonged with a girl I'd once thought I'd never see again, bonded to the men I'd hated for too many years.

"Promise?" Mia growled.

"Yeah, that's a fucking promise," I answered, and Mia nodded firmly, satisfaction rolling through her gaze.

"This might be a long shot, but is there any chance Shawn ever took you somewhere, some place of his outside of town, or even in town?" Rogue asked. "Maybe he mentioned an area or a hideout? Some plan B if he ever had to run?"

Mia frowned as she thought on it then shook her head, making disappointment dash through me. "I didn't leave Rosewood Manor much. We occasionally went to a market out of town every last Sunday of the month. He'd meet his mom there while he sent me off to get groceries with a couple of his men." She shrugged.

"What's the name of it?" Rogue asked.

"The market in Applebrook," Mia said. "I'll leave the keys to this place with Di when I leave on Saturday." Rogue nodded, her brow pinching like she'd just realised that she was going to have to make a decision on what she did with the trailer after that.

"I guess we'll be seeing you," I said, shifting towards the door and tugging Rogue along after me.

"Yeah, or not," Mia laughed but there wasn't much lightness in it. "Goodbye."

I nodded to her as Rogue gave her a one-armed hug while I still had hold of her other hand, and I led her outside.

"Shoot me a text when he's dead," Mia called, and I smirked as I turned back to her.

"When you get a squid emoji from me, that means it's done," Rogue

122

promised, and I sniggered as Mia smiled.

"That's not what a squid emoji means," she said.

"Yeah, I know. That's why it's the perfect code." Rogue grinned.

We left Mia there, heading through the park and Rogue looked wistfully off towards the beach where her friends were no doubt waiting for her. I drew her close, kissing her hard, missing her already as I let her go.

"You're not coming with me, are you?" she pouted.

"I'm gonna go talk to Luther," I said, tipping my head back and groaning.

Rogue tiptoed her fingers up my chest and flicked my adam's apple. "Are you gonna give him a big cuddle?"

"Something like that," I muttered, and she gasped, gripping my hair and yanking my head down to make me look at her. Which I didn't mind at all. In fact, it gave me ideas about taking her somewhere and burying myself in her for a while before I had to go and be a grown up and all that boring shit.

I took out the gun stashed in the back of my jeans, slipping it into the purse she had hanging from her shoulder. "Stay safe."

"You're being such a cutie pie today," she said, pecking me on the lips while I gave her a flat look.

"I'm not a fucking cutie pie. And I'll prove it to you when I eat your ass later on." I spun her around by the hips and spanked her on said ass, making her squeak in surprise as I sent her on her way. She flipped me the finger, and I chuckled, watching her go as my cock begged me to follow her, but it wasn't in charge right now sadly.

"I'll pick you up later or send one of your bitch boys to get you," I called.

"Same difference," she sang back at me, and I cursed her under my breath, but couldn't wipe the smile from my lips as I walked back out of the park to where I'd left my bike.

I even shot another look over my shoulder at her, chewing on the inside of my cheek as I watched that fine ass disappear, and I missed her in an instant.

I got on my bike, heading back to Harlequin House as the sun beat down on my back, and I thought of my youth, up to no good on these streets, always getting into trouble. I felt like that kid again now as I loosed the throttle and took corners at speed, arriving back home with my heart racing and a desire to see my boys building in me.

Fuck, Rogue was right. I was going soft. Had to watch that. *Better pound on JJ.*

I left the bike in the garage, jogging upstairs and walking through the halls towards the sound of people talking in the kitchen.

"Dad – quit it," Fox growled.

"Sit still, will ya?" Luther demanded and I walked into the room, finding him pushing Fox down onto a stool at the island, rubbing Arnica cream onto his neck.

Fox was shirtless, pouting like a little kid as Luther worked to keep him in place while tending to his bruises.

Mutt yapped at Fox like he was playing soldier for our father, and I scooped up the little dog, earning myself a bite to the thumb as I scruffed his head until he grumbled his way into submission, liking the way I stroked his ears too much to complain.

"Morning," I grunted, a slight awkwardness in the air.

We still didn't know how to do this. Fox and I weren't kids anymore, and I'd spent too many years at war with them both for things to just slide back to normality easily. But I knew I was the one holding back the most, keeping a certain distance. I finally had to face up to it, because if things were going to be good again in this house, then I had to let go of the anger I was still holding on to. Though it wasn't easy by any means.

I placed Mutt on a stool beside Fox and he sniffed at the bandages around my brother's waist before giving them a tiny lick. By the time Fox looked down to see what he was doing, Mutt had sat back on his seat, looking away like he'd never given him a moment of affection.

"Where've you been?" Luther asked.

"Is Rogue with you?" Fox added, looking past me, but our father shoved his head back again to gain access to the nasty colouring under his ear.

"She's with her friends."

"Alone?" Fox hissed. "What about Shawn? What if he's-"

"Calm down, Foxy boy. Shawn's run off and between the cartel and the Harlequins, there's no way he's getting back into town without being caught," I said firmly, but the tension didn't leave his posture. "She's a big girl, and I gave her a gun."

"I'll send some Harlequins down that way to watch her," Luther murmured as he took his phone from his pocket and I nodded, figuring that wasn't such a bad idea.

"See? She's good." I knocked my knuckles against Fox's cheek, and he batted me away, still looking anxious. "Where's JJ and Chase?" I looked out to the patio, spotting Miss Mabel there set up on one of the sun loungers, propped up with lots of cushion and some iced lemonade in the shade of a parasol.

"They went surfing," Fox said with a look of longing that said he wished he could have gone too.

When Luther was done texting his gang, he went back to rubbing Arnica cream into Fox's bruises, a furrowed line on his brow. He'd clearly rubbed in plenty already, but the old man couldn't back off, and I could see the need in him to try and fix what had happened to my brother.

Fox looked to me with a plea for help in his eyes as Luther continued smothering his skin in cream and I caught his arm to stop him, giving him a firm look.

"That's enough," I said, and I felt the tension in my father's muscles as he met my gaze, a terrified man looking out at me from his eyes. "He's alright," I told him, needing to banish that fear in him.

I'd never seen anything come close to breaking Luther Harlequin, not in all the years he'd dealt in blood and fury, but standing here before the son he'd almost lost, I could see that his death would have done it. As I glanced down at Fox with his unruly blonde hair and bright green eyes, I saw him as a kid again and knew without a doubt that I would have broken too.

"Dammit, why isn't there a reset button on life?" I muttered, angry at it all. At how we'd gotten ourselves here and how so much of it could have been avoided.

Luther sighed as I let him go, sliding his arm around my shoulders, and fuck if that didn't feel nice. I couldn't let go of the rigidity to my muscles though, too many years of shutting him and everyone else out ingrained in me. It just wasn't natural anymore, and maybe it never could be again, but I had to try.

At the end of the day, this was the only family I was ever gonna be offered, and we'd hurt each other deeper than anyone ever should, but we were still blood. Real blood it turned out, even if I didn't like the source of my origins, I knew it didn't change the way Luther felt about me. There was something rare about that too. No money in this world could buy that kind of unconditional love. Through all the hate and blind anger I'd thrown at him over the years, alongside the bullets I'd hurled at his gang and the trouble I'd caused in his home, he had never once cut me off, never turned his back on me. He'd waited me out, assured that I'd come back one day. And fuck if I hadn't thought he was delusional, but it was pretty hard to call him that now when he'd been damn well right all along.

That was a part of why this was so hard, letting them back in, because I wasn't one who took being wrong easy. But was I really gonna let my stubbornness leave this wall up between me and my family so we'd never truly be whole again? So I'd always be left on the outside, at a distance to the love we'd all once shared.

I searched for the right words, but nothing came. The silence wore on and Luther continued standing there with his arm around my shoulders while Fox stroked Mutt, and all the bad blood we had between us sat there stagnating.

How was I supposed to clean it out? What was it gonna take to fix this once and for all?

I thought back on my childhood, a time when we'd been good, then to the years when we grew into teenagers and Luther started pushing the gang life on us.

It wasn't bad though. Yeah, we had our fights, Fox and I fought back against Luther's demands, rebelling whenever we could. But that was the way of teenagers, wasn't it? We'd still had our good times during all that. Luther had taken me off occasionally, training me up with guns and knives. He'd brought me on gang business sometimes too, let me see the darker side of his life, and honestly? I'd liked it. I was made for it just like he said, even if I didn't wanna admit that back then. Because no kid wanted their life planned out for them, especially when I had plans of my own with my friends.

We'd dreamed of something bigger for ourselves but had never worked out quite how we'd all get there. And in a roundabout way, I guess we'd made it now. Or at least, we had a chance for it. Didn't we all say once that we'd live in a big house together and chase every dawn into existence, live like those kids did, always?

This was it. Our arrival into that, the opportunity finally waiting with open arms. And yeah, maybe some of us had gotten here by travelling separate paths, our feet dirtied by the roads of despair and suffering we'd ended up on, but the point was, we *were* all here now. So I had to seize this chance with all I had, for the kid I'd once been, because I owed him that much.

My tongue loosened at last, and I drew in a breath as I fought through my stubbornness, hoping this would heal us.

"I want a fresh start," I announced, and Luther raised his brows, but I barrelled on before he could speak. "I want camping weekends, and sailing in the afternoons, I want to ride in your truck and go shooting tin cans out in the woods. I want to stay here in this house, and I want it to be my home again. I want to stay here, Luther." I looked him dead in the eye, my throat tightening around these next words as heat burned a line up the back of my neck. "And I want you to be my dad again. And you, my brother." I jerked my chin at Fox as his eyes widened too. "I want the happy family we're owed. I want our day in the goddamn sun to come again, and I wanna stay basking in it for the rest of our lives, because fuck letting the world take it from us. I want today to be the first day of countless days where we're just, fucking, *good*."

"Yeah, son. Let's start over," Luther said with emotion in his voice, drawing me against his chest and I melted like a fucking snowman in the sun against him.

Fox stood, joining us, and I swear I'd had so many group hugs lately, that I really was gonna go soft if I didn't do something particularly masculine today to counteract all of this mushy shit.

Mutt jumped up from his stool, placing his paws on my back with a happy yap and Luther slid his arm around me in a headlock, scrubbing his knuckles down on my head.

"Hey," I barked, shoving him back with a smirk and Fox backed up with a laugh as Luther swung a punch at me.

I narrowly avoided it, diving at him and forcing him back against the kitchen side as we fell into a furious wrestle like we had when Fox and I were boys, and he was training us to fight. Only now, he had his work cut out for him in beating me. I was just as big as him, and a meaner bastard than him too.

"Maverick?" Mabel called as my laughter grew louder. "Is that you?"

I shoved away from my dad with a grin and headed out to see her, the flowing white dress she was wearing fluttering around her in the breeze as she sat up on the lounger. "Ah, there you are." She smiled at me as I dropped down beside her, and she reached out to take my hand. "Have you found that brute yet? Have you brought home my diamonds?"

"Not yet," I sighed. "But soon. I promise."

She smiled, squeezing my fingers in her tiny, wrinkled palm. "They're yours, you know? I want you to have them. To use them to build the life of your dreams, sweet boy. I'm sorry I couldn't bring them to you myself, sorry for all this damn hullabaloo."

I frowned at her, shifting closer on my seat as something sharp twisted in my chest. "I don't care about some fucking diamonds, Mabel. I'm just glad you're safe, and that you're away from that asshole."

"Yes, it is so good to see the sun again," she sighed, titling her head up to look at the sky before turning back to me. "But those diamonds are yours, I kept them safe for all those years, and I didn't do that for some scoundrel to take them and steal the Rosewood fortune. I hate to think of them in his greasy palms."

"I'll get them back," I swore, seeing how this was eating her up inside. "For you."

"No, for *you*, my boy." She reached up and carved her fingers over my cheek. "Goodness, you do look like her in ways, I can see it now. My dear Rhonda."

My pulse ticked a little faster and I felt an urge in me to know more about my mother. My father could rot in hell for all I cared, but Rhonda Rosewood was someone I wanted to know more about. Well, I hoped I did.

"What was she like?"

"Oh gracious," Mabel sighed, a smile gracing her lips as some memories danced in her eyes. "She was beautiful, kind, generous, a real business woman too. Oh, she had such a fierce streak in her, I see that in you too. She would have done anything for the ones she loved, and I suppose she did in the end." She gazed sadly at me, a croak to her voice and my heart cleaved open in my chest.

"Tell me more," I insisted, and she nodded, settling herself back against her pillows.

As she started talking, I got lost building a picture of my mother, discovering who she was and who that might mean I was too. I'd spent most of my life wearing armour and becoming the strongest, fiercest creature I could be, but there was light to my dark. And it was time I let it in again.

ROGUE

CHAPTER TEN

"Are we sure about this?" I asked as I tugged on the hem of the little silver dress I was wearing, knowing full well that my attempts were doing very little to stop my ass cheeks from falling out of it.

We were in the backstage area of Afterlife, music thumping through the club so loud that the walls were vibrating with it while the strippers hurried around us, putting on their costumes for the first performances, slicking their bodies with glitter and baby oil until it looked like a Pegasus had puked on the entire place.

It had been three days since the blowhole, the hanging, all of it. Three days of enjoying the sunshine and bathing in the company of my boys while every Harlequin in town hunted for any sign of Shawn and failed to find so much as a hair that belonged to him.

We'd spent a lot of time recounting stories from our youth and falling back into the bond we'd always shared so easily, and of course this new dynamic had included a whole lot of nakedness that I had absolutely no complaints to.

Not with Fox though. He kept his distance whenever the others sought out the pleasures of my flesh, and I knew he was struggling to adapt to this new way of being. But he didn't leave, and never seemed hurt by my time with them either. And I was just so glad to have him be a part of this even if we were taking things slow.

The threat of Shawn never left us. The feeling of his presence never lifting. He was up to something. Had to be. But we just had no idea what that could be.

We couldn't just keep laying low and none of us had ever been the kinds to cower in fear anyway. So if we couldn't find Shawn, then our plan was to let him find us. Which meant going out in public and taking more chances, giving him the opportunities he would need and making him believe he might catch us off guard.

"The plan is to draw him out, beautiful," Rick purred in my ear while Chase shifted on the edge of JJ's dressing table, his gaze flicking around the room while he glowered at it like he thought Lyla or Di might pull a bazooka from between their ass cheeks and fire on us at any moment. "Not much chance of that if we're hiding out at home now, is there?"

I pursed my lips, knowing the truth of that even if it didn't stop me from wanting to drag all four of them back there to hide away from the world with me.

I knew we had to do this, had to make Shawn believe he had a shot at me and lure him out by acting like we thought we'd already won. I just hated putting my boys in danger like this.

"You'll feel better when we cut his heart from his chest and lay it at your feet," Chase added in a low murmur and the corners of my lips lifted at that visual.

"I'm going to go check out the crowd," Fox said as JJ started warming up for his time on stage, dropping into a set of press ups beside Texas, the two of them racing to a hundred while they got their pump on. My gaze lingered on

JJ as his muscles bulged and the oil on his body highlighted every hard line of his athletic form. Fuck me, he was edible.

"Maybe we should all go," I suggested, reaching for Fox as he took a step back, not wanting any of them out of sight.

We might have taken a few days to lick our wounds and most of my cuts and bruises were well on their way to healing, but I knew Fox needed longer to recover than he was allowing himself.

The last few days had been so full of plans to take on Shawn that there had been little time for anything aside from eating in between them, and with both Mabel and Luther constantly in the house, the two of us hadn't managed to get a repeat of that first night. To say I was aching for it would be an understatement.

The way Fox's green eyes roamed over the scrap of material I wore for a dress let me know that he was just as hungry for round two as I was, but short of dragging him into the supply closet, there wasn't much we could do about it here. As I thought of that, I couldn't help but glance between my other boys hopefully and the look Rick gave me said he knew exactly what I was thinking.

"Let me do a sweep first," Fox insisted, ever the alpha.

I relented, mostly because the bruises surrounding his throat looked worse than ever after having a few days to bloom, and I knew what it was taking for him to remain standing with us despite the pain he had to be in between that and the stab wound in his side. He was on painkillers, but even so, there weren't many people I knew who'd be up and walking about so soon after what he'd been through.

"Okay," I said, my throat thickening at the thought of him heading into that crowd. But he was Fox motherfucking Harlequin, so I knew I had to trust his instincts on this. If he said he could manage, then he could. Not that that would stop me from playing nurse for him later.

I caught his shirt as he made a move to step back, fisting it tightly and tugging him into me in a clear demand.

Fox didn't resist me, catching my jaw in his firm grip and taking my mouth with his, forcing a gasp from me that parted my lips and gave him full access to ravage my mouth.

His tongue swept across mine, painting lines of sin all over my body as I got lost in thoughts of him doing that exact thing between my thighs.

A moan rolled up my throat and I tiptoed even though the heels I wore were already pushing me to the limit of my long legs. But Fox Harlequin was big in all the ways that counted, his physical form, his aura, his damn energy, and I needed to meet the demands of so much all at once.

Fox drew back, smirking down at me as he held me back by his hold on my jaw, his mouth dipping to my ear and making a shiver roll down my spine as he spoke into it.

"I bet you'd beg so prettily, hummingbird," he growled, his grip on me tightening as I bit down on my bottom lip. I was a strong, independent woman, but shit, I had one hell of a tendency to submit when these men of mine went alpha on me. "You'd beg for me to fuck you right here in front of all these people, wouldn't you? With just a little push, I think you'd beg so convincingly that I'd give you what you wanted too. I'd push you back, spread your legs and watch you take every inch of me while you pleaded for it all."

My teeth grew close to drawing blood, my nipples hardening with need as I slipped the hand gripping his shirt down in the direction of his waistband, nodding in agreement to his accusation and making him chuckle darkly in my ear.

"Well, that will have to wait," he said firmly, stepping back and releasing me, his eyes full of the lust he'd awoken in me. "Because I want you all alone when I have you again. No eyes on you but mine. Got it?"

My gaze cut to Rick as he snorted obnoxiously, while Chase just shrugged, not seeming to mind what Fox was demanding even if he clearly had nothing against sharing himself.

"Okay," I agreed, understanding that what I had with Fox was going to be different in that sense. He was too jealous to be able to watch me with the others, too possessive. And though he clearly accepted what I had with them now and made no attempt to get between me and them, it was obvious that he wanted what happened between me and him to stay behind closed doors. I could respect that, even if it might cause issues when it came to the way I'd split my time. But JJ had already been making more than a few jokes about sex rotas and sleepover schedules, so I guessed for now they were still good with us figuring it out.

"Foxy talks a big game, doesn't he, beautiful?" Maverick asked loudly as Fox took a step away from me, causing him to pause. "I gotta say though, it sounds a whole lot like an inferiority complex to me."

"What are you talking about?" Fox scoffed and the malicious grin on Rick's face made it all too clear he was looking to bait him.

"I'm just pointing out the fact that you can talk up a storm about fucking her senseless behind closed doors and making her beg for your dick on her knees, but when it comes down to it, you're just all kinds of vanilla."

Chase snorted a laugh before quickly covering it with a cough as Fox shot a glare his way.

"How do you figure that?" Fox asked irritably.

"Because you can't handle the idea of watching the rest of us fuck her in real life even though you get hard watching the videos of that reality whenever I send them to you. Admit it, Foxy. You couldn't handle watching me fuck her while she sucked your dick at the same time. That kind of thing has got way too many flavours for you; it's all strawberry and chocolate with a dollop of pecan and a shit ton of sprinkles on top. But that just isn't the life for you. You like your ice cream nice and tasteless in a plain white colour, don't you? I bet you'd take it in a cup so you don't even have to deal with a cone."

"You're full of shit, Rick," Fox growled, stepping up to him while Maverick pushed off of the table beside us and stepped close too, making sure their chests bumped as he glared eye to eye at his brother, this game glimmering in his gaze and letting me know he had no plans of backing down.

"Stop it," I said firmly, moving to push them apart and huffing impatiently when they refused to step back.

"Prove it, Foxy boy," Rick taunted. "If you're cookie dough these days, then why not come find a dark corner where you can watch her scream for me then?"

"Just because I have no interest in that doesn't mean I'm vanilla," Fox insisted, a sneer lifting his upper lip and I lost my patience with their boy drama.

"I need something to hit them with." I held my hand out for some kind of weapon and Chase obligingly tossed one my way, the thick, purple dildo vibrating in my hand as I caught it before taking a swing at Rick's head.

He cursed as he was forced to either duck aside or take a rubber cock to the eye and I swung it at Fox next, forcing him to back up.

"Stop it," I commanded, wielding the dildo again threateningly as they both watched me with amusement, Rick raising his hands in surrender as he took another step back.

"You heard the lady," JJ barked, striding towards us with his chest gleaming from his workout, his muscles fully pumped and primed to dry my entire mouth out. "Go do whatever you were doing. My first set is about to start anyway."

"Fine," Fox said. "The three of you need to check out the crowd before heading out there," he added, glancing between me, Chase and Maverick. "When you're confident it's clear then head out and let yourselves be seen. We want Shawn to think we're dropping our guards, returning to our old routines and thinking ourselves the winners in this war, but we don't need to take unnecessary risks. We'll stay until the end of the set and no longer. Got it?"

"Yes, boss," Chase and JJ replied automatically before they both realised how easily they'd fallen back into the roles that had once been set for them in the crew, and awkward laughter covered their embarrassment.

"Yes, sir," I added, dipping my voice, and letting him make of that what he would. I was in no way objecting to the idea of playing nice when we were alone again.

Fox nodded, his eyes hooking on me for a final moment before he turned and strode out of the dressing room.

"The space to the left of the stage will be left empty for the three of you," JJ said, adjusting the gun holstered at his hip to complete his soldier costume. That had been my genius idea – it meant he could have a real gun with him while he was up on the stage without anyone questioning it, plus I got to indulge in fantasies of being a damsel he'd rescued from the midst of battle, willing to repay him for my life with full use of my body. "You can stand up there, hidden by the lights and the curtain while we're dancing. You'll be able to see every face in the crowd, see if there's anyone out there who might be connected to Shawn."

"Okay," I agreed. "But maybe later you bring that costume home."

JJ grinned at me, licking his bottom lip and backing away from me as the rest of the dancers headed towards the stage. "That's a promise, pretty girl."

I grinned as we followed him, Chase and Maverick sticking either side of me, their eyes skipping around the room, reminding me of the danger we knew could be lurking anywhere and making me feel at least a little reassured thanks to all the weapons I knew they were carrying.

We headed into the shadows to the left of the stage, watching as JJ, Texas, Adam and the rest of the dancers all made their way out onto it, getting into position while the lights stayed off and a hush of anticipation rolled through the crowd.

The music dropped and Fancy by Iggy Azalea and Charli XCX blasted from the speakers, lights flooding the stage to the screams of the crowd as the dancers each took turns isolating individual moves designed to flood panties and line the stage with dollar bills.

I found myself dancing to the beat as my eyes remained glued to Johnny

James, his gaze flicking my way as he rolled his body in a move so freaking sexual, I swear I felt it between my thighs.

Chase stepped close behind me, his arm snaking around my waist as he tugged my body back against his and I leaned into him, feeling the press of his muscles surrounding me while I continued to dance, grinding my ass back against his crotch.

"Bad idea, little one," he warned, nipping on my ear to warn me to stop, but I really hadn't ever been good at knowing when to stop anything.

Bad habits came all too easily to me, and my boys were probably the worst one of all, but my addiction ran too deep, my habit far too ingrained now, so I wasn't going to waste time on trying to resist them.

I kept my eyes glued to the sensual movements of Johnny James's body as I watched him, unable to spare any attention for the crowd I should have been searching. Rick was on it though, his huge frame concealed in the shadows right beside the curtain as he peered out for any signs of trouble, meaning I could enjoy the show all I liked.

I caught Chase's hand, moaning softly as I drew it down the front of my body, leading him to the hem of my too-short skirt before hitching the material over his fingers and letting him explore between my thighs.

"Fuck," he groaned in my ear as he dragged his fingers through my wetness, finding me bare and aching for him. "I can't believe you aren't wearing panties with this thing."

"That's because I knew one of you would rip them off before long anyway," I reasoned, sucking in a breath as he continued to tease me, and JJ tore his shirt off on the stage.

I rolled my hips against Chase's hand, feeling the huge bulge of his cock driving against my ass through his jeans, releasing a soft whimper of need as he continued to toy with me.

I tried to link my fingers with his, but Chase chuckled, catching both of my wrists with his free hand and pinning them to my chest to stop me.

He stroked his fingers over me several more times, making me pant and moan in his arms before circling my clit with his thumb and driving two fingers deep inside me.

Maverick jerked his head around at the noise I released, his lips curling into a delicious smile as he took in what Chase was doing to me, and he pulled his phone from his pocket.

I didn't have it in me to object as he clearly started recording us, my mind swimming from the sensation of Chase fucking me with his hand. My eyes remained fixed on the sinful gyrations of Johnny James's hips as he danced on the stage, his movements getting more and more salacious with every beat of the bass, his eyes shifting to us repeatedly as he enjoyed the show we were putting on too.

"More," I panted, my inner walls squeezing Chase's fingers as I felt an orgasm rising up inside me, desperate to break free.

Chase walked us forward suddenly, pushing me over a huge speaker sitting to the side of the stage and shoving his pants down in the same movement.

I sucked in a breath as he pulled his fingers from me, but I was instantly relieved from the empty feeling by him driving his cock deep inside me in their place, burying himself to the hilt as his fingers bruised my hips.

JJ toyed with the waistband of his cargo pants on stage, running his hands down the lines of the V dipping beneath them, turning me on even more as Chase began to fuck me with the power of a demon freshly unleashed from hell.

My moans were swallowed by the heavy beat of the music as the song transitioned into another, but I couldn't even concentrate enough to figure out what it was, my entire mind consumed by the feeling of Chase's cock slamming into me with brutal force.

But just as my body began to squeeze and clench his shaft in the most beautiful of ways, he drew back, his cock jerking from me, leaving me bereft in its absence as he released his hold on me and just left me there, bent over the speaker which continued to pound with the beat of the music beneath me.

I twisted, tearing my eyes from Johnny James and looking over my shoulder to find Maverick's hand on Chase's shoulder, the feral look on Chase's face enough to let me know that he'd just been dragged off of me.

His cock stood proud and glistening with the evidence of where it had just been, and I let out a pathetic kind of sound which demonstrated just how much I needed him back.

"I think we can do better than that, beautiful," Rick said in rough growl, tossing a bottle of lube to Chase that he must have taken from the dressing room.

My eyes widened as Chase's frustration turned into a heady kind of lust and Rick strode towards me purposefully, his phone now propped on another speaker, aimed right at me.

Maverick unbuckled his belt as he came for me, moving to stand at my back and taking my hands into his grip before looping it around them both. I made no attempt to stop him, my eyes returning to JJ as he dropped to the floor, rolling his hips in the most sexual display I'd ever seen and causing a bunch of women in the audience to scream in appreciation.

But even as jealousy punched me in the chest, he turned his head my way, the fire in his eyes proving that all of his desire was only ever aimed one way and that was right at me.

Maverick yanked me upright, shoving my dress higher so that it bunched above my thighs before grabbing two solid handfuls of my ass and lifting me against him.

He turned us, sitting on the speaker with his back to the stage while making me straddle him, the belt cutting into my wrists behind my back as I tried to tug against the restraint before quickly giving up.

Maverick smiled darkly, positioning his cock at my entrance and holding my hips to keep me there as he leaned closer, his teeth sinking into my neck before moving to graze my ear.

"I'm going to feel how tight you get while Chase fucks this pretty ass of yours, beautiful," he growled. "I'm going to feel you take both of us at once while you get off on watching Johnny James out there on the stage. The sight of you taking the two of us is going to make him come right there in front of all those people he's putting on a show for, and you'll scream so loud that they'll hear you even over the music."

"Yes," I panted tipping my head back to keep my gaze locked on JJ while he ripped his pants off, my eyes locking on the straining fabric that let everyone in this entire club see just how hard he was. But it wasn't for them. That was all for me.

Maverick chuckled in that obnoxious way of his before yanking the top of my dress down hard enough to free my tits from it, biting my nipple right as he drove my hips down and impaled me on his thick shaft.

The moan that spilled from me was loud enough to draw a couple of the other dancers' eyes our way and Texas laughed loudly as he spotted us, not missing a single step of his routine before turning away again and carrying on with the show.

I sucked in a breath as Rick held me there, forcing me to feel every inch of him while his hands moved to grip my ass, parting my cheeks for Chase who I could feel closing in behind me.

The cold slick of the lube ran down my skin a moment later, fingers massaging it in, dipping inside me to test how ready I was and only making me whimper again.

"I need you," I said, turning my head to meet Chase's eye as he pressed closer behind me, the corner of his mouth curling up in satisfaction at the honesty of my words.

"You've got me," he swore, his hands landing on the speaker either side of my knees as he braced himself, his cock dragging between my cheeks and making everything inside me clench in anticipation.

I looked back to the stage as JJ ran his hands down his chest, teasing them over the huge bulge in his pants and making the audience scream again while my mouth watered with desire.

Chase drove himself into me with the same brutality as he had the first time, a cry spilling from me at the shock of his entrance, the impossibly full feeling of having both of them inside me at once making me curse as Maverick bit down on my nipple again.

My hands flexed where they were bound at the base of my spine, but I was helpless to release them, forced to relinquish all control as Rick took hold of my hips and began to set a punishing pace.

Chase matched him easily, the two of them finding a back and forth which meant I wasn't left empty for a single moment, my body utterly overwhelmed by the power of them and the total dominion they had taken over my flesh.

JJ faltered mid step, his heated gaze locking on all of us for a moment too long and causing him to stumble. He recovered quickly, following the pattern of the music as it changed again, another routine starting up while he wore nothing but the tight boxers that revealed almost all of him to the crowd.

I knew this was the final set of this routine, the one which would end with him ripping those off too, baring himself to everyone, me included and I was rampant with the anticipation of seeing every glorious inch of him in the flesh.

This felt so forbidden, knowing how many people lay just out of sight, and how all the dancers could see us if only they turned our way. There was only one of them I cared about though, the one with eyes the colour of honey and sin, who could move like a god of seduction and lust, and I swear I felt every roll of his hips joining Rick and Chase's as Johnny James cast looks in my direction.

I came with a wild cry, my body exploding around both Rick and Chase as my head tipped back in ecstasy, and I swear only the press of their bodies surrounding me stopped me from falling to the ground in a heap.

They didn't slow for a second, ignoring the commands of my body which tried to force them to fall with me while they continued to fuck me with a savagery that I needed more than air itself.

Rick barked a command that I was too far gone to understand, but they switched their pace and suddenly they were both driving into me in sync, an orgasm exploding through me again before the first had even subsided, my cry of bliss so loud I was certain it was carrying beyond the curtain and over the music, but I couldn't find it in me to care.

Their hands were gripping me as they continued to slam into me and within moments, Chase snarled something in my ear, the hot spill of his cum filling me just before Maverick fell apart too.

Even through my release, my eyes remained locked on Johnny James, and I caught the flash of fire in his expression as he watched me come for all of them, the need in him burning right through me and making me yearn for his touch too.

Rick and Chase's grip on me was bruising, the tightness of the belt around my wrists so punishing that I knew it would be leaving fresh bruises, but I welcomed them. I wanted them to mark me as theirs like this. I wanted the entire world to be able to see who owned me.

JJ was still watching us, and a look passed across his face that made my pulse fall to a frantic rhythm as he stopped mid routine and strode from the stage, leaving the other dancers to finish while he closed in on me with purpose.

Chase moved back first, and Rick grinned like an asshole as he turned his head to see what had caught his friend's eye.

"Didn't I say you were going to make him come in his pants, beautiful?" he taunted, but the look on JJ's eyes said he was in the mood for anything other than playing.

"Finish me, J," I begged him, my body feeling spent and hungry all at once. But I couldn't ignore that need in him any more than I could deny how much I wanted him to take what he was hungering for.

JJ tugged me off of Rick, kissing me hard as he pushed me down onto the speaker, my bound hands crushed beneath my spine as he shoved his boxers down and stared at the trail of mess the others had left between my thighs.

"Such a bad girl," he growled, taking my ankle in one hand and propping it over his shoulder while his other twisted through the cum they'd left behind.

I groaned with need as he scooped it back inside me, driving his fingers in deep as he pushed it in, his honey brown eyes seeming dark as pitch while he watched me squirm beneath him.

The moment he pulled his hand free, his cock was there in its place, one hand locking around my calf to keep my leg over his shoulder as he sank into me slowly, forcing my body to flex for him while my eyes remained locked with his.

I moaned at the feeling of him filling me, knowing that my wetness was more than just mine, loving how free and filthy we all were with one another, how turned on he clearly was by knowing that too.

JJ gave me a smile that was nothing like the usual grins we shared. It was all dark potency and wicked promises, and as his other hand locked around my throat, I knew he intended to keep every one of them.

The music pounded through the speaker beneath me as he pulled back so far that he almost withdrew from me completely, but as he plunged back in, I knew he wasn't going anywhere until he'd had his fill of my flesh too.

I was helpless beneath him, my body bent to his desires while my wrists remained bound, and I watched him fuck me hard and deep as my tits bounced, my pussy tightening around him almost instantly.

Johnny James knew how to fuck in all the best ways, his hips moving to a rhythm that matched what he'd been promising out there on that stage and then some, my body falling to ruin for him almost immediately.

But just as I started to come for him, his grip on my throat firmed, my air cutting off and that feral look in his eyes brightening as he pumped his hips harder, taking and taking from my flesh while I remained locked at his mercy.

I was trapped there by the power of his body and the pleasure of mine, blackness sparking around the corners of my vision as an explosion of impossible pleasure came crashing through me like a tsunami.

My spine arched, pussy clenched, and a scream of unbridled bliss escaped my lips as I came hard and fast, forcing him to follow me into oblivion with a few more solid thrusts of his hips into mine.

JJ finished with a masculine groan that made my toes curl, his body falling over mine and his mouth stealing kisses from my breathless lips as he finally released his hold on my throat.

My face tingled with pins and needles from the lack of oxygen, my brain firing off like a firework as every piece of my soul seemed to tremble in the wake of so much pleasure. I was left lying there beneath him feeling like every piece of energy inside me had just been stripped away.

Before I was ready to escape the moment, JJ drew me upright again. He seemed to realise that my legs had absolutely no chance of supporting me as he heaved me into his arms and carried me back towards the dressing room without a word.

Rick and Chase closed in around us, making me feel like a princess surrounded by devoted guards, and I closed my eyes as I bathed in the afterglow of being destroyed by three of my men.

I had taken on a hell of a lot by claiming them for my own, but I was definitely thriving at the challenge posed by keeping them all satisfied.

"You walked out on the end of your set," I muttered, and JJ smirked devilishly.

"I had something far more urgent to see to. How am I supposed to resist you, pretty girl? When I've missed you for ten years and wanted you for the entirety of my existence?"

He set me on my feet, and I opened my eyes, finding us in the showers backstage, my heart still thundering with the sweetness of his words.

"I'll grab you something else to wear, seeing as this asshole tore your dress," JJ said, as he released my wrists from the grasp of the belt, bobbing his chin at my exposed tits, making me take note of the tattered material that had once been hiding the goods.

"Okay," I agreed, moving to peel my dress off, but Chase was there already, unzipping it and helping me out of it before dropping to one knee so that he could pull my stilettos from my feet to.

I smiled at him as he set the water running, my body still able to feel the stretch of where he'd been inside me, the reminder making me bite my lip.

"Foxy boy will enjoy that one," Rick said, drawing my attention to him as he sent what I was guessing had to be his latest sex tape of the four of us to Fox.

"He's made it clear he doesn't want any part of this side of things," I said with a frown, flinching a little in surprise as hot water hit my stomach and I found Chase holding the shower head as he began to wash me clean. He had an attentive look about him, like he was wrapped up in some duty to me and I brushed my fingers through his curls, adoring him for that.

"Nah," Maverick said dismissively. "I assure you he's just a sad little snow cone wishing for some flavour other than vanilla to fill him up. Problem is, he's a stubborn snow cone too, which means he can't quite bring himself to invite some new flavours to come fill him up. Instead, he watches these little home movies we keep making and jerks off to them angrily, hating himself for how much he loves watching you take all of us and refusing to admit to anyone what it is that he really wants. Don't you worry though, beautiful, he'll crack eventually."

I probably should have been arguing further in defence of Fox and what he wanted, but the idea of Maverick being right about that sent a thrill through me that I couldn't deny.

The only thing that would have made what the four of us just did better would be adding Fox to the mix and making it all five of us. So as unlikely as that little fantasy of mine seemed to be, I was going to allow Rick to encourage

146

it unless it seemed to be genuinely upsetting Fox.

But he had made his choice. He wanted to be all in with me and he knew that I was all in with the others too. He claimed to have accepted that and even be glad of it, so I guessed this was just a test of how much truth there really was to that oath.

Chase finished cleaning me up just as JJ returned with a towel and a black dress that I guessed belonged to one of the other girls.

I took both gratefully, quickly drying and changing while working to get my mind firing on all cylinders again following on from that earth shattering sex.

I slipped my shoes back on while my boys waited for me, and JJ pressed a hungry kiss to my lips, murmuring apologies about needing to get back to the stage.

I laughed, wondering if anyone hadn't heard the lust fuelled cries of pleasure from just beyond the edge of the stage, and I had to imagine that every woman in the crowd would be feeling all kinds of jealous of whoever had drawn him away.

The sound of the other dancers heading backstage broke our moment and JJ ushered me towards the bar before I would have to endure the taunting I could already hear booming from Texas as he closed in on us.

"Where is that dirty dog hiding?" he called loudly, but I was already slipping away into the bar with Rick and Chase, so at least I didn't have to listen to any more of his thoughts on what we'd all just done in clear view of him and the rest of the dancers.

Chase tugged me along through the crowd and I eyed the bar hopefully, needing a stiff drink to help me recover from that damn near poetic mind melt I'd just experienced.

Unfortunately for me, before I got there, Fox appeared through the crowd looking hot in the face, his furious expression locked on Maverick.

"Asshole," he snapped as he shoved between the bodies.

147

Maverick called something in reply, but it was lost to the music, though the look on his face made it clear that he was only exacerbating the situation.

Chase forced his way between them, and I rolled my eyes at the macho nonsense I'd been dealing with since I was a kid, turning away from them in search of that drink.

I pushed my way through the crowd towards the bar, waving to Di as I spotted her serving and she beckoned me towards an empty bar stool in front of her.

I hopped up, my smile widening as she slid one of those cherry cocktail things I'd grown to like so much across the bar, as if she'd seen me coming from a mile off. I instantly drained the glass before tapping the rim to request another.

"Good thing JJ says you drink for free, huh?" she teased as she made me another and I nodded.

"I think he knows I'd be dipping my fingers into the pockets of every fucker in here to pay for them if he didn't."

A man sitting on the stool beside mine cleared his throat pointedly, shifting his arm aside to reveal the police badge hooked onto his belt.

I cocked a brow at him, and he inclined his head. "Off duty. Still, best not to regale me with tales of your illegal activities."

I laughed easily. "Do I look like I'm seriously capable of pickpocketing anybody?" I scoffed as if it had all been a joke anyway, my tongue always fast with a lie when it needed to be.

His eyes ran over me slowly, not in a creepy way, more assessing while I took in his appearance too. He was a little older than me, with slightly curling brown hair that fell to the nape of his neck, his clothes neither cheap nor expensive, the kind of guy who had probably taken the job as a cop for the pension and career perks instead of any real desire to better the world if his slightly scruffy appearance was anything to go by. He nodded as he turned back to his drink.

148

"I'd say you look capable of all kinds of things." He spoke into his glass but didn't say anything further, and as the lights dipped and the music started up for the next performance, I turned away from him, wanting to watch Johnny James get dirty all over that stage again.

Di headed away to serve some other girls further down the bar and I was left to my ogling in relative peace.

Wellerman by Nathan Evans filled the air, the guys heading onto the stage dressed as sailors now, the pristine white clothes only marred by the filthy looks on their faces.

I whooped loudly, reaching behind me blindly as I grabbed my drink, lifting it to my lips and drinking the entire glass once more. My limbs were still shaking a little thanks to all the orgasms, so I was claiming medical requirement for my shots.

JJ moved to the front of the stage as the chorus hit, rolling his hips as he thumbed the buttons open down the centre of his chest, making my heart flutter as the perfection of his body was revealed once more. I really was one lucky bitch to have claimed not one but four stunning specimens such as him. And their personalities weren't even all that terrible either.

I cheered loudly, getting to my feet with a whoop of excitement which somehow caused the world to tilt and my feet to fall over themselves.

A strong hand caught my arm before I could faceplant the floor and I twisted to see the cop helping me up while my brain swam with dizziness again, the drinks hitting me harder than normal and making me wonder if Di had thrown a few extra shots into the mix.

"Thanks," I muttered, half falling back onto my stool as he steadied me with a concerned expression.

"Are you alright?" he asked but I just waved him away, blinking to try and clear the blurriness that was clouding my vision.

"I just need to find my boys," I muttered, turning to look for them through the crowd, my eyes only finding JJ where he was dancing on the stage.

But with the lights shining brightly in his eyes, I doubted he could see much of me all the way back here by the bar.

The dancers all swarmed together at the centre of the stage, and I looked around again, hunting for one of the others as my head swooped.

"Shit," I bit out, turning to look for Di instead, but just as I did the music and lights cut off abruptly, shrieks of fright breaking out throughout the club as we were plunged into darkness.

Holy fuck.

I pitched forward, pushing my fingers to the back of my throat and heaving violently, realising what was happening even though I knew it was already too late to stop it.

The drinks I'd consumed burned all the way up my throat as I vomited them out, swiping the back of my hand across my mouth as I shoved to my feet and tried to stumble in the direction I'd last seen Chase, Rick and Fox.

A hand latched onto my arm, the darkness making it impossible for me to tell who held me, but my fight or flight instincts were going wild even as my head spun so violently that I knew I was in danger of passing out.

"Getoffame," I slurred, trying to yank my arm away again, but the man's grip only tightened as he started tugging me through the press of panicking bodies.

"Come on," the cop barked as he yanked on me harder. "I'll get you somewhere safe."

The word tasted like a lie even as he forced it past his tongue, both of us knowing he was doing no such thing.

"They'll kill you," I warned him as he hauled me towards the side of the building, my feet tripping over themselves in my stupid heels as I tried to make my legs work the way they needed to.

This was bad. So, so bad. Why had I strayed away from my boys? Why the hell had I been so stupid?

The cop – or more likely fake cop – practically dragged me through a side door where the fresh air of the night washed over us and I stumbled across the concrete.

I shook my head to try and clear it, letting him pull me along while taking in where I was. This was the opposite side of the club to the main parking lot, nothing here but the dumpsters that lined the alley and the single car which had been parked at the far end of it. A cop car he was hauling me straight towards. Maybe he wasn't a fake cop after all.

"Why?" I hissed, stumbling along with him while letting him think I was growing weaker, when in fact I was summoning all my strength so I could make a single attempt at escape and hope to fuck it paid off.

"I got debts," he grunted. "And I know what you are. The life of one lowlife whore ain't nothing compared to the price that diamond will fetch me."

"Diamond?" I asked, my mind whirling as the man coughed out a laugh.

"Yeah. Fat as a grape and worth well more than you, no offence. But I'll take the payment all the same."

I knew there were answers in his words, but I didn't have the brain power available to me to be able to focus on them right now. I needed to get away before he got me in that car.

I could scream, but with the panic from the blackout still causing shrieks and cries within the club behind me, I knew that was unlikely to do anything other than piss him off. I could wait for my boys, hope they found me before he managed to get me in there, but I just wasn't wired that way.

I sucked in a deep breath, scrunching my eyes shut as I tried to focus, banishing the dizziness for a single second. I dropped like a sack of shit, crumpling to the floor at his feet and feeling my knees tear open on the sidewalk as I hit it with a thump.

"Ah, shit," the cop cursed, dropping my arm and moving to lift me off the ground, but I'd already torn the stiletto from my foot and with a furious scream, I swung it at him with all my strength.

The cop lurched back but not fast enough and with a sickening crack, the sharp heel of my shoe imbedded itself in his temple.

Blood spilled and he roared in agony, falling back onto his ass in front of me while I tried to scramble to my feet, tripping as the effect of whatever he'd dosed me with sent me off balance again and I cursed myself as I tried to break into a run.

His weight collided with me before I could get more than a few steps, darkness filling my head as I fell beneath him. I smacked into the ground so hard that I almost blacked out entirely.

"You little bitch!" the cop roared, shoving me over and back handing me, my shoe still lodged in his temple, the rainbow rhinestones swimming in and out of focus as I looked at it.

He smacked me again as a laugh bubbled from my lips, some mixture of terror and hysteria rising in me as I focused on that shoe.

"You really think you can get away from me?" he snarled and when he hit me that time I felt my lip split, blood coating my teeth as I trembled from the shock of my fall and whatever the drugs in my system were causing.

I laughed again, my fingers opening and closing as I focused on regaining control of myself before managing to slam my knee up into his crotch with a satisfyingly loud smack.

The cop bellowed as he lurched away from me, but I followed, my gaze fixed on that shoe as I lunged for it, managing to regain my feet through some miracle and grabbing hold of it with a triumphant yell.

I ripped the thing free of his skull, throwing my weight back as I yanked it out and blood sprayed me instantly, coating me from head to toe.

The cop's eyes went wide, his pupils dilating as the blood continued to piss down the side of his face for several seconds. I just stood there panting with the effort of staying upright, the shoe held tight in my hand like it was all that kept me on my feet as I watched death come for him on swift and violent wings.

He stared at me in disbelief for a lingering second, like he couldn't really believe the fate that had befallen him because of me. Then he fell back to the floor with a sickening crash and the door to the club burst open at the far end of the alley.

I raised my eyes from the corpse, finding all four of my boys racing towards me like a vision from a dream. They'd come to save me. It just turned out I'd saved myself first.

My lips pulled up into a smile which had to look all kinds of grim with the amount of blood that covered my face, but then darkness rushed in on me all at once and this time, I gave in to oblivion.

CHAPTER ELEVEN

"Rogue!" I bellowed, outsprinting the others as I crashed to my knees in front of her, my fingers going to her pulse on instinct. Alive. And no obvious injuries stood out across her body as I examined her. "She's alive," I said for the others, though terror still rocketed through my heart as she failed to respond.

Fox's shoulder rammed into mine as he hit the ground at my side, cupping her cheek in his palm while her head lolled against my knees.

"Wake up, hummingbird," he commanded in his most ferocious Harlequin Prince voice, but Rogue defied him even now, staying still and lifeless in our arms, though she was definitely still breathing.

Panic was taking hold of me, setting adrenaline coursing through my veins as I looked from her to the dead cop who Maverick and Chase were standing over, my ears roaring with noise that wasn't there. Some of his blood had gotten onto the hem of my white sailor pants and I frowned at it briefly as I took in what she'd done. My pretty girl was a damn fighter that was for sure.

"What do we do?" I barked at Fox, fisting my hand in his shirt and yanking him closer. "Tell us what to do."

He nodded, his throat rising and falling as his eyes met Maverick's and the two of them took control of the situation.

"Should we get her to a hospital?" Chase asked urgently.

"No," Rogue croaked, her eyes fluttering open. "Date rape," she croaked before passing out again and we all shared a look of abject fury over that. This motherfucker had drugged her, had been planning to do God knew what to her.

"Fuck," I spat, anger exploding through my chest again while the others cursed furiously.

Fox slammed a kick into the motherfucker's side, and I heard a satisfactory crack I wished he'd been alive to feel, just so we could end him all over again. But of course, my beautiful, fierce girl had finished him herself.

"She'll recover. He won't though. Chase, fetch a blanket from the club," Maverick commanded, eyeing the cop with a grim rage in his eyes. "Big enough for the cop."

Chase nodded, racing off without a moment's hesitation while I clutched Rogue tighter against me, feeling her pounding pulse beneath my fingertips to assure me she was okay.

"I'll get her in the car," Fox said, lifting Rogue into his arms and picking up the high heel she'd clearly used to kill the man who was currently laying there in puddle of his own blood.

"No," Maverick cut in, shoving his hand in the cop's pocket and taking out a bunch of keys. "We take the cop car, ditch it somewhere."

Fox looked ready to argue out of sheer stubbornness, but then he saw reason and nodded, running over to the cop car with Rogue in his arms while Rick unlocked it.

I got to my feet just as Chase returned, laying out a blanket beside the dead cop while opening up a bottle of bleach he must have taken from the backstage restroom in the club. He poured it all over the ground and the strong scent of it burned my eyes.

I left him to that, helping Rick roll the body onto the blanket, focusing on what had to be done and pushing away the anxiety in my chest. I was used to this kind of work now, and I couldn't let my fear over Rogue let me make mistakes that could cost us in the end.

"What if he called for backup?" Chase hissed.

"Then we need to be fucking gone before they show up," Maverick said firmly, and we nodded.

I knew the drill. Roll the dead guy up tight, check for evidence, then get the fuck out.

I left Chase and Rick to finish tying the blanket in place, taking out my phone and sweeping the ground using the flashlight on it. A little unmarked bottle caught my eye and I swiped it up, my muscles bunching as I realised this must be the date rape he'd dosed our girl with.

I shared a look with my boys, and I knew they were thinking the same as I was, praying they'd gotten a little more time with the asshole in this world so they could make him suffer for daring to drug Rogue.

While they lifted him into their arms, I ran to the cop car, pocketing my phone and ducking my head into the back of the vehicle.

Fox was working to wake Rogue up while he held her against his chest and her legs lay draped over the seats. She was now wearing his shirt instead of her dress, and I could see a grocery bag tied up by his feet where he must have put it. I could see the shape of her shoes pressing against the inside of it too, and knew that bag was gonna have to be destroyed before the night was done.

Fox's dark green gaze snapped up to meet mine, full of the sort of explosive fury that could have levelled an entire town. "She had some vomit on her dress," he said. "Maybe she figured out he drugged her and tried to puke it up."

"That's good," I said heavily, and Fox shifted her further over his lap, jerking his head in an order for me to get in just as the car bobbed with the weight of a corpse landing in the trunk. He took a moment to make a call to one of the Harlequins, ordering in a clean-up crew to fix the mess out here.

As he killed the call, the trunk snapped shut and Maverick got in the driver's side while Chase moved to the passenger side.

"Chase, take our car back to Harlequin House." Fox tossed him the keys and Chase's eyes fell on Rogue like he couldn't bear to leave her. "You can come meet us after, just make it look like we left this place together and went home. Cover our tracks."

"Alright," Chase agreed, clutching the keys tighter in his fist and retreating from the car before jogging away towards the parking lot.

I dropped into the back seat and tugged the door closed while Maverick started the engine and drove us out of the lot, pulling on a cop's jacket he must have found somewhere as he did so.

"Come on, pretty girl," I said urgently, stroking her hair. "Come back to us."

"We should head to the cliffs, set the car alight somewhere up there once we've dealt with the body," Maverick suggested.

"We can't do that," Fox said, his brow lined with tension. "He's a fucking cop. He's gonna have people looking for him. There'll be a proper investigation. This shit isn't gonna go unnoticed for long."

"Jesus fucking Christ, has Luther got anyone who can cover this shit up?" Maverick asked.

"He's got a few cops in his pocket, but no one that would sort this shit for us," Fox growled.

"Ain't your daddy a cop, JJ?" Rick asked suddenly.

"So?" I snapped. "He's clean, he's not gonna fucking help us."

"Didn't he say he'd do anything for his boy? Didn't he say to call you if you ever need anything?" Rick pushed.

"Shut up," I growled. "We're not going to *Gwan* of all fucking people."

"He's been keeping your secrets at the club for years," Fox said. "He's been protecting you. He wouldn't let anything happen to you, that's clear as fucking day."

"No," I hissed. "Not. Him."

"Yes, JJ," Rick demanded. "Call him."

"No," I barked. "I don't even have his number; I threw it away."

"Then call your mom, she'll have it," Fox ordered.

"No!" I roared, but Fox leaned over, snatching my hair in his fist and forcing me to look down at Rogue.

"You see her? She's going to fucking prison if we don't cover this up, Johnny James," he growled, his voice raw and gravelly from his throat injury. "Do you hear me? We've gotta be as clean as we can with this, and the best way to do that is to have someone in law enforcement covering our tracks. Someone who paid a whore for sex while he was working undercover around twenty-eight years ago and got her pregnant as a result. Someone who might just be loyal to us for good reasons, or might be loyal because we hold the key to his downfall in your DNA. Either way we need him – *she* needs him, and you're making that fucking call."

I opened and closed my mouth, my argument dying as I stared at Rogue, a little murmur leaving her in her sleep. I brushed my fingers through her rainbow hair and sighed, knowing this was a risk, but maybe they were right. Maybe he would cover for me, and I'd do anything to ensure Rogue wasn't caught for this.

My jaw locked as I nodded stiffly, taking out my phone and making the call to my mom.

"Hey baby," she answered a little breathlessly. "Everything okay?"

"No, Momma. I need his number," I said tightly.

"Whose number?" she asked.

I hesitated on saying his real name. His stupid fucking name.

"Gwan's," I bit out and she paused, the sound of glasses clinking reaching me down the line.

"Gwan's?" her voice came out a little high pitched.

159

"Yeah, the motherfucker who claims to be my sperm donor. I need to speak to him. I wanna…" My lip curled as I spoke the next words which were a complete lie. "Get to know him better."

"You do?" she gasped.

"Yeah," I said, hearing Rick sniggering at me despite our current circumstances. "So? Can I have it?"

"Um, yes baby, but the thing is…well, the thing is-" she cleared her throat and I frowned, sensing something was off here.

"What?" I pushed.

"Well, um, Gwan is here at the house. With me."

A cold stone fell into the pit of my stomach and my hand tightened around my phone in an unyielding grip.

"What?" I questioned in a deadly tone. "Tell me that's a joke. Tell me you aren't seeing Gwan. Tell me my mother isn't currently with a man who used to run his moustache all over her back during the fucking summer I was consummated."

"I think he should regrow the moustache, I quite liked it," she said, and those words cut me deeper than any other possibly could. "Please don't overreact, baby. Why don't you come to the house? You want to get to know him, so do it here. We'd love to see you."

"I really would, JJ," Gwan's Gwanish voice came down the line, and I realised I must be on fucking speaker phone.

The betrayal made me shudder and I killed the call before I could start cursing his stupid fucking name with every cuss word I knew. I had to now pretend I wanted to get to know him, play the part of a fucking fatherless boy who gave a damn where his DNA had come from.

I started punching the metal mesh that divided the front of the car from the back, shaking the whole thing as I pictured Gwan and tried to rip it to pieces.

"JJ for the love of fuck, calm down." Fox pressed a hand to my chest, forcing me back into my seat.

I almost lunged for him then, but Rogue stirred between us, blinking up at me groggily and my chest caved in.

"Johnny James?" she breathed, wetting her lips. "What's going on?"

The rage went out of me, and I pushed my fingers into her hair, relief gilding my heart at seeing her awake.

"We got you, baby," Fox said, and she turned her head, smiling dreamily at him.

"Is the dead guy still dead?" she murmured, the drugs she'd been slipped clearly still fucking with her head.

"You made an ugly mess of him, beautiful," Maverick said, staring at her in the rear-view mirror. "You did a perfect fucking job of caving in his skull. He's deader than dead."

She released a breath, sagging against me and I pulled her closer, her head nestling against my chest.

"Fucker drugged me," she muttered. "I made myself puke. Wasn't gonna let him take me from you."

Pride made my chest swell and I gripped her hand in mine, squeezing tightly while Fox pressed a kiss to her head.

"That's our girl," he growled. "You always were the savage among us."

"Never needed a white knight," she agreed on a breath of laughter. "Though having you clean up my messes is always handy."

Her gaze flickered with a dark memory and I knew she was thinking of Axel, that motherfucker who had tried to rape her all those years ago and sent all of our lives into a tailspin. We'd needed help then too, but none of us had wanted to risk asking Luther Harlequin for it. None of us had trusted him, but I realised now that we should have. We should have trusted in the love a father held for his children and the lengths he would go to to protect them. *Goddammit, now I have to trust in Gwan.*

"We're gonna handle this," I promised. "Just rest."

"I thought I got most of it up, but I feel all…splooshy," she mumbled, breathing me in. "You smell like sex and glitter."

I exhaled a note of amusement, taken off guard as I glanced down at my fucking sailor outfit and pressed a kiss to her forehead. I still had the fucking hat on too, though I made no move to take it off while she was looking at me the way she was. "That a good thing?"

"The best," she whispered, then fell asleep again and I brushed my fingers up and down her spine soothingly as Maverick took turns that were leading us closer and closer to my mom's house.

"Better park up in one of the alleys nearby and walk there," Fox said darkly as we closed in on our destination.

We'd hardly passed anyone on the roads, and Maverick knew all the streets to avoid that had security cameras, so I wasn't too concerned about being caught out that way. It was the dead cop's friends I was most concerned about. And if anyone had caught sight of him and Rogue outside Afterlife…

I looked to Fox, finding his face shrouded in darkness, the occasional streetlamp casting a dull orange glow across his features and lighting up the expression I'd witnessed from him so many times whenever we were on a job. This was where he shone, calming the doubt in everyone around him as he took control of the situation, and I relaxed back into my seat.

I was with Fox and Maverick Harlequin. They knew what to do, because they always knew what to do. It was like that time we'd gone camping in the forest out beyond Sterling and Chase had jumped into the river right where a furious waterfall met the water, and he hadn't come up again. While I'd been shouting his name and not knowing what to do, Fox and Maverick had already dived in, pulling him out of the force of water pressing him down beneath the falls, working together as a unit of muscle and determination to save him.

I always acted better under direction, and hell, I'd be the first to jump in that water if the order was barked in my ear, but in the initial moment, I often hesitated in what action to take, worrying too much over making the wrong choice and not making the right one quickly enough.

I'd learned a long time ago that following the commands of those I trusted when it was needed suited me far better than taking the lead myself. So that was what I was going to do. Because if anyone knew the right choices to make in a desperate situation like this, it was Fox and Rick.

Maverick pulled into an alley and killed the engine, darkness falling thickly over us like a sheet.

I helped Rogue sit upright and she came to again, looking at me through the gloom before turning to Fox and squeezing his arm.

"Are you angry with me, badger?" she asked in a whisper.

"No, baby." He stroked the side of her face, sitting forward to place a kiss against the corner of her lips. "You killed him good."

"Fucking Shawn sent him," she growled, seeming to wake up a little more.

"That cunt," Maverick spat, twisting in his seat to look through the mesh at us. "What did he tell you?"

"That Shawn's offering one of the diamonds for me," Rogue said venomously with a slight tremor to her hands, and I took hold of one of them, threading my fingers through hers.

Hatred spilled through my chest as I felt the presence of that motherfucker hovering over us once more. It seemed like we could never escape him, that prick determined to ruin our lives even after his gang had been all but destroyed by the cartel and he'd been chased out of town with his tail between his legs.

"Well, you know what, beautiful?" Maverick hissed as he took a vicious looking flick-knife from his pocket, whipping it open. "I'm glad he hasn't run. And I'm glad he's still in the game, because though I'd chase him to the ends of the earth to pay him his dues, I'd much rather meet him on the battlefield and cut him down man to man."

"You're happy he's sending dirty cops after Rogue?" Fox snarled.

"No, Foxy boy, but I'm sure happy she's capable of smashing in the skull of anyone who attacks her," Maverick said, looking to Rogue with a twisted smile and she bit down on her lip.

"Come on," I urged, wanting to diffuse the tension in the car.

I pulled Rogue out of the door after me, keeping my hand tight on hers as she stood barefoot before me.

"Are you okay, pretty girl?" I murmured, cupping her chin in my hand, and checking her over for wounds. Her skin had seen far too much damage for my liking lately, and I couldn't bear to find more injuries on her now.

"I'm okay, J," she promised as I spotted the raw grazes on her knees, but my shoulders sagged a little as I found strength burning in her eyes. There was blood speckling her cheeks, and as Rick moved to my side and pulled off the cop jacket he'd found in the car, I took it from him and used it to wipe it away.

They all waited patiently while I cleaned her off, though the split in her lip and slight swelling to the side of her face wasn't so easily wiped away. A mixture of fury and pain twisted through me as I realised that motherfucker had hit her at least once.

"I killed him," she reminded me, like she could tell what I was thinking and I nodded, finding relief in that statement as I accepted it.

"Yeah, you did," I said proudly.

"Let's move," Fox encouraged, and we fell into step behind him and Maverick as they led the way forward.

I tossed my arm over Rogue's shoulders, keeping her close as we hurried along, sticking to the shadows before taking a little set of stone steps that ran between a couple of houses down onto my mom's street.

When we were standing on her porch, I took the lead, moving to the front of our group, carving my fingers through my hair and slapping on a casual expression before knocking.

"Johnny James," Momma gushed as she opened the door in a tiny blue dress that was tight and showed off way too much tit.

She hurried forward to hug me, tottering on her stilettos and I indulged her, though I couldn't fight off the rigidity in my muscles at knowing Gwan was here, and who fucking knew what he'd been up to, running his clean-as-a-whistle cop hands all over her.

"I'm so happy you've decided to get to know him, baby. You have no idea how much I wanted to tell you we've been seeing each other again," she said, stepping back and looking up at my scowling face.

"Just because I want to get to know him, doesn't mean I want him to get to know you again," I hissed. "I told you to stay away from him."

She opened and closed her mouth, looking confused and Maverick's fingers prodded me hard in the back.

I knew it was him because he always jabbed right under the ribs in a way that made my whole body jerk. I got the message though, huffing out a breath and trying to calm myself down.

"Can I just talk to him?" I asked and Mom nodded, letting me into the house while pausing to greet the others.

"Where are your shoes?" Mom asked Rogue in concern.

"One of my heels broke," she sighed.

"Can you lend her some sneakers, Ms Brooks?" Fox asked like the polite little sausage he always was with her.

"Of course," she said as I stalked into the house, my eyes whipping up the stairs and narrowing as I hunted for shadows shifting up there. If Gwan was here, he'd better not be up there, Gwanning around in my mother's bedsheets.

"Wait, oh my God," my mom gasped, and I twisted around, finding her looking up at Maverick as she suddenly realised who he was. "Rick!" She lunged at him, practically hanging from his neck as she hugged and patted his head like she used to when we were kids. "Johnny James, do not storm into my house without explaining this," she demanded and I sighed, turning to them.

"It's obvious, isn't it? Rick is back. He's one of us again." I knew I sounded like a huffy little child, but something about being around my mom always brought that out in me. Maybe if she stopped bringing strange men into

165

this house, I'd have less to be huffing about. But as she currently had a man here who not only claimed to be the reason I walked on this earth, but who was boringly ordinary to the point of offensive, I was well within my right to be pissed off. And now, I was going to have to pretend I gave a fuck about getting to know him.

What was there to know? That if he was a vegetable, he'd be an average-sized, average shaped potato? Yeah, no thanks. I was a butternut squash, or a dragon fruit. Something that if you fed it to your grandma, she'd say 'Ooh, that's unusual.' Not something that was a staple with every meal, who people only noticed if it was deep fried, curly or saturated in salt and ketchup. I didn't need seasoning. I brought the pizazz to every meal. The kind of delight you indulged in occasionally, and only if you could afford it. I could not be sired by a root vegetable.

I heard someone shuffling about in the lounge and marched that way, leaving my mom to get reacquainted with Rick who was playing Mr Funny and winning her over just like always. No doubt she'd already let herself forget the fact that he'd been in prison for years and had been up to fuck knew what since his release. Luckily, I'd never had the heart to tell her about it when we'd been at war with him, so I guessed to her this was just a fun reunion with a heavily inked felon. She always did have a blind spot for my friends.

I stepped into the lounge and was horrified by what I found.

Gwan stood there, hovering over a pot of coffee set out on a tray, placing down several mugs beside it and pouring a packet of cookies onto a plate. And not just any cookies, oh no. Gwan had to go the extra mile to offend me, because those were Oreos. My favourite cookies.

This was a trap, a damn dirty trap to try and win me over, and the worst part about that was that I was going to have to go along with it. Because I needed him, and as sick to my stomach as that made me, I would do anything to help Rogue, so I had to suck this up.

"Oh, hello." He straightened suddenly as he noticed my arrival. "Your mother said-"

"Look, let's get some things straight here," I growled, marching toward him and pointing at his face, and his dark, silky hair that had the same sheen as mine and those eyes, motherfucker had my eyes too. Dammit, it was getting harder and harder to deny the truth. I could see it plain as fucking day. How had I missed it before? He had a look of me about him for sure, oh fuck, it was the other way around. I had a look of *him*, because he was my DNA donator, my dear old daddy, my clean nosed pappa. "I might wanna get to know you, but I'll be drawing the line with how far I mean that. I might ask one question and be done, do you hear me? And you don't get to say I'm being unreasonable, you don't get to backchat me one bit, even if we're in the middle of the ocean on a little rowing boat under the sun, if I say I'm out, I'm gonna dive off that boat, swim back to shore and leave you there for the seagulls, you got it?"

"I got it," he said, his eyes brightening as he stepped past the coffee table towards me. "I'm just so glad you're giving me this chance."

"Well, it ain't for free," I warned, and his brow pinched, his aura shifting to something more serious as he moved into my personal space. He was as tall as me, broad too. But I had the muscle where he'd gone soft, and I knew I could hurl him out the window if the desire took me.

"Are you in trouble, Johnny James?" he asked, reaching out to rest his hand on my upper arm.

I let my gaze fall down to where he was touching me, glaring at his hand until he retracted it. Was he being...fatherly? This goodie two shoes cop, with his lack of criminal record and well-filed taxes. Ergh. It made me sick.

"Yeah, I'm in trouble," I lowered my voice, hating everything about this, laying my trust in him of all people. But he looked at me with his big, puppy-dog eyes and I saw Tom Collins standing there too, the man who'd propped up my club on more than one occasion, the man who'd turned a blind eye to countless crimes right under his nose, all because I was connected to them. Would this be too far for him? Maybe. I guessed I was about to find out.

"What's happened?" he asked, his voice deepening, a sort of professionalism falling over him that commanded respect. It took me by surprise as I frowned at him, assessing how he might react to this as I shot a look over my shoulder, hearing the others still chatting in the hall, keeping my mom distracted.

"Not in front of Mom," I said. "We're gonna tell her we're taking a walk to hash shit out. Just you and me, okay?"

"Okay," he said, nodding firmly and I led him out into the hall.

"We're gonna take a walk around the block," I announced, and Mom turned to us, grinning big.

I chewed the inside of my cheek as she ran to me, hugging me tight. "Thank you, Johnny James."

"And then we'll be setting some ground rules about when he's allowed to see you, because I swear to God, Mom, if he's come here to try and flirt you up to your bedroom, I'll kill him. Straight up. Right here."

"JJ," she gasped at my ferocious tone, looking flustered, her cheeks pinking and making my eyes narrow in suspicion. She hadn't let him into her bed, had she? *Had she??*

"He's just joking, aren't you J?" Fox said, partly through his teeth as he hugged Rogue against his hip.

I said nothing but as my gaze fell on Rogue and I remembered what that cop had done to her, I released a laugh that was super false and clapped Gwan on the shoulder hard enough to send him stumbling into the wall.

Gwan looked at Rogue too, a stillness falling over him as his gaze roamed from her bare feet to her borrowed shirt, the split lip and the swelling to the side of her face in a cop-like way that said he was taking note, tallying things up, copping away. Mom was too distracted by Maverick's appearance to have fully taken in any of that, and I suspected she'd had a glass of wine or three too, but not Gwan. No, Gwan was all eyes and ears and drinking in the details.

"Yeah, just a little joke. Come on, Gwan." I grabbed his arm and hauled him past my friends, not wanting him to study Rogue for a moment longer.

I snatched the car keys from Maverick as I moved to the front door, tossing it wide and dragging Gwan down onto the sidewalk. *Fuck, I can't believe I actually have to call him Gwan.*

I headed off at a march as Mom called goodbye to us, and I let Gwan run to catch me as I set a fierce pace.

"Please, tell me what's wrong," he asked, and I glanced over as he made it to my side. He looked concerned, a deep crease between his eyes that was all because of me.

"You won't like it," I said, lowering my tone as I turned us down an alley and upped my pace again.

"Whatever it is, I won't judge you for it. I can help," he swore, hurrying to keep up as he started to get a bit breathless.

I rounded on him in the alley as the shadows hugged us, forcing him to stop as he bumped into my chest and backed up a step to create some space again.

"You sure you're not gonna snitch on me to your cop friends? Because this is bad, Gwan. Next level shit, bad. Like, I'm going to prison for the rest of my life if I get caught for it bad."

Gwan's eyes widened, and fear danced across his expression, but not like he was afraid of me, like he was afraid *for* me. "Whatever it is, I can help you. I swear it."

I frowned, not knowing how to respond to that, unsure if it was a lie or if Gwan really did care about me enough to cover my tracks. But I hadn't told him what I'd done yet, and outside of my family, most people I knew would sell you out quick for a tidy little bribe. Why would this guy stick his neck out for me when it could cost him everything if he was discovered?

"I killed a cop," I said, letting off the bomb right there in his face. Obviously I wasn't going to let Rogue take any blame for this, and I knew the price of those words if this came out. I'd be the one taking the fall for it. But for my pretty girl, any fall was worth the leap.

"What?" he gasped.

"He was dirty," I went on. "He attacked Rogue, drugged her too, and tried to kidnap her. So I did what any man would do for the woman he loves and cracked his skull open. He took a bribe from our enemy, a man offering a diamond in exchange for Rogue. I guess the motherfucker figured she was worth the trouble."

Gwan stared at me in shock, his mind clearly spinning with all the pieces I'd offered him, the evidence he'd seen on my girl backing up my story even if I'd changed that one detail to incriminate myself. He jerked toward me suddenly, grabbing my arm.

"JJ, what are you wrapped up in? Who's your enemy? Maybe I can help-"

"The only way you can help is if you can get rid of that cop's body in the trunk of his own car, the car itself, and all the evidence sitting inside it." I took the keys to the vehicle from my pocket, dangling them in front of his eyes. "We could dispose of it all, but this man is gonna have other cops chasing his tail soon, maybe they're already looking for him. If we try to cover it up, it's not gonna be enough. They won't stop looking for him. So we need someone who can cover his tracks from the inside as well as the outside."

Gwan didn't react for a long moment, and I half expected him to produce handcuffs from somewhere and try to get them on me. But instead, he moved forward and wrapped his arms around me, patting me on the back.

"Alright, son, I'll deal with this. Don't you worry."

"Don't call me son," I muttered, trying to hold onto my anger, but it was damn difficult when this man was putting everything on the line for me.

"Sorry," he said, stepping back and giving me an awkward smile. "I just want to help. I won't let anything happen to you."

"Seriously?" I narrowed my eyes at him. "I killed a cop. You did hear that part, right?"

He nodded slowly, tension lines rolling across his brow. "Yes, I understand, Johnny James. I do. But I trust your word, and if this man did what you say he did, then…well, it was self-defence."

"Aren't you going to suggest I hand myself in and try to convince a jury that was the case then?" I asked suspiciously.

"No," he laughed humourlessly. "I know how the system works. No one would believe you, and if they started digging into your background, they'd find a whole host of crimes to send you down for. You'd never see freedom again." His throat bobbed like the idea of that hurt him far more than learning his son was a killer.

He took the keys from my hand while I remained standing there like a confused cucumber and he stepped past me, tugging on my arm to make me follow.

"Show me where the car is."

I led him to it, not looking back at him as I frowned the entire way there, unsure why this was going so smoothly, why he was agreeing so damn easily. I'd pictured an argument, a few threats, maybe even a punch or two, but this… this was too simple.

We reached the car in the alley and Gwan opened the trunk, looking in at the dead body and flipping the blanket off of his face to get a look at him.

"He's not from my precinct," he muttered, almost to himself, tilting his head and taking in the hole Rogue had punched in his temple. "What did you use to kill him?"

I stumbled over my answer for a moment before remembering and blurting it out. "A stiletto. I was wearing them for one of my acts."

Why the fuck did I just say that? God, Gwan was a super cop and this was precisely why I never made any comment when I came into contact with the law.

Gwan's eyes dropped over me, landing on the shoes I was very clearly wearing and clearing his throat. "A sailor in stilettos? Must be a new act."

Dammit, I forgot I was dressed as a fucking sailor.

"I didn't say I was wearing them, I said Rogue was and I took one from her and used it," I backpedalled quickly, snatching the fucking hat from my head as Gwan's eyes rested on it for a moment.

"You...took a shoe from her foot during the fight?" he questioned and I shook my head furiously.

"No, obviously that makes no sense. She'd kicked them off while trying to run from him and I picked it up and threw it at him."

"You threw it at him hard enough to embed it in his temple? And you managed to aim a stiletto that well in the middle of-"

"It was a lucky shot, Gwan, what do you want me to say?"

Gwan stared at me for several seconds, something in his gaze softening like he saw the truth and liked what he found, but he knew nothing. Nothing. My story was rock solid. Ish.

He glanced back down at the body then flipped the blanket over the cop's face again before closing the trunk and clearing his throat.

"Go back to your mom's place. Tell her I was called into work. I'll send her a text to apologise," he said.

I took a step back, planning to just leave but I hesitated, too many questions running through my mind. "Why are you doing this? What do you want? Because you can't just have my mom back, you know? If you want her, you'd better court her like a proper gent, I swear to God."

"I'm not asking for anything," he said, and my suspicions only heightened.

"Yeah, you are. Spit it out, what are you gonna demand I do for this? You want cash? I've got cash. I'll give you cash."

"I don't want anything, Johnny James," he reiterated.

"Because you're just that good of a guy?" I scoffed.

"Well...I suppose." He shrugged like he didn't know, and I spat a growl.

172

"No. You don't get to be Mr Perfect, with your free favours," I hissed. "Can't you just be a little bit dirty? Can't you have some grit about you?"

"I'm covering up the murder of a cop for my son who I know full well is a pimp and a sex worker and runs illegal drug money through his business," he said in a low whisper. "Is that not dirty enough for you, Johnny James?"

I gaped at him as he unlocked the car and dropped into the driver's seat, starting up the engine just like that.

Fuck, he was right. He was dirty by association. I was the shit stain on his perfectly clean record, and holy hell, did that feel weirdly good.

"Fine, I'll hang out with you to keep you sweet on this," I said dryly as he lowered his window.

"I didn't ask you to," he said, and I tsked.

"You didn't have to, I can see it in your manipulative eyes, Gwan. And if it'll keep you quiet about this, I'll do it."

"Really, Johnny James, you don't need to do anything you're not comfortable wi-"

"Stop trying to mess with my head. I'll pay the price. I'll ask you questions and shit to make sure you keep up your end of the bargain, yeah?" I thrust my hand through the window in an offering, not wanting to do it at all, but what choice did I even have?

He gaped at me for a moment before slowly taking my hand and shaking it firmly. At least it wasn't a wet fish of a handshake, I supposed he had that much going for him.

"Alright," he agreed, a smile playing around the corner of his lips. "Perhaps Saturday afternoon?" he asked hopefully.

"Yeah, yeah, whatever." I turned my back on him, walking out of the alley.

As if I cared what day of the week we hung out, or for how long, or where we might go. Like the beach, and the shake shack, and maybe even that little ice cream parlour off of Palm Street. I'd probably get mint chocolate chip, or maybe double chocolate. Not that I cared. Not that I was looking forward to it. In fact, maybe I'd cancel on him last minute, so he was left standing alone on the beach in his little sun hat and shorts. Ha, yeah. That'd show him for sniffing around my mother again like a hungry stray cat.

Better turn up though. Wouldn't want him to rat me out to the cops. *Fucking Gwan.*

CHAPTER TWELVE

T he door banged open, and I looked around from where I was curled between Fox and Rick, JJ's mom, Helena, practically bouncing in her seat as she stared towards the door.

My head was pounding, but I slapped on a smile as I looked for Johnny James, my gut twisting with the knowledge that my actions had forced him into this situation. If it wasn't for me, we wouldn't have had to come here, and I hated knowing that I'd taken away the choice he had over seeing Gwan again or not.

JJ strode into the room before Helena could make it out, his eyes holding a blend of confusion and relief in them. I sagged back against Fox even before he shot a quick nod our way to confirm the situation was being dealt with.

"Where's Gwan?" Helena asked as she looked beyond her son, her shoulders drooping and hurt flashing in her eyes as she realised Gwan wasn't with him.

"He had to go back to work," JJ muttered, his jaw ticking with a host of repressed emotion.

"Johnny James," Helena said fiercely, pushing to her feet just as Rick pressed what seemed like the tenth Oreo into my hands. "If you've scared him away from me, I swear to God, I will banish you from this house!"

"I didn't send him anywhere," JJ growled. "I told you; he had to go to work. Cops do that kind of thing all the time, punching in, punching out, filing papers, ticking boxes-"

"Don't you sass me," she replied, raising her chin and the rest of us remained entirely silent, though I did chomp down on my cookie, the sugar helping some with the dizziness from the Rohypnol in my system.

"God, mom, stop being so dramatic. He's just another dude who likes to sniff around you. You know he's after the same thing as all the rest, so why do you even care if-"

Helena strode forward and slapped JJ so hard that his face wheeled to one side, his eyes widening in shock at what she'd just done, and I could feel myself gaping too. I'd known his mom my entire life, and I knew for a fact that she had never once hit him before. She was the softest of all the boys' parents, the sweetest and the most caring. I used to love coming over to his house and letting her play mother with me while she braided my hair and told me stories about her childhood. She'd been the one who had eventually helped me figure out the whole period saga once I'd calmed down enough to let JJ bring me to talk to her, and she'd even shown me the best brands of sanitary products to steal when I needed them each month.

"Do you know how many years I've been missing that man?" she hissed, her eyes brimming with tears she seemed to be fighting back. Fox, Rick and I were stuck watching the show, silent and staring as she broke down right before us. "Do you know how many men ever treated me with an inch of the respect and attention that he does?"

"Mom-" JJ began as the tears brimmed over and she drew the hand she'd slapped him with back to her chest, fingers trembling as she clutched it to her like she couldn't believe what she'd just done.

"I'm lonely, Johnny James," she choked out. "You were all I ever had besides him and now you're all grown up, and I'm just here in this house with nothing to do and no one to need me. And Gwan…well, I suppose it doesn't even matter now, does it? You've seen him off just like all the rest."

She turned away but JJ moved to her, dragging her into his arms despite her resistance.

"I'm sorry," he breathed as he crushed her small frame against his. "I'm sorry if it's my fault you feel alone. I didn't mean to cause that. I only wanted to protect you from assholes who were trying to use you, like that moustache-wielding prick Greg."

"Gwan isn't like Greg," she hiccupped, and he sighed, nodding in acceptance even though I got the impression that he didn't want to accept it at all.

"I know," he agreed. "He's a…good guy." JJ grimaced but Helena didn't even seem to notice, a gasp tearing from her as she jerked back and stared up at him, her eyes widening with hope and making my chest tighten as I watched them.

"You mean that?" she asked, her fingers knotting in his shirt like she expected him to turn and run, and I had to admit that he did seem like a flight risk.

JJ looked like he was inclined to choke on the words he forced out next, and I had to hide a smile as I watched him. "He seems…*nice*. And we're going for ice cream on Saturday."

"Mint chocolate chip?" Helena asked excitedly, dashing her tears away with the backs of her hands while Rick chuckled like the asshole he was, and Fox punched him for it behind my back.

"Yeah. Probably. Or double chocolate," JJ muttered, his eyes shifting to the side like he didn't even want to admit to thinking about that, but it was out there now, shining for the whole world to see. He was going on a dad date with Gwan.

Helena burst into tears again, throwing herself into JJ's arms and choking out an apology for slapping him but he just shook his head.

"I think I might have deserved that one," he admitted, rubbing at the pink handprint on his cheek ruefully. "And if you…want to keep seeing *Gwan…*" JJ paused like even uttering that name made him shudder. "Then you should… continue to spend short periods of time in his company while fully clothed and ideally in public."

Helena's sobs grew out of control, and I bit my lip on a grin as JJ accepted her hugs while still looking all kinds of uncomfortable over the situation.

Fox's phone began to ring in his pocket, and he took it out, showing me the caller ID before answering to Chase.

"Hey…yeah, okay, we'll be out in a few." Fox cut the call and got to his feet, taking my hand in his and drawing me up with him. "Chase is outside to pick us up."

"This has been so great, Mrs B," Rick purred, the devilish look in his eyes promising JJ that he would be getting all kinds of shit over this situation for a long while yet.

"Thank you for the cookies," I added, moving to walk past her but she released JJ suddenly, grabbing me instead and squeezing me tightly.

"I never thought you'd choose him," she breathed in my ear, making my skin prickle. "I was always fearing the day you broke his heart and when you were gone, well, the man he became wasn't the boy I'd reared. But now, with you back, I can see that light in him again. I can see what he means to you, what they all do, and I just wanted you to know because you can't ever leave him now."

"I won't," I swore, the promise spilling from my tongue all too easily because it was the truth, and there was never any denying it now. Me, my boys, and this place were meant to be, written in the sand and stolen by the ocean, an oath that could never be taken back and I wouldn't ever want it to be. Of course, she probably didn't realise I was dating all of the Harlequin boys, not just her son, but I figured it might be too much of a bombshell to drop on her right now.

Helena released me and I moved to JJ, feeling the turmoil in him and wanting to settle it as I wound my arm around his waist and his own arm instantly came around my shoulders to draw me in.

"Maybe you could come over for dinner the week after your ice cream date?" Helena called to him as we went. "Have some food with me and Gwan and-"

"Mom," JJ ground out. "Can we just get through the ice cream and see? I can't be making plans for happy family dinners like this man is my daddy when all he is right now is some goody-goody stranger with my fucking eyes."

Helena nodded in agreement, tiptoeing up to kiss him on the cheek in goodbye and the four of us headed back out into the balmy night air.

"I really liked those rainbow heels," I sighed as I leaned into JJ, my legs wobbling a little beneath me and my eyes drooping as the damn drug still clawed at me.

"I'll get you a new pair, baby girl," Rick promised. "But the next time you kill with them, I want to have my way with you before you clean the blood off."

I snorted in reply to that, knowing he wasn't even joking and shaking my head at his barbaric tendencies.

Fox stayed close on my other side but when I stumbled, JJ just whipped me up into his arms, tugging me close and letting me breathe him in.

I let my eyes fall closed as we got into Fox's truck, Chase's lips pressing against mine as he leaned in to greet me. I smiled against them, running my hand down the scarred side of his face lovingly before snuggling in closer to Johnny James.

I dozed all the way back to Harlequin House, the low rumble of my boys' voices filling the space while Maverick made a hundred Gwan jokes, and Fox grumbled threats to Shawn's life. They all seemed concerned about the price he'd put out for me, but I wasn't afraid. Not while I was surrounded by the four of them. We were untouchable when we were together like this.

Soft sheets brushed against my legs and I moaned softly as I peeled my eyes open, finding myself being placed in my bed.

Mutt was licking my toes aggressively like he could tell I'd come close to danger tonight and I giggled, jerking my feet away and catching hold of JJ's wrist as he made a move to leave.

"Where are you going?" I asked him and he paused, tucking a lock of hair behind my ear as he pulled the sheets up around me.

"The boys want to discuss our plans going forward."

"So let them," I said, pushing the sheets aside and patting the spot beside me as I looked him over in his sailor outfit. "I want you close to me tonight."

JJ hesitated, glancing back towards the door, but I could tell I'd already won him over as his hands dropped to his belt and he began to unhook it.

"No cheating," I said as I rolled onto my side, blinking my eyes to force them to stay open, wanting to watch him do his thing. "You put that outfit on with the intention to strip for a hungry audience. So come on, Johnny James, show me what you've got."

I could see the weight pressing down on him over what we'd found out about the price on me tonight, the drugging, the dead cop and of course all of that daddy drama he had to be drowning in. So I needed him to see that I was fine.

"I don't know if I have a dance in me tonight, pretty girl," he admitted, his voice catching as he looked down at me. "We could have lost you," he breathed, and I sat up, shaking my head.

"No chance of that. I fought like a hellcat to stay with all of you, and there is nothing on this earth that will stop me from doing so every damn time. It's us against the world, Johnny James. I don't care if he offers all five diamonds in payment for me, no one will ever manage to claim that pay day because I'm here, and I have all of you, and I'm not going anywhere ever again."

JJ moved forward like he wanted to kiss me, but I pressed a hand to his chest, shaking my head.

"I came here for a show," I insisted, and Mutt moved to lay beside me, crossing his front paws as he looked up at JJ expectantly too.

Johnny frowned at me, but he caved quickly enough, standing upright again and pushing his fingers into his hair as he tipped his head back and began to slowly undulate his body.

There was no music, but he didn't need any, creating a beat all of his own as he slowly moved his hands down the sides of his neck before finding the buttons at his throat and unhooking the white shirt of his sailor outfit one by one.

I bit my bottom lip as I watched him, a groan of longing rising in my throat as his bare chest was revealed to me, the perfect cut of his abs beyond any reasonable level of believability. All of my men were insanely hot, but JJ's definition was rivalled only by the original Adonis, his dedication to the sculpture of his flesh undeniably paying off. Where the others were bigger, their muscles more suited to brute force and strength, he was all perfect lines and that fucking edible V.

JJ shrugged out of the shirt as he finished unfastening it, flexing his body while he let it slide down his arms to pool on the floor behind him. Undressing really shouldn't have been able to look that good, but Johnny James made it seem effortless.

He ran his hands down his thighs and jerked his hips forward, a grin lifting his lips as he ripped the Velcro fastenings free of his trousers, the things coming off and sailing away over his shoulder.

He kicked his boots off last, leaving him in a pair of form hugging white boxer briefs and the little blue tie thingy that was still around his neck.

He came to me then, his body moving over mine and making my breath catch until he'd crawled to the other side of me.

I rolled over to face him, smiling as he laid his head on the pillow beside mine, our gazes meeting and something so much deeper than lust passing between us.

I wriggled closer to him, my shins pressing to the tops of his thighs as I curled myself up and he moved onto his side too. I took hold of the sheet and drew it over our heads, leaving us in the shadows beneath it like we used to do when we were kids and I'd sneak into his house for a sleepover.

"I love you, Johnny James," I whispered, his exhale feeding air into my own lungs as I drew it into myself. "And I'm not going anywhere. So stop looking at me like you think I might vanish if you dare to look away."

"I just want that motherfucker dead and buried," he growled. "I want him gone and our freedom returned."

"We are free," I replied, not wanting to talk about fucking Shawn right now. I was sick of him taking up so much of our time and thoughts. "Tell me what happened with your dad," I said softly, tangling my fingers with his as I watched him withdraw into himself at my words.

"Gwan," he corrected, a little bite to his tone. "The man who let me think he was a punter for years, allowing me to make sexual suggestions to him regularly while knowing I was his secret lust child of shame-"

"I don't think that's fair," I said, and he scowled at me, but he didn't pull away. "He was trying to be there in whatever way he could after finding out about you far later than he'd have liked."

JJ blew out a harsh breath. "Too little too late."

"Is it?" I asked earnestly, shifting closer to him beneath the sheets until our noses were almost touching. "Because I can remember the two of us laying beneath your bed sheets like this when we were kids, talking about the fathers we both knew we had out there somewhere, wondering if they might sweep into our lives and rescue us some day."

"I mostly remember how hard my dick was because I had you in my bed and the panic I felt over the thought of you accidentally bumping into it or spotting it tenting the fucking sheets," he replied and I laughed, smacking his chest.

"Liar."

"Never. I have countless memories of me trying to hide my hard-ons from you, pretty girl. And even more of me thinking about you while I banished them."

"Jesus, JJ." I slapped him again, blushing furiously as I thought about what my sixteen-year-old self would have thought about that if I'd known, refusing to acknowledge any of the times when I'd relieved myself of the same urges while thinking of the four boys who owned my soul. It had been a secret then, something I didn't let myself admit to and only ever experienced when I found my hands between my thighs, my thoughts clinging to them no matter how hard I tried to deny the reason for it. I'd convinced myself that it was because they were the only boys I knew, not because I actually wanted them in that way. Back then, it would have had to be a choice, and it wasn't one I ever could have made.

"Fuck, I love it when you blush like a virgin for me," he groaned, his hand moving to my hip, his thumb circling against the dip just inside it that led somewhere so much more interesting.

"Stop trying to change the subject," I hissed, my hand moving to his chest like I planned to push him back, but it just stayed there, feeling the heavy pounding of his heart instead.

"What was the subject again?" he teased, and I pouted.

"We used to talk about our dads showing up one day, admitting they were secret millionaires who'd always wanted us but had never even known we existed. Now, I'm pretty sure Gwan is no millionaire, but-"

"Are you seriously telling me that if some dude rocked up here tomorrow in some fancy pants suit with a well-groomed moustache and proclaimed himself to be your long-lost daddy, you'd be all over that? You'd actually want it now? We're not kids anymore, Rogue, I'm almost thirty, I don't need-"

"You have such a hate for moustaches," I pointed out, cutting off his whole spiel because I got it and I didn't need it spelling out for me.

"Everyone knows you can never trust a man with a moustache," he growled, and I breathed a laugh.

"In answer to your question – yes. If my long-lost daddy showed up and wanted to get to know me then I would say *yes*, Johnny James. Not because I need looking after or wanted to go play catch at the park. But because I've always wished to have parents who loved and wanted me, and it wasn't something I ever got a taste of."

"Rogue-"

"This is my pity party, JJ, I didn't invite you to it, so just hush up and listen."

He snorted at me, and I grinned.

"My point is that I'm the daughter of a drug addict who fucked around in order to pay for her next high. From what I've been told, she didn't even know the number of guys she'd offered herself up to in return for a high, let alone their names, so even if my daddy wasn't just some other drug-addicted loser and actually was a stand-up guy who might want me if he ever found out about me, it doesn't matter. He might as well be Santa Claus to me because he isn't ever going to come find me. And that's cool. I made my peace with that a long time ago, just like you did when you thought you were the product of a broken condom from one of many paying customers who were faceless to your mom. But Santa Gwan is real, J. He's real and he's here and he's offering you that thing we both wanted so much. So, I get that you're scared, but it's fucking dumb of you to reject him purely because of that."

"You think I'm scared?" he balked, and I smirked at him.

"Yeah, JJ. I think the big, bad gangster is scared of letting a little love into his life."

"I love you," he pointed out indignantly. "And Chase, Fox, Rick-"

"We don't fucking count and you know it. You're stuck with us whether you like it or not. Same goes for your mom. But Gwan is different, Gwan is new, Gwan is a decision that you actually have to make and-"

"Please stop saying Gwan," he begged and I laughed.

"I will," I said, giving him a firm look and he huffed.

"If?"

"If you give him a shot. A real one. No bullshit. Let him be your Gwan-daddy."

"Fuck you."

"Any time," I replied, biting down on my lower lip as I ran my gaze down what I could see of his body in the shadows.

"Rogue," he groaned, closing his eyes as he drew in a deep breath. "You were attacked and drugged tonight. I'm not fucking you. You need to recover."

"But I have a headache," I said with a pout. "And you know that the best cure for headaches are orgasms."

JJ licked his lips, his eyes landing on my mouth before he grunted, shaking his head in refusal.

"No. I'm all worked up and I'm not going to take that energy out on you. I'll pin you down and make you scream for me when you're not feeling like shit thanks to that drug if that's what you want, but right now you need to sleep it off."

"Boo," I complained, reaching for him regardless but he simply grabbed my wrist then flipped me over, putting my back to his chest and spooning me like we were just two kids again.

I groaned in frustration, grinding my ass back against his very hard cock and he cursed me, holding me tighter to try and make me stop.

"Pretty girl, I'm trying to be a nice guy here. And I'm absolutely not going to fuck you while you're under the influence of that stuff."

"But my headache, JJ," I complained. "What am I supposed to do about that?"

"Take some pain pills?"

"No more pills," I growled, pressing my ass back into him again and he swore once more.

"Stop, please," he growled, and I huffed as I gave in, snuggling into the pillows and simply enjoying the feeling of him holding me like that, his lips pressing to the back of my neck as he got as close as he possibly could to me.

"Promise you'll give him a real shot," I said sleepily as I let my lids fall closed and he sighed before agreeing with a grunt.

"Okay. But in the morning, I'm going to show you how nice I'm not and remind you and Maverick that I'm about as sweet as a lemon when I want to be."

I laughed into my pillow and gave in to the call of sleep as it pulled at me, the feeling of JJ's arms around me making it more than easy to do so. I was safe here with him, them, all of us. So Shawn could choke on his diamonds for all I cared, because we'd be ready for anyone he sent after me, and so help them if they dared to try.

CHAPTER THIRTEEN

When Rogue was so deeply asleep that not even World War Three breaking out would wake her, I shimmied out of bed and walked into her bathroom, taking the piss I'd needed for the past twenty minutes while refusing to let go of her until she'd drifted off.

My head was a fucking mess after the night I'd had, and the last thing I needed was to wrestle my hard cock into submission before my bladder gave out and I pissed in my own face. But here I was, cock in hand, thinking of poor, sweet old Miss Mabel in the room downstairs to try and get my boner to subside while pushing Johnny D down hard enough to draw a growl of pain from my lips.

Wow, this really was my lowest point of the night, and that was saying something when I picked through the hell that had fallen on us. Why couldn't we just live normal lives, where the biggest drama that happened in a day was the mailman mixing up our letters with the neighbours'? That sounded like a damn boring existence actually, and I was pretty sure I'd crave the chaos of our family if I lived like a suburban housewife for even a week.

I could use a bit more balance though, and far less enemies hunting down our beautiful girl, trying to drug her, kidnap her, kill her. Jesus Christ, it seemed we were cursed to live in dangerous mayhem, and the more we tried to stay in our happy bubble, the more fucking Shawn tried to pop it with a kitchen knife.

Death - that was the answer. A nice tidy bullet between Shawn's eyes would do the job, but the others wouldn't want it to be that clean. I'd have settled for anything so long as he ended up firmly in hell, but I could see their desire to make him suffer too. I'd be all for that so long as I was sure the asshole never got free again. That was the problem with him; he was a zombie, and only a headshot was gonna take him out.

That was also why I'd be the one who got us all through a zombie apocalypse. While they were all out, smashing skulls and enjoying the carnage, getting way too close to being bitten, I'd be stashing supplies, taking over a mall and locking that shit down fast. They might have mocked me for my safety equipment and well-planned survival tactics, but they wouldn't be laughing when the zombies came, and I was the one with riot gear already tucked away in my secret bomb shelter. I'd told Fox outright that I was buying the plot of land that had come on the market just beyond Carnival Hill and having one dug in, but had he believed me? Nope. He'd barely even listened, thinking I was making jokes, but I had one alright, and he'd be begging to get inside it when the bombs started dropping, or the zombies showed up at our door.

I finally got my dick to do my bidding and relieved myself with a piss that made me sigh audibly, my head dropping back.

By the time I returned to the bedroom, Mutt had taken my place, snuggling down into the warm spot I'd vacated and keeping our girl company. I knew she was safe in his little paws, so I slipped out of the room and followed the sound of voices to Fox's office, nudging the door open and finding the three of them gathered around the desk with a map laid out between them and a lamp lighting it up.

192

They glanced around as I entered, and Fox's brow dipped in concern. "Is she good?"

"Yeah, she's sleeping. Mutt's watching her," I said as I knocked the door closed behind me and jerked my chin at the map. "What's the plan?"

"Applebrook market," Maverick said as he leaned back in his seat. "Mia mentioned it and I think it's worth checking out as it's the only lead we've got. We'll head there in a couple of weeks and scout it out, hope they show up."

"That's it? Hope for the best?" I said anxiously. "What if more of those assholes wanting to score a diamond come here looking for Rogue in the meantime?"

"We don't let Rogue out of our sight." Chase clawed his fingers through his dark curls.

"Yeah," Fox affirmed with a sharp nod. "And I've already told Luther to double security here at the house. Whenever we head out, he's got a group of Harlequins that will follow when we want them too. We can't ever let our guards down, don't let strangers near her. If we're out and she needs a piss, we go with her, got it?"

We all nodded, and I sagged against the door, rubbing my eyes as tiredness pressed in on me alongside a thousand worries.

"Have you heard from your dad yet?" Rick asked.

"Don't call him that," I muttered.

"Sorry. Have you heard from the man who's biologically related to you and who you hit on countless times at your club yet?" he corrected with a taunting smirk, and I launched myself at him with a snarl, colliding with him in his chair and sending him crashing backwards onto the floor.

"I didn't know!" I snapped as Chase hauled me off of him and Maverick's obnoxious laughter filled the room.

"Chill, man," Chase said, locking his arm around my shoulders and keeping me tight against him.

I glared at Rick as he shoved to his feet, not seeming the least bit

193

concerned about me having just thrown him to the ground.

"Have you heard from him or not?" Fox asked and I shook my head.

"Not yet," I sighed, and Chase released me as he felt the tension run out of my body.

"Well, we should probably get some rest. It's on him now," Fox said. "All we can do is trust he comes through for us."

"Wake me up if you hear anything," Chase said through a yawn, and I nodded.

He slipped out the door and we all trailed after him. Chase headed straight into Rogue's room and Fox followed, the open door letting me see them climbing into bed with our girl and nestling in around her. Mutt growled half-heartedly, but didn't do any more than maintain his position right next to our girl as they got comfortable beside her.

Maverick rested a hand on my shoulder, lingering next to me.

"You know I love you, brother. And feel free to take a few swings at my daddy in return, the psychotic brother of my adopted father who killed Foxy boy's momma. How's that for click bait?"

"Fucking hell, Rick," I muttered, but he just laughed like it didn't matter to him. I knew it did though. He rarely talked about the subject, but it probably would have done him good to let it out. Maverick liked to swallow his pain like acid, until one day it burned a hole in his gut and rage poured out in its place.

"You going to bed?" Rick stepped toward the bedroom, but I retreated a little, feeling wide awake with endless thoughts still cycling through my head on repeat.

"Nah…I thought I might steal a couple of Chase's cigarettes and finish off the last of the margaritas in the fridge."

"That sounds like a date I can't refuse," Rick said with a grin, walking downstairs before I could make any suggestion that I wanted to be alone. Not that I did really, but I might have told him that to avoid having to talk about all the bullshit I was feeling over Gwan. And I had a feeling that was exactly what

Rick was angling for.

I followed him down to the kitchen where he was already taking the pitcher from the fridge, pouring us out two large glasses before swiping Chase's box of cigarettes from the pocket of his leather jacket hanging on the back of one of the stools. I took one of the glasses as we walked out to the patio where the moon was bathing the pool in silver light, everything so perfectly quiet that it was hard to believe this was the same night that Rogue had almost been kidnapped.

I took a long swig of my drink as I dropped down on the edge of the pool beside Rick, letting my feet hang in the water as he kicked off his shoes to do the same.

By the time I'd drained half my glass and had a cigarette dangling from my lips, I felt a mile better. Although I knew this wasn't the healthiest way to take the edge off, I didn't really give much of a fuck.

"How many assholes do you think Shawn has offered that diamond to in exchange for Rogue?" I asked darkly, drawing the nicotine into my body through a deep toke, where it hugged me from the inside with its new friend Margarita.

"Fuck knows," Maverick gritted out, toking on his own cigarette. "But I'll kill all of them, one by fucking one."

I nodded and silence settled between us. It was the comfortable, familiar kind, but there were secrets laying in it too, things going unsaid.

"So you're Augustus Rosewood, huh?" I breached the silence.

"Yeah, and you're Gwanny James Junior."

"Fuck off," I snorted, kicking my feet in the water and he released a low chuckle.

"I think you got the better deal, J," he said, and I clucked my tongue.

"Rogue thinks so too," I murmured.

"Well, that girl is always fucking right, so I say you'd better give him a chance."

"Says the guy who held a grudge against Luther for ten years," I pointed out.

"Well, I thought he'd sent a bunch of Harlequin guards to beat me night after night before locking me up with a rapist, so…" He shrugged and my heart clenched in horror.

"Why'd you always do that?" I growled.

"What?" he snipped, angrily stabbing out his smoke on the ground beside him, sending sparks into the water where they hissed out of existence

"Play things off like they're nothing, saying such awful shit so fucking deadpan." I shuddered, hating what he'd been through, hating fucking Shawn to his absolute core for orchestrating it. He was the villain in all our stories, the monster in the dark who painted our nightmares for us, and I was so tired of being haunted by him.

"Because if I act like it's nothing, maybe one day it'll become nothing," he said, so quiet I almost missed it and I turned to my friend with a frown and an ache in my soul.

"It'll never be nothing," I said, though it hurt me to say it, and he looked to me with that same hurt reflected in his eyes. "It's your past and it's full of far more cruelty and deception than you ever deserved, Rick." I laid my hand on his back and was surprised when he leaned into me, accepting my sympathy instead of withdrawing from it, shutting down and slapping on an uncaring mask like he usually did. "But that kind of pain is sharp enough to forge a weapon from. You're unbreakable, Maverick Stone, don't ever fucking forget it."

His lips twitched then he tipped his head back to look up at the bright crescent moon above us. "Harlequin," he said.

"Huh?" I frowned.

"Maverick Harlequin." He looked down at me, dead in the eyes as a smile pulled my lips wide. "But don't you dare go telling Fox or Luther that."

Saturday arrived and I stood before the mirror in my bedroom in my navy board shorts while Rogue danced around me, trying to pick out a shirt for me. Mutt followed her everywhere she went as she took nearly every shirt from my closet and spread them all out on the bed, climbing up on the end of it and gazing down at them thoughtfully.

"Hmm, which one's the most dad date-ish?" she mused while Mutt yipped at her from the floor.

"I don't care," I drawled. "I just need to get going, pretty girl."

She came hurrying over to me with a red tank that had a naked woman's silouhette down the centre of it and I shook my head, grabbing it from her hand and tossing it away.

"Not that one," I clipped.

"So you *do* care," she accused with a wild smile before sprinting back to the bed. "That was a test, Johnny James, and you failed. I can see your squishy heart now, all skipping and jumping, excited to see Daddy Gwan."

"Rogue," I warned. "I'm just going to fulfil my end of the deal. Nothing else."

Gwan had pulled through for us hard, not even a single scrap of evidence left over what had happened to that cop, though he wouldn't give me any details on how he'd dealt with it when he'd called me. Just that it was done, and I didn't have to worry. I still didn't trust him, half expecting to have the cops burst into Harlequin House one day and arrest us, but for now there was no sign of that happening, so I guessed we were in the clear.

"Sure, you are," she said lightly, snatching up a white tank top with a wave curling through the centre of it in blue. "Here."

She moved in front of me, tiptoeing up as high as she could and I smirked as I raised my arms and let her try to get it onto me. Eventually, she had to pull over a chair and as it fell down to cover my chest, I grabbed her by the waist, throwing her over my shoulder and launching us onto the bed in the sea of shirts. Mutt barked at us as I pinned her down, locking her arms above her head before stealing a kiss from her laughing mouth.

Her body arched into mine and I drew back with a groan. "If only I could stay and play."

I kept her wrists in my hands, admiring her, my gaze trailing over her body to where her shirt had ridden up to expose her stomach. I leaned down, running my tongue around her belly button and making her wriggle and scream as I tickled her with my mouth. Fuck, she tasted like heaven, but I had to go.

I released her, realising it was Rick's t-shirt she had on and I grabbed it, tugging it off of her and pulling the dark blue wifebeater I'd worn last night over her head instead, making sure she was smothered in the scent of me.

"Mine." I flicked her nose with a smirk, her grin widening at me playing possessive, though we both knew I was just doing it to fuck with Rick.

"Don't go getting all badger on me," she said, and I chuckled as I got off the bed, dropping down to pet Mutt goodbye and he licked my palm in a rare kiss instead of a nip.

"You like a bit of badgering," I said as I reached the door, hooking my wallet off the side and pushing it into my pocket before checking my hair in the mirror one last time. Not that I cared what it looked like or anything.

"Pfft, says who?" she demanded.

"When we got home from surfing last night, Fox told you to go get washed and changed like a good girl, and you gave him this face." I swung around so my back was to the door, clasping my pecs and squeezing them hard while biting my lip dramatically.

"Fuck you," she laughed, picking up a pillow and throwing it at me.

"You went running off to that shower to finger fuck yourself over the Duke of Badgerton," I accused, and she laughed harder as I pretended to finger myself and moaned in an overexaggerated woman's voice, grinding my ass against the door.

"You're such an asshole." She leapt off the bed, running into battle and I threw out my hands to catch her before she went for my dick like a little savage.

I twisted us around, shoving her against the door and ground against her, crying out loud enough for everyone in the house to hear – except Miss Mabel. Or at least I hoped not Miss Mabel.

"Badger me, Badgerton!" I moaned, rolling my hips as she tried to fight me off, while unable to contain her laughter.

Rogue got her hand between us, grabbing my dick in a vice and my attempt at girlish moans were choked out of existence as she grinned up at me like a wicked, cock-wielding witch.

"Now what are you gonna do?" I croaked.

"Maybe I'll twist it off and make myself a nice new dildo out of it."

"Johnny D is nothing without me attached to him," I said powerfully, and she cracked a smile as she released my cock which was starting up a party in my pants even though she'd tried to wrangle him like a deadly snake. I guessed Johnny D liked any attention from her, and I couldn't really blame him.

"Are you ready or what, J? We're all waiting down here!" Chase's voice called from downstairs, and I frowned, resting my forehead to Rogue's.

"Please tell me you're not all planning to drive me there."

"Okay, I won't tell you that, but it won't make it any less true," Rogue said, and I cursed, grabbing her hand and pulling her out of the room as Mutt bounded along behind us.

I walked downstairs, finding Fox, Chase, Maverick and goddamn Miss Mabel dressed up and ready to go.

"Oh, come on," I pleaded, looking between them all standing there, Fox's truck keys dangling from his finger, looking all fatherly as he smiled at me.

"It's your big day," Fox teased, and I huffed as Miss Mabel tied her straw sun hat into place with a pink ribbon under her chin.

Rick was holding her purse which seemed to be packed to the brim and it didn't look like Mabel had any intention of taking it back.

"I helped Fox make a picnic," Mabel said keenly, and Chase lifted the cooler box to show me.

"I'm not going on a picnic," I said, shaking my head. "I'm going to see my Gw- no - my da- I'm going to see someone."

"Yeah, yeah, Johnny James," Rick said, hooking the purse onto his shoulder and letting Miss Mabel loop an arm through his. "We'll keep outa your way while you go on your dad date."

"But if you need anything, we'll be right there," Rogue said brightly, stepping past me.

"And the picnic is to make sure Rogue doesn't start brawling with seagulls over stolen French fries when she gets hangry," Rick added in a low tone she definitely heard.

Fox caught Rogue's hand, twirling her in against his side before the two of them gazed at me all fucking cute-like.

I huffed a breath as my gaze flicked to the clock on the wall and I realised I was going to be late if I didn't leave now.

"Fine," I gave in, and Fox and Rogue led the way towards the garage.

"Did you change your shirt, beautiful?" Rick called after Rogue, and I sniggered as I fell into step beside Chase while Mutt weaved between all of our legs.

"Kinda," she sang non-committally and Rick shot me daggers like he knew I was the culprit.

"Ready for your big day?" Chase asked.

"It's not my first day at school, what's with the entourage?" I muttered.

"Oh, come on, J, I have a shit stain for a Dad, Rogue's is probably some deadbeat drug addict, Rick's is Luther's psycho brother who's six feet under, and Luther's a gang leader with years of blood on his hands. I think we're all dying to see what a functioning father looks like," Chase replied.

"I bet he's handsome," Mabel declared as we made it into the garage. "Johnny James is so handsome."

"Thanks Mabel," I murmured as we all piled into Fox's freshly fixed up truck. The guys at the garage had given the whole thing a new coat of spray paint so the red colour of it shone metallically.

Maverick helped Mabel into the passenger seat after Rogue, and I climbed into the truck bed with Chase before Rick joined us and Mutt dove in to sit on our girl's lap.

The drive to the beach was predictably full of endless taunts about how I'd flirted with my dad at the club, and we were all sporting fresh bruises by the time Fox pulled up at the edge of the beach near the Shake Shack.

I froze, spotting Gwan waiting there in the shade the shack was casting, wearing cream khaki shorts with a pale green shirt tucked into them, a belt cinched tight around his waist, paired with a cream khaki baseball cap that matched his shorts. But it got worse. So much fucking worse, as my gaze fell down to his legs where two mid-calf socks stood proudly against his untanned skin, and on his feet were, of course, fucking sandals.

"Oh God," I groaned. "Fuck, no." I swiped a palm over my face as Rogue and Fox got out of the truck, helping Miss Mabel down.

"What's up?" Chase asked, shifting closer in front of me.

"He looks like such a fucking...dad. I can't do this, Ace." I looked up at him frantically, grabbing hold of his shoulders and shaking my head. "Look at him. Look how fucking practical he is. I bet he has a wallet chain, and every inch of skin is smothered in SPF fifty."

"What's so bad about that?" Chase asked, and my throat clogged up as I continued to shake my head, feeling the truck bounce as Rick jumped out of it.

"He's too normal, he's too nice," I said urgently, and Chase clasped my head in his hands, making me look at him before I went into a full-blown panic.

"You're worthy of him," he growled, and I stilled, feeling those words down to my bones, settling some broken thing inside me that I hadn't even realised lived there. "Do you hear me?"

"Yeah," I whispered, gazing into his unseeing eye, and thinking of all the moments I'd spoken these sorts of words to him, demanding he value himself the way we all valued him. And that was what this all came down to, wasn't it? I wasn't good enough for Gwan. I was his dirty little secret, the one he probably never breathed a word of to his real friends, to anyone in his real life. He snuck down to the grubby end of town and made himself feel better for never having been in my life by inserting himself into it now, into my club.

But it was probably just a hobby to him, an amusing little game, because in what world did fancy, uptown people want anything to do with people like me in the long term? I was the thing they bought for a night and tossed away by dawn. I was everyone's pretty fantasy, but when reality came knocking, I was the first thing to get shoved aside. Gwan would do the same once his little father-son daydream popped and he realised I was still just a street kid with a life paid for in sin. He'd retreat to his real life and forget all about me and Mom.

"Give him a chance," Chase cut through my thoughts. "That's all you have to do. You don't owe him anything, and if he disappears on you or you wanna tell him to fuck off out of town, then we'll deal with it, J. But if you run away now, you'll never know all the answers to the questions in your head."

I swallowed hard, knowing he was right. That cutting Gwan off now was something I'd regret forever, because I had to know one way or the other if he really gave a fuck about me.

"Okay," I agreed, and Chase clapped me on the shoulder before hauling me to my feet.

"You got this, Johnny James," Rogue called to me, and I spotted her down on the beach where Fox and Rick were setting up a parasol and sun lounger for Miss Mabel.

I nodded to her, twitching a smile at Chase before jumping out of the truck and heading up the boardwalk towards Gwan. He hadn't noticed me yet, his gaze fixed on a seagull that was eating an ice cream it had probably stolen from a toddler, squawking smugly.

I cleared my throat as I came up beside Gwan and he looked around, a smile spilling across his face.

"JJ," he said in relief, like he'd half expected me not to show up. "Or would you prefer I call you Johnny James? Whatever you're comfortable with."

"JJ's fine," I said tightly, flexing my fingers at my sides, my gaze sliding to the vendor in the shake shack who had a whole display of ice cream spread out before him. I cleared my throat, shuffling in that direction a little. "Did you want to, um…"

"Cone or cup?" he asked. "I always say an ice cream's not an ice cream without a cone. But if you're a cup man, then-"

"No, I'm a cone man through and through," I said, and his smile got even bigger as he nodded and led the way over there while I took in all the different flavours and wondered what Gwan was going to choose.

"Double chocolate for me," Gwan said and dammit, Gwan, that was a good choice.

"Same," I said like I didn't really care, but if I was gonna get ice cream then I was gonna do it right.

The vendor handed over our ice creams and Gwan got his wallet out before I could get to mine – and of course it was on a chain. He paid before I could object, and I was forced to thank him. Fucking Gwan. Showing off. Making a fool of me. But okay, I supposed I appreciated the gesture. Didn't make up for him coming to my club night after night while I treated him like a horny customer. Occasionally I'd swung my hard, naked cock in his direction up on stage an extra few times to ensure he had a good night too. This was the thanks I got for that.

Fuck my life.

We started walking along The Mile and I ate my way through my ice cream in silence as Gwan did the same, taking in the view as we just sort of strolled along.

"So how long have you been a cop?" I asked, not that I was particularly bothered, but the silence was stretching and if I had to go through with this whole date thing, I guessed I'd better pretend I was interested.

"I went to the academy straight out of high school," he said. "It was all I ever wanted to do. My parents are in the force too. Or they were."

Great. More cops.

"They're dead?" I asked.

"Retired," he said. "They moved down to Cabo a few years back."

"Do they…know about me?" I asked, my chest tightening as I wondered how much of a secret I really was in Gwan's life. But I couldn't help but be interested in the idea of having a Gwanpa and Gwanma out there somewhere. Not that I'd call them that of course. Unless I did. Which I wouldn't because that was as ridiculous as Gwan. Oh God, they chose the name Gwan for him – what the hell was I supposed to think of that? I bet they had terrible names. Like Crust and Jedwin.

He looked to me with a frown. "No, they don't."

"Ah, there it is," I said dryly, releasing a cold laugh. "Couldn't bear to tell them about your shameful little discrepancy, huh Gwan?"

"It's not that," he said firmly. "It's your choice whether you want them to know. I'm not taking any of those decisions out of your hands."

"Oh yeah? Well, how come you took away my choice over what kind of relationship I had with you when we first met? How come you let me treat you like a damn client at the club?" I hissed, shuddering at the memories. Oh lord, the memories. Too many times were coming back to me of when I'd made filthy suggestions about him riding my cock, or me kneeling down to suck his. I'd once put a little dick straw in his Tom Collins and told him to suck on it like a good boy. Why hadn't he said something then?? That seemed like a *very* apt moment to say something.

Gwan's cheeks burned brighter, and he cast his eyes to the ground as shame swept over him. "I wanted to. I really did. But I thought you'd tell me to go, I was afraid you wouldn't want me in your life. And it felt so, so good to be a part of it, JJ. I never took any of the flirting stuff seriously, that's just your work persona. And you've done such a great job perfecting it."

"Don't you dare compliment me on how good I can talk up clients. I thrust my bare cock in your direction far too many fucking times, Gwan. Do you know how damn uncomfortable that makes me feel right now?"

"I j-just liked to see your performances," he stammered, shaking his head as his ears turned pink too, just like mine did when I got flustered. "You're such a wonderful dancer, truly, it's a gift. And I don't care about your willy, JJ."

"Oh God," I cringed. "Don't call it that."

"Sorry, your penis," he backtracked.

"No, that's fucking worse. God, Gwan." I looked away from him, taking a massive bite out of my ice cream to try and distract myself, and I guess it helped because I got goddamn brain freeze and my whole face screwed up as I fought my way through it.

"Sorry," he repeated. "Is there a better term? Something more modern? Your mother uses the word cock a lot, do you prefer that?"

I recoiled from the mention of my mother and the word cock in the same sentence, and Gwan gazed at me apologetically like he wished he hadn't uttered those words. So why the fuck had he?

"Winkle?" he tried, and I died inside. "Or I've heard the young'uns using the term Long Sherman on occasion-"

"Can we just change the subject?" I demanded and he nodded quickly.

"What would you like to talk about? Is there anything you'd like to know about me?"

"You don't have like...some terminal illness or something, do you?" I asked, panic rising in me. "That's not why you're here, is it? To tell me you're dying and that I've got your death genes and I'm gonna die too."

"No, JJ," he said, his forehead furrowing. "Why is it so hard for you to believe that I'm here simply because I want to know you? That I have missed your mother every day since I left Sunset Cove, and that I have a thousand regrets about never being there while you were growing up?"

My heart thumped painfully hard within my chest as I relinquished the truth, those words my undoing. "Because it's not fair. Because if that's true then I missed out on having a dad for no good fucking reason."

He fell quiet, regrets pooling in those eyes that were so like mine and I got angry all over again.

I pursed my lips. "Then again, if you had been here, if you'd really wanted us, it probably wouldn't have lasted anyway. You would have left eventually."

"Why do you say that?" he asked, hurt lacing his tone and I looked him straight in the eye as I bared my soul.

"Because we're trash. At least, that's what people like you think of us. We're second-class citizens, grimy, the kind people with fancy careers and clean records don't wanna associate with. And if you're thinking 'well, I would have given you both fancy little lifestyles and brought you up right' then I'm not the son for you. This is who I am to my roots. And I'm glad I didn't get taken away from this world, because I've found my family in it. I wouldn't give it up for anything, I wouldn't change my childhood one bit, because it led me to them." I pointed back down the beach and Gwan followed my finger as I looked that way, finding all of them watching us without even trying to be subtle about it. Miss Mabel even had a pair of small binoculars raised to her eyes that she sometimes used for bird watching.

"They're it for me," I said. "They're the ones who were here for me when I had to find somewhere to sleep at night just so I could escape the sounds of my mother's fake moans and the grunting of whatever walrus had paid for her time that night. They were the ones who were there for everything, good and bad. They're mine and I'm theirs."

Gwan's eyes glinted with emotion as he turned to me and tentatively pressed a hand to my arm. I didn't remove it like I should have. I stood there and let him touch me, the desperation in my heart to experience some piece of a father's love keeping me bound in place. Even if it was far too late to have anything real of that now.

"You're not trash, JJ," he said powerfully. "You're the most remarkable person I could ever have dreamed up, and I am privileged to be related to you. Even if that is simply by blood, and you never wish to see me past this day. I want you to know how damn proud I am of everything you've built for yourself in life, how well you've cared for your mother as soon as you were able to. I'm sorry I wasn't there when you needed me, but I'm here now, and if there is anything I can offer you, then it's yours. However much or little you want to know me, it's your choice, and I will respect that choice."

The pinch in my chest sharpened to something so deep and raw, I couldn't ignore it any longer. I was moving before I'd even realised I was doing it, acting out the impossible and crossing the bridge between us in a monumental way.

I nudged the toe of my sneaker against his and stuffed my hands into my pockets as his eyebrows raised in response to that.

"Was that a friendly toe nudge?" he asked in shock, and I shrugged.

"What other kind of toe nudges are there?" I mumbled and he started smiling so big that I wished I could take it back. "You'd better not grow a moustache," I blurted, not wanting that smile to get too large.

I wasn't saying I love you with that toe nudge or anything, I was just opening a door between us, cracking it to let the light in the tiniest amount. If he wanted to peek through it, then I guessed that was okay. And if I wanted to peek back then I guessed that was okay too. And why shouldn't I? I had a duty to find out who he was for my mom's sake, especially if he planned on sticking around town and sweeping her off her feet in the most gentlemanly way he knew how – because if he tried to fuck her under my watch before they were in wedded bliss, I swore on every starfish in the ocean, I would feed him into their tiny, wet mouths and wipe him from the face of the earth.

I supposed if I believed his story, then I had to accept that he didn't just want my mother for her body though, that he'd loved her once, treated her the way she deserved to be treated. Maybe he'd been in love with her this whole time, pining for the woman he'd had to leave behind when his undercover work was done and he'd returned to his real cop life, believing she hated him for his lies. That was actually kind of romantic when I thought about it. Kind of tragic too – for all of us. Not that I *was* thinking about it.

"If it's an issue, I promise my upper lip will remain hair free for as long as you want," he said and dammit, I had no choice now. He'd vowed to live a moustacheless lifestyle just for me, and the pledge made my chest expand with air.

Yeah, I was going to have to let him into my life. And I was going to have to call him Gwan.

CHAPTER FOURTEEN

I sped down the road in my red Jeep with the top down and my rainbow hair billowing in the wind as I made my getaway. My trusty sidekick barked happily from the seat beside me, and I blasted Seaside by Diane Warren, Rita Ora and Sofia Reyes while singing my lungs out.

This was likely to earn me a spanking, but I didn't care. Or maybe I did care, and I wanted the spanking. Either way, I'd made a run for it like the good old days when I'd first come back here and Badger had tried to lock me up to keep me, and it felt damn good to be free.

Not that I really minded the babysitters so much these days, especially when I was laughing or surfing with them or they were making me come so hard I blacked out, but I also needed them to remember that I was no pushover, and I would fly free when I needed to.

I wasn't an idiot. I hadn't forgotten that Shawn had people hunting me. That was why I had a knife strapped to my thigh, a shotgun on the front seat and a pistol in both the glove box and my car door. But I wouldn't need them when I got where I was going. The Temple was just as safe as Harlequin House if not more so and I needed to have some girl time with Tatum.

A horn blasted behind me, and I laughed as I spotted JJ's bright orange car in the rear-view mirror, Chase in the passenger seat as they raced after me.

He definitely had more horsepower than me, but I had the advantage of knowing they wouldn't put me at risk, so when he made a move to overtake me, I just casually swerved all over the road until they backed off again.

I hit dial on the handsfree, calling Tatum as I sped down the road that led to her mansion, and she answered with a bark of laughter.

"Saint is losing his shit over 'hoodlums racing in our neighbourhood'," she said. "We can see you from the bedroom window."

"This is what happens when you fraternise with people of low breeding," Saint growled in the background, and I barked a laugh.

"Can you open the gate?" I asked as we shot towards it.

"Already open," she replied, and I grinned wider.

"See you soon." I cut the call and accelerated the rest of the way to their house, turning into their drive and slamming on the brakes the moment I crossed through the gates.

I unbuckled my seatbelt and moved to stand on my seat so that I could look back at Chase and JJ who had been forced to stop on the road outside the gates that were now swinging closed again.

"Don't wait up!" I called, waving sweetly as they both got out of the car and started towards me.

"You know Fox is going to lose his shit over this, pretty girl," JJ warned.

"And Rick will punish you for it," Chase added.

"I'm counting on it," I replied, giving them a dirty grin just before the gates shut between us and I was left to my girls' night in peace. I mean yeah, they were probably going to camp out there like little watch dogs, but that was cool with me. It was Saint Memphis they might piss off if they set up a tent that offended his eyes.

I hopped out of the car, grabbing my guns and bringing them with me just in case, and Tats swung the door open for me as I reached it.

"Hello, little hellion," he said with a wide smile, reaching out to take the shotgun from me and inspecting it as I stepped inside. His dark hair was swept up into a top-knot and his white tank top revealed a helluva lot of ink on his body, including a squid wrapped around his forearm.

"Hey, big hellion," I replied brightly.

"You do realise it is not necessary to cause such theatrics in all aspects of your life?" Saint's voice drew my attention to the stairs, and I squealed excitedly as I ran past him to embrace Tatum, Mutt scampering after me at my heels. "Oh good. You brought a dog without asking," he added, sounding way less than amused.

Tatum squeezed me tightly, stepping back and tugging me towards the kitchen. "Ignore him, he's in a mood because of some magic money thing that none of us understand."

"Bitcoin is not magic money, and the threat that could be posed to it by the use of online-"

"Hey, Saint, wanna come help me sort my closet out?" Tats interrupted before he could start on a tirade that I could already tell would go straight over my head. "I've been trying out a new system and I don't think it's working."

"That is because your system is nothing but a heap on the floor that I am continually reorganising," Saint huffed, but he headed towards the stairs all the same, clearly intending to do it.

"Actually," I called before he could leave. "There was something I was hoping you could help me with. Something I was thinking we could keep from my boys for now."

"And there I was thinking that a girl with a verb for a name would be incapable of intriguing me," Saint said, arching a brow as I gave him a shrug.

"Better than having an improper noun for one."

Silence hung between us, and Saint barked a laugh suddenly, beckoning me after him as he started up the stairs.

"Let's conduct this in my office before Tatum starts pouring the drinks. It's always better to do business pre inebriation."

"My thoughts exactly," I agreed, trying to keep a straight face as I followed him. The man was seriously uptight, but I was beginning to think he might just like me.

"When you get back here, I'm keeping you for myself though," Tatum called as I followed Saint up the stairs. "We haven't hung out nearly enough recently."

"Agreed," I promised her as I followed Saint to his ridiculously ostentatious office.

I fully planned on getting utterly shitfaced tonight before calling my guys to come scrape me off the floor and carry me home. I just had a little something to deal with first in case this whole thing ended up going to hell. Because if there was one thing I knew about Shawn Mackenzie, it was that we should never underestimate him. And if we were going to take him on then I was going to plan for every possibility. Even if that included my death.

"You really think this will work?" I asked Rick as I climbed off the back of his bike, removing my helmet and taking care not to pull my wig off alongside it. It was finally market day and we were hunting a sadistic motherfucker.

Ruby red curls tumbled down around my shoulders, courtesy of Lyla's performance props, and I raised a hand to double check my hairline as Maverick took my helmet from me and hung it from the bike's handlebars. I was wearing a pale blue maxi dress dotted with little white flowers billowing around my legs in the cool breeze that managed to find us from the sea. It was a little different to my usual style to help make my disguise more convincing.

Rick was dressed like a total tourist too, his white linen shirt clinging to his frame while a pair of matching pants hugged his ass, the look finished off with preppy navy boat shoes that both made him look like a total douche and got me in the mood for some billionaire romance roleplay.

Maybe I could play a mermaid to his prince charming, needing a magical cure to the loss of my voice that could only be found beneath the layers of linen he wore like a shield to protect his poor I-was-adopted-so-I-made-myself-into-a-billionaire-to-help-me-deal-with-my-daddy-issues heart. I was mixing up my romance stories there, but I was also fully onboard with it.

"I'm a pessimist, beautiful, so I'm fully expecting this to go as wrong as conceivably possible, but that doesn't mean you should give up hope too," Maverick said as he opened the storage compartment on the bike, taking out a straw hat to place on his head before passing me a huge pair of sunglasses. Our disguises were kind of obvious, but we weren't looking to win any prizes for them, just aiming to appear different enough to anyone who happened to glance our way.

I rolled my eyes at him, slapping his arm as I turned away towards the sounds and smells of the market to the east of us, but he caught my wrist and tugged me back again.

Rick's mouth claimed mine as he whirled me into him, his other hand closing around the nape of my neck as he pinned me there, the bite of his passion crashing into me as his tongue swept over mine and I melted in the heat of his desire.

"Whatever way today goes, I can guarantee the way tonight will end," he rumbled against my lips. "With you moaning my name as I kiss you five times as filthy as this in a spot much lower down on your body."

"Hopefully while my skin is still wet with Shawn's blood," I replied fiercely, the animal in him always calling to the beast in me. Maverick made it easy for me to lean into the most savage parts of myself without apology, the dark in him thriving on it just as the dark in me did too. And I was done apologising for any of it. This was who I was, who we were, brutal, bloody things, out for vengeance and beyond the point of restraint. I'd even killed that bastard cop, and I hadn't lost a wink of sleep over it.

JJ's dad had come through for us, covering up the crime as smoothly as if it had never happened. I really needed to send him a thank you gift basket full of fancy soaps, or fine wine, or whatever the fuck prim and proper cops liked to enjoy when they were off duty.

JJ said I wasn't allowed to go near him though because he was 'too Gwanly' – whatever the fuck that meant. I knew Johnny James was in a dilemma over his newfound dad, but the way he'd gone all shy and mumbly when he'd come back from his dad date told me he was warming to the dude. And I was too. Gwan had seriously pulled through for us, and yeah, his name was Gwan, but at least it wasn't Twiddlecock or some shit.

"Fuck, I love it when you talk psycho to me," Maverick growled, his mouth moving to my throat where his teeth sank into my flesh, and he sucked hard enough to leave a mark on me.

I gasped, arching against him as I gripped the thick swell of his biceps, my nails marking him right back before we shoved away from each other like we both knew we'd end up fucking in this damn alleyway if we didn't force ourselves apart. There was just something about the energy that Maverick Stone gave off; this frantic, carnal heat that somehow made every second seem so endlessly fleeting, like he knew that the world was going to end soon and was determined to devour every last drop of it that he could get before it was all over.

I flashed him a heated look before turning away and striding further down the alleyway.

I didn't know Applebrook as well as Sunset Cove, but I'd been here often enough in my youth to remember my way through the back streets to avoid the tourists. We used to come to this market fairly regularly as kids, picking pockets and stealing candy or other treats from the busy vendors before riding the bus back home, or piling into Fox's truck once we were older.

"Come on," I called, tossing a look back over my shoulder as I pushed my way into the crowd, my four boys watching me go with those feral looks in their eyes which always promised the best kinds of trouble. "It's a scavenger hunt. Last one back to the fountain in the town square gets tossed in."

I grinned at them as they exchanged competitive looks before turning and hurrying away into the crowd to hunt for my prize. We'd already picked enough pockets to satisfy our desire for cash for the day, so now we just needed to round it all off with a feast. And I was going to provide the best part of any meal – the burritos.

I twisted around bodies, slipping back and forth between tourists who were taking their sweet time inspecting every little thing they came across while heading straight for my prize at the end of the next street.

I hurried past the throng of people, ignoring everyone while I rushed for my goal, knowing that my boys would be going as fast as they could too and determined to make it back to the fountain before them.

I spotted the Mexican food truck up ahead and ran for it, shoving a few slow-bos aside and ignoring their angry calls that followed me as I went.

There were a couple of people already in the line for the truck as I arrived, but I casually slipped in behind the woman who was ordering as the family behind her squabbled over what they wanted.

"Hey!" the woman squawked, but I was already stepping up to the dude who was serving, a sweet smile on my face and a fifty-dollar bill in my fist like I was ready to pay.

"Can I grab five bean and cheese burritos please?" I asked with a big smile, ignoring the outraged woman while her husband shushed her down.

The men working the truck started fixing my order while old squawker gave hers too, and I casually slipped my fifty into the back pocket of my short-shorts before reaching out to grab the bottle of hot sauce which had been left out for customers to use.

I hummed to myself as I unscrewed the cap and the squawky bitch less than accidentally shoulder checked me as she made space for herself beside me.

That made me feel a whole lot less guilty over my plan as I set the bottle down again right in front of her just as the dude in the truck held out a paper bag filled with yummy goodness for me.

I reached for it with a big smile, taking hold of it and oh so accidentally swinging it straight into the bottle of hot sauce.

Squawker shrieked as I knocked it over, the cap flying free and bright red sauce splattering her from head to foot while I nimbly leapt aside with my prize in hand and a cry of false horror spilling from my lips.

"Oh, I'm so sorry!" I gushed as the men in the truck all hurried to help her and she squawked loudly about it getting in her eyes.

The moment that all the focus was on her, I turned tail and ran.

I shoved my way into the crowd once more and took off at a sprint with my bag of sweet -smelling victory food clamped tight in my fist.

A laugh tumbled from me as I raced away, but my triumphant thrill was quickly dampened by the sound of the food truck dude hollering out for me to stop, heavy footsteps pounding the street behind me and making me heart leap.

I cursed, ducking between two market stands and sprinting up a narrow alleyway that led towards the sea and away from the fountain where I needed to meet my boys.

The wind tangled my hair in ghostly fists as I ran on, my legs carrying me so fast that my surroundings sped past in a blur.

The guy yelled for me to stop again just as I made it to the end of the alley and I threw a look back over my shoulder, spotting him running up behind me, though the way he was panting already told me I had this in the bag.

I flashed him a big smile then threw myself to the left as I exited the alley, racing along the sidewalk before crossing the street and heading into another alley which curved further down the hill and back around to the right.

I took several twists and turns before ducking into a deep doorway, catching my breath in the shadows while listening to check if I'd lost him.

I gave it a couple of minutes to be sure then lifted the bag of burritos up to my face, inhaling the scent of victory with a low, hungry groan as my stomach rumbled with need. Mary Beth had banned me from breakfast again this morning in punishment for my continual sneaking out late at night, but she could eat a bag of dicks if she really thought she could stop me from spending all my time with my boys. They were my everything. And even her starvation punishments wouldn't see me cave to her dictatorship.

I ducked out of my hiding place and took off, my stomach knotting for a whole different reason as I broke into a run again, circling the throng of the market and heading to the far end of town where the fountain stood waiting for me.

I ran all the way there while the sun beat down on me, my legs burning and heart thundering as the thought of being last awoke the competitive little beast that lived inside me, making me grind my teeth together.

But as the fountain came into view up ahead and I only spotted two figures sitting on the low wall that ringed it, a laugh fell from me.

"Ah ha!" I cried as I ran straight up to Chase and JJ, holding my bag of burritos up while taking in the two giant slushies, bag of doughnuts, bottle of rum and net of oranges sitting on the floor in the shade beside them. "Wait…" I counted the number of prizes and whipped around just as Rick and Fox closed in on me from behind, grinning demonically.

"Looks like you lost, beautiful," Rick said menacingly, and I shrieked as I turned to run from them, finding the others on their feet behind me, caging me in already, their hands all grabbing me so that I couldn't escape.

"Hang on," I begged as Chase took the burritos from me and I reluctantly let go, knowing I had to save them from my fate even as I fought to try and come up with a way out of it. "You don't understand," I begged but there was no mercy – there was never any mercy.

Fox hauled me off of my feet and I screamed as I tried to fight him, the other three helping to restrain my thrashing arms and legs for all of five seconds before he tossed me straight into the icy water of the fountain. My screams turned to a torrent of bubbles while I sank like a wishing coin tossed to the bottom.

My ass hit the tiles and I shoved myself up to sit there, flicking water from my saturated hair and gasping as I glared at the four of them while they howled with laughter.

"You motherfuckers," I snapped as I scrambled to my feet, ringing water from my white shirt and stomping back over to them with my stomach growling loudly in a demand for burritos.

Their laughter fell away, the four of them suddenly staring at me in a way that set the hairs raising all over my body as the intensity of those looks pierced me through.

"What?" I demanded, noticing their gazes had fallen from my face. Looking down, I found my hard nipples now very much on show through the wet, transparent shirt. "Oh, fuck my life."

I crossed my arms over my chest angrily, scowling at all of them as they seemed to realise that they'd been staring.

JJ's cheeks stained bright red as Chase turned away, running a hand down the back of his neck and Rick muttered, "Jesus," while glancing across the square to the church standing there like the Messiah might appear to save us all from the mortifying reality of me having tits.

"Here." Fox tugged his own black wifebeater over his head and held it out to me as I ungraciously tried to clamber over the edge of the fountain while still covering my nipples.

A lot of people were looking at us now and my own blush rose up so furiously that I could only stare at the ground and wish for it to swallow me.

"Get changed, beautiful, or Ace is going to end up taking someone's eye out with that thing," Rick said.

"Oh, like you can fucking talk," Chase snapped back as the four of them moved to box me in and I snatched the shirt from Fox's fingers.

They all turned their backs on me, hiding me from the world and I quickly tugged my wet t-shirt off before pulling Fox's wifebeater on in its place, the scent of him enveloping me and the feeling of it dragging over my hardened nipples making my blush only rise even more.

"I hate all of you," I grumbled, flicking my wet hair out of the back of my new shirt, trying to wring some water from my denim shorts too before giving in to the inevitable afternoon of chafing that awaited me now.

"Will you still hate us if we let you take first pick of the haul?" JJ asked, his back very much to me though Rick wasn't anywhere near as gentlemanly, and I caught him trying to throw a glance over his shoulder.

"I'm done," I said firmly, letting them all break apart and turn to face me once more. I grabbed my sopping wet shirt from the ground and tossed it straight into Maverick's face. "That's for trying to steal a look, asshole."

"I can't help it if I want to see your-"

Fox punched him in the gut hard enough to send the air crashing from his lungs and Chase leapt on him too, the three of them falling into a fight instantly which no doubt scandalised the surrounding onlookers even more.

JJ sidestepped them as they fell to the ground, grabbing one of the slushies for me and handing it over before taking the lid from the rum and pouring a large measure into it.

"Better?" he asked, taking a long swig of the alcohol too while still avoiding my eye.

"I want a burrito," I muttered petulantly, leaning down to take a slurp of my drink and enjoying the burn of both the alcohol and ice as it raced down my throat.

"Done." JJ picked me one from the bag I'd stolen, then offered up a doughnut too. I accepted both, holding everything awkwardly and ripping into the burrito paper with my teeth before spitting it aside and taking a bite out of the real deal.

I moaned in appreciation, tipping my head back and forgetting my everlasting embarrassment in favour of enjoying my food.

"Did Fox steal the oranges?" I asked through a mouthful and JJ snorted. "You know he did."

"We should all be eating more fruit," Fox grunted defensively as he continued to roll about on the floor with Rick and Chase.

"So long as it comes after the booze, sugar and greasy take out, I'm all for it," I agreed, and Fox's huff of irritation only made me laugh. "Come on, assholes, I'm sick of standing around here making a show of ourselves. Can we just go be alone somewhere now?" I asked when their fight seemed like it was going to continue for a while yet.

"Yeah," Rick agreed, shoving Chase hard enough to put him on his ass before rearing up to his feet and grabbing the rum from JJ. "Let's go be alone."

I looked back at the huge man who had always understood that the only kind of alone that mattered was the one that included the five of us, and smiled as I led him past that same fountain, the quirk at the corner of his lips letting me know he was recalling the same memory.

"I jerked off over thoughts of you dripping wet in that see through shirt for months," he said boldly as he easily caught up to me with his longer stride. "Worth every punch Fox gave me for it and more."

"I still hate you," I said, the memory of how mortified I'd been that day rushing beneath my skin, even though he'd seen and done far more to my body since then.

"Yeah, but the hate sex makes it worth it, doesn't it, beautiful?" he slapped my ass, and I slapped his right back, the linen pants allowing me to get a good enough strike in to make me think he might have been left with a handprint.

Rick slipped a pair of sunglasses on to complete his disguise then dropped an arm around my waist, drawing me close to him as we rounded a corner and found ourselves on the outskirts of the marketplace.

We merged with the crowd, and I led the way to a stall selling fruit and vegetables, making a show of picking between things while Rick scanned the crowd around us for any sign of Shawn or his mom.

My skin tingled like ants were creeping all over my body, adrenaline trickling through me and hunting for an outlet that I couldn't give it.

"Ace is in the shadows by the street band," Maverick murmured as I selected a punnet of fat strawberries and handed over my cash like a nice, respectable woman, wondering if I had ever actually paid for anything from this market before now.

The man serving passed them to me along with my change and I plucked one from the punnet as we moved away from his stall, biting into it and moaning softly at the sweet taste before lifting it to Rick's lips so that he could have a bite too.

His lips grazed my thumb as he accepted the strawberry and I smiled up at him while the simplicity of our pretence made my chest lighten.

"You like this," he accused as we moved through the crowd.

"Like what?" I questioned innocently.

"Us. This. A couple out for the day being all…normal." The word both wrinkled his nose and made a smile hitch the corner of his lips, and I snorted.

"We can play at normal from time to time," I said. "There's no harm in that. It's not like it'll suddenly make me want to head home to our four bed, picket fence house and have vanilla sex for five minutes before going to sleep at a reasonable hour."

"That sounds like a very particular kind of hell," he agreed, taking a strawberry from the punnet, and lifting it to my lips for me. "Far better I take you back to our gang stronghold, tie you to my bed and take turns fucking you with the rest of our pack of heathens while we fight to see which one of us can wear you out first."

"Good luck with that," I said, licking red juice from my lips and enjoying

223

the way he watched me do it. "We should be focusing on the job at hand," I added.

"Just because you're panting all over me doesn't mean I've forgotten, beautiful. I just spotted Johnny James drinking an espresso over by that la-dee-da barista truck, pulling off the pretentious prick look like he was born to it."

I looked over to see for myself, amusement tugging at me as I found JJ wearing cargo shorts and loafers along with a flat cap that made him look like a total asshole and nothing like the man I knew right down to the fabric of his essence.

"I can't wait to get these clothes off of all of you," I muttered, my eyes sweeping the crowd again as Rick and I moved down the street and I pointed out a jeweller selling handmade items with carved wooden beads and cut-glass pendants.

I started examining the items with interest, giving Rick the opportunity to hunt the area once more, every second that passed without us spotting Shawn feeling like an impending doom slipping ever closer.

My phone pinged in my back pocket right as Rick's did and I glanced around at him as he pulled his out to check the message, his face lighting with the kind of demonic smile which could only mean one thing.

"Looks like Foxy picked up the scent," he murmured, making my heart leap with a mixture of excitement and anticipation. Something was going right at last. "Let's go."

He tugged on me but as I made a move to turn away from the stall we were at, I spotted a leather bracelet. It had five threads twisting all together with gold weaved through it and a little clasp with a skull on it. I instantly thought of Chase, unable to take my eyes from it even though we needed to get moving.

"Wait," I demanded, grabbing the bracelet from the display, and drawing the attention of the market trader who began to babble about what a beautiful piece it was and what fabulous taste I had.

"I'll take it," I interrupted her, dipping my fingers into Rick's pocket and taking a fifty from his wallet before he even noticed I was robbing him. I slipped the bracelet over my wrist, waving off her offers of a gift box and telling her to keep the change before turning away and letting Rick guide me back into the crowd.

"Where?" I demanded, my eyes scouring everyone that surrounded us.

"Just past the flower stall," he replied, picking up the pace as I tiptoed up to look over the heads of the crowd and hunt for the stall at the far end of the street. "And you owe Foxy boy fifty dollars now, beautiful."

"Fox?" I frowned.

"Yeah, I slipped that out of his wallet this morning." He boomed a laugh and I snorted. Asshole. Though I guessed I was an asshole too, so c'est la vie.

Movement caught my eye from my left, my instinctual bond with my boys making me turn to see Chase slipping through the crowd there, his phone to his ear as he pretended to speak to someone while moving faster than everyone around him and heading to where Fox had directed us.

His bright Hawaiian shirt and dark sunglasses worked alongside the topknot I'd managed to force his curls into to form his disguise, and though none of us were exactly unrecognisable, I was confident that we'd done enough to make it difficult for anyone to easily realise it was us.

Our phones went off again and this time I took Rick's from him to read the message Fox had sent.

Fox:

They're heading towards the next street over

I curled an arm around Maverick as we upped our speed, gritting my teeth as we were forced to keep our pace measured so that we didn't draw any attention, but the knowledge that we were so close had me on edge. My fingers brushed against the gun which was hidden beneath the fabric of his shirt, the knowledge of its presence settling me even as he wound his fingers through mine and drew them away from it.

"That's a last resort, baby girl," he reminded me. "I want to feel his bones crack beneath the force of my fists long before he gets any kind of mercy in the form of a bullet."

The mental image of that helped calm me a little, my fingers squeezing his as I nodded.

"I can't wait for him to see what true power is," I growled, turning us away from the crowd.

I spotted an alley we could use to cut across to the next road where there were more street vendors, artists and touristy stalls.

Bright sunlight shone in my eyes as we stepped out between a fish stall and a dairy stall. A long crowd of locals who were waiting to purchase fresh produce forcing us to slow as we made our way through them.

I noticed Fox to our left, the familiar prowl of his walk drawing my attention despite the wash-out black dye in his hair and the bright Green Power Ranger shirt I'd lent him. He was just lucky I'd bought it in a men's size so that I could curl up in it.

But just as thoughts of the GPR threatened to distract me from my goal, my eyes landed on a far less appealing sight and I fell still, stumbling as Rick continued to draw me along, holding onto him to keep my feet.

"There they are," I hissed, bobbing my chin towards a stall filled with inflatable pool toys that Shawn and his mom had just stepped around.

"Where?" Rick asked, but I was already moving again, towing him along as I hurried to catch up to the asshole who had taken so much from us, the need for vengeance burning through my limbs.

"Remember we just need to follow him," Fox's voice almost brought a scream to my ear as he snuck up behind us and I found him on my other side.

"You scared the shit out of me," I snapped, smacking his chest to tell him off while still hurrying on towards the place where I'd spotted our prey.

"You look like a woman on the hunt," he growled, keeping up easily. "But we can't just grab him in a marketplace full of witnesses with his mom looking on. We need to be smart about it, follow him, remember?"

"Yes, I remember," I growled as I tried to recall which of them had been tasked with leaving a vehicle towards this side of town. "Is Chase getting his bike?"

"Yeah," he replied. "If Shawn makes a break for it, we're ready."

I nodded, my focus going back to hunting the motherfucker again as we rounded the inflatables stall, finding ourselves surrounded by clothes stalls that wound away from us in three directions.

"Split up," I hissed.

"No fucking chance," Rick replied instantly, holding me tighter.

"We don't know which way he went," I snapped. "And if it's too crowded here for us to snatch him then he'll be facing the same problem with us. We need to find him so we can tell Chase where he needs to be, so stop treating me like I'm not just as capable as the rest of you motherfuckers and get on with the job."

I gave Maverick a shove to force him to release me, then took off up the righthand path between the clothes stalls without giving either of them the chance to argue.

I glared back over my shoulder at them as they hesitated and they were forced to give in to what needed doing, peeling away down the other routes that Shawn might have taken.

I slipped my hand into the pocket of the flowing dress I wore, palming the flick knife I'd stashed there and keeping my fingers wrapped around it just in case.

The street headed up the hill ahead of me and my thighs began to burn as I moved up it quickly, my hopes sinking as I glanced between the racks of clothes before spotting the long white sheets and towels hanging from the vendors stalls ahead of me.

Shawn could be right there, just beyond a single piece of fabric, or he could have taken a different path, following his mother's whims as she shopped.

My phone pinged and I took it out, looking at the message from Rick saying he'd seen them just as one came in from Chase who was moving his bike closer to their position.

I turned, meaning to head back to re-join Rick, but as I did, movement between the white sheets hanging to my left made me flinch aside.

Shawn lunged for me, his hand catching my wrist and yanking me towards him, the hanging sheets meaning that we were almost invisible to the surrounding market goers, but I knew I only had to scream to change that.

"Looking for me, sugarpie?" he leered, his eyes going over my shoulder as he checked around us for any sign of my boys coming to help me. But that was his mistake because I was no fucking damsel in distress.

I drew the flick knife from my pocket with my free hand, not bothering to engage with him for even a second, swiping it at him with a furious snarl.

Shawn cursed loudly as my blade swept across his forearm, forcing him to release me as his blood splattered the white sheets at our side.

"Bitch," he snarled.

"Better run, Shawn," I replied, holding the knife between us threateningly, making it clear that I didn't give a fuck if we were surrounded by witnesses or not. He looked off, his eyes a little sunken like sleep was evading him and the bandages peeking out between the open buttons at the top of his shirt told me he was still recovering from the bullet Travis had put in him. "The sharks are out hunting and now you've got blood in the water."

"You and I have a date with the Devil, pudding," he warned me, backing up a step and making me frown as he retreated just like that. "He'll come calling for ya real soon. Me and him have been making all kinds of plans, I had quite the epiphany just today about what I'll be doing with you when you're mine again. It's gonna be worth the wait, sugarpie, I promise you that."

He ripped a sheet from the stand beside me, hurling it in my face as he turned and shoved his way out between more sheets hanging at his back, escaping while I was forced to stow my bloody blade away as I was revealed to the people behind me.

I quickly dialled the group as I took off after him, losing myself in a world of white cotton before bursting out on the other side of it.

"He's here," I said as the call connected, both Fox and Chase on the line while it still waited on the others. "Heading up the hill towards Banyan Street."

"Did he see you?" Chase demanded, the roar of his bike letting me know I was talking to him via the headset in his helmet.

"Yes," I growled, pissed at myself for allowing that to happen.

"Did he touch you?" Fox barked.

"He grabbed me, but I cut him then he just took off," I said, confused as fuck by that. "I'm following but I can't- wait, no I can see him, he's still heading towards Banyan, he has his mom with him now."

"Stay back," Fox growled. "Chase has this from here, he needs to think he's lost you."

"I need to be sure he's still going that way," I argued, pushing between the throng of bodies as I fought the urge to break into a sprint.

Rick joined the call before anyone else could reply, his gravelly tone rumbling through the speaker. "Fuck, I was wrong, it wasn't him, I-"

"Rogue found him," Fox interrupted. "She's chasing him towards Banyan Street even though I told her to stop."

"We can't just let him get away, Fox," I snarled, pushing between a pair of tourists who shouted at me angrily.

I gave up on any attempt at subtlety and broke into a run.

"I'm coming up that way now. I've got her," Rick said like I wasn't even involved in the conversation, and he hung up before I could call him out on his macho bullshit.

"I'm closing in on Banyan," Chase said over the sound of his bike engine. "If he gets in a car, I'm ready to follow."

"Leave it to him from here, Rogue," Fox demanded, the harsh breaths escaping his lungs letting me know that he was running now too, most likely coming after me.

"I know the plan," I snapped, fisting the skirt of my dress as my feet caught in the long material, trying to keep sight of Shawn through the thick crowd, but he'd ducked behind a pet food stall, and I couldn't see him or his mom anymore.

I pushed between more people, making it to the stall and whirling around as I failed to spot him.

"What's going on?" JJ's voice finally joined the call, and I ignored their back and forth as Chase explained what he could.

"I don't know if he's still heading to Banyan," I interrupted them. "I can't see him now and he might have headed towards Fenway instead."

"My car is parked on Fenway, I can be there in two minutes," JJ said, referring to the unremarkable sedan he'd brought for this purpose.

"Should I head that way too?" Chase asked, but I didn't know what to say, my head whipping back and forth as I tried to hunt for any sign of the slippery motherfucker.

"I don't know," I admitted, anger at myself over losing him colouring my words as I continued to look all around us for some sign of the man we were hunting.

I spotted a huge form running up the road towards me, a mixture of irritation and relief filling me as my gaze met Rick's but before he even got close, Fox barrelled into me, damn near sweeping me off my feet as he practically carried me to the side of the street where we'd have more cover.

"Where did he go?" he demanded and I didn't even have the energy to spare for irritation with him as I just shook my head hopelessly, searching the heaving crowd for any sign of him.

"I'm at the car but I can't see anything," JJ said, and my grip on the phone grew tight enough to bruise my fingers.

"I've got nothing either," Chase agreed, and I swore loudly.

"He's going to get away," I said bitterly.

"It's not over yet," Rick disagreed as he reached us, lifting his arm to point up the hill towards the far end of the market and my breath caught as I finally spotted Shawn and his mother.

"Come on," I snarled, taking off instantly and barking orders at Chase and JJ to head for Terrance Street.

It was just a dead-end road that no one really made use of, and Shawn clearly didn't realise we were about to have him cornered. A surge of triumph swooped through my chest as I pushed myself on, vengeance humming through me as I thought of finally watching Shawn die, of making him hurt and scream for everything he'd done to me and my boys.

We pressed on, Fox and Maverick having no choice but to let me go or keep up with me as I gripped the knife in my pocket so tightly it was leaving an imprint on my palm.

Shawn threw a glance back our way, whooping excitedly as he realised how many people were still blocking us from him, making it impossible for us to make any kind of strike at him.

"Fuck him," I hissed.

"He's running straight into a trap, hummingbird, Chase and JJ are ready," Fox reminded me, and I nodded, though I didn't slow down.

"I'm waiting right by Terrence Street," Chase confirmed over the phone.

"And I'll be there in thirty seconds too," JJ agreed.

I nodded, losing sight of Shawn as he hauled his mom behind a line of market stands and disappeared out of sight.

"Where is he?" I snarled as I ran up the hill, sweat rolling down my spine.

"We've got this, pretty girl," JJ promised but it was hard for me to believe that.

231

"Trust them," Fox urged but I didn't slow.

"I do trust them. It's fucking Shawn I don't trust."

They couldn't argue with that, so they just kept pace with me instead, the three of us sprinting up the hill while hunting left and right for signs of the asshole who was fleeing from us.

I glanced towards the direction Shawn had just been and cursed as I spotted him dragging his mom into a black SUV, his gaze meeting mine in a malicious grin that promised this wasn't over.

"He's getting into a car on Blackthorn Street," I gasped into the phone, which was still clutched to my ear, knowing that meant JJ would have to turn around and Chase would have to double back on himself.

"I can't wait to rip his face off and feed it to Mutt," Rick snarled as he put on a burst of speed, overtaking me as he ran for the car.

Fox swore, charging after him too, unable to resist the competition with Rick the moment it presented itself. And now he was pretty much healed from his injuries, he was able to go full badger again.

"I'm coming, little one, he won't get away," Chase said through the phone, and I could hear his bike now, the engine growling as it hurtled this way, ready to take chase.

"Me too, I'm right behind you, Ace," JJ agreed, and I tried to take comfort from that, but I knew I wouldn't feel any better until I knew for a fact that we had Shawn in our grasp and this thing was done at last.

Rick and Fox closed in on the SUV but the engine roared before they could reach it and it tore away from them, Shawn's excited whoop calling back from the open window as he went.

I refused to let my hope fade though, my eyes landing on a motorbike parked up in an alley to our left, a black helmet hanging from the handlebars, just begging me to take it.

"I'm coming with you, Ace," I said as I turned for the bike, hearing the roar of his engine approaching the end of the road we were still running down.

"Pick me up."

"Don't you fucking dare," Fox barked, his head jerking to me, his green eyes flashing with fury. "You are not getting on the back of a fucking motorbike while it chases down that motherfucker."

"Not your call to make," I snapped, grabbing the helmet from the parked bike and shoving it onto my head as I dropped my phone back into my pocket.

Fox yelled my name as he turned and started running for me instead, but Chase skidded to a halt in front of me before either he or Maverick could get close.

"Come on, little one, we have some vengeance to dole out," Chase growled as he spotted them too.

I was already leaping onto the back of the bike, my thighs hugging his and my arms coiled around his waist, so there was no chance of them stopping me unless he refused to drive.

"Are you ready to watch him bleed?" I asked excitedly while Fox bellowed another command for me to get off the bike and the black SUV sped further away from us down the street, making Chase hesitate, but he knew as well as I did that we were owed this vengeance, and not even the commands of the great Fox Harlequin would rob us of it. "Shawn is going to get away if we waste any more time."

"Then let's make sure he doesn't." Chase exchanged a heated look with me, our need for revenge burning hot between us before he whirled around and I tightened my hold on him. He revved the engine and we shot away at speed, my stomach lurching as the powerful bike sped down the road.

I twisted in my seat to see Fox bellowing my name in fury while Rick turned towards the car that Johnny James had just pulled up in. The two of them leapt in with him, Fox ending up in the back and I turned my attention to the road as Chase pushed the bike to its limits, tearing after the man who had hurt both of us so much.

The roads were busy with traffic and Shawn had managed to get ahead of us in it, but the bike zigzagged between cars, trucks and buses with ease – even if my heart did threaten to leap right out of my throat more than once at the tightness of the gaps we sped through.

But Chase had the same need in him as I did, the same desperate urge to spill the blood of our enemy and make him pay for all he'd done to us, and I trusted him implicitly as he pushed the bike to its limits.

I needed to watch the light fade from Shawn Mackenzie's eyes, watch him pass from this place in misery and agony, and know without a shadow of a doubt that he would never again darken my door or my thoughts with the cloying thickness of his presence.

JJ couldn't keep up in his car and I soon lost sight of them behind me, focusing on the asshole ahead of us instead and the need in me to see him bleed.

Shawn turned out of the town, heading towards the mountains and away from the coast while I clung to Chase and felt the heavy pounding of his heart beneath my hand with every inch we gained on him.

The roads began to empty out as we sped further inland, giving Chase the opportunity to really let the throttle loose and we shot after our quarry with the intense relief of knowing that we had him now.

"Hold on tight, little one!" Chase yelled over the snarl of the engine, and I latched my arms around him, adrenaline coursing through me as the wind whipped at the thin fabric of my blue dress and the long strands of the red wig I wore beneath the helmet.

A truck shot past us on the other side of the road, leaving the way clear ahead as Chase turned us and tugged the throttle back, sending us shooting up the outside of the traffic, overtaking the cars separating us from Shawn one after another, the colours of them blurring together until all I could see was the black SUV.

Shawn yanked the car around just as we closed in on him, turning off the main road and onto a mostly dirt road that headed into the trees and disappeared among them.

I screamed as Chase took the hairpin turn at speed, the bike leaning wildly, my fingers digging into his chest as the back wheel skidded out.

I closed my eyes, expecting a wipe out, but I should have known better than that. Chase barked a laugh as the bike righted itself again, the engine bellowing loudly as we took off down the dirt road too, refusing to let Shawn go.

Dust billowed up around us, making me cough and blocking our view of the black SUV as we pursued them, and Chase swore as the bike struggled with the uneven terrain, its wheels unsuited to it, causing the back end to slide out more than he wanted as we took corners at speed.

We kept going all the same, chasing the cloud of dust ahead of us and squinting into it as we tore on, Shawn's wheels kicking it up so thickly that my eyes stung, and my throat burned with the taste of it.

The trail turned a sharp corner ahead, a spray of gravel joining the dust as Shawn took it fast, and I flinched against the assault of the tiny missiles as they bounced off of my exposed skin, drawing sharp lines of blood and leaving fresh bruises.

Chase coughed as he followed, taking his gun from his belt and firing wildly into the plume of dust, but before he could even get the third shot off, a shadow loomed in the dust cloud in front of us and a scream ripped my throat raw as I spotted the car there, stopped right in the middle of the dirt road, a trap waiting to end us.

Chase jerked the bike aside as death flashed before my eyes, the crash seeming inevitable, the pain of us colliding with the back of the car brushing against my skin before it had even happened.

But by some miracle, it didn't. The bike skidded on the dirt, more of it sweeping up all around us as we lurched aside and instead of colliding with it, we spun out and hit the ground.

I was launched from the bike at speed, tumbling across the dirt and stones into the trees beside the dirt road and rolling down a small hill before landing hard on my back, gasping like a fish out of water as I fought to catch my breath.

Pain radiated through my body, but it only took me a couple of seconds to realise it was nothing life threatening, merely the memory left in place by every stone, root and bump I'd just tumbled across when I fell, the helmet saving me from any headwounds.

I rolled onto my hands and knees just as Chase started shooting from behind a tree to my left, my eyes meeting his as he beckoned me to him. There was blood running down his shoulder, staining his shirt around a visible tear in the material, but the cut didn't appear to be too deep.

"Today ain't the day, sugarpie," Shawn called, his mom's shrieks of fear coming from somewhere a little further away.

I risked a glance around the edge of the tree I was using for cover to search for him, but I couldn't see anything beyond the cloud of slowly settling dust.

"We'll put a pin in this reunion for a day when I am feeling more myself. But don't you worry – I've got all kinds of fun planned for you when the time is right!" Shawn shouted.

Two shots rang out in quick succession, and I lurched back behind the cover of the tree, Chase's hand finding mine as our eyes met as we looked at each other through the visors of our helmets.

I could tell what he was thinking by the way his grip tightened around mine and how he lifted his gun with intent. I held on tighter, shaking my head.

"Wait," I hissed, knowing that Shawn had to be up to something and fearing what would happen if we risked breaking cover for even a moment.

But before I could second guess what the motherfucker had planned any more than I already was, the sound of a car door closing called out to us, quickly followed by the rev of an engine before the black SUV took off up the dirt road and raced away.

I sucked in a breath, the two of us peeking out to confirm what we already knew, climbing to our feet slowly as we risked approaching the road once more.

There was nothing there as we climbed up onto the dirt road, only Chase's bike lying in the dirt, both tyres shot out and hanging limply from the wheels, making it clear that we wouldn't be using that to get out of here, let alone to continue our hunt.

"Fuck," I cursed, tearing my helmet off and hurling it into the trees in frustration as the sound of the SUV's engine disappeared into the distance.

Chase tossed his helmet aside too, letting it thump to the floor and roll away before he caught my face between his hands and kissed me hard, demanding all of my attention.

His touch helped drag me away from my furious disappointment in having come so close to ending this, only to have it all torn away so fast.

"That was our only lead," I said, my voice hitching as our failure threatened me with tears that I blinked back furiously. I wouldn't cry for Shawn Mackenzie. Not ever.

"Doesn't matter," Chase said roughly. "None of it matters but this." He kissed me again and this time I gave in to it fully, fisting my hand in his now filthy Hawaiian shirt while he knotted his fingers in the red wig and tugged it off me.

My own personal rainbow fell down around us, the strands tangled and sweaty, but Chase didn't seem to mind that at all as he pushed his fingers through them and kissed me deeper.

There was an entire ocean in that kiss, one tainted with the pollution of all that we'd survived to get to this point, while still brimming with life and hope and beauty at the same time. His tongue was a tide that crashed against mine, the power of us brutal and unstoppable, endless, and merciless.

"I love you, Chase Cohen," I murmured into his mouth, wanting him to taste the words on my lips and feel the truth of them as he devoured every one of them.

My hand trailed up his cheek, caressing the scars he bore in payment for loving me in return. The darkness in me grew deeper, the need to reset the scale and end this torment driving down into my veins and beyond.

"I don't deserve your love," he breathed out, though the way he clung to me made it clear he wasn't giving it up either. "But I will. I'll earn it every day that I have left to me and make myself worthy if it's the last thing I do."

"Stop," I protested, hating when he talked about himself like he held less worth than he did, but he only shook his head.

"The Last Time by Taylor Swift and Gary Lightbody," he said, moving his mouth to my ear and making me shiver as the lyrics of the song rose from my memory and made my entire body shiver with pleasure. "And I love you too."

CHAPTER FIFTEEN

"Hurry up, JJ!" I barked as he drove down the dirt road, the car bumping and jostling furiously over every ditch and hump in the road.

"I'm going as fast as I can," JJ snarled.

"Miss Mabel could drive faster than this," Maverick hissed at him from the passenger seat, his arm hanging out the window with his gun primed to shoot.

"Fuck you." JJ pressed down on the accelerator even more, throwing us back in our seats and I braced myself on the back of his chair as I hunted the dirt road for any sign of Rogue and Chase.

My heart was beating out a frantic tune in my chest, thrashing against my ribcage in an effort to break free and get to the two people it so desperately needed to see were okay.

The car swung around a sharp bend and dust kicked up all around us as my gaze landed on Chase and Rogue half tearing each other's clothes off as they kissed with all the fiery passion of the sun.

My heart lifted at seeing them unharmed and I threw the door open as JJ slammed on the brakes and we spilled out of the car, racing toward them, praying I'd see Shawn's lifeless body laying beyond them. But all I saw was Chase's bike on the ground with flat tyres.

Chase and Rogue were ignoring the fact that we'd arrived as he pushed her off the dirt road and pinned her against a tree.

"Chase," she moaned, her hand sliding between them, grasping at his cock and making him groan deeply in response.

Maverick's shoulder met mine on my left and JJ's brushed against me on my right as they joined me, and I realised I'd come to a dead halt, my gaze locked on the way Chase was touching her, the way she arched so perfectly against him as he hitched her dress up around her bronze thighs.

"Enjoying the show, Foxy boy?" Rick muttered to me in a mocking tone and my upper lip peeled back in a snarl, but I still didn't move, my eyes riveted to Rogue's movements as Chase held her at his mercy and started unbuttoning his fly.

"Are we gonna just stand here then?" JJ murmured, looking to me for direction.

My lips twitched and I snapped out of my frozen state, clearing my throat and marching straight towards them again.

"What's happening? Where the fuck is Shawn?" I asked, though it didn't come out in anger like I'd initially expected it to.

Seeing them kiss like that, lost within a trance of one another had reminded me of the wounds they shared, some dark and sacred thing they were both caught in the grasp of. And it fucking killed me knowing the piece of shit that had laid those scars on them was still walking this earth.

Rogue's head snapped around and Chase buried his face in her neck with a groan of disappointment.

"Five more minutes," Chase begged. "Go for a walk or something."

"Ten more." Rogue thumped him on the arm, her cheeks flushed with colour as he laughed into her flesh.

"How about you carry her to the car, and we take her somewhere we can all play this game?" Rick suggested and my hands balled into fists at the thought of them all disappearing off without me somewhere.

"Shawn?" I pushed and Rogue untangled her legs from Chase, giving in to the inevitable as he let her go too and rearranged the huge bulge in his pants with a look of aggravation crossing his features.

She started walking towards us, but he kept hold of her hand, keeping her close like a wolf guarding its kill. Though as I looked between them and noted the strength in Rogue's eyes, I realised it was more like a wolf guarding its mate.

"He ran off," Rogue sighed. "He said something about not being ready for me yet."

"He's still injured," JJ said with a note of satisfaction in his voice over that.

"Good," Rick grunted. "But he ain't injured enough for my liking. Which way did he go?"

He looked further down the dirt road that split off in two directions, his muscles flexing with the need for blood.

"He's long gone," Chase sighed. "These dirt roads run all over the forest out here for miles and let out onto roads all over the place."

I nodded, knowing he was right. He used to practise driving up here a lot, and we'd had a few dirt races against the local kids here too. It was a maze of trees and farmland, and wherever Shawn was going, we had no chance of predicting it.

"He didn't run just because he's injured," Rogue said, moving between all of us, her eyes skimming across us one after another like she was reassuring herself we were all okay. "He's got something planned. He wouldn't have just given up an opportunity like that so easily. I don't like this."

"None of us like any of this and we won't until he's dead and buried,"

Chase agreed, and unease settled over us as we all gave that some thought, wondering what the hell Shawn could be planning that would make him give up an opportunity to get his hands on Rogue like that. Not to mention the questions that raised about why he'd sent someone after her if he didn't even want her yet. Fuck knew what he was up to, but it couldn't be anything good.

My gaze fell on a bruise rising along Rogue's arm and I frowned as I shifted forward, gently tracing my hand down it. "Are you hurt?" I asked, my fingers finding another fresh bruise on her shoulder.

"I'm good," she said, goosebumps following the line of my touch as I checked her over.

I pulled her into my arms, kissing her forehead and breathing a sigh of relief at knowing she was okay.

"Are you about to go full badger?" she asked into my shirt.

"I dunno, what's me going 'full badger' look like?" I asked dryly and the others chuckled at me.

"You're gonna lecture me and Chase on safe behaviour, then you're gonna send us all home and bark orders at us to never run off on our own again," she sighed like she was already exhausted by what she expected of me, and that admittedly hurt. Especially as it was exactly what I would have done in the past, but Rogue clearly hadn't gotten the message that I'd changed. Or at least, I was trying my damn hardest to.

I slipped my hand under chin, tilting her head back so she could see the honesty in my eyes as I spoke my next words. "I'm never going to control any of you again. Yeah, it fucking terrifies me when you do crazy shit like disappear off on the back of a motorbike in pursuit of a goddamn psychopath, and I'm always gonna try and protect you whenever I can. But I'm trying my best to let you all make your own decisions, because trying to force my will over you all made me almost lose every single one of you." I looked to the others, finding them drawing closer, and even Rick stopped smirking as he met my eye.

"I've had a taste of the world without you as a part of it, and let me tell you, it's fucking bleak. I know I had the right balance once, back when we were kids, and I'm trying to rebuild that. Is that…the Fox you want?" I asked.

Rogue's bright blue eyes blazed at me like a summer sea, and I loved her so fiercely in that moment that I could feel it buzzing through my flesh.

"Is that the Fox you want to be?" she whispered, reaching up to brush her fingers through my dyed black hair where it had fallen forward to shadow my eyes.

I nodded, a lump rising in my throat as I stared at this beautiful creature before me. "More than anything."

"I love all versions of you. Even the badgeriest of badgers," she said with a grin lifting her mouth. "And I know how hard you're trying to make this all work, even if it doesn't fit the fantasy you had of us once. But I don't want it to mean you're in pain, Fox." Her brow creased as she rested her hand over my heart, her smile faltering. "Does it hurt to see me with the others?"

I felt all of their eyes on me, the weight of that question hanging between us. Then the sound of car approaching made us turn and my heart jolted as a cop car appeared, rolling along the dirt road towards us.

"Follow my lead," I muttered as I slipped my hand around Rogue's and the cop got out of the car.

She was a short woman, but had a stocky kind of build and a look in her eye that said she was more than capable of taking us all on single handed. "Everything alright down here? There's been reports of illegal racing."

"No racing here, ma'am," I said politely. "My friend's tyres were blown out by some sharp rocks, so we came here to pick him up." I pointed to the bike and the cop narrowed her gaze.

"Uh-huh, and how do you plan on removing that bike from here, sir?"

"We were just trying to figure that out, ma'am," I said smoothly.

Her gaze travelled over us, and she nodded slowly. "I see. And whose bike is it?"

"Mine, ma'am," Chase said. "I was just taking a shortcut through to the road."

"Mmmhmmm," she hummed like she didn't believe him one bit. "Do you know this is private land, sir?"

"Yeah, it's Rafe Gunder's land," Chase said smoothly, and I looked to him surprise. "He's a friend of mine. I'll call him, if you like?"

"You know Rafe?" she asked, her eyebrows arching.

"Yeah, and his wife Sobrene who own that big old farm out here. They were real good to me after the accident," Chase said and JJ gave him a sympathetic look, playing along even though we had no idea where this story was going.

"The accident, sir?" the cop asked.

"Yeah...it was a long time ago. I used to play out in their crop fields, but I was such a small kid, and I guess they didn't see me that day." He took a shuddering breath.

"What day?" the cop pressed, clearly sucked in by the promise of his story.

"Rafe was driving the combine harvester when I got tangled up in it." Chase lifted his shirt, gesturing to his scars, then his eye and the cop gasped in horror while I bit back a laugh. "I was real cut up, and I couldn't get out of the mechanism. I can still remember the smell of all that grain." Chase held a hand to his throat as he shook his head. "I can't eat oatmeal to this day."

"That's terrible," the cop breathed, resting a hand to her heart as the rest of us worked hard not to crack up.

"Yeah, but Rafe and Sobrene were so nice to me after. They paid all my hospital bills, and said I could come onto their land whenever I liked. Only..." He dropped his gaze to the ground and shuffled his feet back and forth.

"What is it, sir?" the cop asked gently, and he lifted his head, a tight frown pinching his features.

"They don't like to be reminded of what happened that day. It's the guilt, you see? So, I don't visit them anymore, but I think they like knowing I come and go across their tracks sometimes. I think it soothes some of those bad memories, but whenever they hear my name, they shudder. So, you won't have to tell them I was here, will you? They'd be all kinds of upset if they heard I had a crash, that I got hurt again on their land. I'm not sure poor old Sobrene's heart could take it."

The cop hesitated before nodding and holy fuck, Chase Cohen was just as good at this as he had been when we were kids. "Of course not. And if it's any comfort to you, they're planning on selling this land anyways. You all head along now. And I'll tell you what, my boy has a truck and he lives not five minutes from here. If you give me the address of where you want the bike taken, I'll be sure he moves it there for you."

"Really? You'd do that for me?" Chase asked, giving her the puppy dog eyes and combined with his scars, his pretty face and his sob story, she melted for him right there and then.

"Yes, sir, just write the address down here for me." She took a notepad from her pocket and he walked forward to take it, writing down what was no doubt one of the Harlequin's addresses, or possibly the workshop where my truck had been fixed up.

"Alright then, you'd best get along," the cop said, taking her notepad back from Chase and he smiled at her before beckoning us after him toward the car.

We all piled in and the moment we were on the road with JJ driving us back in the direction we'd come, we burst out laughing.

Rogue clambered into Chase's lap, kissing him and cupping his face in her hands beside me in the back of the car.

"Do you wanna get tangled up in my combine harvester, Ace?" she joked, and I laughed. But then he bit down on her lip, sucking it into his mouth before they started kissing like animals and I cursed as they butted up against me. Rogue met my gaze as I watched them, my throat thickening as his hands squeezed her ass and she ground down over his lap.

She broke the kiss, giving me an apologetic look before slipping back into the seat between us and I felt like an asshole for being the one setting boundaries.

"Kiss him if you wanna kiss him," I muttered.

"It's okay," Rogue said, patting my knee and I kinda hated that, feeling like I was being pitied for not being able to handle seeing her with the others.

"It's fine," I pressed, but she shook her head.

"I made you a promise," she said.

Maverick met my gaze in the rear-view mirror, mirth lighting his eyes.

"What?" I snapped at him, feeling his eyes driving right under my flesh and trying to dig out some truth that wasn't there.

"Nothing, Foxy boy," he said lightly. "You just seem awful insistent for her to continue."

"I don't wanna cage her," I said irritably.

"Yeah, sure. That's what it is," Maverick said tauntingly like he knew better.

Rogue was distracted as Chase whispering something no-doubt filthy in her ear, his fingers sailing higher over her thigh on top of her dress.

"When we get back," she murmured in response, gripping his hand to stop him, though they shared a dirty look that was a promise of what was to come, and I shifted a little further away from them, hating that I felt like I was suddenly on the outside of the group again.

But I guessed that was how it was always going to be, considering the rules I'd set for this relationship. Though as Rick mouthed the word *vanilla* in the mirror, my muscles tensed with the challenge that sparked in me, and I pushed it back down as hard as I could, my hands fisting on my knees.

I wasn't fucking vanilla just because I didn't wanna have an orgy with my best friends and the girl I loved. Now I was healed, the next time I got

248

Rogue to myself, I was going to damn well prove how un-vanilla I was when it came to fucking. And there didn't need to be a second, third or fourth cock in sight for that to be true.

I'd spent most of the day at the Oasis Club House with Dad making plans against Shawn while he tried to convince me to re-join the Harlequins. He was like a dog with a bone, but I'd told him straight I wasn't going back to that life. Although, when I was absorbed by planning, surrounded by men who listened to every word I spoke and followed my orders without question, I had to admit that it did feed into my need for control in the world. But that was my problem, wasn't it? And if I leaned into it for too long, maybe it would corrupt me all over again, make me want to exert that same power over my friends and ruin everything.

That thought quickly quieted any niggling desires I had about returning to my old position. Yeah, it was tempting, especially because I was getting an idea of what life could have been like ruling beside my brother now. Maverick slotted into the role of the intimidating leader as easily as breathing, and the two of us had found a balance with giving orders, intuitively allowing the other room to take charge as well. He still had the Damned Men doing his bidding, and made them cooperate with the Harlequins despite their confusion over our renewed alliance, but in true Rick fashion he didn't give a damn about explaining anything to them.

We were born for this, born to rule together, to stand at each other's sides and be kings of the world. But I had a far more important world to protect now which was made up entirely of the people I loved, and I wasn't going to allow the Harlequin Crew to come between me and them again. Not ever.

I rode in Dad's truck beside Rick, the three of us perfectly content in each other's company, all of us falling back into old routines, yet building new ones too. We were a family again, one that had taken all the good pieces of our past and used them as a foundation to build something even better, and perhaps even stronger too. It was hard to marry this version of Rick with the one who had hated me and Luther so viscerally, and I guessed I could say the same of myself. The storm cloud that had rained down acidic hatred on us for so many years, stealing all sunlight from our lives had finally passed on, and I was starting to believe it wasn't coming back.

I was looking forward to getting home, and damn glad that no one had realised what day it was because I hated celebrating my birthday. It hadn't always been that way, but since Rogue had left all those years ago, it had become a marker of another year passing by without her. Sure, she was back now, but I couldn't shift the anxiety that had been ingrained in me over this day. The memories of me drinking myself into a coma or seeking out a girl who looked vaguely like her to bury myself in for the night. It had all been made worse by the good memories I'd had of my birthday as a kid, playing on the beach with my friends or causing chaos out on the streets of Sunset Cove. I remembered the cakes made out of sand and the little sticks Rogue would place in the top of them before Maverick lit them up and the group of them chanted my name until I blew them out.

One year, Maverick had dipped the tips of those sticks in gasoline, and I'd nearly lost my fucking eyebrows when he'd lit them up while I was leaning over them, ready to make a wish. My wishes back then had always consisted of the same thing, wishes that we'd always stay together, and wishes of her. Of having her love me the way I loved her.

Years later, with blood on my hands and my soul firmly in the hands of the Devil, I'd finally had all of those wishes come true. Just not in the way I'd once imagined it.

It was why I'd been holding back with Rogue since the first time we'd claimed each other, and though she'd invited me close to her body plenty of times since, I'd always felt the presence of the others there like an unspoken thing. I didn't know how to do this in the way I was being asked to do it. I wanted to learn, I just didn't know how. But tonight, I was going to steal her away for myself and let out this pent-up energy because I was going mad thinking about having her again. And now I was healed, there was no reason for me to hold back.

As we pulled into Harlequin House where the sunset painted the sky in deepest pink, anticipation rushed through me over seeing Rogue.

JJ and Chase said they'd be out at the club tonight and Rick was heading on with Luther to go pick up a shipment of guns from the dock. That left me and Rogue alone after Mabel got her usual early night, and I was dying to have her to myself at last.

Maverick started chuckling to himself as Dad pulled up by the front door to let me out and I looked to him with a frown, especially when Dad cracked out a laugh too.

"What's so funny?" I asked.

"You," Maverick sniggered.

"What about me?" I looked between them in confusion as they continued to laugh.

"You thinking we forgot your birthday," Rick said, flipping his arm over and showing me the tattoo woven into the beautiful ink there, and I couldn't believe I'd never noticed it before. A fox was running between two trees and a date was inked subtly into the bark of the one on the left of it. My birthday.

"Fuck, when did you get that?" I asked.

"Well, I planned on marking your death date on the other tree," Rick said with a dark laugh and Dad tutted disapprovingly, making me look to him.

"When have I ever forgotten your birthday?" Dad asked with a smile, reaching out to scruff my hair and I just let him, kinda liking it.

"Nothing over the top, right?" I asked uncertainly, my hopes of having Rogue alone fading before my eyes.

Maverick just boomed a laugh and got out of the truck while Dad darted after him and beckoned me to follow them.

Great. This didn't bode well.

I took in a breath and focused on the positives. At least I'd spend the night with my family, and I wouldn't be drowning myself in the most toxic alcohol I could find to try and forget Rogue. No, she was here for this one. Finally. And that made me feel a whole lot better about it.

I slipped out of Dad's truck, heading after them through the front door and a bang made me draw my gun, adrenaline bursting through my veins before I realised confetti was tumbling down over me from a party popper.

"Surprise!" JJ cried, colliding with me, and wrapping his legs around me too so that his whole weight was hanging from my neck and my back slammed into the door behind me.

"Fucking hell," I half laughed, half snapped.

"Did you almost shoot me in the face?" JJ gasped as he dropped down, noticing the gun in my hand, and shaking his head at me.

I didn't have time to answer that as Rogue ducked under his arm, squealing her excitement, and shoving a cupcake into my mouth.

"Happy birthday, badger!" she cried while I choked on lemon icing – my favourite – and before I could get mad, she dropped the cake and started kissing me, devouring the icing and my mouth along with it.

I groaned, having missed her all day and I hoisted her up by the ass, sinking my tongue between her lips while a little dog bit my ankle and barked at me in fury. Though he quickly became distracted as he realised there was an abandoned cupcake on the floor and he dove on it possessively, growling like he expected us all to try and take it from him.

"How comes I didn't get that treatment?" JJ muttered and Chase laughed somewhere close by, but I couldn't stop tasting my hummingbird and the way she was pulling at my hair made me want to walk her straight upstairs and steal that alone time I was craving with her.

But it wasn't to be as she finally broke the kiss and wriggled her way out of my arms, picking up Mutt and placing him in my hands instead as he swallowed the last of his cake. I took in the tiny rainbow sequin dress Rogue was wearing with my cock throbbing, her ass almost peeking out of it and her high heels making her calves look so fucking good, I wanted to lick every inch of them. Her makeup was darker than usual, her eyes smoky, giving her a sultry look that I knew I was going to obsess over all night.

Luther and Maverick had disappeared, but Chase and JJ were clearly already in full party mode, the two of them dressed in nice shirts and shorts.

"We got you a gift," Chase announced as I was herded down the hall while Mutt licked the last of the icing off of me.

We reached the kitchen and Rogue leapt in front of the island, waving her hands around the gift on top of it dramatically. Holy shit, it was a giant inflatable badger fit for the pool.

"Where the hell did you get that?" I balked.

"Custom made," Rogue said, taking Mutt from my arms. "Now go get changed, everyone's gonna be here in five minutes."

My heart sank like it had struck an iceberg. "People?"

"Yes, people," JJ laughed. "Go get ready, man." He shoved me and I sighed, wishing it could have just been us for the night, but no. I was going to have to be…sociable. Shudder.

I headed upstairs, finding Luther in my room trying on one of my blue shirts. "This one's better than the one I had on. Can I borrow it?"

"You looked just fine in that one." I gestured to the black one he'd left on the bed with a shrug.

"That one's less fitted," he muttered.

"So?" I pulled off my own shirt, tossing it into the laundry basket before stepping into my closet to grab something else. When I was changed into a pair of jeans and a dark red shirt, I headed into the bathroom to fix my hair. But by the time I returned to the room, Luther had changed into another one of my shirts. This time, a white one.

He'd rolled the sleeves back to reveal the ink on his forearms and was working to flatten a stubborn strand of hair that continued to stick upwards every time he tried to keep it down.

"Fucking stay down, you motherfucking piece of shit," he was growling under his breath, and I gave him a confused look.

"Since when do you give a fuck about the way your hair looks?" I asked as he grabbed a comb and started fixing his beard. What the fuck was going on?

"It's your birthday. And it's a big one too."

"I'm twenty-seven, how is that a big one?" I asked, scratching the back of my neck as I moved toward the door.

"Just go to the party," he demanded, and I raised my hands in surrender, laughing as I slipped out the door.

Music carried from downstairs, and the sound of new voices joined those of my family.

Maverick stepped out of Rogue's room across the hall in a dark green shirt and jeans, his hair pushed back from his eyes and ink crawling out from a couple of loose buttons at his throat.

"Happy birthday. I got you something," he said, reaching into his back pocket.

My eyebrows raised and I moved closer.

He brought his fist up towards me, closed around something but as I reached out for it, he slammed his knuckles into my gut, making me wheeze and buckle forward.

"Motherfucker," I rasped as he laughed loudly and slapped me on the back.

I took a swing at him as I righted myself, but he ran away down the stairs, still laughing as he went, and I released a breath of amusement as I followed him. A punch like that from Rick was always code for I love you, still made him an asshole though.

I headed out onto the patio where the lights were low and That's What I Want by Lil Nas X filled the air. Rogue's friends from the trailer park had arrived alongside the dancers from JJ's club and a bunch of other people he worked with. They were already doing shots and my eyebrows raised as JJ jumped up on a table with Rogue, swept her into his arms and twisted her upside down while Lyla poured a shot in her mouth, her rainbow hair swinging wildly beneath her and her skirt slipping up her thighs, almost revealing her panties.

A possessive growl left me as I took a step in that direction, needing to make sure no one got a view up her dress, but someone jumped into my way and I found a tiny woman there with her dark hair pulled up into pigtails with silver stars stuck all around her eyes. She wore a skin-tight cream jumpsuit with a fluffy tail somehow standing up tall from her ass. Brooklyn looked as unhinged as ever, but the big ass smile on her face reminded me of how much I liked her. Though when I remembered the dick jar incident, I wondered if my like for her was misguided.

"Rah!" she growled. "Happy birthday! I came dressed as you."

I frowned, noticing the ruff of red fur around her neck and the whiskers painted up her cheeks. "You did?" I asked in confusion.

"Yeah, I'm Lion Harlequin." She did a twirl. "Isn't it great?"

"Um…" I tried to think up a way to tell her that wasn't my name, but she'd clearly gone to so much effort on the costume that I just didn't have the heart to do it. Fortunately, I was saved from having to as her boyfriend called out to her.

"What will you have to drink, chica loca?" Mateo was standing at a table that had been set up outside stacked with every drink imaginable.

He had the huge dog Brutus on a chain wrapped around his wrist and the big guy's arm kept getting yanked sideways every time the monstrous dog took a snap at someone's legs.

"Something pink and fizzy, oooh, and something with sparkles in it too. Oh – oh! And something that pops and fizzes and bangs!" Brooklyn got excited, running over to the table to join her boyfriend while the guy looked between all the drinks with a frown that said he was figuring out how to make such a thing.

"You're the one who took my dog's meds," a deep Irish voice made me wheel around and I found a huge, tatted guy standing there sipping a blue cocktail full of umbrellas and straws. He had blonde hair and a look about him that was all danger, even though he had our pink flamingo ring sitting around his waist, his bare chest scrawled with endless ink.

"You must know Brooklyn and Mateo," I said, offering out my hand and he slapped his into it, shaking mine.

"Sure do. Name's Niall O'Brien. Mateo's a little cunt of a donkey by the way, but Brooklyn's as sweet as a pie in a crow's nest. Speaking of which…" He took out a birthday card, handing it over to me and my brows lifted as I tore open the envelope and took out the card which had a lion cub on it and was address to 'Lion Harlequin', signed from him and Brooklyn, though I wasn't sure what that had to do with a pie in a crow's nest. "So, Lion-"

"It's Fox actually. Fox Harlequin," I said, and his lips popped open.

"Holy fuck, I know who you are. Your daddy's got a murderous reputation. Fuck, is he here? I wanna ask him about the time he gouged a man's eyes out with a spork."

"Who told you he did that?" I asked, never having heard such a thing before.

"Oh lad, you don't know half the things your black hearted father has done. You only hear it when you're in the circles like I am. Dark, dark circles with all the monsters of the world. He's a fucking legend where I hail from."

"Ireland?" I questioned and he laughed like I'd made a joke, though I definitely hadn't.

"Anyway, happy motherfucking birthday to you. I've got a date with your pool." He walked straight off the edge of the pool, dunking into it and sloshing his cocktail over his chest as he bounced upright within the rubber ring.

I fixed my gaze on Rogue again as the Afterlife crowd started cheering and I spotted JJ dancing erotically with her up on the table, his hands climbing under her skirt and giving the whole party a glimpse of her ass.

"Fucking Johnny James," I growled as I headed that way, but my path was blocked again as Chase appeared carrying a beer, holding out a Red Solo Cup for me to take that was full of it.

I noticed he had an eyepatch on now and I wondered how long it would be before Rogue stole it from him, though there was something about the look that suited him, especially paired with his fitted black shirt that gave him a pirate vibe. Rogue would lap that right up.

"Thanks, man," I said, my eyes slipping over his head to where Rogue was now lying flat on the table while JJ ground over her in one of his signature stripper moves.

She was laughing, clearly enjoying herself, and I released a breath as I tried to let go of the monster in me that wanted to go and snatch her away from all those onlooking eyes.

I drained my cup of beer as Chase and I were joined by a bunch of Harlequins who were playing kiss ass with me, and I was relieved when the doorbell rang and I had a chance to slip away to answer. Though the pleading look Chase gave me as he was left behind with them made me feel a little guilty. Not enough to turn back though.

I headed to the front door but was nearly bowled over by Dad as he shoved his way past me, making it there first.

"What the-" I started, but my words died as he yanked the door open, and Carmen Ortega appeared there in a stunning violet dress that was slit up one thigh. Diamonds dripped from a necklace around her throat and her dark hair was gathered into a perfect bun with a single coil pulled purposefully loose to hang down and caress her cheek.

She had a champagne glass in her hand and the huge man to her right took a bottle of fucking Dom Perignon from an ice bucket in his hands and refilled it for her. To her left, was Travis, his muscular frame filling out a crisp cream shirt and highlighting the deep brown colour of his skin. He looked to Dad, raising his chin ever so slightly and my dad's muscles flexed in response.

"Good evening, chico tonto," Carmen said, kissing the air nowhere near Dad's cheeks before sweeping forward to place air kisses closer to me, her subtle perfume rich and sweet. "Happy birthday, Fox. Show me the way to the party."

"Er, sure," I said, taken off guard by the sudden command and turning to lead her back through the house.

"Can I get you a drink, Carmen?" Dad asked as he moved to walk at her side, offering his back to Travis as he followed.

"Are you blind as well as stupid, Luther?" she asked lightly.

"No," he grunted.

"Then you can clearly see I have brought my own drink. Though I am quite weary of holding it." She moved to pass the glass to Pepito, but Dad swiped it into his grip before he could take it and Carmen arched a single brow at him, the only suggestion that she was surprised.

Dad gazed hard back at her like he'd won something, and her mouth twitched at the corner as she continued on without remark, allowing him to keep hold of it.

I led them out to the patio, feeling like this already wild party might not be the kind of place Carmen Ortega would choose to spend her time, especially as I spotted Miss Mabel standing up on a deckchair near Rogue, dancing with Texas from JJ's dance troupe. My jaw went slack as Texas ground up behind her and Mabel laughed raucously, grinding back into him like she didn't have two false hips and sixty odd years on him.

Carmen paused to take in the mayhem, and as two Harlequins tore their shirts off and dive-bombed into the pool close by, Pepito dove in front of her like he was taking a bullet, shielding her from the spray of water and taking a full splash of it to the face.

Carmen stepped past him like nothing had even happened, moving over to speak with Mateo while Brooklyn bobbed on her toes and stared at Carmen like she was a goddess. And in a way, she was in this town. She was certainly getting a lot of attention, people pointing and muttering while Dad shadowed her around and Travis slinked off into the crowd, clearly doing a security sweep of my property.

I looked for Rogue again, the table where she and JJ had been dancing now empty and my lips parted as I spotted her.

She was yelling at Maverick who was on the ground, trying to pull him off of Texas who was being beaten to hell by my brother. Miss Mabel was clutching the pearls at her neck, still standing up on the deck chair as I ran forward to intervene.

"She asked me to!" Texas cried.

"She's. My. Fucking. Grandma!" Maverick enunciated every word with a strike of his fist and Rogue desperately tried to pull him away.

I got hold of Rick's shoulder, tugging him off so he and Rogue fell in a heap on the ground and Texas was left panting on his back, his shirt half torn off of him while Mabel hopped down to check he was okay.

"Augustus Rosewood," Mabel used the name Rick was born with over his true one, raising up to her full height – which wasn't all that high at all – planting one hand on her hip while pointing directly at my brother. "If I want to be manhandled by a fine specimen such as this man, then I will absolutely be manhandled. Do not come defending my honour when it is my honour to hand away into the wind if I so wish it." She leaned down, clapping Rick around the ear and he pursed his lips as Rogue covered her mouth to hide her laugh.

"Now come here, young lad, you come with Miss Mabel, and I'll get you a stiff drink for your troubles." She tugged on Texas's arm, and he got to his feet, looking sheepish as he glanced from Rick to Mabel.

"Go then." Rick waved them off and they headed towards the drinks table where Mutt was now sitting while Brooklyn carefully fixed a tiny party hat onto the dog's head – though where she'd gotten that, I had no idea.

"You got told off by your grandma," Rogue taunted Rick, letting her laughter fly free.

I helped her to her feet, tugging her skirt down at the back so her ass wasn't on show, though I skimmed my knuckles over the smoothness of her right cheek before I did so. She looked up at me, biting down on her lip and I gave her a wicked smile that told her how much I was dying to get a moment alone with her.

"How many minutes can you spare the birthday boy?" I murmured in her ear, already towing her backwards away from the crowd as Chase used Rick to escape from the Harlequin ass kissers.

"At least five," she said teasingly.

"How about fifteen," I bargained.

"How about ten?" she countered.

"But what I can do to you in ten minutes, I can do three times in fifteen," I said, and she caught my hand, tugging me into the kitchen where more Harlequins filled the space and were blocking the way to the stairs.

I pulled her through the house to the back door, towing her out onto the beach where the night air whipped around us and the sound of the party still thrummed in the air, but here, we were alone.

"Do you like being watched, hummingbird?" I asked, locking her to my side as I led her towards the jetty at the end of the beach.

She shrugged innocently and I carved my fingers over her waist and down to the hem of her skirt, tugging it up a little.

"I think you do," I growled. "I think you liked dancing up on that table with your panties flashing the crowd while Johnny James showed everyone just how he'd fuck you if he had you alone."

"And did you like that?" she asked, a raw hope in her voice that made my mouth dry.

"No," I said, though it tasted like a lie. "It drives me to insanity. And you know it."

"Maybe that's why I do it."

"Mm," I grunted, walking her down the jetty underneath the light of a million stars and leading her straight onto the speedboat bobbing in the water at the end of it.

"Everything about you torments me," I said, pushing her back against the wheel and kicking her ankles apart so I could stand between them. Her back bowed as I pressed forward, making the position uncomfortable for her and forcing her to cling to my shirt so she didn't fall down against the control panel. "So maybe you've earned yourself some tormenting."

I gripped her jaw in one hand, making her look at me while I spread her legs wider with mine and reached between us, forcing her to perch on the wheel which sat at an angle on the control panel.

I ran my fingers up her panties, finding a wet patch and smirking as I rubbed my hand over it. "Is this for me or JJ?"

"Both," she said breathily and my need to dominate her attention made a growl build in my chest.

"But it's *my* birthday," I said, my mouth so close to hers I could taste her excitement as I rubbed at that damp spot between her legs, making her even wetter. "And I want all of your attention."

"So selfish," she accused as she panted, trying to grind her pussy into my hand and take more from me, but I gave her just enough to drive her crazy without giving anything more.

"Yeah, I'm selfish, baby. So fucking selfish when it comes to you. I want you moaning my name while I slide the first inch of my cock inside you, and I want you begging for all of me until I'm so deep in your pussy, you can't think of anyone else. Because I'm the Harlequin Prince." I squeezed her jaw tighter as her eyes fluttered and started to close, making her attention sharpen and her eyes focus on mine. "I'm so fucking jealous when I see you with them, I feel this urgent need to make you see me, because when you're looking at them, you're not looking at me. And I can tolerate it, I'd tolerate anything to have you, but that hungry, envious demon in me is never going to die. I've gotta feed it, baby. I've got to show it you're mine too, and I've waited too long now. I need to make you shiver and moan and I need to feel you come over and over on my fingers, my cock, my tongue. And every time I make you fall, I want you to say my name, you got it?"

She nodded and I slipped my thumb between her parted lips, watching as she sucked and swirled her tongue around it, making my cock thicken just for her. "Good girl."

I dropped my hands to her hips, flipping her around and tugging her dress up over her sides, revealing the little pink frenchies she was wearing which had lace along the edges.

"Hold onto the wheel," I commanded, and she did as I ordered while I dropped to my knees behind her and shimmied her panties down her legs, lifting each of her feet in turn to remove them. I skimmed my fingers up the backs of her calves before climbing higher to her thighs, her body bending forward like she could sense what I wanted before I even asked for it.

It was so us. The way we'd always been in tune with one another, even when we fought, we were two fires burning in the same pit.

I took in this perfect view of my girl as little shivers ran through her body from my touch. I squeezed her ass cheeks in both hands as I returned to my feet, caressing, and kneading them before I took my right hand away and spanked her hard enough to leave a mark.

She cried out, her voice echoing across the water, swallowed by the waves as they crashed against the shore.

"Do you miss me when you're fucking them?" I asked, my heart pounding fiercely as I rubbed the reddened mark on her ass and prepared to do it again if her answer made me angry.

"Yes," she admitted. "I wish it could be all of us."

I spanked her and she cursed colourfully while I caressed the handprint I'd left on her this time, my jealousy piquing.

"Do their cocks not satisfy you, Rogue? Do you really need more?" I moved up behind her, grinding my hardness against her so she could see what she was doing to me, and she moaned, her ass pushing back needily before I moved away again.

"It's not about that," she said. "It's about all of us being together. I can't explain it unless you try it."

I spanked her once more as I bared my teeth. "You expect me to fuck you while another man is inside you? My friend?"

"You can just watch if that's what you prefer," she offered.

I spanked her on the back of her thigh this time and she cried out as I pressed a hand down on her spine to keep her in place. She wasn't escaping my wrath tonight, and she knew it. I was letting this jealous creature in me out at last because if I didn't, I'd snap in a far worse way than this.

"I know you like it," she panted. "I know you watch the videos Rick sends you."

I grabbed her hair, yanking as I leaned over her and spoke in her ear. "Watch your mouth, hummingbird, or I'll think of a way to keep it busy."

"Why can't you admit it?" she growled, pushing her ass back against me. "Why don't you admit that you're hard right now because you saw me dance with JJ? Because when I'm with them, you get angry and jealous, but you get so fucking turned on too, Fox."

"That's a lie," I snarled, pushing her down harder beneath me while freeing my cock. She inhaled sharply as she realised what was coming and I gave her no time to prepare as I shoved myself inside her, fully sheathing myself in her soaking pussy and making both of us swear at the same time.

She was so tight and hot around me that my thoughts scattered, and I turned into nothing but an animal as I let myself enjoy her, fucking her hard and fast as I held her at my mercy, doing this only for my pleasure. But the moans that left her told me she loved that, that she was getting off on me taking from her and I drove into her more punishingly, her moans tangling around us in the air as her pussy clenched and I felt her orgasm cresting already.

I let her have it, reaching around to rub her clit in time with my thrusts and she came, shuddering beneath me as I fucked her through her pleasure and waited to hear my name fall from her lips.

"Maverick Stone," she garbled, and a vicious, furious rage tore up from the depths of my being.

I fucked her harder, sucking my fingers before placing them back on her clit and urging another climax out of her. It was barely another minute before she finished for me again and the tip of my cock ached with the need to explode too, but not until I was done with her.

"Johnny James Brooks," she moaned, and I pulled out of her, flipping her around and yanking her toward me by her hair.

"Say *my* name, Rogue," I ordered as she stared up at me in a haze of desire, but her eyes sparked with the game, and I should have known she'd be anything but obedient.

"I'm saying the name of the guys who've made me come harder than you," she taunted, and a snarl ripped from my lips.

I picked her up, tossing her over my shoulder and carrying her to the bench at the back of the speedboat, making her sit there while I knelt between her legs and shoved her thighs wide for me. I buried my face between her legs, licking and sucking her clit while she ground her pussy against my mouth. I pushed three fingers inside her, stretching her and making her mine as she clawed her hands through my hair. She tasted so goddamn sweet, and I wished we'd done this sooner. We should have been fucking for years, we should have been each other's firsts, and I despised the fact that I could never have that from her. But it spurred me on now, because I had plenty of time to make up for, and I'd be sure to brand her with so much pleasure, she'd forget about anyone who had her before the Harlequins reclaimed her.

Besides, I may not have been her first, but I was the last man to join the group, which made me the last first she'd ever have. And that was a little crown I was more than happy to place on my head.

I rubbed her g-spot in perfect circles, curling my fingers inwards and running my tongue over her clit in fast flicks that had her coming for me again in seconds.

"Chase Cohen," she moaned this time, and the game really was pissing me off now as I looked up at her, my fingers still deep inside her and my mouth wet from her desire.

I slowly drew my fingers out, making her whimper for me as I stood up, gazing down at this girl who was so infuriating and so captivating at the same time.

I sucked her taste from my fingers and her lips parted as she watched me, her hand moving to tug her dress down over her pussy, but if she thought I was done with her, she was going to find out how wrong she was.

I scooped her up under her thighs, dropping down in her place on the bench and lowering her over my lap so she faced me. I took hold of her wrists, holding them in one hand at the base of her spine and she perched her knees on the bench, her forehead pressing to mine as she raised up enough for me to line my cock up with her entrance. Then she drove her hips down and I was in heaven again, the two of us moaning loudly as we joined and I took full control of her riding me, capturing her mouth with mine and nipping her tongue as she kissed me.

I kept one hand on her thigh, massaging her clit with my thumb and feeling her tighten around my shaft, knowing I was going to freefall this time too. Between bites and kisses, our movements become more frantic, and I released her hands so she could steady herself on my shoulders, holding both of her hips and fucking her deep and hard until her pussy tightened, and she climaxed with a cry of pleasure. I was drawn into ecstasy right after her, spilling myself into her and groaning into the flesh of her neck as we clung to one another, riding out the wave of bliss that kept us in its grip.

I sagged back against my seat as Rogue flopped against me, my arms wound tight around her as we fought to catch our breath.

"Fox Harlequin," she purred in my ear. "Fox motherfucking Harlequin."

A stupid ass smile split across my face and the roaring monster in me finally went back to sleep as I bathed in that victory, reminded that she was mine and I was hers. There was no changing that.

When we'd finally recovered and were fully dressed once more, I towed Rogue back to the house and let her slip away to the bathroom.

I floated back to the pool area in my freshly fucked daze, pouring myself a strong rum and coke and draining half of it in one long gulp.

"It's not dramatic," Dad was saying to Pepito close by.

"It is a very dramatic thing to say," Pepito countered as he kept one eye on Carmen who was speaking with Brooklyn.

"Look at him and tell me you wouldn't die for him," Dad said, pointing and I followed his line of sight to Mutt who was now wearing a little bowtie along with his party hat, nibbling on a cookie someone had dropped on the ground.

"I would not die for that dog," Pepito said with a head shake.

"Well, I would," Dad muttered just as a drunk guy came stumbling towards Mutt and the little dog grabbed the cookie and ran off with it like he thought someone might steal it.

"What are you smiling about?" JJ asked as he appeared, then his eyes widened in realisation as he reached me. "You had sex." He accused, pointing right at my cock in my shorts and I batted his hand away.

"JJ," I laughed, sipping my drink.

"You did," he pushed. "How'd you do it?" He moved closer, looking excited. "A finger in the ass while you pounded her from behind?"

266

"JJ," I growled this time, anger slipping into my voice.

"Oh sorry, bro, I forgot you're touchy about being part of a whole… reverse harem."

"A what?" I muttered.

JJ rolled his eyes, swiping a beer from the table and twisting the cap off. "Please tell me you're not *still* reading that series of books I lent you."

"It's five books and they're huge," I said.

"I gave them to you weeks ago. You're such a slow reader, man."

"Well maybe I stopped reading after book three."

"What?" he gasped, looking horrified as he grasped my shoulder and gaped at me. "You're joking, right? Book three was a huge cliff-hanger."

"She chose one of the guys," I said with a shrug. "And not the one I was rooting for."

"Oh my God," he groaned. "You're so stupid. This is why you're not getting it."

"Not getting what?" I frowned.

"Us." He pointed between us then to Maverick and Chase on the other side of the pool. "We're her harem."

"Uhuh," I said dryly.

"God, you're such a Gabe." He walked away from me, leaving me with that nugget of confusion to chew on.

I swallowed the last of my drink just as Rogue reappeared with a glint in her eyes that spoke of our secret. I watched her moving through the crowd, talking to people while her gaze slipped to me time and again and I chewed on the inside of my cheek. Fucking perfect she was. I couldn't get enough of watching her, of knowing what I'd just done to her, and knowing I was the sole cause for that flushed look about her. It made me feel goddamn high.

"Help! Someone – help! Mutt is stuck!" Di cried in alarm, pointing down a narrow gap behind the shed for the pool heater.

"Mutt!" Luther cried in a panic, but I got there first, racing past him, and dropping to my knees to look down the gap behind the shed where Mutt had gotten wedged, his ass aimed my way and his little body shaking as he tried to back up but couldn't. A weight slammed into my back as Rogue clambered on me to see.

"Mutt," she gasped. "Come here, come on baby. Back your tiny butt up, you can do it."

Mutt whined, trying to move, but he couldn't seem to get out. Rogue reached for him, her fingers almost grazing his tail, but her arm wasn't long enough.

"I'll do it," I said, and she moved back off of me so I could manoeuvre.

I rolled onto my side so I could get my arm down the gap easier and shimmied forward so my head was in the gap too, my hand closing around Mutt's little body.

I tugged on him and he grunted but came loose and I managed to draw him back towards me.

The little asshole started fighting to get free though and with every twist of his body, he farted right in my face. I spluttered, screwing up my eyes as I struggled to hold onto him and held him over my head for someone to take.

"For the love of fuck," I growled as he farted again, and I tried to shrink away from it while he barked excitedly.

I squinted out at him where Rogue was now hugging him to her chest and Luther was petting his head with a relieved look in his eyes, squeaking Mutt's favourite plastic broccoli toy.

"Here's Mr Squeakeasy, good boy," Dad cooed.

I scrambled my way back to my feet and Rogue looked at me like I was a hero, lunging forward to try and kiss me. I jerked backwards though, shaking my head and she gave me a questioning look.

"Be right back," I said grimly. "I need to wash the fucking dog farts out of my eyes."

CHAPTER SIXTEEN

No, no, no, this would not do. I could not let this lie.

I was pacing outside the trailer, the woods around me full of bird chatter and too much damn noise. I swung a pistol in my grip, anger gnawing up the centre of me like an infestation of ants housed in my flesh.

Fucking Harlequins.

I'd been stewing on how close they'd come to getting their claws into me ever since it had happened a week ago. They'd come too damn close, they could have got holda my momma, or worse, me.

The birds continued to sing, and I spat a growl, kicking at the dirt around the fire I'd built out here. I was verging on full health now; I didn't need to be hiding out like a rat under a rock. My injuries were healed at last, and I no longer had to lay low like a wounded animal from its predator.

I hadn't been wasting time though, I had a plan now and it was coming together real nicely. So I needed to get back in the game, I needed to play Devil with the Harlequins, get my girl, take her away from them and leave their hearts bleeding in her wake. Yeah, I was ready now. But they were gonna gut me good if I didn't get the jump on them first. They'd come sniffing too close to my hideout, and I'd had to uproot myself again, disappear into a woodland further east away from the coast.

I was enraged over it all still, those assholes making me flee like that. Fuck, I did not get beat. I did not lose, especially not a game I'd started.

The birds grew louder still, and I aimed my pistol at the canopy above, firing off three rounds as a roar of anger ripped from my lungs. The birds took off in a rush and silence fell at last as they left me in goddamn peace.

I shoved the pistol into the holster at my hip, huffing a breath through my nose and contemplating the world in front of me.

Okay. Let's take a deep, meditative breath and think over this.

I was Shawn Mackenzie, I just needed to regroup and get my plans moving along quicker. I had to mark out my weaknesses, lock 'em up tight and press forward. I had to stay on the move, that was for sure. And now my wounds were healed, I had no problem managing that. But then what? Could I keep my momma safe travelling town to town? Outa the paws of those dirty dog Harlequins while I finalised my arrangements?

Maybe, maybe.

I still had the hit out on Rogue, sending any and every asshole who took the bait her way with the promise of one of my diamonds as payment. I doubted any of them would actually manage to get their hands on her, but it would sure keep her and her boys busy while I worked on my end of the plans. And if one of them did manage to bring her to me all tied up in a bow then I was sure I would figure out a way to make that work, even if I wasn't fully prepared. I'd find a game or two to play with her and maybe I'd let her escape me, prolong the hunt, let them think they were winning before I had all my ducks in a row and came sweeping in to claim her again for my endgame.

I took a pack of cigarettes from my pocket, pushing one between my lips and lighting it up with Chase Cohen's pretty little Zippo lighter. I ran my thumb over its smooth surface, smiling at the memory of cutting the soul right outa his flesh. He wouldn't be rid of me, even now. His brain would be circling with my dark and mighty words, reminding him of the disgusting rat he was. He was nothing and no one, just a conquered creature left in my dust. Boy, did I love breaking the tough ones. He'd be reminded of me every time he saw those scars on his skin, every time he looked in the mirror, and even better than all of that, he'd be reminded of me every time he looked at *her*. And she'd see me when she looked right back. Yeah, that did something to assuage this anger in me. It felt real good knowing they walked this earth with my taint on them, two of my finest accomplishments.

Of course, I wasn't quite done with Rogue's destruction. I planned on breaking her so good, she'd beg for death when I slipped a pistol between her pretty lips. She'd never know when that moment was gonna come, but it surely would, and when I had her, I'd make sure she feared it during every minute of her last night on earth. Then…*boom*.

Mm, it'd be a damn shame to see her pretty skull shatter under the force of my bullet, but hell would it feel good too, knowing what her death would do to those Harlequin boys. One little bullet in that girl's head and they'd all fall like dominoes, suffering under the weight of her loss forevermore.

There was no time for playing long games anymore, I'd decided. So when I made my final move and I was ready to play a game or two with my sugarpie, she would already be on the clock, those seconds ticking away down to her final moments. After it was done, I'd build myself up nice somewhere with another gang around me. I might even come back one day and seek out the Harlequins deaths too if the urge was roused in me.

I released a plume of smoke from my lips, relaxing as I thoughts of death and blood and carnage did something to sooth my fury. See, I was a man of logic, and I wasn't one to let emotion get the better of me. That kind of instability belonged to women, not to powerful men with empires to build. As if to emphasise that thought, a sob croaked sounded from my momma within the trailer and I sighed, flicking my cigarette onto the ground and crushing it with my boot.

I turned, walking up into the trailer and finding her on the little couch with her head in her hands as her shoulders shook, tears spilling through her fingers like little drops of rain.

"Come now, Momma," I said gently. "Don't be crying. There ain't no need for all that."

"I just feel so terrible about all that's happened, bubba," she said, looking up at me through reddened eyes, her makeup smeared and making her look like a real mess.

"Fix ya makeup," I encouraged. "You don't wanna be looking like trash. Have some dignity, would ya?"

She hiccupped as she nodded, her cheeks flushing with embarrassment. "Of course, bubba. I'm so sorry, I didn't mean to make a mess of myself. What kind of woman does that make me, falling apart like this?"

"It's the way of your kind," I said sympathetically as she stood, moving into the little restroom to fix her makeup in the mirror.

I followed her, standing behind her and drawing her red hair back over her shoulders, picking up a brush and combing it through for her. She smiled at me through watery eyes, and I smiled back. Poor, sweet Momma. She was just a woman after all, I couldn't go blaming her for all this, she wasn't fit to handle the world the way men were.

"There we are now, all better, huh?" I asked and she nodded, her eyes brightening as she turned to me and cupped my face in her palm.

"You deserve so much more than this," she said, and I nodded, leaning down to kiss her cheek.

"It's okay, shh, shh," I cooed as I saw the tears welling in her eyes again and I drew her into my chest, humming The Lady In Red by Chris de Burgh as I led her out of the bathroom and made her dance with me.

I placed my hand on her back, rocking her side to side and hugging my tiny momma to me as she rested her ear against my heart and relaxed in my arms.

"There now, that's better ain't it?" I asked and she nodded, releasing a long breath. "No need to be hysterical."

"I'm sorry, bubba," she whispered.

"And I forgive you," I said, twisting a lock of her bright red hair between my fingertips. "You've always been good to me, you're one of the few people who knows how to look after me, Momma."

She patted my arm. "You're a strong man with lots of business to conduct, you need someone cooking and cleaning for you, so you don't have to worry about those things."

"Yeah," I agreed. "And I'm thinking when Rogue comes back to me, she might like to take over in all that, what do you say?"

"I could teach her," she said brightly, excited by that prospect. That fantasy I painted for her was nothing but a lie though. Rogue wasn't going to be playing house with me again, even if she begged for mercy. It was unfortunate that I wouldn't get to fuck that tight pussy again, but she had to go. She was the only weakness of the Harlequins, so her death was fated now.

"I'd like that," I said, taking out my phone and picking out Momma's favourite song on it as I set it down on the side.

Copacabana by Barry Manilow filled the trailer and I cranked it up nice and loud as I smiled at Momma and her face lit up.

"Oh Shawn, I do love this song," she gushed. "You remember that summer we spent down in Mexico, and they played this every night at the local bar?"

"I remember," I said with a smile.

I'd laid low down there for a while after a particularly nasty string of murders had drawn the attention of the feds up north. I'd scarpered outa there until the dust had settled and thankfully my name never came up in the investigation, even though I had absolutely been the perpetrator of those

275

bloody crimes. I'd had a fall guy take the hit and a few dirty cops keeping my name out of the judge's mouth, so it went down smoothly.

Momma had loved the Mexican heat, but I'd enjoyed the women and the tequila best.

I spun Momma under my arm, dancing through into the little kitchen while she sang along, as happy as a clam full of pearls.

I danced with her, grabbing her waist and spinning her again, before pressing her back against me. Her laughter filled the air as the song came to an end and it felt so good to see her happy like that, all the joy of a lifetime shining in her eyes.

So that was when I snatched the sharp little knife from the block on the counter and drove it deep and hard into the fleshy spot at the base of her skull. She gasped the moment it pierced her flesh, her eyes widening, shock crossing her features for the most fleeting of seconds before hot blood spilled over my hand and she jerked once before going limp in my arms.

"I love you, Momma," I breathed, driving the knife in a little deeper to ensure the job was done, but the hollowness of her eyes was clear. "But you were gonna fuck this all up if something wasn't done about you."

I laid her down gently on the floor, tugging the knife from her skull and tossing it in the kitchen sink with a heavy breath leaving me.

I washed my hands then grabbed a comforter from the bed and started rolling her up in it, binding her in there good and tight with some rope too. Copacabana had started playing on repeat, the music filling my head and I sang along as I worked, sad in some ways, but mostly relieved. I wasn't gonna be disrespectful, I'd given her a good death, now I'd give her a decent burial too. She was my momma, after all. But the truth of the matter was, she was a liability. A weakness. My only weakness if I was counting them, and truly, it was time I was free of it. Of her. There was something therapeutic in that.

She'd already been used against me once, and I'd still have Rogue if it wasn't for her, if I hadn't had to trade her out for Momma to those Harlequins.

And now her shopping habits had almost come round to bite me in the ass too. Enough was enough. It was time I made the decision of a true leader. I had to let her go. She was dead weight, an anchor holding me down, one that could trip me up at any moment.

I scooped her into my arms when she was wrapped up tight and carried her out of the trailer, walking off into the woods.

Dusk was falling now, and it would take me a while to dig a deep enough hole to keep the night critters from clawing her outa the dirt, but I'd do it. For her. I could admit my previous experience with burying my problems in shallow graves made me more cautious now and I wouldn't be making that same mistake again. Rogue mighta risen from the grave to come back and haunt me, but this time I would be certain the thing was done right.

When I found a place far enough off into the trees, I laid her down and returned to the trailer for my shovel, whistling softly as I went. I'd have to clean up the trailer and get outa dodge. This wasn't pretty work, but there was definitely something cathartic about it. I felt freer now, my final shackle released.

Perhaps a man could not be a king until he'd shed himself of all binds. There was certainly something buzzing in the air following that most final of acts, like a promise of what was to come, my ascension just waiting to be grasped.

I felt all-powerful, a master of life. And when I was done putting my momma in the ground, I'd leave this place for good and play the Harlequins at their own game. One that would land Rogue right back in my lap where she belonged. I already had the chessboard set, I just needed to get my pieces into motion.

CHAPTER SEVENTEEN

A tickle against my cheek made me swat my hand as I slept, a mumbled curse escaping me as Chase's soft laughter fell against my ears, urging me to wake.

"Nooo," I pleaded, rolling over and driving my head beneath the pillows even though that left me with my ass exposed.

Predictably, I felt the sting of a smack to my rear but the sound of Mutt racing to my defence filled the air as feral growling met with Chase cursing and the feeling of his weight scrambling from the bed.

"Ah, you little asshole," he muttered while Mutt continued to snarl at him, two tiny paws coming to rest on my spine as he took up position as my guard dog.

"Come back in a few hours and wake me up with your cock," I muttered, the call of sleep singing my name as I went towards it willingly, dreams of my Harlequins promising all kinds of blissful oblivion without the added cardio that accompanied the reality of those ideas coming to fruition.

"As tempting as that offer is, it's past eleven and we have somewhere to be," Chase replied, clearly not planning on leaving and taunting me with words of morning.

"Where?" I grunted.

"Remember when we were kids, and every day was just another adventure?" he said, and I knew he was trying to lure me with his words.

"Maybe."

"Well, I was hoping that I could tempt you out on another one? Just you and me? JJ has club business to see to, and Luther wants Fox and Rick to spend some time with him today, so I thought we could take the boat out to the Mariner's shipwreck, maybe get some paddle boarding in, keep an eye out for turtles…"

"And coincidentally stay far out of Shawn's reach and any assholes who may be after me thanks to the diamond he's offering in payment for my kidnap?" I suggested, rolling over and knocking the pillow aside so I could look up at him.

He stood over me in a black t-shirt and a pair of grey boardshorts, curly hair pushed back from his face and his eyepatch nowhere to be seen, though I didn't miss the twitch of tension that crossed his face as my gaze roamed over his features hungrily.

I gave him a sleepy smile, biting down on my bottom lip and trailing my hands down my front as I tugged the thin white tank I was wearing flush to my body, my hands caressing my breasts through it before sliding lower.

"Help wake me up before we have to leave then," I said, parting my thighs, and his throat bobbed as his gaze moved to my hands which were heading between my legs.

"We don't have time for that," he said, though the way he was looking at me told me he was questioning that statement.

I pouted at him, tugging my shirt up and out of the way as I made a move to start on myself, but he lurched forward, snatching my wrists, and stopping me.

"We really don't," he said firmly, eyes on mine, grip tight. "But we'll have all day together once we're out on the water."

"Boo," I complained half-heartedly, and his gaze slipped to the left side of my face for a moment before he gave a soft snort of amusement and reared back, hauling me to my feet.

Mutt barked irritably from the bed but made no further attempts to savage Chase now that I wasn't actively trying to resist him.

He steered me to the closet and motioned for me to pick something out and I gave in, able to tell this wasn't going to be optional anyway, and unable to summon a shit to give about that.

I wasn't a prisoner to this house anymore, but I sure had felt like one recently. Ever since the incident with the cop dosing my drink at the club, I hadn't been anywhere without at least one of my boys right beside me, and it was usually two of them or more. And since I'd escaped to Tatum's for a night of drunken antics that ended with us both drawing squids on our ass cheeks and pressing them to the window of Saint's music room while he was playing piano, I hadn't managed to escape again. Saint had even called Fox to come collect me like he was my damn dad or something.

I loved them and I loved being around them, but it was starting to feel a hell of a lot like being babysat, not to mention the fact that more often than not, we didn't even go out at all. It was safer at the house. I got it. I just didn't like it.

More than anything, I wanted to be out on the open sea for the day so I wasn't going to make a fuss over the idea now that it had been presented to me.

I picked out a glittery, rainbow bathing suit with a Pegasus on the front of it, the words 'Horny for the horn' written just beneath the flying unicorn bringing a smile to my lips. Then I chose a transparent white kaftan with white flowers embroidered onto it, tossed them down on the bed and turned away towards the bathroom.

Chase hounded me inside, planting his ass against the sink, his bulk blocking the mirror as he folded his arms and waited for me to do my business.

"Have you developed a pee fetish I didn't know about?" I asked as I sat on the toilet, my brow arched at him while performance anxiety made my over full bladder struggle to let go.

"I'm not sure yet," he teased. "I thought I'd watch you go and figure it out."

"Has there been some new threat made?" I asked, hearing a dip to his voice which indicated there was some sort of lie in his words beyond just trying to wind me up. "Some reason you want to stick to me like glue?"

"No, little one," he replied softly, realising he was worrying me. "I can go if you want? I only wanted to spend the day with you."

"Peeing and all?" I asked with a snort, and he just gave me a boyish grin in reply, the look reminding me so clearly of the kid I'd known my entire life that I decided to give in to his odd choice of game. "Fine. Stick to me all you like."

I closed my eyes and managed to relieve myself, glad I only needed to pee because I would have been drawing the line at anything else. When I opened my lids again, I found him looking away anyway, clearly not at all interested in taking a golden shower and I had to admit that I was glad of that. I mean, I'd have totally mustered up the courage to do it for him if that was what he wanted, but urine play really wasn't a kink of mine.

I flushed the toilet and moved towards him, meaning to wash my hands in the sink, but he shook his head, still blocking it with his broad frame and stepping forward to meet me.

"I think you need a shower, dirty girl. You can just wash your hands in there."

"What?" I asked, my brow pinching but he'd already stepped into me, his rough hands skimming my sides as he peeled the white shirt from my flesh, and I was forced to lift my arms to oblige him.

Chase kissed me the moment he had me naked, his hands going to my hips as he walked me backwards until he bumped me into the wall beside the shower. He switched the water on for me, his hands moving to lift my hair for me, holding it up as he pulled his lips from mine and nudged me towards the shower.

"You're acting very strangely today," I commented as I moved into the shower cubicle, and he grabbed the head from its stand, directing the water at my body so that I didn't get my hair wet.

"Maybe I'm just in the mood to get a little revenge," he replied, his eyes sparking with mischief.

"How so?" I asked and in reply he dropped the shower head until the spray was directed between my thighs, the heated water crashing against my clit and making a surprised moan tumble from my lips.

"You have me aching with need for you whenever you want," he replied with a shrug, bobbing his chin towards the bottle of shower gel in a command for me to make use of it. "I figure I can let you have a taste of feeling the same."

"You think you can make me beg for you, Chase Cohen?" I questioned, realising his game, and quite liking the sound of it.

"I like my chances," he admitted, his blue eyes blazing as he watched me massage soapy suds all over my skin and I made sure I put on a good show, enjoying the way his fist tightened in my hair, making my scalp burn from his grip and my mind wander to thoughts of feeling my lips wrap around his cock.

Before I could do any more than consider that option, Chase finished rinsing the suds from my skin and abruptly shut off the water.

He grabbed a large white towel from the hook and quickly wrapped me in it, bundling me back out of the bathroom and scrubbing me dry from head to toe.

"I have a gift for you," I said suddenly, breaking him from his regimented orders and making him frown at me in surprise.

"Why?"

"Wow, you're so suspicious," I muttered before heading to my nightstand

and retrieving the bracelet I'd gotten for him in the market before Shawn had come and fucked everything up, driving it from my mind entirely. After that I'd just been waiting for the right moment to offer it up to him and apparently, I'd decided that moment was now.

Chase shadowed me, making me bump into him as I turned back around, and I laughed before taking his hand in mine and quickly pushing the new bracelet onto his wrist alongside the others he'd bought to represent the rest of us so long ago.

"I told you, you needed one to represent you," I said as he looked down at it mutely, his throat bobbing with some repressed emotion that made me grin with satisfaction. "Go on; say it. I'm the best."

"Rogue...this is..." Chase really wasn't great with the emotional gooiness, but the kiss he gave me stole my breath from my lungs and made my heart race to an unrelenting beat.

I moaned in pleasure, trying to tug him closer as I dropped my towel, but he jerked back with a rueful grin, realising what I was trying to do.

Chase snapped his fingers at the clothes I'd picked out and left lying on the bed. "Get dressed, Rogue, we have plans."

"You're very bossy today," I muttered, dressing like he'd requested and kicking on some white sneakers too.

"Don't pretend you don't like it, Easton," he replied and dammit, I did.

Chase grinned like an asshole, reminding me a whole lot of Rick and I remembered how the two of them used to get when they egged each other on as kids, the machismo rising off the scales until I had to escape them entirely to protect my ovaries from contamination, usually by seeking out J or Fox, or even by just heading out to surf and leaving them to it. I got the feeling those tricks wouldn't work out so easily for me these days though.

He grabbed my hand and hauled me out of the room, tugging me down the stairs at a jog where the scent of cooking eggs hit me, and my stomach roiled.

"Shit, Fox, that smells bad," I said, wrinkling my nose as we made it to the kitchen and he looked up at me from where he was slaving away like a domestic goddess, his dad and Rick sitting patiently on the other side of the breakfast bar awaiting their meals.

"You think so?" he asked with a frown, looking down at the pan of eggs.

"Err, yeah, those eggs are definitely off," I said, the rotten taste practically coating my tongue.

"They do smell kinda janky," Rick agreed but as he turned to look at me, a bark of laughter escaped him that he quickly cut short.

"What?" I asked as Luther looked our way too, his brow lowering and head shaking as he turned away again, muttering something about us still acting like dumb kids half the time.

Rick hesitated a beat then shrugged, turning back to watch as Fox dumped the eggs out into the trash. "Mutt just wiped his ass all over the bottom step," he said and I looked around to find Mutt sitting on said step looking as innocent as pie.

"Come on," Chase said loudly, tugging my arm again. "No time to hang around with these assholes all day. Fox already packed us a picnic so you can eat on the boat."

"So long as there aren't any of those stanky eggs in there I'm sold," I agreed and Fox threw me a scowl like he was the hen responsible for squeezing those suckers out of his ass.

"Eggs wouldn't exactly keep fresh in a picnic hamper," he began but Chase was towing me away and I had no desire to hang around his stinky kitchen any longer than necessary, so I just blew him a kiss and let my feet follow on towards the back door.

Rick stood, striding out after us as Chase led the way onto the beach and down the private jetty, the air thick with heat and sun shining brightly in the endlessly blue sky above.

I tipped my head back to enjoy the feeling of it kissing my skin, listening

285

to the gentle sound of the waves as they caressed the shore at the edge of the golden sand.

Chase released me as he untethered the luxury speedboat that belonged to Luther, and I grinned at the thought of racing out across the waves on it.

Maverick grabbed a handful of my ass as he dragged me against him, kissing me filthily in a goodbye that was designed to imprint the feeling of him on my flesh until we saw each other again and I smiled into it as I tasted him.

"Be bad," he said as he released. "And take lots of photos," he added to Chase. "I want you to capture every moment."

"Don't worry, I will," Chase agreed, the two of them exchanging a look that spoke of all kinds of chaos, and I groaned, wondering what fresh hell they'd cooked up now because I'd seen that look before and it only ever equalled trouble.

"What are you up to?" I asked them suspiciously but they both just played innocent, trying to convince me that I was insane to even ask while I scowled between them.

Maverick leaned in to kiss my left cheek without giving me an answer, telling me to look after my ass because he had plans for it later and Chase hauled me onto the boat behind him a moment later.

I gave up on trying to figure out their game as I dropped down onto the soft cushions at the back of the boat, tipping my head back to soak in the sun while Chase started the engine and we shot away across the waves.

The day passed in a blur of sun kissed moments filled with flirting, snorkelling, sunbathing and whale watching as the two of us let go of our pain and fears, allowing nothing but the moment we were in to own us.

This was the life I'd dreamed of in the years I'd been gone. The simple pleasures of the sun on my back and sea salt in my hair, my boys laughing with me and the beauty of our private little paradise taking me hostage and giving me the best kind of Stockholm syndrome a girl could ever dream of.

Chase kept photographing me throughout the day, grinning broadly every time he did so while getting me to pose for him, though he refused to let me see any of the pictures he took, insisting he wanted us to enjoy looking back through them later. I didn't understand why he kept refusing selfies with me, but I was starting to suspect it had to do with his insecurities and that just pissed me off.

"Why won't you take any photos with me?" I grumbled as he took yet another one of me while I climbed up the little steps to get back onto the boat, water streaming from my body and slicking my rainbow hair back as I moved closer to him.

"I just don't feel in a very photogenic mood," he replied with a shrug, though his gaze cut from mine, and I narrowed my eyes.

"If you start up that shit about your scars again, I swear I'll-"

"It's not that," he replied quickly, though I noticed the way he shifted his weight at the mention of them, his hand opening and closing at his side like he was considering grabbing a shirt to cover himself with.

I narrowed my eyes, stalking closer to him, my attention roaming over his muscular body, before I pushed up onto my toes and took his mouth with mine.

Chase reacted instantly, dragging me against him and parting my lips with his tongue, his cock hardening between us as I ran my hands down his body with a hungry moan.

He broke away suddenly, a snort of laughter breaking from him that made me frown as he backed up, taking a seat on the large seating area at the rear of the boat and looking up at me with his eyes glimmering.

"What?" I asked, brushing a hand over my left cheek as his attention shifted to it for a moment before darting back to my eyes and his smile grew.

"Nothing," he insisted. "I just can't believe I have you like this sometimes. I wanted you for so long and now here you are."

He waved a hand at me like I'd just appeared from nothing, and I rolled my eyes at him, slinking closer until I was climbing into his lap, straddling him, and rocking my hips over his.

Chase wrapped his fingers around my throat, making me arch my spine and look skyward before pulling on the strap of my bathing suit and tugging my breasts free of it.

I gasped as he sucked one of my nipples into his mouth, his teeth grazing the hard point of it while I rocked my weight over the length of his cock once more.

"I've been wanting to feel you inside me all day," I panted as he continued to torment me, wetness gathering between my thighs and a moan of need riding up my throat.

"Insatiable, aren't you?" he replied, biting down on my nipple just hard enough to make me gasp.

"Yes," I agreed because for the four of them it was the truth.

I couldn't get enough, my body always aching for more, my thoughts always filled with the things they'd done to me or the things I wanted them to do. This bond between us had formed something that made us all high with the power of it, and I swear that the more we indulged in our addiction to one another, the more powerful and intoxicating our concoction grew.

I pushed up onto my knees, shoving his swimming trunks down to free his cock and moaning as I took in the length of him, the tip beaded with moisture, proving he was just as in need of me as I was of him.

I knocked his hand from my throat, leaning down to kiss him again but as his eyes met mine, a laugh spilled from him.

"What?" I demanded, leaning back as my eyes narrowed with suspicion and I sensed some game here.

"When I tell you, you'll be pissed," he replied, his grin so full of mischief and amusement that it was hard for me to maintain my indignation. This was my Chase. The boy I had loved for the entirety of my existence. The one who was full of smiles and confidence no matter what shit life threw his way. This was the man who had been lying beneath the jaded layers he had built in the years since I left this place, the one who Shawn had tried to destroy for good.

But out here, all alone in the middle of the ocean where there was no one to see us or judge us, I'd found him again.

I pursed my lips, wondering what the hell he was up to before deciding I had more urgent matters that I wanted to attend to first.

"Fine. If you won't tell me willingly then I'll just torture it out of you."

I climbed from his lap, my heated gaze holding his as I rolled my bathing suit the rest of the way off of my body, exposing every piece of myself to him beneath the power of the afternoon sun and loving the feeling of his eyes moving down to take it all in.

"Your turn," I purred, biting my bottom lip suggestively as I looked at his hard cock, my need for him making me salivate as he did what I wanted and removed them for me.

Chase's cock stood proud and thick before me, his fist wrapping around it tightly as he slowly worked himself over, his eyes on my body and his desire more than clear.

I stepped forward, wanting to take control and ride him, pushing him to the edge of release before drawing away again and demanding the answer to whatever game he was playing, but he shook his head as I did so.

"Give me your mouth, little one," he said, reaching for his phone which had ended up wedged down the side of one of the cushions.

"I thought Rick was the one obsessed with making sex tapes," I questioned as I watched him stroke himself again, his pumps slow and languid, his eyes fixed on my body and not raising to my face.

"Maybe I plan on sending him one of my own," he replied with a shrug. "He needs to be reminded which one of us makes you scream the loudest after all."

I licked my lips, not minding the sound of them making that into a competition in the slightest and I shrugged.

"Okay then, but I expect you to live up to that claim, Ace."

"No worries about that," he agreed, but there was amusement in his voice which didn't belong in this moment and only made my suspicions rise.

I was distracted from trying to demand answers by the sight of him continuing to pleasure himself though and decided to attack instead of defend, moving forward and dropping to my knees in front of him, pushing his thighs wider to give me space.

I was half aware of him moving the phone around to my left as he started recording me, but I had to admit that the idea of him sending that to the others only turned me on more, making me want to put on a real show for them that would probably result in more pleasure for me once we returned to them again.

I ran my tongue up the side of Chase's cock, following the thick line of a vein there, moaning softly as he released his grip on himself to give me room and instead pushed his fingers into my hair.

I lapped at the salty liquid that coated his tip, teasing and tempting him with my tongue without once taking him into my mouth.

"Fuck," he gasped, his grip tightening in my hair as he lifted it away from my face to give the camera a better view.

I took him in then, not slowly or carefully, simply opening myself to him and taking every single inch all the way to the back of my throat with a moan of satisfaction as his hips bucked into me.

His grip tightened in my hair, and he pushed me down onto him again, another curse falling from him as he took control, fucking my mouth and making me moan loudly as I loved every second of it.

But my moment of triumph came crashing down around me as Chase suddenly burst out laughing, his fist in my hair dragging me off him so that I could look up and see what was so fucking funny.

My lips parted as I stared at his phone, the camera flipped on the video call he had going so that it was showing me myself while a little box in the corner showed Maverick and JJ on mute while howling with laughter.

"I warned you I'd get revenge for drawing on my fucking eyepatches," Chase said as I stared at my face which was covered in drawings of penises. A huge cock dominated my entire left cheek, drips of cum spotted down to the corner of my lips in sharpie which clearly hadn't even begun to wash off in the damn sea.

"Have I looked like this all day?" I yelled in outrage, trying to think over what we'd been doing, remembering those fishermen who had been laughing their assess off when we sailed past them earlier and all the fucking photographs Chase had been taking all day.

"You deserved it," Chase replied, clearly not the least bit sorry and I narrowed my eyes at him as I shoved to my feet.

"Well, the joke is on you, Chase Cohen, because I'm not going to suck your dick anymore."

"No?" he laughed, tossing his phone down onto the seat beside him before standing suddenly, dominating me with his sheer size alone and making my breath catch. "I mean, to be perfectly honest, I was having other ideas about that anyway, because as much as the feeling of you sucking me off is something close to heavenly, little one, it was damn hard not to laugh the entire time while looking at that shit scrawled all over your face while you gave me the come fuck me eyes."

I took a swing at him, but he only laughed again, catching my fist and using my momentum to spin us around before pushing me face first down on the huge seating area he had just been sitting on.

"Asshole," I snapped but he just laughed again, dropping down over me and letting his cock press to my ass.

"Yeah. But like I said, you deserved it. Now, I want you to beg me to push your face down into these pillows and fuck you good, little one. And I want you to admit that you deserved this punishment or I'm not going to let you come and I'll just get myself off instead. Got it?"

"Get fucked," I hissed, bucking a little beneath him but all that did was make his cock shift until it was slipping through the wetness as the entrance to my pussy and a breathy moan escaped me despite my feelings on the issue.

"I fully intend to. But like I said, you're gonna have to beg for it."

I wriggled and squirmed some more, only really achieving more friction between the two of us and turning me on even further.

I really did have such big intentions to be a dominating force of nature when it came to my men but shit, I couldn't help but love it when they took control.

Chase leaned forward, his teeth grazing the back of my neck before biting down and a wanton moan spilled from me.

"You like that?" he taunted, doing it again while shifting his hips so that the tip of his cock pressed to my opening, his hands spreading my legs further apart to give him the room he would need to take me like that if I only said the word.

"I just remembered why I hated you so much when I first came back here," I hissed and he shifted his hips again, teasing my entrance before taking my wrists in each of his hands and pressing them down to the cushions either side of me, making a cross with my body I would gladly die upon.

"Why's that?" he murmured, nipping at my ear lobe, and making me gasp again.

"Because you're an arrogant, infuriating, egotistical piece of shit," I panted, my spine arching as he teased me with his cock again, urging him to just do it already.

"Nah, those qualities only make you want me more," he replied with a chuckle. "They make you want me even when you've spent the day with a face full of sharpie and I got full revenge on you for the shit you've been pulling with my eye patches. In fact, I think I could make you scream every one of those words like praise if only you gave in to the inevitable here."

"Never," I hissed defiantly, though my body was screaming *yes* with everything I had.

"Fair enough. I guess I'll just finish what you started for myself then." Chase released my right wrist, moving his hand to his cock and rearing back enough to fist it as he began to jerk himself off, keeping his solid dick precisely where it was so that every pump of his fist made the head of it drag along my core from clit to ass and back again.

"Fuck," I moaned, trying to tilt my hips so that he would find my clit more often, urging him to release the building storm within my veins.

My free hand clawed at the fabric I was pinned to, my pussy growing so wet that the emptiness inside of me was almost painful while Chase's breathing grew heavier. He wasn't going to give in. The stubborn bastard would come all over my pussy without finishing me and I wouldn't be surprised if he would hog tie me to stop me from finishing myself too. Not that I had any interest in using my own hand right now because I was aching for the fullness of his cock. It wasn't a want; it was a need. And with a moan that spoke of my own failure while fully accepting that I was okay with giving in for this, I broke.

"Fuck me," I panted. "I need you inside me, Chase. *Please.* Show me all the reasons you have for that big fucking ego and make me scream so loud that Rick can hear it right across the ocean."

"Well, as you asked so nicely."

Chase took his hand from his cock and thrust into me with a savagery that had a scream instantly tearing from my lips as the blissful thickness of his cock filled me just as deeply as I'd been aching for.

"You feel so much better than my fucking hand, little one," he groaned, holding himself there for a moment before returning his hand to my wrist and pinning me down once more.

"More," I begged, giving in to my submission now and loving every moment of it. "I need more."

"Always," he agreed and then he started to move.

My cries spilled out across the open water that surrounded us, scandalising every dolphin, sea urchin and starfish for miles around as he fucked me hard and fast, driving himself in so deeply that it stole my breath with every pump of his hips.

I was crushed to the cushions beneath me, the rough friction dragging against my clit and making me come for him within minutes, his name clawing from my throat as I pulsed and spasmed around his length.

He didn't even pause to let me catch my breath, fucking me harder and harder, like an animal set lose from his cage, tasting freedom at last and unable to get enough, he used my body for his own pleasure, taking and taking while I just cried out at his mercy, loving every moment.

I came again, pushing back against his thrusts as I took all he could give, my face scraping against the cushions as he fucked me through it, resisting his own release with all he had.

The third time I fell for him, he was forced over the edge with me, the roar that left him filling my soul just as deeply as his seed filled my body and he collapsed on top of me, panting and sweating, his weight so beautifully intense.

Neither of us moved for several long minutes, the swaying of the boat the only thing reassuring me that the world was still out there beyond us while every fibre of my being focused in on him and him alone.

Eventually Chase drew his body from mine, rolling onto his back beside me and hauling me over with him so that he could look at me.

"You're every dream I ever dared wish for myself, you know that?" he asked as he took my hand, entwining his fingers with mine and raising them above us so that we were looking at nothing but them and the open sky beyond.

My gaze caught on the five bracelets that sat around his wrist, and I smiled as I watched them bob with the current.

"Even when you have to fuck me face down to stop yourself from laughing at all the cocks you drew on my face?" I asked and he barked a laugh which made my heart leap and swell.

"Especially then. I wished upon a star for that particular fantasy to play out."

"Good," I replied with a sigh, closing my eyes, and just feeling the strength of his body wrapped around mine. "Because I'm thinking of getting them all tattooed there permanently."

Chase's laughter surrounded me as we continued to bob on our little boat in the middle of the sea I loved so dearly.

I soaked in everything about that moment, tucking it away inside my heart and keeping it there so that when the darkness came for us again, as I knew it would, I'd have this to hold on to. Just me and Ace in the sun, without any fear or pain in sight for miles all around.

MAVERICK

CHAPTER EIGHTEEN

The bang of my gun firing sent a shot of adrenaline into my blood as my bullet blasted another tin can off of the log in the woods ahead of me.

"That's five in a row. Pay up, old man." I held out my hand as Luther moved closer beside me, taking out a twenty dollar bill and shoving it into my palm.

"You're giving that back to me if I get more than five," he insisted. "And stop calling me old. I'm not even fifty yet. And you know what those extra years bought me on you?"

"What's that?" I asked with a smirk as Foxy boy moved to line up the cans again on the log.

"Pure skill." Luther fired as Fox got out of the way, taking down one can then another and another. Motherfucker took down eight before he missed one and I cursed, handing the twenty back to him.

"You got lucky," I said as Fox laughed at me, stepping forward to have his go.

"Practise makes you lucky in this life. You work on something long enough, you'll be the luckiest man alive in that field," Luther said, perching himself on one of the camping seats we'd brought up here.

The tailgate at the back of his blue truck was down and he had a mini fridge there full of beer and snacks. He took one of the beer cans, cracking it open and taking a long swig as I moved to sit in the seat beside him, grabbing my own as we watched Fox take down tin cans like they'd personally insulted his cock.

"Your knees hurting you?" I asked my dad, and he gave me a dry look over the top of his beer.

"You're asking for trouble, kid," he warned. "I'll beat your ass if you keep goading me."

I let out a low laugh as I took a swig of my cold beer, resting my gun on my knee.

"How's it going with Carmen?" Fox asked as he finally shot down a can he'd missed three times, walking over to join us and dropping down on his seat.

"Why would you think there's anything going on with me and Carmen?" Luther bit out quickly and I arched a brow at him as Fox coughed a laugh.

"Because she's forcing you to help her out in payment for saving my ass…" Fox said and Luther blinked at him before forcing a laugh.

"Right. Yeah. Of course you meant in that sense." Luther passed him a beer, scratching the back of his head, taking a damn long time to continue. Was he flustered? Did the old man have a thing for the ice-cold queen of the cartel? Fuck me. "Well…that's kinda why I asked you boys up here."

"What do you mean?" Fox asked with a crease forming between his eyes.

I shifted in my seat, eyeing Luther closely, sensing I wasn't gonna like what he was about to say.

"I've gotta go outa town for a while," he said.

"Where?" Fox demanded immediately.

"Just out of town," Luther repeated, and I leaned forward in my seat towards him.

"Where?" I echoed Fox, not letting him avoid this.

"I can't say. And it'll be for a while. I'll come home when I can, but...I don't know how long it's gonna take all in all," Luther said, drinking a long drink of his beer while Fox and I exchanged a glance.

"How long what is going to take?" I pressed.

"You know I ain't gonna bring you boys into this, I told you that," he said firmly, and I sighed, knowing he wouldn't relent.

"I don't like this," Fox said, chewing the inside of his cheek as he gazed at our father. "She's got you doing something dangerous."

"My work is always dangerous," he said, though I didn't miss the darkness in his eyes that said this was one of the riskier things he'd done in his life. And I didn't like that one bit.

"Is there anything we can do to help?" I asked and Luther looked between us, measuring up his next words.

"There is as a matter of fact," he said.

"Anything," Fox said.

"Oh yeah? That a promise?" Luther asked and Fox frowned while I narrowed my gaze on our dad.

"What is it?" I growled before Foxy boy could go signing us up for something I didn't ask for.

"I need you two to step up and take leading roles in the Harlequin Crew," Luther said.

I wasn't rendered speechless often in my life, I could usually think of some inappropriate joke to crack no matter what the situation, but right now I had nothing, shock stealing all my words away.

"What?" Fox gasped. "Why?"

"I told you, I've gotta go outa town. And frankly, you boys have been running the Crew just fine for weeks now. Fox, you half ran it anyway with me for years. Rick, you've been running your own gang too, you've got this. If you want it, that is." Luther looked between us, and I sat back in my chair, draining my beer as Fox stared at our father in shock.

"I told you I'm out," Fox said, though the words didn't have the same conviction in them that they used to.

"Is that because you still wanna be out, or because you're a stubborn asshole?" Luther asked him and Fox pressed his lips together, but it did kinda look like he was thinking on his answer.

"You're handing us the keys to the kingdom just like that?" I asked and my father nodded, his eyes bright and full of that unwavering faith he had in us. I didn't know how he kept it up. I'd given up on myself once, yet somehow, he hadn't, always waiting for me to come back like he'd known I'd find my way home.

"Well I'm in," I said easily, shrugging as Fox's jaw went slack, staring at me with a flare of fury in his eyes. "Guess that makes me the Harlequin King. You wanna be my errand boy, Foxy?"

"Fuck you," Fox snapped.

"Fox," Luther growled, and my brother huffed out a breath as he looked to him.

"I said I was out. I don't wanna be that man again," Fox said, pain flashing in his green eyes. "Why do you have to ask the one thing of me I swore I'd never do for the sake of my family?"

He shoved to his feet, tossing his half full can of beer into the grass before stalking off into the trees like an angry little tiger. Luther sighed sadly, watching him go with an ache in his expression.

I rolled my eyes at all the drama, sinking the rest of my beer and crushing the can in my grip before tossing it into the truck bed.

"You owe me one for this, Dad." I pushed to my feet, starting after Fox, but Luther called after me.

"What did you call me?"

Fuck.

I stopped walking, hesitating before looking back at him and shrugging my shoulders. "That's what you are, aren't you?"

"Am I?" he asked like the desperate little dodo he was.

"Yeah," I exhaled. "Only one that matters."

Sunbeams shot out of his eyes, and I waved him off before he could come seeking a cuddle or some shit, striding after my brother into the trees.

Fox had walked all the way down the dirt road that led out to Carnival Hill, standing on the grass as he gazed across the town to the glimmering ocean beyond. The sun was setting over the water, casting the sky in rivers of deep gold and orange light that gilded Fox in its glow.

It was all very fucking melodramatic, and I clucked my tongue as I moved to my brother's side. It was damn impossible not to appreciate that view though. Even the ruin of Sinners' Playground looked magical in that light, the last pieces of it standing out in the water like a ghost of its former self. I still felt the loss of that place every day; a part of our home had been carved away from us and turned to ash, and there was nothing that could ever replace it.

"Would you go back in time?" I asked Fox, pondering on that question myself. "Would you trade in today for all those perfect yesterdays we once had?"

The silence stretched and I wondered if he might not answer, but eventually he did.

"No," he said. "I used to wish for that so fucking hard. I'd dream of it so often, it made real life feel like a waking nightmare."

"It was," I grunted, and he nodded, shooting a sad glance my way. "But now?"

His mouth turned up in a smile. "I think if I spend any more time thinking about what could've been, I'll miss out on what is. Would I take away all the pain everyone's suffered through? Fuck yes. But I can't. I used to think I could prevent more bad from happening too if I just wrapped up everyone I loved in cotton wool, but then I became the bad thing happening to them instead."

"I learned something when I was in prison at the hands of a monster," I said, my voice low and fraught with tension, and though I felt Fox's gaze on me, I kept my eyes firmly on that breath-taking horizon. "I learned that control is an illusion. That there's no order in this world, no grand plans designed by something bigger than us. Life is anarchy, and the moment you surrender to it, you're free. Free of society's rules and demands. Free of guilt, of regret. Sure, it ain't easy, but once you let go…" I breathed in deep through my nose and let it all out through my mouth. "It's peaceful, brother. It's how it should be. We don't need to wield the power of the ocean; we only need to catch the waves and enjoy the ride."

"You're right," Fox said, pushing his fingers into his hair. "Fuck, you're so right."

"Always am," I said, my taunting tone back in place and he laughed, shoving me in the shoulder so I stumbled sideways a little. "So? What are you gonna do? The ocean's sending a big wave your way, Foxy boy, are you gonna catch it with me?"

"Shit, are we definitely ready for this?" he asked.

"We got this," I said. "And if the power starts going to your head again, I'll put you in line."

He grinned and that smile just kept getting bigger.

"I knew you wanted your crown back," I mocked. "Are you sure your big head will fit into it this time?"

"Fuck you," he drawled and I slung my arm around his shoulders, looking out over the town we were officially about to rule side by side. "Is this our Lion King moment?"

"Yeah, Foxy. Kumbaya."

"Do you mean Hakuna Matata?" he muttered.

"That's the one," I snorted.

I felt Luther arriving behind us, wrapping us in his arms and pushing his head between ours as he looked out at the view.

"What's the verdict, Fox?" he asked. "Will you lead at your brother's side?"

"Yeah…I'm pretty sure that's how it was always meant to be," he said.

"Kings of Sunset Cove," I said, liking the sound of that.

I broke away from the others, tipping my head back to the sky and howling like a wolf, the sound echoing away across the hill. Fox joined in next, and Luther laughed before howling too, my Harlequin blood heating and telling me I was exactly where I should be in the world.

Luther left town just after midnight, dropping Fox and me at home in his truck before heading away towards an unknown fate. Anxiety wrapped around my heart as I got the uncomfortable feeling that he might not return from whatever mission he was on, but I pushed it away, laying my faith in him and the strength he possessed.

I fell into the bed where Rogue was curled up with Chase, JJ, and Mutt while Fox took the place on the other side of them. I didn't think I could sleep in a dog pile like this without the air conditioning keeping us cool, and honestly if we kept at it, we were gonna need a bigger bed.

Sleep found me quickly as it often did in their company, stealing me away into the dark and into one of my sweeter memories, coaxed back to life by the closeness of *them*.

"Would you rather have eight tentacles for legs, or huge crab claws for arms?" Rogue called to us as she led the way along the stony beach at the foot of the cliffs. The tide was low which meant we could walk out here for now, but it wouldn't be long before this beach was swallowed whole again by the ocean.*

JJ adjusted the nerd-pack on his shoulders which carried all kinds of survival gear in it that we wouldn't need. Except the brownies he'd swiped from his mom's kitchen, the rest of the shit jangling about it there was simply causing him effort for no reason.

"Crab claws," Chase answered easily as he walked at my side, a fresh bruise lining his jaw today, though he hadn't breathed a word about the man who'd obviously put it there. "What use are fucking tentacle legs? I could cut someone's head off with giant crab claws."

"Fuck yeah," JJ agreed, and Fox and I nodded.

JJ's foot slipped on a slimy rock, and I caught his arm before he went nerd-pack over tit and I righted him beside me, his bag jangling furiously as all his gear shifted around inside it.

"What have you got in there, J?" I sniggered. "A fucking crockery set for a tea party?"

"I've got all kinds of survival stuff, asshole," he said. "And you'll be glad of it if we get into trouble."

I laughed, shaking my head at him. "What are you gonna do? Get out your Swiss army knife and whittle us a whistle if we get stranded here?"

"Shut up, man," JJ growled, and I shrugged, jogging past him to catch up to Rogue at the front of our group.

"Would you rather be bald or have a furry ass?" I asked her and she laughed beautifully for me, that sound lighting me up inside.

"On a scale of one to yeti, how furry would my ass be?" she asked, stroking her long dark hair protectively.

"Full yeti," I said, smirking as her nose scrunched up while she thought on it.

"Furry ass," she sighed. "I just can't give up my hair."

I roared a laugh, leaning back to look down at her ass and picturing hair bursting out of her shorts. But my laughter died away as my gaze got caught on the movement of her ass in that tight denim, the perfect roundness of it and the way it jiggled a bit with every step she took. Damn...

"Rick," Fox barked at me.

I looked up, snapping out of my stupor and I shrugged at him as he gave me a death glare.

"We're here!" Rogue cried in excitement, and I realised she was right as we spotted the cave we'd seen from the boat we'd taken out this way yesterday. The tide had been too high for us to approach then, but we could walk right into it now.

"Flashlights," JJ announced, taking five from his bag and handing them all out to us.

Alright, so maybe they were sort of useful, but I could bet whatever else he had in there was pointless.

Fox took the lead, and I only didn't barrel after him to try and go first because Rogue linked her arm with mine and gave me a look that set my heart pumping. Did she want big, bad me to protect her in there?

My chest puffed out, though it deflated a little as I realised she was just using me for support so as not to slip on the wet rocks lining the floor of the cave as we picked our way inside. Still, she'd chosen me to hold onto, so that had to count for something.

"Woah," Chase breathed, the place commanding quiet as we headed deeper into the dark.

The flashlights picked out the murky green colour of the cave roof and the glinting minerals in the stalactites that hung down from it. It was clear the sea would fill up this entire cavern when the tide was high, but for now it was our own secret place to explore.

"Do you reckon a pirate stashed treasure down here?" Chase wondered aloud.

"Pirates didn't stash treasure, that's a myth," JJ said.

"Says who?" Chase shot back.

"Says Mrs Peterson," JJ said.

"Oooh, Mrs Peterson," I mocked him over our history teacher. She

305

always wore tight dresses with her tits half hanging out, and more than half of the assholes in our class had a hard on for her, though I always found the things she wore more disturbing than hot.

"Dude." JJ grimaced. "I'm not into Mrs Peterson."

"You sure?" Rogue asked a little sharply and JJ looked to her.

"There's only one girl for me, and that's you, pretty girl," he said, a teasing lilt to his voice, but I narrowed my eyes at him suspiciously, knowing there was more to it than that.

"Shut up, J," she laughed.

"Hey look!" Fox called from somewhere up ahead and we ran to catch him, the cool air in this place making goosebumps rise on my arms.

"Is it treasure?" Chase asked excitedly.

"I told you, there's no such thing as pirate treasure," JJ insisted.

"Sure there is," Rogue chimed in.

"Why would a pirate bury his treasure and not come back for it? It doesn't make sense," JJ said.

"'Cause he died after he killed everyone who knew about it, duh," Rogue said.

"That's just story stuff," JJ argued as I pulled Rogue past him to catch up to Fox, finding him around a tight bend in the cave system, pointing his flashlight at some words carved into the rock face.

M.R. & L.O. We're the wild in the darkness.

"Who do you think they are?" Fox whispered and Rogue cocked her head to the side, examining the jagged heart carved beside the words.

"I dunno, but I think they lived a good life." She brushed her fingers over the marks. "Maybe they're still out there living it."

"We should add our names," JJ said, taking out the Swiss army knife I'd just known he had smuggled away in his nerd-pack.

306

Rogue took the bag from him, snagging the brownies as JJ began carving all of our initials beneath the other markings. I swiped myself a brownie too as we settled ourselves on the rocks, drips of water sounding around us as they fell from the ceiling onto the damp cave floor.

Between the sugar in my mouth and the company around me, I was pretty sure this was another perfect day to add to my collection. And as JJ backed up to let us see the finished product, I grinned at the words he'd engraved beneath our names.

We're the darkness in the wild.

I didn't know what the fuck that meant, but I liked it. In fact, I reckoned I might just like it enough to ink it onto my flesh one day.

I stirred within the sheets as I tried to stay with that memory, but a more persistent one was creeping in, one that fell upon me like something corrosive against my skin.

I felt his hands winding around my body, making me feel so goddamn small as I was bent to his will. A splinter of pain made me flinch and I fought against it, trying to break free, but he was too strong. Always so fucking strong.

I thrashed as I felt him taking possession of my body, owning me, violating me. I was sick to my stomach and the bile burned all the way up until I tasted it.

Hands clasped me, pushing me down further and I shoved at them with a roar, my eyes flying open and finding the soft hue of brown irises staring back at me.

I hurled the man away from me with a bellow, but then a little dog collided with my chest along with a girl whose hair was painted all the colours of a sunset. I saw her and came back to the room in a rush, my chest heaving as the nightmare tried to hold onto me, but she brushed her fingers over my cheeks, keeping me present.

"I'm here, it's okay," she promised, and I didn't dare blink, afraid she'd vanish and I'd never find her again.

Mutt nestled in against my body and the frantic thumping of his tiny heart kept me grounded. I raised my hand, stroking him and finding peace in the movements as Chase moved closer again in my periphery, while Fox and JJ leaned over Rogue's shoulder to check on me.

"It's fine," I bit out. "Stop looking."

I shoved the sheets off of me, keeping Mutt in my arms as I slipped away, realising I was trembling as I stormed out of the room.

I felt Rogue following as I pushed into Fox's bedroom and walked straight out onto his balcony to get some air.

The moment the oxygen slid into my lungs, the chains of my past loosened on me further and I found safety closing in on me once more. Rogue hugged me from behind, resting her cheek to my back and I bathed in the closeness of her as Mutt licked the ink on my bicep, right where the words from my dream were now tattooed around it.

"I got you," Rogue whispered, her lips pressing to my back and the darkness slid away easier than it usually did.

I hung my head, glad I wasn't descending into one of my worse episodes where only violence could bring me down from that state.

"I love you," I told her, and she squeezed me tighter.

"I love you too," she answered.

I smiled, rubbing Mutt's head, glad of his presence as he looked up at me with a small whine.

"I made a vow that I'd tried to beat Fox's letter," I said with a sigh. "I wanted to put into words how much I adore you, but I'm fucking shit at writing it down."

I turned to her and she frowned up at me, her nose scrunching in that familiar way. "You don't need to do that. I know how you feel."

"I wish I could say it better," I said in a growl. "I wish I could tell you that I love you as catastrophically as the loss of you broke me. That this kind of ruin is a far sweeter destruction to endure, and that I would never choose any other downfall but this."

She shook her head at me, smiling cutely. "You just did, Maverick."

CHAPTER NINETEEN

After Fox and Maverick had taken us to The Oasis Clubhouse and announced they were stepping in as the rulers of the Harlequins, we spent the rest of the day celebrating their coronation at home.

Maverick had announced The Damned Men's official integration into The Harlequin Crew and threatened anyone who opposed him on that with pain of death. Unsurprisingly, there had been no words spoken against them, and the elders of the Harlequins took it all so neatly in their stride that it was clear Luther had given them the heads up already before he left.

"You realise me and Ace are the new princes of The Harlequin Crew now, right?" JJ said, shooting me a grin across the patio table.

"How's that work then?" Rick asked at my side, mirth glinting in his eyes.

"You know exactly how it works," JJ said. "If you and Fox die, we get to take over."

"What about me?" Rogue said. "I wanna be next in line."

"You're already queen consort," I said.

"Pfft, fuck consorting. I wanna be the royal bitch boss," she decided, and we all chuckled.

"You can be anything you want, baby," Fox said through a wolfish smile as he laid a kiss on her cheek.

"You rule us all anyway, Queen Harlequin," Rick said.

"Fuck, I like the sound of that," JJ said gruffly, and I had to agree.

"No consorting?" she asked Rick, biting her lip seductively.

"No consorting. Well, actually, you can consort with my cock sometimes, how about that?" Rick reasoned and she laughed, picking up an olive from a bowl in the middle of the table and tossing it at him. He caught it in his mouth, chewing through it victoriously.

"That sounds preferable to all that gang shit anyway. Their meetings are so dull and there are never enough snacks," she said and Rick and Fox exchanged an amused look. No doubt if she actually wanted a real role in the gang, they'd hand her her crown and watch her grow into it, but we all knew that wasn't what Rogue wanted. She wanted the sun on her skin, the sand between her toes and laughter on her lips while the sound of the sea crashed all around her. Simple. Beautiful. And exactly what we all planned on making sure she had her fill of for the rest of our damned lives.

My phone buzzed and I huffed a breath as I took it out of my pocket, finding another message from my dad's carer. That was the third one today. I just wanted to relax, enjoy the company of my family, and keep making up for the time we'd all lost together. But apparently the universe had other ideas.

Alice Bevlin:
Please, Mr Cohen. I know you're not fond of your dad, but he's messaged me three times begging for someone to come help him and I can't get there today. I'll have to call 911 if you won't go.

I ran my tongue over my teeth, the sound of my family talking fading to a din around me as I made the decision to go. I could almost feel his shadow drawing over me like a veil, making me feel two sizes smaller, just a boy summoned home where a punishment was waiting.

I pushed to my feet, my teeth grinding at the flare of pain in my leg. The effort of surfing yesterday had caused some inflammation in it that was a real fucking bitch, and though I accepted the painkillers Rogue gave me at night, I didn't like taking more than that.

"I've gotta go see my dad," I told the others bluntly, and they all stopped talking, looking to me in surprise.

"Everything okay, man?" JJ asked, stroking Mutt who was perched on his lap.

"Yeah, just the usual shit. His carer's away," I muttered. "I'll be back in a bit."

"You want company?" Rogue asked.

"Nah," I waved her off.

"He never does when he visits him, hummingbird," Fox said quietly. I walked as straight on my bad leg as I could, not wanting the others to see that my limp had temporarily returned as I walked inside from the patio. I made it halfway to the garage before Rogue appeared, darting past me and planting herself in my way with her arms stretched wide. She had white denim booty shorts on today and a baby pink crop top that showed off her waist. Fucking perfect as always.

"I'm coming," she announced. "And don't go giving me some honourable, going-it-alone bullshit. That's Red Power Ranger talk, and we don't speak of him in this house. I'm Green, and you're Pink."

"I'm not Pink," I growled.

"You're Pink, Ace. Through and through." She pinched my nipple and twisted it and I cursed her, batting her off while she danced away as I tried to grab hold of her. My leg fucked with my plan, sending me stumbling sideways into the wall. It rarely gave me much trouble anymore, but anytime I overdid it in the water or working out, I was reminded it wasn't entirely back to normal.

"Argh," I growled.

"Arrrr, me matey," Rogue teased. "How's your peg-leg, Captain Ace?" She moved back towards me, slipping her hand around my hips and pressing herself flush against me.

"Bad move," I warned her, sliding an arm around her back and fisting her little crop top in my grip. "I've got you now, and you're gonna pay for the pirate joke."

"Oh yeah? What are you gonna do to me, Captain?" she purred, the lust burning in her eyes telling me she really was into this pirate roleplay shit. Crazy little one. "Are you going to make me service your long plank? Scrub your dick – I mean decking."

I didn't crack a smile, leaning down so we were nose to nose and running my palm down the length of her spine. She shivered deeply for me, and a dark smile twisted up my lips at how responsive she was to my touch. I swear I was still living in a daydream, the knowledge that she was finally mine not ever feeling real. But one thing that had always been easy between us was the way we played together, mocking the ever-loving hell out of one another in a game of back and forth that never ended. Right now, we were just kids going toe to toe with one another, and it was my favourite game in the world.

I slid my hand down the back of her shorts and her breath hitched, her pupils dilating with want, but then I dropped my other hand to join the first, gripped her tiny G-string in my fists and yanked it right up to her tits.

She screamed to high heaven, punching the hell out of me to try and make me let go, but the material was surprisingly stretchy and as her arms flailed about, I managed to hook each side over them and snapped them down to sit right up on her shoulders.

"My ass!" she cried, trying to struggle her way out of the G-string as a laugh exploded from my chest. But suddenly I found myself at the end of three guns as Maverick, JJ and Fox spilled into the hall with Mutt charging along at their heels, her scream having summoned a fucking army.

JJ burst out laughing as he realised what I'd done while Fox launched into rescue mode, producing a knife from who knew where and slicing through the G-string in two quick slices.

Rick was at her side in the next second, shoving his hands down her shorts and tugging the ripped material out with a roaring laugh.

Mutt barked ferociously, savaging my ankle like he knew I was to blame, and I cursed him, nudging him away with my toe until he stopped.

"Good one, Ace," Rick laughed, casually pocketing the G-string.

"No, not 'good one, Ace', you asshole." Rogue punched Rick in the arm hard enough to make his eyebrows raise. "I think he's cut my butt."

"Oh no," JJ gasped seriously.

"Oh come on, I haven't cut your butt," I said dismissively and she glared at me with a furious vengeance in her eyes that I knew she was gonna deliver.

"Come on then, beautiful. Shorts down, bend over. Let's take a look," Rick ordered, trying to manipulate her body into position but she started smacking his arms to keep him away.

"You good, baby?" Fox asked in concern, picking up Mutt who looked to Rogue with his ears pressed down and a whine in his throat.

"I don't know, badger," she growled, then looked to JJ. "Johnny James, you're the only one I trust with my butt right now." She held out her hand for him in a demand for him to follow her and he moved between us with a proud kind of smirk like he was the king of the butt, and that actually kinda pissed me off.

He took her hand, leading her into the little restroom off the hall and we gathered around it, pressing our shoulders to the wall as Rogue yanked the door closed behind them.

Rick reached for the handle, but a click sounded it locking and we shared a look over her betrayal.

"How come *he* gets to go?" Fox growled.

"Because he's an ass expert, badge," Rogue called, and Fox frowned like he was working out how he could become an ass expert too. He always had to be the best at everything, even asses.

"Stand on the toilet seat," JJ instructed.

"Okay. Like this?" Rogue said.

"That's it. Here," JJ replied, and we all pressed our ears to the door, listening to the sounds of shuffling and what I guessed were Rogue's shorts hitting the floor.

"Bend forward, pretty girl," JJ encouraged. "And part your cheeks for me."

"This is like listening to a low budget porno," Rick muttered.

"Is she okay?" Fox asked urgently.

"It doesn't look good, pretty girl," JJ said in concern and my stomach dropped, the thought that I'd actually hurt her horrifying me.

"Fuck, maybe I should call the Harlequin doctor," I said.

"Lemme in," Rick insisted, banging his fist on the door as his brow pinched.

Rogue gasped and my heart jolted.

"Rogue, I'm sorry. I didn't mean-"

Her gasp turned to a moan followed by another and another.

"Oh my god, JJ," she said breathily, and Maverick started to try and break his way in for a whole other reason. "Yes, J, *yes*."

I moved closer to the door as Rick tried to get it open and Fox backed up, muttering something about JJ being an asshole before walking away entirely.

"She's fine," JJ called to us. "But just to make sure…"

Rogue cried out, the sound making my cock jerk to attention.

"Open the door, beautiful," Rick encouraged.

"Nah, she's already a goner," JJ said, though his voice was muffled, and a second later Rogue started gasping and moaning her way through an orgasm.

I breathed a laugh; glad she was taken care of.

"See ya later, Rick." I turned and headed for the garage, jogging down the steps and grabbing the keys for JJ's car off the hook. *Yoink motherfucker.*

I dropped into it, starting her up and liking the way she purred beneath me as I pressed the button to open the garage door. But before I made it out, Rogue came running into the garage, pointing a finger gun at me and I raised my hands, playing along with her little grand theft auto game.

She yanked the car door open, pressing her finger gun to my chest. "Bang."

"Wow, you just killed me straight up. I would've given you the car, little one," I said, and she grinned, lifting her finger gun to her mouth, and blowing the end of it.

"I know. I'm just a psycho like that."

I grabbed her hips, dragging her into the car on my lap and she started pretending to shoot me as I tickled her. She squealed as I got hold of the hand forming the gun and forced her fingers into her own mouth.

"Bang," I said, and she slumped across the seats, pretending to be dead.

I laughed, shaking her, but she stuck to the role, not moving an inch, but now her stomach was exposed, and she was in trouble. I poked my finger straight into her belly button and she squealed, lurching upright, and aiming a punch at my face. I caught her hand, biting down on her knuckles as I smiled wickedly, and the game turned to something more depraved as our eyes locked and my free hand trailed between her thighs.

I took a breath, blinking out of the hypnosis this girl always cast on me and threw her roughly into the passenger seat. "Don't look at me like that, little one. I've gotta go."

She scrambled upright on her seat, looking like she'd enjoyed me tossing her around like that. "Can I look at you like that after you've seen your dad?"

"Definitely," I said. "You can look at me like that all over JJ's car, maybe on the hood of it too."

"Are you going to take me up Devil's Pass?" she asked huskily.

"Yeah, I'm gonna take you right up the Devil's Pass," I agreed, and she tossed her head back as she laughed, looking wild and free and just like the woman she was born to grow into. My girl as she was destined to be. And that gave me a sense of peace like nothing else in this world could.

I tugged my door shut and took off out of the garage, the engine roaring as I drove us up to the Harlequin gates and they were opened wide for us.

Rogue whooped as I took the turn out onto the road hard, a thrill dancing through me as she buckled herself in for the ride, knowing I'd give her a good one.

I took corners at speed, following the quieter back streets so I could really enjoy the horse power behind JJ's GT and Rogue smiled during the whole ride.

The thrill wore off as I closed in on our destination, and my mood was soured entirely as I drove down the dirt road toward my dad's house. My heart sank in my chest, weighted down by a thousand bad memories. It always felt like this, coming here. It wasn't home, it was hell.

Rogue reached for my hand as I parked up but I withdrew it, pushing my fingers through my hair and not meeting her gaze as a line of heat burned along my neck.

I loved her for her empathy, that she saw right through to my soul and knew I was suffering, but I hated it too. Because it exposed me, that little boy I'd once been revealed like her eyes were peeling were back the layers of my flesh and she was looking right at him. The one with the bruises he tried to hide, the one who had lived in between the walls of this house.

"It's okay," she said.

"It's not," I growled. "It never is when I come here, that's why I wanted to do it alone."

"And that's exactly why I'm here," she said, reaching for me again and this time I let her pull my hand into her lap and caress my fingers with hers. "I'll stay in the car if you say you don't want me in there with you Chase

Cohen, but I don't think you're going to say any such thing, are you?"

I sighed, gazing at her and shaking my head, causing a dark curl to fall forward into my eyes. "No, little one. But it's still hard to let you see me as that kid again."

She reached forward, brushing my hair back and smiling sadly at me. "I love that kid. He was the bravest boy I knew back then, because he fought wars every day even when he had no chance at winning them." Her gaze slid beyond me to the house where my dad resided, a coldness filling her expression. "He's your monster, Ace, which makes him my monster too."

I drew her closer to me across the seats, kissing the corner of her mouth and breathing in the sweetness of her. It calmed my anxiety to have her, my little ray of sunshine.

"Always Forever by Cults," I murmured the song that I'd picked out for her last night.

"I love you too," she whispered, and I held onto her for far too long before sucking up the fate awaiting me and opening the door, drawing her out after me.

I pushed open the broken gate, the metal creaking and groaning in protest at my entrance like it was warning me to turn back. But it was too late now.

I walked up to the door, slipping an eyepatch out of my pocket and putting it on while feeling Rogue's glare burning into me from the side.

"Don't ask me to take it off," I muttered and her lips tightened before she gave in and nodded.

When my dear old father didn't answer the door, I shoved it open and the scent of sweat, booze and the worst time of my life filled my senses.

I pushed through the urge to retreat, squinting through the gloom as we walked into the lounge. I spotted the back of my dad's chair with a tightness in my stomach, but it was clear he wasn't sitting in it.

"Where are you?" I barked into the house, everything too quiet.

Hope shifted in my chest as I realised he might be dead, that some demon greater than him had finally managed to tear him from this world. But then the roughness of his voice carried to me from above and a grimace formed on my face.

"Up 'ere."

There was a command in that voice for me to come to him and I resisted it with all the rebelliousness of my youth, but I had to go to him. That was why I was here, and why come at all if I was going to leave now?

"I hate this place," Rogue whispered, wrinkling her nose at the room and every trace of my father within it. She hadn't come here often when we were kids – none of them had for obvious reasons, but she'd snuck in with me once or twice when I was certain he wouldn't be here, and the place had hardly changed at all in all those years. Same yellowing walls and ratty brown carpet, same stink of PBR beer and cigarettes hanging from the same furniture and tarring the ceiling. It was like stepping right back into my own personal hell every time I walked through that door, like stepping into the skin of the boy I'd been when I had been forced to call this house a home.

I nodded in agreement, giving her a dark look before leading the way upstairs and walking along the narrow hallway to my dad's bedroom.

I nudged the door open, the light low in the room as I hovered in the doorway with the old rules of this house holding me back from entering. I wasn't allowed in there. It was a place for him and my mom, a place he took her that I couldn't reach her thanks to the locks on the inside of the door.

A lump thickened in my throat at the weight of guilt that placed on my heart. As a man, I saw the logic of those memories, that I was just a boy who didn't know how to save his mommy. But I still couldn't shake the feeling that I could have saved her if only I'd tried harder, if I'd stood my ground more firmly, fought back more fiercely.

"Get in here, boy," he growled, his voice gravelly and full of cancerous tar.

I despised how deeply I felt his claws in me whenever I was here with him, all the worst parts of my childhood crawling out of the woodwork around me like termites come to feast on my fears.

"You're a waste of good oxygen." The voice found me from the past, my father's cruel words as cutting as they had been then. And what made it worse, was how Shawn's voice followed in my mind.

"Look at that gleam in your eyes, it's almost as if you believe you're worth something. But don't worry, I'll remind you what you are, Chase Cohen. You're just dirt that grew legs."

Rogue's hand slid into mine and I was brought sharply back to the moment, the warmth of her fingers in mine reminding me of the life I had now. I wasn't a prisoner of either of those soulless men anymore, at least not in any physical way.

"You got this, Ace," she growled, and I drew my strength from her, this stunning creature who was filled with the power of the ocean. With her at my side, anything was possible.

I stepped into the room, my chin high, though the scars across my body prickled with the intensity of my dad's gaze on me. He hadn't seen me since Shawn had tortured me, and as much as I wanted to pretend that I didn't care what he thought of my appearance now, I couldn't ignore the part of me that wanted to hide.

"Someone finally give you what you had coming to ya?" my dad mused, chuckling as he took in my scars, and ice dripped down my spine. "Look at the state of you. Ugly on the outside as well as the inside now."

My teeth ground together in my mouth as I tried not to feel those words, but they sliced in deep.

"He's one of the most beautiful men I know. And if you laugh at him again, I'll make you regret it," my girl warned, and my heart beat harder at those words.

"Who's 'at?" he grunted at me, jerking his chin at Rogue as he drew the covers higher over his body.

He was propped up on the sweat-stained pillows, a thin tank top revealing the sun-baked skin of his arms and the faded anchor tattoo on his left bicep. His hair was grizzled and lank, hang around the sagging skin of his cheeks as he peered over at Rogue with a sneer on his lips. And that was all I needed to find the monster in me, my shoulders pressing back as I released her hand, moving forward to place myself between them. He didn't deserve to lay his eyes on her, and he certainly wasn't going to fucking sneer at her.

"Get that look off your face," I hissed. "This girl is a fucking queen, and if you don't treat her with respect, I'll leave you here to rot."

My father glowered at me with years of loathing behind his eyes. His hate for me had been born the day I was, though I'd once tried to make him love me, when I was small and innocent and had no idea why my flesh and blood looked at me with so much contempt. I felt angry for that little boy now, the rage of it all building up in me and choking the air out my lungs.

My dad clucked his tongue, but said nothing more, raising his hand which was bound with a white shirt and waving it at me. "I cut my hand on a fucking tin can so get on with fixing me up, or are you gonna waste more of the oxygen in this room?"

"Watch your mouth," Rogue snarled, stepping around me and glaring down at my father in his bed. I looked to her in surprise. "You speak to him with respect, or you don't speak at all. We can turn around and walk out of this house whenever we damn well please, but I don't think you can say the same, can you?" She kicked his cane out from where it was leaning against the nightstand so it hit the floor and rolled away across the room.

My father's face twisted in rage like he couldn't believe she'd just spoken to him like that, and a grin pulled at my mouth. His lips parted, but he swallowed whatever he wanted to say, jerking his hand toward me again.

I leaned down, ripping the makeshift bandage off his hand with little care, making him curse in pain. The jagged wound ran up his thumb, the blood leaking from it enough to tell me it needed stitches.

"Have you still got a suture set in the house?" I asked, remembering the time he'd thrown a lamp at me and some of the broken pieces had cut my forearm. He'd stitched it up roughly without letting me go anywhere near a hospital – or painkillers for that matter – and I'd been in agony the whole way through. It was a perfect example of why I tried not to let the memories housed within these walls to have airtime in my head, but now I was within them again, it was impossible to block them out.

My father nodded stiffly. "Cabinet in the bathroom."

I left the room to get it, trying to pull Rogue after me but she shook me off and remained there, her arms folded as she gazed coldly down at my father.

I found the box with the suture set inside it and grabbed a bottle of white rum from the kitchen too before returning to the bedroom, finding the silence thick and Rogue's stare just as hard. I could see the contempt in her eyes, and I loved every spark of fire in her gaze, knowing it was there because of me.

I sat on the edge of the bed, pulling my father's hand into my lap, and making him snarl in pain, and that pain was about to get a whole lot worse. I cleaned the cut with the alcohol before sticking him with the needle, drawing a hiss of pain from him that brought a smile to my lips.

Yeah, I was gonna enjoy this, and fuck if I cared that that made me a sadistic piece of shit. I came from one after all.

I took my sweet time stitching him up, adding more stitches than necessary to ensure I got my fill of revenge on his flesh. When I was done, I stood up, wanting to increase the distance between us once more as he reached for the cigarette packet on his nightstand.

He lit one up and the acrid smell of my own bad habit wrapped around me as smoke filled the air, my craving for this same affliction rising in me. It was a tie between us, one of our few commonalities, though sometimes I feared there were more within me. Parts of me that were purely born from him, a nastiness that I could never carve out.

"Mrs Bevlin will be back tomorrow," I told him as I moved to the door, guiding Rogue with me.

"Fix the back door before you leave," he sniped at me. "Some asshole kids kicked it in last night and there was a fucking coyote in my kitchen this morning. I had to chase it off with my cane."

I smiled at that image, slinging my arm around Rogue's shoulders as I led her out of the room and called back to him, "I came to fix your hand, not your door."

"Don't you backchat me, boy," he snapped, but as I looked down at my girl, I didn't feel the bite of those words, my heart didn't flinch in fear. He was just an old man in his bed, unable to rise and hurt me like he once had.

"Let's go, Ace," she whispered, and I remembered the life waiting for me outside this place.

I didn't need to stay here any longer, I'd done my time in this hell, and I wanted to forget it again just as soon as I could.

"Hey! You listenin' to me, boy?" my dad shouted.

"No," I answered, walking away down the hall and not bothering to look back. He was my past, not my present. And the only thing that mattered to me now was the girl who looked at me with sunshine in her eyes and the men waiting for me in our home. This place was a prison, but it wasn't my prison anymore. It was his. And he'd rot away in it with only his sins for company.

ROGUE

CHAPTER TWENTY

The sun beat down on me as I lay on my towel, my fingers trailing through the sand and my board drying beside me. It was a stunning day, clear blue sky all around and only the sound of seagulls and the waves perforated the air.

I was taking full advantage of the stretch of privately owned Harlequin beach by sunning every inch of my naked body and topping up on my tan. I was going to be one wrinkly old woman if I kept this up, but I couldn't find it in me to stop. I just loved the sun-baked feeling too much to care about it. Besides, what were a few wrinkles in payment for a life well led?

Distant laughter let me know that my boys were enjoying themselves out on the water. All of them were still surfing aside from Rick who was keeping watch over me as usual, and I knew that he was keeping a very close eye on me even while I had my eyes closed.

"You're making it damn hard to pay attention to anything other than you, beautiful," he grunted from his position on his own towel beside me.

"You could always strip off and experience the full body tan for yourself," I pointed out.

"If I get naked with you then I'll end up inside you within minutes," he replied firmly. "And as much as I find the idea of fucking out here in the open where everyone can see and be reminded of who you belong to, I don't think I would be doing a very good job of keeping watch in that scenario."

I smirked to myself as I opened my eyes, lifting a hand to shade them from the sun and blinking up at him innocently.

"Think of all the sand," I replied. "Beach sex has to involve a lot of sand ending up in the wrong places."

"Yeah. The sand is what puts me off," he deadpanned, and I bit my lip as I looked him over where he sat sideways on a deckchair beside me, his bare feet in the sand and damp board shorts straining over his clearly hard cock.

I pushed myself to sit up, my gaze roaming over Mutt who was curled up on his own deck chair beneath the shade of a parasol then out to the water where Chase, Fox and JJ were riding the swell as they moved to catch a wave.

"Fifty bucks says I can make you come before they ride that back here," I said, shifting closer to him on my knees and licking my lips seductively.

"Fifty bucks says Foxy boy loses his shit when he sees you're naked out here," Rick replied, his dark eyes moving from me to our surroundings as I shifted closer to him.

"No deal. That's guaranteed. But as much as Fox likes to protest to my naked sunbathing, he also enjoys taking pleasure in my evenly tanned skin, so he will be tamed by it just as easily as you were."

"You think you tamed me?" Maverick scoffed, pushing his shorts down to reveal his solid length and making my mouth water as I eyed the ink coating it, the desire to taste him consuming me.

"Yeah," I replied cockily even as he reached out and fisted my rainbow hair in his inked fingers, trying to take control as always. "I think I snuck out to your secret island and let you think I was your captive while taking you as mine all along."

"Oh, I'm going to enjoy fucking this lying little mouth of yours, baby girl," he purred, tugging me closer and I obligingly ran my tongue over the head of his cock tasting the precum there with a moan of desire rolling from my throat.

"And I'm going to enjoy taking control of you all over again and proving my damn point," I replied, my eyes meeting his as I swirled my tongue around him again and he cursed.

"Only a true queen can rule me from her knees," he muttered, his love for me burning between us and making me want this even more.

I was addicted to these four men. There was no other excuse for it. No matter how much I took or gave, I was always hungry for more, wanting to make up for the time we'd missed and needing to make every second with them count for the time we wouldn't get back. Nothing seemed certain anymore. Shawn was still out there, hunting us, hating us, working to destroy us. So I was going to make every second we had extra memorable just in case. And even if we did manage to take Shawn down and survive his wrath, I wouldn't stop seizing the moment like this, because every single one that I had with them was precious and I wouldn't take a single one for granted.

I placed my hands on Rick's knees, bracing myself as I shifted forward, knowing how he liked it and preparing for his brutality when he began to fuck my mouth. There was nothing gentle or soft between me and him, but I loved it when he took control the way he did. I loved feeling the raw power of his desire and being the sole owner of his pleasure. The savage in me demanded it, seeking out the actions of its counterpart and needing him to give me his all every damn time.

But as I moved to take the full length of him into my mouth, my cell phone began to ring.

I hesitated a moment, looking up at Rick who growled in frustration and that single look was enough to let me know that he wasn't willing to press pause on this now.

I gave in to what he needed, taking him into my mouth and loving the feeling of his fist tightening in my hair as he pushed me down over his cock, making me swallow every inch of him. I drew back with a moan, sucking on his tip before taking him in again, his hips thrusting up this time, making my eyes prickle.

I moaned again, my head bobbing up and down in his lap while he took complete control of me, fucking my mouth and growling my name between thrusts.

My phone stopped ringing then started again, my attention catching on the sound for a brief moment between thrusts but the feeling of Rick's cock between my lips quickly tore all of my focus back to him again.

I sucked and licked while he pumped his hips up to meet me and I felt his fist tighten to the point of pain in my hair a moment before a deep growl escaped him and he came hot and fast down my throat.

I swallowed greedily, wanting every drop and looking up at him from my knees as he withdrew. His inked chest was heaving where he blocked the sun above me, a bead of sweat rolling down his tattooed chest and over his abs which only made me want more.

The sound of my phone ringing cut out again and I smiled in satisfaction at the look of pure bliss on Maverick's face while he released my hair and ran his thumb along the swollen curve of my lips.

"So fucking beautiful," he murmured and I grinned at him, twisting my head to bite down on the pad of his thumb, making him curse me as he jerked his hand away. "And so fucking violent."

My phone started ringing again and I frowned as I turned to look for it, spotting my purse where I'd wedged it beneath Rick's sun lounger and tugging it out to see who was so desperate to get hold of me.

I frowned at the unknown number in surprise, answering it quickly before it could ring out again and meeting Rick's gaze as I spoke.

"Hello?"

"Took you long enough," a rough, male voice spoke in reply and I stilled, glancing around quickly and putting the call on speaker so that Rick could listen too.

"Who is this?" I asked as Maverick picked up on the shift in my mood and gave his own attention to scanning the empty beach too. There was no sign of anyone being out here aside from us though, so my focus remained fixed on the call.

"Let's call me Wolf," the voice replied. "And you can be my Little Red Riding Hood."

"I'm not innocent enough for that," I scoffed and the man on the other end of the line snorted a laugh.

"No. I assumed not. Either way, we have a game to play, and I have your granny all ready to cut up for my dinner."

"What?" I breathed, my head snapping around towards Harlequin House where Mabel had been snoozing in her favourite chair before we'd left. But the place was crawling with Harlequins, and I couldn't see how anyone possibly could have gotten to her there.

"Well, maybe this one is a little young for a granny," the voice said. "But I have it under good authority that she is incredibly important to you. Then again, if that was the case then why did you leave her out there in that trailer park unprotected and so easy to get to?"

"Fuck," I breathed, rocking back onto my heels as my heart began to pound, fear for Di, Lyla and Bella thundering through me as I tried to figure out which one of them he had gone after. I hadn't seen any of them in a couple of days so there was no way for me to be sure.

Mutt leapt up and hurried over to me, a low growl building in his chest as he looked around in search of whatever had me on the verge of panic.

"Yeah," the voice agreed, and Maverick took my hand, stopping me as I made a move to get up, clearly reading the panic in my eyes and sensing that I was going to do something impulsive.

"Cut the shit and tell us what you want," Rick growled, and the voice laughed softly in reply to him speaking.

"There they are," Wolf said. "The pack of dogs I was warned about."

"I take it Shawn put you up to this?" Rick asked without bothering to respond to that comment. "Promising you a diamond which you seem to think is worth dying for."

"If you'd seen the diamond then it's likely you'd agree," Wolf said. "But I'm not a foolish man, which is why I have taken precautions. So here's how this is going to play out. I'll give you an hour to confirm that I really do have your granny here, then we are going to find out how cold hearted you really are Rogue Easton. Because either you will be turning yourself over to save her or I'll be live streaming her demise directly to you before coming at you from another angle. And another. And another. Until I find a granny who you care about enough to trade yourself for."

"Trade myself?" I asked, my frown burrowing deep onto my face while Maverick's grip on my hand remained firm, grounding me, and making sure I didn't lose my shit altogether.

"Yeah," Wolf agreed. "So, call me back when the hysterics are done with and you're ready to hear my terms."

The call cut off and I instantly moved to redial the number, but Rick snatched the phone away.

"Deep breath, beautiful," Rick commanded, his voice powerful and allowing for no arguments while Mutt whimpered and nuzzled against my ankles.

"He has one of my friends," I said, a plea in my voice which begged for it not to be the truth.

"And we'll get her back. If it's even true."

"You think he could have been lying?" I asked, hope spilling through me at the prospect.

"I think he could have let her speak if she was really there. I also think we'd be dumb as fuck to just take his word for it. Call them. See if you can find the truth."

I nodded, taking the phone and quickly dialling Di's number while Rick took my white sun dress from my bag and stood, pulling it over my head to cover me up again.

He turned to wave out towards the water, beckoning the others back to the beach while the unending ring of the phone echoed through my head and I bounced up and down on the balls of my feet, silently begging Di to answer and be okay.

The call rang out and I cursed, quickly switching my focus, and calling Lyla instead.

"Come on," I growled, starting to pace as Rick took off down the beach towards the others, telling them what was happening as they made it out of the water and hurried over to us.

Lyla's phone rang out too and I cursed, my heart hammering wildly in my chest as Fox raced over to join me.

"Any luck?" he demanded, and I shook my head, dialling Bella.

"They're not picking up. But he said he had one of them, not all. So how am I supposed to figure out who it is?" I asked, my voice raising in pitch as panic drove into me.

"We'll figure this out, hummingbird, just try to stay calm," Fox commanded and JJ, Chase and Rick joined us too. "We'll drive over to the trailer park. We'll figure it out. You just concentrate on trying to get hold of them."

I nodded, my entire focus zeroing in on the sound of the ring tone which droned on endlessly in my ear as Bella's phone rang out too.

My boys all stripped out of their wet shorts around me, pulling on dry clothes quickly and hurrying to gather our shit.

Maverick grabbed my hand and drew me into a run as we took off up the beach and I let him lead me as I made call after call, trying to get one of them to answer me and let me know they were okay. But every time a call rang out, my hope dwindled a little more, my worry for my friends raising with every step I took as I began to fear all the worst things. What if he'd taken one of them but hurt the other two to show me what he was capable of? That was the kind of twisted game Shawn would have played. Was I going to find two of my friends dead when we made it to Rejects Park, their fates forcing me to take him seriously with whoever was left alive?

"Fuck," I hissed as I followed the others into the house where they all grabbed guns before taking off down the stairs into the garage.

We piled into Fox's red truck, my heart hammering a mile a minute as JJ drew me onto his lap and we crushed ourselves into the cab together.

Fox barked orders at the Harlequins on the gate to check all around the house and post a few men inside to watch over Mabel then we were off, tearing away down familiar streets while the heated air of the California sun billowed around us through the open windows.

The truck skidded to a halt, and I scrambled for the door handle, leaping out and taking off in a sprint without even looking to check if the others were following me.

I gasped as I spotted McCreepy's door ajar at the top of the hill, my spine prickling as I headed that way, my instincts telling me that something was wrong.

Chase barked my name and I glanced around in time to catch the gun he tossed me, giving him half a smile in thanks as I moved towards the door, flicking the safety off.

My gaze instantly caught on the puddle of red just inside the door, my throat working on a swallow as I tiptoed closer, ignoring Fox's command for me to let him go first as I reached out and knocked the door wide with the muzzle of my gun.

Joe's body lay in a twisted heap on the floor, the bullet hole in his chest and the glassy look in his eyes leaving no question over his fate as he stared unseeingly towards the sky.

He was dead. And as I raised my eyes to the open cupboard to the right of the door, the reason for his death became all too clear. The hooks that should have held the keys to all of the trailers had been ransacked, hardly any of them remaining on their hooks while a jumble lay in the bottom of it, making it impossible for me to tell which of them had been taken. But I already knew. This had to be the work of the man who had named himself Wolf.

"Shit," JJ muttered as they all made it to me and took in what I'd found.

I turned and bolted before they could say any more, worry for my friends eating me alive as I raced away into the depths of the trailer park, rushing between the sea of trailers while heading straight for Lyla's place which was closest.

The others cursed me as they followed, but none of them tried to stop me. It was clear that we were too late anyway. Whatever I was going to discover here had already happened and I couldn't do a damn thing about it, but I still needed to know.

I made it to Lyla's trailer, my stomach rolling as I found the blue fairy lights on to indicate she was with a client. I ignored them and ran up the steps anyway, hope building in my chest as a sound from inside caught my ear.

I wrenched the door open and tumbled through the door with my gun raised, my eyes falling straight on my friend who was riding a guy who looked barely in his twenties while his terrified eyes shot to me.

"Fuck," he squeaked, his word descending into a groan as he came, and Lyla whipped around to stare at me in shock.

"Jesus, give a girl a knock before you bust in like that," she chastised, getting to her feet like there was nothing at all unusual about her clambering off of a man she'd just been fucking while the dude on the bed hastily grabbed a cushion to hide his condom wrapped cock as it began to deflate.

"You're okay," I garbled, lunging for her, and hugging her tightly despite her nudity, causing a surprised laugh to fall from her lips.

"Why wouldn't I be?" she asked but I just shook my head, looking back to the door where JJ was peering in at us now too.

"She's okay?" he confirmed and I nodded.

"You need to come with us," I said, tugging on Lyla's hand and drawing her towards the door.

"Hold your damn horses, I need to put something on first," she said, though I could tell she'd picked up on my urgency and was taking me seriously.

Lyla turned back to the bed, grabbing a black silk gown from the end of it and wrapping it around herself before holding her hand out to the guy in the bed.

"Was it all you ever dreamed of, sweetie?" she purred as he hurried to grab his jeans from the floor and pulled out three hundred-dollar bills for her.

"Yeah," he said, looking at her like she was some kind of goddess before glancing my way and clearing his throat. "You, er, mentioned something about a regular deal..." He trailed off and she grinned widely.

"You got it, baby," she replied. "I'll drop my price to two hundred a turn if you come more than once a week and we can work on building up that stamina of yours alongside teaching you a few tricks. You'll be fucking like a demon in no time."

JJ snorted a laugh as he ducked out of sight again and I shook my head, beckoning her after me urgently and making sure she followed.

"Don't let her out of your sight," I demanded of JJ as I passed him and he agreed before I took off again, racing between the trailers in search of Di.

My breath caught in my lungs as I found her sitting out on her front deck with Bella right beside her, the two of them indulging in a midday cocktail and looking more than a little alarmed by my frantic arrival.

"What the fuck?" I breathed as I looked between them, my brow pinching as I tried to figure out what I was missing here.

"Maybe he was just bullshitting you, baby?" Maverick asked as he caught up to me, his arm going around my shoulders as he tugged me in against him. "They're all fine."

"Then what about Joe?" I asked, shaking my head. "He didn't just shoot himself."

"Joe's been shot?" Di asked in alarm, getting to her feet and moving closer to us while Bella just looked utterly confused.

"Yeah, he's dead," I confirmed, reaching out to take Di's hand as I reassured myself that she was okay. "Some guy called me and said he had a friend of mine and that he'd kill her if I didn't cooperate with him. But you're okay, and Lyla…" I trailed off as Lyla caught up to us with JJ and Chase, all of us grouping together now while Mutt stayed close to me like he could sense that there was something wrong.

"What's going on?" Chase asked, clearly as lost as I was, and I just shrugged.

"Maybe this was a trap," JJ said, looking around us with his gun in hand as a shiver ran up my spine and I looked about too, hunting the shadows between the trailers for signs of anything amiss.

"I can't find anyone hanging about here waiting for us," Fox called as he appeared at last, his brow low and his body language laced with violence. I sure as shit wouldn't want to cross him when he was looking like that. "We should get out of here to be certain though."

"Call him back and find out what the fuck he's up to," Maverick said before Fox could usher us away.

I tugged my phone from my pocket, glancing about nervously as I opened up my call list and hit dial on the unknown number.

It only rang once before Wolf answered and a shiver passed through me at the calculating sound of his voice.

"Well?" he asked.

"Who have you taken?" I demanded, thinking of Tatum and suddenly finding myself with someone else to worry over, though I had to believe it would be impossible to get to her through the barriers put in place by her men.

"You haven't figured it out yet?" he scoffed. "And there was me thinking you'd care a whole lot more about your own flesh and blood."

"My what?" I asked, utterly lost now because I didn't have a single blood relative who he could be referring to and I never had done.

"Your sister," he drawled and before I could ask what the fuck he was talking about again, the sound of a shrill cry came from somewhere in the background of his call.

"Rogue! Is that you?" Rosie goddamn Morgan sobbed, and my lips parted in a mixture of relief, surprise, and the knowledge that I was an utter asshole for being glad that it was her.

But honestly, of all the people who he could have taken to use for this, Rosie Morgan wouldn't have once even entered my mind as a possibility though I guess she had been insisting on referring to us as sisters just because we'd been in the same group home as kids, but that was utter horseshit and we both knew it.

There was the sound of a smack and Rosie cried out again before a door was slammed and the sound of her loud wails was cut off.

"Clock's ticking," Wolf growled menacingly. "I'm gonna send you an address and you're gonna come swap yourself for your sister or I'll have to start cutting pieces off of her. Don't worry – I have no intention of hurting you. I only plan on trading you for that big fat diamond. So we can all be winners here."

"Wait," I began but he cut me off.

"No, don't make me wait," he said firmly, and he cut the call before I could get another word out.

I stared dumbly down at my cell phone as the others all shifted closer to me, each of them looking far more concerned than I felt.

"He has…" I hesitated, looking at Chase and remembering all the vile things she'd said and done to him, my hatred for her building up to the point where I had to actually consider whether or not I was just a total bitch. "Rosie,"

I said, shrugging at the surprise on all their faces. "He thinks I'll trade myself for her because she's been telling everyone we're sisters."

There was a beat of silence before Rick burst into laughter and I bit my lip to stop myself from joining in too.

"Let's just let the fucker keep her then," he said in amusement.

"No way we're gonna risk you for that cunt, pretty girl," JJ announced, and I could tell that they were all feeling pretty relieved over the identity of Wolf's captive.

"Shit, does it make me the worst person alive if I agree with you on that idea?" I asked, looking to Chase who was trying to smother a smile of his own. "I wished all kinds of bad karma on her just for fucking you," I said to him. "And after the shit she said about your scars, I have to think she deserves this, at least in part."

"I'm certainly not risking any of our asses for hers," Fox agreed, his lip peeling back at the thought of Rosie, and I let him draw me into a hug as I allowed myself to fall into this relief.

"I think we should do something about the girls while this shit is still going on though," JJ said, glancing between Lyla, Di and Bella as they all looked more than a little confused about what was happening. "He could come after them when he realises that Rosie means nothing to you."

I nodded, looking to Fox with my biggest eyes. "Maybe they can all come stay with us while-"

"No," he said before I could finish that thought. "The house is already a big enough target, and we don't have the room to take even more people in, let alone the security risk of adding three more bodies to the mix."

"I hardly think they're a security-" I began, but he cut over me again.

"They can stay at the club house with Dad," he said before I could argue. "It's safe there and there's far more room. They can work the bar or whatever they want to for money."

"Err, I'll be taking Harlequin D all day long for cold hard cash, thank you very much," Lyla announced quickly. "And the three of us might even put on a strip show or two for the whole gang."

"I'm sure there won't be many complaints to that," Rick snorted, and I felt my chest deflating at the thought of them there surrounded by an entire gang for safety.

"Okay," I agreed. "So long as the three of you are alright with that?"

"I think I'm gonna need some more information, but I understand the whole 'not wanting to get kidnapped' concept, so I think I can deal," Lyla said, and I nodded, relief finding me as I realised that we should have done this sooner. We were just lucky that it had been Rosie who got targeted.

"I'll take them to get their shit together and get some of the gang to come collect them," Fox offered, and I agreed, letting the others shepherd me away towards the truck once more while accepting the fact that I probably shouldn't be hanging around here where some other fucker after a diamond might know to come hunting for me.

I glanced down at my phone as it buzzed with a message from the same number that Wolf had used to call me on.

Unknown:

Come alone. Get out when you arrive and walk east until I come for you.

The message was followed by another that contained GPS coordinates and I pursed my lips as I let Chase tug me into the truck with him.

He took the phone from my hand and looked down at it, reading the messages and pulling up the coordinates on a map as he studied it, leaving me with the opportunity to study him in turn.

I reached up to pull the baseball cap he'd been wearing from his head, hating the way he used it to try and shadow his face when we went out in public like this. I leaned up to press a kiss to the scar that marred the side of his face, the skin there smooth and soft beneath my lips.

Chase turned at the feeling of my mouth on his flesh, his lips capturing mine in a sweet kiss which took me off guard and made my heart race for all the best reasons.

"I love you," I breathed as we broke apart, feeling his smile against mine as I lingered close to him like that, and we all waited for Fox to return.

I sighed, thinking of that pain in the ass trout, Rosie, and the vile things she had said to Chase after we got him back from Shawn, and I found I really was tempted to leave her ass to rot with the man calling himself Wolf. But, on the other hand, leaving her with him would hardly help our situation.

"As much as I couldn't give a flying turd about that bitch," I began reluctantly. "At least we know where this asshole is going to be later. I'm not planning on walking my ass out there like he wants, but maybe we can make this into a trap of our own?"

"Let me see." Maverick took my phone from Chase, examining the open, grassy area where Wolf wanted me to give myself up to him with a scowl. "There isn't much up there, but we can assume he has some kind of hideout prepared. That, or he'll be in a car somewhere in this area." He pointed to the grassy area which would be most easily accessed from the road, and I nodded, wondering how we could get the drop on him.

"We need a helicopter or some shit," I muttered wistfully, and JJ sat up suddenly, a grin on his face as he leaned in closer.

"That…or a flashy as fuck drone," he said.

"Okay, and where are we going to get a drone from?" I scoffed at his excitement, but he didn't seem the least bit put off.

"From your bestie's whacko boyfriend," he said. "Saint Memphis."

The Temple

CHAPTER TWENTY ONE

The sound of Beethoven's Moonlight Sonata (First Movement) filled the large room I used for my office as I sat at my desk, my eyes on the screen of my computer as I directed my drone out across the sun beaten landscape of western California.

The corner of my lips lifted into a smile as I watched the feed from the camera attached to it, the powerful piece of military grade equipment easily scanning everything beneath it and giving me a god's eye view of the world.

I had been tempted to refuse this request, or at least bargain for a grander payment, but of course my siren had seen to it that I agreed on the simple basis of friendship.

I wasn't entirely certain why I was supposed to take her relationship with every waif and stray she came across so seriously, but she had formed an attachment to the rainbow haired hellion, and I was always weak for anything that made her smile, no matter how confounding I found the cause of it.

Besides, I hadn't had much reason to use this drone for an actual task like this before now, and I had to admit that there was something of a thrill to be had by doing so. Even if I couldn't deploy any of the attached hardware. Missiles being fired upon American soil were likely to cause an uproar of some sort after all. And I might have been a god among the masses of this hugely underdeveloped land, but even I wasn't that far above the law. More's the pity.

The door banged against the wall, and I released a breath through my nose as the rabble poured in, Tatum giggling as no doubt one of them pawed at her indecently.

I didn't turn their way as they piled into my space, only raising the volume of my classical music to remind them that I needed to concentrate on this task.

Tatum shushed the others insistently, the sound of chairs dragging painfully across the floorboards following her instructions for quiet, and I closed my eyes for a moment as I prayed for patience. But as the only deity I worshipped happened to be in this room, it was a fairly pointless venture.

"If I cannot concentrate on this, then I cannot help your band of ruffians," I commented lightly, and the others worked harder to silence themselves while Tatum moved her chair up directly beside mine.

"Have you found anything yet?" she asked, her interruption allowable as she placed a hand on my thigh over my chinos, her fingers exerting just enough pleasure to light a fire beneath my skin.

"I am closing in on the coordinates given," I told her, my eyes slipping from the monitor to take in her stunning features, the spill of endless blonde hair which tumbled down over her shoulder and the tiny bikini top she had coupled with a pair of denim shorts to combat the heat.

I chastised the others endlessly about their lack of proper dress, but Tatum always managed to rise above those rules by the simplicity of looking so edible in her undignified clothing.

"Where are Rogue and the others?" she asked, her gaze moving from me to the screen, and I followed her attention there too.

"They are to the south of here in two vehicles, ready to deploy as soon

344

as I give the command to do so."

"Deploy?" Kyan scoffed at my back. "Who the fuck do you think you are, Corporal Squiddington?"

I sighed in irritation, the squid haunting me as always as I battled with the desire to ask what it meant. The most infuriating thing of all was that I had thought I had it figured out. I had come to the conclusion that it was entirely designed to rile me and had no further meaning than that. But it had become all too clear that the depths to its meaning went beyond that. There were nuances and tenses that shifted the meaning and above all else, it was still beyond my comprehension. There was depth to the squid. Depth which I was as yet, still unable to fathom.

I ground my teeth at that endless mystery and focused on the task at hand as I spotted several things at once upon the screen.

"You see that?" I asked as I switched the view to take in the thermal imaging, the corner of my lips twitching as I spotted the tell-tale heat of a body huddled in the corner of an almost entirely hidden shack on the edge of a patch of woodland.

"You think that's the Wolf?" Tatum asked, leaning in, the scent of her enveloping me and setting my pulse racing.

"If you keep moving into my personal space, I will become quite distracted, siren," I warned her, letting her know that I would be forced to act if she continued as she was.

"Is that so?" she asked innocently, though we all knew there wasn't an innocent bone in her body.

I turned back to the screen, knowing that despite her teasing, she needed me to complete this task well before I indulged in my favourite activity of all with her.

"I believe the man describing himself as the Wolf is currently getting into that vehicle," I pointed out, shifting the drone through the sky far above the head of my prey and watching as a large figure got into a black four wheel drive a little way down the hill from the cabin.

"I love it when you go all evil villain on the world," Tatum cooed as I reached for my phone so that I could inform the band of ragamuffins of the information they required.

"Dominion does hold a certain appeal," I agreed and the sniggers and muttering from the men at my back made it clear that they were in the mood for tolerating a little dominion of their own.

"What now?" Tatum asked, shifting closer and pressing her mouth to my neck. She knew what she was asking for with that behaviour, and my pulse grew stronger as the dark in me came out to play.

"Now I think you had better get on your knees for me, sweet siren," I purred. "Because when I'm done exerting my power over the world, I fully intend to exert it over you."

I pressed call on my cell phone as she obediently dropped down to her knees beside me, the others all shifting with excitement at my back while Kyan made a crude remark or two. I'd have them all bending to my will after this though and they knew it. I just needed to complete my task first.

CHAPTER TWENTY TWO

We were all sitting in Fox's truck just over a mile to the west of where Wolf had told me to come meet him alone, waiting for our plan to come together.

My phone was on silent, but I felt the vibration of it ringing the moment Saint called, answering it instantly and lifting it to my ear.

"Took you long enough," he drawled down the line and I scoffed.

"I answered the second it started ringing," I replied.

"Did you now?"

Silence hung for a moment as I wondered whether or not this was the moment to get into an argument with a megalomaniac, but it was damn hard to bite my tongue when I knew he was full of shit.

Fox plucked the phone from my grasp before I could commit to taking the conversation one way or another, and I huffed as I leaned in to be able to hear Saint's words too.

"So far as I can tell, he has left the hostage in a small cabin to the northwest of your location while travelling down a southerly road where he will have a clear view over the terrain where he asked you to approach. He's carrying a long-range rifle – a Mossberg MVP Precision, though I would have opted for a Ruger Precision Rifle if I was in his position as it is the far superior weapon in my opinion," Saint said, sounding more than a little judgmental and I arched an eyebrow not only at the fact that he had recognised the exact gun our enemy was carrying but that he was looking down on him for it too. Saint Memphis really was his own brand of psycho. "He also has a handgun – a Glock 17," Saint scoffed lightly and I couldn't help myself from questioning him on that reaction.

"What's wrong with a Glock 17?" I asked, glancing at Fox who had the exact same gun himself.

"It's just so very…mainstream," Saint said, and I swear I heard him shudder.

"Or would you call it basic?" Rick asked, his eyes alight with amusement as Saint exhaled a breath and Fox looked kinda pissed.

"That would be a good adjective," Saint agreed. "And I would always prefer class, style and excellence over mass popularity and blending in with the crowd. But what do I know?"

Maverick boomed a laugh and Fox flipped him off before turning the conversation back to what mattered. "What else?" he demanded.

"He is also carrying what I assume is a hunting knife of some variety, though I couldn't get a clear enough view to assess the branding on it within the holster at his belt." Saint's voice was tinged with bitterness at the fact that he hadn't locked down an exact brand on the knife Wolf was carrying, and I shook my head in disbelief.

I glanced up at the sky, hunting the endless blue for any sign of the drone he was using to see so much, but the thing was damn high up and either I needed my eyes tested or it was impossible to spot from down here.

"Alright. We'll head around behind him now," Fox said.

"I have sent the locations to your phones. The coordinates he forwarded to you were inaccurate to say the least," Saint replied, though they couldn't have been that far wrong as he'd clearly managed to use them to find the fucker for us. "I'll keep watching until it's done."

"Thank you," Fox said.

"Thank Tatum. She's the one who keeps convincing me into these situations." Saint cut the call and I breathed a laugh.

"That guy has some serious issues," I muttered, and Fox nodded, his attention fixed on my phone as he studied the locations Saint had just sent over.

"Looks like Rosie is being held about three miles to our northwest," he said slowly. "And Wolf is set up on a ridge just over half a mile from here."

"Let's get going then," I said, climbing across him as I reached for the door handle, but he caught my waist to stop me, a frown creasing his strong brow.

"I think you should head for the cabin with Johnny James and Chase," he said. "Rick and I can handle-"

"No," I said simply, cutting him off. "I've told you, Fox, I'm one of you or I'm not. No special measures, no me and the rest of you. I'm all in. You said you were too, so which is it? If you're happy to take Maverick with you to kill that asshole, then you can take me too. Besides, you're the ones who are coming with *me*, not the other way around. He's after me and he took that stupid trout Rosie in an attempt to strike at me. Which means he's mine."

I drew the apparently overly popular Glock 17 from his waistband and looked him in the eyes, daring him to take it back again.

"So what's it to be?"

The others stayed silent while Fox and I stared each other down, my gaze lighting with a determined fire while his smouldered with the desperate desire to protect me and keep me away from harm. But it was far too late for that.

"I'm not some fragile creature who you can shield from the worst of what this life has to offer us," I reminded him. "I was born on these streets the same as you and I clawed my way through dirt, blood and suffering to claim my place standing on them. I won't be caged, Fox. Never again. Not by cruel words or hateful intentions and not by a suffocating kind of love either."

"You'll be the fucking death of me, you know that?" he demanded, and I grinned because I knew I'd won then.

"Not if I can help it."

I kissed him hard then drew back just as fast, reclaiming my phone from him, opening the car door, and jumping out.

I looked at the location marked on the phone and took off across the scrubby landscape, heading straight towards the man who had thought he could outsmart The Harlequin Crew and get away with it.

My men fell in at my back, the four of them keeping in a close formation around me while I was the tip of the arrow, leading the way on beneath the blazing sun.

There were some trees we used for cover as best we could, and as we drew nearer to our destination, we slowed our pace, being careful to hide our approach from our prey.

JJ got back on the phone to Saint, saying nothing while listening to every observation our friend in the sky made about our prey and making sure he wasn't expecting us.

As we drew close enough to spot him beneath the trees ahead, laying on the ground with his rifle aimed and ready, Fox shot a message to the Harlequin who he had ready to drive up the dirt road where Wolf was expecting me, rainbow wig and all.

I held my breath as we waited, the weight of the pistol in my hand feeling like a promise of the turning tide until we heard the low rumble of a car engine drawing closer.

Wolf shifted in his position, looking down the sights of his gun and as if they had somehow silently communicated their intentions, Fox and Maverick both took off running at once.

I gasped in alarm as Wolf jerked around at the last second, the huge man spotting my boys as they ran for him and a gunshot went off, causing a scream to tear from my throat.

Rick and Fox leapt on him in the next heartbeat, the rifle having blasted a hole through the trees somewhere above them and their fists and boots slamming into him over and over again as the realisation that we had already won grasped him.

Chase and JJ moved so close to me that their arms brushed against mine as we strode closer, our guns held ready and adrenaline singing through my veins as I went.

Rick punched Wolf in the face so hard that he crashed back onto the rocks unconscious with blood splattering the sun-bleached ground around him.

I strode closer, raising my pistol as my jaw ground with fury over the fact that this motherfucker had sought to ruin our lives over nothing more than some fancy gemstone.

Fox stepped over him, pulling the knife and pistol from the man's belt and tossing them out of reach before slapping him hard enough to wake him up again.

Wolf gasped as he was hauled up onto his knees before me, my men circling like sharks all around us as I raised my pistol and aimed it at his head.

"Do you know where we can find Shawn Mackenzie?" I asked coldly, needing that answer before I ended this.

Wolf's eyes lit with fear as he realised the truth of his reality and the clock ticked down the seconds to his final breath.

"I can help you find him," he said quickly, eyes darting between my boys one after another before landing on me like he'd just realised which one of us was making this call. "We only spoke online, but I can tell him I have you, arrange a meet-"

"What arrangements did you have in place for if you caught me?" I asked coldly, not interested in any bullshit.

"I…he…I was going to leave you in a shipping container bound for Mexico. He had a man who would have taken you from there, I think. Then-"

"So, you had instructions to leave me somewhere for him to collect, which means he had no intention of ever meeting up with you directly and you have no idea where to find him," I surmised, and his mouth opened and closed like a fish on land as he began to shake his head.

"Let me send him a message. Let me arrange a meeting. I can-"

"No," I replied calmly. "You can't. Shawn isn't interested in meeting with you. He has his own plans and no doubt we'll figure them out soon enough. Unfortunately for you, that means you aren't useful to us anymore."

"Make him bleed, baby girl," Maverick purred, and a dark smile grew on my lips.

"This is a kindness," I said as Wolf began to tremble, garbled pleas spilling from his lips as he looked from me to my men, hunting for a sympathetic soul among a pack of hell hounds. "If I let them have you it would take so much longer and hurt so much more."

"Wait," he begged but I was done giving our enemies the chance to strike at us a second time. He's made his choice when he'd chosen the value of a diamond over the value of my life. Which meant my choice was already made too.

"No," I replied, and I pulled the trigger.

We left Wolf's body for the crows until the Harlequin clean-up crew could come to remove all evidence of our involvement and dispose of him. Saint signed off, leaving us to locate Rosie on our own and flying his drone back home or wherever the fuck he kept his highly illegal shit like that.

It took us a little while to locate the cabin where she'd been hidden away, but the sound of her squealing and crying loudly drew our attention to a thicker patch of trees eventually and JJ spotted it lurking within.

Chase took the lead as we quickly checked the area for traps but all we found was a locked door and a sobbing, hog tied girl with tear tracks through her heavy makeup and her platinum blonde hair so tangled that I doubted even a bird would want it for a nest.

I took a flick knife from my pocket as I approached her, cutting away the filthy rag that had been tied around her mouth and regretting it almost instantly as her sobbing just got louder.

"Chasey, baby, you came for me," she gushed, staring up at him while I took my time cutting the rope that held her hogtied away.

"Actually, I voted to leave you out here," he said with a sneer, stepping back as she started to scramble towards him the moment her ropes were cut.

"I knew you'd come," she sobbed through the tears and snot that coated her face, apparently not hearing him and I quickly sidestepped into her path to block her access to him.

"Rosie," I said firmly. "Chase isn't yours, so you don't get to lay a hand on him," I growled, thoughts of him and her ever having been together making me want to punch her even if she had been through hell. Or maybe it was him I wanted to punch because gah.

"He...what?" she asked, blinking at me in confusion. "We're destined. Always have been. You were the only thing that ever got between-"

"Stop talking shit, Rosie. Chase is mine," I said possessively, ready to slap the realisation into her if she tried to deny it.

She gaped at me for several heartbeats then turned to Chase abruptly and her words set a fire in me that would not be put out. "I've been looking into surgeons who can fix you, baby. I think we can find a way to get us back to how we were-"

"We don't have long," I said suddenly, grabbing her arm and tugging her towards the exit at a fast pace. "The man who kidnapped you is on his way

355

back. He'll kill you if he finds you've gotten free."

"What?" she squeaked in alarm, and I nodded firmly, dragging her out into the sunshine again and setting a fierce pace towards Fox's truck.

My boys all followed us, throwing me a few confused glances while I just shrugged in reply and kept dragging her on. I knew they'd go along with whatever I wanted anyway, and I had just realised that I was done with her shit. So this was the end of the line for her.

"Don't you get it?" I asked her in a low tone, glancing around like I was nervous. "That man has been stalking you for months. He's obsessed with you. He wants to make a coat out of your skin and wear it forever."

"He what?" she gasped, and I nodded seriously. "But all he kept asking about was you."

"Yeah, because he wanted me gone," I said like that was obvious. "Doesn't want a sister around to get between you and him – at least until he makes his coat. I saw plans for a hat made from your face too."

"And a cock ring braided from your hair," JJ added, grinning at me as he began to play along.

"Kitchen utensils carved from your bones," Rick added, and Rosie whimpered in fright.

"So, what are we going to do? Will you guys keep me safe while you hunt him down?" she asked, looking to my boys but fuck that.

"No," I said firmly as we made it back to the truck. "We will do what we can to take him out, but he's too much for us. It isn't safe here for you anymore, Rosie."

"It's not safe?" she parroted, and I nodded.

"You'd better hide in the back in case he spots us on our way out of here," I said, pointing her towards the truck with a look of deep concern on my face.

Rosie looked to the truck bed in disgust, but Rick had already moved to heave her off of her feet and he tossed her in among the wet surf boards before using Mutt's stinky dog towel to cover her up.

The rest of us stifled laughter as we all leapt into the front of the truck, and I set a destination on the GPS with a broad grin.

Fox shook his head, muttering something about never wanting to cross me as he started driving and Chase tugged me into his lap, pressing a kiss to the side of my neck that sent shivers right through my body.

"You're a fucking savage, little one," he said, biting down on my ear lobe as JJ leaned in to kiss the other side of my neck too.

"She deserves it," I breathed, keeping my voice low so that Rosie wouldn't hear us.

Fox managed to find every bump and pothole along the entire journey and every time the back of the truck bounced over one, Rick laughed loudly and obnoxiously, clearly enjoying every second of this.

We finally pulled up at the old railway yard on the outskirts of Sterling where the freight was loaded up for transport across the states and I smiled as I hopped out.

I climbed into the back, whipping the dog towel off of a particularly battered looking Rosie and she cried some more as I gave her a bit of a push to get her moving.

"What am I doing here?" she breathed as JJ led the way to the wire fence which blocked off this end of the train yard and quickly found a hole that would admit us.

"It's the only way to keep you safe," I said firmly. "You don't want to become a skin coat, do you?"

Rosie shook her head violently and I patted her arm sympathetically before giving her a little push to get her walking.

We made it through the hole in the fence and I led the way to the freight cars which were already locked up and ready to go. Further up the platform, a few workers were loading the last few cars, but they didn't look our way or maybe didn't even care about us if they did, because no one tried to stop us as we headed over to the train.

I moved along the freight cars one at a time until I heard the low mooing and smelled the barnyard scent I'd been hoping for.

"In here," I said firmly, climbing up and managing to slide the train car door open before peering in at around thirty large cows who stood about on beds of straw while chomping food from the buckets lining the far side of the space.

"With the livestock?" Rosie blanched but I nodded seriously.

"They suck all of the oxygen out of the other train cars to make it move faster. It's the only option."

"They do?" she squeaked and the boys all hastily agreed with me. Honestly that girl was still as dumb as a box of rocks.

"Quick," I urged as the men on the platform started closing the last few train car doors, making it clear the train would be leaving soon.

Rosie allowed me to usher her towards the door, dragging me into a hug that took me off guard and I awkwardly patted her on the back.

"Goodbye forever, Rosie," I said, feigning sadness. "You'll have to call yourself Gertrude Salamander and start a new life wherever the train ends up. It's the only way to be certain no one will ever find you."

"Gertrude Salamander?" she echoed, tears swimming in her eyes.

JJ moved forward to clasp her shoulder as I escaped her clutches. "It really suits you," he agreed. "Goodbye, Gertie."

She lunged towards Chase with her lips puckered but Maverick got to her first, heaving her off of her feet and tossing her in with the cows. Her puckered lips hit the ass of a particularly large heifer on the way down and the cow kicked out its hind leg in anger, striking Rosie in the tit as she hit the ground. "Ah!" she wailed, her hand sinking into a cow pat as she tried to get up.

"Bye, Gertie!" Rick called loudly and Chase moved to lock the door behind her.

"We just weren't meant to be," Chase said as the sound of the engine and cows mooing drowned out whatever she shouted back to us.

We backed up, fighting our laughter as the train pulled away then finally falling apart fully as we watched it and the girl who had always tried to fuck up my life head off towards a destination somewhere in the middle of nowhere in central Nebraska.

One of the men who worked in the train yard finally spotted us, yelling something and we all took off running like a bunch of kids up to no good again.

JJ grabbed my hand and Fox ripped the fence aside as we all raced away before leaping back into his truck and gunning it out of there at top speed.

"Shit, we are terrible fucking people," I gasped though my laughter.

"A bunch of utter assholes," JJ agreed.

"Total cunts," Rick said proudly.

"I couldn't even give a fuck," Chase laughed.

"Wouldn't have it any other way." Fox grinned between us and right there and then I knew that I had my boys back again. The five of us. Just like it always should have been.

CHAPTER TWENTY THREE

"I'm trying to understand why my time is being wasted by you right now, Luther Harlequin," Carmen's voice came from the video chat Dad was having with her while he paced around my office at The Oasis Clubhouse. "You should be back here by my side, fulfilling your promise to me rather than in Sunset Cove checking up on your little prodigies. They can handle one man; they do not need the entirety of the cartel at their disposal. And if they cannot handle him, then perhaps that is a far deeper problem which you should be addressing."

Dad was back for the weekend after he'd gone dark on me and Rick, off doing work for Carmen while I was left feeling like the concerned parent for once. He still wouldn't tell me a single thing of what he'd been up to either, and it was seriously fucking hard for me to just place my faith in him and not try and push him for answers. I had to trust him though. My dad was a goddamn powerhouse and I knew he could look after himself, but I guessed I was only human.

Shawn had gone to ground, and after the Rosie bullshit, we were back to chasing shadows and following hunches that always led to dead ends. Dad was asking for more help from Carmen, but it didn't look like he was gonna get it.

"This isn't just any man," Dad growled. "Shawn Mackenzie is a fucking monster, and he has made yet another attempt to kidnap my boy's girl."

"Yes, and from what you told me, the rainbow child placed a bullet between that man's eyes and cast him into damnation, so perhaps it is her help you should be asking for, not mine."

"She's the one that asshole is after," Dad scoffed while I folded my arms, watching him with a frown.

There was tension lining his features that hadn't been there before he'd left Sunset Cove, and I feared what she had him involved in to pay off his debt to her. I hated that I wasn't privy to whatever she had him doing, but Dad was clearly never going to allow me to assist him.

I just hoped he wasn't getting into something he couldn't handle. Though there was no challenge I'd ever seen the great Luther Harlequin fail at. I'd idolised that about him as a kid, and now, as a man, I respected it. It still didn't make me any less worried about him after he'd disappeared into the clutches of the cartel, only making the odd video call home which showed the shadows in his eyes and sometimes fresh wounds marking his flesh. I hoped whatever Carmen had him wrapped up in, he would be out of soon, because the claws of the cartel dug deep, and I wanted my father out of them as soon as possible.

"Precisely," Carmen answered then she released a soft moan that made my father stiffen, his eyes sharpening on the screen.

"What's going on?" he demanded in a dangerous tone that set my blood pumping.

Why the hell was he talking to her like that? Like he had any right to question her reasoning for anything. She'd killed men for less as far as I'd heard.

"Pepito is giving me a foot massage, chico tonto. Believe me, if it was anything more intriguing than that I wouldn't want to be wasting time speaking with you," Carmen replied. "Now if you are done acting like a caveman in a forest fire, I'll return to my day." She moaned softly again, and Luther pulled at the collar at his neck to give himself more room to breathe. I wasn't sure I'd ever seen my dad distracted by a woman before, but even he was affected by the power of Carmen Ortega.

"If your men hear anything of Shawn's whereabouts-" Dad started, the authority in his tone cracking just a little as he watched Carmen intently on the screen.

"Yes, yes, I have agreed to this once already. If you make me do so again, I will have to reconsider that offer, Luther. And I've also given you a piece of advice now that I encourage you to take if you wish to succeed in finding the leech."

"What advice?" Dad scoffed. "You've said nothing."

"Oh, chico tonto," she tutted at him like he was a kid. "Perhaps God ran out of intelligence the day she made you, so she gave you extra strength and beauty to make up for it. Goodbye, Luther."

"Wait," Dad growled, but Carmen had already hung up and he crushed the phone in his fist, raking a hand through his blonde hair, his bicep bulging with the tension in his body.

"Beauty?" he muttered, dumbfounded and I broke a laugh, making him round on me as he remembered I was still in the room. He pushed his phone into his pocket, clearing his throat and narrowing his eyes on me. "What was she talking about? What advice did she give me?"

"To use Rogue," I said slowly, a frown drawing my features down.

"We're not putting her at risk," he said, and I nodded once in sharp agreement to that.

"Never," I said. "But Rogue knows Shawn, perhaps she's the best person to figure out his next move."

"She's part of the gang. She can come to the Crew meetings any time," Dad said.

"She says they're dull, ineffective and lacking snacks," I said, a grin twitching my lips at that last one.

"Well, she's not wrong there," Dad sighed, leaning back against his desk and running a palm down his face. He looked tired, exhausted actually, and I wondered if he'd been out last night working for Carmen again.

"How's it going with the cartel?" I asked carefully, hoping I might get more out of him this time, though I wasn't banking on it.

A darkness crossed his features for a moment before he blinked it away and smiled warmly at me, the kind of smile a father gave his child when he didn't want him to know something was wrong. But I wasn't a kid blinded by false smiles anymore. I saw the truth, and it concerned me.

"Everything's in hand," he said.

"Dad-" I started, desperate to press him for more information, to insist I start coming with him on whatever jobs Carmen had him pulling.

"I said it's in hand," he growled ferociously in full Luther Harlequin mode.

My shoulders dropped as I gave in, seeing the impenetrable wall in his eyes there would be no getting past.

"Just stay safe," I said.

He nodded, moving forward and gripping my shoulder as he turned me towards the door. "It's getting late, go home and see your girl. There's nothing more we can do today now the men are off hunting again. I can hold down the fort here, and I'll call you if I get any leads."

"Alright," I said, lingering close to him for a moment. Every time I said goodbye to him lately, I had this horrible feeling it might be the last time. Because whatever it was that Carmen had him doing, I could be sure of one thing; it wasn't picking daisies in a meadow.

"Love you," I said in a low tone, and he smiled wide and true at me.

"Love you too, kid." He slapped me on the back, and I went on my way, leaving the clubhouse behind and taking my truck back to Harlequin House.

When I got home, I found the place quiet. Miss Mabel was napping, and the others were all out on the beach, so I took the opportunity to clean up before I joined them, falling into my old routine while listening to their laughter carrying from outside. My heart was full at that sound, knowing they were safe, happy. There was no greater feeling in the world than that.

I carried the laundry basket upstairs, moving from room to room as I put everyone's clothes away and ended up in Rogue's room last, stepping into her closet and hanging up some shirts and dresses. The space was pretty small, but she'd managed to fill it with a lot of clothes since she'd arrived here. All of them were so typical of her, her fashion sense varying from loud to wild, to sexy as fuck. Though Rogue could have worn an old potato sack and I still would have been as hard as hell for her.

The sound of footfalls carried up the stairs and Rogue's breathy laughter turned to a moan as the weight of several bodies slammed into a wall close by.

I stilled as I listened, my heart jack-hammering in my chest as I realised what was going on.

"Fuck, you're so wet for us already," JJ growled.

"Let me feel," Chase said darkly, and Rogue moaned louder a second later.

My cock started to throb in my shorts and my teeth locked together as Maverick's voice joined theirs.

"In your room," he commanded, and the door banged open before I could do anything about my position in the closet.

Thankfully they couldn't see me as the door had swung over behind me, but as the sound of several bodies moving onto the bed reached me, I realised I was in trouble. Big fucking trouble.

"On your knees, baby girl," Rick said, and I shifted closer to the door, pressing my back to the shelves, and peering through the crack that let me see out into the room.

Rogue moved onto her knees on the bed in her little linen shorts and blue bikini top, her rainbow hair spilling around her shoulders as she looked back at the men kneeling behind her, biting her lip so seductively that I got even harder.

Chase took hold of her shorts, drawing them down her sun kissed legs along with her bikini bottoms and Maverick and JJ gripped her thighs, spreading them wider as Chase tossed her clothes onto the floor.

JJ ran the palm of his hand over the perfect curve of her ass, and I wetted my lips as I watched, jealousy and lust twisting into something potent and wild in my chest.

He rode the curve of her spine with his palm, and she arched into his touch like a cat, the three of them admiring the way she lit up for him before he skilfully undid her bikini top. It fell away to the bed, revealing her perfect tits and the tight buds of her nipples, making my cock so solid it ached.

"What now?" she asked them huskily, playing into the hungry looks in their eyes. "Are you going to keep staring or are you going to do something useful?"

Maverick chuckled wickedly, reaching between her thighs while stroking the thickness of his cock through his shorts, his fingers sliding into her pussy and making her gasp.

"God, you look so good," Chase groaned, squeezing the head of his dick in his pants while JJ moved up the bed, pushing his fingers into her hair and stealing a dirty kiss from her mouth.

He shoved his shorts down while their mouths were locked and my pulse raced, my eyes unblinking as my gaze remained riveted on this act before me. One that had me captivated beyond any of the fucking videos Rick had sent me of them doing this, because this was real, happening right in front of me, and I didn't know how I felt about it, only that I had to keep watching.

JJ raised up onto his knees, breaking the kiss and offering her the tip of his cock instead. She took it between her lips with a greedy moan that had my own cock tenting my shorts, my hand lowering to try and choke the life out of it, because I was not fucking into this. I didn't want to see my friends touching her, didn't want to see their mouths on her skin or their cocks driving into her body, but as JJ thrust in deeper between her lips and Maverick pumped his fingers in a teasing rhythm that made her drive her ass back to meet his pace, I lost all sense of myself and shoved a hand into my shorts, starting to jerk myself off in time with their pace.

Chase watched patiently for only so long, his resolve breaking as he lay down sideways on the bed, shuffling beneath her and lapping at her clit to help bring her to ruin.

Rogue moaned around JJ's cock and the sound made my own dick twitch in my grip as I pictured her lips around it just like they were on his. My mind was in turmoil, and I was conflicted as fuck, but I kept stroking my cock, so hard and so damn hot over this that I couldn't do anything but keep my gaze stitched onto them.

Rogue released JJ's cock from her lips as she came, her head tipping back as she ground her pussy into every movement of Rick's hand and Chase's tongue, her back bowing so beautifully that I groaned.

I swallowed the sound, lifting my fist to my mouth and biting down as I ran my thumb over the bead of moisture on the head of my cock and pleasure rippled along the length of it.

Fuck, what was I doing?

They could catch me here. They could find me lurking on them.

But none of them seemed to have noticed my groan, all of them too busy as they moved into different positions to claim our girl and they shed all of their clothes.

JJ grabbed a bottle of lube from Rogue's nightstand, wetting his cock in it before laying across the bed and pulling Rogue on top of him, her back to his chest. He masterfully spread her legs with his and she lifted her hips as he lined his cock up with her ass, sliding in slow and deep while she writhed on top of him, pawing at her tits.

Heat was burning a trail up my spine as I leaned one arm against the wall beside the door and worked my cock harder, biting down hard on my tongue to keep myself from making any noise.

Chase took position on top of her, his thick cock driving deep into her pussy as he spread her legs even wider by hooking her knees up over the crook of his elbows. Maverick watched as JJ and Chase fell into the same rhythm, fucking her together as she was pressed between their bodies, her moans for more making me want to storm in there and give her what she needed. But how could she want more? She was already so full, weren't they enough for her?

Rick moved to the side of the bed and JJ shifted his head aside so Rogue's could drop backwards over the edge of it.

Maverick took immediate advantage, running his fingers along the length of her throat as she opened her mouth for him.

He slid his tattooed cock between her lips, and she hummed her approval as he drove in inch by inch, the muscles in his stomach tightening as a heady curse fell from his tongue. When he was all the way in, he started moving in slow, deep thrusts that she took with apparent ease. Chase circled his hips as he fucked her deeper and the moans that left her had me losing my mind, my cock so hard in my grip it was like iron.

I was about to come, and from the sounds of everyone in that room, they were too.

I couldn't stop. I was on a runaway train and there was no way to stop it. I fucked my hand with all the vigour I wanted to fuck her with, fighting back the sound of my panting breaths falling from my lips.

I was going to give myself away if I didn't end this madness, but I couldn't now. I was lost, too deep into this crime to stop. And as Rogue cried out with another orgasm and one by one, the others fell with masculine groans and growls, I came apart too, grabbing one of Rogue's t-shirts and spilling myself into it with a feral noise I couldn't contain.

Pleasure ripped through me as I emptied myself into that shirt then balled it up in my fist, working to catch my breath without making any more noise.

Thankfully I hadn't been heard while they were all caught up in their own passion and I watched as they unfurled themselves, all collapsing in a heap on the bed, painting her skin with kisses and caresses as they continued to shower her with attention even as they tried to recover.

I remained quiet, my eyes trailing over the blissful look on her face as she ran her hands over each of the men surrounding her while a slight ache in my chest made me want to go to her and be a part of this. But that was insanity. I couldn't do that. If I even tried to be a part of it, I'd want to tear all of them off of her and claim her for my own. Still, I couldn't exactly deny what I'd just done, what I'd silently admitted to myself. Because this had made me feel so fucking good, even if I felt conflicted now as I tugged up my shorts and scrunched the shirt up tight in my fist.

Fuck…

Mutt bounced into the room, the tip-tapping of his claws on the floorboards a familiar warning of his arrival. The little dog started barking and my stomach clenched as I realised he was at the closet door, peering in at me through the crack.

Holy shit – no!

"Come here, Mutt," Rogue called, and I prayed the little asshole would listen, but instead he gave me what I could have sworn was a smirk before barking again and pushing his nose into the crack to try and widen it enough to get in.

I tried to nudge him back with my toe, but he scrambled his way inside and kept barking.

I cursed the dog in my head with every savage word I knew, trying to turn him around and send him back the way he came, but before I could even try and fix this, the door yanked open.

Maverick stood there pulling his shorts up, his eyebrows zipping towards his hairline and making me want to punch him square in the face.

I shook my head, begging him with my eyes not to tell the others while his gaze moved to the shirt in my fist then back up to my face as everything clicked together and his expression shifted into a taunting grin.

"Well look what I found. A fox in a rabbit hole." He grabbed my arm, yanking me out of the closet and presenting me to the others.

I snatched my arm out of his grip, colour burning along my cheeks as I stood there like a fucking asshole and refused to look at the other three people in the room, my gaze settling on the floor instead. *Great, now I'm a pussy too.*

I forced my gaze up, finding them pulling clothes on and Rogue's eyes darting between mine as she hurried off the bed in Chase's shirt, reaching for me.

I stepped back, raising a hand to warn her off, but it just so happened to be the cum-filled t-shirt wielding hand, so that was just fucking great.

"Fox, wait," she said, predicting my next step, but I was already gone, tossing the fucking shirt to the floor between us and striding from the room with too much testosterone, rage and embarrassment shifting through my flesh to think straight.

"Is that my dolphin shirt?" I heard Rogue ask in a low tone and I died a little more inside.

Maverick's booming laughter followed me, and I moved faster, half running down the stairs as Rogue's bare footfalls rushed after me.

"Fox!" She caught my hand as I made it into the kitchen and I whirled on her, anger coursing through my flesh, needing an outlet. And I exploded, unable to hold it back.

"What?!" I bellowed at her but instead of shrinking from me, she donned her fucking armour and struck right back at me.

"Don't you shout at me," she snapped. "You were the one hiding in my bedroom."

"Hiding?" I scoffed. "I was doing the damn laundry and got stuck in there while you had a fucking orgy!"

"You could have come out of there before we started," Rick said, appearing behind her and resting his shoulder against the doorway as he gave me an amused look.

"Stay out of this," I snapped, but lo and be-fucking-hold, he didn't. Not only that, but JJ and Chase appeared behind him.

"Rick has a point," JJ said, smiling encouragingly at me. "I think you liked it."

"Fuck you," I snapped, feeling cornered as they all examined me. Like I didn't even know my own truth, but I knew it, they were just deluded into thinking I could be like them, that I could do any of that shit they'd just done.

"I have a sexth sense about these things," JJ said mysteriously, and Chase nodded seriously like he really thought JJ was some sort of magic sex wizard.

"We'll your senses are way off base with me," I hissed. "I'm not into any of that, I just got trapped in there."

"Why'd you come all over Rogue's shirt then, man?" Chase asked in a soft voice like I was the only one who could hear him.

Rage ricocheted through my chest, and I shoved my way through them, marching towards the garage and pushing through the door. I needed to get out of here. This was bullshit. They didn't know shit about my feelings on this, and the whole shirt thing had just been a confusing accident. It didn't mean I was into gang banging my girl alongside my friends.

I rubbed my eyes, missing a step and stumbling my way down into the garage, grabbing my truck keys and jumping into it.

Before I could start her up, Maverick appeared, dropping smoothly into the passenger seat in his board shorts and t-shirt, giving me a look that said I'd have to try and fight him out of there if I wanted him to leave.

"Get out, man," I snarled.

"Make me," he said, casually putting on his seatbelt.

"You're an asshole," I hissed.

"And this is surprising to you? That's cute." He smirked and I spat a curse before pressing my foot to the accelerator and opening the garage door as I went, taking the motherfucker with me just so I didn't have to stay in this house with the rest of the accusing stares from the others.

Because yeah, I'd been caught out, and fuck if I knew how to act now. I was on the defensive, and I didn't plan on letting go of my stance on this. I'd come one time in one closet, so fucking what? It didn't mean anything. It didn't change anything. Maybe I'd been jerking off in there before they showed up – they didn't know if I had or hadn't. Just like they didn't know shit about what turned me on or what I was curious about participating in or not. Fuck them.

Maverick smoothly linked his phone up to the dashboard and started playing It Wasn't Me by Shaggy and he gave me a goading look.

"Seriously?" I deadpanned as he started mouthing along to the words, aiming them at me and I huffed out a breath. But as he continued and started dancing in his seat like a fucking idiot, I bit down on the inside of my cheek to hold back a smile.

He punched me square in the chest and I coughed out a breath. "What the fuck?" I snapped and he started laughing.

"That's for being a proud motherfucker. Now let it go, and admit the goddamn truth, Foxy boy."

"There's no truth to give," I said through my teeth and Rick sighed dramatically like he was tired of my lies. And dammit, they were lies. Because deep down, I knew the truth. It was impossible to deny, especially when there was a cum stained dolphin t-shirt in Rogue's bedroom as evidence.

"Fuck," I exhaled.

"There it is," Maverick said in satisfaction, leaning back in his seat and manspreading his legs. "Finally."

"I didn't say shit," I muttered.

"You're about to," he said. "Because your back's against the wall, you were caught cock handed and you can't deny it anymore. So come on, say it. Say I was right, say that you've been fucking your hand over every video

I sent you and now you've seen a live performance you know you'll never experience true satisfaction until you've fucked her alongside the rest of us."

"Shut up," I gritted out, my shoulders tensing and my grip on the wheel tightening.

"Why is it so hard for you to admit? No one's judging you. It's what Rogue wants. It would make her seriously fucking happy, so why can't you just say you want it too and give it a go?"

"Because maybe I can watch, Rick, but that's not the same as doing it. Not the same as being right there, involved in it while my friends fuck my girl. I'll snap, I'll try and take her from all of you, and I never, ever want to be that person again."

He frowned at me as the truth spilled from my lips, brutal, raw and wholly honest. There it was. My fear exposed. And I refused to look at him while he processed that, and silence fell between us.

"You know…as much as it kills me to admit this, you're not actually as much of an asshole as you think you are."

I tsked, expecting some joke to come from him next, but when it didn't, I glanced over at him, finding him looking back with no bullshit in his expression.

"You want this, Fox. I know you better than anyone, but your problem is you've always been afraid of what'll happen if you let go of control. But I know you won't try and take her from us, because you've seen how happy we make her, and that's all you ever really wanted. The rest of the shit was just a bunch of defence mechanisms you built in yourself after she was gone. But she's here now and she's not gonna leave again."

"She might," I said quietly. "Maybe not you three, but she might leave me."

The honesty ripped my chest open inside and I felt all that fear spilling out and surrounding me now. Because that was what it all came down to really. I'd driven Rogue away when I was a kid, then I'd done it again when she'd come back by trying to hold onto her too tightly. I wasn't going to get another chance; this was my last shot. And if I fucked it up, I'd never forgive myself.

"I can't lose her," I whispered. "And the jealousy I feel when I see you all with her like that...I'm not sure it's ever going to go away. So, I have to keep my distance when you're all together, because otherwise one day, I might..."

"You won't," he said before I could come up with the end of that sentence. I wasn't even sure what it was. That I'd attack the others? That I'd try and take Rogue away? I'd done those things before; these very hands had struck blows against my brothers over her. They'd also hogtied her in the back of my truck and they'd locked her up in my house countless times too. I didn't want to ever be that man again, a man who controlled his friends, and didn't let them think their own thoughts.

"I wanna be what she deserves," I said, the darkness within me deepening. "But I'm afraid of how much I love her. It's not something sweet or pure, it corrupts me to the point of insanity. There isn't anything I wouldn't do for her, there is no ring of hell I wouldn't journey to for her. Being a villain is far too easy if it means I can keep her another day. And now that she's mine, I can't go back. I can't relinquish her, not to you, not to anyone."

"But you can share her," Rick growled, and I realised he was right, because I'd done just that in all ways except one. "You'll share her with the three sinners who run this twisted playground." He looked out at the town around us, and I nodded, knowing that was true right down to the roots of my soul. "Because she's the idol we were born to offer ourselves to, and we may be corrupted by our love for her, but she's safe within that love too. It's built on a foundation of torment, but upon it, we can find nirvana."

CHAPTER TWENTY FOUR

I crept beneath the jetty within the mottled shade cast beneath the wooden planks that lined it, my dark hair twisting in the breeze and whipping across my face.

Soft fingers caught the wild strands and wrangled them for me, JJ giving me a sheepish smile as he tucked them behind my ear, and I swallowed around the lump that his touch had lodged in my throat.

"Thanks," I whispered, and his cheeks coloured as he shrugged, turning back towards the water and picking his way across the sand.

"We're never going to get away with this," he hissed, and I could tell he was nervous about this whole plan. "And I'm definitely not the right man for the job here either."

I scoffed, hurrying forward a few paces and taking hold of his hand, making him jump a little in surprise as he glanced down at the place where our fingers twisted together, and I tiptoed up to speak in his ear.

"Don't let the others get in your head. You're the smart one, J. They only rib on you for it because they all have rocks for brains," I whispered *conspiratorially, and he breathed a laugh.*

*"I still think I'm better at the distraction part than the grand theft bit,"
he pushed, and I shook my head, tugging him to the edge of the water and
wading out into it while we remained hidden beneath the jetty.*

*"Bullshit. You and me are gonna pull this off, and our names will go
down in history for the rest of time for this one."*

*JJ grinned at the thought of that, keeping up with me as the sound of
Maverick's voice reached us from up on the jetty where he was talking to the
dude who sold the banana boat rides, questioning the vastly overpriced tickets
he was touting for the tourists. I'd always wanted a go on one of those things,
but it was too much money for me to waste what I could steal on a turn. And
after years of hearing me intermittently complain about it, JJ had made the
brilliant suggestion that we just take the fucking thing for a joyride for the
afternoon, hence our current position sneaking along beneath the jetty.*

*When we'd started figuring out which of us should run which part of the
con, Rick and Fox had predictably put themselves in position as the thieves
while me and J were to play the part of the distraction. Again. So I'd decided
to call time on their macho shit and demanded to be the one to pull the actual
theft today, forcing Johnny James to join me in my rebellion even though I
knew he was far happier to let them take the lead with this kind of thing. But I
for one was sick of the two of them showboating about, claiming they had the
hardest part to play in every con we ran, and I was ready to prove to them that
we could make their accomplishments look like dog shit in the face of ours. It
was poetic really. Or at least it would be once we pulled it off.*

*We started swimming while Rick kept the guy distracted on the jetty and
I peeked up between the boards to see Fox and Chase positioning themselves
on the banana boat while he haggled over the price.*

*Chase threw me a wink that made my stomach flip over as he spotted me
swimming closer to the boat, and I grinned at him before looking to JJ again.*

"Ready?" I breathed and he nodded, releasing my hand so we could

both swim more freely.

I dove beneath the surface and kicked my legs to propel myself beneath the speedboat the banana boat was lashed to, swimming hard and fast as adrenaline raced through my veins and JJ kept close beside me.

We surfaced on the other side of the white boat and JJ gave me a boost as I reached for the side of it, giving me the extra height I needed to grab the side rail and hoist myself higher.

Maverick made a show of getting his wallet out while loudly accusing the guy who ran the rides of daylight robbery, clapping him on the arm and making him laugh loudly, covering any sounds we made while we got onto the boat behind him.

I helped tug JJ up and he quickly scrambled for the mooring rope while I held my hands out to catch the keys which Chase had pickpocketed from the boat owner before he'd gotten into place on the huge inflatable banana attached to it.

I stifled an excited laugh as I caught them and ran for the helm, looking back over my shoulder and meeting Rick's gaze to make sure he was ready before starting up the engine with a roar.

The boat owner jumped, whirling around to stare at me and JJ in alarm, and Rick snatched the guy's wallet from his hand before shoving him hard enough to send him crashing back into the sea with a cry. He could keep his hair on though – he'd get his boat back when we were done with it. We'd just dump it somewhere when we disembarked, and he'd be back to ripping tourists off in no time.

I whooped in triumph as yells went up from the other tourist-conning boat owners nearby, and Maverick broke into a run just as JJ dumped the mooring rope at my feet and kicked us away from the jetty.

Rick leapt onto the back of the banana boat, Fox catching his arm to steady him as he took hold of the handle in front of him and I loosed the throttle the moment I was certain he was in position.

The frantic yells of the boat owner were soon drowned out by the growl of the stolen engine, and I slapped JJ a high five while cheering wildly and setting a course for open water.

By the time anyone came after us we would be long gone, way out to sea where we could spend the day banana boating to our hearts' content for the much more reasonable price of sweet fuck all.

"I think my fucking heart is going to leap right out of my chest," JJ exclaimed while the others all whooped and cheered from their positions clinging to the big yellow banana we were dragging away over the waves, and I just had to hope they could cling on long enough for us to make it far enough away from the dude we'd just robbed.

I grinned up at JJ as the sun half blinded me and my pulse thundered adrenaline through my body.

"Best feeling in the goddamn world," I agreed.

I woke suddenly in the night with my stomach swirling and tension lining every muscle in my body. It took me a few minutes to figure out where I was in the dark, the shadows of the room both familiar and all wrong at once. It was late, the middle of the night if the dark was anything to go by and I had vague memories of screaming at Fox not to take me from my Power Rangers after I'd started dozing off while watching old reruns of my favourite episodes.

They were dated as fuck now and I could practically hear the nineties calling my name with every outfit that any of them wore outside of Ranger costumes, but I still loved it. It was my comfort show. Nostalgia in a twenty-minute bundle of joy that put me straight back into my childhood, and memories of curling up with one or all of my boys while arguing over this being the best show out there. They were always wrong with their arguments for Pokémon or Rugrats or Sabrina the Teenage Witch, but I always put them right in the end.

Fox and Rick had been gone for the rest of the afternoon following the incident of him jerking off into my dolphin shirt while indulging in some secret voyeurism, and by the time they'd returned, I'd managed to convince both

Chase and JJ not to give him shit over it.

In all honesty, the idea of him watching us and touching himself like that had been making me all kinds of hot ever since I'd gotten over the shock of it and I'd been seriously tempted to offer him a repeat performance while he watched from somewhere I could see him and feel the weight of his eyes on me. Or better yet, actually get involved himself.

But when he'd returned it had been pretty obvious that he didn't want to discuss it, so instead of having the orgy of my dreams, I'd tempted all of them into an icebreaking TV night watching my favourite show with me and I'd obviously passed out at some point after the awkwardness was forgotten.

I was snuggled up on the couch with Mutt by my feet and I had to assume that my starfish position and blanket hogging had been enough to chase off the others. I couldn't even remember the last time I'd woken up without being wrapped around one or more of them and a sad little dependant part of me had to admit that I missed that feeling.

I yawned, stretching as I got to my feet and wrapping the blanket around me as I headed off in search of a bed to crawl into.

Mutt just rolled over where he was, earning a quick belly rub from me before I left and wagging his tail in one solid thump before falling straight back to sleep again.

The churning feeling I'd woken with didn't let up as I walked, and my heart beat faster as I realised that something was off. A muffled thump from upstairs made me jump a little as I strained my ears to listen for any sounds and it was soon followed by a low yell of fear.

"Fuck," I cursed as I took off at a run, my bare feet pounding up the stairs as I raced towards mine and Maverick's room, the sound of him caught in a nightmare pushing in on me and making me feel like utter shit for falling asleep downstairs.

He hadn't been having them so often lately but there was no instant fix for the kind of trauma he'd lived through in prison, and I knew his demons would always hold the most power over him in the night.

I made it up onto the landing and realised with a start that Fox was already at Rick's door, his hand on the knob as he hesitated there, clearly uncertain of what to do.

"I should have known that even Sleeping Beauty would wake when one of her boys needed her," he murmured, stepping aside for me and I offered him half a smile before hurrying into the room.

The lamp crashed from the nightstand, shattering on the floor as Maverick bellowed something in his sleep, the sound a mixture of rage and pain and I started towards him quickly.

I was jerked to a halt suddenly as Fox grabbed hold of my wrist, his eyes fearful as Rick thrashed in the bed, sweat beading his tattooed torso and his demons fully haunting him.

"He doesn't know what's happening," Fox warned, looking from Rick to me fearfully. "Let me go to him first. I don't want him to attack you like he did to Chase last time."

"No," I said firmly, pressing a hand to his chest to stop his advance as he tried to step around me. "When he realises it's me, he'll stop, but if it's you trying to pin him down in the dark then it's only going to put him back there again. It has to be me, Fox."

Fox's eyes filled with pain over what his brother had endured in that hell, and I raised my chin, refusing to let myself fall into that feeling too. Maverick didn't need pity, he just needed to know that he was here with us now, the people who loved him more than anyone else in the world could ever even strive to.

Fox released me though I could tell it took him a lot to do it, and I instantly moved to the bed.

Maverick bellowed something again, his fist colliding with the headboard and making it rattle violently.

I moved onto the bed, shifting towards him without fear and reaching for his arm, my fingers meeting with his sweat slicked skin as he continued to thrash violently.

Maverick yelled something unintelligible, whirling on me so fast that I found myself pinned beneath him before I'd even registered the fact that he'd grabbed me.

His hand locked tight around my throat as his eyes snapped open, the darkness in them boring into my soul while his grip cut off my oxygen and held me at his mercy.

"Hey!" Fox yelled from behind him, but he might as well have not existed because I could tell that there was nothing beyond me in that moment for my dark warrior.

"You," Rick growled, his lip peeling back, fingers flexing around my throat, and I nodded, reaching for him even as he pinned me like that because I knew what he needed to sate this hate in him. He needed love. He needed to feel it and experience it and remember it again.

I ran my hand down his ink-stained abs until I met the waistband of his boxers and threaded my fingers into the material.

"Let go of her!" Fox demanded, moving closer to us and I tried to shake my head in warning, knowing that I was safe here with Rick even as he choked me. It didn't matter. I was his and he was mine, and he would never really hurt me.

Fox grabbed Rick's shoulders, trying to heave him back and Maverick roared furiously, twisting around and throwing a punch with such force that it knocked Fox back against the wall, splitting his lip open.

Maverick released me, moving to follow Fox, but I caught his arm, my fingernails biting into his flesh as I fought to hold him back.

"Give it to me, Rick," I demanded. "Use it on me."

Maverick jerked around to stare at me again, the panic in his eyes still raw and endless, the evidence of his nightmares pressing closer all too clear. He needed to lose himself in something pure and real and honest. He needed me.

I yanked the large tank I'd been wearing over my head, revealing my body in offering to him as I pushed myself up onto my knees in nothing but my panties, hoping to draw that savagery into an outlet that both of us could use to help us heal.

Maverick stared at me for several seconds and I reached for him, knowing what he needed, knowing I could handle it. And the dark inside me rose to the surface of my skin, hungering for this release too. My broken pieces and my damaged fragments hungering for a reminder of who we were and where we were. The brutality that Maverick and I shared demanding an outlet which always worked so masterfully to bring us back to who we were.

"Come on," I insisted but Fox was moving towards us again.

"Rogue, don't," he growled. "He's not himself. Just move away from him and-"

Maverick lunged for me before he could even finish that thought and I let him shove me down onto the bed beneath him, flipping me onto my front as his teeth sank into the side of my neck.

"Rick!" Fox barked, but Maverick ignored him, his fingers moving to my panties as his weight pressed me down into the bed firmly, keeping me where he wanted me.

I gasped as he yanked on the thin material, making it cut into my skin as he tore it off of me and shoved his own boxers aside.

Maverick thrust into me instantly, no fanfare or foreplay or gentle caresses, he took what I'd been offering without messing about, and began to fuck me brutally before I even had a chance to catch my breath.

"Fuck," I hissed as he slammed into me harder, faster, his fingers gripping my ass and digging in as he took and took while I gave him everything he needed and more.

"Jesus, Maverick," Fox snarled, moving to grab his shoulder again like he wanted to pull him off of me.

"No," I gasped, craning my neck around to look at them while Rick growled at him like a feral dog. "I want it, Fox, please, I-"

My words cut off with a raw moan of pleasure as my pussy tightened around Rick's cock, the broken, shattered parts of me needing this kind of release just as much as Maverick did sometimes. It was cathartic, like reclaiming some piece of myself by allowing him to use me like this, giving over all of my control to him and trusting him to help me fight off my own demons.

"We aren't all vanilla like you, Foxy boy," Maverick snarled, his eyes on me as he continued to fuck me so hard that every thrust stole my breath. "Living in a perfect little world where we all stay in our boxes and fuck quietly behind closed doors. Me and her need more than that. We need to be reminded that we're alive."

"You think forcing her beneath you and fucking her like an animal is what she needs?" Fox sneered, but as I continued to look back at the two of them, I couldn't miss the heat in his eyes or the way he watched me either.

"I do need it," I panted, a cry spilling from me as oblivion purred my name and I fisted my hands in the sheets.

"See, Foxy?" Rick grunted, "Our girl needs a whole lot more than vanilla in her life."

"I'm not fucking vanilla," Fox hissed, looking like he wanted to leave, though his hungry eyes stayed fixed on me, and I couldn't help but moan louder at the feeling of his gaze fixed on my skin.

"Sure, you're not," Maverick scoffed, thrusting his dick into me so deep that I cried out, his hand clapping down hard on my ass and making me come for him in an explosion of heat and colour as he roared his release too, filling me with his seed and giving us both a taste of what we really needed.

My head fell forward against the mattress as my body came apart for him, my fingers knotting in the sheets and every inch of my skin trembling with the power of our connection.

Rick held my hips tightly, his cock still buried deep within me like he wanted to maintain that connection for as long as physically possible.

I whimpered at the feeling of him still inside me, my greedy flesh wanting more even though he'd just blown my mind with that orgasm and had left me a quivering mess on the bed beneath him.

"That's it, walk away," Rick mocked from behind me at the sound of retreating footsteps. "Leave her wanting and go fantasise about some missionary bullshit where you tickle her with feathers and let yourself believe you have any real flavour about you."

"Rick," I warned, though my voice wasn't fully working yet so mostly I just made a garbled noise.

"What do you want from me?" Fox demanded angrily and I turned my head to find him standing in the doorway, his hand on the knob as he prepared to leave, and my heart twisted with longing for him to stay.

"I don't want anything from you," Maverick replied scathingly. "It's Rogue who you're leaving wanting."

Fox's eyes moved to me, the green in them a turbulent sea which roiled and frothed and hunted for something he wasn't putting any words to.

Fox lingered there, seeming caught between staying and going, and I bit my lip as I waited to see what he would choose.

"Come on, Foxy boy," Maverick purred. "I know how often you've been jerking off to those videos I send you. We all know you were fucking your hand while you watched us from that closet yesterday too. You're all kinds of curious to taste the fucking rainbow, so why not leave your vanilla at the door and come show our girl what it's like to be owned by you too."

Fox wetted his lips, his grip on the door handle tightening and I knew he was on the verge of leaving, but the thick ridge of his cock straining through his boxers made it all too clear that he was aching to stay too.

"I need you, Fox," I breathed, wanting him to make the decision that was right for him while at the same time desperate to feel him claiming me too. "If you want this, then just come and take it."

Maverick pulled out of me suddenly, making me whimper at the loss of him and I looked around, finding his huge cock already semi-hard again, making it clear that he was in no way done with me yet.

"Go on, Foxy. I dare you."

Fox's eyes flashed at the challenge, his hand falling from the doorknob as he came for me with purposeful strides, and I pushed myself upright to meet him.

Fox drew me up to my feet and I stood on the bed, only a little taller than him even with this advantage and he drew me closer to kiss him, the pressure of his mouth on mine making it more than clear how excited and angered he was by this.

"We don't have to-" I began but he fisted my hair and tipped my head back, making Maverick chuckle like an asshole as he kissed his way down my throat and sucked my nipple into his mouth.

I gasped at the harshness of his touch and the sound of his boxers hitting the floor came a moment before he grabbed the backs of my thighs and lifted me into his arms.

My legs instantly went around his waist and the urgent press of his cock against my core let me know he'd already made his decision on this.

I moaned into his mouth as he kissed me again, shifting my hips so the tip of him pressed into me just enough to make my entire body throb with the need for more.

Fox gripped my ass, his mouth taking mine possessively as he thrust into me, and I moaned into the space between his lips as I felt every inch of him driving inside me.

He stepped away from the bed, moving towards the wall, but Rick got there first, his hands wrapping around my waist as his mouth carved a line up the back of my neck.

"What are you doing?" Fox snarled.

"This ain't some turn-taking shit, asshole," Rick replied, and I gasped as something cold splashed against my ass, his fingers smearing into it a moment later as he massaged the lube between my cheeks, making me moan loudly.

"You're getting the full chocolate chip experience with sauce on top and everything."

Fox met my eyes, reading the desire there all too clearly and he arched a brow at me.

"You want that, baby?" he asked me, his voice all rough grit that made my toes curl as he rocked his dick back and forth inside me.

"Yes," I gasped as Maverick pressed his chest to my spine, pushing forward until Fox's back was hitting the wall.

"Last chance to run for the hills," Rick warned, his fingers finding my ass and pushing in just enough to make me squirm.

Fox watched me for several seconds, his own desire clear on his face and a groan leaving him as he clearly felt how much tighter I was with just Rick's fingers inside me. Curiosity and desire burned through his gaze and a throaty moan left me which seemed to solidify his decision as he nodded once in acceptance of this.

"Let me show you how I make her scream then, motherfucker," Fox growled and suddenly he was pressing forward, his cock driving so deep within me that I cried out.

He turned all of us so fast that by the time Maverick realised what Fox was doing, his back had already slammed against the wall, and he found himself pinned behind me with my spine to his chest as Fox fucked me against him, using him to steady me there.

Fox drove me against the solid plane of Rick's chest as he thrust into me harder and I cried out while Maverick chuckled darkly in my ear, his hands supporting my ass as he bounced me up and down Fox's shaft, making me take him as deep as I could and stealing my fucking breath.

"Let the games begin," Rick said, lining his cock up with my ass as the splash of more lube spilled across my skin before he tossed the bottle aside.

It was all I could do to cling to Fox's shoulders as he continued to drive himself into me roughly, kissing me so hard he stole my breath away and making my pussy throb with need around the thick length of his shaft.

Maverick bit down on my neck half a second before pushing his dick into my ass and I cried out loudly, my head falling back against his shoulder while Fox cursed as he felt the increased pressure too.

"I love you," I gasped, my words for both of them, as a moment of hesitation passed between us, then suddenly they were both moving inside me and all I could do was hold on for dear life while I remained pinned between their powerful bodies.

They both fucked me like they were trying to prove a point, their huge cocks filling me so completely that I found it hard to draw breath between my moans of ecstasy.

This was heaven. Pure and simple. The thing I had been put on this earth with the power to excel at above all others, and I loved every depraved and filthy second of it.

I reached around to grasp the back of Maverick's neck, my nails biting into his skin and Fox's where I still gripped his shoulder.

I fought against the rising tide of my orgasm as it built and built in me, holding it off while I bathed in this feeling, panting their names between thrusts, and loving the feeling of owning both of them.

When I couldn't take another moment, a cry tore from me that was so loud I knew the entire household had to have heard it as my body exploded into untold pleasure, every muscle inside of me flexing and contracting in the most delicious way.

I forced the two of them to come with me, their masculine groans of pleasure merging with mine as they filled me with their cum and I accepted it greedily.

Somehow, the three of us ended up on the bed, falling in a heap as we panted in each other's arms and Maverick's soft laughter brought a satisfied smile to my lips.

My eyes fell closed as I lingered there, bathing in the afterglow of my ecstasy and enjoying the heat of their bodies pressed close on either side of me. But just as I was beginning to drift off, I felt Fox remove himself from our dog pile and get out of the bed.

I blinked my eyes open, calling out to him as he headed for the door, but he just kept going, closing it softly behind him and leaving me there with Rick.

"Shit," I muttered while Maverick just chuckled again, pulling me closer to him and kissing me roughly.

"Go on," he said, giving me a push. "Go check that the baby isn't sobbing over his first taste of chocolate."

"You're an asshole," I muttered.

"Yeah. And I fuck like one too. That's why you love me."

"Among other things," I said, rolling my eyes at him as I moved to get out of the bed.

Rick swatted my ass as I went, and I hissed at the small sting before hurrying into the shower to quickly rinse off the results of their pleasure. I loved fucking my boys more than anything in this world, but they left me in one hell of a mess when they were done with me.

I cleaned off as fast as I could before grabbing one of Rick's tanks and pulling it on, the black material showing my hardened nipples through it and leaving a whole lot of side boob on display too, though maybe Fox would appreciate that.

"Are you okay now?" I asked Maverick as I moved across his room towards the door.

"You know me, beautiful," he replied with a shrug. "All that dark just finds its way outa me from time to time. But I always find my light again between your pretty legs."

"And there was me thinking you loved me and not just my body," I teased.

"I love you in spite of your body. That thing causes me no end of trouble. I'm hard all the fucking time thanks to you, though I don't hate working through that issue with you as often as necessary."

I rolled my eyes at him, moving over to kiss him softly and looking into his eyes to make sure that dark really had been banished. He gave me a rueful grin, letting me see that he was back to himself, and I brushed my fingers down the rough stubble on his jaw before turning away, leaving him to deal with my other boyfriend. I was going to be kept seriously busy for the rest of my life with these men.

Fox wasn't in his room and after checking around the house I quickly realised that he wasn't inside either. I pursed my lips as I paused, trying to figure out where he would have run off to before the faint sound of the sea lapping at the shore drew my attention towards the windows.

I slipped through the house, giving Mutt another tickle and patting my thigh to invite him along which he responded to with a happy little yip as he leapt up and trotted after me.

I unlocked the back door, heading out onto the sand and nodding to the few Harlequins who were posted out here keeping watch through the night where they sat around a fire lit on the beach. One of them bobbed his chin to my left and I gave him a grateful smile as I spotted the footprints heading away from me in the sand, letting me know where my badger was hiding out.

I walked along with the cool air blowing around my bare thighs, lifting the hem of the tank I was wearing for a dress as I went and putting me in danger of flashing my ass at the men I'd left sitting on the beach.

Fox had passed Harlequin House by and headed on down the beach, though in the dark I couldn't make out any sign of him up ahead. I upped my pace, Mutt trotting along faithfully at my side and making me feel more secure about coming out here without any weapons as his little doggy ears perked up at every sound, letting me know he was on high alert.

I upped my pace, realising I needed to if I was going to have any hope of catching up to Fox, and Mutt happily went with me while I held my tits in place as I ran oh so glamorously along the sand with zero support for them.

I finally came to the end of the trail of footprints, about half a mile down the sand from Harlequin House where the first of the boardwalk stores sat at the beginning of The Mile, and I cursed as I made it onto the wood, losing my trail.

I looked around, spotting a single open store a little way down the boardwalk, selling booze and snacks to anyone out late enough to need more in the middle of the night. I took a step towards it then paused as the scent of cigarette smoke carried to me on the wind.

Mutt took off as I turned my head towards one of the little alleyways that led up into town, his tail wagging furiously as he went and confirming my suspicions.

I took off up the alley too, treading carefully now that my bare feet were on asphalt instead of sand, knowing all too well how likely it was that there would be broken glass on the ground around here.

I spotted Fox in the darkness as I rounded a corner into an open little area where a couple of beach houses backed onto the stores, their tiny yards ringed with low walls. Fox had perched his ass on one of the walls, toking on a cigarette as he leaned down to tickle Mutt's ears in greeting.

"I should have known you'd come after me," he said, and I was forcibly reminded of all the times this sort of scene had played out when we were kids. He and Rick would get into it, beat each other up a bit and Fox would eventually storm off so that he could go and cool down. I'd follow him and we'd talk shit about the world over a cigarette while he got himself together and had an epiphany which allowed him to get over himself, meaning we could re-join the group in peace. Rick never needed time to cool off. He was hot or cold. No in between. So all it ever took was Fox's reappearance and everything would be back to normal.

"Just like old times," I agreed, taking a seat beside him on the cold ass wall and picking up the bottle of rum which was wrapped in a paper bag by his feet. "This is classy," I commented, taking the top off and sinking a healthy measure of it.

"Only the best for you, hummingbird," he said, his eyes roaming over my features slowly and making me blush at his intensity.

I offered him the bottle of rum and he took it, lifting it to his lips and drinking deeply.

"So...what was it? The fact that you shared me or the fact that you wanted in my ass?" I asked casually and he choked on his drink as he yanked the bottle away from his lips, making me laugh while I gave him a heavy thump on the back to help bring the rum back up out of his lungs.

"Jesus, Rogue, you have no fucking filter, you know that?" he asked as he got control of himself, and I grinned.

"No shame more like," I replied with a shrug. "Because I'm not ashamed, Fox. I like sex. I like dick – four dicks to be precise and that is because I happen to be in love with the four assholes who own them. I like coming and I love making all of you come too. Why should I be ashamed of that? Why should we be unable to discuss the way the two of you just fucked me until I screamed my throat raw and filled my body to the brim with your massive cocks while I loved every damn second of it? I feel like I should be shouting it from the rooftops, not trying to hide it."

His lips twitched as he looked at me, but he tore his eyes away, swiping a hand down his face.

"I just...I dunno."

"Say it," I demanded, reaching over to steal his cigarette and inhaling deeply on it.

"Well, I guess I just spent so many years imagining how you and me would be if I ever found you again that I'm having trouble accepting the way it really looks. Like reality and fantasy aren't lining up and I can't get my head around it."

I nodded, trying to listen to his words without letting myself fly off the handle as I all too often did with him, and I passed the cigarette back as I exhaled my smoke.

"This isn't something I ever imagined either. If you can believe it, I really did just want to carry on hating all of you when I first came back here. I certainly didn't want to fuck any of you – at least not that I would have admitted to. But that pull between us we all remember from being kids is still here, stronger than ever, and now it has an outlet too. I can honestly say I never had fantasies of fucking more than one man at once before coming back here. I had fantasies of finding some way to feel happy again and that was about it. I liked sex because it helped me to forget the rest of the shit in my life, at least for a little while. But sex with the four of you doesn't make me forget anymore. It makes me wake up and keeps me burning right in that moment, feeling so alive and full of bliss that I can't imagine ever getting enough of it. And yeah, I want to fuck all of you, and yeah, I have begun to dabble in the art of doing that with more than one of you at once and I have to say, badger, I like it. I like it a whole fucking lot. But if you don't like it then that's cool. I'm happy to take your lead on that side of things. If you want sex with us to just be you and me, and you're happy for me to do whatever I like with the others in groups or otherwise then that's okay. This has to work for all of us."

Fox was silent for several seconds as he took a drag on his cigarette, and he tipped his head back to the sky as he exhaled.

"And what if, despite everything I had previously thought about the idea of sharing you, it turned out that Maverick had a point?" he asked in a low voice. "What if I have been jerking off to those fucking videos he sends me so often that my cock is raw from all the attention I've been giving it? What if I was so turned on when I was watching you from inside that goddamn closet that I would have come in my pants if I hadn't jerked off anyway? What if feeling how tight you were with two of us inside you, and watching you enjoy the worship of more than one of us was the hottest thing that I had ever experienced in my entire life and all I can think about is doing it again. With Chase and JJ too. Watching you get everything you deserve from all the men who love and worship you and making sure you're taken care of as thoroughly as possible?"

I bit my lip on a moan as his words made energy race through my body in a potent cocktail that had my chest heaving and my pussy growing wet at the mere thought of that.

"If you're shitting me right now then I am going to lose my mind," I warned him, looking into his green eyes in the darkness and hunting for a lie. "Because I have been having all kinds of fantasies about how much I want to fuck all four of you at once, and I tell you now, Fox, that if this is some bullshit designed to-"

Fox leaned in and kissed me hard enough to shut me up, the cigarette falling from his fingers as he pressed his tongue between my lips and tasted the desire on my tongue in return.

His hand moved between my legs, and I parted them for him instantly, moaning as he found my clit with ease and began to stroke it in the most perfect way.

Mutt barked suddenly, yanking us out of our lust filled haze and Fox slammed into me, throwing me over the back of the low wall and rolling as we landed so that he took the impact of the hit onto the concrete there.

A plant pot in the little yard we had landed in shattered as a bullet hit it and the supressed sound of another bullet being fired made my heart leap in fear.

"Stay down," Fox commanded as he grabbed another small plant pot from the windowsill behind us and hurled it back towards our attacker.

There was a cry of pain as the sound of the plant pot shattering filled the air and Fox launched himself over the edge of the low wall with a furious roar before colliding with the man who had tried to shoot us.

Mutt barked viciously and I scrambled to my feet, finding Fox locked in a fight with some bastard wearing a ski mask to hide his face.

The gun had been knocked to the floor by their feet and I leapt over the low wall, running for it before our attacker could get an opportunity to grab it again.

Fox threw his weight forward, forcing the other man back as he rammed him against the graffitied wall of the alleyway before taking hold of his ski mask and ripping it off. I didn't recognise him, no doubt just another goon who'd come here to try his luck for that diamond Shawn was offering in exchange for me.

I grabbed the gun, backing up as I raised it at the man, but Fox didn't pay me any attention, his lip peeled back in a feral snarl and nothing but the animal in him on show now.

The man threw a violent punch at Fox's face, but he surged forward even as blood ran down his chin from the wound, snatching a fistful of the man's hair before slamming his head back against the wall.

There was a loud crack and blood splattered but Fox didn't stop, slamming his head into the wall over and over again until there was absolutely no doubt that he was dead, blood and gore everywhere and his lifeless eyes staring back at us.

Fox dropped him in disgust then turned to me, his eyes still wild with bloodlust and that feral heat in them making my heart hammer to an uncontrollable rhythm.

"You look so fucking hot right now," I breathed, and his eyes flashed with desire before he was on me.

Fox turned me around, knocking the gun from my grip and pressing my palms to the blood splattered stone wall as he bent me over and shoved my tank up to give him access to what he wanted.

I whimpered needily at the sound of him shoving his shorts down and he was inside me within the next breath, my pussy so wet that he thrust in to the hilt in one swift jerk of his hips and continued to pound me brutally from there.

"Next time we do this I want all of them here too," he growled, and I moaned at the thought of that. "I want you to have all of it, hummingbird, every last piece of us, and I'm going to make damn sure that you get it."

CHAPTER TWENTY FIVE

"Wait, what?" I balked as Rogue and Fox retold the story of the attacker last night.

"Fox was like - bam!" Rogue cried in excitement, holding a watermelon and bashing it against the fridge.

"Yeah, I got that part," I said, folding my arms. "It's the next part I'm questioning."

Rogue bit her lip while Fox laughed, returning to making us pancakes like he wasn't a savage murderer who'd fucked our girl against a wall after killing a man with his bare hands.

"What can I say? I have a thing for a bloodstained psycho who just saved my life." Rogue's gaze dipped to Fox's ass in his shorts, clearly lost to the memory of it all again as colour touched her cheeks.

Maverick took a vicious bite out of a nectarine, the juices dripping down his jaw as he glared at Fox like it was his head he'd just taken a bite out of.

"What's up with you?" JJ nudged him, still smirking from Rogue's story.

"Nothin'," Rick snarled in a way that said the exact opposite.

"Are you jealous, baby?" Rogue taunted him and Fox glanced over his shoulder, arching a brow at Maverick and laughing as he realised Rogue was right.

"Fuck off," Rick muttered, but Rogue didn't let it go, tiptoeing around the island, giving me a view of her ass as she rested her elbows on it and the shirt she wore rode up a little.

I finished the orange juice in my hand, placing the glass down and moving to stand beside her while she gazed across the island at Rick and gave him a teasing look.

"Do you wish it was you in that alley?" she asked. "Your hands wet with blood while you fucked me against a wall with the brutality of a wild man?"

"You should start writing this shit down, pretty girl," JJ said. "You could make a killing with romance novels, you've got me rock hard already."

"Only if you narrate them JJ," Rogue purred.

"Nah, I can do you one better than that. I know a married couple who create pure magic when they narrate together. Once you've been ear fucked by the Bordeauxs, you'll never go back."

"Can we just shut the fuck up and eat our breakfast now?" Rick growled.

"Damn, you're a moody little jellyfish this morning, Rick," Rogue said, climbing up onto the kitchen island and crawling towards him across it in the sexiest fucking display I'd ever seen. Her ass was fully out now, her little white panties on view and I wetted my mouth as I watched her approach Maverick with a seductive look.

Fox forgot the pancakes, turning to watch the show and JJ casually pressed play on his phone, his music hooking up to the Bluetooth speakers in the kitchen so Love Nwantiti by CKay filled the room.

"Fuck me, pretty girl," JJ breathed, leaning back on his stool to get a good look.

Maverick kept his expression flat, hiding the interest he clearly had in her as she leaned in for a kiss and he offered her his cheek.

I laughed, taking a seat as she moved onto her back, arching between us and scrunching the shirt up against her stomach so we got more glimpses of her body beneath.

"Fox, I'm changing my breakfast order," I said, but as I reached for her, she slapped my hand away and I retracted it with a grin.

Maverick folded his arms, continuing to look bored while our girl arched and writhed on the island, getting me seriously worked up as I took in her beautiful body.

"Touch me, Rick," she commanded while slapping my hand away again, making me laugh.

"Go on, Maverick," JJ urged while I reached out to skim my knuckles over her ankle, earning me a kick from her.

It was tempting to grab her and pin her down, all of us easily able to take control of her if we wanted, but there was something so right about her authority in this room. Whatever she wanted, she got. And right now, she wanted Rick.

Maverick bared his teeth, pushing out of his seat as his eyes ran all over her, looking conflicted.

"Maverick," she said breathily, her back arching again as she carved her palm between her tits then down to rub her pussy.

I groaned, rising to my feet too, but Rick grabbed her legs and yanked her towards him, leaning down and burying his face against her thigh. He bit her hard enough to make her scream and Mutt woke from his bed, yapping in fright, but his barks died away as Rogue started moaning, reaching for me and grazing her hands up my abs. I caught her wrist, biting down on that too and making her moans deepen as we marked her with our teeth, the wolves descending on her flesh.

"JJ, Fox," she encouraged now that she had Rick under her control, her legs moving to wrap around his neck as he bit her higher up her thigh.

Fox moved to bite the soft skin of her shoulder, while JJ leaned in to bite

401

her stomach and this crazy act got me so fucking hot for her as she fell prey to us.

One by one, we released her from our teeth and she sat up to examine the marks, none of us having bitten that deeply, though Rick's bites looked like they might bruise.

She glanced between us, her rainbow hair hanging around her shoulders as she brushed her fingers over each of the bites.

"Are we insane?" she whispered, a little laugh leaving her as the scent of burning pancake mixture filled the room.

"I've seen a lot of people's secret fantasies, and trust me, everyone's insane," JJ said. "We just wear our insanity on the outside."

I grinned as Fox ran to try and save the pancake which was on its merrily way to hell. I dropped back into my seat as Rick tugged Rogue over to him by the ankles, his desire for her all too clear, and I really hoped we were about to play out some more twisted fantasies with our girl.

"I get the next kill," Rick insisted. "And I get to fuck you while I'm bloody and fresh from the fight."

"Deal," she said, and his demeanour went from arctic to volcanic just like that, a smile turning up the corners of his mouth before he leaned in to kiss her like a starved beast.

She shimmied off the counter onto his lap, winding herself around him, and Maverick's expression turned to something softer that I rarely saw on him. He rested his chin on her shoulder and I saw more of the truth behind his anger. He'd been worried about her, knowing that some asshole had tried to take her again last night and come close to killing his brother too. I knew it because I felt the exact same way, only it was harder for Rick to express because he still defaulted to rage whenever he was confronted with a deeper emotion.

It reminded me that Shawn was ever-present, still out there making his plots and schemes while we had to remain constantly on guard to try and prepare for whatever angle he might strike at. It was draining, and always kept the darkness around us no matter how hard we tried to push it away. That was Shawn all over, getting in our minds, leaving a mark on us even when he was nowhere to be seen.

"Will they even miss you, pretty eyes? Or have they already forgotten you exist?"

My pulse pounded at the memory of his words, the terror I'd felt within the clutches of them as I believed him. He'd latched on to my insecurities as if they were a gift handed to him from a deity, and I'd fallen for every word he'd spoken to me. Even now, with my family surrounding me, it was sometimes hard to remember those words were lies. My worth lay with them, and every time Rogue kissed me or smiled at me, or I tussled and joked with my friends, I remembered that I was loved. That I meant something in this world. But I feared how easily those destructive beliefs could sneak back in. Each day I got with my family was a gift, and I was working to accept the fact that it was a gift I deserved, but it was a damn hard thing to achieve.

Miss Mabel walked into the kitchen in a light purple dress which floated down to her ankles, a little straw sunhat on her head and a brown purse over her shoulder.

Rogue slipped off of Rick's lap and tugged her shirt down, but Mabel waved a dismissive hand at them. "Oh don't worry about all that. I did plenty of dongle dancing in my day. Goodness, I even had an amorous tryst with an Irish mob boss once who really rocketed me to the moon, if you know what I mean. Liam O'Brien still visits my dreams to this day, I can tell you now." She laughed, patting Rogue on the arm and moving to stand at the head of the island, looking to us all like she was waiting for something.

"Everything okay, Mabel?" I asked.

"It's Sunday the fourth," she said with a bright smile, waiting for us to do something again but I just shared a look with JJ that said, 'what the fuck is relevant about that?'.

"So?" Mabel pressed, tucking her purse higher over her shoulder. "Shall

I wait in the car?"

"Oh shit," Rick said in realisation and Mabel smiled.

"Oh shit, indeed," she said keenly. "You made me a promise, Maverick, and I am making good on it now."

Maverick groaned, then pointed to all of us. "All of you assholes are coming too."

"Coming where?" Fox asked as he plated up our pancakes.

"There's a yarn festival in town," Maverick sighed.

"Yarn?" I frowned.

"Yeah, like wool and shit," Rick grumbled.

"For my knitting," Mabel explained. "I always wanted to try my hand at it. I'm currently knitting you all scarves. Rogue's is a rainbow pattern of course."

"Oooh," she cooed.

"But we live in endless sunshine," JJ said forlornly, like he knew without a scrap of doubt we'd all have to wear Mabel's scarves no matter how hot they made us, or how ridiculous we'd look.

"You can never be too prepared," Mabel said. "Besides, I'm sure you can come up with a great bit for your show using them, Johnny James. I can knit entire costumes for your dancer friends once I get the knack of it. Oh! I could knit you a nice little willy warmer to wear for the big finale!"

"He'd love that," I agreed, fighting back my laughter and JJ shot me a death glare.

"I don't want a woolly cock sock, Johnny D needs air flow," JJ groaned, but if Mabel heard him, she didn't let on.

"It's settled then," Mabel said, and Rick barked a laugh.

"Now that's a show I'll be front row for," Fox taunted, and JJ scowled at him as Mabel bustled her way out of the kitchen with a clear intention for us to follow.

"I guess we're going to check out some yarn then," I said, and Mutt yapped his goodbye as we left him to have free roam of the house while we were gone.

Rogue beamed. "I *woollen* miss it for the world."

I now knew more about yarn than I'd ever wished to know in my life. Turned out, you could have a forty-minute conversation with a man who never once lost a beat of enthusiasm for explaining the various uses for yarn, and my ears hadn't even fallen off. I'd come damn close to blowing my own brains out though, or his.

I hadn't realised how much violence knitting could inspire in me, but here we were. I was convinced I'd only kept my hand away from my gun thanks to Rogue showing up in her little lemon sundress with a bag full of fucking knitting patterns under her arm and the proclamation that she was going to attempt to make a blanket for Mutt.

She'd led me to a surprisingly good tiki bar at the far end of the outdoor fair where JJ and Fox had been holing up. There, I had found my salvation in the bottom of three sex on the beaches and now I was actually feeling quite merry - thank you very much, Mrs Vodka and Mr Peach Schnapps. Yeah, they were married to other people, but that was why they fucked so well when they came together in my glass. It was the forbidden nectar, the danger juice – *fucking hell, I'm drunk.*

"Well, what a day that was!" Mabel cried as she appeared with Maverick who was laden down with bags. He had a green woollen hat on his head with a little sheep sticking out the top of it, and it was one of the best things I'd ever seen.

"Say one word and you're dead," Rick growled at us as Rogue swallowed her laughter by sucking on the end of her straw which only caused a loud gurgling noise seeing as her glass was empty.

"Nice hat," JJ said, snorting and we all cracked up, making Rick's glower turn murderous.

"Well, I've had the most wonderful day," Mabel lamented, and I noted the band of Harlequins Fox had rounded up to secure this place were lurking close by. "And didn't we learn a lot about yarn? What's the best fact someone discovered?"

She looked between us all and flashbacks of my forty-minute conversation about yarn played on repeat in my head – or my near-death experience, as I would be calling it from here on out.

"Wool yarn is stronger than cotton yarn," JJ supplied.

"Is it strong enough to hang yourself with, I wonder?" I muttered, and Rogue drove her elbow into my ribs, burying her face against my shoulder as she laughed.

"Marvellous, isn't it? All this yarn," Mabel sighed, looking around the stalls and vendors on the street which had been closed for the fair. I felt a little guilty at how little I'd enjoyed the yarn then, because Mabel had been stuck in that basement for so damn long, she deserved a day out doing something she loved. Though why there was even a yarn festival in southern California, I'd never know.

"I can't wait to see what you make, Miss Mabel," I said, and she waved a hand at me with a wide smile.

"Oh, Chase Cohen, you are a sweetheart," she said.

"JJ's particularly looking forward to your work, he's been talking about it all afternoon," I went on and Mabel lit up, pulling out some knitting patterns she'd bought and showing him a range of willy warmers on them.

"Look, Johnny James, there's even one shaped like an elephant. Your willy can be the trunk," Mabel said in delight.

"Please stop saying willy, you're as bad as my dad," JJ said, and we all fell quiet in shock at what he'd just called Gwan.

Rogue gasped, pointing at him with the straw from her cup. "You dadded him."

"No, I didn't it. I didn't mean to say that," he said hurriedly.

"Totally did, man." Fox drained the ice out of his cup into his mouth, crunching through it while JJ narrowed his eyes on him.

"He's just Gwan," JJ insisted, though he definitely had another dad date lined up with him soon and I was here for his growing relationship with the guy. He seemed like he really cared for JJ, and it was cute as fuck to see my friend get all boyish around him.

My phone buzzed in my pocket, and I lost my chance to jump into the game of taunting JJ while I took it out, finding my dad's carer Mrs Bevlin calling.

I sighed, standing and moving away from the tiki bar so I could hear her better before answering.

"Mr Cohen," she said frantically, and I frowned at her tone.

"Everything alright, Alice?" I asked.

"No. Not at all. Oh god, oh god," she said in a panic. "You need to come to your father's place. It's...oh Mr Cohen, I wish I didn't have to tell you this."

"What?" I ground out, the phone locked tight in my grip as she took a moment to collect herself before she spoke again.

"He's dead," she whispered. "I just found him. I've called an ambulance, but it's too late. It's too late, Mr Cohen. He's gone."

"Gone?" I echoed, frozen in time as shock kept me from truly processing what she was saying.

"Yes, I'm so sorry. He was in quite the state – his body that is – oh I don't want to upset you with the details. The ambulance will be here soon. They'll move him. You won't have to see."

"I'll be there soon," I said fiercely, then hung up, looking to the others, finding their gazes already moving my way like they sensed something profound had happened.

Rogue was at my side in a heartbeat, holding my hand and asking for an explanation, but my mouth wouldn't work to give her one. I gave a single command and that was for them to follow me, and we were soon out on the road piling into a cab while Mabel was taken home by the Harlequins.

"Ace, what is it?" Fox pressed urgently beside me while Rick looked back at me from the front of the car, the woollen hat still on his head.

"I just need to see. I need to get there and see," I said, and they didn't press me again for answers.

I couldn't voice it, not unless it was true. I couldn't let that hope rise in me, let it pour out and fill every void in my soul, not if it was a lie. Not if he was somehow still walking on this earth, and hell my dad had been known to crawl back from the brink of death far too many times. Maybe Mrs Bevlin was mistaken. Maybe the paramedics were resuscitating him right now.

When we arrived, the ambulance was blocking the dirt road leading to my father's house, and I didn't wait for the cab to bump its way down it, I threw the door open and clambered out, running for the house and leaping the fence.

I ran past Mrs Bevlin who was ashen faced, sitting on the porch, calling something out to me about 'the coyotes', but I ignored her, barging past two paramedics in the doorway and finding him there. My father. Right there on the floor where a man in a green uniform was checking his pulse despite the fact he was obviously long dead, and I pulled my shirt up over the lower half of my face as the scent of death crept into my nose.

He was at the foot of the stairs, his face twisted in a horrified, pained grimace that spoke of an agonising demise. His cane had snapped beneath the weight of him when he'd clearly fallen down the stairs, his arm twisted at an angle that told me it was broken. But that wasn't the worst of it, there were fingernail marks in the floorboards, signs of distress where he'd tried to drag himself along, and it was clear why when I looked at his legs.

They were mangled, chewed by some animal and the blood staining the floor around him told me all I needed to know about how starkly alive he'd been when the creature had begun to eat him. I remembered his complaint about the back door being broken and it all clicked together. Coyotes.

"Holy fuck," Rogue's voice sounded behind me.

"Sir, are you a relative?" the paramedic asked me in concern. "It may be better if you wait outside while we move him."

Rogue's hand slipped into mine and I looked back, finding her there with three brutes at her back. My family, my true family.

It all came crashing together in such clarity that this house suddenly meant nothing to me anymore. It was a keeper of pain and abuse, but the master of it was dead, torn from this world in a slow, torturous death like he'd deserved. Now he was gone, his hold on me was gone too, the chains woven so deeply into my flesh cracked and turned to ash. He wasn't my monster anymore, he was nothing. All his bitterness, his hate, his destructive cruelty, it had gone with him into death, and I was free of him forever.

I fell on Rogue, crushing her to my body as a sob left me that was full of so much relief, it nearly broke me. And then I was laughing, laughing and fucking laughing as the world finally gave me an end to his reign over my mind, my thoughts. I could no longer hear his voice, because he wasn't in this realm anymore, he'd vanished from existence and I remained here, solidly present and standing at the foot of a future which was sweeter than anything I could have imagined up for myself.

Rogue kissed my cheeks, finding tears there that I hadn't even realised were falling, and she hugged me tight, feeling this too as she began to cry in relief for me. Fuck, I loved her even harder for that.

My brothers surrounded us, holding me tight between them, and while the paramedics no doubt assumed we were grieving in some fucked up way, we knew the truth of it. This was joy in its purest form, an enemy fallen and conquered before us. This was a new beginning, one they all shared in, and I decided to shed every part of it from my flesh in that moment.

"I'm no longer a Cohen," I vowed. "I'm Chase Harlequin. If you'll have me?" I looked to Fox, and he nodded, smiling and cupping my jaw in his cheek.

"You were always a fucking Harlequin, Ace," he said, kissing me on the forehead. "We ran our own Harlequin gang long before we were bound into my father's."

"True," Rick said, his lips twitching up. "So I guess it's a good time to tell you I'm Maverick Harlequin again."

Fox smiled like a kid and Rick shrugged like it was nothing, even though we all knew that wasn't the case.

"And I'm Johnny James Harlequin," JJ decided, raising his chin as the power of us claiming each other bound us with new chains, the kind that were made of all things good in the world.

We looked to our girl, wondering if she might choose this path, if she wanted to be one with us in this way too.

"Rogue Harlequin," she announced, her sea blue eyes so full of light I felt like I was standing before the intensity of a blazing furnace. And I felt a belonging among them that had been lost to me for far too many years.

"Never have I ever bought a mermaid tail and gotten one of my friends to record me swimming with it out in the cove because I was convinced that I could star in the mermaid show at the Weeki Wachee Springs Park in Florida if I practised enough," Rogue said, the game demanding that whoever actually had done that, had to drink. And the fact that it was so damn specific made me certain she had a target in mind.

"That was *one* summer, and I swore you to secrecy, Rogue," JJ hissed before aggressively sipping his rum and coke out of his plastic cup while the rest of us fell apart laughing and Rick ripped into him.

The sun was long past the horizon, the sky now a star-spangled expanse of forever hanging above us while we sat on the beach around a fire. We were only a stone's throw from my father's house, now drunk on cheap, store-bought rum which was the same brand we'd sometimes drunk as kids whenever we could get our hands on it.

This moment tasted like the sweetest days of my past, and I wondered if I was a lucky enough man to have reclaimed that time again for good. Maybe it would always be like this now, the five of us free to do whatever we liked, whenever we liked, and it just so happened that all we wanted to do was roam the streets of our hometown and rub shoulders with chaos. It was even better than being a kid when I really thought about it, because as of today, I no longer had a hateful father who despised me, and we no longer had to do what anyone told us to do.

Even Rosie Morgan was long gone. Fuck, somehow, I'd landed in the dream we'd all had for ourselves once upon a time, and I was so terrified that it might vanish into thin air, that I didn't wanna fall asleep again for as long as I could hold off.

"Your go, J," Rogue encouraged as JJ stopped pouting about his long-lost mermaid dreams and laughed it off instead.

"Fine, pretty girl. But you've just made this game a hunting ground and now I'm out for blood," JJ said, shifting closer beside me and giving Rogue a pointed look on my other side.

Rogue refilled her rum and coke with a look that said game on, and I wondered how many of us were about to fall in this war, because hell, I had a few secrets of my own which I didn't need being brought to light. Being a teenager had come with way too many fucking embarrassments as I tried to navigate the world as a man for the first time. There really should've been some sort of handbook, especially when your dad was a sack of shit, and I'd rather have cut my nipples off than asked his advice on anything.

"Never have I ever…" JJ started, gazing around at the four of us as he decided on his target. He clearly wasn't going straight for Rogue's jugular in retaliation, no, he was going to bring us all down with him. "Had a sex dream about Luther Harlequin."

"Oh, fuck you, man," I cursed as JJ struck me down and I drank a gulp of my rum and coke. "I knew I shouldn't have told you about that."

"Wait, what?" Fox barked while Rick barked a laugh.

"What was it like?" Rogue asked with a snort of amusement.

"Hey, what do you care what it was like?" Fox sniped at her, and she wrinkled her nose.

"Ew, I'm not into your dad," Rogue scoffed.

I was glad the attention was being drawn away from me, and I took the opportunity to shoot JJ a venomous look but he just shrugged innocently.

"That's the game, man," he said.

"You're gonna pay for that one," I warned.

"Hey, Rogue just outed me as a mermaid, how much further can I fall?"

"Oh, you can fall further alright," I started but Rogue thumped me in the arm to get my attention.

"Tell us about the sex dream," she insisted.

I groaned but gave in, knowing she wouldn't give up until I offered details. "It was like two years ago, it was just one of those weird things – it's not like you can control who shows up in your dreams."

"And rails you?" JJ asked and I shot him a death glare.

"This is so sick, but I can't stop listening," Rick said.

"I don't wanna fucking hear it," Fox muttered.

"Did he bend you over and call you pretty?" Rogue asked. "Did you call him Daddy?"

"Fuck off," I snipped. "It was all very…exotic."

"*Exotic?*" Rogue echoed as her amusement spilled over.

JJ lost it and Fox flinched away, covering his ears so he didn't have to hear any more.

"Please tell me you didn't enjoy my old man dream-fucking you?" Rick asked, roaring a laughing of his own. "Are you bi-curious, Acey baby?"

My throat tightened as my gaze locked briefly with JJ's then I quickly took a long drink from my cup to avoid answering that.

"Your go, Ace," Rogue said, covering for us and Fox dropped his hands from his ears as he realised I'd stopped talking about his dad.

I still didn't know how exactly to let Rick and Fox in on the secret about me and JJ. Not that there was a 'me and JJ', but sometimes we did stuff with Rogue that definitely crossed lines I hadn't crossed before with a guy. I wasn't in love with him or anything, it was Rogue I wanted like that. But the three of us together…well, I didn't even know why, but I liked pushing those boundaries and I liked the way it felt when we did. Though how I was supposed to explain that to the other two men in our group, I had no idea.

I locked my eyes on JJ, vengeance shifting my expression into a dark, dark thing and his big ass smile fell right away. "Never have I ever fucked Rogue with a loaded gun."

"Ah shit," he said under his breath, his eyes flicking to Fox who was scoffing like I'd make a joke.

"That would be insanity. You can't actually think any of us would do that, Ace," Fox laughed, but no one else laughed. Well, except Rick.

I gave JJ a look that said drink up and he scowled at me before taking a sip.

"WHAT?!" Fox bellowed and Rogue looked to JJ like a naughty school girl who'd been caught out, but also like she didn't really give a fuck.

Fox went into a ten-minute-long rant at JJ about the stupidity of what he'd done, and only stopped when Rogue climbed into his lap, pressed her fingers to his mouth and kissed him deeply, distracting him from his tirade and ending it just like that.

Rick took the reins next as Rogue slid back out of Fox's lap, and I wondered who was gonna be the next victim of this game.

413

"Never have I ever double dicked Rogue," he said, looking right at Fox like he was taunting him, and I felt kinda bad for him as Rick, me and JJ all took a drink. Fox stared at Rick the entire time, his jaw ticking before he raised his cup to his lips and drank.

"Wait, was that a drink for the game or a drink for thirst?" I demanded as JJ pushed up onto his knees, his head swivelling from Rogue to Rick to Fox like a meercat on guard.

"Oh my god," he breathed. "How did my sexth sense miss this?"

"You don't have a sexth sense, J," Fox said with a tut.

"Don't you deflect," JJ growled, pointing right at him while Rogue bit her lip and gave away that this was absolutely the truth. "You did it! You fucking did it."

"With Rick?" I asked in surprise and Fox shrugged, but that was all the admission we needed.

JJ jumped up, leaping across the motherfucking fire and colliding with Fox as he hugged him, scruffing his hair in celebration.

"So you're gonna join us in our orgies?" JJ asked excitedly.

"Maybe," Fox said stiffly, and JJ whooped, jumping back to his feet and doing a circle of the fire before falling down beside me again.

I looked back over my shoulder at my old home, palm trees curving up around it and weeds climbing the walls. The window my father always sat staring out of gazed back at me like a dark void, all lights off within that place. And that was how it should stay.

"I'll be right back," I murmured as the game descended around me into a tit for tat, and Fox and Rick started competing to see which of them could outdo the other in outing their secrets.

I pushed to my feet, jogging away from them across the sand and walking up the dirt road at the side of the house, pushing through the rusted gate to get in. My old bike was still there, laying tangled in the long grass and I smiled at that one good piece of this place. My escape.

I walked into the house, the floorboards creaking and groaning as I moved through the quiet space, the air putrid with the scent of death and old cigarettes.

I headed into the kitchen, checking one of the drawers where my dad had always kept his cigarettes and found a near-empty box of Marlboros inside with a lighter pushed inside it too. It was gold with a pop art naked woman in it, squeezing her tits. The same lighter my father had used to burn a mark into my arm once to see 'how much of a pussy I really was.'

I'd gritted my teeth and refused to show a flinch of pain, thinking I'd won something by doing that. But there were no victories where my father was concerned, I saw that clear as day now. Except maybe today. Today, there was a victory, justice too. Because the old bastard had finally gotten what was coming to him, and I was satisfied that the final years of his life had been lonely and miserable like he deserved.

Even now as I pocketed my dad's cigarettes, I felt my heart quickening, my instincts heightening as I expected to be caught out. But all that lived in this house now was silence, and a breath fell from my lungs, a smile of relief capturing my mouth as I fully processed the fact that no one was coming. I could do whatever I liked in this house; it was mine now, I guessed. But the only thing that really came to mind was wiping the whole place from existence.

I returned to the beach, my family turning to me as I dropped back down between Rogue and JJ, pulling out the cigarettes and rattling the box at them. "One last theft from my Daddy," I said with a smirk.

I flipped open the top of the packet, finding five cigarettes inside and Rogue shuffled closer, peering into it. "Why don't we make it our last?"

"Last theft?"

"No way," she snorted. "Our last cigarette. There's five here. One each."

"No more smoking?" I questioned a little forlornly.

"Pretty girl's right," JJ said, moving closer. "That's fate right there. One last smoke each."

"I'm down," Rick said. "The only vice I need is her." He gestured to Rogue, and she waved him off like he was joking, but he had a damn good point actually.

"Fox?" I asked.

"Hey, I've been trying to get you all to be healthier for years. I'm fully down for this," he agreed.

"Do you think you can stop just like that, Ace?" Rogue asked me and I brushed my knuckles up her throat as I leaned in, stealing a soft kiss from her mouth. "I know you need them."

"They help me hold onto the past, but I think it's time to let go," I said, feeling power in those words. We had to stop clinging onto what was gone and start nurturing what was right here in front of us.

I leaned back, passing a cigarette to each of them before perching one on my lips and lifting my dad's lighter up, igniting it with the flame. Rogue took it from my fingers to light her own and I inhaled a lungful of smoke, the taste of it reminding me of that naïve, reckless little kid I'd been once. He was always going to be a part of me, and it was easier to look back at him now with sympathy than it had ever been. He'd needed love and he'd found it elsewhere, and as I looked around me, I realised he'd held onto it too, regardless of all his mistakes. My mistakes.

I wore a long-sleeved shirt despite how damn hot it was today, but I didn't want my friends seeing the fresh burn mark on my arm which my Dad had put there with his lighter last night. It was bright red and had turned into an ugly blister that was pretty noticeable. It wasn't like I could always hide the marks he left on me, but I tried, preferring to pretend like they didn't exist as often as I could get away with.

I cycled to Sinners' Playground, racing down The Mile, the boardwalk rumbling beneath the wheels of my bike as I weaved between the people walking along it.

I cycled so fast, I drew a lot of angry gazes and a few people shouted at me when I almost collided with them. Key word: almost. I was skilled at this, and there was no chance of me cycling into anyone unless I wanted to.

I sped along to my favourite place in the world, leaving my bike at the gates of the pier and running down onto the beach to climb the makeshift ladder which we'd carved up one of the struts. But before I could place one hand on the first rung, Rick called my name.

"Ace! We're going surfing. Come join."

I spun around, finding him, Fox and JJ stripping down to their board shorts further down the beach. My stomach knotted as I walked over to join them, not wanting to take my shirt off and let them see the burn on my arm.

"Where's Rogue?" I deflected, looking for my little one.

"Mary-Beth's giving her shit for getting home after midnight last night and waking her up," Fox said with a scowl. "If she's not here in thirty minutes I say we go over there and break her out."

"Definitely," JJ said, taking his phone out of his pocket and tossing it into the backpack between them. But doing so had dislodged three condoms from his pocket and they scattered into the sand at his feet, making him curse as he moved to grab them. Rick got there first though, snatching them up in his fist and staring at them in confusion.

"What the fuck are you doing carrying condoms around?" he demanded, a bite to his voice for a second like he suspected something. My mind pin-wheeled to Rogue as I caught onto his suspicion and my knee-jerk reaction was to punch JJ in the face. Though I held that in and waited for JJ's explanation first.

"My mom keeps sneaking them into my pockets," JJ huffed. "She says she's 'excited for me to explore my urges, so long as I do so safely.'" He shuddered and relief washed through my chest as I saw the truth in his eyes.

I noticed Fox's hands were balled into fists, but they relaxed at JJ's explanation.

"Does she make you roll them onto bananas at breakfast to practise?"

417

Rick taunted him. *"Or is it mini cocktail sausages so it's more realistic?"*

"Fuck off," JJ shoved him, trying to snatch the condoms back from him, but Rick pocketed them. *"I've got a bigger dick than all of you."*

"Bullshit," I scoffed.

"Second biggest, maybe," Fox said smugly.

"Is that what you were doing when I found you with Dad's tape measure the other day in your room and you punched me in the head?" Rick asked his brother as he laughed. *"You know you can't measure from underneath to add inches, right? It doesn't count unless it's done from the top."*

"You haven't used that tape measure for that, have you?" Fox grimaced.

"Maybe," Rick said with a laugh. *"Every guy measures their dick, it's important to build statistics to know where you rank in the world. So come on, gimme numbers. I'll beat you all easily. Though you all have to subtract three inches because I know you measured from your ass cracks."*

"Or we could just pound on you," I said, leaping at him and punching him in the chest.

JJ and Fox leapt in to join me and we soon had Rick beneath us on the sand, beating on him as we all started to laugh.

"Come on, let's go surf." JJ jumped up, heaving me after him while Rick and Fox continued to wrestle a little longer before calling a truce.

"I'll watch you guys," I said, tugging at my sleeve, and my friends peeled off into the water with their boards. Two more lay on the beach that Fox had brought here in his truck and I sat myself down on the one he always brought for me, the design of a blue swirling wave curving over a shark worn in places from use. Rogue's had a sunset on it in pastel colours and all of our names were written on the base of it too.

She suddenly appeared, dropping down beside me, out of breath as she flopped back to lay on her board.

"You alright?" I asked and she nodded, resting a hand on her stomach as she fought for breath. She was wearing denim shorts and baggy white tank

top that was ripped purposefully in places, places my gaze was instantly drawn to.

"I - punched – Rosie – in – the – tit," she panted, and I grabbed a bottle of water out of the guys' backpack, tossing it to her. She gulped it down as she sat up again and finally recovered enough to tell me the rest of the story. "Mary-Beth saw me do it and I ran away, but she got in her freaking car and chased me half the way here."

"What did Rosie do to deserve the tit punch?" I asked with a frown.

She scowled. "She took my phone. She's obviously been watching me enter my damn passcode because she got into it and went through all my photos. She sent a bunch of them to Mary-Beth that showed me doing graffiti on the walls in town, plus....well, there may have been a dick pic on there."

"What?" I snarled so fiercely that her eyes widened. "Who the fuck sent you that?"

"Sammy Coplin," she sighed. "It's fine. It was months ago. He kept texting me, asking me to meet up and I ignored him constantly until he finally sent me that. I don't know what the hell he was trying to achieve with it. It looks sort of like a swollen turtle head, is that normal?" She glanced down at my crotch before her eyes quickly flashed back up to mine, a blush lining her cheeks.

"No, it ain't normal," I said in a growl, glancing out at my boys on the water who were definitely gonna want to hear about this. "Forward me that photo, little one."

"Why?" she frowned.

Because I'm gonna threaten to send it to everyone in school when I beat the shit out of him.

"Just do it," I urged, and she shrugged, taking out her phone and sending it to me. "You got it back then?" I nodded to her phone, and she grinned mischievously, the look setting my pulse racing.

"Yeah, it was just after the tit punch. Then I ran like my ass was on fire when Mary-Beth started screaming at me," she said with a light laugh. "I'm gonna be so dead when I get back later."

"Stay here tonight," I said instantly, pointing to Sinners' Playground. "I'll stay with you."

"Okay," she agreed, jumping to her feet and pulling her top off, unveiling her bikini top.

Tits.

My mind got stuck on that word as she dropped her shorts too and picked up her board. "You coming?"

I nodded mutely, pulling off my shirt a beat before I remembered why I hadn't gone surfing before. Rogue's eyes found the mark instantly and she dropped her board in the sand, lurching forward and gripping my wrist as she gazed down at the burn.

"Ace," she breathed, pain lacing that word.

"Don't," I begged, and she looked up at me with an ache in her eyes.

"I hate him," she whispered. "Sometimes I hate him so much I wanna burn your whole house down with him locked inside."

My cock stirred at the darkness in those words, and she glanced up at me again, her jaw tightening and guilt flashing in her eyes.

"Not that...I didn't mean-" she started, fearing my reaction, but I cut her off.

"It's okay, little one," I said, stoking that darkness in her as my own darkness crept up to meet hers. "I dream about that too."

My cigarette came to an end and I didn't even have any lingering desire for it as I flicked the butt into the fire, watching it vanish into the flames. The others finished theirs too and there was a finality to the act which I knew we wouldn't go back on. That part of our lives was done. No more smoking, no more tar in our lungs. And I felt damn good about that.

We drank more and more as the night wore on, and after another couple of hours, Fox and Rick laid down and passed the fuck out. The two of them had been going head-to-head in our drinking games, and I wasn't surprised they were the first soldiers to fall with how much rum they'd consumed.

My head was a daze of pure happiness as I propped myself back on my elbows and listened to JJ and Rogue talking across me. I tipped my head back to look up at the night sky and wondered if all the dark days I'd had had been payment for this. There had to be a balance, right? And we'd all faced so much of the bad, maybe that was it now. Maybe all that was left for us was good. But just in case that wasn't true, I wanted to squeeze the goodness out of these moments even more.

I caught hold of Rogue's hand, tugging her down onto me and cutting her off mid-sentence as I kissed her. She instantly melted into me, swinging one leg over my hips to straddle me and I cupped her ass beneath her little dress, drawing her flush against me as I kissed her in slow, greedy movements of my tongue. It only took a few rocks of her hips to have me hard for her and between the rum and my girl, I was already fully persuaded into an outdoor fuck that could get us done for public indecency. Of course, it was seriously late and I doubted anyone would come wandering by now, but there was always the chance of some junkie blowing off the streets this way.

Rogue's tiny sundress was already around her hips and JJ moved up behind her, drawing it over her head and showing me what I'd suspected all day long was true. She wasn't wearing a bra.

I captured one of her nipples between my teeth, growling ferally and making her gasp and arch her back, her hips still rocking as she ground her pussy over my firm cock.

JJ knelt behind her over my legs, pulling her hair aside and wrapping it around his fist as he kissed her neck, making her moans increase.

I met JJ's gaze and we shared a smirk as he moved his free hand to tug and play with her other nipple. I could see he was swimming in a haze of alcohol and she was too, and I felt no barriers between us this time as my hand slid smoothly up onto his bicep and drew him forward, our mouths meeting over her shoulder.

His tongue brushed mine and I met his strokes with my own, our stubble grazing as we crushed Rogue between us and the three of us moaned like we were one creature.

I turned my head a little and JJ took my cue, drawing Rogue into the kiss as the three of us sucked and licked and nipped at each other's mouths. It was carnal, without thought, just this natural coming together that drove us all to claim one another.

My thumb circled her hard nipple and made her whole body quiver with need. JJ growled at the sight, tugging on her hair, and sliding his tongue deep into her mouth, making her whimper for us.

JJ's gaze met mine and my own need for him heightened, this new desire awakening once again as I leaned forward to feel his body pressing to mine. Excitement rippled under my skin as his fingers ran over my abs and I knew we were back to pushing boundaries, finding out just how much we wanted each other like this.

Rogue's throat rose and fell as she looked from him to me, panting a little as she took in our lust for one another.

"Does it bother you?" JJ asked her roughly, grazing his thumb over her lower lip. "How we want each other too?"

"Is it just sex, or more than that?" she asked, glancing between us and I met JJ's gaze again.

"It's like...friends with benefits," I said, trying to put it into words.

"Yeah," JJ agreed. "This is hot as fuck, but you have my heart, pretty girl."

"And mine," I assured her, and she smiled.

"Well, if it makes you both happy, I'm happy too," she said.

"You wanna push some more boundaries then, Ace?" JJ asked me, closing the distance between us and my heart raced as I nodded.

My dick was hard, I knew it was up for everything, especially as JJ's hand came down on my shoulder and pushed me onto the sand. He was the first guy I'd done anything like this with, and it wasn't like I hadn't had the odd thought of guys before, I'd just never really explored it until this desire for him had roused in me.

Rogue slid off of me, kneeling at my side and JJ dropped over me, his legs spreading my knees apart as he kissed me again, his chest pressing down on mine. I pushed my fingers into his hair as I accepted his tongue into my mouth again and the solid shaft of his cock rubbed against mine through our shorts.

He started to grind against me and I groaned, meeting the movements of his hips as I raised my knees either side of him and fisted a hand tightly in his hair. He felt so different to Rogue, all muscle where she was so soft, though I liked both in different ways.

I pulled at his shirt, tearing it over his head and Rogue gripped mine with an excited noise escaping her, pulling mine off too and tossing it away somewhere in the sand.

JJ dropped his mouth to my throat, kissing down to the scars on my chest and Rogue shifted closer, my eyes meeting hers and devouring the lust I found there.

"Take your panties off," I commanded, and she nodded, rising to her feet and drawing them down her legs, so I could get a good look at her. She returned to her knees, and I gasped a little as JJ's tongue circled my nipple before dragging lower still, leaving a trail of fire across my skin.

I moved my hand between Rogue's legs and found her soaked pussy ready and waiting for me, slipping two fingers easily inside her tight hole.

"Look at me," I demanded, and she sucked her lower lip as she met my gaze. I watched her closely as I pumped my fingers in and out of her and dragged my thumb over her clit, enjoying the pleasure I could see in her eyes.

She moaned softly and my cock jerked in response, especially as JJ reached my waistband and started dragging his teeth across the sensitive skin above it.

"Fuck," I exhaled as Rogue rode my hand, her eyes pinned on JJ as he tugged my shorts off, freeing my cock and wetting his lips as his gaze flicked over to meet Rogue's.

"You like that, pretty girl?" he asked, taking my cock in his fist and I cursed as his thumb rolled over the tip in the most perfect fucking way.

"Yeah," she said huskily, her voice making my cock twitch in JJ's grasp as he held me in suspense.

"Ace?" he asked me, a smirk dancing on his face as he applied more pressure and my hips thrust up on instinct to try and take what I needed.

"Fuck. Just do it, man," I insisted, and he laughed like an asshole before starting to stroke and rub my cock in corkscrew movements that blew my fucking mind.

I drove my fingers deeper into Rogue's pussy, making her moan too and I shot a glance over at Fox and Rick by the fire, wondering if we should try and shut up or move somewhere else. But the rum was saying fuck it, and my cock was in absolute agreement as it got worked over by JJ's large hand.

"You feel so good," Rogue panted, her pussy tightening around my fingers as she braced one hand on my chest and continued to ride them. "More."

"You want more too, Ace?" JJ smirked at me and I nodded, biting down on the inside of my cheek as I watched him.

He lowered down, sucking the head of my cock between his lips before I had a second to prepare and the noise that left me was all animal. His tongue flicked and danced across the head of my dick in an incredible pattern, his fist still jerking off the length of me in a tight grip.

Rogue started to come, the tell-tale pulsing of her pussy letting me know she was falling into bliss. I fucked her harder with my hand as she came with a shudder and a cry that carried right out across the beach, making a dark smile pull at my mouth.

I shot a look at the others as I withdrew my fingers from her, fearing they might wake, but that fear was forgotten as JJ took my cock deep into the back of his throat, placing his hands either side of my hips in the sand and sucking like a fucking pro.

"God," I rasped, half sitting up to steal a kiss from Rogue's lips as she caught her breath, but she broke the kiss quickly, turning her head to watch JJ instead and I chuckled at her, resting back on my elbows as I watched him too, pleasure rippling up through my cock with every stroke of his tongue.

But JJ didn't let me finish, releasing me from his lips and directing Rogue to lie on her back on the sand. She obeyed easily, amusement glinting in her eyes as she fell under his instruction, and I was more than happy to play along too.

"Get inside her, Ace. Don't keep our girl waiting any longer," he said, and I didn't need to be told twice, rolling over onto her and pushing her legs wider with mine.

She gripped my shoulders as I lined myself up with her tight entrance and I pushed inside her in a fierce movement that made her cry out again. Her nails dug into my back as I fucked her into the sand, her pussy so wet and so damn perfect as her body gripped my cock. I kissed her hard, tasting the lust between us and groaning into her mouth.

JJ's hand suddenly wrapped around my balls, something wet and slick against his palm as he did so.

"What is that?" I gasped as he started massaging them and pleasure rocked through my dick as I started to fuck Rogue even faster.

"Travel lube," JJ said. "I never go anywhere without it now."

"*Yes,*" Rogue moaned, her legs wrapping around me tightly as I pounded deep inside her, hitting the perfect spot.

I didn't put one and one together on what JJ had said until his fingers slid up between my ass cheeks and started rubbing lube between them in a soft movement that held a question in it. I slowed my pace, looking back over my shoulder at him, finding his shorts gone and his hand on his cock as he stroked himself.

"Pretty girl?" His eyes met hers. "You fancy feeling the power of me in Ace's thrusts?"

I swallowed the dry lump in my throat as I looked down at her, falling still as I wondered what she thought of that, and hell, what I thought of that too.

She nodded mutely, biting her lip as lust swirled in her eyes, the idea of it clearly igniting a fire in her. But did it light one in me?

I looked back at JJ again and he arched a brow, asking me the question with that single look. And suddenly I was nodding, agreeing to this madness and not knowing why, only that I wanted to try it. YOLO and all that shit.

JJ pushed me down over Rogue again, but drew my hips back a little as I knelt up in the sand, my cock throbbing inside our girl as it ached for me to move.

JJ's fingers slid up and down between my ass cheeks then he teased a finger inside me, making me shiver as he curled it, finding some seriously good-feeling spot and rubbing.

Rogue urged me to move, clinging to me in need, but JJ kept me still, gripping me firmly as he replaced his finger with the head of his cock.

I knew there was no going back from this, that we were crossing a line that would become an immovable wall behind us the second we were over it. But I wasn't sure I cared. I just wanted to feel them both at once.

He eased inside me, stretching me as I growled and took the bite of pain, pushing my hips back into his movements. Rogue moaned as she watched, playing with her tits, her hips bucking and driving me crazy as we shared in this insanity together.

When JJ was fully inside me, he pushed my head to one side so he could see Rogue beneath me, his chest pressing to my back and lighting my skin up as he started to move in a slow, heady rhythm.

I drove inside Rogue to the same pace as he became the ruler of my thrusts, and I melted down over her, my hands pressing into the sand and my muscles tightening to ensure we didn't crush her as JJ settled his weight over me too.

Then he was fucking me, her, both of us and we were just slaves to his power. Every thrust of my cock into Rogue was full of both of our strength and she started making noises I'd never heard from her before, her hands reaching for both of us and holding us close as we fell into this slow, euphoric rhythm that drove us all towards what was sure to be an explosive climax.

JJ drove into me deeper and started grinding against a spot that made me see more stars than the ones in the sky above.

I kissed Rogue between groans as JJ's thrusts pushed my cock deeper inside her, and she started screaming for us, her pussy spasming as she came, and my balls tightened before I spilled myself into her. JJ took over from my thrusts fully, making my ecstasy go on and on as he fucked me and her, and Rogue garbled both of our names as her own pleasure was prolonged.

When the two of us were spent, JJ slid out of me and I rolled onto my back beside Rogue while he stood over us, stroking his huge length and finishing on the two of us, across Rogue's tits and my chest.

He was a god of sex, and he'd cast us into fucking oblivion before marking us as his conquests. And I didn't give a fuck that he'd just owned me, because there was something right about it I couldn't even deny.

JJ smiled at us like a heathen who'd just committed the seven sins, and Rogue nuzzled into me as our chests heaved and JJ bathed in his victory over us.

"There's an inlet over there, come on," JJ ordered, and I got to my feet, pulling Rogue up too.

She still didn't quite have control of her legs as we followed him to where a pool of sea water was carved into the sand, and I kept hold of her so she didn't fall.

We slipped down into it and washed the marks of pleasure from our bodies before resting back against the bank of sand at one edge of the cool water side by side with the water still lapping up and over our waists.

Rogue's fingers found mine beneath the surface and I shut my eyes as I bathed in the afterglow of what we'd just done.

"So when exactly will we be telling the others that you guys like fucking each other?" Rogue asked casually and JJ snorted a laugh while a smile curled up my lips.

"Only when you're there with us, pretty girl," JJ said and I nodded firmly, because there was something instinctual about that. Me and him were an extension of her and us, not something outside of it that we'd want to do without her. She was the one we loved.

"How do you think Fox and Rick will take it?" I mused.

"Maybe they'll wanna play too," Rogue said with a note of hope in her voice, and I barked a laugh.

"No chance. It's definitely an us thing, right J?" I asked, but I knew it was true. Not only were Fox and Rick highly unlikely to be into this side of things, but I just didn't have those urges towards them the way I did with Johnny James.

"Yeah, I dunno what it is. But it works, doesn't it pretty girl?" he asked.

"Fuck yes, it works," she said, a hint of desire in her voice again.

"I think I'll do the fucking next time though, man," I told JJ, looking over at him with a smirk.

His returning smile skewed into a frown suddenly and he let out a roar of pain, jerking away from us violently and making my heart leap in alarm.

"What the fuck?" Rogue gasped. "Are you alright?"

"No! – Ah – motherfucker!" JJ started punching the water and I stared at him in shock as he beat the living hell out of the surface and droplets sprayed everywhere. He winced in pain and I lunged toward him, grabbing his arm.

"What's wrong?" I demanded in fright, but he shoved me off, climbing out of the water before dropping down onto his back and clutching his cock as he rocked from side to side on the sand.

I climbed out too with Rogue right beside me, looking down at him in concern.

"What's going on?" I demanded.

"Something bit my cock," he rasped. "Oh god, fuck, fuck, fuck."

I dropped to my knees, shoving his hand aside, terrified I might find his cock bitten right off, but there was no bite there. In fact, in the darkness I couldn't see much wrong at all.

"There's no bite," I said in confusion.

"Get a light," I urged Rogue and she ran away back to the fire, returning a beat later with her phone, pulling on her dress as she moved.

She switched the flashlight on and angled it down at JJ's cock, and we all looked at it, the sight making my stomach clench. A circle of wavy red lines ran around the length of his shaft and up onto his pelvis.

"Jellyfish sting," I said in horrified realisation. "Holy shit, man. Are you alright?"

"No, I'm not fucking alright, my cock feels like it's on fire, Ace!"

"I'll wake the others," Rogue said in alarm.

"No," JJ gritted out, grabbing my arm and tugging me closer. "I need you to pee on my cock like a good best friend."

I gasped, shaking my head. "No way."

"Yes way. Fucking do it," he insisted.

"I'm not sure that even helps a sting. You need a warm bath."

"Yeah, in your pee. Now come on, Chase Harlequin. You are gonna man up and piss on my cock."

I gaped at him, shaking my head again then looking to Rogue. "You do it."

"I'd have to squat! Besides, I have no pee. Do you have pee?" she asked, and I tried to say no, but dammit I did, and she knew it.

"Ace, please," JJ begged, and I could see how much pain he was in, so I felt my resolve melting away.

I nodded, frowning deeply and angling my dick towards his. He shut his eyes and I shut mine too before trying to calm my mind enough to get a flow going.

"Why's it taking so long?" JJ groaned.

"I've got performance anxiety," I hissed. "Just shut up so I can concentrate."

I squeezed my eyes shut tighter and Rogue started making whooshing noises.

"What is that supposed to be?" I cracked an eye at her.

"Sea noises?" she said like she didn't really know.

"I can hear the sea, Rogue. It's right fucking there." I jerked my head in its direction and she gave me a guilty look before miming zipping her lips.

"Come on," JJ begged. "I'm in cock agony."

"Alright, alright, just shut up," I growled, shutting my eyes tight again and taking a deep breath.

The flow finally came but as I let loose, JJ roared in anger and I stopped peeing instantly, opening my eyes, finding I'd forgotten to aim, and the pee had not only hit his chest but splashed him in the face.

"Why aren't you looking?!" he bellowed.

"Fuck, sorry. You weren't looking and I didn't wanna look so-"

"I'm allowed to not look! I'm the one being pissed on, but you *have* to fucking look." He pointed right at me as he wiped the piss from his cheek. "You have to look right at where you're pissing, Chase, that's your goddamn duty. Do you understand?"

"I wanna go home," I said anxiously. "I don't like this JJ."

"None of us like it," he growled demonically. "But we're here now and we're going through this, so you'd better focus, and you'd better focus good, because I need you to piss on my cock."

"You can do it, Ace," Rogue said, slapping me on the ass like I was a football player and she was my coach. "Pee on that cock."

"I hate you," I muttered before looking down at JJ's cock and the sting marks on it. I sighed, aiming my dick at his and unleashing my flow.

JJ kept his eyes shut, falling down in the sand like a wounded soldier and I peed right on him. I'd thought being fucked in the ass was as far as my boundaries would be pushed tonight, but no. Here I was, being forced to piss on my best friend's cock while he writhed on the ground like a beached dolphin.

"Huh, this says pee really doesn't help with jellyfish stings," Rogue said, looking down at her phone just as my stream ran out.

Silence stretched in the wake of those words and Rogue looked up at me guiltily before looking to JJ who flung an arm over his face.

"Just go," he whispered. "I need a moment alone."

"You need to get home and soak your dick in a warm bath," Rogue said quickly.

"I told you," I said.

"Just. *Go,*" he demanded, and Rogue took hold of my hand, towing me away from him while I tried to process what we'd just done and realised him fucking me wasn't going to be the sharpest memory that stuck with me from this night. Because I was harrowed by that last experience. Harrowed down to my bones and beyond. And I prayed this secret was never brought to light in a future game of never have I ever.

"You know how some nights just get really fucking crazy?" I muttered to Rogue as we made it back to the fire and I picked up my shorts, pulling them on.

"Yeah," she said, gazing back across the beach to where I could just make out JJ laying on the sand with an arm flung over his face. "This is one of those. Remember that time JJ got stung on the nipple by a bee and you just sort of leapt on him and tried to suck the stinger out, Anthony Bridgerton style?"

I sighed. "Thanks for bringing that up. I'd wedged that memory firmly into a void in my head never to be looked at again, but I'm so glad it's been brought back to the light," I said dryly, and Rogue clapped a hand to her mouth to stifle her laughter.

"Why'd you even do that?" she snorted.

"I dunno, it was a weird instinct. I just went for it. Can we change the subject now?" I grumbled.

She stifled her amusement, picking up the bottle of rum and taking a long drink of it. "So…welcome to the butt sex club."

"That's it." I dove on her, tickling her sides and she squealed as she laughed, trying to escape me, but I was after vengeance for her little taunts, and it was coming in the form of tickle torture. I got her onto the ground, pinning her down on her back and tickling her as she held the rum in the air, working not to spill a single drop even as she tried to fight me off.

"Gimme that." Rick appeared, taking the rum from her outstretched hand and we both fell still as we looked up at him drinking from the bottle. "Did I miss much?"

"Yes," Rogue said as I said, "No."

"Argh goddammit," Rick huffed. "You all fucked."

"Yup," Rogue said brightly. "My world was rocked while you snoozed your little head off, Rick."

"Where's JJ?" he asked with a pout.

"He had a jellyfish incident," Rogue said, and I shot her a look that warned her against telling him about the pee-to-cock business. JJ didn't need the added embarrassment, and honestly, I wasn't exactly proud of my involvement either.

I spotted JJ out in the sea as I hunted for him, standing up to his waist in the water with his hands on his hips, looking like he was contemplating life. Or maybe just his cock, I guess we'd never know.

"Is he alright?" Fox asked through a yawn as he pushed himself up on the sand.

"He'll be okay. I'll go bring him his shorts." Rogue grabbed them and jogged off in his direction.

I swiped the bottle of rum from Rick's hand, taking a drink, the burn rolling all the way down my throat. This night had gotten wild, and as I glanced up at the nearly full moon in the sky, I decided to embrace the madness and finish it off with a bang.

"Who wants to burn down my daddy's house?" I asked as I shoved to my feet.

"Fuck yes," Rick said excitedly.

Fox shook sand out of his hair which was sticking up in places from his nap as he grinned like a kid. "Let's do it."

I whistled for JJ and Rogue and they came back hand in hand, JJ now in his shorts, walking a little awkwardly.

"You good, man?" I asked. "Did the seawater help?"

"A little," JJ said quietly.

"Where did the jellyfish sting you?" Rick asked, looking over JJ's body for signs of a mark.

"You know what, Rick." JJ snagged the bottle of rum from my hand, draining a huge gulp of it before shoving the bottle back into Rick's hands. "I'm gonna leave that to your imagination."

"We're gonna burn down my dad's house," I said to save him from more questions and JJ's eyes brightened.

"We are?" he asked and Rogue whooped.

"Yep," I said. "Let's go find some gasoline."

"Hell yes," JJ agreed, starting after me as I led the way up the beach.

"It was your cock, wasn't it?" Rick called after JJ, but he didn't answer. "It was definitely his cock," he said to Fox who cringed and rearranged his own cock like he was getting sympathy dick pains.

We were all soon inside my dad's house, hunting the cupboards for flammable liquids and after a few minutes, we had bottles of liquor, lighter fluid and one jerry can of gasoline lined up on the kitchen table.

"Ready, Ace?" Rogue asked me with a wild expression.

"So goddamn ready," I said, grabbing the jerry can and starting to splash gasoline around the kitchen.

The others grabbed bottles of their own, tossing alcohol and lighter fluid everywhere while Rick played Burn The House Down by AJR on his phone.

When the house was fit for a bonfire, we gathered by the front door and I ignited my dad's lighter, dropping to a crouch and lighting up the liquid by my feet which trailed away into the lounge.

It went up like fucking jet fuel. We all lurched backwards out onto the porch as the fire caught and we watched as it swallowed up the furniture, the heat of the flames washing against my skin.

"Holy fuck," I breathed, my heart pounding erratically as I watched all the places my father had hurt me go up in fire and ash.

I threw my dad's lighter into the flames and it exploded as the heat hit it, the pieces lost among the carnage.

My friends pressed close either side of me and a smile gripped my lips as we continued to back up, the fire growing and growing. My foot bumped into my old bike as we reached it where it leaned against the porch and I took hold of it, moving it away from the fire and stealing it away from this place for good. I'd keep this one piece of my past from this house, fix it up and make it new again. Just like my family had done for me.

And with that, I turned my back on my childhood hell, never to look back again.

CHAPTER TWENTY SIX

A long soak in the bath and some help from Johnny James to wash my hair had released some of the tension from my body following our night of debauchery while we danced around the pyre of Chase's childhood home.

Johnny James had even laid me on the bed and massaged away the knots in my back once I was clean, the firm pressure of his hands making me feel all the best kinds of relaxed while the attention of his tongue had made me come so hard, I saw stars.

He hadn't taken it any further than that though – probably in part because his cock was still in jellyfish recovery - promising me a day of pampering as he whisked me downstairs where he had gone on to show me the latest routine that he'd been working on in a private setting while feeding me a 'breakfast of dreams' – his words.

Fox, Rick and Chase had been gone when I woke, the three of them following a tip off that might lead to Shawn, and though I'd been all kinds of salty about being left behind while I slept, JJ was doing a damn good job of treating me like a queen to make me forget about it.

Not that I could fully relax while knowing they were all out there hunting down the most vindictive man I'd ever known. Shawn may have been in hiding for a while now, but I wasn't foolish enough to believe he really was gone for good.

My morning of pampering had turned to a lazy afternoon of swimming and watching some of mine and JJ's favourite childhood movies. I'd had a pretty damn relaxing day - so far as a day fearing for the lives of three of my boys could go - but the others had all kept in touch often enough to reassure me they were okay.

It didn't seem like they were going to find Shawn from the updates they'd given me, but they had it on good authority that he'd been staying in an RV up in the hills beyond the town limits, and they were determined to scour every inch of that land before they came back to me. I might be missing the hunt, but I knew they'd make sure I was there for the kill if they found him, that much they had promised me.

"Rogue," the sound of Johnny James calling my name had me hurrying to finish up getting ready for our evening plans, and I quickly dressed in a pair of booty shorts and an oversized white GPR tank which I loved with the intensity of a mother with her new born. Probably. I had no real point of reference there, but this was a damn nice shirt.

I quickly left my room and jogged down the stairs, leaping from the bottom step and pouncing onto JJ's back where he stood in the kitchen, filling up a hamper with food for our date night.

"Give it to me now," I demanded, my lips brushing his ear as I remained on his back like a limpet.

"Can't you just wait until we're out on the water?" he asked with a breath of laughter, and I swiped for some of the food he was packing into the bag with a feral snarl.

"No, JJ. I need it now. Give it to me. Put it in my mouth."

438

"No." He swatted my hand like I was a buzzy little fly and I hissed at the tiny sting, snatching my hand back while he took the opportunity to close the picnic hamper and leave me hanging.

"Oh, fuck you," I growled, trying to lurch over his shoulder for the food but he just swung around with a laugh, backing up until my ass hit the work surface of the island and dropping me onto it.

"Don't tempt me, pretty girl," JJ said, turning around.

He dropped his hands to the work surface on either side of me as he stepped between my legs, his mouth moving in until the space between us was almost nothing.

Mutt barked angrily as I tilted my head back in anticipation of his kiss and JJ cursed as his ankles were savaged, shifting away from me while he fought off a tiny terrier who was working damn hard at trying to bite him.

"Ah, stop," he commanded, backing up while Mutt followed, giving his shoelace the death shake treatment.

I laughed as I watched them before giving in and calling Mutt off as JJ gave me an imploring look.

"You should have fed me," I pointed out and JJ shook his head.

"What's the point in taking you out for a sunset dinner on a speedboat if you eat the dinner before we even leave?"

"I could double dinner," I suggested. "I'll take one now then another in the boat. You know I can take it, Johnny James, stop resisting the inevitable."

He snorted a laugh, still shaking his head in refusal as Miss Mabel appeared in the room wearing a long white dress and a sun hat.

"So are we heading out or not? Let's not dilly dally – I don't want to be in bed too late, it plays havoc with my digestion if I'm not horizontal by ten."

"You're coming with us?" I asked in surprise and from the look on JJ's face that hadn't been what he was expecting either.

"When Johnny James told me all about it, I couldn't very well refuse, despite my hips not being suited for vessels of the sea these days. He's a sweet boy, trying to make an effort, and I wasn't going to dash his hopes to impress me."

I glanced at JJ, wondering if she hadn't spotted him standing in the room as she casually spoke about him like he wasn't here.

"You know JJ is right there, don't you?" I asked, pointing to him and she barked a laugh.

"And you're right there, I am right here, and the dog is pissing in the potted palm. Want to point out any other obvious facts or should we all get our asses onto that boat?"

I looked around to find Mutt innocently kicking some soil over the offending piss patch in Fox's potted palm and snorted a laugh.

"Come on then," I agreed, jumping up and linking my arm with hers as we headed for the back door.

I glanced back at JJ who gave me a rueful grin, not seeming to mind our date crasher joining as we headed out back towards the Harlequin private beach and the jetty beyond.

Mabel began to complain about sand getting in her crannies if we lingered on the beach too long and I agreed with her, telling her about the way it got lodged in every damn place all too easily for my liking.

JJ moved past us and onto the speedboat first, picking the larger of the two vessels which were currently docked there, offering Mabel his hand as he helped her onboard.

I hopped on behind her with Mutt right at my side, and we made ourselves comfortable as I looked out across the sea towards the setting sun with a smile on my face.

"I love it here," I stated as I drank in the last rays of sunshine to grace the day.

"It ain't half bad," Mabel agreed.

JJ set the picnic basket down and untied the boat from its mooring before he moved to the helm.

It had been a beautiful day and there were lots of boats out on the water, sails raised or engines powering across the waves, some people were out on jet skis and others on paddle boards, everyone drinking in the peace and beauty of the west coast as another perfect day came to an end.

We headed away from land, the spray from the boat's passage across the water speckling on my arms and cheeks as I leaned over the edge to hunt for dolphins in the brilliant blue water.

Once we were far enough out that the land was nothing but a green and yellow blur on the horizon and most of the other boats had been left behind, JJ cut the engine and moved to open the picnic basket where our dinner awaited us.

I shifted closer greedily, eyeing the food he'd prepared with my stomach growling so loudly that I almost didn't hear the purr of a jet ski as it tore across the waves close by.

JJ started getting things out of the hamper, his focus on the task, but I raised my head to look as that engine noise drew closer, my gaze falling on the blue jet ski which was moving at high speed in our direction.

It was hard to make out much about the man riding it with the sun dipping down to caress the waves at his back and my vision distorted by it, but something about the way he was headed right for us set my pulse rising.

"JJ," I said as I moved to grab a pistol from the pocket on the side of the hamper, and Mutt started barking as he picked up on the concern in my voice.

JJ whipped around, grabbing his own gun too, getting to his feet again as he turned to face the jet ski speeding right toward our boat without any sign of slowing down.

I raised my weapon, planting my feet as the jet ski sped even closer, adrenaline spiking through my body as I saw the inevitable crash coming.

JJ fired off several warning shots and the replying whoop of laughter from the man riding the jet ski made my blood run cold as I recognised fucking Shawn's voice.

"Did you miss me, honeypie?" he roared over the sound of the engine.

I replied by firing several bullets his way as JJ started aiming to kill too, spitting a snarl of fury.

Shawn dropped low over his machine, and I let out an involuntary scream as the collision drew closer, but Shawn yanked the jet ski aside at the last second, sending a wave of water crashing over all of us and making Miss Mabel shriek in alarm as we were drenched.

"Get us moving, pretty girl," JJ barked as he shifted to the other side of the boat, firing again, the harsh sound of gunfire filling the air.

Miss Mabel threw her hands over her head as I ran for the helm and Mutt moved to stand over her protectively, barking loudly while he kept his attention fixed on the jet ski as it circled us.

I gritted my teeth as I started up the boat, raising my pistol and firing at Shawn again as he circled around in front of me, evading my bullets like the luckiest asshole in the world.

"What's wrong, baby doll?" he hollered over the roar of the jet ski's engine as I missed yet again, and he lifted a shotgun with one hand to aim it our way. "You didn't go convincing yourself of anything silly, like thinking I was gone for good, did ya? You had to know that ain't my style. We got things to finish, you and me. It's time for the endgame, sugarpie."

"Fuck you," I spat, releasing the throttle, and holding on tight as I turned the boat towards land and took off at speed.

JJ fired more shots and Shawn whooped in excitement as he took chase, the jet ski weaving back and forth through the water and making it damn near impossible to hit him with a bullet.

The jet ski smacked into the left of our boat and Miss Mabel started screaming curses as she was almost knocked from her seat by the impact.

JJ fired twice more, trying to take advantage of how close Shawn had come and I fired my last bullet his way too before throwing my gun aside in frustration and concentrating on driving us the hell away from him.

Shawn laughed and hollered as he swung the jet ski around to the other side of the boat and I clung to the wheel as he rammed us again, my heart leaping in fear as the speedboat lurched violently, tipping right up on one side.

A huge splash made me whip around and I screamed as I spotted JJ in the water, yanking on the wheel as I turned back for him, my heart in my throat as Shawn sped away and began to turn too.

"I'm coming, J!" I bellowed, cursing the boat as it swung around in an arc that was too damn big while the jet ski manoeuvred all too easily and Shawn sped straight for him.

JJ dove beneath the surface as Shawn raced at him and I screamed as he shot right over the spot where JJ had just disappeared.

The boat was aimed their way now though and I urged it on as I closed in on them, Miss Mabel hurling insults at Shawn as he whirled away again, laughing obnoxiously.

I put the boat in neutral as I made it to the spot where JJ had disappeared beneath the water, running for the edge of the boat while the roar of the jet ski closed in on us once more.

JJ breached the surface right in front of me, his dark hair plastered to his scalp as he reached for me and I practically threw myself over the edge to grab hold of him, hauling him closer as he clung to me.

My fingers bit into his skin as he reached for the edge of the boat, trying to pull himself up as fast as possible.

The boat lurched violently, and I almost lost my grip on JJ, while Mutt snarled ferociously and Miss Mabel screamed.

"Rogue," JJ gasped, his eyes widening on the man who had stepped up behind me and I felt fate closing in on us without mercy as my chest cleaved in two with the realisation of our failure. Shawn was onboard.

"I love you, Johnny James," I said, a sob catching in my throat as I met his honey brown eyes, and he shook his head frantically as he realised what I was going to do before I even did it.

I released my hold on him half a second before something collided with the side of my skull and I was thrown down into the bottom of the boat while JJ fell back into the sea, the cry of my name on his lips turning into a stream of bubbles as he sank beneath the waves.

Mutt leapt over me, diving on Shawn's ankles as he fought to protect me, and I rolled away from them both as I hunted for something to use as a weapon.

"Not so fast, sugarpie," Shawn mocked, swinging his shotgun at me again and forcing me to fall on my back to avoid the blow landing.

His boot stamped down on my chest before I could even attempt to move away, and Mutt squealed in pain as Shawn hit him with the barrel of the gun instead of me.

Miss Mabel shoved to her feet behind him, lunging at him with a knife from the picnic hamper and Shawn laughed as he smacked her arm with the gun too, making her wail in pain as the knife was knocked from her hand and sent flying into the water.

"Let's not be hasty now," Shawn cooed as he loomed over me, casually pointing the gun at Miss Mabel and making me fall still in my attempts to get free of him. "Put the mutt in the picnic hamper or I'm gonna see how many pieces I can blast him into with this here gun."

Miss Mabel cursed him as she began to do what he'd commanded and the moment his focus fixed on her, I bucked beneath him, managing to unbalance him and make him fall back into the chair to the side of the boat as I rolled away.

The boat rocked again as JJ grabbed hold of the side of it and tried to haul himself up, but Shawn recovered too fast, lunging for the throttle, and sending us speeding away without even bothering to give any attention to steering us.

JJ clung on with a snarl of determination and I scrambled to my feet as I lurched towards him, my hand outstretched with the intention to pull him back onboard.

Shawn swung around and fired at him before I could get there and he was forced to let go, falling into the ocean, left far behind in a heartbeat while the edge of the boat splintered from the spray of shot that struck it.

Shawn grinned as he met my gaze and I snarled at him before diving for the anchor sitting on the floor to the rear of the boat.

I grabbed hold of it just as Shawn threw his foot into my side and I coughed out a breath at the pain of the strike.

I didn't slow though, whirling on him with a determined yell and swinging the anchor at him with all my strength.

The heavy metal slammed into his thigh, and he bellowed in pain before smacking me around the side of the head with that fucking shotgun again.

I fell back to the deck once more and he was on me a moment later, his fist damn near ripping the hair from my head, his mouth hot against my ear as he forced my spine to arch painfully beneath the weight of him.

"I'm gonna so enjoy watching you die, sugarpie," he growled, his other hand moving to my throat, and I spat in his fucking face as he leered at me.

"Better do it quick then, motherfucker," I hissed through the tightness of his grip. "Because when my boys catch up to you, you'll be praying for death to release you from their power."

Shawn laughed loudly then slammed my head back against the deck so hard that the world was stolen from me in the space of a blink, and I was left with his words ringing in my ears and a desperate hope in my heart that my boys would come for me quickly.

"Game on, sugarpie. It's time for us to see this story end."

CHAPTER TWENTY SEVEN

My arms powered through the water, cutting a path towards Shawn's jet ski, gasping down breaths only when I ached for them.

The open water spread out around me in every direction and there was no other boat close enough to call out to for help. I was alone, left behind while my girl was taken by that fucking monster and there was nothing I could do but try to go after her.

She's gone. She's fucking gone.

I forced those painful words from my mind, fixing my gaze on the jet ski as the sunset turned the sky a deep and unforgiving blood red above me. Darkness was already coming for the world, and the moment it did, I'd lose sight of her in that speedboat for good. I'd never find her.

My hand finally latched around the side of the jet ski and I hauled myself up with my muscles burning, seating myself on it and starting her up. She roared beneath me, and I took off, my gaze set on the speedboat which was rapidly disappearing into the distance, bouncing over the waves as Shawn stole the girl I loved, and my heart was wrenched apart in her wake.

"Rogue!" I bellowed, pushing the jet ski to its top speed, tearing across the water and closing the distance between us only a fraction. But so long as I kept my eyes on them, so long as I kept going, all hope wasn't lost.

The engine stuttered and the power in the throttle choked out, the jet ski slowing to a halt as I looked down at the gas tank and found a knife sticking out of it, precious fuel spilling away into the ocean and leaving me with nothing.

Fucking Shawn.

"FUCK!" I yelled, my voice echoing out across the vast ocean, but even that wouldn't be loud enough to reach her.

I hunted my pockets, patting myself down as I searched for my phone, but it was gone. Lost to the boat or the waves, I couldn't be sure.

My head was in a chaotic spin cycle, panic closing in on me as I thought of Rogue and Mabel and Mutt. I'd failed them. I'd brought them out here to their deaths and I'd never, ever forgive myself for it.

I ran a palm down my face, trying to think, struggling not to let myself fear the worst. Shawn hadn't shot them there and then; he was too fucking psychotic even for that. No doubt he'd want to play with Rogue first, make her hurt, suffer. I knew that was by no means a good thing, but it meant that she was still alive, that I had time, even if it was only a little bit.

A wave of nausea gripped me, my hands shaking as I watched the little speck of white that marked their boat vanish into the distance.

I turned my head to the far away shore and knew there was only one choice left to me now. I had to get back to my boys, I had to gather every weapon we owned and hunt that motherfucker down to get our girl back before it was too late.

It was a long swim, and I didn't know how far away Fox, Rick and Chase were off on their pointless hunt for Shawn right now, but what else could I do?

I dove into the water, swimming with all the might left in my body, hating myself for failing her.

Time was my enemy now, and I had to go as fast as I humanely could, because I could almost hear the ticking of the seconds in my ears, counting down to the moment when Rogue was stolen from this world by Shawn Mackenzie.

I vowed to get to her and save the girl who was owed a lifetime in the sun for all she'd been through. And I'd make damn sure that she was there to watch it rise tomorrow.

MAVERICK

CHAPTER TWENTY EIGHT

I tore along the road on my motorcycle, chasing after the black SUV ahead as it took corners at speed, winding along the narrow dirt roads that criss-crossed the cliffside up here. But Shawn was a fucking fool to have come out here because me and my boys knew this place like the map of it was etched into my soul, and as he took another corner ahead of us, Fox's truck tore out of a road to the left, blocking his way forward.

Shawn slammed on the brakes, and I skidded to a halt, twisting my bike around at the back of his vehicle to block his retreat, dust and muck kicking up around me, swirling in the beams of my headlights.

The dusk was red and thick in the sky, a perfect night for blood to be spilled, and I ached for it as I swung my leg over my saddle, my boots hitting the ground as I strode around Shawn's car with purpose. We'd been out hunting the town and surrounding hillside all day since our men had spotted this car driving through Sunset Cove, the very vehicle we'd chased out of Applebrook weeks ago.

We'd finally gotten another call saying the car had been seen again heading towards the cliffs and raced here to find it just in time.

Shawn had made a ballsy, stupid fucking move and now it was going to cost him his life. And I wasn't gonna make it pretty. But first I planned on wrapping him up in a bow for Rogue.

I aimed my gun at the driver's window as I took the coil of rope from my hip, winding it around my fist as I bared my teeth. The dust was still settling around me in the air as nothing but idling engines growled in my ears.

I could taste it, this victory. The drumming of fate starting up in my chest as we finally succeeded in finding the motherfucker who'd tormented our girl, who'd tortured Chase and who was responsible for the hell I'd been through in prison. His penance would be paid in pieces of his flesh until there was nothing left of him but bones, and even those I would crush beneath my heel.

Fox and Chase stepped out of the truck, sharing a predatory look with me as they surrounded the car, blocking all exits as they raised their guns higher, all of us ready to shoot the asshole if he tried anything.

"Get out of the car, real fucking slow, Shawn," I ordered as I planted my feet and squinted into the gloom of the vehicle.

The rattle of the door handle sounded, then the door was pushed slowly open and a boy who couldn't have been more than fifteen years old stepped out of the car, his hands raised in the air while he shook with terror.

"Please," he begged, looking up at me through fearful eyes, his gaze locking on the barrel of my gun as my heart jolted in my chest. "Please don't shoot me."

"Who the fuck is this?" I spat while Chase rushed forward, tugging the passenger door open and ducking down to look inside for anyone else, his gun primed to fire at any sign of movement.

"Empty," he confirmed as he stood back upright, slamming the passenger door shut with a curse.

Rage hit me like an arrow between the eyes and I lunged at the boy before me with a roar, grabbing his throat and throwing him against the side of the car. I pinned him there, pressing my gun to his forehead as he screamed in fright.

"Where is Shawn Mackenzie?!" I boomed, feeling Fox and Chase moving closer, though they continued to look around as if suspecting a trap to descend on us. And wouldn't that just be Shawn's style after all.

"I-I don't know," he stammered. "I don't know wh-who that is!"

"This is him," Chase growled, lifting his phone to show the kid a photo of the fucker.

The boy's eyes widened with recognition, and he nodded quickly.

"Start talking, or I'll start breaking fingers," I hissed.

"Rick," Fox warned. "He's just a kid."

"Just a kid who works for fucking Shawn," I spat.

"Please, man," he begged. "I just wanted the cash. I never hurt nobody. He told me his name was Ben."

"Ben?" Chase asked with a frown.

"Yeah, but he made me call him Mr Dover."

"Ben Dover?" Chase confirmed and that shit almost would have been funny except that fucking Shawn had got one over on us again.

"What did he say to you?" I snarled, releasing his throat but keeping my gun firmly pressed to his head.

"H-he gave me a couple hundred bucks to keep tabs on you. I m-met him last week at the drive-thru on Shade Avenue. H-he said he wanted to know if you were planning any days out, where you might be going. I-I followed you down to the beach a couple of times, that's all."

"And what did you report back?" I demanded, heat blazing along my limbs, the need for a kill sharpening in me.

"Nothin'," he said and I cocked the trigger on my gun, making him gasp in terror. "I mean, nothin' until today. I-I heard your friend say he was gonna take the girl out on a boat at sunset. That's all I heard, I swear."

My throat closed up, and I shot a look at Chase beside me, feeling Fox move nearer at my back.

"So what about this car?" Fox growled as my mind started piecing this all together too fast.

"H-he asked to meet me on the edge of town. He gave me the car and another couple hundred bucks to drive it through town and hang around the cove all day. He said to head this way if it looked like anyone was following me, so when you showed up and started chasing me, I-"

"Fuck," Chase growled, snatching his phone from his pocket and dialling JJ's number.

He hit speaker and the sound of the phone ringing and ringing came before it cut out, then he tried Rogue's and the same damn thing happened.

"We've gotta go," Fox said urgently, terror lacing his tone as he yanked my arm back so my gun fell from the kid's head.

He dragged me away from him, but I raised the gun again, firing off a shot into the car beside him, making him cry out in alarm as glass shattered. "If you've cost me my girl's life I'll hunt you to the ends of the earth, boy!"

He shrank away in fear and Fox grabbed my shoulder to make me look at him. "Get on your bike. Get home. Find her."

I nodded, twisting away from him and shoving my gun into its holster as I threw my leg over my bike and started her up, turning her back down the dirt road. I let the throttle loose, anger, hate and fear clashing inside me, making me into a monstrous beast. If he'd gotten to her, if Shawn had her now-

I spat a snarl, unable to finish that thought and focusing on driving as fast as I possibly could back down the winding cliff roads towards home.

CHAPTER TWENTY NINE

Cold water crashed over me and I gasped in shock, jerking awake and finding myself tied to a chair in a dimly lit space with the scent of grain hanging in the air and a chill digging into my bones.

I coughed as I squinted up at Shawn where he stood over me, his shotgun slung over one shoulder and the metal bucket I assumed had held the water now drenching me hanging from his other fist.

"Wakey, wakey, Sleeping Beauty," he purred looking all too pleased with himself as he surveyed me and I spat at his feet, my upper lip curling back as I surveyed him right back.

"You look like you think you've won already," I muttered, taking in the way he was smiling down at me, his black shirt unbuttoned around his throat and his black jeans spotless. I guessed he'd had the time to get changed since we'd arrived wherever the fuck this was, but it was hard for me to guess exactly how long it had been since the boat.

"That is likely because I *have* won, sugarpie," he replied smoothly. "And now I'm just looking forward to watching this night play out and having a pretty little rainbow haired corpse to dispose of at the end of it."

I scoffed lightly, like I wasn't tied to a chair in the middle of fuck knew where with blood plastered to the side of my head, and no weapons in sight to fight back with even if I could figure out a way to get free.

I looked up, squinting into the dark as my eyes got used to it a bit more and realising that we were in some rusted old silo, the metal walls curving around me and towering up endlessly towards a curved roof that offered no chance of escape. There was a hole in the roof there, a black sky littered with unhelpful stars clueing me in to the time which must have passed since Johnny James had been left at sea and I'd been kidnapped by my own personal nightmare.

"Smile for the camera, won't you?" Shawn held a cell phone up between us, illuminating the flashlight on it and making me recoil, my eyes screwing up against the assault of the glare as he stepped closer.

He chuckled as he moved around me slowly, making me tilt my head away from him as the light continued to batter my fragile brain.

"Look at what I caught," he said to the camera as he kept circling me. "A pretty little whore who's been used a time too often."

Shawn reached out to grab my chin, forcing my face up to look at the camera and I lunged at him, sinking my teeth into his thumb. He cursed as I ripped into his flesh and he yanked his bleeding thumb back with a snarl, leaving me with a chunk of skin as a reward which I spat out again like a savage.

He backhanded me in return for that and the chair I was tied to almost fell over from the force of the blow as my head snapped sideways. But it had been more than worth it to see him bleed.

"Now it has been said that I am a cruel man," Shawn went on as if that hadn't happened and there wasn't blood running down his hand, dripping onto the dusty floor. "An unfair one even, though I would simply refer to myself as an opportunistic one. Either way, I am a man who doesn't take being crossed lightly, and you boys have crossed me time and again for this tempting piece of ass."

I realised what the point of this little home movie was and raised my head defiantly as he began circling me again, refusing to allow any fear to show on my face in case this really was my end, and this was the last time my boys ever got to see me alive. I didn't want that. Hell, the idea of leaving them after we'd just found each other again was a particular kind of torture, but in my current predicament, I wasn't certain if there was any alternative to that fate.

"Don't get me wrong. The girl fucks like she was born for it and I, myself, fell for that appeal too. So I understand your obsession with her, but where you went wrong is simple – you went and let your cocks addle your brains. It's easily done for a lot of men, I know. But inexcusable all the same. A nice, wet, eager pussy can beguile the best of men, especially when it comes with a smart mouth and pretty face for a bonus, but it is still a failure to fall prey to such a tempting honey trap. And the only real cure to such an ailment is to cut out the source of the problem at its root. Wouldn't you agree?"

Shawn took a sharp little knife from his pocket and moved closer to me, running the blade along my cheek bone just lightly enough to avoid cutting me while he smiled the whole time.

"Remind me of how you used to beg me for my cock, little whore," he purred. "Remind me what it was I liked so much about you when I found you all broken and alone, wanting to die just so you could try to figure out what it felt like to live again."

My eyes moved over his face, the features I'd once found handsome now twisted with all the ugliness I knew resided within him. I couldn't unsee that anymore. I couldn't see anything other than the monster he was, and I knew exactly what that monster needed. Power. Worship. Devotion. Shawn's ego was his only motivation for anything he did, and his superiority complex was a fragile, shallow thing.

"Please," I said, my voice low with lust, the pretence of desire coating it roughly as I licked my lips like I couldn't even taste the blood on them. "Give it to me," I begged, and his grin widened like he thought he was winning something here, but my lips curved into a mocking smile, and I started laughing at him before he could get any dumb ideas about the reality of those words. "I lie so fucking prettily, don't I baby?" I mocked him and he stilled as his gaze moved over me. "Did it make you feel good when I moaned while you fucked me? Three minutes of faking it for the big, strong man before finishing myself off while you tried to convince yourself that I was just getting off again instead of doing the job you couldn't."

Shawn snorted, rearing back and shaking his head like he was shaking off my words. "Whatever makes you feel better, sugarpie. All I know is that you were always more than willing to spread those sweet thighs for me whenever I came calling."

"You're the one who was obsessed with me. Not the other way around."

"How do you figure that?" he spat.

"You followed me here, Shawn. You came at me and my boys time and again, and even after you were beat and you knew staying here would be your death, you didn't leave. It's pathetic really. Just a little boy trying to play dress up. But we both know the shoes you're trying to fill with this big man bullshit are too damn big for you. You could have just let me go, left this alone and run for the hills. We wouldn't have found you if you'd run far enough and you know it. But your obsession just wouldn't allow for that. Would it?"

Shawn stared at me for several seconds then barked a humourless laugh before driving the little blade he held straight into my shoulder.

I gritted my teeth and bit down on the scream that tried to tear from me as the blade hit bone and he leaned in, yanking my head back by my hair and twisting the knife cruelly until a cry broke free of my restraint and a sadistic smile spread across his lips.

"You and me have a game to play," he said, spittle peppering my cheeks as he leaned over me and I bared my teeth at him in reply.

"I'm not playing any fucking games with you anymore, Shawn."

"Tut, tut, you don't even know the rules," he protested, tugging the knife out of my shoulder and casually wiping my blood on the hem of my white GPR shirt, staining it as more blood began to flow from the wound and run down my arm.

"Spit it out then," I ground out, my chest rising and falling rapidly as I tried to block out the pain.

Shawn grinned broadly, shoving me away from him again and backing up as he held his arms out wide and spun in a slow circle.

"You may have noticed that our current location is not featuring too many home comforts," he said before coming to a halt facing me and stamping his foot down on a metal hatch which banged dully, making it clear there was an open space beneath it. "But then again, I didn't buy this place with any sort of comfort in mind."

"Get to the fucking point, Shawn, I'm sick of hearing the sound of your damn voice," I growled, forcing my mind away from the agony in my shoulder as I worked to find something I could exploit here, something I could use to turn the tables on him.

Shawn laughed good naturedly like we were two old pals ribbing each other and just went on with his long-winded bullshit.

"Well, you may recall that night many moons ago when I hung myself a little Fox from a bridge in payment for your life and the life of your other little boy toys. You know, when you turned one of my own men against me and effectively destroyed my entire gang in the course of a single stroke by bringing the Castillo Cartel into gang warfare?"

"What of it?" I hissed but Shawn didn't seem to care that I wasn't enjoying his monologue, still blathering on endlessly for what I had to assume was his own benefit.

"After that debacle I was left with something of a dilemma. It was just me and my sweet old momma – God rest her soul – and I had not a man to follow me, nor a place to run to where you didn't have someone on the lookout for me. It was quite the conundrum. Especially as I had no intention of leaving our quarrel unresolved and-"

"What happened to your momma?" I asked, clinging onto that little bit of information and forcing him to pause in his ongoing ramblings. I was started to think that I might even be able to keep him talking long enough for my boys to have a chance of showing up before he got any further with whatever bullshit he had planned. And of course, he answered my question because the asshole just couldn't resist listening to the sound of his own voice as often as possible.

"My momma?" he asked, touching a hand to the void where his heart should have resided and sighing as if he had one. "After that little escapade in the marketplace where you came so close to catching up with me, I realised there was a problem there which needed resolving. That was the second time you and your boys managed to use that sweet, foolish, predictable woman to strike at me and I couldn't allow such a problem to stay present. All the time she was breathing, she was leverage waiting to happen. And I am not a man who can allow anything to be used as leverage over me."

"You killed her?" I gasped, uncertain why I was even shocked by that, but the one and only person in this world who I had ever known this heinous, villainous man to show any kind of affection or tenderness toward had been her. He'd traded me for her. Loved her enough to run from us when me and Chase had caught up to him after chasing them from the Applebrook market instead of falling into a fight where she could have been caught in the crossfire – or so I'd assumed. "When?"

"Not long after that whole car chase affair. I have to say, pretty eyes can be quite nippy on a motorcycle when he needs to be, even with that lack of depth perception. But that was the final straw."

"So why not just take me then and there? Or kill me?" I frowned because it made no sense if it hadn't been to do with his mom being there, but the way his eyes brightened at my question let me know he was damn proud of his answer to it.

"Because, I didn't have this place yet. I needed time to finalise the purchase and prepare it for your arrival. I'd been busy making my offer that day in Applebrook when you showed up all too soon. But it's ready for you now, sugarpie," he said, throwing his arms wide once more and thumping his foot down on the metal hatch again so that the banging sound of it echoed all around the empty silo.

I swallowed thickly as I looked around again, trying to see something more to this place than just some abandoned farm building, but there was nothing to it aside from it being creepy as fuck and damn cold in here.

"I see you are confused, so allow me to explain. I need you to pay the price of what those boys of yours have cost me. And if I'm being entirely honest, a part of me just wants to watch you bleed for me too. So I took the money I had from running The Dead Dogs and ploughed all of it in to this place – I didn't even have to give up one of my precious diamonds for this land, or even you in the end. There is no one around here for miles and miles. No one to hear you crying or screaming and most importantly, no one to scent your blood on the air either."

"What's down there?" I asked, eyeing the trapdoor he still stood on, making it clear that he intended for me to go down there.

"I'd sure as shit love to say monsters," Shawn purred. "But unfortunately, I do not live in some magical land filled with dragons and suchlike, so I had to make do with what I could. Shall we call it a maze?"

"A maze?" I asked and the way his eyes glittered said it was way more than that.

"Yeah. And at the end of that maze – if you make it that far you will find a set of stairs that will lead you on up into a barn where another game awaits you. If you manage to survive that one too, I will encourage you to join me in the farmhouse where I will be waiting for you with dear old Miss Mabel who I am fully prepared to kill in the most brutal way I can imagine if you refuse to play with me."

"What the hell is wrong with you?" I asked in horror, but he only shrugged, clearly so far gone down this path that nothing would see him turn back from it now.

"I did wonder whether or not you would take me seriously in that threat, so I figured I could make it plain and clear how far I am willing to go."

Shawn strode towards me, spinning the small knife in his hand and making me stiffen before he dropped it into his pocket, tossing me a wink as he passed me by.

He kept walking and I turned as best I could, craning my neck to try and see what he was doing behind me, but it was no use.

Shawn began to whistle some creepy tune and I could tell he was getting off on these fucked up mind games just as much as he would over whatever awaited me beneath that trap door.

He reappeared before I could freak out too much, swinging JJ's picnic hamper in one hand and carrying a can of gasoline in the other. Little doggy whimpers came from within the basket he'd tied shut with a piece of string, and I cried out as I realised Mutt was still in there.

"What are you doing?" I gasped as Shawn set the hamper down right in front of me, just out of reach even if I hadn't been tied in place like I was.

I began to struggle as he ignored my question, panic tightening my chest.

He straightened, taking his sweet time unscrewing the cap from the can of gasoline and I started screaming Mutt's name as I thrashed against the restraints holding me in place, desperate to break free of them and save my little friend.

"Stop," I begged. "He's just a dog. He hasn't done anything to you. He doesn't matter to you – please!"

"That's the point though, sugarpie," Shawn said as he poured the contents of the can all over the picnic basket, his eyes wild as he watched me the entire time he did it, drinking in my terror, my horror.

Mutt was going frantic inside the basket, barking and whining, scratching against the woven walls of it as he tried to escape it too, making the whole thing rock and shake, but he was unable to break the string which tied it closed.

"It ain't about the dog mattering to me," Shawn went on as he took a matchbook from his pocket and struck a match with a wicked gleam in his eyes I knew I was only feeding as I screamed in desperation for him to stop. "It's about it mattering to *you.*"

The bitter scent of smoke met with the pungent aroma of the gasoline in the air and my heart free fell in my chest as I watched an unavoidable fate come barrelling towards me in utter terror.

The scream that escaped me as he flicked the match down onto the picnic basket was filled with more agony than I had ever felt in my life. The entire thing was engulfed in flames within a heartbeat and as Mutt began to shriek in terror within it, I felt something tearing apart deep inside me.

Tears spilled down my cheeks as I roared Mutt's name loud enough to tear something within my throat and I threw myself forward with everything I had.

The chair tipped up and I went crashing to the floor, colliding with the burning basket and smashing one side of it somehow as I fell, breaking a hole into the woven material while the flames greedily licked at my arm in payment for stealing its intended prize.

Mutt tore free of the gap in my next breath, bursting from the blazing basket and leaping from the flames with a yelp of terror before racing away as Shawn pulled a gun from the back of his jeans with a curse.

"Run!" I bellowed as I twisted my head to look at my little friend from my position still tied to the chair.

Mutt threw a terrified look back my way just as Shawn took a pot-shot at him and I flung my weight sideways, knocking against Shawn's legs to force his aim off.

My little dog howled in fright as he dove for a tiny gap at the base of the rusted metal of the silo wall, while I wrenched myself away from the burning basket before it could burn me anymore than it already had.

Mutt kicked and scrambled at the hole, the few flames clinging to his white coat smothered by the dirt as he forced his way into the tight space and just as Shawn took another shot at him, he made it out to freedom.

"Run boy!" I roared as sobs of relief escaped me and Shawn cursed loudly as his kill was stolen from him.

The basket still burned just in front of me, but the flames couldn't take hold on my saturated clothes and a relieved sob caught in my chest as Mutt's close call with death sent adrenaline and relief spilling through every vein in my body with unrivalled power.

Shawn cut the ropes tying me to the chair, my limbs tingling as the blood flow returned to them in a rush and he heaved me upright, sneering in my face.

"I don't think the old woman can run that fast, sugarpie," he growled in warning. "So, I suggest you get on with what I want before I decide to burn her alive too."

"Fine," I spat, letting him shove me towards the hatch and stumbling as I fought to keep my feet.

I glanced around quickly, hunting the space for anything I might have been able to use as a weapon and cursing my luck as I failed to spot anything within the circular tower aside from the sadistic motherfucker who had brought me here.

Shawn grabbed the handle on the edge of the hatch and yanked it open, revealing nothing but darkness and cold air in the dark space beneath.

I drew in a deep breath as I looked for a ladder or something to help me climb down there, but found nothing.

"You're gonna have to jump," Shawn purred, but before I had a chance to do that, he gave me a shove and I fell to the bottom of it with a cry of fright, rolling in the dirt I found there as bruises blossomed along my spine.

I rolled onto my back, staring up at the space above me as Shawn sneered down in return, lifting the hatch and smiling at me in that taunting way of his.

"Don't forget what I said about you playing nice," he said, aiming his phone down at me once more and taking a photograph of me laying there at his mercy. "Miss Mabel is counting on you to keep her breathing." He took something from his back pocket and I frowned at the little travel alarm clock as he set a timer on it.

"What is that for?" I breathed.

"You're gonna sit tight down there until this here thing goes off. I have cameras down in the dark to watch your progress once I'm nice and comfy back in the farmhouse and I wanna be sure Miss Mabel is close by in case I need to follow through on my threats. So don't you move a muscle until it rings, got it?"

He threw the little clock down at me and I flinched aside as it struck my knee, picking it up quickly and frowning at the thirty-minute timer he'd set.

"Good girl," Shawn purred, moving to close the hatch and my heart leapt at the thought of that.

"Wait," I gasped, realising I was running out of time to stall him here and wanting to do anything I could to keep him with me instead of letting him return to Miss Mabel and do fuck knew what.

"This here is the time for action," he replied with a firm shake of his head. "See you at the other end, sugarpie."

The hatch swung closed above me and I was plunged into darkness with no choice left to me now but to go along with his twisted games and hope to hell I could figure out a way to win.

MAVERICK

CHAPTER THIRTY

Inearly crashed three times before I made it home in record speed, the Harlequins opening up the gates for me as I sped through them and skidded to a halt outside the front door. There was a fancy ass mom mobile parked outside the house, but I didn't pay it any attention as I unlocked the front door and ran inside with intention.

"Rogue!" I roared, just in case she was here somewhere, praying she and JJ had just left their phones somewhere and were off together fucking or swimming or anything except what I feared had happened to them. "Miss Mabel?!"

There was no sound of scampering paws, no sign Mutt was here or anyone else. The lights were off and as I made it to the back door, a bang made my heart lurch in my chest.

I snatched my gun from its holster, raising it at the back window where a dark silhouette slapped wet fists against the window, looking like a goddamn lake monster as bits of seaweed fell from his hair. He was half naked, his feet bare and a look of terror in his eyes.

"JJ?" I gasped, running forward and unlocking the back door.

He half collapsed as he fell on me, soaking wet and clinging to my arms, drawing in ragged breaths, but he managed to get three words out that drove a hatchet into my chest.

"Shawn. Took. Them."

"No," I gasped in fear.

"Yes, indeed." A posh voice sounded behind me and I wheeled towards it, keeping one arm around JJ as I raised my gun.

"Who the fuck are you?" I demanded.

A figure stepped into the darkness of the hallway, approaching us through the gloom and flicking on a light switch. Saint Memphis looked like he'd come straight from some fancy ass office, wearing a black designer suit with shiny little fucking cufflinks.

"What are you doing in my house?" I snarled, on edge as I tried to figure out what to do.

JJ was still gasping down air, dripping water all over the floor and clinging to me like his legs were about to give out on him.

"I was waiting outside, but when you ignored my presence, I followed you into your home and here I am. Tatum is in the car waiting for me to return with you all in tow, and we have wasted precious moments on these words already. So, I will increase efficiency by explaining as we move."

"Explaining what?" I spat.

"I have the location of your girl," he said, giving me an intent look before turning his back on me and sweeping out of the room.

"You do?" I begged, latching onto the certainty in his voice even though I was still confused as fuck as to why he was here. "Where is she?"

I hurried after him, dragging Johnny James with me and clinging to those words, unsure how this asshole could know any such thing, but he'd pulled through for us before, so I had to trust him.

Fox and Chase appeared, running through the front door and Saint lifted a hand, circling his index finger in the air in an order for them to turn around.

"What's going on?" Fox demanded.

"Shawn has Rogue. He ambushed us on the water," JJ panted, and the blood drained from Fox and Chase's faces.

"I have her location," Saint suppled cryptically again. "Let's keep moving, shall we? Keep the questions for the journey. Efficiency saves lives. Chop, chop. I have an arsenal of weapons in the trunk, no need to round up any of yours."

"Oh my god," Chase breathed in terror as Fox turned sharply around, shoving Chase along as his shoulders bunched with tension, clearly deciding the best thing to do right now was follow Saint's orders. And if he really knew where our girl was, I had to agree.

I grabbed a bunch of clothes for JJ out of the laundry as we went, shoving them into his hands and he mumbled a thanks as we ran over to Saint's huge mom-mobile.

Someone threw open the side door from inside to let us in and I found Tatum there, dressed in a fitted black jumpsuit, beckoning us inside.

"Hurry," she urged, but she didn't need to do any such thing, the three of us leaping inside quickly and dropping into a row of seats while Tatum shut the door.

Saint got in the front, taking off out of the drive while JJ stripped out of the last of his clothes and yanked on the dry ones in less than a few seconds.

"Tell me what the fuck is going on," I demanded.

"Where's Rogue?" Fox snapped, a ring of command in his voice.

"Keep hold of that anger," Saint said calmly from the front. "It will be key when you arrive there, but you need to listen to what I'm about to tell you."

"Arrive where?" I growled, starting to doubt if we should even be trusting this guy.

"I implanted a tracker on Rogue when she came to us a few weeks back. Upon request, I did not divulge that information to you before now-"

"You did what?" I hissed.

"I put a tracker under her skin, do keep up," Saint said, and Tatum shot me a look that told me to be patient with his bullshit.

I took a deep breath, trying to do just that, so he'd give me the damn information I wanted.

"So you really have her location?" Chase questioned, an ache in his voice.

"Yes," Saint swore. "Rogue believed it was inevitable that Shawn would get to her eventually. I reminded her nothing in life is inevitable other than death, but the statistical probability was concerningly high, so I offered her what I have offered my own girl. A way to find her if she was ever taken."

I realised this may have just saved Rogue's life and a heavy breath left my lungs. "Thank you."

"It is Tatum you should thank. As always," Saint said, glancing at his girl in admiration using the rear-view mirror and we all looked to her in gratitude.

"So where is she?" Fox said in desperation.

"Show them, siren," Saint instructed, and Tatum took an iPad from a rucksack on the floor, bringing up a map on the screen, a blinking light on it showing me where my girl was.

I snatched the iPad, taking in the location as Fox, Chase and JJ leaned closer around me to see.

"That's Rafe Gunder's farm," Chase said in realisation, and a breath of relief left me as I stared at that tiny blinking light.

She was right there, still reachable.

Unless she's dead already.

I winced at the intrusive thought, pressing my fingers into my eyes for a moment as fear carved out a hole in my chest.

"How do we know she's still alive?" I asked, my throat thick.

"The implant monitors her heart rate too," Tatum said, pointing to a heart in the corner of the screen which was flashing fast, showing me how furious Rogue's heart was working right now. Shawn was almost certainly causing it to beat like that, and I wished she could sense we were on our way to her now and that we'd move heaven and earth to save her.

I ached for Shawn's death so deeply it burned, it was written into my flesh. And tonight, I would find a way to secure it. No more failures, no more close calls. Fucking Shawn was going to bleed and scream and beg as he fell prey to my merciless hands.

"It seems an anonymous buyer purchased this land several weeks ago," Saint said. "The moment Rogue went off the perimeter set for her on her tracker and didn't respond to the texts Tatum sent, I knew she was in trouble. I deployed my drone, and it has been returning images to me ever since it arrived at this location."

Tatum leaned over to tap on the screen, bringing up those images. They were taken with night vision, showing the farmland from above, and anxiety warred in my chest as I saw the high metal fences ringing the land.

"It seems Shawn has taken measures to secure the place, and unfortunately, it seems he has given a tip off to the local law enforcement and they will now cause us an obstacle or two during our approach," Saint said.

"There's cops on every road leading up to the farm," Tatum said, tucking a lock of blonde hair behind her ear, an anxious line forming on her brow. "Saint managed to hack their radio systems and-"

"I didn't hack it, siren, I bought a police scanner on the black market and tuned into the right frequency," Saint said.

"Same difference," Tatum said.

"It absolutely is not the same difference. And you know how I feel about that phrase. It is a non-sensical abomination."

Tatum sighed, shaking her head and I caught her wrist, making her look at me.

"Tell me what you know," I said, a bite to my tone and she nodded firmly, tugging her hand away and reaching over to bring up a recording on the iPad.

"Saint recorded this ten minutes ago," she said, and we all fell quiet as she played it, the sound of a male cop talking across a crackling radio surrounding us.

"The Harlequins are gonna try and seize more territory tonight. We've had a tip off that they've purchased a large quantity of guns and are planning to clash with The Dead Dogs somewhere beyond here. Any sign of disturbance and we arrest on sight. Let's make sure they can't get past us and start any shit on our watch."

The sound of assent came from several responding officers, and I shared a look with Fox beside me.

"Shawn has used his cunning to wield them against us, and frankly they are going to arrest first and ask questions later if you're caught," Saint said.

I brought the map back up on the iPad, working out the best route to take which would help us avoid the cops. But apart from taking a seriously long ass walk through the forest on the east side of the property, I couldn't see an easier way. And that was gonna take far too fucking long.

"This is bullshit," I snarled.

"Yes, quite," Saint said. "But I have prepared for all eventualities and have already deployed two teams to the location to distract the police and allow us to approach."

"Teams?" Fox frowned. "Who?"

"My family, plus Kyan's uncle, Niall, will be leading his own team. I believe you have met Brooklyn and Mateo. They will be joining him, and though I wouldn't usually employ such volatile people, I believe this occasion calls for some volatility. They will be perfectly suited to causing enough mayhem to allow you safe passage past the police."

"Okay," Chase said heavily. "Just get us as close as you can."

"I intend to," Saint said. "We will be arriving in precisely thirteen minutes if my calculations are correct."

"They always are," Tatum sang.

"I know," he said. "But I've left a margin of error of one minute in case there is an unexpected interference."

Fox's phone buzzed and he took it out while I flexed my fingers, anxiety warring in my blood. There was a message there from an anonymous number and rage coiled through me at the words on the screen, knowing exactly who they'd come from.

Unknown:

Time to pay for your sins, boys.

A video was attached and JJ gripped my arm as Fox clicked on it, terror seizing up every muscle in my body as I waited for it to play. Was I about to see my girl and my grandmother die? Was it already too late?

Shawn had her in some dark room, the camera angled down at her face as he pressed a knife to her cheek, his fucking voice drawling in my ears as furious words exploded from my lips. Promises of death that were echoed by my boys, but as Shawn drove that knife into her shoulder, I lost all sense of everything, throwing fists into anyone I could around me as JJ and Fox locked me in their grip and forced me back into my seat.

The phone started ringing and my blood turned to ice as I grabbed it from Fox's hand, answering it myself and hitting speakerphone. "You're dead," I snarled. "So fucking dead."

"Well now, that ain't no way to greet an old friend," Shawn chuckled. "Listen here, you're gonna keep this call live the entire time while we play this thrilling game of mine. If the call cuts out, I'll give you thirty seconds to reconnect it, understand? If not, then I'm afraid someone's gonna die. It might be Rogue, or it might be your little old grandmomma."

"Maverick!" Mabel cried in the background. "Don't you worry about me, you just get to Rogue, you come for her and-" A smack sounded and Mabel groaned in pain, making me spit a stream of colourful curses.

"Get your filthy hands off of her!" I bellowed.

"She's sure got fire in her belly, that old girl. Now don't you go turning me into a monster. I don't wanna kill no old ladies if I can help it, but I will, so help me, Maverick Harlequin. I will kill her slow and cruelly if you don't pay attention, alright?"

I heaved in several breaths, lifting my gaze to the others who gave me frantic looks in response.

"There now, breathe in through the nose and out through the mouth," Shawn said. "That's a good boy. You really should take up meditation, it's done wonders for my mentality. You really can't appreciate the world until you learn mindfulness. There are so many ripe fruits to be enjoyed, so many bright skies and pretty little screams to indulge in." He exhaled low and long, making my teeth grind as I waited for him to get to the fucking point. "Okay, now turn your camera on, I wanna see all those handsome faces staring back at me."

I moved the phone away from my ear, rigidly doing as he said in an effort to protect Mabel and Rogue.

Shawn's face came into view and he smiled wide for us. "There you all are, now aren't you a picture?" He took a screenshot, laughing to himself as we glared at him.

"Where's Rogue?" JJ growled and Shawn's eyes shifted to him.

"Oh ho, if it ain't the dancer boy, how was your swim back to shore? See any dolphins on the way there?"

"Fuck you," JJ hissed. "Where is she?"

"She has gone for a deep dive down into my horror hole." He swivelled the phone around, showing us a row of camera feeds on a large television screen set up before him.

I spotted Rogue on one of them, crouched down in what appeared to be a dark, muddy tunnel, clearly unable to see as she patted the ground in front of her. But she was alive, even if she was in the clutches of this asshole's game, she was still breathing. And that was Shawn's first mistake.

"Enjoy the show, Harlequin boys, it's about to get nasty." Shawn set the phone down on something so the camera feeds filled up the screen.

I cracked my knuckles, tasting bile in my mouth as I sank into a depraved, wicked state of mind. And there I would stay until this night was done. I didn't care what fresh sins tarnished my soul come dawn, so long as those I loved were safe once more.

Fucking Shawn may have been a monster, but he was summoning a far greater one to his door, and tonight it was going to feed.

Rejects Park

ROGUE

CHAPTER THIRTY ONE

Darkness pressed in all around me so deeply that I almost felt more comfortable with my eyes closed than I did with them open.

It was cold down here. Cold and damp with the scent of wet earth filling my nostrils.

The weight of the entire world was pressing down above me, trapping me within this too-small iron box and making my heart thunder pointlessly against my ribcage.

A sob caught in my throat, making me cough as dust settled in my lungs and the distant sound of banging echoed down to me.

I tried to call out but it only resulted in more coughs ripping from my lungs and I fought another sob as I got lost in thoughts of me dying down here, lost forever in this hell, my boys long gone and my heart forever broken.

I blinked away the memories that this tight space kept rousing in me, reminding myself that I'd made it out of the wreckage of The Dollhouse. That I'd survived that, and I would survive this too. Whatever it took.

My stabbed shoulder burned with the force of a thousand suns after my fall and I hissed out a curse as I pressed my hand to it, the wet warmth of my blood steadily running from the wound.

I pressed my back to the dark wall of mud behind me, drawing in a shuddering breath as the cold sank deep into my bones and I listened to the ticking of the alarm clock as I waited for my cue to move. I wasn't a fool, and I wasn't going to take risks with Mabel's safety, so I'd just been sitting here alone in the dark, waiting for the time to run out without doing a single thing since Shawn had left.

"Where are you?" I breathed, running my thumb over the almost undetectable bump in my upper arm where Saint had placed the tracker inside my flesh for this very reason.

I knew what Shawn was through and through. I knew he'd never stop. I'd known this day would come eventually. He was single minded and focused so intently on what he wanted that I'd never known him not to seize it for himself one way or another. He'd fixated on the idea of taking me, so the tracker had seemed like an obvious choice.

I hadn't told my boys about it because I'd known how they would react. They'd have gone all caveman, swearing that they could protect me just fine and promising me the world while resisting me having the implant inserted, not wanting me to need such a thing.

Saint had come up with a simple plan for me to make the best use of it. He'd set a perimeter alarm to alert him if I left the streets of Sunset Cove and I just had to shoot him a text to confirm that I'd left intentionally to reassure him. If he didn't receive a message from me, then he would let my boys know about the tracker and give them the information they'd need to find me.

I could tell we weren't in the town anymore. There certainly weren't any old silos on the streets I grew up in and if I had to hazard a guess, I'd say we were somewhere in the farmlands to the east of the paradise I called home. Not that I had anything to go on aside from an agricultural building, but as Shawn had been lurking on us this entire time, it only made sense to assume he hadn't ever strayed too far from us.

A distant cry made my eyes snap open, and I looked into the gloom surrounding me in alarm as I imagined all the worst things he might do to Miss Mabel if I didn't play along with this shit. So I had to get moving.

I wetted my parched lips, feeling a welt on one that Shawn had no doubt given me while he smacked me about. I clenched my teeth as I thought of that man and all the bad he had brought into my life ever since I'd had the misfortune of meeting him on that rooftop two years ago.

I almost wished I'd just jumped that night, saved my boys the pain of me having returned here with that demon lurking in my shadow. But then I thought of all the ways the five of us had reunited, how broken they'd been when I first came back and how much they'd needed the love we had all rekindled in that time. So I couldn't really wish for that reality to have been the one I was gifted. Because Sunset Cove, the beach, the sand, the sun, and most importantly, the men I loved, would always be my home.

The clock rang loudly in the dark, the sound of the alarm making me gasp in surprise and I quickly located the button to stop the noise.

I got to my feet, not wanting to hesitate for a single second as I took a step forward, moving my hand across the damp soil surrounding me as I traced a wall to my left then my right, before a light breeze across my legs made me move forward.

At first, I was at a loss, finding another wall before me but then I realised I could still feel that hint of a breeze across my shins and I dropped down into a crouch instead.

I ran my fingers down the wall until they fell into a gap, a crawl space opening up before me which made my heart patter wildly as I hesitated in the mouth of it.

It was equally dark within that small space, and I was going to have to banish pointless fears of monsters lurking within the shadows as I reminded myself that the only beast here would be waiting for me at the far end of this passageway.

I swallowed a lump in my throat and moved onto my hands and knees as I began to shuffle forward.

My shoulder screamed in pain every time I put weight down on my left arm and I gritted my teeth against the agony as I forced myself to ignore it as best I could and kept going.

Still, the dark pushed in on me, whispers coiling through my mind that sounded an awful lot like Shawn's taunting words mocking me as I went. There were so many times back when we'd been together that I'd bitten my tongue against the things he said and did. I'd been such a fool, letting him treat me like that, staying and staying no matter how far he pushed me, because he was just so goddamn manipulative that it was impossible for me to break free of him.

"Silly little whore, stop trying to do things better suited to men."

"Just sit there and look pretty. If I wanted intelligent conversation, then I wouldn't have come to you."

"Don't ask questions, sugarpie, it only makes it clearer to everyone in ear shot how little you have going on in that pretty head of yours."

"A woman should be grateful for the things a man provides her, isn't that right, sugarpie? Come get on your knees and show me how grateful you are then."

"Such a pretty face for such an empty vessel."

"Look how sad you are. Don't ask me why, but that hollow look in your eyes only makes me harder for you, and I don't ever want it gone."

I shook my head to dispel him, refusing to fall into the trap of hating myself for having put up with so much of his shit. He had wanted me vapid and broken and willing. He'd found me at my lowest after spending years fighting for my own survival while dreaming of four boys who had hurt me so deeply, I'd feared I'd never find true happiness again. Shawn had wanted a pretty plaything, and I'd let him use me as such while I used him right back, putting a roof over my head and keeping food in my belly. So maybe that did make me a whore on some level, but I wasn't going to feel shame for exploiting what I had and creating my own power with it. Because whether Shawn wanted to admit it or not, I did hold power over him. It was why we were here after all. The obsession he'd built over a girl who had forgotten how to feel anything until returning home. The need in him to own me when he'd never stood a chance of doing so. He'd wanted to break me and become my whole world, but he'd never come close to meaning anything to me while I had my boys to hold up in comparison.

Well fuck him and his obsession with me. I was done with it. And that meant that no matter what he tried to throw at me now, I wouldn't stop fighting back. I'd play his game and so help me, I'd win it too and prove to him that I was so much more than he had tried to make me believe.

A hiss of pain escaped me as something sharp cut into my palm and I reared back, lifting my hand before me and finding a lump of broken glass protruding from it as I ran my other fingers over the wound.

I cursed as my eyes were still robbed of sight by the pitch darkness in here, but when I checked around me, I found nothing to help illuminate the way on. All I knew for certain was that there was no way back now.

I pulled the piece of glass from my hand then hesitated, my mind turning over Shawn's sadistic tendencies and my heart sinking into my stomach as I tossed the piece of glass out ahead of me.

"Fuck," I cursed as the tell-tale sound of more glass clinking together reached me and I realised what he'd done, coating the ground ahead of me in shards of sharp, shattered glass I'd be forced to crawl through if I ever wanted to get out of here.

I fought the desire to back up, focusing my mind on Miss Mabel who needed me to finish this and who had been locked up in the dark for far too long.

I tentatively reached out with the hand that wasn't bleeding – thankfully my right so that all my injuries remained on one side of my body for now – and

I swept the back of it across the mud, knocking more shards aside as I carved something of a path between them.

I moved on as it was cleared, setting a gruellingly slow pace as I continually paused to brush the glass aside before moving forward again, and despite my efforts, I still felt the sharp sting of the shards piercing my skin over and over.

My knees and legs took the worst of it so I could place my hands with more care, and there was nothing I could do besides grit my teeth and insult Shawn endlessly beneath my breath while I continued on through it.

I felt like a puppet, letting him pull my strings, and the thought of being under his control again set a fire burning inside me that wouldn't go out.

I was angry. No, I was more than that – I was fucking furious. How dare he decide that I was his to toy with? How dare he come for me time and again then threaten my dog and the only woman who had ever loved me as a child?

Well, he was going to be sorry when I made it to the end of this tunnel, and he realised that I was no pet to tame and punish at will.

I was a wild beast hunting my enemy. I was a hellcat sent to destroy him. I was Rogue fucking Harlequin, and if he knew what was good for him, then he would be best served to run.

FUCKING SHAWN

The Dead Dogs

CHAPTER THIRTY TWO

All in all, I was having one hell of a day.

Power was brimming in my blood, and I finally felt like the king of the world again. Yeah, this was where I belonged, at the top of the food chain toying with my prey. Rogue was gonna die so prettily tonight, and I had a front row seat to the Harlequin boys' hearts breaking as they tried to race to her aid. They might find this land, I didn't put that past them. They weren't to be underestimated, which was why I'd taken the precaution of tipping off the local cops about a Harlequin gang movement. That was sure to keep a bunch of lawmen ready and waiting for those boys if they showed up on my doorstep.

Meanwhile, little old me could keep the game running, and keep them watching it all play out before their sad eyes.

"How you holdin' up, boys?" I called to them as I stood behind the phone where it was mounted in a stand, angled at the television screen that was receiving a host of live streams from across the farm. I used my iPad to maximise one of the feeds that showed Rogue crawling through the broken glass I'd scattered along the muddy tunnels I'd dug down there that would lead her right to where I wanted her.

Streams of curses came from the phone and I laughed, turning to Miss Mabel where she sat in an armchair, one of the few pieces of furniture in this here farmhouse that had a little class about it. She was an old biddy after all, so I'd happily given up my seat so her tired legs could take a rest. I was a gentleman like that.

I picked up my rifle, loading it slowly, enjoying the kiss of each bullet against my fingers as I slid it into the barrel, preparing for the next round in this game.

"I didn't mean for you to get so wrapped up in all this, Mabel," I said tenderly, sliding another bullet into my gun. "That's the way of the world sometimes though, ain't it? We don't always land where we'd like to when we take leaps in life. But you've lived a good one, I can see that. You're far older than my daddy was when I blew his brains out, and far more deserving to be here too, I'd imagine. Did I ever tell you about that man? The one who beat me and my brother bloody? He was a cruel person, Miss Mabel. A real cruel person. There ain't a man in this world who's made me feel as small as him since. But I learned something real valuable from him, see? You wanna know what that was?"

"Go to hell," she snarled, and I tossed my head back as I laughed.

"You sure got a sharp tongue on ya," I said, cocking my rifle hard and making her flinch at the sound. "But I can see you're intrigued, it's glittering in your eyes. Well, the thing about my daddy was that he knew how to inspire fear in people. It was a real, goddamn gift that. He could walk into a room and everyone in it would feel his presence."

I paused for effect, the power he'd wielded back then sweeping around me now as Mabel shrank before me. "I still remember the way his boots sounded on the front porch when he got home, that tell-tale jingle of his keys in the door. Oh boy," I paused, clutching my chest as my heart raced. "Yeah, he knew how to frighten ya. And I was terrified, just a poor little nothing boy who hid under his bed from his mean old daddy. But he didn't let me hide for long, Miss Mabel, no he did not. He'd drag me and my brother outa our room and take us on a nice long walk through the woods. He'd take us huntin', but his kills were never clean. No, he'd keep 'em wriggling then make me and Nolan finish them off real slow. I didn't like it at first, but I got a taste for it after a while. Funny how that happens, ain't it? The way humans can adapt to anything…"

I mulled over those memories for a moment, rubbing at the stubble on my chin as I reflected on my daddy's teachings. "I hated him, don't get me wrong. He made my life miserable, he made me feel pain like no other person in this world has ever managed to. But the day I took his gun and blew his brains to kingdom come, something changed in me. I stole his power, took it within myself and I became this." I pounded my fist against my chest. "This all-powerful being that no man, no woman, no creature on this earth can conquer. And my dear momma was grateful to me for that, she saw my strength, she stoked it like a good woman does and placed me on the pedestal I'd earned. But there's something about people I learned later in life, Mabel, something you know about too, 'cause I see that rebellion there in your eyes. Not all of them come to heel, not all of them sit in my shadow where they belong. Some of them bite the hand that feeds, and I got a real taste for breaking the spirits of people like that, asserting my dominance, proving my power time and again. I have a long, long list of conquests, but Rogue Easton…" I shook my head, a growl burning its way up my throat. "Damn, that woman is persistent. I had her right where I wanted her for a while, kneeling for me, opening those sweet lips and taking my cock between them whenever I pleased, always begging me for more. But then she went and did something none of the others have ever done, Mabel. Not only did she come back from the fucking grave I put her in, she came back with more spirit than she ever had before. And woo-wee." I laughed a little wildly, striding closer to Mabel as I swung my rifle up to rest across my shoulders. "That is one hell of a way to cause an addiction in me. It's like these." I slipped a box of cigarettes from my pocket, sliding one between my lips and lighting it up with Chase Cohen's lighter with a smile. "She's my nicotine, Mabel. The hit I need, and I've gone too damn long without it now. And she's right, I'll admit, I have come to obsess over her in a way I have never obsessed over any woman in my lifetime. It's that damn fire in her that keeps burning. I have to snuff it out, Miss Mabel, don't you see? It will be my most prized accomplishment."

A whimper of pain sounded from the camera feed alongside the Harlequin boys calling out to Rogue and I turned to watch as she pulled a shard of glass out of her calf.

"Damn, that gets me hard," I muttered, my dick jerking to attention. "Power is a real good aphrodisiac, don't you agree, Miss – ah!" I yelled in pain as Miss Mabel punched me, driving a screw into my arm as she locked it between her knuckles.

I threw my fist out, slamming it into her chest and knocking her back into her seat, making her wail and curl in on herself. The screw fell from her grip, bouncing across the floorboards at my feet, blood dripping from my arm where it had impacted.

"You crazy old bat," I snapped, lifting my arm and sucking on the bloody cut she'd sliced into my skin. "You've thrown me right off my goddamn story."

I tore off a piece of my shirt at the bottom, wrapping it over the irritatingly deep cut she'd managed to land on me.

"Mabel!" Maverick shouted from the phone in desperation, and I smirked.

"Now where was I?" I sighed, trying to realign my thoughts. "Ah yes, women with too much spirit." I gazed down my nose at Mabel and she peered back at me with hate in her eyes.

"You're going to die at the hands of that girl, Shawn Mackenzie," she growled, a touch of prophecy to her voice that I didn't like one bit, and my smile dropped into a dark glower.

"No, Miss Mabel. You're wrong," I purred, leaning down and breathing a plume of smoke into her face. "And I'm gonna prove it when she's right here breaking in front of you. My name will be the last word to ever leave her lips while I claim all the power from her flesh and absorb it right into my own. Just like I did with my daddy." I took a coil of rope from the table beside her and started to bind her hands together. "Up you get, old gal. It's time for phase two."

CHAPTER THIRTY THREE

The tunnels beneath the silo had seemed endless, dead ends and countless turns making me lose all sense of direction as I was forced to crawl up and down them over broken glass while strips of razor wire hung down from the ceiling ready to cut into me if I didn't stay low enough.

It was exactly the kind of fucked up bullshit I would have expected from Shawn, though he must have spent a whole lot of time down here in the dirt setting it up just so he could get off on watching me cut myself via the little cameras he had hooked up down here. I'd been more than a little tempted to rip the fucking things down while the blinking red lights on them taunted me through every cut and sting the glass marked my flesh with, but doing so only would have given him an excuse to hurt Mabel and I couldn't risk that.

I shoved to my feet as the tunnel finally opened up above me, brushing the bits of broken glass from my knees and pulling one jagged shard out of my shin as I cursed Shawn loudly and colourfully.

I blinked at the space around me as I realised the darkness had receded a little, and as I peered towards the larger tunnel ahead of me, I was almost certain there was a sliver of light coming from that direction.

I drew in a deep breath, pressing a hand to my still bleeding shoulder for a moment as I tried to centre myself. I needed to stay sharp, focus and get through this while I waited for my boys to get here. And they would get here. The little microchip in my arm promised me that much.

I stepped cautiously forward, squinting in the dim light as I hunted for any more sharp and deadly things, but the further I went, the lighter it got and there wasn't so much as a single pointy stick aimed at me.

The tunnel turned a corner and I fell still as I found a dead end waiting for me with a ladder leading up somewhere above my head. At the top of the ladder, the flickering flame of a fire gave away the source of the light that had spilled down to me, and I hesitated, trying to gauge what else awaited me up there.

It was impossible to be certain, so I drew in a deep breath and moved to start climbing.

The shoulder Shawn had driven a knife into hurt like a bitch as I gripped each rung and heaved myself higher, but I ground my teeth and carried on, knowing there was no other choice.

I emerged in a large wooden barn with holes in both the roof and walls, the scent of rotting hay filling the air and cobwebs clinging to every corner in thick swathes filled with dust.

A cool breeze swept in from the door standing ajar before me, and the only real light came from the burning torch which had been wedged in the ground at the top of the ladder.

I took a step towards the door but fell still as the sound of an old-fashioned telephone ringing broke through the space and made me flinch in surprise.

I looked around for the source of the noise, knowing I had no choice but to play along with this bullshit as I spotted the red phone sitting on a three-legged stool to the left of the door.

I lifted the heavy handset, my eyes moving over the rotating dial as I tried to figure out where in the hell Shawn had found that thing, let alone how he'd managed to get it working.

"Yes?" I answered coldly as I pressed the handset to my ear and prepared to listen to his bullshit.

"Well now, that is no way to address the keeper of your life, is it sugarpie?" Shawn cooed from the other end of the line, his voice crackling over the old handset and setting me on edge. "I deserve a proper greeting from my dear beloved, do I not?"

"Just tell me what you want, Shawn, I'm not going to play pretend with you. We both know you're just toying with your food here, so tell me what the fuck you want."

"Okay, okay, keep your hair on," he sighed. "Though perhaps I should have shorn it all off considering the offensive multicoloured hue of it."

I gave him nothing in reply to that, simply waiting for him to get to the damn point already.

"Fine. Be that way," he muttered. "This part of our fun is fairly simple. You see that there farmhouse on the far side of the cornfield?"

I stepped to my right and tentatively pushed the door wider, looking out across the wild cornfield, which was illuminated in silver tones thanks to the moon, and spotting a large farmhouse lit up on the far side of it.

"I see it," I confirmed.

"All you gotta do is get there in one piece."

"I just have to get there?" I asked uncertainly, narrowing my eyes on the farmhouse as I tried to figure out what more there was to this, because there was no way it was some simple task.

"I do believe that you care enough for dear old Mabel to come either way, but just in case you are in need of further motivation, I buried land mines along the possible exit routes to both your left and right. The only way to avoid them is through the cornfield and straight to me. Got it?"

I pursed my lips, wondering if there was any chance he really had buried landmines out there and seriously doubting it, but in the end it was irrelevant because I wasn't going to try and run from this. Miss Mabel needed me, and even if she hadn't, I was done running from fucking Shawn. This was going to end tonight one way or another, and I sure as hell knew which way I was hoping it would go.

"Got it," I confirmed, and Shawn cut the call just like that.

I looked around at the empty barn, hunting for something I might be able to use as a weapon and cursing as I failed to find so much as a single piece of old farming equipment.

I moved towards the wall as I gave in to the fact there was nothing for me to use here, and took hold of a piece of wood that was nailed into place against a beam where all the rest of the wood had rotted away to leave a hole behind it.

I swore like a sailor as I was forced to brace my foot against the beam and heave my entire weight back to break it free, my shoulder burning with agony the entire time, but my efforts were rewarded when it finally ripped its way off.

I stumbled back as I almost fell on my ass, grinning to myself as I was left with a solid bit of wood which had a few nails sticking out of it for a weapon.

It wasn't much, but it felt like power as I tested the swing of it in my right hand and made a move towards the door once again.

I took a breath of fresh air into my lungs, tightened my grip on my makeshift weapon then darted out into the night, heading straight for the cornfield ahead.

My bare feet slapped against the cool mud outside, thorns and bits of gravel cutting into them as I ran, and my gut twisted sharply as I got the feeling I was being watched.

I jerked to the right on instinct and a scream tore from my lips as gunfire

496

cracked through the air, a bullet striking the ground where I'd just been which simply had to have come from fucking Shawn.

I dove into the cornfield and almost fell over as I started running as fast as I could, the hard stalks and sharp leaves slapping against my skin as I forced my way through them with my heart in my throat.

I started weaving from side to side as I ran, knowing the way the cornstalks were shaking around me would be giving my position away all too easily. Once again, gunfire lit the air and a bullet tore through the plants to my left. I swallowed a scream, my heart jack-hammering as I fought to keep down, keep my quiet, keep the cornstalks from moving as much as possible.

Holy fuck.

The ground was wet here, like it had rained at some point recently, maybe while I was trapped underground, and my feet slipped and squelched in the mud as I sprinted on.

I couldn't help but scream every time another shot was fired, my hands going up to shield my head as I fought against the desire to just curl up in a ball and hide.

There was one way through this. One way only. I had to get to that farmhouse.

My foot snagged on something as I ran and I lurched aside as a snare was triggered, a noose yanking tight on the ground where I would have been if I'd kept going straight and another shot shredded the cornstalks to my right as I stumbled away from it.

I sucked in a sharp breath and ran on, having no choice and unable to slow despite realising there was more within this field than just the fear of a bullet.

I sped on and on, refusing to drop my newly found weapon even as I feared it was slowing me down and I shoved more stalks aside.

It was disorienting in the depths of the field, nothing to tell me which direction the farmhouse was in, and every time I was forced to leap aside, I worried I was turning off course.

An excited whoop reached my ears and I recognised Shawn's voice, making me think I had to be getting closer to the house. I ran towards the sound even though every piece of me begged to run in the opposite direction instead, my panic drowned by my determination to finish this.

I leapt between another row of cornstalks and a shriek of fear escaped me as I spotted a beartrap right in front of me, my momentum propelling me straight towards it like fate had already decided to lay its bets against me.

I swung the piece of wood at it as I tried to throw my weight aside and I hurled it from my grip, snapping the trap a moment before my bare foot landed right where it had been. The sound of the wood shattering made my heart knot up with terror as I skidded in the mud, hesitation costing me several seconds.

Another gunshot rang out and I lurched aside, my movements too late as a blaze of fire ripped across my thigh, the bullet carving a lump of flesh from my body as it skimmed me and a cry of pain parting my lips.

I broke into a sprint once more, almost certain I could see the lights of the farmhouse up ahead of me as my eyes burned with tears I wouldn't let fall.

Pure terror unlike anything I'd ever known threatened to eat me alive. Adrenaline swallowed away some of the pain of my injuries, but I could feel the tears and cuts in my flesh all the same, the scent of my own blood hanging beneath my nose.

I burst from the edge of the cornfield with a sob of relief and Shawn's mocking laughter reached me as I sprinted for the front door which was open wide to welcome me in.

The door swung open at my touch, and I tripped as I burst over the threshold, crashing to my knees. This place offered me both safety and the promise of worse to come all at once.

I trembled from the adrenaline of that run as I fought to catch my breath, and the heavy sound of footsteps approaching from the stairs let me know my tormentor had come to bathe in this moment already.

"Up you get, sugarpie," Shawn cooed as he snapped the door shut behind me and locked it for good measure. "We've barely even begun."

CHAPTER THIRTY FOUR

Saint abruptly turned off the road which led to the farm and I sat up straighter in my seat as he trundled down a short, dead-end dirt road and killed the engine, plunging us into darkness.

"What are you doing?" I demanded in a growl. "We need to move."

Saint calmly checked his watch and looked back at me through the gloom of the vehicle. "Trust me, Fox Harlequin. Have I let you down yet?"

I swallowed the string of angry orders I wanted to unleash on him, knowing I had to place my faith in him tonight. He'd gotten us this far, and the dude was like an American Sherlock Holmes on speed, so I'd be a fool not to trust him.

I released a heavy breath, sharing an anxious look with the others before my gaze was drawn back to the endless feed on the iPad screen. But Rogue wasn't in sight now since Shawn had recorded her running out into the cornfield and my heart couldn't take the stress it was under as I feared she was in his grasp.

She was fierce enough to face him, but she was unarmed, and I didn't know how much longer he was going to keep this up.

"Please, man. I've got to go to her," JJ begged, and Chase nodded anxiously while Maverick continued to furl and unfurl his right fist.

Our desperation was tangible, and Tatum gave us pitying looks, a tight frown furrowing her brow.

"Saint knows what he's doing," she whispered. "I swear he won't waste a single second in his plan. He *will* get you to her."

It was hard to draw any comfort in her words when Shawn's feed remained dead, and I didn't know what was happening to my girl. It was suffocating, this fear, this dread. I just had to find a way to reach her and sitting here in this car doing nothing was agony.

A bang sounded then a flare of red sparks cascaded above us, the tinted glass sunroof giving us a view up to the sky where the firework had exploded. Another joined it then the honking of a horn back on the road drew my attention that way and I realised I could see out to it through the trees as headlights lit up the tarmac.

The beeping continued then a bright pink Jeep appeared, dragging a trail of tin cans behind it on strings and making a load of clatter. The back door was open, and Brooklyn sat on the edge of it, throwing fireworks out into the night with whoops of delight leaving her.

The sound of a cop's siren carried this way as it took chase after them and my eyebrows arched in surprise.

"Holy fuck," Chase gasped as all of our attention locked on the carnage.

A huge, tattooed guy was driving the car, his arm hanging out the window as he fired his pistol blindly behind him, his loud laughter filling the air before another enormous bang sounded a firework exploding above us. A shower of colourful light illuminated the sky, and the Jeep went zooming off down the road as Brooklyn continued to hurl fireworks out the back of it.

A cop car came racing along behind them, firing shots at them as the siren blared and the flash of red and blue lights added to the colourful chaos.

They shot past us too, taking chase after the Jeep at high speed, swerving to avoid the rockets which were veering left and right across the road before they went up in showers of sparks.

"That's Kyan's uncle, Niall," Saint explained, and I recalled the tatted guy I'd met at my birthday party. I also recalled Brooklyn showing me a photo on her phone of him with his cock out and wished my mind would just forget that image instead of presenting it to me right now. "Entirely unhinged, but always reliable when it comes to causing anarchy." His eyes remained fixed on his watch for several more seconds before he started the car up and turned us back onto the main road, leaving his headlights off as he accelerated fast between the trees arching over us.

"Come on, come on," JJ said under his breath, his nails digging into his palms as Chase checked the phone feed again.

"Where is she?" Rick growled, looking to it too.

"She's not dead," Tatum breathed. "He'd make you watch it like he said." She looked at us guiltily for those words, but she was right, and my shoulders relaxed a little. They tensed right up again as I checked the iPad and spotted the little dot marking my hummingbird inside a building at the centre of the farm. She had to be with him now, and I just prayed he kept fucking talking until we could get there.

"We're coming, baby," I vowed, touching my fingers to that dot as violence shifted under my skin.

Saint finally stopped the car right beside a high, chain-link fence. I wrenched the door open and got out of the car, meeting Saint outside as he strode around to open the trunk. He unzipped a large black duffel bag, showing me the guns and knives stashed there alongside a handheld circular saw. Rick grabbed that, strapped a machete to his hip and slung a rifle over his shoulder before running to the fence and starting up the saw to cut through the metal.

"Tatum and I will come back and pick you up here when you have her," Saint said. "We will be helping with distracting the law enforcement officers

503

in the meantime."

"Alright," I said as I finished strapping weapons to my body and took off towards the hole in the fence that Rick had finished cutting and he gave the circular saw back to Saint.

Rick led the way through the gap and JJ and Chase moved at my back as I followed him into the dark trees beyond the fence. Then we took off running, checking Rogue's location on the iPad only once before we set our gaze ahead and sprinted into the night as fast as we could possibly go.

"Hold on, pretty girl," JJ said anxiously as he pounded along at my side, our breaths falling furiously between us. "We're almost there."

Mariner's Grave

NIALL

CHAPTER THIRTY FIVE

"Bam, bam, bam, kablam!" Brooklyn yelled as the sky lit up red, blue, and green behind us, the echoing bang of the fireworks making my heart thump in time with the explosions.

A whoop of excitement escaped me as I yanked the wheel hard and sent the pink Jeep skidding out as we took a corner at speed.

"Hold on tight, little psycho!" I called to her, my Irish accent thickening with my excitement and she screamed like we were on a rollercoaster as she gripped the headrest of the closest seat to make sure she didn't go flying out the back of the car.

Sirens wailed and the flash of ren and blue lights chased us as the cops came flying down the road at our backs, perusing us into the night.

I fired a few half-arsed pot shots back at them as we took the corner, grinning widely at the alarmed looks on their faces as they raced after me in their funny little cop cars.

The road stretched out endlessly ahead of us, but this wasn't my first rodeo, and I knew they'd have their buddies out there, ready with a barricade and maybe even one of those fancy tyre-popping sting traps.

No thank you.

A dirt road met the road to our right, leading away from the farm where all the drama was apparently taking place tonight. I felt the devil in me, urging me on as I yanked the wheel around and took the turn at speed.

"Yippee ka yay, turtle humper!" Brooklyn yelled, her laughter lighting me up inside as she clung to the back seats, and I looked around at her to make sure she was doing alright.

"Did you remember to wear your big girl knickers tonight, love?" I called and she whipped around to look at me, the little black ears of her headband making her look all kinds of cute as she blinked at me in alarm.

"Was I supposed to?" she breathed, her voice almost lost to the roar of the engine and the howl of the sirens as they continued to pursue us. "Because I wore my bad girl ones instead."

I chuckled darkly, forcing my eyes back to the road as we thumped and bounced along it. "They'll do," I assured her. "Point is, this here is about to get all kinds of messy. Are ya ready?"

"I was born ready, Hellfire," she promised me, and by God, she was right about that.

"Keep 'em busy then," I urged, and she grabbed some more fireworks from the box.

She flicked the lighter in her hand to set the fuses burning, hurling them at the cop cars before they could go bang in her fist.

More cops had joined the chase now, clearly coming from further down that road like I'd known they would, their little trap made pointless by us taking this turn and we now had five of them on our arses.

Brooklyn tossed another firework and an explosion of pink and white sparks collided with the cop car closest to us, the Catherin wheel managing to lodge itself in the windscreen wipers and stick there. The frightened yells of the lawmen inside the vehicle brought a fucked-up kind of joy to my soul as they swerved all over the dirt road behind us and effectively blocked the other cops from getting any closer to us.

"Ah! Ouchie," Brooklyn cried, as she lit another firework and I glanced around to see she'd dropped the bastard thing, the fuse lit and burning down fast as it rolled around by her feet.

"Get that thing outa here!" I roared at her, and she spun to glare at me, sucking two of her fingers into her mouth before spitting them out again just as fast.

"It burnt me," she snapped, the firework rolling closer to her as I took the next corner blindly, just hoping I was staying on the dirt road because my eyes were fixed on her.

"Now, Brooklyn!" I demanded, adrenaline spiking through my veins as that fuse hissed its way towards an explosion.

She kicked it at the last second, knocking the rocket out of the open back door and it exploded into red sparks half a heartbeat later.

"Better?" she snapped angrily, glaring at me.

The car smacked into a rock at the side of the road before I could reply, the whole thing leaping into the air for a moment before slamming back down again and giving us all a jolly good fright.

"Get your arse up here, woman," I barked. "Let me see that ouchie."

Brooklyn huffed but obediently started climbing over the seats to get to me. She dropped into the passenger seat a moment later, the skin-tight grey leotard she wore making me get all kinds of ideas as I glanced at her bare legs, tracing the line of them all the way down to her neon green leg warmers and back again.

The car hit another rock and I snapped my focus back to the dark road as we sped down the dirt road and further into the trees, the gap between us and the cops widening as they got stuck behind the fella with the firework stuck in his wiper blades.

"Let me see," I demanded, holding a hand out and Brooklyn obediently offered me her hand.

I dropped my focus to her fingers, tilting them side to side to inspect the small burn on two of them and sighing.

"I may have to cut them off," I mused, and she tried to snatch her hand back, but my grip just tightened, and I gave her a devil's grin as she gasped in alarm.

"You wouldn't," she said, and I met her electric blue eyes with my crocodile greens as I let her see that I very much could while flattening my foot to the gas – the road was pretty much straight ahead from what I could recall anyway.

"You sure about that?" I asked, tugging her closer and drawing her wounded fingers into my mouth, sucking on them, and making her moan.

"You're a bad, bad man," she hissed, shifting closer to me, her hand falling onto my thigh and making me lose all sense of the world.

My Jeep slammed into a much bigger rock this time and Brooklyn screamed as the fucking thing tipped up onto two wheels, a huge bang letting me know at least one of the tyres had just seen its death.

Brooklyn screamed as she snatched her fingers back out of my mouth, fisting my shirt instead while I yanked on the wheel, trying to fight against the inevitable as the car swerved violently before clipping a tree which fucked us five ways 'til Thursday.

I gave in to fate, releasing the wheel and grabbing my woman instead, tugging her against my chest and winding my arms tight around her, my hand over her head as I locked her against me and worked to cradle her body with mine.

The car flipped and the airbags exploded as I was thrown into my seatbelt, my grip on Brooklyn so firm it was bruising as I crushed her against me and refused to let go.

The car rolled twice more, glass breaking, metal screaming and all the time I kept hold of her, shielding her with my body while her fists gripped my shirt and she clung on like my own little limpet.

The Jeep finally stopped rolling, bouncing down on burst tyres and leaving me to cough out dust from the airbag as I shoved it away from us and let Brooklyn sit up.

"Holy crap, Batman, can we do that again?" she breathed, her eyes wild and full of life.

I barked a laugh before unclipping my seatbelt and opening the car door.

"No time, love. We've got a booby trap to build," I growled.

I set Brooklyn on her feet, the howling sirens closing in on the road just up the hill from us, the red and blue lights flashing through the trees and letting me see a bit better.

I whistled sharply to draw Brooklyn after me as I moved around to the side of the Jeep, pulling open the back door with some difficulty thanks to it being battered to fuck then grabbing a box out from the footwell where it had miraculously remained through the crash.

"Line 'em up, little psycho, we ain't got long," I urged her as I cracked the box open and she hurried to help me as we lined up the last of the fireworks, all pointing back towards the road in a happy little row.

These fellas were bigger than the ones Brooklyn had been tossing at the cops so far and they were fifty shades of illegal too. I certainly wouldn't wanna have one of them pointed at my face.

I grabbed the coil of fuse I'd packed just in case of emergencies and made quick work of connecting my little line up to it before running the end of it to lay in the dirt just in front of my feet.

The cop cars skidded to halt up on the road as they spotted the destruction of our vehicle and I jerked my chin, directing Brooklyn to come stand at my side and watching her with heat in my blood as she skipped closer, readjusting the ears on her head.

"Do you think we did enough to help Racoon get his rainbow girl back?" she breathed, accepting the gun I handed her and jamming it into the back of

511

her leotard, so that it was pressed to her arse cheek outa sight.

"I'd say so," I agreed as I took a smoke from the pack in my pocket and lit it up, casual as a duck on a dinghy. "Nice work tonight, by the way."

"You too, Hellfire. You did some crazy hot driving," she said, her eyes trailing to the wrecked Jeep behind us as the cops started moving down the hill, yelling commands for us to show them our hands. "Until you crashed."

"Thank you kindly. I suppose I'll have to buy us a new Jeep now though," I said, inhaling deeply on my cigarette as I raised my hands, innocent as a lamb. No one needed to know about the two guns I had tucked into the back of my jeans, let alone the grenade in my pocket.

Brooklyn held her hands up too, giving them the doe eyes, which made her seem so sweet and harmless. Lies, lies, lies.

"Get on your knees," a cop barked as she took the lead, inching through the trees with seven of her buddies spread out behind her, all of them aiming guns our way.

"What was that, love?" I asked around my cigarette, smoke spilling from my lips as I spoke. "My ears are ringing something chronic from the crash."

"I said get on your knees!" she yelled, getting all antsy and red in the face. She wanted to watch that. High blood pressure was as much of a killer as me, and that was saying something.

"My knees?" I questioned innocently and Brooklyn cocked her head like she didn't understand either.

"Do it now or we'll shoot," the cop snarled, and I nodded.

"Alright, alright, keep your knickers on straight, no need to yell," I barked.

I dropped down to one knee and then the other, Brooklyn following suit beside me as I kept my inked arms up high where the cop could see them plain as day.

I turned my head to look at my little psycho, loving that hungry fire in her eyes and offering her a wink as I let the cigarette fall from my lips in a cascade of burning embers.

Brooklyn inhaled sharply, her teeth sinking into her bottom lip as her eyes traced the cigarette's fall to the ground. I watched in the reflection of her pupils as the fuse lit just like that and began to burn its way through the grass at lightning speed.

"Sorry," I said, turning my eyes back to the cop as she stalked closer, taking a set of handcuffs from her belt, and eyeing me like she might a cornered lion, which was about the only smart thing she'd done since her arrival. "But there's only one woman in my life who I allow to perform cavity searches on me."

"Aww," Brooklyn sighed, and I grinned widely at her right as the fuses burned out and the fireworks exploded with a boom that damn near put me on my arse in the mud.

The cops screamed as they were bombarded by them, and I grabbed Brooklyn by the back of the neck as I tugged her to her feet. The two of us took off running into the trees, leaving chaos and carnage in our wake just like always.

We'd call my nephew's girl for a ride outa here and be back home before dawn, celebrating the best way we knew how – naked and bloody from a fresh kill.

CHAPTER THIRTY SIX

Shawn strode away from me as I scrambled to my feet, bloody, bruised and splattered with mud from the cornfield, not to mention the way my freezing, wet clothes and hair clung to me like I was some kind of drowned rat.

"It all began when I was a boy," he said calmly, not even looking my way as he swung the rifle he'd been using to take pot shots at me up and over his shoulder while he swaggered into the next room.

I glanced at the stairs, trying to figure out where Miss Mabel was being held and Shawn whistled for me like he was calling a dog.

"Keep up, sugarpie, or I might have to motivate you," he warned, forcing my feet to follow him.

The farmhouse looked like it hadn't been lived in for a while, though there was still furniture lining the walls. There was a musty smell to the interior and the décor was dated, the seventies wallpaper peeling in places while dust coated pretty much everything.

A trail marked a path across the floorboards through the dust, making it clear that someone had been in and out of here pretty frequently recently, and I guessed Shawn had taken his time planning this out.

The low growl of a generator let me know how the lights were on, but nothing else looked like it functioned in this place.

I glanced towards the closest window hopefully as I passed it, but there were wooden boards haphazardly nailed over it. They hadn't been put there carefully enough to block the light from spilling out into the darkness, but there was no gap big enough for a person to fit through, and there were enough nails in each of them to let me know I wouldn't be moving any of them easily.

I tried not to limp as I put weight on my right leg, the burning pain from the bullet that had clipped me flaring every time I moved, but I didn't want Shawn to know that. I wasn't going to give him the satisfaction of seeing me flinch.

"As I was saying: it started when I was a boy. Just an innocent little whelp, looking out at the world through big, overly comprehending eyes."

"What the fuck are you talking about?" I hissed as I trailed after him, blood dripping from the wound in my shoulder and splashing against the well-worn floorboards beneath my battered feet.

"The origins of this need in me, of course," he replied, looking back over his shoulder at me like I was dense in the head. "The reason for your demise, sugarpie. Don't you want to understand your death before it comes to take you?"

"Death is just death, Shawn. I don't care if you think adding torture and pain into it makes it something special. I don't even care if you cut me apart bit by bit for me daring to run from you. You can't own people, and that's what this really comes down to. You're just a little boy spitting out his bottle because he can't accept the way the world is. I'm not and never have been your plaything, Shawn. I don't exist because you allow it. And the truth is, that you were never anything more to me than a way to pass the time while I was stuck living in the purgatory of my solitude from the only men who I have ever truly felt anything for."

"Liar," Shawn barked, whirling on me, and pointing the rifle straight at my face, my heart lurching as I gazed down into the dark barrel.

"It won't make you a big man to kill me," I replied, standing before him in my beaten state while letting him see the honest truth in my eyes. He was nothing to me. Just a blip. A mistake. A regret. "This obsession of yours was only ever about you trying to prove you held power over me when the reality is that you don't. You can't control my mind or my heart even if you enforce power over my flesh. So beat me if you have to. Cut me, rape me, call me all the worst things you can think of and kill me too, but it won't change a thing. I belong to the Harlequin boys, always have, always will. And there is a power in that which you can never come close to because you simply don't compare in any way."

Shawn's face broke into a feral snarl, and he lunged for me, tossing his rifle aside and grabbing my throat as he slammed me back against the wall so hard that my head spun, and his face slipped in and out of focus for a moment.

"Oh, sugarpie," he growled, cutting off my air and putting me right back to the last time he'd tried to kill me, when he'd buried me on Harlequin turf and left me to rot without realising I wasn't even dead at all. Who would have suspected that would turn out to be the best thing that had happened to me in ten long years? "You really should have just let me tell you my fucking story."

He released my throat then punched me right in the stab wound he'd given me in the shoulder. I screamed, unable to hold back the agony of that attack as I doubled over and clutched the wound.

Darkness flickered across my vision as I sucked in a breath, trying to force my focus from the pain and Shawn grabbed hold of my hair, yanking it so hard that I fell to my knees before him.

He began to drag me across the floor of the decrepit kitchen, and I thrashed and kicked and screamed as I fought to break free.

His grip was unrelenting, and he was chastising me in that patronising voice of his, but I refused to let the words pass my ears, continuing to scream and fight him every step of the goddamn way.

Something clattered across the floor as my bare foot collided with it and as if fate had just rolled the dice and changed sides, a jagged piece of what looked like a broken plate knocked against my fingers.

I snatched it into my grasp, taking a swing for him that he didn't even pay any attention to and missing as he continued to drag me by my hair.

I kept fighting as he yelled something about women never knowing when to be quiet, and I kept the piece of pottery tight in my fist as I swung it his way again and again. But the way he was dragging me along by my hair made it impossible to hit him with it while my feet scrambled along the floor, my other hand constantly bracing myself to stop me from falling.

A door banged hard against a wall, and I was momentarily distracted by the sound of Miss Mabel calling my name, relief tumbling through me at hearing her voice even though I wished she was anywhere but here.

I craned my neck against the pull on my hair and spotted her, her hands bound where she was sitting on the lid of a toilet seat in a grimy bathroom with mould lining the edges of the white tiles.

I spotted the freestanding white bathtub before me and had half a second to suck in a breath before Shawn grabbed hold of me and threw me into it on my back. Freezing cold water engulfed me as he forced my head down first then flipped my legs in too, my entire body submerged and my hands flying out to press against the edges of the tub as I tried to fight my way back out of it.

I dropped the shard of broken porcelain in shock, the world seeming to flip around me as I lost my place in it while I was driven further beneath the surface.

My lungs began to burn, Shawn's fingernails biting into my scalp as he held me under the water for a few more seconds before releasing me suddenly.

I flipped around, my hands finding the sides of the tub as I lurched upright, gasping down a breath of air.

Mabel was yelling something but I couldn't concentrate to hear it, her terror only feeding into mine.

"You always said you liked water, sugarpie!" Shawn yelled as I tried to scramble back out of the bath, but the back of his hand collided with my face, dislodging my hold on the tub's edge as I was knocked back down again.

I sank beneath the cold water and Shawn snatched my wrists into his grasp as I tried to grab the edges of the tub again. He yanked me up by them, my weight hanging from my arms and making the stab wound in my shoulder roar with a blinding agony that forced a scream from my lips. Shawn looped my wrists in a rope so fast that I barely had time to try and jerk against him before he was yanking it tight enough to bruise, knotting it tightly around the taps behind my head.

My feet kicked wildly as I fought to push myself up enough to keep my head above the water, the huge tub so long that only my toes could reach the far end of it. I was forced to stretch myself out painfully just so that I could continue to breathe.

"What the hell are you-" I began, but Shawn's hands landed on my shoulders before I could do more than suck in a terrified breath.

"Let's see how much you really like the water, huh?" he asked with a feral grin and I cried out in fear, only making his blue eyes blaze with excitement as he held me there at his mercy.

Shawn shoved me down with the full force of his body and I screamed as I was submerged, the rope holding my wrists cinching tight and sending blinding pain through my shoulder as my back hit the base of the bathtub.

Mabel's cries for mercy disappeared until all I could hear was the echoes of my legs slamming against the edges of the tub as I tried to fight back and the roar of my own scream as it tore from my throat, bursting into bubbles all around me.

CHAPTER THIRTY SEVEN

We ran furiously through an overgrown field, carving a path through the long grass, the ground rising sharply beneath our feet.

It wasn't much further. Just beyond this hill and we'd see the building she was in.

Maverick was at the front of our line, his rifle gripped in one hand as he ran like there was a fire at his back. And the rest of us kept behind him, moving as a unit as we made a bid to get to our girl in time.

I felt Shawn's presence even before we crested that hill, like his breath was on the back of my neck as I pushed myself to my limits, his words in my ears and poison sliding beneath my skin.

"Worthless, ain't ya? The weak link that always let everybody down."

I snarled as I forced his voice out of my head, refusing to fall into the trap of his words. I was here for Rogue, and I'd damn well be strong enough to save her from that monster's ire.

My hate for Shawn was poison in my blood, and I knew the only antidote to it was bringing death down upon his head. Tonight, I'd see it done.

We made it over the hill and suddenly the land was sloping away beneath our feet down, down, down towards a large farmhouse below, an endless cornfield beyond it while an unkept lawn spread out before us. Lights glimmered in the windows of the old brick building, and I knew with all my soul that she was in there with him. Her nightmare.

I wanted to call out to her, but kept my lips sealed as we closed in on that house, needing to keep our approach silent so we could get the jump on that asshole. We'd end this thing on our terms while snatching our girl right back out of his arms in the process.

But as I raced on, the ground disappeared beneath me with no warning, making my heart drop into my stomach as I crashed through the false surface of the trap that had been set for us. I stifled a cry as I fell, my arms flying out to try and catch myself, but there was nothing there to grab onto.

I crashed to the bottom of a dark pit, something scraping painfully against my side and forcing me to throw my body away from it. The solid weight of JJ's bulk landed on top of me as he fell into the pit too and I grabbed his shirt in my fist, yanking him away from whatever had nearly skewered me.

"Fuck," I growled, rolling JJ off of me as my eyes widened on the sharpened wooden spikes which had been driven into the base of the pit, facing skyward. There were four of them spread out in the side space and fuck only knew that luck had to have been smiling on us because we'd narrowly missed being impaled by one of them.

I scrambled to my feet, taking JJ's hand to haul him up too and giving him the once over in the darkness of the pit to make sure he was okay.

"Holy shit, Shawn's insane," he said, looking to the spikes in horror of what could have happened to us.

"You're just figuring that out now?" I said, tipping my head back to look up at the top of the hole above our heads. It had to be ten foot deep, and we were fucking lucky that the ground had been soft enough to cushion our fall, not to mention how we'd tumbled into the right of the pit where no sharpened stakes had been close enough to kill us.

Fox and Maverick appeared above us, their silhouettes highlighted before the night's sky and their features cast in darkness as they looked down at us.

"Fuck," Rick cursed as he noticed the spikes, terror crossing his features.

"Are you okay?" Fox asked frantically as he dropped to his knees, leaning down into the pit to try and reach us.

"Yeah," JJ grunted and I agreed.

"Just help us get the fuck out of here," I said.

"Grab my hand," Fox demanded, reaching for me and I leapt up, catching hold of him and kicking against the soil wall as he hauled me up, Rick gripping his shoulders to help anchor him.

I scrambled onto the grass, turning to help pull JJ up after us, my hand locking around his as I heaved him skyward. He was soon kneeling at my side, panting as he shoved to his feet and swiped mud from his chest.

"Shoulda known there would be traps," Maverick growled darkly as the four of us took a moment to examine the ground ahead of us, wondering what else that motherfucker had lying in wait out here. I could only imagine it was going to get worse.

"Well, I can't say I'm surprised," Shawn's voice spoke out of the phone in Fox's pocket, making me flinch in surprise and I cursed myself for the tendril of power he still held over me.

Fox tugged the phone out with a growl of hatred and held it up between us so we could all hear him clearly. There was a load of splashing carrying down the line too and I frowned as I tried to figure out what the fuck he was doing, wondering why he'd decided to turn the fucking video feature off now and hating him for his fucking mind games.

"You just activated the motion sensors on my land, boys," Shawn purred. "So I know precisely where you are, and you're right in time for the big finale."

"Where is she?" Fox snarled and I shifted closer to the phone in desperate need of that answer too.

"Fox!" Rogue cried before her voice was cut off and the sound of splashing carried in the background.

I took off, not pausing a second longer as I heard the fear and desperation in that single word. She needed us. Rogue fucking needed us and I wasn't ever going to let her down again.

I ran down the hill as fast as I could go, Rick right at my side as we sprinted towards the house, looking out for more traps but mostly just focused on getting to her and rescuing her from whatever hell Shawn had cooked up in that fucking house.

Gunfire rattled through the air and Rick and I split apart, diving for cover in opposite directions.

I sank down behind a rusted old tractor fifty yards from the house while Rick leapt behind a shed, his back pressed to it as he prepped the rifle in his grip.

I raised my pistol, but I knew I wouldn't fire unless I had my eyes locked on Shawn. I couldn't risk shooting Rogue or Mabel by accident.

Fox and JJ did a wider circle around the house, and I lost sight of them as they kept low in the long grass.

I chanced a look past the cab of the tractor, but a bullet slammed into the window and glass showered over me as I ducked down once more, swearing colourfully as I found myself trapped.

A familiar bark made my heart lurch with surprise, and I looked around with wild eyes, staying in the cover provided by the huge rear wheel of the tractor and spotting a little bundle of white and brown fur scampering across the grass to my right, coming straight for me.

"There's that motherfucker," Shawn spat, the sound of his voice so close making my muscles lock with tension. "Here, puppy, puppy!"

"Mutt!" Rogue screamed from within the house and the fear in her voice sent my murderous instincts into overdrive.

The sound of Shawn's rifle firing shot after shot made my blood run cold and huge clods of mud were blasted into the air behind Mutt as he ran at full pelt in my direction, a yelp of fright escaping him as fury burned through me at the realisation of what Shawn was trying to do to him.

I released a furious cry, getting to my feet without worrying that it put me at risk, refusing to allow him to take that brilliant, violent little bastard of a dog from this world if I had anything to do with it.

Mutt darted to the left and a gunshot set off a bear trap right in front of him. He leapt into the air as high as he possibly could, the trap snapping closed just beneath his outstretched paws and he landed beyond it, making a harsh breath of relief fall from my lungs.

I started firing at the house to give Mutt a chance to get to me, not caring that it would pull Shawn's attention to me, just needing to take it from that dog who Rogue had found when she needed someone to love her more than anything.

Shawn whooped with excitement as he swung his gun towards me, firing my way once more and forcing me to duck as more glass shattered from the windows of the tractor. But as I fell to my knees, a little bundle of white fur collided with me and I broke half a laugh as Mutt leapt up and licked me right in the damn mouth.

"Hey, boy. Where the fuck have you been?" I muttered, pulling him under my arm and noticing the scent of burning hair that clung to him as I fired another couple of shots back towards the house blindly, keeping Shawn's attention on me.

Rick took the opportunity to run closer to the house, a bullet slamming into the ground beside him as he skidded across the mud to avoid it before scrambling under a truck only a stone's throw from the house. Shawn wheeled the gun towards him, blasting the windows to shit and puncturing the tyres of the truck and my heart stopped working as all fell quiet.

"Did I get ya, big boy?" Shawn called and panic cleaved apart my chest when Rick didn't answer. Rogue started screaming for him, and my gut knotted with distress.

"Rick?!" I bellowed in panic and my friend's obnoxious laughter rang out, making my heart squeeze with relief.

"Today's not my last day on earth, Shawn," Rick called. "It's yours."

"Unlikely," Shawn sang, and I peered around the edge of the tractor's wheel, trying to spot where he was firing from.

Movement drew my gaze to a window on the bottom floor which was pushed up, and I spotted his rifle sticking out through a line of boards there. *Got ya.*

I raised my gun, placing Mutt down behind me as I lined up my next shot and caught sight of his smirking face between the boards. I squeezed the trigger and Shawn cried out as the window above his head exploded in a spray of glass.

"Motherfucker!" he cried, assuring me he wasn't dead, and anger curled through me at my failure. Shawn fired off more rounds and I was forced to take shelter again, hugging Mutt to my side as he trembled wildly.

"Hey, pretty eyes, I see you out there," Shawn called as his gunfire stalled. "Why don't you come in and play with us? Tell you what, you gimme your other eye and I'll let the old lady go," Shawn taunted.

An explosion suddenly rocked the ground and my head whipped sideways, spotting the blast ripping a hole in the hillside near to where I'd last seen Fox and JJ. Fear bloomed in my chest for them, and Shawn hollered in excitement.

"Holy moly, who set off one of my land mines? Did I blast myself a little Fox?" he called, and I shoved away my terror for my friends, using the distraction to make a move.

I grabbed Mutt, tucking him under my arm, ducking low and darting out around the tractor.

I powered along with Mutt held close, and no bullets fired my way as I ran towards Shawn, passing by the truck Rick was taking cover beneath.

Harsh breaths fell from my lips as I caught sight of Shawn as he squinted in the direction where the fire was blooming in the long grass.

I raised my gun, trying to get a clean shot, but his gaze suddenly whipped sideways, locking with mine.

"Woah there, pretty eyes!" he shouted, turning his rifle on me and I swore, firing at the exact same moment he did.

A weight of muscle knocked me down before Shawn's bullet could take me out of this world and Fox shielded my head as the bullet whizzed past us. We rolled onto our fronts and Fox shoved me along, Mutt yipping in fear as I clung onto him.

The two of us crawled fast under the truck where Rick was taking cover, his wide eyes meeting mine as a rain of bullets slammed into the vehicle. But none made it close to us as we huddled together in the dark.

"Where's JJ?" I hissed in terror, thinking of that landmine that had gone off.

"Round back," Fox said and a breath. "He's gonna get in, we've just gotta keep Shawn distracted on this side of the house."

"Did you set off that mine?" I asked Fox.

"Yeah, I almost stood on the damn thing, but I noticed the soil was all dug up around it, so I got outa the way and tossed a few stones at it until it went off. Figured it might distract Shawn enough for me to get over here."

"Well it worked," I said, squeezing his arm. "But now what?"

"I've got a plan," Maverick growled, rolling onto his back and taking a hunting knife from his hip.

He severed the truck's fuel line, squeezing the pipe to keep the gasoline inside before looking to us as he slid a lighter from his pocket. Rick was one crazy asshole, but the crazy in his eyes right now might have just been at an all-time high.

"I'm gonna light this truck up. The fire will fuck with Shawn's vision out here, and give us a shot at getting to him," Rick explained, and Mutt barked like he was agreeing with the lunatic. "Now get running, assholes. It's gonna go up fast."

"Crazy motherfucker," I gasped as he shifted aside and let go of the fuel line so the gas poured over the ground.

Rick shifted back so Fox and I could army crawl past him to the other side of the truck, dragging ourselves out from underneath it and moving into a crouch to keep behind it out of Shawn's line of sight. I tucked Mutt tighter against me while raising my pistol, sharing a look with Fox.

"Ready?" he breathed, and I nodded, swallowing the lump in my throat.

"For Rogue," I said, and we both stood up, firing blindly back in the direction of Shawn and keeping our heads low as we ran towards the far end of the house.

A bullet whistled past my ear and I swore, glancing back at the scent of burning in the air, spotting Rick charging after us away from the fire blossoming beneath the truck.

"Go!" he roared, racing after us and Fox and I fired over his head, forcing Shawn to duck for cover while our brother ran to meet us.

The fire caught quickly, consuming the truck in a hungry blaze and just as we made it to the far corner of the house, an explosion ripped through it that blasted the whole thing apart.

We were thrown to the ground and Mutt yelped as I squashed him, my back arching to keep my weight off of him and the three of us scrabbling through the mud to get around the corner of the house.

We made it, breathless as we sat side by side with our backs to the wall, my ears ringing from the explosion and my hand stroking Mutt's head mindlessly.

Rick got to his feet, smashing the nearest window and starting to work on breaking the boards which barred it from the inside, but they were fucking huge and nailed heavily in place.

"We need to distract Shawn to give JJ time to get in," Fox hissed at his brother.

"Go have fun with that. I'm not wasting another second out here." Rick shoved his weight against the boards, trying to force them out of his way, but they wouldn't give in.

"Fuck it," Fox growled, moving to help Rick.

I joined them too as I placed Mutt by my feet, the three of us working together to try and break in, but they wouldn't budge.

"I wouldn't do that, I might just get trigger happy with our girl here," Shawn purred from Fox's phone, and he slid it out of his pocket so that we could see the asshole's face on the screen.

Shawn flipped it around to show Rogue tied in a bathtub beneath him, my heart squeezing at the sight of the cuts lining her skin, blood colouring the water she was struggling to keep her head out of.

"Bad, bad boys," Shawn taunted. "Now let me see all four of you standing right there on the screen or I'll cut her throat as deep as I can go. Ten seconds. Ten…nine…"

"Fuck you," she spat at him as he leaned down over her, twisting a knife in his hand to show it off to the camera.

He pressed the blade to her throat and dug it in, drawing a thin line of blood on her neck that made panic flourish in my chest while she stared up at him defiantly with hatred flaring in her ocean blue eyes.

"No!" I yelled in fright.

"JJ!" Fox bellowed. "Get here right now!"

"Eight," Shawn quickened his pace, wetting his lips in excitement. "Seven, six, five, four," he said quickly as I heard JJ's footsteps pounding this way and we turned to run towards him.

"Go – go!" I urged in alarm as Shawn laughed loudly.

"Three... two..."

We collided with JJ around the back of the house and Fox angled the phone so we were all on screen.

"We're here," Fox snarled. "All of us."

"Phew, that was a close one. I was real ready for it too," he said, withdrawing the knife before taking hold of Rogue's hair and dragging her closer to him, leaning down to lick away the blood on her neck.

"Don't fucking touch me." She tried to headbutt him, but he whipped his head away with a laugh, his eyes shifting back to us.

"Now you sit tight right there and watch," Shawn ordered. "If you move so much as a goddamn muscle, I swear to Lucifer, I will stab her so many times, she'll be Swiss cheese before you even step a foot inside this house."

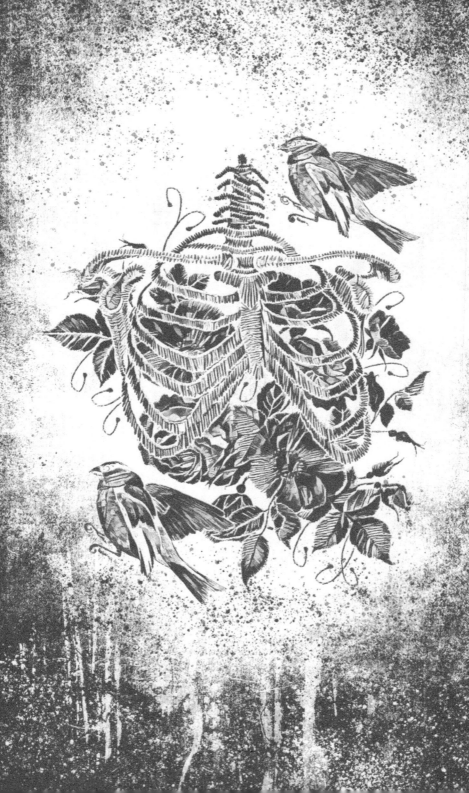

FUCKING
SHAWN

CHAPTER THIRTY EIGHT

I pushed my phone into my shirt pocket, the camera still offering a view of my actions to the demons at my door as I took my knife and cut through the rope securing my sugarpie in the bathtub, done with this part of my game.

She cursed and fought me as I hauled her out of the water, her saturated clothes wetting mine as I heaved her into my arms and with a furious scream, her fist slammed into my face.

I bellowed in pain as agony tore across my cheek from the blow, my blood spattering the dirty white tiles as something sharp in her fist cut me open and made me howl in unbelievable pain.

Rogue came at me again as I stumbled back from her attack, but I was ready for her this time, running at her instead of trying to escape, my body colliding with hers before I slammed her back against the tiled wall with enough force to put one hell of a lump on the back of her head.

"Let her go!" Miss Mabel wailed from where she was still perched on the toilet seat.

Rogue cried out, the weapon in her hand scoring a line of bloody heat along my spine as she managed to strike me again, and I snatched her wrist into my grip before she could do it a third time. I smacked her hand against the tiles with enough force to make her drop whatever she was using to attack me, the sound of porcelain clinking against the tiles as it fell, and I glanced down to see a shard of what looked like a broken plate there.

"Bitch," I hissed, spittle speckling her cheeks as we both panted in the wake of that little drama.

My bulk flattened her to the wall as I raised my knife and pressed the blade to her heart in warning before she could get too feisty.

"Damn right I am," she snarled back at me, a lock of wet hair fluttering before her lips as she glared right into my eyes.

I inhaled her air, her essence, that strength I planned on plucking right out of her brutalised body and claiming for my own when all was said and done tonight.

Blood dripped from my cheek to stain the front of the white shirt she wore and fury burned into me at the knowledge that that would likely scar.

My hand shook as rage flooded me, the point of the blade cutting into her flesh just a little as her chest continued to rise and fall rapidly and I kept her there at my mercy.

It would be so fucking easy to give in to that rage. To stab and stab and stab her. Cut into her flesh a hundred times, carve my name into it and bathe myself in so much blood that I wouldn't even be able to see the wound she'd given me anymore.

A shuddering breath escaped me as I battled that impulse and won, knowing it wouldn't be enough. That it would be too fucking quick.

I forced myself to retreat a step. Then another. My upper lip curled back in a snarl as the two of us continued to stare at one another, death hanging between us as we both acknowledged the fact that one of us wouldn't survive this night. Though the fact she seriously still thought she might be the end of me was laughable at this point.

I tore my eyes from that fucking defiance which wouldn't abandon her and looked into the stained mirror, clenching my jaw as I examined the jagged cut which scored a wide line across the left side of my beautiful face. It hurt like a motherfucker and was ugly as sin, the sight of it bringing my demons to the edges of my flesh.

"You're gonna pay for that." I was losing patience and I wanted to move on to the real fun here.

I turned my attention back to Rogue while Mabel struggled fruitlessly against her binds.

"You look like shit, sugarpie. Why don't you ring some of that water outa your hair and try to make yourself look pretty for me again?"

"Like I could give a fuck about looking pretty for you," she hissed, making no move to do as I instructed and I sighed heavily, backing up until I was pointing my knife at dear old Mabel's face and arching a brow, the threat clear.

Rogue bared her teeth at me with that disgusting defiance yet again, but she obediently wrung her hair between her fists followed by her shirt, and I licked my lips as I admired the way the saturated material clung to her curves.

She looked like shit, no doubt about that with the bruises I'd put on her face, blood and mud staining her clothes and that abomination of a hairstyle all lank, wet and sticking to her cheeks, but damn, the girl still had some sex appeal to her which wouldn't even be dampened by the state she was in. Not that I had the faintest intention to fuck her before I was done with her. No. I didn't get my kicks from that kind of torture. I wanted my women willing even when they had no reason to be so. I wanted them worshipping me and bowing to my every whim, and it was beyond clear that I wasn't going to be able to get that from this little problem of mine, so the act held no appeal. But it wasn't hard to see why she had enthralled those monsters out there with the taste of heaven she kept locked away between those long legs of hers.

"That's better," I commented, though in all fairness she still looked much the same. "Upstairs we go then. Come on, you too Mabel." I shoved Rogue ahead of me and aimed my rifle at her back.

I tugged Mabel up from the toilet seat, locking her against my hip while sliding my knife into its sheath. I listened to the dulcet tones of the Harlequin boys cursing me out from the phone in my pocket while they continued to watch us, my heart rate settling as I regained control over the situation and got my plans right back on track.

Hell, I'd even enjoyed a bit of gunslinging, and those explosions sure did add the kind of flare I was known for. So all in all, this night was going well – except for the cut on my face, that was. But a little plastic surgery would fix that right up, and I certainly had the funds for that what with five plump diamonds to my name. Diamonds which were currently sitting snuggly in my pocket, always close where I could feel their constant presence. That was where I liked my favourite possessions.

"Hands behind your head, sugarpie. And keep walking." I jabbed my gun into her back and she did as I said, her body dripping wet, making her white shirt turn transparent and cling to her body real sweetly.

"Mm, I have to say, you are looking a picture tonight all cut up and bleeding for me," I said.

"Get fucked, Shawn," she snarled.

I chuckled, licking my lips as I jabbed her towards the stairway with my gun and followed her up the creaking wooden steps, all the way to the third level.

I directed her along to the master bedroom which I knew had a wide balcony overlooking the back of the house. And that seemed like the perfect place to make my getaway when what was done was done.

The room held a stronger scent of must to it than the rest of the house, likely from the sheets which still lined the king sized bed in the centre of the room, even though it had clearly been a long damn time since anyone had slept in them. The previous owners of this place hadn't lived on this part of the property in years. After their money had dried up and they couldn't afford the repairs the farmhouse needed, they'd been forced to abandon the house and move into a trailer instead.

I'd gotten this land for a steal, befriending them and using my way with words to talk them down to a fair price. Well, fair for me. I'd undercut them by a mile, but they were old, and their minds weren't sharp no more, so it had been all too easy to convince them this land was worth nothing but soot, and my offer was the best one they'd ever get.

Dark wooden panels lined the bottom half of the room while the top held peeling floral wallpaper which held stains indicating damp now. There were some heavy pieces of wooden furniture about the space but no personal belongings remained, just the ghosts of the people who had once lived here creeping close to watch what mayhem I was bringing into their domain.

I kept Mabel against me as I closed the door at my back, locking it tight and removing the key, stuffing it deep into my back pocket. The old bird seemed to be in shock, though she still grumbled a few curses at me as I offered her a shark's smile.

"Push that chest in front of the door, darling," I commanded Rogue, pointing to it with my gun and she sneered at me before doing as I told her, her thighs flexing beautifully as she heaved it into place.

I watched the way she gritted her teeth against the pain of that little stab wound in her shoulder and, my oh my, I had to say I enjoyed that a whole lot. I wondered how much she could take before she just gave in and started screaming? Or better yet, sobbing and begging for mercy.

"Good girl. Ain't you just so good at taking orders? Do you do that for them too? Do you spread those thighs at the click of their fingers? Or do you play hard to get? Because that's all it would be, sugarpie. Just a part you played before the inevitable, because I know a whore like you couldn't ever really keep away from being fucked too long."

"Shut your filthy mouth," she snarled. "You don't know anything about the love my boys and I share."

"In fact, I do," I disagreed. "I know they've been in every one of your holes while high fiving each other over how easily you take their cocks, how you let them defile you in any way they see fit for their pleasure."

"And mine," she said, jerking her chin up. "That's the part you forgot about when we fucked, Shawn. The part where I got off too. My boys never forget that bit. They're real men. Powerful men. The exact opposite of you."

"Shut your whoring mouth." I wheeled the gun towards her face and was satisfied when fear danced in her eyes, but she still had that defiance. That fucking look of superiority and I was so goddamn done with it. I was going to carve it out of her before this was done, mark my words.

"Please," Mabel croaked as I knocked her down into an armchair. "No more of this."

"It's almost over, Miss Mabel," I promised as I narrowed my eyes on Rogue. "On the bed, sugarpie," I growled, all lightness slipping from my voice just like that.

She'd enraged the beast in me one too many times and I had slowly sunk deeper and deeper into insanity for her.

She wanted to goad me? Make me prove my power over her? Then so be it.

CHAPTER THIRTY NINE

"What now?" I asked as Shawn's eyes raked over me hungrily where I knelt on the musty bed, a street dog in need of a kill. There was no lust in his eyes, but there was desire there, the need to break me, destroy me, finish this once and for all and end his obsession in the most brutal way he could imagine.

Miss Mabel gazed at me from the armchair behind Shawn, her nails tearing into the arms of it.

Shawn licked his lips, eyes moving from me to the window before he rolled his shoulders back.

"They're gonna get in here, you know?" I taunted, seeing the fear in him even as he tried to hide it. He was twitchy, volatile, backed into a corner and ready to snap. In short – damn dangerous. And it was almost certainly a bad idea to rile him up. "They'll break down the door or smash through a window and then they'll come for you. What do you think they'll do when they get here?"

"Likely start sobbing over your bloody, butchered corpse. But no need to skip to the good part too soon. I think we have time for one last game." He placed his rifle down by the window and prowled towards me.

I backed up, shuffling onto the bed away from him, my muscles tensing in anticipation of the inevitable. This wasn't a large room and Shawn was a big man. If this became a chase then it wouldn't last long, but that didn't mean I planned on making any of this easy for him.

"No one would sob over *your* body though, would they Shawn?" I taunted, moving onto my knees as I continued to back away from him across the bed. "In fact, I don't think there would be a single person in this world who would even so much as notice if you were snuffed out of it. No one to attend your funeral. No one to even remember your name."

"That's where you're wrong," he replied, reaching the end of the bed and pausing to see where I'd run to next, leaving me in limbo as I hesitated with my back to the headboard. "I would live on in the minds of those I bound to myself. Like you and that pretty eyed boy toy of yours. All the lost souls who came to me with pain in their hearts and need in their souls. The ones who let me slip through the cracks in their minds and become their everything."

I scoffed, shaking my head at him. "You know as well as I do that you were never my everything. Oh, you tried to make yourself into that alright. You hissed your poison in my ears and made use of willing flesh when I was using you to try and feel alive, but you could never reach me like that. It's why you're so fucking obsessed, isn't it? I'm the one you couldn't break. The dolly who didn't play the way you wanted me to. I didn't surrender to your need to own me, and I was never devoted to you in the way you craved. I was beyond your capabilities, Shawn, I was never truly yours and you know it. It eats you up, doesn't it? Knowing that I never fell for you, never let you twist me up inside and never broke for you."

Shawn's jaw ticked with the truth of those words, and he leaned towards me, placing his hands flat on the mildewy sheets at the foot of the bed as he stared me down.

"Well now, sugarpie, that's where you're wrong. You aren't unbreakable. I just ain't done with you yet." He grinned this dark and depraved smile which set fear prickling a trail up my spine.

I bared my teeth at him, letting him know I was no frightened girl. I was wild, savage, Harlequin. A breed all of my own.

Movement behind Shawn had me falling still and I sucked in a sharp breath as Miss Mabel raised the rifle he'd placed down, pointing it right at his head and steadying it against her shoulder as if she weren't some tiny little whisp of a thing and that gun wasn't almost as big as her.

"I've met a few wrongguns in my lifetime," she growled, her eyes flashing with a maternal kind of fury as Shawn fell utterly still, realising his mistake, and I swear for a moment I could see the woman she'd been before I knew her, the strength she'd owned and the power she'd commanded. "But I can't say I ever wanted to watch one bleed quite so much as you."

Shawn whirled around and she pulled the trigger in the same movement, the echoing bang seeming to take up the entire room as Shawn's cry of pain lit me up from the inside out.

Shawn roared furiously, the bullet having torn through his arm and Miss Mabel stumbled back as the recoil almost knocked her off of her feet.

"Take that, you rotten beast!" she cried with the tenacity of a far younger woman, one who had faced demons before and won.

"You old bat!" Shawn bellowed and in the next breath, he whipped the little dagger from his belt and slashed it across Mabel's throat so violently that blood splattered the walls and ceiling before I'd even fully comprehended what he'd done.

My heart fell still in my chest as I stared at her, my brain taking too long to catch up with what I'd just witnessed as shock held me captive and grief came barrelling towards me like a freight train.

An agonised roar fell from my lips as her wide eyes met mine, time coming to an absolute halt as I tried to wield it, force it to undo what had just been done. But I was helpless to this fate as Mabel staggered and dropped to the floor, her body going limp as blood pooled all around her, barely giving her a moment to realise what had happened.

Death came swiftly for her, stealing her away from this world and leaving me far behind with nothing but pain left in the space she'd occupied.

Horror echoed throughout my body, time starting up again as the reality of her loss ricocheted throughout my limbs in an endless cycle of memories filled with hazy sunshine and the kind of affection I had never known before her.

I heard the echoes of our shared laughter as we sat on her porch at Rosewood Manor, sipping lemonade as life promised us endless days together. At least, that was how it had seemed back then. A pocket of time that I'd thought would never come to a close, but I'd learned in the bitterest of ways that all good things withered eventually. Summer passed to fall, and winter waited at its edges. Miss Mabel was one of the sweetest, purest things in Sunset Cove, and she'd become a pillar within my family. And now, winter had come to steal her away at last in the most brutal way imaginable.

Pain ripped a hole in my chest and agony made its home in me as the grief I felt over losing her tore through all sense and reason, leaving nothing but the cold, hard slap of reality in its place along with a desperate need for vengeance I planned on gaining no matter the cost.

Shawn whirled on me as I remained frozen in shock, the blood of the woman I'd loved coating him, and death making his eyes flash with an untold power as he bathed in the pain he'd caused me, my suffering his sustenance.

"I think it's time we went at it, don't you? Just you and me like that fire in your eyes says you want to," he challenged, shoving the bloody knife into the sheath on his belt.

Something in his words snapped me out of my shock and back to my reality. The one where a devil ran loose throughout my life causing carnage and misery, and I needed to exorcise him before he could do any more harm.

Shawn lunged for me, and I leapt right back at him instead of running like he expected, fuelled with all the rage and despair I felt over Mabel's death.

A shriek escaped me as we collided, and my height on the bed allowed me to throw my knee into his face with all my strength as his arms locked tight around my waist.

He hurled me down onto my back as he cried out in pain, the old mattress making me bounce as he aimed a punch into my side, trying to rear over me, but I ignored the agony of the blow in favour of kicking him in the balls as hard as I could.

"Fuck!" Shawn bellowed, lurching back and I rolled aside, getting to my feet on the far side of the bed, grabbing the nightstand, and hurling it at him as he instantly came for me once more.

Shawn knocked it aside, flinching as the bullet hole Miss Mabel had put through his arm clearly caused him trouble.

I hunted all around me for something else to use as a weapon, but Shawn slammed into me before I could locate anything, his weight throwing me back against the wall as he aimed a punch at my face. I lurched away from it, causing him to hit the wood panelled wall behind me instead with a crunch.

He snarled at me, pinning me there with his weight as he tried to grab me by the throat, but I threw my head forward, pain rattling through my skull as my forehead collided with the bridge of his nose and he howled in agony as it cracked from the blow.

I threw a punch of my own, aiming straight for his gunshot wound and making him release me once more. I grabbed an old lamp from the desk beside me, swinging it at him and smashing it over the back of his head, causing broken shards of glass and porcelain to rain down over us.

"You little bitch," he snapped, swinging a punch that caught me right in the jaw and sent me flying towards the bed.

My bare feet slipped in the puddle of Miss Mabel's blood and a noise of grief and agony tore from me as I fought to stay upright, gripping the edge of the mattress and scrambling aside as Shawn bellowed like a beast and ran at me again.

His arms locked around me despite my efforts to escape, and he threw me to the floor so hard that white spots burst before my eyes as the back of my head collided with the floorboards.

Shawn threw his booted foot into my side, making me cry out in pain as he kicked me again and again, something snapping beneath the force of his blows and a scream tearing from my lips.

He laughed hollowly, shoving me onto my back with the toe of his boot while I writhed in pain beneath him, trying to drag myself backwards.

"There she is," he jeered, as he dropped down to straddle me, his weight pinning me to the floor as he took his phone out of his pocket and aimed it right at my face. "The creature who cast a spell on all of you and committed you to the eternal damnation her so-called love required."

I tried to look away, not wanting my boys to see me like this, but Shawn gripped my jaw in his bloody fingers and forced my head around so that I had no choice but to look.

They were there. All four of them, yelling and screaming my name in the dark. Over the hammering of my own frantic pulse, I heard them in reality too, so fucking close and yet so far away.

"I love you," I breathed as Shawn's hand moved to my throat and his look grew feral and desperate, the need to finish this flaring in his eyes. I knew he was done playing with me.

"Endgame, sugarpie," he purred, dropping the phone and wrapping his other hand around my throat too, forcing me to look at him and only him, wanting my final moments all to himself.

"I love you," I forced out again, speaking to my boys, but my words weren't a goodbye. They were a promise, pure and simple.

If the sun rises tomorrow, we'll watch it together. But if this was my final sunset then I was going to make it count.

CHAPTER FORTY

The moment a fight had broken out between Rogue and Shawn, we'd run forward as one, tearing at the boards that kept this window locked up tight, shoving and kicking and fighting to get in.

Shawn's cold taunts fell over me from Fox's phone and I slammed the full force of my body into the boards we'd been working to get loose, the wood splintered and cracking from our efforts. They finally came free as I collided with them, clattering into the room beyond in broken pieces.

I hauled myself into a dusty old lounge with Chase, JJ and Fox spilling in after me, all of us panting with exertion. Mutt was clutched to Chase's chest, but he wriggled and fought until he put him down, and the little dog zoomed over to the closed door that would let us out of here, scratching at it furiously, seeming to grasp the gravity of the situation.

I ran after Mutt to the door, finding it locked and my heart splintered, the most visceral kind of terror holding me in its fist. I collided with it, a roar leaving me as I tried to escape this dark, dusty room, cursing as the door held before throwing my shoulder against it once again.

A scream pitched through the house, echoing out through Fox's phone too as my boys all fell in around me.

"We're coming!" Chase called to her, and I prayed she could hear us, that she knew we would be there in moments.

My girl was dying. My beautiful, perfect goddess was in the grip of a hellion, and I would die this very day too if she left the world without me. But before that fate dared present itself, I would fight with every scrap of strength in my bones to save her.

The hinges rattled as Fox rammed it with me on the next attempt, the wood groaning and splintering under the power of our blows.

Mutt barked as if giving orders to strike it once again, Rogue's miniature soldier ready to run into battle for her as always.

"Rogue!" JJ roared, trying to get near enough to help, but there was only room for two of us to ram the door at once. And it was pointless anyway because on the next strike, the thing busted open, and we spilled through into a dark hallway. Mutt shot off like a bullet, his little claws tip-tapping furiously across the floorboards, while he yapped angrily as if in a command for us to follow him.

"Say my name, sugarpie," Shawn's voice purred out of Fox's phone and a snarl ripped from my lips as we ran for the stairs after the dog. "Give in to me. It's all over now."

"Fuck you," she growled, and I stole an ounce of hope from the strength still in her voice.

We were so close, she just had to hold on.

"Hummingbird!" Fox cried in fright as the four of us sprinted up the stairs, our footsteps hitting the floorboards heavily.

Mutt had vanished, so I started throwing doors open at random as we all split apart to hunt for her, listening for our girl, but I could only hear Shawn's taunting coming from that phone in low growls that made me see red. Pure, murderous red.

"You'd better run!" I bellowed. "I'm gonna tear your body apart with my bare hands when I find you Shawn!"

I prayed he'd fear me, that he'd turn tail and leave her before her final breaths were stolen from her lungs, but panic rose in me as Shawn gave no response.

"When I have you, Shawn, you'll wish you were never fucking born into this world! I'll cast you from it in more pain than you ever imagined you could feel!"

Mutt began barking somewhere along the hall, and the fury of his little voice made me swing around in his direction.

"This way – Mutt's found something!" JJ shouted and we raced after him across the landing and down a dark corridor where Mutt's barks were coming from, my pulse drumming on the inside of my skull.

I could feel the grains of sand slipping through the hourglass of Rogue's life, each one drawing her closer to the inevitable. No matter how fast I was moving now, it felt all too slow, my limbs as heavy as iron as I felt the certainty of this fate closing in around me.

It was insufferable, feeling this failure taking hold of me and telling me it was too late. But I would never, ever give up on her. I'd follow her into the ocean of death if I had to, dive as deep as I could go and take hold of her hand, never to be parted from her again.

CHAPTER FORTY ONE

Shawn's grip crushed the air from throat as he leaned down over me, groaning like my death was the sweetest thing he'd ever tasted.

He dropped his mouth to my ear as I thrashed beneath him, fighting to buck him off of me even as he kept his weight planted heavily over my hips. I didn't claw at his arms though, my fists driving into his sides instead, nails tearing at his chest, reaching, hoping.

"You're all mine, now," he growled. "Your power, your soul, your darkness, it's all gonna become a piece of me which I will carry with me always, sugarpie. I'll keep you locked up in the dungeon of my heart and bring you with me everywhere I go from this day forth. It'll be all kinds of beautiful."

The wet pad of his tongue landed against my cheek, and he licked the mixture of blood and tears from my face with a sigh, his body dropping over mine fully and allowing my hand to find exactly what I'd been hunting for.

My fingers locked around the little dagger he'd used to kill the woman who lay dead beside us, and I snatched it free of his belt with a surge of adrenaline.

He felt what I'd done and tried to jerk back. But not fast enough.

"No," he gasped, a hint of fear cracking his voice.

I stabbed the blade into his side, one, two three times, making him roar in pain as he threw his weight backwards and fell off of me. The hot splash of his blood urged me on and awoke a violent darkness in me.

I sucked in a sharp breath as my lungs finally expanded with air once more and my vision sharpened as oxygen flooded my brain.

I wasn't letting him run again. He had escaped this fate far too many times through luck and chance, but I was the ruler of his destiny now.

My lips peeled back over my teeth, and I pounced at him as he tried to get up, his hand locked to his side to try and keep the blood in his body instead of splattering to the floorboards. But he couldn't undo what had been done; I'd stuck him too damn good.

I slammed into him, my fist locked tight around my weapon as I aimed for this throat, but the knife slashed across his chest as he lurched backwards just in time, and I carved a bloody line across his body instead of bleeding him out like I'd wanted.

"You fucking whore!" Shawn bellowed, punching me hard enough to knock me off of him and I fell back into the puddle of Miss Mabel's blood with a gasp of shock. Horror froze me for a heart shattering second as warm blood sank into my clothes, and I was painted in death and grief for the entire universe to see.

Shawn was on his feet before I could recover, spitting curses and tightly gripping the stab wounds at his side as his boot landed on my wrist to immobilise the knife. But I didn't need it. I just needed his death.

I twisted beneath him, throwing my foot up towards his dick in a solid kick, forcing him to throw himself backwards to avoid it and allowing me to yank my arm out from beneath his boot, though I lost the knife in the effort it took to do so.

Shawn lunged for it, and I threw myself at him, colliding with his side while he was doubled over and sending us both crashing to the floor once again.

I ended up on top of him and I punched him in the face as hard as I could, becoming a rabid animal as I fought to keep the upper hand.

Shawn snarled at me as he threw a punch of his own, striking me in the stab wound to my shoulder and making agony explode through the entire left side of my body. But the physical pain was nothing compared to my grief over Mabel, and I just screamed as I punched him again.

The door rattled as my boys made it to the other side of it, their yells lending me strength as I punched Shawn for a third time before he bucked me off of him and sent me tumbling towards the bed.

I landed on my front, raising my head and spotting a pair of men's shoes beneath the bed, snatching one into my grasp as Shawn grabbed my ankle and dragged me back towards him across the floorboards.

I flipped myself onto my back, aiming kicks at his face with my free leg which he struggled to avoid while trying to clamber over me again, the need for my death burning in his feral eyes.

As my boys threw their weight against the door again, the heavy wooden chest that Shawn had made me shove in front of the door slid forward just a little, the sound of their voices yelling my name offering me more strength than they could have known, and my lungs heaved with the determination to survive this for them.

I swung the shoe I held at Shawn like it was a damn battle axe and he let out a whoop as it smacked into his shoulder with about as much use as a wet fish.

He came at me again, knocking the shoe from my hand and aiming another punch my way as he fought to try and pin me down once more. I avoided the strike, but he managed to knock my other leg aside, scrambling to get his weight over me and pin me down while I continued to thrash and kick like a wild thing, halting his advance.

"They're gonna be too late," he taunted, determination blazing in his eyes. "Too fuckin' late and so fuckin' broken."

"Rogue!" my name fell from their lips as they fought to force the chest aside and I could see their arms pushing through the gap they'd forced open, but the thing had gotten wedged against a raised floorboard and there was no way in hell it was going to budge another inch without someone in this room moving it.

Shawn landed on top of me, his hands locking around my throat again while I hissed and fought like a damn alley cat, every fucked-up thing he'd ever done to me and the men I loved playing through my skull on repeat as my own rage, hatred and need for revenge ate through my flesh like a ravenous beast.

A ferocious bark sounded as Mutt forced his way through the gap my boys had made between the door and the chest, and I spotted him racing towards us across the blood-soaked floorboards a moment before he leapt at fucking Shawn and sank his sharp little teeth straight into his arm where Mabel had shot him.

Shawn wailed in agony, rearing backwards and throwing Mutt clean across the room with such force that I screamed as he hit the wall, his howl of fright and pain ripping something apart inside me as he smacked down onto the floor again and fell still.

But the opening he'd given me was all I'd needed, my foot striking Shawn in the centre of his chest and throwing him off of me, his head hitting the edge of the nightstand with a sickening crack.

"Fuck," Shawn cursed, trying to get up but I was already on him, my fist smacking into the bloody gash I'd cut into his face earlier before I snatched his hair in my fist and slammed his head back against the nightstand again. And again.

I refused to stop, throwing my fists into him over and over, my body fuelled by fear, grief, adrenaline and the most potent kind of hatred that any creature on this earth had ever felt. I cried out furiously as he fell still beneath me, but continued to batter him with all the strength remaining in my body.

I didn't know if he was dead or not and I couldn't stop either way. This man had taken so much from me, from my boys and from everything I had ever held dear.

He was my enemy, and I was his obsession, and finally, this cycle had come to an end. In blood and gore and violent demise, I was exorcising my demon and he was falling to the wrath incurred by his own lust for things which had never been his to claim.

CHAPTER FORTY TWO

"Rogue!" I roared, shoving my weight against the door, bruising my arm to shit with how furiously I'd been attacking it.

Whatever was blocking us gave way suddenly as someone shoved it aside and I stumbled into the room, my gun raised and pointing right into the face of the girl I'd loved my entire life.

Alive. Her bright blue eyes captivating me as I stood before this woman who I thought I'd lost. I forgot how to breathe, how to function at all as I soaked in the reality that she was really standing there at the end of my gun, the strength of a warrior burning through her expression.

I felt the others at my back, pressing forward in preparation for battle and falling still as they saw what I did.

Rogue raised her chin, bloody, defiant and victorious. One glance beyond her proved Shawn was dead and I cracked apart, my soul tearing up the middle as I dropped my arm, the gun slipping from my fingers and hitting the floorboards.

I fell to my knees at Rogue's feet, wrapping my arms around her and burying my face against her stomach as a noise of relief and fear escaped me. I just let myself hold her as I took in the fact that this was finally over, and she was still here.

She held me tight as the others closed in around us, sharing words I couldn't hear as the adrenaline in my body turned to a warm rush of relief. My boys threw their arms around her too and the five of us were locked in a tight embrace that contained so much love it nearly ruptured my heart.

"I shouldn't have doubted you. Of course you fucking killed him," I said.

"You did it, little one," Chase said in relief as he kissed her cheek and she leaned into his touch, shutting her eyes for a moment to savour it.

"Rick," she croaked, pushing her fingers into my hair. "I'm so sorry."

I looked up at her, confused as to why she'd say that as I found tears running down her blood-stained cheeks. Fox was peering over her shoulder and as he looked down at me, pain sliced through his expression.

I slowly rose to my feet, stepping past Rogue as I saw what he had found, and JJ and Chase took my place before Rogue, wrapping her tighter in their arms.

Miss Mabel lay on the floor in a pool of blood so wide that it was clear she was long gone, her throat slit. Death had taken her far beyond my reach.

Numbness swept over me like an icy flood as I walked towards her, my knees hitting the floorboards as a noise of grief left me, a piece of my heart tearing off for her.

I gently turned Mabel's face towards me, brushing my thumb over her pale cheek. Her eyes were open and wide, but there was triumph written into them in death.

Fox's hand pressed to my shoulder, and I turned my head to look up at him, grief flaring in his eyes.

"I'm so sorry, brother," he breathed, and I nodded mutely, turning back to look at my grandmother.

The woman I'd not had nearly enough time to know in this life. But if there was a next life, I'd seek her out there and thank her for everything she'd done for me and my family.

A lump built in my throat as I placed a kiss on her forehead then my gaze lifted, falling on Mutt's still body by the wall as the others rushed toward him. Rogue released a sob as she dropped down and swept the little dog into her arms, hugging him to her chest.

My hands trembled as Chase shook him gently, trying to coax life into his body while Rogue started to rock back and forth on her knees.

"Please come back," she begged of him, but the dog's head only lolled as she stroked it.

"I'm sorry, baby," Fox said, his voice tight with pain as Mutt didn't stir.

"He saved me," she sobbed, tears rushing down her cheeks and dripping down onto Mutt's white fur.

"He loved you more than anything in this world, pretty girl." JJ slid his arm around her, gazing down at Mutt before looking to Mabel and so much grief passed between us all, that I couldn't find it in me to move.

"I failed them," she sobbed as she looked to Mabel then buried her face in Mutt's fur, her shoulders shuddering.

Chase wrapped her in his arms, and Mutt was pressed between them as she clung to him. Fox crouched down at my side, gripping my arm and meeting my gaze.

"We have to get Rogue out of here, brother," he said in a low tone. "Can you carry Mabel?"

I nodded, flexing my fingers to stop them shaking and forcing myself to get up while Fox braced me. I stole some of his strength, shutting my emotions down and tearing my eyes from my grandmother's lifeless body and onto Rogue as she broke apart.

A little whimper made all of us fall quiet and Rogue's head snapped up as she gazed down at Mutt through watery eyes. "Did he just…"

Mutt let out another little whine, his limbs flexing as he came to and JJ quickly moved forward on his knees, stroking his back to encourage him.

"Hey, boy," Fox said, hurrying over and I staggered after him, all of us ringing around the little dog who belonged among us, hope cresting in the air like a rising wave.

"Mutt," Rogue rasped in relief as he blinked and looked up at her, and she crushed him to her chest with a cry of joy.

"He must have been knocked out cold," Chase said as Mutt started licking Rogue's hands before leaping up to lick her face.

"Good boy," she said as she cried for a whole new reason, relief coating her words. "You're such a good boy."

I glanced at JJ as he stood up, moving across the room to Shawn where he lay by the nightstand, nudging him with the toe of his boot to check he was dead. My jaw tightened as the barest movement in Shawn's chest told me he was still with us, and a sinister darkness coiled through me as I strode towards him.

"Fuck, he's alive," JJ announced, and the others got to their feet, immediately on guard.

"Then I'll kill him," Rogue snarled, striding forward as Mutt yipped his agreement, but I caught her arm to stop her.

"No, beautiful," I said, my voice low and full of malice. "You broke him good. But I've had far too many dreams of having this man at my mercy, and now he's here on a silver platter, I ain't gonna waste the opportunity to make him hurt for you."

Rogue looked up at me with parted lips, nodding as shadows darkened her eyes, that wicked streak in us coming to the surface.

"He's going to suffer," Chase said as he moved to my side, leering down at the man who'd tortured him. "I'll make sure of that."

"We'll do it for all of us," JJ said, and Fox nodded, looking hungry to spill Shawn's blood, but there'd be time for that. As much time as I could buy us.

I stepped forward, crouching down beside Shawn and fisting his hair in my hand. His eyes were still closed, but the furrows on his brow told me he was present, and he was in a world of pain.

"You're gonna wish my girl sent you into death," I hissed and a low groan from his lips told me he'd heard me. I patted him down for weapons, making sure the bastard couldn't come back at us again and my palm met with a bulge in his pocket.

He released a murmur that sounded like a beg for me to stop as I slipped my hand into the pocket, finding the diamonds there in a little black pouch alongside Chase's zippo lighter. Of course he hadn't parted with his trophies.

Shawn twitched as if in an effort to try and take them back from me, but I was already slipping them into my own pocket, the small triumph doing little to ease the anger washing over me. But there was one thing that would ease it…

A sadistic smile twisted my lips as my mind lit with every single vicious thing that I was going to do to him in penance for everyone's suffering in this room. "It's my turn to play a game."

"You'd better run!" I bellowed. "I'm gonna tear your body apart with my bare hands when I find you Shawn!"

I prayed he'd fear me, that he'd turn tail and leave her before her final breaths were stolen from her lungs, but panic rose in me as Shawn gave no response.

"When I have you, Shawn, you'll wish you were never fucking born into this world! I'll cast you from it in more pain than you ever imagined you could feel!"

Mutt began barking somewhere along the hall, and the fury of his little voice made me swing around in his direction.

"This way – Mutt's found something!" JJ shouted and we raced after him across the landing and down a dark corridor where Mutt's barks were coming from, my pulse drumming on the inside of my skull.

I could feel the grains of sand slipping through the hourglass of Rogue's life, each one drawing her closer to the inevitable. No matter how fast I was moving now, it felt all too slow, my limbs as heavy as iron as I felt the certainty of this fate closing in around me.

It was insufferable, feeling this failure taking hold of me and telling me it was too late. But I would never, ever give up on her. I'd follow her into the ocean of death if I had to, dive as deep as I could go and take hold of her hand, never to be parted from her again.

CHAPTER FORTY

The moment a fight had broken out between Rogue and Shawn, we'd run forward as one, tearing at the boards that kept this window locked up tight, shoving and kicking and fighting to get in.

Shawn's cold taunts fell over me from Fox's phone and I slammed the full force of my body into the boards we'd been working to get loose, the wood splintered and cracking from our efforts. They finally came free as I collided with them, clattering into the room beyond in broken pieces.

I hauled myself into a dusty old lounge with Chase, JJ and Fox spilling in after me, all of us panting with exertion. Mutt was clutched to Chase's chest, but he wriggled and fought until he put him down, and the little dog zoomed over to the closed door that would let us out of here, scratching at it furiously, seeming to grasp the gravity of the situation.

I ran after Mutt to the door, finding it locked and my heart splintered, the most visceral kind of terror holding me in its fist. I collided with it, a roar leaving me as I tried to escape this dark, dusty room, cursing as the door held before throwing my shoulder against it once again.

A scream pitched through the house, echoing out through Fox's phone too as my boys all fell in around me.

"We're coming!" Chase called to her, and I prayed she could hear us, that she knew we would be there in moments.

My girl was dying. My beautiful, perfect goddess was in the grip of a hellion, and I would die this very day too if she left the world without me. But before that fate dared present itself, I would fight with every scrap of strength in my bones to save her.

The hinges rattled as Fox rammed it with me on the next attempt, the wood groaning and splintering under the power of our blows.

Mutt barked as if giving orders to strike it once again, Rogue's miniature soldier ready to run into battle for her as always.

"Rogue!" JJ roared, trying to get near enough to help, but there was only room for two of us to ram the door at once. And it was pointless anyway because on the next strike, the thing busted open, and we spilled through into a dark hallway. Mutt shot off like a bullet, his little claws tip-tapping furiously across the floorboards, while he yapped angrily as if in a command for us to follow him.

"Say my name, sugarpie," Shawn's voice purred out of Fox's phone and a snarl ripped from my lips as we ran for the stairs after the dog. "Give in to me. It's all over now."

"Fuck you," she growled, and I stole an ounce of hope from the strength still in her voice.

We were so close, she just had to hold on.

"Hummingbird!" Fox cried in fright as the four of us sprinted up the stairs, our footsteps hitting the floorboards heavily.

Mutt had vanished, so I started throwing doors open at random as we all split apart to hunt for her, listening for our girl, but I could only hear Shawn's taunting coming from that phone in low growls that made me see red. Pure, murderous red.

CHAPTER FORTY ONE

S hawn's grip crushed the air from throat as he leaned down over me, groaning like my death was the sweetest thing he'd ever tasted.

He dropped his mouth to my ear as I thrashed beneath him, fighting to buck him off of me even as he kept his weight planted heavily over my hips. I didn't claw at his arms though, my fists driving into his sides instead, nails tearing at his chest, reaching, hoping.

"You're all mine, now," he growled. "Your power, your soul, your darkness, it's all gonna become a piece of me which I will carry with me always, sugarpie. I'll keep you locked up in the dungeon of my heart and bring you with me everywhere I go from this day forth. It'll be all kinds of beautiful."

The wet pad of his tongue landed against my cheek, and he licked the mixture of blood and tears from my face with a sigh, his body dropping over mine fully and allowing my hand to find exactly what I'd been hunting for.

My fingers locked around the little dagger he'd used to kill the woman who lay dead beside us, and I snatched it free of his belt with a surge of adrenaline.

He felt what I'd done and tried to jerk back. But not fast enough.

"No," he gasped, a hint of fear cracking his voice.

I stabbed the blade into his side, one, two three times, making him roar in pain as he threw his weight backwards and fell off of me. The hot splash of his blood urged me on and awoke a violent darkness in me.

I sucked in a sharp breath as my lungs finally expanded with air once more and my vision sharpened as oxygen flooded my brain.

I wasn't letting him run again. He had escaped this fate far too many times through luck and chance, but I was the ruler of his destiny now.

My lips peeled back over my teeth, and I pounced at him as he tried to get up, his hand locked to his side to try and keep the blood in his body instead of splattering to the floorboards. But he couldn't undo what had been done; I'd stuck him too damn good.

I slammed into him, my fist locked tight around my weapon as I aimed for this throat, but the knife slashed across his chest as he lurched backwards just in time, and I carved a bloody line across his body instead of bleeding him out like I'd wanted.

"You fucking whore!" Shawn bellowed, punching me hard enough to knock me off of him and I fell back into the puddle of Miss Mabel's blood with a gasp of shock. Horror froze me for a heart shattering second as warm blood sank into my clothes, and I was painted in death and grief for the entire universe to see.

Shawn was on his feet before I could recover, spitting curses and tightly gripping the stab wounds at his side as his boot landed on my wrist to immobilise the knife. But I didn't need it. I just needed his death.

I twisted beneath him, throwing my foot up towards his dick in a solid kick, forcing him to throw himself backwards to avoid it and allowing me to yank my arm out from beneath his boot, though I lost the knife in the effort it took to do so.

Shawn lunged for it, and I threw myself at him, colliding with his side

554

while he was doubled over and sending us both crashing to the floor once again.

I ended up on top of him and I punched him in the face as hard as I could, becoming a rabid animal as I fought to keep the upper hand.

Shawn snarled at me as he threw a punch of his own, striking me in the stab wound to my shoulder and making agony explode through the entire left side of my body. But the physical pain was nothing compared to my grief over Mabel, and I just screamed as I punched him again.

The door rattled as my boys made it to the other side of it, their yells lending me strength as I punched Shawn for a third time before he bucked me off of him and sent me tumbling towards the bed.

I landed on my front, raising my head and spotting a pair of men's shoes beneath the bed, snatching one into my grasp as Shawn grabbed my ankle and dragged me back towards him across the floorboards.

I flipped myself onto my back, aiming kicks at his face with my free leg which he struggled to avoid while trying to clamber over me again, the need for my death burning in his feral eyes.

As my boys threw their weight against the door again, the heavy wooden chest that Shawn had made me shove in front of the door slid forward just a little, the sound of their voices yelling my name offering me more strength than they could have known, and my lungs heaved with the determination to survive this for them.

I swung the shoe I held at Shawn like it was a damn battle axe and he let out a whoop as it smacked into his shoulder with about as much use as a wet fish.

He came at me again, knocking the shoe from my hand and aiming another punch my way as he fought to try and pin me down once more. I avoided the strike, but he managed to knock my other leg aside, scrambling to get his weight over me and pin me down while I continued to thrash and kick like a wild thing, halting his advance.

"They're gonna be too late," he taunted, determination blazing in his eyes. "Too fuckin' late and so fuckin' broken."

"Rogue!" my name fell from their lips as they fought to force the chest aside and I could see their arms pushing through the gap they'd forced open, but the thing had gotten wedged against a raised floorboard and there was no way in hell it was going to budge another inch without someone in this room moving it.

Shawn landed on top of me, his hands locking around my throat again while I hissed and fought like a damn alley cat, every fucked-up thing he'd ever done to me and the men I loved playing through my skull on repeat as my own rage, hatred and need for revenge ate through my flesh like a ravenous beast.

A ferocious bark sounded as Mutt forced his way through the gap my boys had made between the door and the chest, and I spotted him racing towards us across the blood-soaked floorboards a moment before he leapt at fucking Shawn and sank his sharp little teeth straight into his arm where Mabel had shot him.

Shawn wailed in agony, rearing backwards and throwing Mutt clean across the room with such force that I screamed as he hit the wall, his howl of fright and pain ripping something apart inside me as he smacked down onto the floor again and fell still.

But the opening he'd given me was all I'd needed, my foot striking Shawn in the centre of his chest and throwing him off of me, his head hitting the edge of the nightstand with a sickening crack.

"Fuck," Shawn cursed, trying to get up but I was already on him, my fist smacking into the bloody gash I'd cut into his face earlier before I snatched his hair in my fist and slammed his head back against the nightstand again. And again.

I refused to stop, throwing my fists into him over and over, my body fuelled by fear, grief, adrenaline and the most potent kind of hatred that any

CHAPTER FORTY THREE

THREE WEEKS LATER…

Maverick wiped the blood from his hands onto a rag as I lay on a cold metal table, tied down and twitching through the aftermath of what he'd just done to me. This one knew how to keep me breathing, lead me to the edge of death only to pull me back to consciousness to suffer all over again.

I didn't know how much time had passed since the Harlequins had taken me to the dark basement of Rosewood Manor, but my blood joined that of Chase Cohen's on the dark concrete now and my screams had coloured this room far more times than his ever had.

When Chase had taken my right eye, I'd thought that was the end, I'd prayed for death to take me, but it was in alliance with the Harlequin boys, obeying their every word.

"Wait, give me water," I rasped as Maverick shed his shirt, using it to wipe his face clean of my blood.

He paused, looking my way with a sneer as I jerked against my restraints.

It was a futile movement; there was no freedom left in this world for me now unless it was offered to me by *her*.

My face was butchered, half my teeth removed and what few fingers I still had weren't even the kind good enough to pull the trigger of a gun. Johnny James had taken some of them away, promising to feed them to some pet starfishes he owned, and the crazy glint in his eye told me it was no joke.

"You don't give orders in this world no more," Maverick said, and the clank of a door let me know someone else was about to join us.

I heaved in a breath, shivering against the ice-cold metal, terrified of being left alone here. The waiting was almost as bad as when they returned for me, the long hours in the dark, the cold, only my pain for company. It had broken something deep in me that I knew could never be repaired. I wasn't a man anymore; I was stripped back to nothing but flesh and bone and agony.

Rogue appeared as she always did after they were done playing with me. Sometimes she made me hurt too, but mostly she just liked to watch, and I swear those bright blue eyes were seared against the inside of my skull now. They were my god, the decider of life and death for me, no other deity existed but her.

She came closer to examine the damage her boy had done to me this time, taking it all in with a dark kind approval.

"Water," I begged of her, my throat so dry, it was a torture of its own.

She moved to the pail where Rick had washed the blood from his hands, lifting it up and dumping it over my head in one go. I opened my mouth, trying to swallow it down and get what moisture I could into my body.

"You're merciful," I said. "Thank you, sugarpie."

"What did I say about using that name?" Maverick spat, moving up behind her like a looming shadow and I shuddered, trying to shrink away into the metal at my back.

"S-sorry," I stammered. "I won't utter it again. Don't take my tongue. Please, please." I broke into a sob and Maverick tutted, walking away and leaving me there with his girl as she studied me, her head cocked to one side.

"Rogue," I begged as I met those ocean blue eyes, shivering under the intensity of her power. I'd lost it all, every scrap of strength in my body belonged to her now. Her boys had torn it from my flesh and placed it in her palm. And I so wanted to please her, to gain her clemency. "Haven't I suffered enough? Haven't I paid the ultimate price?"

Her gaze raked down my bare chest which was littered with open wounds before she looked back to my face and the gaping hole where my right eye had once been.

"I-I can go soon, can't I?" I begged.

She leaned down, her upper lip curling back as she gazed at me. "You will remain here until me and my boys have made you feel how we have felt on the inside because of you. You will suffer for them and for me and for all you have taken from us. We're only taking from your flesh, be thankful of that."

"No," I croaked. "It's more than that and you know it." A tear washed down into my hair as I shattered beneath the queen of my ruin. "You're in my head."

Her lips parted in surprise and my gaze roamed over that beautiful face of hers, seeing what I hadn't let myself see all those years. How could she not know that she had carved herself onto the inside of my flesh as well as the out? How could she not see that she was the mistress of my being? The dictator of everything I was and ever would be from this day forward.

"I've been a fool," I told her. "I see the truth now."

"And what truth is that?" she growled, and I quivered from the roughness of her tone.

"You're more powerful than I ever was. You're stronger than I realised. I didn't understand it, didn't see what those boys saw all along. But I see it now. I see it, Rogue Easton."

"Harlequin," she corrected in a snarl.

"Harlequin," I agreed, that name binding me to death and beyond. It was branded in my skin, carved permanently into the flesh of my chest by Fox's hand. It was a reminder of their unending reign, the five of them the rulers of an empire of their own making.

I had never stood a chance. I saw my arrogance now, I saw where I had failed, the moment I should have run far, far away and never looked back. But it was all too late for regrets, I'd made my bed and now I had to lay in its icy, unwelcoming embrace.

"I bow to you," I told her. "If I could kneel at your feet now, I would. Please accept my apologies. Please forgive me for my misgivings, Rogue Harlequin."

She leaned over me, her rainbow hair falling forward and a lock of it brushed my cheek, making me shiver.

"No," she whispered and even the lightness of her breath against my face stung my wounds.

She withdrew from me, offering me her back and sliding her hand into Maverick's as she led him from the basement. I thrashed, calling out her name as they switched the light off and left me in the dark. The door closed with a bang, the sound of the lock clicking making my bones tremble with fear.

"Rogue!" I called her name into the void I was suspended in, pain driving into me from every angle as I jolted my injuries.

She was in me now, her voice in my head, whispering the truth of who I was. And I was nothing, no one, a man who'd be forgotten when they were done with their torture. I'd be cast from this world as soon as she decided it, and the terror of not knowing when that day would come held me in a state of despair.

I was alone, left here with nothing but my failings and the memory of those blue, blue eyes staring at my soul. And as the sound of their footsteps receded and they left this empty, lonely house once more to return to the sunshine together, I was given nothing but regrets to feast on.

"Momma?" I whispered into the dark, a sob hitching in my throat as

I wished to feel the closeness of the only woman who had ever loved me, while knowing that I was the very reason why she couldn't answer my calls. "Momma!"

CHAPTER FORTY FOUR

TWO MONTHS AFTER THAT…

Mabel's funeral had been quiet but perfect all the same. The five of us all standing around her casket as it was lowered into the ground and recounting our favourite stories about her. She had been the one adult who had shown me love as a child and I'd needed and appreciated that more than she ever could have known.

We'd laughed, sobbed and gotten wasted in her honour, toasting her in the afterlife where we hoped she was causing a right old ruckus and scandals galore.

It had taken time for us to process that grief and to heal from the wounds we'd received the night we'd taken Shawn down, but like the pain of her passing, my bruises had faded, and I was able to think back on the best times now with joy instead of my grief colouring them all too darkly. I had loved her, and I wanted that love to go on, not be forced aside by my inability to process her passing.

My hair was freshly dyed, the pastel colours vibrant and styled to perfection, and I pulled on my rainbow sequin dress with a pair of ridiculously tall platform sneakers to finish of the look before painting my lips baby pink and smiling at myself in the mirror.

My skin was flawless, no more mottled bruises marking my face and the pain from my cracked ribs had gone too. I had some new scars on my thigh and shoulder, but I'd already dealt with those. The word Harlequin was now inked over the scar the bullet wound had left on my thigh, five roses blooming behind the letters, the centre of each holding a tiny skull to represent each of us.

On my shoulder, where Shawn had stabbed me, I had a pair of dancers locked in an embrace, the woman's leg hooked around the man's hips as he dipped her backwards, the image contained with a stylised ace of spades symbol so that I incorporated my last two boys within it, meaning I had a tattoo for all of them now.

There was a knock at the door, and I turned to find Johnny James there waiting for me, a devilish smile on his face which promised all the baddest things and set my pulse hammering just like always.

"Are you sure about this, pretty girl?" he asked as he held a hand out in offering, and I checked out his white shirt and navy shorts combo, appreciating the way they clung to his body.

"It's time," I said firmly, taking his hand and letting him lead me away down the stairs. "I'm ready to start our lives again."

"Well, you won't get any complaints from me about that."

"Are the others meeting us there?" I asked as we made it downstairs and I found the house empty, the darkness of night sweeping away beyond the windows as Johnny James led me towards the back door.

"Yeah. You know Rick; he wanted to have the last of his fun while he still could."

I snorted, keeping my imagination away from that particular line of thought because I didn't need the mental images, and tiptoeing up to steal a kiss from JJ.

He tugged me closer instantly, groaning into my mouth and flattening me against the wall by the door, his hand shifting up my thigh and making me wonder if we had a few extra minutes to spare.

"I'm sure they wouldn't mind if we were a little late," I breathed, thoughts of his wicked mouth on my flesh making me forget about our plans for the night in favour of something even more tempting.

"I wish we could be, pretty girl," he groaned, drawing back from me reluctantly as he shook his head. "But I just had a call from Fox telling me to hurry up. We might miss it if we don't go now."

I realised what he meant by that and huffed, irritated at the others for putting pressure on us by getting over excited in their games. No doubt they'd gone all caveman and started competing with each other, and now we were going to be lucky to get there in time for any of it.

"I'm tempted not to go at all," I muttered, and JJ laughed.

"You'd be pissed if you missed it."

"Fine," I huffed, following him as he opened the back door and heading down the private beach towards the jetty where the speedboat awaited us on the bobbing waves.

Moonlight painted the tips of the ocean in silver as we closed in on it, and I sighed as I drank in the beauty of this place, knowing in my soul there was nowhere else in this world I would rather be than right here.

JJ hopped into the boat, taking my hand so he could guide me in too, and I took to the helm as he untied us from the dock.

I turned the boat out to sea and let the engine loose, heading in the direction of Dead Man's Isle in the distance and the Mariner's Grave to the north of it.

JJ moved to stand beside me as I drove us out across the waves, gently massaging my neck to relax me as we went and dropping his mouth to place kisses behind my ear, setting my entire body buzzing with want.

I swallowed down my desire for him though, focusing on what we needed to finish as I spotted the old fishing boat out ahead of us.

"Is that it?" I called over the noise of the engine, and JJ checked his phone before nodding as he confirmed the location of the others.

I headed towards the fishing boat, slowing my speed as we approached it and smiling as I spotted Fox, Rick and Chase there, the three of them standing at the back of the boat where the fishing lines were hitched and buckets of chum were lined up along the deck.

Chase waved and I waved back, guiding my boat closer as the three of them moved to greet us.

"Having fun?" I asked as my boat bumped against theirs, and Fox and JJ moved to lash them together.

"More now that you're here," Maverick replied smoothly, offering me a hand as I climbed up into the fishing boat.

He pulled me against him, taking a kiss with a rough kind of heat that let me know just how much his blood was up and clued me in on what they'd been doing before we got here.

I drew back reluctantly, looking down at my hand as he released me and frowning at the blood now staining it.

"Lovely," I said dryly, making him laugh and Chase passed me a cloth to wipe it off again.

"We might have gotten a bit too into it, hummingbird," Fox admitted as he stepped closer to kiss me too and I didn't miss the blood splatter on his cheek.

"Sounds like we almost missed it," I said, and Chase grinned.

"We patched him up good enough to buy us a few more hours – depending on how much longer you want to keep this going for?" Chase replied.

I pursed my lips, uncertain of the answer to that question as I moved away from them towards the rear of the boat.

The scent of death and carnage clogged the air despite the sea breeze as I closed in on the reason for this trip out into the middle of the sea. I cocked my head as I took in the figure who lay bound and gagged on the floor, distaste curling my lip back.

Shawn was a shell of the man he'd once been. He was gaunt and hollow in the cheeks, the countless wounds my boys had given him with their various forms of torture leaving his body broken beyond repair, every shred of arrogance and false charisma stripped away until he was nothing. Which was exactly how it should have been.

He was as pathetic on the outside now as he had always been on the inside, and the last few times I'd gone to see him had only confirmed to me that every piece of the malicious, twisted villain who had once been so present in him had been crushed away.

He was nobody anymore. Not a gangster or a heathen, not a sinner or an abuser. Just a forgotten soul with a broken spirit and nothing left to live for beyond suffering for his sins.

There was a lot of blood on the deck and the ripe scent of burnt skin showed me where they had cauterised the wound which would have killed him before my arrival.

"I came to watch a monster die," I said, making Shawn jerk as he recognised my voice, his head snapping in my direction and that creepy devotion which had been there all too often recently brightening his blue eyes. "But all I see here is a dog that's been kicked too many times. Though maybe that's an insult to dogs."

Shawn tried to speak around the confines of his gag and Chase looked to me for approval to remove it, which I gave with a soft nod.

"Have you come to end my suffering, sugarpie?" Shawn wheezed and Rick took a purposeful step towards him which I stopped by placing a hand to his chest and shaking my head.

"He doesn't get to call you that," Rick growled but I just shrugged.

"It's just a name. A name whispered on an ill wind which will soon be forgotten when the sun returns to banish it."

"I meant nothin' by it," Shawn murmured, flinching as he looked to Maverick, and though his fear had once settled something inside me, I felt numb as I witnessed it now.

"I'm tired," I announced, looking between my boys, and letting them see the truth of that. "And as far as I'm concerned, this has gone on for more than long enough."

"I agree," JJ said instantly, and Fox nodded, though I could tell he would never stop if I wished this suffering to be endless, but I was done, and I just wanted to move on with my life.

"Rick?" I asked softly, ignoring Shawn as he began to whimper, shuffling towards me on his knees like he seriously thought I might save him now.

Maverick's eyes darkened and I knew he was back in that prison cell, feeling every moment of suffering that he'd endured there thanks to Shawn's intervention in his incarceration. I may have been satisfied by what that monster had endured until now, but I wasn't the only one of us owed this vengeance.

"The only place I wanna be is in the sun with you, beautiful. And the rest of these assholes too I guess," he said roughly, and I nodded, knowing that despite the torture he had relished handing to Shawn since we captured him, he was ready to move on from this too. He'd already lost years of his life to one prison, and he didn't need to be trapped in another one now, locked in this eternal cycle of trying to destroy his demons by destroying the man who gave them to him.

"Ace?" I asked, looking to him last of all.

He wasn't wearing an eyepatch now. In fact, I couldn't remember the last time he'd worn one, and the sight of his gorgeous face gilded silver by the moonlight made me feel like a hopeless little girl again, endlessly in love with the boys who surrounded her and uncertain of what to do with such powerful feelings.

"Yeah," he said finally, looking to Shawn with a sneer. "I'm done wasting time on this too."

I smiled at him, nodding firmly and he stooped to pick up a bucket of chum before tossing it into the sea at the back of the boat. The flash of a fin let me know there were more creatures than just us on the hunt tonight, ready to take their kill.

"Please," Shawn croaked from his knees before me and I flinched as he reached for my leg, stepping aside so he couldn't touch me.

"What?" I asked, not even glaring down at him as I just looked on impassively. I didn't even feel hatred towards him anymore. I was just done. And he would be too before long.

"Tell me I mattered, sugarpie. Tell me, you've taken my strength for your own."

I paused as I considered his words, shaking my head at Rick as he tried to step closer once more.

"Mattered?" I asked him incredulously as JJ and Fox both threw buckets of chum into the water too, the sea churning with movement as more predators were called for their feast. "I've already forgotten you, Shawn. You're nothing but a stain on a dress I don't wear anymore, and in the moment of your death, I'll cast that overworn garment into a pit of fire and exhale the last of you like smoke from my lungs. My mind will never drift your way again. Not one of us will give you so much as a passing thought. We will be whole and fulfilled and loved while the world forgets that you were ever even here to mark it with the taint of your ungodly soul. So, for now, I'll enjoy listening to your screams, then when you finish bleeding out, I'll celebrate your demise with the four men who love me more than life itself. Then the sun will rise tomorrow and we will watch it as one, forgetting you were ever here to darken the brightness of our world. We will all be free of you and everything about you ever after. You're nothing. You always were nothing, and now it's time that you face that fact at last."

Shawn's face paled as he stared up at me, finding no mercy or pity there. In fact, there was nothing at all left in me for him beyond the desire to see him die and know that it was done.

"Ten long years ago, our girl killed a man who tried to hurt her," Fox said as he stepped between me and Shawn, looping a rope around his wrists and binding them tightly while the man who had once dominated my nightmares just quivered beneath him, no more fight left in him. "The four of us helped her cover it up. We came out here to this very patch of water on a boat not so unlike this one and we tossed him in for the sharks to feast on."

"Trouble was," Rick added, reaching up to catch hold of the hook that hung from a small crane above our heads and hooking it through the ropes at Shawn's wrists, forcing his arms to raise above his head and a soft whimper to escape him. "Back then, we didn't realise that it ain't as simple as just tossing a body in the sea."

"You have to create a feeding frenzy," JJ agreed, hitting a button on the remote which controlled the crane hoisting Shawn up as the hook was retracted, and his wild gaze met mine as he was dragged to his feet then off of them, blood running down his skin from the many injuries my boys had inflicted upon his flesh.

"You gotta make sure they can smell plenty of blood in the water," Chase agreed, taking the crane remote from JJ and making the crane extend out above the water so Shawn was left hanging there, his feet just brushing the tips of the waves as he trembled in fright.

He seemed to be out of things to say at last, no more monologuing bullshit, no more poisonous words. Nothing. Just his blood dripping down into the sea and offer the circling predators a sample of the feast to come.

"Sorry, sugarpie," I said coldly as Chase passed me the remote and Rick tossed the last bucket of chum into the water, making the sharks frantic. "It ain't personal."

I pressed the button and Shawn screamed as the crane began to lower him into the water, the fearful cries turning into shrieks of pure agony as the sharks attacked and I watched as he begged and cried my name, the dark water coloured red as their feast continued, and I didn't once consider backing out of this decision.

I didn't draw my eyes away until the sharks had had their fill and his screams had long since stopped, every scrap of flesh devoured and every whisper of poison he'd ever spewed dying with him, washed away into the sea I had always loved so dearly. And with his death, our souls were scrubbed clean of the taint he'd left on us, freeing all of us from him forever.

"If the sun rises tomorrow, we'll watch it together," I said as my boys closed in around me, the weight of our victory pressing down on us solidly, their arms falling around me and each other, the five of us bound together like we were always intended to be. "And the next day and the next day and the next…"

CHAPTER FORTY FIVE

ANOTHER TWO WEEKS AFTER THAT…

Freedom.

The kind that made every breath of air in my lungs taste so goddamn sweet. This was heaven, no two ways about it. Fucking Shawn was dead and every day since was the new greatest of my life.

There was just one thing left on my agenda to solidify this lifestyle I was signing up to, one that I never could have pictured when I'd dreamed of having Rogue as mine as a lovestruck teenager. But now we'd found our way to it, I'd finally realised this was exactly what I'd wanted. To keep her and keep them too. It took some getting used to, and my boundaries had been seriously pushed as I adjusted to this new way of living, but tonight I planned on pushing them to their limits.

I finished loading the dishwasher, listening to Rogue and the guys talking out on the patio as they sipped tequila sunrises, and my heart began to drum as I tried to figure out how to approach this situation. I'd been tidying the kitchen for nearly thirty minutes now, procrastinating as I tried to come up with a way to initiate this situation. With just Rogue, it was easy, but it wasn't just Rogue. It was all of them, and I didn't know what the protocol was for starting an orgy.

Did I just go out there and take my clothes off? Or should I kiss Rogue, make my wants clear to her before giving the others the side eye? Both of those ideas seemed really fucking awkward, and as I met Mutt's gaze where he sat in his fluffy bed by the door – actually using it for once instead of rejecting it - I swear the little shit knew what I was thinking, giving me a judgemental glare.

"You'd better go make yourself busy, I don't want you there looking at me while I figure this out," I muttered to him, making myself a tequila sunrise, and draining half of it as the dog continued to glower at me.

I inhaled deeply, tossing back the rest of the cocktail and placing my glass down, the alcohol giving me the kick I needed to go out there and do this.

Outside, Rogue was lazing on a sun lounger in a little red bikini, while JJ, Chase and Maverick played cards at the table beside her in their swimming trunks.

"So erm…" I cleared my throat and they all looked to me while I carved a hand down the back of my neck and tried to figure out the rest of that sentence. The warm night air swept around me as the silence thickened and I came up short on what to do.

JJ turned the music down using his phone, smiling at me as he waited for me to go on, and that just made this awkward as fuck. I cleared my throat as Rogue sat up, her brows arching with intrigue as I hovered there like a lost fruit fly.

Why was this so difficult? I was a damn pro at being a bossy asshole. But ordering them all to do this seemed like the wrong way to handle this, so I just sort of…stood there.

Chase's gaze slid to Rick across the table, and my brother sniggered, making me press my lips together.

"I wanna try group sex," I said, just facing my fucking fear and getting it over with.

Rick burst out laughing and Chase looked to Rogue as she worked to flatten her smile, while JJ swiped a palm down his face.

"You did not just announce an orgy," JJ said, shaking his head at me as heat blazed up my spine.

"Well, I don't fucking know how else to do this," I growled.

"You need the orgy trumpet," Chase joked, though my features remained flat. "Give it a good blow and our cocks will rise like an army ready to invade Rogue's realms."

"You're such a fucking idiot," Rick continued to laugh at me, and my upper lip curled back, my hands tightening into fists as JJ and Chase cracked up too.

"Fine. Fuck you all." I turned away, striding back inside, feeling like a stupid prick.

"Wait – badger!" Rogue called, chasing after me and she caught my hand before I made it inside.

I let her turn me around, keeping my eyes on her instead of the snickering assholes at the table behind her.

She bit her lip, fisting her hand in my shirt and drawing me down as she tiptoed up to kiss me. I let her work to please me before melting into her touch and kissing her back, figuring I'd just steal her away while the others remained here. Because fuck them. I was officially cancelling the orgy – not that I'd gotten it underway at all, but still.

Her hand sailed down my chest, riding over my cock and getting me hard in seconds as our kiss turned to something more carnal.

I felt the others' eyes on us and instinctively tugged Rogue away from them into the kitchen, but she broke our kiss, keeping hold of my waistband as she backed up, pulling me in their direction instead.

Their laughter had stuttered out and they watched us now with heat in their eyes as my heart beat fiercely against my ribs.

Was it happening? Did I just go with the flow now and let the orgy unfold?

"Come on," she urged, and I gave in to her wants, letting her pull me outside where the others were getting to their feet.

Rogue released me, keeping her eyes on mine and backing up into JJ's arms as he came up behind her, squeezing her tits and biting down on her neck as she tilted her head to one side to give him access.

Chase closed in on her other side, brushing his fingers down her stomach. I watched her reaction as he slid his hand into her bikini bottoms and she started to moan for him. Rick stepped closer to her too, enjoying the show as he lowered his shorts, taking his cock into his fist and starting to stroke himself over the performance the others were putting on.

"How ready for us is she, Ace?" Rick asked and Chase chuckled as he withdrew his fingers from her bikini bottoms, pushing them between JJ's lips who sucked them clean.

"Come over here and find out," Chase encouraged Rick and he moved forward, undoing the strings of Rogue's bikini bottoms so they fell to the ground and exposed her pussy to us all.

Rogue's gaze shifted up to meet mine as Rick kneeled down and slung her right leg over his shoulder while Chase looped an arm around her waist to steady her.

Rick buried his face between her thighs with a hungry growl and Chase lifted Rogue by the hips, pushing her other leg over Rick's shoulders, and between him and JJ, they held her there for him while caressing her tits and nipping at her neck.

Her moans carried up into the night and I stood there, rock hard and aching as this all played out before me, but I didn't know how to insert myself into it.

It seemed so natural to all of them, one of them moving, causing the others to respond until they fell into this effortless rhythm which I didn't know how to match.

"Fox," Rogue breathed, looking to me through hooded eyes, holding a hand out in encouragement.

I moved forward, my leg knocking into Rick as I tried to get closer and I moved sideways instead, my hip hitting Chase's.

Rogue caught the back of my neck, drawing me in for a kiss and my hand landed on Chase's back, making me move away again with an apology.

"It's fine, man," Chase said. "Don't worry about it."

"I just er…need to find a position." I moved sideways again, and my knee jammed into Rick's head, forcing him off of Rogue and he glared up at me in frustration.

"What is your problem?" he snapped as Rogue slid her legs off his shoulders to stand upright.

"There's not much space," I growled, and he rolled his eyes at me, standing up and hitching Rogue into his arms by her ass, carrying her away from us.

Chase hurried after him, sweeping all the cards off of the table so it was clear as Rick laid Rogue down on it and her hips bucked with need. Chase untied her bikini top, pulling it off and leaving her complete bare to us.

JJ gave me an encouraging smile, slapped me on the back and headed over to join them again. But dammit, now what was I supposed to do? I'd just found myself a position and they'd gone and moved elsewhere. I felt like a cock bandit trying to slip my way in the back door. Or the front door. *Shit, I need to claim myself a door.*

I felt someone's attention on me, and my gaze shifted to the full-length window where Mutt was glaring out at me with narrowed eyes. I swear he even shook his head judgementally. But what was I supposed to do? Dive into the fray like a dolphin chasing a fish?

I cursed the little dog, turning away and hurrying forward to try and find a spot for myself before they were all taken. A quick mental math of dicks and holes said someone was going to be left high and dry, and I didn't want it to be me so soon into my first orgy.

Maverick feasted on Rogue's pussy again and she moaned, arching her back as JJ reached down to slide his fingers in too, resting one hand on Rick's back as he leaned over him.

She came with a cry, her whole body flexing as she finished, and Rick laughed his victory as he stood upright and wiped his mouth on the back of his hand. He caught hold of her hips, yanking her forward and as he lifted her off the table, Chase moved smoothly to sit beneath her. He dropped his shorts and kicked them away as Rick held Rogue above his cock by her ass, and JJ handed out lube like it was perfectly normal to carry little bottles of the stuff around in his pockets.

JJ squirted some into his palm and casually rubbed it along the length of Chase's cock, making my lips part in shock and Rick looked between them with a knowing smirk.

"I knew it," he muttered, and JJ shrugged before leaning in and sinking his tongue between Chase's lips.

I gaped at them, dumbstruck by that as I watched them kiss, and JJ's hand started to glide up and down Chase's cock, lube dripping between his fingers.

"Wait, is this what we all have to do?" I asked, though my voice didn't carry that far. "Do I have to do that?"

Rogue looked at me over Rick's shoulder, a laugh leaving her as she shook her head. "No, badger. Only do what you're comfortable with."

"But is that like, part of this?" I asked in confusion as JJ's mouth broke from Chase's and he looked back at me.

"It's something we like. You don't have to do anything you're not into, man," JJ said.

"Can we hurry up, I'm dying here," Maverick growled, and they all turned their attention back to Rogue.

Rick guided her hips back and JJ held Chase's cock in place as he drove into her ass. Both Chase and Rogue swore as she settled into his lap and Rick tipped her chin up, making their eyes lock as he spread her thighs and slowly pushed inside her too.

JJ leaned in to lick and suck at both Chase and Rogue's flesh while the others started moving, groaning, pawing at each other, and I just stood there like I was in line at the grocery store, dick in hand like a discounted sausage.

JJ looked over at me, jerking his head in encouragement for me to join in and I forced my legs to move, taking up the opposite side to him and leaning down to kiss Rogue's neck, but Rick shifted her forward at that moment and my mouth landed on Chase's shoulder instead.

I reared backwards, my elbow slamming into Rick's arm and Rogue looked around to see what was going on, her head moving so fast that she knocked heads with me.

"Ow," she laughed, and I backed up, aware I was ruining this whole thing. "Badger," she said, seeing the decision in my eyes before I shook my head and turned away. "Wait – ah," she moaned as Rick started fucking her furiously.

"Let him go. He's not cut out for this, baby girl," Rick taunted, and I spat a snarl as I walked inside, finding Mutt pissing in one of my potted palms.

"For the love of fuck," I snapped as he gazed coolly at me, daring me to do anything about it before kicking his little back feet and sending soil across my nice clean floor. I must have changed the soil in those pots a hundred times to combat the piss smell, and I was starting to think I needed to just cut my losses and get rid of the damn things.

I turned my back on him too, striding upstairs in anger, marching into my room and heading straight out onto my balcony in frustration. I leaned my forearms on the railing, gazing out over the view with a huff.

Maverick was right. I wasn't cut out for this. I should have known that. It just made me feel like I was letting Rogue down, and I hated that. The others could fulfil her in ways I couldn't, and that made me more goddamn furious than anything else about it.

"You're overthinking it, bro," JJ sang as he stepped out onto the balcony like a mystical sex guru with a new client. And yeah, I supposed he was that. So maybe it was worth hearing him out.

I looked his way with a frown as he moved to lean his arms on the balcony railing beside mine.

"Maybe some people just aren't made for orgies," I said.

"Hey, don't you talk like that," JJ said firmly. "Everyone can have an orgy if they really want one. The problem is you're doing this for her, not you. So, what does Fox want?"

I gave him a dry look, but he just cocked his head and awaited my answer. I blew out a breath, giving into his sex demon stare.

"I want her to be happy."

"That's great and all. It is. But you've gotta be in this for you too. You can't just shut your eyes and jab your cock back and forth 'til it's over."

"Nice," I drawled, and he snorted.

"You've gotta want it for *you*. You've gotta like it."

"I don't think I can, not when there's so much going on. There're cocks everywhere and I don't wanna cock block one of you, or touch dicks by accident."

"Look, brother." JJ rested a hand on my back, and I turned to him with a deep frown pulling at my brow. "Sometimes our dicks are gonna touch, and that's okay. It's no big deal."

"But I don't wanna fuck you, man," I said. "You're great and all, but I'm not into guys."

"You don't have to be into guys. Ignore me and Ace. If we start kissing or touching or fucking-"

"Fucking?" I rasped and he waved a hand like it was nothing. Was it though? Two of my best friends liked fucking each other, and I wasn't supposed to be surprised by that? Or thrown off my game when they went at it? It was a lot to get my head round.

"You just need to focus on you. Get in there, dude. Dive deep. Go for gold," he said with an encouraging smile.

"It doesn't feel natural to me. You're all so in sync," I said, and he frowned, thinking on that.

"Well, that's because you're not bringing Fox Harlequin to the orgy," he said in realisation.

"What do you mean?"

"Back there, you were like this bumbling, awkward dick jangler," JJ said with a pitying look.

"A dick jangler?" I echoed sadly.

"Yeah," he said with a morose expression, patting my shoulder. "But it's okay. That's not you. You're one of the Harlequin Kings, you control ruthless gangsters day in and day out. You command every room you walk into, so walk into that orgy with the same energy you rule the Harlequins with, okay?"

"I'm trying to hold back on my bossy shit," I muttered.

"That's your issue though. You're trying so hard to hold in a piece of you, but it's a part of who you are. And fuck, Rogue loves when you tell her what to do. I'm not opposed to it either. You wanna tell me how to fuck our girl? I'd be fully down for that."

I arched a brow, not minding the sound of that. "I can be bossy?" I asked hopefully.

"Yeah, you can be the bossiest motherfucker in town. Rick will bite back, Rogue will get off on you trying to fight for power, me and Chase will work to appease all of you and it'll be like old times. Just with orgasms involved and lots of lube."

I nodded decisively, amped up now that I had a new game plan in mind, one that felt far more comfortable to me. This was who I was, and JJ was right. I needed to be part of an orgy in a way that felt natural to me, and this was how.

589

I knew it.

"If I go too far, if I get super fucking possessive or some shit-" I started anxiously, but he cut over me.

"We'll keep you in check," he said with a grin. "Trust us."

I nodded, really wanting to try this because it was a part of me, and I couldn't keep it away forever. Maybe this was the best outlet for it anyway.

"You finished that book series, right?" JJ asked. "Ruthless Boys of the Zodiac?"

"Yeah," I said with a grin, finally understanding what JJ had been angling at with getting me to read it. I had to admit it gave me a damn good insight on how to make this five-way business work, though I was seriously fucking surprised at how things had gone down in the end.

"So you've read detailed, explicit, seriously hot orgy scenes already," he said proudly. "Just draw on those for inspiration."

"Okay," I said, nodding firmly. "I can do that."

"Come on then, before they wear our girl out." He turned and led me back through the house while I unleashed the possessiveness in me which I'd been working to keep caged. It set my heart racing and I placed my faith in myself. I wanted this. I'd been aching to see her fall to ruin between all of us at once, and if I could make that fantasy become reality while telling them exactly how to go about it, then I was more than down for that.

I followed JJ back outside, finding Rogue cresting towards climax as Rick fucked her deep and hard while Chase drove up into her from below, her moans of ecstasy making me rock hard again instantly.

I smirked darkly, striding toward Maverick and yanking him off of her, making him stumble back in surprise. I shoved my shorts down as he hissed a snarl and Rogue gasped as I drove myself inside her a beat later.

She cried out at the sudden change, coming right on my cock and I groaned as she squeezed the length of me, feeling like perfection as always. "Hey, hummingbird."

"Badger," she moaned and fuck I liked the sound of that name right now.

"Kiss our girl and tell me how she tastes while she's coming for me, Ace," I commanded and Chase gripped her hair, turning her head and pushing his tongue between her lips as she rode out the wave of pleasure I'd stolen from Rick.

JJ moved behind Chase, giving me a thumbs up and a wink, and I fucked Rogue harder as Rick approached from my other side. I was doing it. No, scrap that. I was killing it. I was the fucking orgy king, and I'd make damn sure they all knew it by the time I was done.

I could feel Chase's cock pumping into her ass and groaned, unable to deny how good that felt as I let myself relax into this and enjoy it.

"She tastes like heaven," Chase said as she broke the kiss with him, turning to kiss Rick on her other side and he palmed her tits as he drew her closer.

JJ kissed Chase's scars, making him tip his head back in pleasure, sweat rolling down between his pecs before he drove up deep inside Rogue and stilled, finishing with a low groan that JJ swallowed with a kiss.

Rick took hold of Rogue, lifting her so Chase could withdraw, and my cock slipped out of her as he forced her onto her knees on the table.

"JJ lie beneath her," I commanded as I pushed my fingers into Rogue's hair, and she looked up at me under her lashes before moving forward to take my cock between her lips.

I sighed in pleasure, wrapping her hair around my fist to hold it back while JJ positioned himself beneath her and pulled her down so he could start fucking her.

Rick moved up behind her, the perfect height to enter her ass as he slathered his cock in lube before easing himself inside her. With every thrust of his hips, my cock pressed to the back of Rogue's throat, and I groaned in delight as I realised I'd finally let go and found the rhythm all of them were a part of.

It wasn't long before I came, finishing into her mouth with a deep groan only a few seconds before Maverick finished too, spanking her hard on the ass and making her shudder and moan.

JJ was left with her as me, Rick and Chase all dropped into chairs around the table and watched the work of art that was her and JJ fucking. He moved like he had no goddamn bones in his body, every thrust of his hips like a dance move as he rolled them over and hooked her right knee over his arm. She came twice more before he let himself finish inside her, smirking as he claimed her in front of all of us and left his mark on her just like the rest of us had.

JJ dropped down to sit beside us and Rogue lay there panting and carving her fingers across her skin as we admired her destruction.

Mutt appeared in the doorway once again, his eyes moving between us one at a time before settling on me, and unless I was hallucinating, the little fucker gave me a nod of approval before huffing out a breath like this entire thing was a drain on his energy as he disappeared back inside.

"You satisfied now, beautiful?" Rick asked.

"Never," she panted, rolling onto her front and observing us with heat in her seductive gaze.

I started to get hard again and one look at the others said they were raring to go already too.

"Are you still hungry, Fox?" she asked breathlessly, searching my eyes to see if I'd enjoyed that, if I wanted more. There was no denying it. I'd found my place in this den of sin, and I knew how to wield my power within it now.

I rose to my feet, snapping my fingers at Chase and JJ and they stood to attention, ready to take my orders while Rick laughed devilishly.

I cupped Rogue's jaw in my palm, smiling at her as her blazing eyes shimmering with life.

"Ravenous, hummingbird. Now do exactly as I tell you."

CHAPTER FORTY SIX

SEVERAL YEARS AFTER THAT…

I tapped my fingers against the bar while Estelle wiped it down, the club at Afterlife quiet this early in the day, and while JJ did some paperwork in the back office, I lounged about like a lady who lunched – sans the lunch.

"Can I get you a sandwich?" Estelle asked me fondly like she'd read my damn mind and I looked up hopefully. "I've got some stuff here that I can slap together for you. The bread is fresh, and I have some cheese…" She trailed off as she stuck her head in the fridge to check out the options, grabbing the ingredients she found and placing them on the bar.

My gaze fell on the cheese and suddenly I didn't feel so hungry anymore. My stomach turned at the thought of that and I grimaced.

"Err, I dunno," I began, and she looked up at me sharply.

"I may not know you well, but I ain't ever seen you turn down a snack when it's offered," she said, narrowing her eyes on me and I snorted, wondering if I should be offended by that observation before deciding I was cool with it if it earned me extra snacks – so long as they didn't include any of that cheese.

"I want the snack," I said firmly, but I shuddered as the cheese tried to catch my eye again. "Just maybe some bread and butter instead of making a full sandwich?"

Estelle pinned me in her gaze, shoving aside the ingredients she'd just gotten out of the fridge and leaning in closer to me as I found myself trapped there within the knowing look in her eyes.

"Oh, I've danced this dance before, poppet," she said slowly, her eyes travelling from my face, down my body before hopping back up to meet my eyes once more. "How long since you had a bleed?"

"A what now?" I asked with a frown.

"A bloody mary. A week of respite. A whore's vacation?"

"Huh?"

"Your period, poppet, don't be coy with me. I've seen it all around here. How late are ya?"

"Late?" I squeaked, shaking my head as I realised what she was suggesting. "No."

"No?" she asked, arching a brow. "That ain't an answer to my question. You think saying no undoes the amount of times you've fucked those fellas of yours without a condom? You do know that sex was designed for making babies, right? Not just blowing your socks off."

"Babies?" I squeaked again because apparently I was a squeaker now, shaking my head more vigorously, but just as I did that cheese gave me a look and I lunged to my feet, hurrying away to the bathroom because I was pretty damn sure that her line of insane questioning was going to make me puke.

Estelle's high heeled steps followed me through the club and down the corridor, but she didn't appear as my knees hit the tiled floor of the bathroom and I started heaving over the toilet.

I gripped the edge of the porcelain rim while my stomach tightened and I heaved some more, but nothing actually made its way up and out of me.

"Pretty girl?" JJ's concerned voice found me, and I looked around, finding him standing over me, pale faced and concerned, his hand landing on my shoulder as he brushed his fingers across my skin.

"Estelle has gone crazy," I hissed in a low voice before realising she was right behind him, one heavily pencilled eyebrow raised as she looked at me where I knelt on the floor of a strip club bathroom, shame heaving without even having had a single drink.

"No, poppet, you're just in denial. Here." She held out a handful of what I thought were tampons but as Johnny James robotically reached out to accept them, I realised there was something else in those little thin packets.

"I don't need to take one of those," I protested.

"Well, you can always live on in denial until you're in the hospital trying to force that thing out of your hoo-ha, but I have to think a little forewarning is preferable," Estelle said matter of factly.

"JJ?" I pleaded, needing him to tell the crazy wombat to stop with her nonsense before I lost my shit.

Johnny James seemed to snap out of some sort of trance, and he reached for my hand, tugging me to my feet in one swift movement which almost felt like one of his dance moves.

"We should go home," he said, not looking directly at me as he tugged me along with him and turned for the exit.

"Congratulations," Estelle called after us as we went, and I craned my neck to look back at her in alarm. "Or commiserations. Whichever you need." She cackled a laugh just as JJ tugged me away through the club and before I knew what was happening, we were out in the blazing sunshine and JJ was directing me into the passenger seat of his bright orange Mustang GT.

He got in too, reaching over to carefully fasten my seatbelt for me before turning his eyes to the road and pulling away without another word.

I eyed the handful of pregnancy tests sticking out of his shirt pocket and my pulse began to hammer against my ribcage so hard that I fought to control

597

my breathing.

"You've been taking your pill, right?" he asked after way too long and I nodded.

"Yeah. Sure." I frowned a little though, because in all honesty I kinda forgot about them half the time. "Mostly."

JJ made a sound like a dying cockroach, and I looked to him with concern.

"We stopped using condoms," he breathed like it was a prayer or maybe a curse, and I bit my lip.

"I don't like condoms," I muttered, sounding like a petulant child but there it was.

"We've had so much sex," he said, his face so pale now that I was half convinced he was going to puke too.

I shook my head, watching the world go by as we sped back towards home.

"I'm not pregnant," I said firmly because if I put that out into the universe then it would clearly manifest.

"So much fucking sex," JJ breathed again, and we stayed silent the remainder of the drive back while I tried to think when the last time I'd had my period was, because it sure as shit hadn't been any time in the last few months.

Fuck.

CHAPTER FORTY SEVEN

"What the fuck is going on, JJ?" I demanded as he stood outside the bathroom in the hallway with Mutt sitting on the floor at his feet, watching the door intently.

He gave me a look which he'd never given me before, something between terror and confusion, and I slowed to a halt in front of him with a frown.

"J?" I asked, my tone softening as a flicker of fear brushed my heart. "Is Rogue okay?"

"Yeah, man," he said hollowly, pointing to the door. "She's in there."

"What's happening?" Chase asked as he appeared with Fox.

JJ visibly swallowed as we surrounded him, hungry for answers and he finally relinquished them.

"Rogue's taking a pregnancy test," he said as Mutt whined.

Those words should have made sense when they were all put in a line like that, yet somehow my brain was struggling to comprehend them.

"Which is impossible to do when you're all standing out there listening to me trying to pee," she called, and JJ herded us further along the corridor.

"She's pregnant?" Fox asked as the world darkened around me and a ringing started up in my ears, but I noted the hope in his tone.

"No, she's not," Chase said immediately, a manic sort of laugh leaving him as he looked to JJ. "This is a joke, right? It's a shit joke, but it is a joke, right J?" He tried to continue laughing but it trailed off as JJ shook his head, and I knew without a doubt, he wasn't joking.

No, this shitstorm of a possibility was really swirling around us, and it was choking all the air out of my lungs.

"She's on the pill," I blurted, and JJ frowned at me.

"The pill isn't one hundred percent effective," he muttered, and I shook my head, retreating until my back hit the wall.

"Come on, this isn't so bad," Fox said, smiling at us, fucking smiling like this was a great goddamn thing to have happened. Did he even know who we were? We were a cutthroat bunch of fucking sinners. We killed people and ripped them off and thrived on all the bad in the world. Where did he think a baby would fit into that?

"Not so bad?" I hissed, shoving my palms into his chest and he frowned at me.

"I know it's a shock," he said. "You just need a minute-"

"She's not even got a positive result yet, Fox," JJ said firmly. "This could be a false alarm."

"I know, man. I'm just saying," Fox said.

"Well don't just say," Chase said, dragging a hand down his face and Fox clucked his tongue at us before moving along the hall and gently knocking on the bathroom door.

"Are you good, hummingbird?" he asked.

"Yeah," she said, the door clicking as she unlocked it and stepped out, and I was so relieved to see her that it took the edge off the shock I was feeling.

"It's two lines. That's negative, right?" she said, a little nervous laugh leaving her.

"I think so. Thank fuck for that," I said heavily as Fox took the pee stick from her and she hurried forward to hug JJ who was closest.

He kissed the top of her head, still looking pale faced from this whole shitshow and Chase moved forward to hug her from behind.

A breath of relief left me as Rogue met my eyes and I smiled. "Well, that's another bullet I've dodged in my life."

"Don't be an asshole, Rick," JJ muttered, but Rogue knew I always fell back on dark humour in times like this, though her pursed lips said she didn't find it so funny. Probably shouldn't have made a joke about my Russian Roulette days right now, but hey ho, that was how I rolled.

"Er...hummingbird?" Fox said, clearing his throat and we all looked over at him where he was now tapping something on his phone. "I just looked up the instructions and um..." He compared a picture on his phone to the pregnancy test in his hand. "C'mere a sec, baby." The gentleness in his tone made my heart jerk violently and I looked from him to Rogue as she slipped from the others' arms and walked toward him.

"What?" she asked.

"I think it's one line for negative, two for positive," he said in a low voice, showing her the phone and the stick again.

"Oh fuck," she breathed, and my pulse started to pound uncontrollably in my ears. She lunged into the bathroom, returning with even more pregnancy tests, checking them all, one after the other against the instructions on that screen and tossing them aside each time she found two lines marking them.

One slapped me in my slack jawed face and I cursed as I took the splash of urine like a slap from reality. Even the universe was mocking me now.

"What's happening?" JJ asked in fright, clawing his fingers through his hair, his other hand latching in Chase's shirt and drawing him closer.

"They're all positive," Fox announced, looking bright eyed and fucking merry while the rest of us stared on in horror.

"What the fuck are we supposed to do with a baby?" I demanded in anger, though it was fear that really had me in its grip. I couldn't be a dad. I was a fucking murderer. I didn't do sweet or soft or gentle. And those were all things babies needed. I was destructive. I'd break it, hurt it.

"Raise it?" Fox suggested, happy as a fucking clam at a mermaid party.

"No," I said in a panic, backing up down the hall as Rogue met my gaze, tears swimming in her eyes. And for the first time in my life, I didn't go to her when she needed me. I kept retreating, needing to get myself away from her and the child I was going to taint with the darkness in me if I stayed too close. Because protecting her now meant staying the fuck away.

Rogue broke a sob, darting back into the bathroom and slamming the door, shutting us all out as she locked the door. Guilt hit me in the chest, but I couldn't go to her. I had to leave. I had to get the fuck out of here.

I ran down the hall like a prime asshole, spilling through the door into the garage while Fox barked an order for Chase and JJ to get me. I felt them hurrying along at my back, but they didn't try and stop me when I took Fox's keys and leapt into his truck. They got right in it alongside me. And suddenly we were running away like fucking cowards into the wind.

CHAPTER FORTY EIGHT

I stared into the toilet, wondering if I might read a vision of my fate there among the water destined to carry shit away down the drain and finding myself lost in thoughts of my own failings.

I wasn't cut out for this. Plain and simple. I didn't know what being a mom looked like. Between the five of us, only JJ had ever really had one of those and though Helena had loved him and cared for him the best she could, I knew he hadn't had it easy watching strange men come and go from her bedroom every night while she used her body to pay for the things he needed to survive.

My amount of experience with loving, maternal figures was precisely zero. My own mother had been a drug addict so incapable of caring for me that I'd been taken from her the moment of my birth and placed in the system. She'd never once come to try and claim me back, and I'd always assumed she must have been relieved to be rid of me. That stung, but it was an old wound, one which had long since healed over and was mostly forgotten these days. Except now it wasn't so easy to forget it. Because the only hope I'd ever had of figuring out the whole mom thing had chosen her next hit over the chance of having me in her life.

Here I was with no fucking idea of what I was supposed to do and four boyfriends who were clearly just as lost as I was about this entire thing. Not to mention the fact that they all seemed about as horrified as possible by the prospect too. Well, all of them but Fox.

"Rogue?" my loyal little badger hammered on the bathroom door, and I hiccupped a sob, brushing absently at the tears which painted my cheeks as I failed to answer him yet again. I wasn't crying because I was sad. I was fucking terrified.

A heavy thump made the door rattle and I gasped as I whipped around to look at it just as Fox slammed into it for a second time, breaking the lock as he forced his way into the room.

"Hummingbird," he growled, dropping down and scooping me into his arms without giving me a single second to adjust to his sudden appearance. His mouth found mine, a heated kiss searing my lips before he drew back again. "I'm taking you to hospital to get checked out," he said firmly as Mutt yapped like he agreed, my tiny dog jumping up so he could lick my bare toes where Fox held them suspended above his head.

"Hospital?" I squeaked, wanting to refuse because I knew that would mean this was real. There would be tests and scans and questions, and I really didn't think I could cope with that. "Fox, I think I just wanna eat chocolate and cry while I watch GPR re-runs," I said but he shook his head, carrying me out of the bathroom and straight towards the door.

"No. This is real, and you can't run from it. Besides, you made me a promise, didn't you?"

"No more running," I breathed, and he nodded firmly, leaning in to kiss the top of my head before he opened the door leading to the garage and carried me down there. I didn't really need him to carry me like a baby, but I had to admit that I liked the feeling of being held tight in his arms, so I just leaned into him and allowed it to happen.

Mutt stayed behind as Fox placed me in the passenger seat of my Jeep and I noticed that his truck was missing and the others were missing right along with it.

"They left?" I asked, my heart aching at the thought.

Fox grunted an agreement, a furious look passing across his features for a brief moment before we headed out onto the road in silence with his hand held tight around mine.

"For the record," Fox said as I looked out the window to the sea which always called my name so hungrily. "If you are pregnant and you do want to keep it, then I'm in. All in. Diapers, vomit, late nights, all of it. And I'll even help you out with the baby too."

I coughed a laugh and he grinned at me even as it turned into something of a terrified sob.

"And if you don't want to keep it, then I'm all in too," he added, his thumb tracing over the back of my hand and making me tremble just a little at the tenderness of this man who could be so brutal when he wanted to be.

"I'm yours, hummingbird. No strings. No conditions. You have it in you to be the most amazing mom a kid ever knew and the rest of us will just figure it the fuck out."

"So you...want it? If there is an it?" I asked, studying his face.

There was no hiding the excitement there as he tried not to grin like he used to when we were kids planning our next great adventure.

"Honestly?" he asked, shooting me a look which said he was worried his answer might make me bolt, but I needed to hear it. "Yeah. Fuck yeah actually. But more than anything I want you. I want what you need and what makes you happy. So, let's just go find out what we're dealing with and then you can make that decision. Whatever way, I'm here for it and I'll stand by you."

"Jesus," I muttered, looking away from his glowing face before I freaked the fuck out.

I focused on the sight of the sea as I tried to remember how freaking small I was in this world, how little anything I ever did would ever really matter, and just how insignificant anything I did really was. Even if that included the entirely earth-shattering prospect of having a small person growing inside me.

Fox pulled into the hospital and parked straight up in a bay which was supposed to be reserved for ambulances like the utter asshole he was.

He got out, jogged around the car and quickly opened my door for me, lifting me into his arms again as if I couldn't walk myself into the hospital. Of course, I had no shoes on, so it wasn't exactly a bad thing not to have to walk, but I did feel a little self-conscious as people started looking at us.

Fox strode straight in, bypassing the line of people waiting at the front desk and cornering a nurse as she made a move to head off somewhere.

"We need a scan done," he barked firmly.

"A scan?" she asked, looking from him to me with a slight frown. "What kind of-"

"The kind that checks for babies. Now."

"Sir, you can't just-"

"Tell me where to go," he demanded and though her brow pinched, she relented under the power of his voice, and maybe there was a little recognition in her eyes too. He was one of the Harlequin Kings now, a ruler of this town, and there were very few corners of Sunset Cove that didn't know it.

"Second floor, turn right out of the elevator. Follow the signs for-"

Fox walked off before she could finish, and I buried my face against his shoulder as I laughed.

"You're such a dick," I muttered.

"Anything to ensure you get what you need," he replied with a shrug.

He hit the button for the elevator, stepping past the people who had already been waiting as it arrived, and I guessed something about him was damn off-putting because not one of them followed us into the thing either. We headed to the second floor and Fox marched us straight up to the desk in the prenatal unit before commanding the attention of the woman who was working there too.

"My girl needs a scan," he said firmly, and the woman looked up with a frown.

"Well, so do half the people waiting in this room."

"We're first," he replied, taking a wedge of cash from his pocket and tossing it down in front of her. "I can get my gun out next if that's what it takes?"

The woman blinked at him for several seconds, glanced around the room then hastily pocketed the cash before anyone else could notice it. She beckoned for us to follow her, and we headed down another corridor into a dimly lit room there where she pointed towards the bed next to an ultrasound machine.

Fox placed me down on it, but I grabbed hold of his hand when he made a move to step back, keeping him right there with me whether he liked it or not, though the smirk tracing his lips said he was all kinds of pleased about that.

"Shut up," I hissed.

"I didn't say anything."

"You're thinking it."

"I'll be sure to stop thinking then."

"That would be ideal," I agreed.

"Okay, we're going to get started," the sonographer said, clearing her throat as she lifted my shirt up and I gasped as she squirted cold jelly over my lower abdomen. "Just relax and watch the screen and we'll see if we have anything to look at here."

I chewed on my bottom lip as she pressed the weird probe thing to my belly, my eyes moving to the little screen and my grip on Fox's hand tightening as I stared at the black and grey granules which shifted about as she moved the thing.

"Okay…here we are," she said as a dark patch appeared in the centre of the screen, a little blobby lump thing sitting in the middle of it which made my heart fall still and a breath catch in my lungs.

"Oh," I breathed, tears spilling down my cheeks without my agreement and Fox sucked in a sharp breath as he leaned forward to see better.

"Holy shit, that's a baby," he said.

I stared at the little thing on the screen, the words of the woman conducting my scan washing over my ears and away as I forgot to breathe, captivated in the reality which had just become mine. My heart raced a million miles a minute, my palms grew slick and I held Fox's hand in a death grip as something deep inside me twisted and planted itself there, growing into an idea I had never once entertained.

Nothing at all had changed and yet everything had all at once, the reality I was in and the one headed my way in a few months' time could suddenly be entirely alien to one another. I had no idea what that might look like or what it would mean, but all these strange and unconsidered possibilities were opening up in front of me.

I didn't know what that meant or what I was supposed to want now, but the truth was sitting right there on that screen, tiny limbs moving and heartbeat pulsing, refusing to let me deny it a moment longer.

That was a baby.

A little, diddy dot of a baby.

And it was mine.

CHAPTER FORTY NINE

I paced back and forth on the beach, the sun beating down on my back as the world kept tipping and rocking like I was on a goddamn boat in a storm.

JJ sat on the ground, watching me pace in front of him while Maverick was still in the truck parked up beside us, his forehead resting against the steering wheel.

"I can't do this, J," I said as I continued to carve a path into the sand, stalking back and forth before him. "I'm not cut out for it."

"And you think I am?" JJ rasped. "I've only recently met my own dad. I can't become one. I don't even know what that looks like. Do I have to wear socks with sandals now? Oh god, I'm gonna be just like Gwan." He buried his face in his hands and Rick finally exited the truck, staring accusingly at JJ as he strode toward us with purpose.

"It's you," he growled accusingly, grabbing hold of JJ and hauling him to his feet. "It's your cock that's done this to us."

"What?" JJ barked, shoving Rick's hands off of him, but Maverick lunged at him again, knocking him from his feet in a football tackle and falling on top of him in the sand. "You always had to double wrap your cock because you know something we don't. You've got super swimmers, admit it! You and your sneaky little ninja cock are responsible."

"Fuck you." JJ fought and punched Rick back, the two of them rolling and fighting in the sand while I watched them dumbly, half aware that I should probably step in while feeling too distracted to do so.

"You're the one who has some sort of fucking voodoo shit tattooed on his dick," JJ snarled at Rick. "How do you know that's not a fertility spell, huh?"

"You're clutching at straws, Johnny James," Rick hissed, grabbing JJ's throat and starting to choke him. "You're the one with the fancy moves, you've probably been dancing your dick right into her ovaries all this time."

I groaned, looking up at the sky and begging the single lonely white cloud above to help us.

"We'll have to get a paternity test," I said. "I can do this, just not if it's mine."

The others fell still, and I looked down as I found them rising, brushing sand off of their clothes as they approached me.

"It can't be mine," I croaked, thinking of my dad, my fucking cunt of a father whose genes needed to die when I did. I couldn't carry on the Cohen line, it was riddled with bad DNA and too much pollution. "I'm not gonna be the reason for a monster being born into this world."

"Ace," JJ said softly, reaching for me and gripping my cheek in his hand. "Don't fucking say that, man."

"Hey, you're not the only member of the bad daddy club," Rick muttered, clearly concerned about the same thing. "At least you turned out alright. I'm fucked in the head." He tapped his temple. "My offspring would be devils with Rogue's perfect fucking face. Do you know how much of a dangerous combination that could be?"

I frowned, not liking him saying that about himself, though I knew I'd be a damn hypocrite if I started defending his potential kids if I didn't defend my own too.

A horn blasted violently, then again and again and I found Fox driving down onto the beach in Rogue's red Jeep, his upper lip curling in utter rage.

He pulled up beside us, spitting sand everywhere and making us cough and back up as he glared out of the open window at us.

"You motherfuckers just walked out on our girl. You'd better get your asses back home this second," he snarled, and guilt descended on me, the accusation in his eyes making me feel like a piece of shit.

"We can't do this, Fox," JJ implored, moving to grip the edge of the Jeep window. "We're not cut out for this."

Fox leaned forward, snatching JJ's shirt into his fist so that he was nose to nose with him. "Rogue feels the same way. She's fucking terrified right now. She needs us. All of us." He gave us all a pointed look and I kicked the sand at my feet, feeling like a fucking asshole. "We'll figure the rest out later. Just get home."

He turned the Jeep around, leaving us in a sandstorm of his creation and Rick coughed out swear words as he left us behind.

We shared a look that solidified our decision and piled back into the truck I'd borrowed from Fox one by one, our heads hanging with the shame of what we'd done. JJ drove us and I sat chewing on my thumb while sharing looks with Rick that told me how worried he was about this whole thing. But Fox was right, this wasn't about us right now. It was about Rogue, and we'd left her when she needed us most.

"For what it's worth, I think you'd both make great dads," I told the two of them, and Rick straightened in surprise while JJ looked over at me with wide eyes. "Not innocent, crime free ones. But good ones," I added. "You'd be seriously protective. You'd make good choices and shit."

"So would you, Ace," JJ said, reaching over to squeeze my arm and I really, really wanted to believe that.

When we were parked back in the garage, we headed upstairs, covered in sand and sheepishly making our way through the house to where Fox was talking in a low voice to Rogue.

"-everything's going to be fine. I promise, hummingbird," he said, and my heart tugged at the love in his words. Fuck, we should have been here saying those very things right from the start, but we'd gone and run like rabbits from a wolf. We had to make this right.

We moved into the lounge where Rogue was sitting in the dark with sunglasses on, a blanket tucked up around her and Mutt nestled in her arms. The Power Rangers was playing on the TV, but she turned to us as we entered and Fox folded his arms, standing upright and giving us a stern look from behind Rogue that told us to apologise.

"Sorry, little one," I took the lead, moving toward her and hoping she'd forgive me. "I panicked."

"We all did," JJ agreed. "Please forgive us, pretty girl."

"It's a headfuck, baby. But we love you. We're here now," Rick added. "And we're not going anywhere."

Rogue nodded, pushing her sunglasses up onto her head, a shadow of fear in her eyes as she produced a sonogram picture from beneath the folds of her blanket.

"This is our baby," she whispered, raising her chin. "And I'm keeping it. I don't know what that means for all of you. I don't know if you can do this with me, but I really, really, really want you to."

My heart cracked open at the worry in her gaze, and I moved forward, sitting down by her feet and taking the picture from her. There it was. I mean, I couldn't really see what was what, but it had a vague shape that looked sort of baby-like.

I knew from the depths of my being that I wasn't going to leave Rogue for anything. I'd find a way to be the right man to deal with this. I'd do it for her. I'd do it for this little unborn baby.

"We've got nine months to prepare, right?" I asked, trying to figure out how I was going to become the dad this child was gonna need. Though I wasn't sure any amount of time was going to turn me into a respectable citizen with good morals. Ergh.

I shuddered. I didn't want to be that. But I could be a man who loved his child with every scrap of his heart, even if that heart was stained with a lifetime full of crime.

"Well, I'm over four months along so it's more like five months to go," Rogue said, and I nodded, my lungs squeezing tightly. *This is fine. I'll be fine. Just fine.*

JJ moved to sit next to me, taking the photograph and running his thumb over it before looking to Rogue. "It's got your blobbiness," he said to her and she snorted a laugh, her eyes brimming with tears.

"And your wiggliness," she said, prodding him in the ribs.

We all looked to Rick where he still stood in the doorway like an angry ghost who wanted to come haunt us, and JJ offered him the picture.

He hesitated before moving forward and Rogue's eyes remained pinned on him as he took it, his eyes falling down to the little being we were all soon going to be responsible for.

"Well, four shit dads have gotta add up to a good one, right?" he said, a small smirk lifting his mouth as he looked to Rogue.

"Er, three shit dads thank you very much," Fox said, and we broke a laugh. "I've been ready for this my whole damn life."

CHAPTER FIFTY

Mount Everest by Labrinth pounded through the speakers in my club, and I danced solo on the stage to the slow beat, the deep blue spotlight swinging around me. This was one of my favourite things in the world, letting the music flow through me, my muscles trained in every movement so deeply that I didn't need to even think about it anymore.

My body worked with the music, my hips rolling sexually before I skimmed my thumb down my shirt and the buttons opened to a chorus of cheers. But I never stripped fully anymore. I came here to dance, but now I was gonna be a dad, I felt it was best to keep my cock for my girl's eyes only. And the guys could have a gander whenever they wanted to be reminded of how pretty my dick was in comparison to theirs.

I finished the dance with a forward flip and a knee skid which sent the crowd wild. Turned out, I didn't even need to get Johnny D out to earn myself hundreds of dollars in tips.

I spotted my dad in the crowd, a Tom Collins perched next to him on the bar and my damn mom there beside him too, clapping and cheering me. And okay, that felt damn good, warmth spilling through my chest at their enthusiasm, but it was a bit awkward when a woman screamed, "I'd die happy if I can just suck on your balls Johnny James!" at the top of her lungs and it carried above the music for all to hear. They didn't seem to care though, and I guessed I kinda liked that about my parents, even if they were embarrassingly supportive of my job sometimes.

Gwan had pulled through for my mom, and when he'd come to me last week and asked if he could propose to her, I'd nearly lost my cool when I'd hugged him. He really was a good guy, and I'd never seen my mom as happy as she was with him, so how could I say no? I didn't even hate his name that much these days, especially because I didn't call him by it anymore. I called him Dad, and fuck if it still made me feel giddy inside. The first time I'd said it to his face, he'd teared up, and I'd tried to pretend I'd called him Brad because Gwan was such a terrible fucking name, and he needed a proper one. But in the end, I'd embraced my newfound love for him.

I headed backstage where Lyla and Di were painting on glitter for their next act together. They'd begged me to let them choreograph something between the two of them, and that had been one of the best decisions I'd ever made for this business. Their talent shone out on that stage, and I was more than happy for them to come up with more dances in the future.

"Oh my god! Oh my god, Ollie, look!" Bella cried, running through the dressing room in a tiny pink thong, her tits bouncing and her nipple tassels spinning as she ran over to Ollie with something in her hand.

"What is it?" he asked, rising to his feet as she waved a shiny gold card under his nose. "Holy fuck."

"Is that another scratch card?" I murmured to Lyla, and she nodded, hurrying over to Bella with Di to see what her friend had won. Bella had been buying the things for years, but she'd never won more than fifty bucks from one.

"What did you get?" Texas asked as he hurried over too and I was caught up in the excitement, rushing over with Adam at my heels to see.

Bella was a little pale faced as she twisted the ticket around to show us, and my heart lurched as I spotted the three matching numbers on it.

"Five hundred grand?" I gasped.

"We can get that little beach house we wanted," Ollie said, jumping up, whipping Bella into the air and spinning her around.

She squealed and they started kissing, clinging to each other and tearing at each other's clothes in a way that told us all to make ourselves scarce.

I barked a laugh, patting Bella on the shoulder in congratulations as my phone began ringing where I'd left it on my dressing table. I jogged over, picking it up and finding Fox calling, my thumb hitting answer as I held it to my ear. But I didn't need to hold it that close apparently, because Fox shouted at me like I was a mile away from him.

"JJ!"

"Fuck, *ow*. What is it?" I asked.

"Rogue's gone into labour," he said.

"What?" I gasped, my heart doing fifty cartwheels in my chest. "She can't be, she's not due for another week."

"She is. We're on our way to the hospital," he said.

"Motherfucking fuck on a fucking dick!" Rogue screamed in the background.

"Argh, don't hit me, hummingbird, I'm trying to drive," Fox said.

"Is she okay?" I asked in a panic, running for the back door already as I grabbed my car keys and broke out into the night air.

"She's fine," Fox said.

"Fine?" she growled. "Is pushing a whole person out of my vagina fine, badger?"

"Of course not, baby. Just breathe like the Lamaze class woman said."

"I only went to one class," Rogue snarled.

623

"Well, you could have gone to more of them, but you said they were boring and lacked snacks," Fox said, then turned his attention back to me as Rogue growled like a demon. "Rick and Chase are on their way too. Hurry up."

"I will," I said, my voice hoarse as my brain tried to comprehend what was happening.

"See you at the hospital." Fox hung up and I dropped my phone into the cup holder as I dove into my car, starting her up and accelerating out of the parking lot.

Holy fuck, I'm gonna be a dad!

I turned my car towards the cliff roads that would lead me to the upper quarter, tearing along as fast as I could get away with. It was late, but it was a Saturday night so there were quite a few people out partying, but as I reached the cliffs, the traffic thinned until there was nothing but open roads leading me towards Rogue and my brand new baby girl.

Maverick had laughed when he'd found out we were having a girl, excited about how many guys' limbs he was going to get to break when she was a teenager and started getting attention from them. It was his new dream, though Fox had been less impressed by that, already talking about curfews and rules. I'd reminded him we'd broken every single one of those when our own parents had tried to put them on us as kids, and he'd wrangled his little badgery soul back in check.

It wasn't gonna be easy, raising this new little person among us all, but after having some time to process her arrival, I was sure we could do it. Chase had read every baby book he could get his hands on, plus attended some freaking therapy to try and deal with his fears over becoming a parent. He'd be a damn good one though, we'd all worked to reassure each other of that. Rogue had woken one night after having a nightmare of accidentally baking her own baby in a pie, and she'd only calmed down when Fox had reminded her that she'd never cooked a thing in her life, and it wasn't likely she'd start anytime soon.

I sped into the dark of the cliff roads, gripping the wheel tight and trying to go over the new baby plan in my head. We had a nursery set up for her at Harlequin House, and Fox had already written out a night time rota for us all. Between the five of us, we were surely gonna be just fine, right? One tiny baby would be a breeze. Right??

A bang made my heart jolt and my GT nearly skidded off the road as the front right tyre exploded.

"Fuck!" I cried in alarm, gripping the wheel and slamming on the brakes, coming to a halt before I lost control.

I took several slow breaths as adrenaline rushed through my blood, then shoved the door open and got out of the car to see the damage. The tyre must have hit a sharp rock because it was absolutely fucked, and I didn't have a spare in my car.

"No, no, no," I said in a panic, carving my fingers through my hair.

I lurched back into the car, grabbing my keys and phone, stuffing the former into my pocket while making a call to Chase. The phone rang and rang, but he didn't fucking answer, so I tried Rick instead. The ringing went on and on, but he didn't pick up either and I spat a snarl in frustration, kicking the flat tyre and cursing as pain ricocheted through my toes.

"Goddammit," I growled, figuring there was no point calling Fox. He was with Rogue, and she needed him more than he needed to be distracted by my current situation.

The road was quiet, no cars headed this way that I could steal a ride off, so I quickly tried to book an Uber on my phone, waiting for a driver to connect with me. But fuck, I had a one-star rating since the first and only time I'd gotten an Uber. The driver had tried to convince me he knew more about starfishes than I did. We'd gotten into such a heated argument that he'd tried to kick me out of the cab before my destination. I'd refused to get out, calling him a crab-eating moustached cunt - because of course he'd had a moustache - and eventually he'd called the cops and I'd made a run for it. Now, my one-star rating taunted me on the screen as no drivers dared pick me up. It had been years since that argument, but it looked like that Uber driver was my arch nemesis now.

I tried to search for a cab company on the internet, but I had zero cell service out here and I cursed as I gave up and started running up the road. My arms powered back and forth, the wind whipping against my bare chest as my open shirt whipped out around me. Thankfully, I wasn't wearing glittery shoes with slippy soles – oh no, wait, I was.

My feet skidded and slid everywhere until I was forced to take them off and hurl them into the bushes with a roar of anger and power on in my socks instead.

There were little flaps covering my ass on the back of these pants and they kept fluttering up in the breeze to reveal my bare ass as I ran, my teeth gritted and determination forcing me on.

I was breathless by the time I reached the top of the cliff roads, and I wasn't anywhere close to the upper quarter yet. I looked down at my phone to check for internet signal, but there was still none, so I could do nothing but keep going, running on into the dark as my lungs heaved from the workout.

When I was dripping with sweat and gasping for water, I shed my shirt, throwing that away too and leaving me in nothing but my ass-flap pants and socks as I continued towards my girl and the baby that was on the way into this world.

"I'm coming," I said heavily. "Daddy JJ's on the way."

Two lights cut through the dark up ahead of me and my heart lifted with relief as I held out my arm, raising my thumb. I didn't care if they were going in the opposite direction, I'd promise them a fortune to get me to the damn hospital.

A pink Jeep came into focus on the road, slowing to a halt and I ran to the driver's window, recognition prickling at my senses about this vehicle, though I couldn't place it in that moment.

"Well hey there, lad. What are you doing all the way out here, all shoeless and desperate like?" the Irish accent made me pause and I suddenly realised who this was.

"You're Kyan's uncle," I said, clinging to the side of his car as he toked on a cigarette in the corner of his lips, lighting him up in a red glow. He had dark blonde hair and was covered in colourful tattoos and some lethal looking scars, his green irises full of untold sins.

"That I am. And you're one of the Harlequin boys," he said, his eyes glittering with knowledge.

"I need a ride to the hospital, my girl is in labour," I said frantically.

"Labour, you say?" he said in surprise. "Sounds like hard work. Did she find out about the baby today, or has she known about it for a while? I only ask 'cause I heard about a woman who was sitting on the toilet once, straining away to take a big ol' dump when out plopped a baby. Imagine that? One second you're having ya morning poo, not even a squirrel around to peep on ya as you enjoy the delights of its passing – then splash! A baby in your toilet bowl, swimming around like a squid in a whirlpool."

"I really need to get to the hospital," I begged, and his eyebrows jumped up.

"Oh don't mind my rambling, lad. In ya get. I'll get you there in time."

"Thank you," I said in relief, getting in the passenger's side and Niall turned around at speed, making me hurry to get my seatbelt on as he took off back the way he'd come at a hundred miles an hour.

"Fuck," I gasped as he accelerated even more, smoke pouring from his lips as he took one hand off the wheel to pluck the cigarette from his lips and flick it out the window.

"How about a bit of music?" he offered, not waiting for my answer as he switched on Stan by Eminem and Dido, immediately starting to sing along.

A bang in the back of the Jeep made me peer back that way and Niall suddenly turned off the road onto a bumpy road.

"Where are you going?" I demanded. "The upper quarter is that way." I pointed, but Niall waved me off as he sped along the unmade road, the two of us bumping wildly in our seats.

I braced myself on the window, wondering if I should have trusted this maniac. I'd heard the rumours about him; he was a hitman for hire and an unhinged one at that.

"Look, I'll just keep walking, man," I said urgently.

"This won't take a second, lad, I'll still get ya there before she has that baby in the toilet."

The banging in the back of the Jeep was familiar enough to tell me what it was, and I rubbed a hand over the back of my neck. "Who've you got in there?"

"His name's Terrence Whistlebee. Sick son of a bitch, lemme tell ya. He was keeping four women in his basement and torturing them to boot, weren't you, you cunt?" he called into the back of the Jeep and Terrence wailed in terror. "He had a best friend who helped him too. My girl's currently cutting him into pieces and painting a picture with his blood for me."

"That's nice," I said tightly as Niall halted the Jeep and leapt out into the dark.

He opened the back door of the Jeep and hauled Terrence out of it, dragging him along by his hair as he kicked and flailed.

"Come on, lad," Niall called to me. "I need help with something."

"I really need to go," I implored, half tempted to steal his Jeep as he'd left the keys in the ignition, but I really didn't think it was a good idea to incur the wrath of this psycho.

I got out of the car, running after him as he hauled Terrence along while singing to the Eminem and Dido song we could still hear from here.

I realised where we were as my eyes adjusted to the dark, and my stomach twisted as we closed in on the blowhole I'd gotten stuck down with my friends.

"I've got you and your family to thank for me learning about this place," Niall called back to me. "I heard you got sucked out into the ocean like a turd down a drainpipe. How was that? Must have been a real ride."

"I almost died," I said as he threw Terrence down at the edge of the blowhole and drew a gun from his hip, casually aiming it at his head as the man started to beg for mercy.

"But ya didn't," Niall said, looking back at me. "That's the fun part, no?"

"No," I said with a frown, and he barked a laugh.

"Well, I guess we're a different breed. I like looking death in the eye and making her my bitch. You haven't lived unless you've almost died, that's what I say. How about you, Terrence?" He pressed the butt of his gun to the man's head and he whimpered in fear. "Now open wide like I'm gonna put a spider in your mouth."

He screamed and Niall swiftly took something from his leather jacket pocket, sliding it into Terrence's mouth.

"Don't worry, I'm not actually gonna put a spider in ya mouth. There we are. Lovely." Niall stood up straight, waving a grenade pin in front of Terrence's face and I noted the grenade wedged firmly in the man's mouth. *Holy shit.* "Now, Terrence, I'm gonna tell ya something you're not gonna like."

Tears ran down the man's cheeks as he whimpered around the grenade.

"You're gonna die, Terrence," Niall said with a firm nod. "That grenade in ya mouth is gonna go off with a big bang. The only thing keeping it in place is your tongue pressing down on that trigger, but that can't go on forever now, can it? It ain't viable if we look at the odds and stack them all up, is it?"

Terrence whimpered again and my heart thundered in my chest as I watched, unable to tear my eyes away from Niall's insane game.

"That'll be karma for ya though," Niall said. "But we can make it fun before you go boom. So I'm gonna place a little bet with my new friend, here – what's your name again, lad?" He looked to me.

"Johnny James," I said hoarsely.

"Aw, I like that. Your momma liked ya so much, she named ya twice." Niall smiled at me, his muscles tightening as he stood up straight, keeping his boot down on Terrence's chest. "Now, Johnny James, how many seconds do you think it'll take before this grenade goes off in Terrence's mouth and sends his brain in every direction?"

Terrence sobbed around the grenade, and I turned my gaze from him back to Niall. I didn't feel bad for some asshole who'd tortured innocent women, and it wasn't like I hadn't seen blood and gore before, though Niall's particular flavour of it was slightly unsettling.

"Five," I said, needing to move this along so I could get back on the damn road.

"I say eight," Niall decided then turned and kicked Terrence right over the edge of the blowhole.

Terrence screamed and just like that the grenade went off and a boom echoed throughout the hole before several splashes sounded the pieces of him hitting the water below.

"Fuck me, did you count that? I didn't even get a chance to say one." Niall roared a laugh, turning back to me and shoving me in the direction of his Jeep. "Right, let's get you on the road to meet that dinner reservation."

"It's not a dinner reservation, my girl is having a baby," I said, hurrying along all the same.

"Right, yeah, that's the one. I could go for some Italian though, could you? We could get takeout on the way. I know a great little-"

"Niall," I growled as we dove back into his Jeep. "I'm having a baby."

He looked me up and down as he dropped into the driver's seat in confusion. "Men can't have babies, you don't have the mechanics for that. Or…wait, are you a woman?" He looked me over, trying to figure it out.

"We need to go," I demanded. "Please, Niall, I need to get to the hospital."

"Alright, alright, keep yer hair on. But I do need you to tell me something while we're driving, something that'll pay for this little trip I'm offering ya."

I frowned, worried about what this man was going to ask of me, but I wasn't exactly in a position to bargain. "What's that then?"

"Where did you get those charming pants with the ass flaps?" he questioned. "My girl would love to see me in some of those. Do you think they make them with a cock flap too?"

"I...er, I'm not sure. They're not mine, but I get a lot of shit like this from a specialist website. I'm a stripper."

"Oh really? Can you write the name of that website down for me?" he asked keenly as we jostled furiously along the dirt road towards the road.

"Sure," I said as he passed me a glittery notepad with a unicorn on it along with a pen that was shaped like a squid.

"I have so many questions for you now. How do you get out of your clothes so seamlessly? I've done a strip show or ten in my time for Brooklyn, but I always end up wriggling outa my jeans like a worm with a bad back, or cutting through them with a knife, but it seems an awful waste."

"Stripper clothes have quick releases on them. They're held together with Velcro and shit," I explained, and he gaped at me in delight, not paying any attention to the dirt road as we sped along it.

"Of course! How did I not think of that before?" He turned his gaze back to the dirt road just in time to spin us out onto the road and relief hit me as he raced along in the direction of the upper quarter at last. "And is there a special technique you use when you're willy slapping girls in the crowd?"

"I don't do that anymore," I said.

"But you have in the past?" he pressed. "Because I tried it the other week with my girl, and she was knocked out cold for four hours."

"Jesus," I breathed.

"The piercing in my cock gave her a nasty gash in her hairline too," he said, looking over at me with a frown. "I feel right bad about that, I tell ya."

I stared at him as I tried to process the insanity of this night, then remembered to speak.

"It's more of a gentle hip movement, don't put any power in it," I said, and he nodded seriously like he was taking mental notes.

"Like this?" He raised his hips in his seat, swinging his hips sideways furiously.

"No, like this." I lifted my own hips, showing him the subtle movement. "Then it'll swing back and forth on its own."

"Oh, look at those fancy hip movements. You must be related to Shakira, because I can tell you're a real pro," he said, mirroring my movements and picking them up surprisingly fast.

My eyes flashed back to the windscreen, and I yelled out in fright as two headlights lit up the space ahead of us and I realised we were on the wrong side of the road.

Niall steered us around the oncoming vehicle at the last second, honking his horn angrily like it was the other person's fault not his.

"There's some crazy assholes out on these roads, ya gotta be real careful," Niall said, shaking his head.

The lights of the upper quarter finally came into view and relief rushed through me as we sailed through the streets of the town, growing ever closer to my destination.

Niall tore into the hospital parking lot like we were in a high-speed chase, and I braced myself against the window as he swung around in front of the entrance and slammed on the brakes.

"There ya are, lad. Enjoy your pizza," he said brightly.

"Baby," I corrected, but I didn't waste any more time as I threw the door open and ran for the entrance.

It was almost an hour since Fox had called and I felt like I was letting Rogue down as I trailed dirt through the foyer in my grubby socks, looking left and right at the signs all around me.

"Can I help you, sir?" the receptionist called to me from the desk.

"Rogue Harlequin," I blurted. "Do you know where she is? She's having my baby."

She checked something on her screen then nodded, frowning at my attire as she directed me to the maternity ward.

I got all kinds of strange looks as I ran through the hospital, shirtless with my ass flaps fluttering, but I didn't give a fuck as I hunted down my girl.

I made it to the ward, and the nurse there took one look at me and pointed me to a room down the hall like she knew exactly where I belonged. I ran there, ready to get Rogue through this, to offer her a hand to squeeze and to time her contractions for her, but as I pushed through the door, I found her propped up in bed with a baby already cuddled to her chest and my three best friends surrounding her.

"What happened to you?" Chase asked in alarm.

"It doesn't matter," I breathed, my jaw going slack as I stared at the impossibility of our daughter being here already.

Rogue's tear-filled eyes lifted to meet mine. "Isn't she perfect?"

The guys' gazes travelled down my attire, questions filling their expressions as I staggered forward and looked down at this tiny little girl who was all ours. She was wrapped in a light pink blanket, and she had a coating of dark hair on her head.

"Oh my God," I exhaled as Fox rested a hand to my shoulder, shifting aside with the biggest ass smile on his face I'd ever seen.

"She's tiny," I said, my voice weak as I took her into my arms, terrified that I might break her. Her eyes were closed but as I held her to my chest, she cracked them open and I was stunned to find them the exact same shade as Rogue's.

"You have to hold her next, Ace," Rick muttered.

"I'll drop her," he said fearfully.

"You won't," Fox said.

"Badger?" Rogue whispered while I continued to stare at our baby, not wanting to blink for a single second in case I missed something.

"Yes, hummingbird?" he asked as she took hold of his arm in my periphery, dragging him down so she could speak in his ear.

"That was the most painful motherfucking thing I have ever experienced. I want to go home and never, ever, ever do it again. Can you go tell the doctors that and make sure they let me leave in the next five minutes before I punch the one who pulled her out of me?"

"Yes, baby," he said obediently, heading straight out of the room.

"How did she arrive so fast?" I asked, looking up at Rogue finally. "Are you okay?"

"No, JJ," she said, swallowing and shaking her head. "She came too fast. I couldn't have any drugs, so I had to feel it all, and she fucking sprinted out of my vagina swinging a baseball bat, I swear to God."

"At least it was fast," Rick said, and Rogue shot him a narrowed eyed look.

"If it took me fifteen minutes to turn your dick inside out using only cocktail sticks, would you think that was fast?" she asked him and he paled, his throat rising and falling.

"No, beautiful," he rasped.

She looked to our little girl, smiling brightly as she forgot all about their argument. "She was worth it though."

I gazed down at our baby again as she made the cutest, tiniest little noise and it made my heart turn to goo. I knew in that second, I would give her anything she wanted the moment she asked for it. I was going to be the softest parent of all of us and I didn't give a damn. She could have the world and everything in it.

Fox stepped back into the room, moving to gather Rogue's bag and giving her a nod that said it was done. No one argued with a Harlequin.

"Does she have a name yet?" I asked. We'd all been arguing about what to call her for so long, we'd all decided Rogue could have final say and that would be that.

Rogue grinned, nodding as she sat up in straighter in bed. "Ranger."

"Like The Lone Ranger?" Chase said in confusion.

"No, not like The Lone Ranger," Rogue scoffed. "Like the Green Power Ranger."

"I weirdly like it," I said as Rick boomed a laugh and nodded his assent.

"Ranger," Fox tried out the name, looking down at her.

"It's got a ring to it actually," Chase conceded.

"That's it then," Rogue said. "It's decided. She's Ranger Harlequin."

Chase leaned forward to tickle her chin. "Welcome to the crew, tiny one."

"Surprise!" Chase said as he appeared out on the back porch, rolling his old bike along with him which was now freshly painted pink with little tassels on the handlebars.

I sat beside Rogue on the outdoor couch as she nursed Ranger beside me, looking up at Chase with her eyebrows arching.

"Wow, that's so cute," she said.

"Maybe Ranger can have a little ride around on it," Chase said.

"She's three days old," Rogue said. "She can't go on a bike."

Chase's face fell then he covered it with a laugh. "Well, yeah, but like in a few weeks or something. Obviously I need to get her a special seat to sit on top of the saddle but then-"

"Dude, that's an adult's bike," I said with a snort. "She's not going on that until she's like thirteen."

Chase's cheeks touched with colour, and he steered the bike against the porch railing, leaning it there.

"Yeah, I know," he laughed a little too loudly. "I was joking."

"You so weren't joking," Rogue said as she cracked up and Ranger was forced off of her nipple as she jolted her. "Oh, sorry, sweetie."

I helped her latch on again, cupping the back of Ranger's head and smiling at the beautiful sight of my daughter in the arms of the love of my life.

A low whining noise caught my attention, and I lifted my head with a frown, spotting Mutt scrabbling up the porch steps with a white mouse in his jaws.

"Shit," I gasped, lurching out of my seat, and moving to take it from him.

As Mutt placed it down, I realised it wasn't a mouse at all. It was a freaking puppy.

I gaped at it as Mutt nudged it towards me with his nose and I glanced back at Rogue and Chase in alarm.

"Did he steal that from some poor dog?" Chase questioned.

"No way, he's no puppy stealer," Rogue said, awe lighting her features. "Is that yours, boy?"

Mutt yapped, wagging his tiny tail and I noticed a scruffy brown terrier peering around the bottom of the porch steps beyond him.

"Hey there, girl," I said, reaching for her and she trembled a little before Mutt barked in encouragement and she came bounding up the steps, sniffing my hand before licking it.

I rubbed her head and she moved to sit beside Mutt and the puppy which was wriggling its way towards her.

"It's really yours?" I asked Mutt like a crazy person, but he answered with a yip of joy, leaning down to lick the puppy.

"We had babies at the same time," Rogue squeaked. "Can I see?"

My girl was still sore from the birth, so I scooped up the puppy gently, carrying it to her so she could meet it. Mutt ran over with his girlfriend in tow, and he jumped up beside Rogue, licking Ranger's head before looking to his own baby.

"Oh my gosh," Rogue breathed, stroking the puppy's head and the mother jumped up too, nuzzling into my hand.

"We're keeping them all," Rogue announced. "That's that."

"What's that?" Fox stepped out onto the porch with a frown that said something was wrong and I immediately straightened. His gaze fell on the dogs and his eyebrows leapt up.

"We're keeping them," Rogue reiterated. "This is Fluff," she decided on the momma dog's name. "And their baby can be Pup."

"Fine," Fox said, seeming too distracted to question that.

"What's going on?" Chase asked, sensing something was off too.

"Sinners' Playground," he sighed, and my heart tugged at those two words. "I've just got word it's going to be demolished in thirty minutes by the prick who bought it. Rick's gone down there to see if he can finally get hold of whoever it was, but it's not looking good."

"Fuck," I growled.

A few months back, some anonymous buyer had bought the place and had started work on rebuilding the thing to reopen to the public as some ugly, modern shopping centre. We would have bought it our damn selves if we'd known it was even on the market, but fuck knew how someone had gotten the jump on us. All kinds of scaffolding and sheeting had been erected on it so we couldn't even see what the asshole was doing to our beloved childhood hideaway. But last week, news had spread that there were structural deficiencies with the whole thing and the owner had decided to demolish it and scrap the entire project.

No one had the name of the purchaser, and not even Saint Memphis had been able to dig up their information when we'd asked him.

"If Rick can reach the owner before it goes down, we might still have a chance to buy it," Fox said. "But I wanna get down there and help."

637

"Me too," Rogue said, getting to her feet and I scooped the puppy into my hand. "I wanna be there if it's demolished anyway. We should be there for its end." There was pain in her eyes and I placed a kiss on her cheek, saddened by that.

"Come on then," Fox said.

We all headed inside with the two adult dogs at our heels, keeping to Rogue's pace, though she never once complained about the pain, only refused to ever go through it again. And honestly, one baby filled my heart to the brim. I didn't need any more or any less than that.

I placed the tiny puppy down in Mutt's bed and Fluff lapped at the water bowl beside it before grabbing herself a chicken treat and curling up with her puppy just like that. Home sweet home.

Mutt bounded up to lick Rogue's ankles and Chase picked him up, bringing our little warrior dog along for the fight.

We had a mom-mobile in the garage now, the huge SUV looking closer to a tank with its khaki green colour and bars on the front of it.

Rogue put Ranger in the car seat, and I got in the back with them as Fox took the driver's seat and Chase sat in the front with Mutt in his lap.

"Is she secure?" Fox asked, adjusting the rear-view mirror, and getting all Dadly about things.

"Yeah, she's in, badger," Rogue said, and he triple checked everyone was buckled in too before putting on his Ray Bans and driving us out onto the road at a snail's pace.

"At least drive at the speed limit, man," Chase said as Fox started indicating to turn, letting car after car go by even though he had plenty of opportunity to make the turn.

"Come on, badge, make the turn," Rogue urged. "We'll be here until sunset otherwise."

Fox still waited until there were no cars coming our way before he did so, ignoring all of us and going full safety mode. I wasn't exactly complaining,

I'd already stocked the car with emergency everything in case of a breakdown.

We finally made it to Sinners' Playground where a TV crew were waiting to film the demolition and a crowd of people were standing on the beach to watch the show.

I spat a curse as I got out of the car, hurrying to the trunk to get the stroller out for Ranger.

When she was snuggled up inside it with her favourite Green Power Ranger plushie, I pushed her aggressively down the boardwalk towards the official looking assholes near the entrance to the amusement park with my family moving along at my back. The pier was covered in plastic sheeting, and no doubt explosives were packed onto the last of it, all ready to blow.

I spotted Rick in a heated conversation with one of the camera crew, the man shaking his head as if he had no answers to whatever Rick was asking him.

Fox whistled to catch his attention and Rick came stalking over to us in a foul mood. "None of these assholes seem to know shit about who owns the place, but apparently they're gonna be here any minute to see it go up in smoke."

He gave Rogue a firm kiss on the mouth in greeting, though the creases on his brow didn't smooth out.

"There's still time," Rogue said. "We can buy it from them here and now."

"Yeah, only if they wanna sell though," Fox said with a sigh.

The crowd started turning and pointing, and we swung around as a black Porsche pulled up at the side of the road. My lips parted as Saint Memphis stepped out, offering his hand to Tatum and drawing her after him.

Saint wore an expensive white shirt tucked neatly into his slacks and Tatum was wearing a flowing baby pink dress. She let go of Saint's hand, rushing forward to hug Rogue.

"How are you? Can I see her?" she gushed.

"Er, yeah, sure," Rogue said, pointing to Ranger in her stroller and Tatum squealed as she looked down at her, then back to Rogue.

"I'm sorry for all the theatrics about this. We just really wanted to surprise you," she said.

"Huh?" Rogue frowned and Tatum bit her lip before looking to Saint.

"It was quite the eyesore, you see?" Saint said. "And I had to get you down here this morning, so I let word slip of the pier's demolishment."

"What are you talking about?" I asked as Rick cracked his knuckles in anger.

"Did you buy that pier? Are you the one blowing it up?" Maverick snarled, jerking towards Saint like he intended to hit him, but Fox caught his shoulder to hold him back.

Saint didn't so much as flinch, smiling instead as he nodded in confirmation. "Yes. I believe Kyan called the press though. He always has to make a production of things, but I think it adds a little something to the event, now that I am here to witness it."

"We'll pay you for the pier, man," I said urgently. "Please don't destroy it. It means everything to us."

"Quite," Saint said, then turned on his heel and walked over to some men standing by builders' trucks at the side of the street.

"What the fuck is going on?" Chase whispered.

"Just bear with him," Tatum begged, and Rogue frowned, nodding to her and giving us all a look that told us to keep calm. But how the hell were we supposed to keep calm when Saint was the one who'd fucked up the remnants of our goddamn pier and was now threatening to blow it to shit?

The builders drove a large truck down to Sinners' Playground's entrance while Saint walked back to join us, casually tucking his hands into his pants' pockets as he reached us.

"Do remain calm," he urged.

"How about you explain what the fuck is going on?" Rick growled.

"I would, Maverick, but I think this will do it for you." Saint raised a hand to signal something to the men and they hurried over to a truck waiting at the front of Sinners' Playground, climbing into it.

I watched in confused fascination as they drove away from the entrance, dragging the huge sheeting after them on a hook at the back of their truck and unveiling the refurbished amusement park beyond it.

The Ferris wheel still stood tall and proud at the far end of the pier, and shock took hold of me as more and more of the rides were revealed, just as they had been before. The whole thing had been restored, looking exactly how it must have done when it was originally opened.

The front gates were brand new and a pastel-coloured rainbow was painted across it. Written through the colours in stylised white graffiti was the name Sinners' Playground. The crowd cheered and the camera crew kept recording it all even though this wasn't what they'd come here for.

"No way," Chase gasped, and Mutt yapped excitedly in his arms.

"Yes 'way', Chase," Saint said, a smirk dancing around his lips as he held out a set of five brass keys in his hand. "One for each of you."

Rogue took them from his palm as Tatum grinned like a kid, glancing between us all as we stood there in shock.

"It's yours," Tatum said. "We wanted it to be a surprise. Saint kept complaining about seeing a glimpse of the burned down pier on the horizon, and I thought, well why not renovate it and give it to you guys after you had the baby!"

"Tatum, this is too much," Rogue said, though she was smiling from ear to ear, lit up like a Christmas tree.

"Not at all." Tatum waved her off. "I hope you don't mind, but I went a little mad on the planning and we converted the whole thing into a liveable home. There's bedrooms and bathrooms, a kitchen, even a pool! Come and see!"

Rogue gaped at her in disbelief, and we all headed after her towards the gates as Saint walked along at my side.

"You didn't have to do this," I told him, still shellshocked.

"I did, Johnny James. I couldn't bear to see it on the horizon anymore. It was an atrocity," he said, and I lunged at him, drawing him into a tight embrace.

He stiffened in my arms like he didn't know how to react to that, but I just cuddled the motherfucker regardless.

When I let him go, he cleared his throat, seeming lost, but then he smiled a little and I knew I'd won him over.

We headed onto the pier and Tatum gave us the grand tour while I stared around in disbelief at the beautiful work they'd had done on this place. It was just as it had been when we were kids, only now it gleamed and shone, everything that had been damaged in the fire, now restored, and anything lost entirely replaced by something in its exact image.

"How did you do this?" I breathed to Saint as Tatum led us into the arcade which had the same domed roof and red and white striped walls outside as always. But inside, it had been converted into a beautiful home.

"I obtained the original plans from the local library and had a team work to restore it," Saint said simply, but it wasn't simple. It was a fucking miracle worked by the hands of a god. "We've gone for neutral tones and furnishings so you can put your own stamp on it."

Saint led us into a bright lounge with windows that looked out over the sea and a massive kitchen off to one side of it that Fox ran eagerly into like a kid in a candy store.

"You may find this of interest, Johnny James." Saint pointed to a large aquarium that ran along the side of the room, full of beautiful fish and a coral. "I took the liberty of moving both of your starfish into it this morning. I have no idea how you kept them alive so long in a tank unfit for their requirements, but this one is more than fitting."

I grinned, running up to the glass and peering in at Sparkle and Jigglypuff in there, happily starfishing about at the bottom of the tank. There was room in here for a whole army of starfish, and maybe some seahorses…and a mollusc called Carl.

"This is incredible," I said in awe.

We were led outside again along the brand-new boards lining the pier and I took in the details of the carvings on the railings, all of them freshly painted in white and given life all over again.

Tatum guided us to an incredible pool area which was built up on a raised deck that overlooked the ocean. There were sun loungers and even a fucking outdoor bar made from one of the old ticket booths.

"The rides at the end of the pier are the original ones, but unfortunately, I was only able to have a few of them fixed up well enough to work again as the parts for such outdated models are near impossible to come by. The Ferris Wheel still doesn't move, but I assumed you would prefer it remained there than to be replaced," Saint explained.

"Yeah, definitely, man," I said, still overwhelmed by all of this.

"What do we owe you for all of this?" Rick asked Saint and Tatum.

"Nothing," Tatum said firmly.

"I would not accept a penny if you tried to force it upon me," Saint added. "This is a gift, and the definition of a gift is something which is given willingly without requirement of payment."

"I like your brand of insanity," Rick laughed, shaking Saint's hand.

"Me too," Tatum said, biting her lip as she threaded her fingers through Saint's, smiling up at her boyfriend.

We eventually made it to the end of the pier and Rogue lifted Ranger out of her stroller, showing her the sea and pointing out a little pod of dolphins jumping through the waves.

I moved up to stand beside her along with Rick, Chase, Fox, and Mutt, as Saint and Tatum gave us a moment alone together.

"Are we really gonna live here?" I asked hopefully and we all looked to

Rogue as an astonished smile gripped her beautiful face.

"What do you think, Ranger?" she asked, nuzzling into our daughter's little head and she cooed softly. "That sounded like a fuck yes to me."

CHAPTER FIFTY ONE

SIXTEEN YEARS AFTER THAT...

I ran down the beach with the wind in my hair and the sun blazing on my back, a laugh tumbling from me as my boys ran with me, the four of them forming an arrowhead with me at the tip of it. They were laughing too, grinning at me as I turned my head to look between all of them in turn.

Fox had a brightness to his green gaze which set me alight like nothing I'd ever known before, the power of his will a burning beacon which summoned us all closer to him with every breath he took.

JJ was laughing the loudest of us all, his big heart and joyful spirit always bolstering the rest of us, lightening the darkest of days and making ones as full as this sparkle like we were all experiencing some magical version of the world known only to the five of us.

Chase pushed a hand through his dark curls, his strength of character always making me feel stronger too, the way he survived the worst of life and still managed to come out on top every damn time, making me feel invincible whenever I was in his presence.

Maverick's gaze was full of dark promises and dangerous desires which were always bound to get us all into the best kinds of trouble, the ones we thrived on and lived for and made us feel like we were on top of the world even when we'd been born at the bottom of it.

I was the wildness in our group, the one without restraint who always pushed us a step further, dared us to take that bit extra and never stopped demanding everything that life could offer us and more.

And together, the five of us were something no one else could touch. We shared a love more powerful than any force on earth that no one would ever be able to tear apart.

We made it to the struts which held up the pier and climbed up the one where we had long ago carved our own personal entrance to our little stolen slice of paradise until we were all standing on the well-worn boards of Sinners' Playground.

I took off running, hardly even remembering what trouble we were racing from or towards this time as the Ferris Wheel at the far end of the peer whispered my name and urged me closer to it like always.

I came to a halt at the foot of it, tasting the sea air on my tongue and listening to the way the waves lapped against the sand beneath us as a sigh escaped me.

My boys were right there beside me, throwing their arms around me and each other, the sound of the gulls crying as they swooped overhead joining the natural orchestra of my favourite place in the entire world.

"I wish we could ride on it for real," I said wistfully, my eyes on a carriage at the very top of the wheel which rocked softly in the breeze, taunting me with an unreal possibility.

"One day we will," one of them said, and I wasn't even certain which because they'd all promised me that more times than I could count, their words never losing their certainty and the sweetness of that impossible promise wrapping around me and making my heart swell with the possibility, even *though I knew it wouldn't ever come to pass.*

"She of little faith," Chase teased as he walked me down the pier with his hands over my eyes, the others' footsteps surrounding us as they escorted me to the end of it to the Ferris wheel they'd spent the last God knew how many years lovingly painting and restoring in their spare time.

"I don't care if it runs or not," I told them for the hundredth time because this wasn't the first time they'd announced that the thing was up and running again only for me to get in it and it not move a single inch when they tried to fire it up. It had become a running joke and a point of pride to them that they truly believed they could do it, and they had refused to get anyone in to help them, but that only made me more certain that this latest attempt was doomed for failure just like all the rest.

"Lies," JJ chastised, leaning in to speak in my ear and making a shiver run down my spine at his closeness. "What did I tell you I'd have to do to you if you lost faith in us again over this?"

"Remind me," I purred, and Rick released a filthy laugh because we all knew it had involved me, them, and my latest roleplaying fantasy which may or may not have run along the lines of being a trapped princess who grew up in a Fae realm where the old gods had long been lost, but were waking up and vengeful in all the best and worst ways. I'd let them pull on my magical hair and make me their somewhat willing servant while they each played the part of either a brutal guard who was duty bound to protect me, but secretly wanted to ravish me senseless, or a street thug looking to steal me away from my palace and teach me how good it could feel to be all kinds of bad. Yeah, I was totally down for that kind of punishment, and they all knew it. It was a game of malice and greed which we indulged in as often as we could.

"Stop smirking like that or I'll come up with my own fantasy to act out on you," Fox added, and I smirked some more because, yes please.

They all laughed, though there was an edge to the sound which made it all too clear how this night would be ending up, and I had to say I held no objections to that whatsoever.

We came to a stop and Chase removed his hands from my eyes, the four of them practically bouncing on the balls of their feet as they pointed me to powder pink carriage which sat with its door open invitingly just ahead of me.

I smiled at the sweetness of this gesture though I still had very little belief that the thing would even start up, playing along and getting into the carriage like they wanted, taking my seat close to the view, and looking out along the beach.

A cry of laughter drew my attention down to the beach and I bit my bottom lip as I spotted Ranger running across the golden sand, her long, dark hair billowing around her as she raced towards four boys who were striding down the beach with their gazes all locked on her.

The Rivers' boys were all kinds of bad news, and I knew it. They had money, power and the arrogance of kings with the superiority complexes to match. They already had a reputation around here, and none of them had even hit twenty yet. I knew deep down that I probably should have been doing the whole mom thing, yelling Ranger's name and calling her back here, warning her away from them and the risks they posed. But she was sixteen and had my wild streak to her, and I knew that if I tried to stop her from going with them, she would only sneak out and go anyway. Besides, I was willing to bet that whatever they were getting up to, me and my boys had done the same and worse a hundred times over, so I wasn't going to ruin their fun while being a total hypocrite. I also wasn't going to be pointing her out to my men.

The carriage I was sitting in lurched suddenly and a gasp tore from my lips as I whirled around, staring at the four of them in delight and surprise as multicoloured lights flickered on around the entire Ferris Wheel and the whole thing slowly began to turn.

Cries of excitement and celebration tore from all four of them and they leapt into the carriage with me a moment later, crushing me between them and planting kisses on my lips and skin wherever they could find it.

We stayed on our feet, calling out to the sea as the wheel turned more, lifting us into the air and hoisting us up high over the ocean, letting the view of our own personal paradise spread out endlessly all around us.

I was filled with a sense of euphoria and peace which made me grin so widely, I feared my face might crack in two.

I looked out at the sunset as it painted the sky in tones of pink and orange, the beauty of this place coiling around us and making me feel at peace with the world.

Just as we reached the top of the Ferris Wheel, the lights all flickered and a low groan sounded from the ride, a cry escaping me as the thing ground to a halt and I grabbed Maverick's arm to steady myself as the carriage rocked wildly.

The lights flickered once more and then everything died, the power cutting out and leaving us there, stuck at the very top of the wheel just as the sun disappeared beyond the horizon.

"Well, fuck," Fox said, breaking the poignant silence which had fallen among us, and I burst into laughter that was quickly echoed by the rest of them.

"Would you rather be stuck at the top of this broken Ferris Wheel together for the rest of our lives or living alone as a billionaire with everything in the entire world at your fingertips?" I asked as I snuggled between the four of them and felt the warm press of their bodies surrounding me.

"Easy," Chase replied, placing a kiss on my hair.

"No doubt about it," Fox agreed, his fingers tangling with mine and squeezing me tightly.

"That's not even a question, pretty girl," JJ added, his arm curling around my back.

"Forever would be empty without you, assholes," Maverick agreed, giving me a savage kiss which still stole my breath even after all this time.

"Yeah," I agreed as he released me, and I looked between each of them in turn. My boys, my life, my world. "I'd be a billionaire too."

Raucous laughter broke out as they all tried to grab me, tickling me and spanking my ass, calling me names and trying to force me to take it back while the carriage swung wildly beneath us.

Our laughter rang out into the sky all around us, stolen by the wind and delivered to the ocean where the waves dragged it down to the bottom of the sea to be locked away with all the best treasures that had been lost throughout time.

That sound would be kept forever alongside the purest magic in this world where the dolphins played, the mermaids ruled, and girls with rainbow-coloured hair and the men who loved them got to live on in their wildest dreams until the end of time, together, the way fate had always intended them to be.

———————————

AUTHORS NOTE

Well hey there, sugarpie, was that all you dreamed of and more?

This story has been one wild ride for us from the moment Rogue woke up buried in a shallow grave and all the way through her reunion with the boys she had always been destined to be with. There was something really special about this group, their bond so pure and endless that it wrapped us up with them and took us on one hell of an adventure. Things may not have always been easy and fucking Shawn certainly did his best to screw it all up, but he got what was coming to him in the end.

We were going to kill Chase.

I said it.

He was gearing up to be irredeemable in book one and you all remember what he did. Fox was gonna take him out and it was going to be all kinds of horrifically necessary, buuuut then that sneaky little shit went and wormed his way into our hearts and we remembered that we live for a good redemption arc, and now it's hard to imagine that we ever had such a terrible plan for him. But don't you worry – there are still lots of characters left for us to kill off in other books so you will get your dose of trauma there.

Honestly, this series has been such fun to write, and we really hope that that fun translated for you too. I mean yeah, there was a lot of trauma and pain and heartache but then there was the jellyfish to the dick, GPR galore, Mutt's general personality and all the would you rathers...

On that note, would you rather live under the eternal reign of a megalomaniac Dragon asshole or be a potato in a magical prison for Fae? Food for thought there for sure.

Seriously though, thank you guys as always for reading our books, our lives have been altered irrevocably by the love so many of you hold for our words, our characters and our stories, and we will never be able to fully convey how grateful we are to each and every one of you for that. We have had so much fun creating the United States of Anarchy world, and I can't believe that we have now completed three stories within this universe spanning eleven full length books and one novella. You may have picked up a hint or two about some more characters whose lives we plan on destroying – ahem – I mean showcasing next and we have such big plans for their stories too, so watch this space.

If you started off with The Harlequin Crew and are wanting to know who the hell Saint, Tatum and co are then you can read their story in Kings of Quarantine, and if you are intrigued by the insanity of Brooklyn, Mateo and Niall than you'll want to check out The Death Club.

Another series bites the dust, and that now only leaves us with a few waiting for completion but don't you worry – we have so many diabolical plans coming your way very soon.

If you want to keep up with all the latest news, info, teasers and new book/series reveals as soon as they happen then you should come join our newsleter – we won't spam you, we just keep you in the know on all things books a couple of times a month, and offer up exclusive competitions and giveaways too. You can also find us in our amazing Facebook group with almost 50k likeminded super readers so you should come hang out with us there if you aren't already. If you'd like to come see us doing stupid shit, skits from the books, and giving you a little deeper insight into our daily crazy world of writing, then come check us out on TikTok too.

That's enough rambling from me – as always we love and appreciate you, and we can't wait to crawl into your brain with another epic romance story very soon.

Love, Susanne & Caroline xoxo

ALSO BY
CAROLINE PECKHAM
&
SUSANNE VALENTI

Brutal Boys of Everlake Prep

(Complete Reverse Harem Bully Romance Contemporary Series)

Kings of Quarantine

Kings of Lockdown

Kings of Anarchy

Queen of Quarantine

**

Dead Men Walking

(Reverse Harem Dark Romance Contemporary Series)

The Death Club

Society of Psychos

**

The Harlequin Crew

(Reverse Harem Mafia Romance Contemporary Series)

Sinners Playground

Dead Man's Isle

Carnival Hill

Paradise Lagoon

Gallows Bridge

Harlequinn Crew Novellas

Devil's Pass

**

Dark Empire

(Dark Mafia Contemporary Standalones)

Beautiful Carnage

Beautiful Savage

**

Forget Me Not Bombshell

(Dark Mafia Reverse Harem Contemporary Standalone)

**

The Ruthless Boys of the Zodiac

(Reverse Harem Paranormal Romance Series - Set in the world of Solaria)

Dark Fae

Savage Fae

Vicious Fae

Broken Fae

Warrior Fae

Zodiac Academy

(M/F Bully Romance Series- Set in the world of Solaria, five years after Dark Fae)

The Awakening

Ruthless Fae

The Reckoning

Shadow Princess

Cursed Fates

Fated Thrones

Heartless Sky

The Awakening - As told by the Boys

Zodiac Academy Novellas

Origins of an Academy Bully

The Big A.S.S. Party

Darkmore Penitentiary

(Reverse Harem Paranormal Romance Series - Set in the world of Solaria,

ten years after Dark Fae)

Caged Wolf

Alpha Wolf

Feral Wolf

**

The Age of Vampires

(Complete M/F Paranormal Romance/Dystopian Series)

Eternal Reign

Eternal Shade

Eternal Curse

Eternal Vow

Eternal Night

Eternal Love

**

Cage of Lies

(M/F Dystopian Series)

Rebel Rising

**

Tainted Earth

(M/F Dystopian Series)

Afflicted

Altered

Adapted

Advanced

**

The Vampire Games

(Complete M/F Paranormal Romance Trilogy)

V Games

V Games: Fresh From The Grave

V Games: Dead Before Dawn

*

The Vampire Games: Season Two

(Complete M/F Paranormal Romance Trilogy)

Wolf Games

Wolf Games: Island of Shade

Wolf Games: Severed Fates

*

The Vampire Games: Season Three

Hunter Trials

*

The Vampire Games Novellas

A Game of Vampires

**

The Rise of Issac

(Complete YA Fantasy Series)

Creeping Shadow

Bleeding Snow

Turning Tide

Weeping Sky

Failing Ligh